The Saga of Satisar

Chandrakanta is one of India's foremost Hindi writers, with over 50 books to her credit. Her work has been translated into many languages. The English translation of her novel, *Ailan Gali Zinda Hai* (*A Street in Srinagar*) was published by Zubaan nd shortlisted for the DSC award for literature in 2011. Among hardrakanta's many other awards are the prestigious Vyas ian (2005) and the Mahatama Gandhi Sahitya Samman (2011) as well as the Subramanya Bharathi award.

Ranjana Kaul teaches literature at the University of Delhi and translates from Hindi to English when she can find the time.

The Saga of Satisar

CHANDRAKANTA

Translated from the Hindi original by

Ranjana Kaul

zubaan

ZUBAAN
128 B Shahpur Jat, 1st floor
NEW DELHI 110 049
Email: contact@zubaanbooks.com
Website: www.zubaanbooks.com

First published by Rajkamal Prakashan in Hindi in 2007
Copyright © Chandrakanta 2018
English translation copyright © Ranjana Kaul 2018

ISBN 978 93 81017 63 0

10 9 8 7 6 5 4 3 2 1

Zubaan is an independent feminist publishing house based in New
Delhi with a strong academic and general list. It was set up as an
imprint of India's first feminist publishing house, Kali for Women,
and carries forward Kali's tradition of publishing world quality books
to high editorial and production standards. *Zubaan* means tongue,
voice, language, speech in Hindustani. Zubaan publishes in the areas
of the humanities, social sciences, as well as in fiction, general non-
fiction, and books for children and young adults under its Young
Zubaan imprint.

Typeset in Adobe Garamond 11/14 by Jojy Philip, New Delhi 110 015
Printed and bound at Raj Press, R-3 Inderpuri, New Delhi 110 012

This story is dedicated to all those anonymous dispossessed children who, even after many years of exile, cannot understand why they cannot return home.

Ackowledgments

I would not have been able to write this novel if my husband, Dr M.L. Veshin and our Bhabiji (my mother-in-law) had not shared their stories with me. Bhabiji is a true descendent of the writer Somadev, a storyteller par excellence.

There were a number of books that I found useful in gaining a better understanding of my state, my country and myself. These are: *Neelmath Puran*, Kalhana's *Rajtarangini*, G.D.M. Sufi's *Kashir*, Jawaharlal Nehru's *Discovery of India*, Sarvepalli Gopal's *Biography of Nehru*, Pandit Anand Koul's *Kashmiri Pandit*, Dr. Kusum Pant's *The Kashmiri Pandit*, Lt Gen. B.N. Kaul's *The Untold Story*, Brig J.P Dalvi's *Himalayan Blunder*, Pyarelal Kaul's *Crisis in Kashmir*, Sheikh Abdullah's *Atish-e-Chinar*, Premnath Bazaz's *Inside Kashmir*, P.N.K.Bamzai's *Cultural and Political History of Kashmir*, Karan Singh's *The Heir Apparent*, Jagmohan's *Kashmir, Samasya aur Samadhan*, Tavleen Singh's *A Tragedy of Errors*, Chamanlal Sapru's *Saffron and Lotus*, *Koshur Samachar* (Delhi).

An Auspicious Moment

It is difficult to say what prompted the great astrologer Anandjoo to decree that Lalli should be sent to her in-laws for the curd ceremony on the third day of the Ashadh Shukla Paksh. Despite the widespread tension and violence in the city, his decision remained steadfast.

Grey clouds had been scudding across the sky for many days. Occasionally a light drizzle would break through, but for the most part the sky remained overcast, the city nestling in the lap of the mountains, a grayish sheet of muslin covering it with the gentle breeze carrying the dust of fear. No sooner had the sun, a conscientious sentinel from morning to evening, disappeared behind the range of mountains, doors and windows in the city would bang shut. As dusk set in, an occasional glimpse of lamplight, of arms adorned with bangles, was all that could be seen. An instant, and they were gone. Afterwards, there was absolute emptiness, with no trace of anyone belonging to the human race.

The learned Pandit Anandjoo had the *Shivstuti* written by Abhinavgupt at the tip of his tongue. When he ordained an auspicious moment, it was as sacrosanct as a dictum from the ancient texts, the Vedas. Who would have the courage to challenge it?

'May Shiva Shambhu protect us. An auspicious moment is an auspicious moment jajmaan. Whether the earth splits or the sky is in turmoil, there cannot be even a second's delay.'

Krishnajoo Kaul, a head clerk in the accounts office, may

well have been the first member of his family to work in an
office but he did not believe in interfering with the rites and
rituals associated with religion. So, with the brief observation
that, 'Whatever happens is ordained by Lord Rama' and 'It is
the will of God', Lalli was sent to her in-laws at the appointed
moment. All rituals, Shagun and Zang, were carried out and
she went laden with the exhortation that she have many sons.
What happened afterwards, however, raised some anxieties and
uncertainties in Saraswati's mind though this was not a time
when women were permitted to entertain any doubts and fears.

'This should not have happened,' she remarked to her
husband as she spun, her eyes fixed on the woollen yarn winding
around the spindle. Her voice seemed to hold an unspoken
question. 'The moment Lalli set foot in the tonga, the clouds
hovering above Hari Parbat poured down, monsoon showers
in the middle of a hot summer! It is Kaliyug, it has to be. And
worse, ruffians and looters accosted them near Berikunj though
we did everything according to Anandjoo's instructions.'

'May God protect us.' Krishnajoo could not attribute the
fears and anxieties of his deeply religious wife to a lack of
faith. She was a woman who began her day in the last watches
of the night after a bath in the Vitasta and obeisance to the
gods. During the day she tirelessly looked after the needs of her
family. But these fears? Foolishness, what else?

Krishnajoo enlightened his wife, 'Lalli arrived home varkar,
safely. Isn't that extraordinary? The rioters had to hold off their
blows. Even the thick cream atop the bowl of curd she took
with her, even the saffron and almonds that decorated it, were
not disturbed. Isn't this a miracle? Can you understand this?'
In other words, you are so dull witted. Didn't think before you
spoke, as usual.

And this miracle? Was it God's doing or Anand Bayu's?
Anand Bayu, whose round turban and salt and pepper beard
were his distinguishing features. Chanting 'Shiva Shambhu,' the

family priest kept his distance from those who did not follow tradition. Not only did he carry the wisdom of the sacred texts in his small head, but his knowledge of the proprieties was such that he was the only individual allowed unhindered access to every corner of the house, from the women's quarters to the men's sitting room. Shaking his head, counting the knobbly joints of his index and ring fingers with his thumb, he'd done his additions and subtractions and he now announced: 'There is only one auspicious moment, just one. The third day of the Ashadh Shukla Paksh. Send Lalli to her in-laws at 5.30 in the morning with a bowl of curd for good luck. At 5.41 the stars change their position, you know what that means – grave danger!'

'May Lord Ganesha bless us,' Anandjoo doesn't forget to hand out reassurance together with guidance.

'Just observe the proprieties, don't collect a crowd.'

So early in the morning. But there was no other choice. What could Anandjoo do if there was no auspicious moment after this? Lalli was completing her seventh month. The Shastras forbad the performance of the curd ceremony in the eighth month, even novices knew this. There was no need to explain anything to Krishnajoo, a descendant of the sage Dattatreya.

Saraswati had spent much of the night pottering about (no wonder her mother-in-law called her the 'mouse queen'!). Not only did she not sleep but she did not let Lalli rest either. She inspected everything again and again, folded and unfolded the clothes, checked that the pashmina was not moth-eaten, made sure nothing had been left out. The blue dariyai cloth from Kabul, the raffal in a deep rich plum colour and the pashmina jamewar shawl. Dulari had been given a pashmina pheran but Lalli wanted a sari, so Babba bought her a coral pashmina sari.

Girls are indulged while their parents are alive. Who will give them anything later? Lalli was an only child, and her uncle's children were very fond of her. They had not been influenced by Kaliyug, so she did have brothers and sisters, in a manner of speaking. But still…Saraswati's hands were busy as her thoughts leapt across centuries. She peeled almonds that had been soaked in hot water, put out cardamom seeds and pine nuts to decorate the bowl of curd. The letter Om was made up with strands of saffron—this was Lalli's second curd ceremony. May the lord Ram grant her a son this time—there is no scarcity in his house. She had already visited the Bhairav and Chakreshwar temples to plead with the gods to grant her wish. If Lalli gave birth to a son, she would also go to the shrine of Rishi Pir with an offering. They say nothing is impossible if one has the blessings of pirs, pandits and powerful emperors.

Nathji, who slept like Kumbhkaran, woke from a deep slumber only after he had been shaken vigorously. Rubbing his eyes, he peered out of the chinks in the window and saw clouds like little balls of cottonwool hovering above the birch leaf roofs of the Khazanchi house. There was not even the shadow of the sun behind the range of mountains. 'Wait a while kakni, dawn has not yet broken.' Leaving his face uncovered, Nathji curled up and pulled the blanket over him.

Saraswati remembered the story of the three lazy men, Temberkas, Sukhi Aas, and Bakwas. When their home caught fire the first one said, 'Douse the fire', the second turned over and said, 'Leave it, be happy'. The third, irritated at having his sleep interrupted, scolded the other two, 'Stop talking nonsense, and go to sleep quietly.' This story, she thought, was Nathji's story.

The situation was delicate—she had to tread carefully. She said, her tone full of affection, 'My dear, please get up. Balai lagai, may all your troubles come to me. Wash your face and get ready. You have to accompany Lalli.' Saraswati wiped her nose on the sleeve of her pheran and wheedled, 'It will get late my precious, and the auspicious moment will be gone. Just get up. I have made some Kahwa for you with lots of almonds. See how the samovar is steaming.'

Krishnajoo had instructed Rehman, the tongawallah, 'This is a delicate matter Rehmanjoo. Lalli is not well and this is the last auspicious moment for this ceremony. You know the situation is quite tense these days...'

Rehman's father had handed the reins of the tonga to his son when he was only ten, so Rehman had been ferrying passengers for the past fifteen years. He had carried coy, jewellery-laden brides to their impatient husbands on the occasion of Dyar dashmi, and taken the old and the infirm and delicate women about to deliver to the hospital, shielding them from bumps and jolts. God knows, he had never given anyone reason to complain. As Lalli walked unsteadily, supported by her mother and Khurshid, her shot silk pheran with its wide brocade armband shining as she moved, the musky perfume of kasturi wafting along with her, Rehman noticed the little belly between the folds of the burqa and understood Krishnajoo's fatherly anxiety.

'Allah is all-powerful. Don't worry.'

'Yes my son. Why should I worry when you are with them?' Krishnajoo said, for the sake of saying something. What choice did he have? In a moment of crisis one was compelled to address even a donkey as one's father. And then, Rehman was a friend of Natha's. He'd been ready and outside their house before dawn. Other tongawallahs wouldn't stir till the sun was high in the sky and they had eaten their fill. Krishnajoo had tried so hard to get an older tongawallah but without success – had he found one, he would have drawn some comfort from that. Krishnajoo had very little faith in young men.

Even so, by the time Rehman had appeared at the corner of the street it was already half past five. Krishnajoo repeatedly pulled his made-in-Switzerland watch with its Roman numerals out of his pocket and looked at the hands of time run by. He could not stop time's passage even though his name was Krishna. Saraswati, however, seemed quite untroubled and Krishnajoo was surprised by her lack of anxiety.

Saraswati, who generally created a big fuss over minor issues, had already sent Lalli's embroidered shoes and handkerchief over to Gash Kaul's house at 5 am as a token, signifying her departure from her father's house. Once this was done, no hour could be inauspicious. Saraswati was more aware than him of the loopholes devised by the elders to cope with difficult situations. Though the 'knowledgeable' men of the house pitied the female mind, the women provided ample evidence of their commonsense.

There was no escape for Nathji. He must accompany his sister Lalli. Cupping some water in his palms he sprinkled it on his face and brushed his teeth. He wrapped a dussa over his pheran and got busy loading the heavy globes of crystallized sugar, the baskets of nankhatai biscuits, the earthenware trays of curds and a small trunk of clothes in the back of the tonga. As her mother and nurse helped Lalli into the tonga, her cousins Radha and Batni placed pillows behind her and affectionately asked her to lean back and be comfortable.

No outsider had been invited for the occasion. Krishnajoo said, 'Take her carefully son. Stop and pay obeisance at the Sheetalnath temple,' thus informing Rehman and Lalli about his anxiety and their duties at the same time. Saraswati reminded them that they had to pick up the shoes and handkerchief from Gash Kaul's house.

Patting the horse's flanks Rehman cajoled her, 'Let us go, Sultana. Move, slowly, tih, tih, tih, don't hurry, we have to take sister Lalli home safely.'

Standing a little distance from Gash Kaul's threshold, Saraswati and Bhadra kept chanting the Sharika mantra and watched the tonga until it disappeared round the corner. If by chance a cat or a woman crossed the path of the tonga or some idiot sneezed, they would worry. Look! There was Sula the sweeper! If he passed the tonga on the right, it would be an excellent omen. Mother Sharika, have mercy, they prayed.

Khurshid waved her hand reassuringly. Have faith in God and remember I am also with her.

Turning around, they crossed the courtyard and stepped onto the threshold of their home. A few drops of rain fell on Saraswati's neck near her zooji, the long embroidered piece of tulle, which hung down from the taranga on her head. She looked anxiously at the sky. It opened its fist and the slow drizzle changed into a torrential downpour. A frisson of fear touched her. This unseasonal rain!

'Dear Shri Ram, My Lalli is in your care,' she said.

Krishnajoo, moved by some premonition of impending disaster, recited mantras meant to keep trouble away. What else could he do?

A little distance away, Rehman looked up at the sky and stopped the tonga to take shelter under the copse of trees near the Berikunj. Nathji helped him wrap a tarpaulin around the tonga, securing it by tying it to the seats so that Lalli, with her bangle laden arms, was protected. Lightning is always attracted to gold. It is feminine after all!

Rehman thought they could shelter under the eaves of Neel Gurtu's house for a while. This was just a momentary downpour, like a spat between a long married couple. The argument would be over in a few minutes.

As they moved again, the horse, spooked by the flashes of lightning, began to race. Khurshid scolded Rehman, 'Are you being chased by dacoits Rehmana? Racing with the wind! Even my back is hurting with all these jolts and jerks and you are carrying this young girl who is in such a delicate condition. At least think of her.'

Khurshid was Lalli's nurse. The pain of the one who nurtures a child is greater than that of one who gives birth. But it wasn't Rehman's fault. The sky and the earth were being lashed by rain. There was darkness all around. Sheets of water made it impossible to see the road ahead. A horse is also a living being after all. It stumbled as it swerved to avoid a hole in the ground and Khurshid started scolding him again. Rehman was in a difficult situation.

But there was worse to come, and it happened soon enough. At the Berikunj mazar 40 or 50 men, shouting 'Allaho Akbar' suddenly appeared from behind a little hillock and leapt towards the tonga. First only their dark shapes were visible and then the entire band of ruffians appeared, completely drenched by the rain.

'May Allah have pity on us,' Rehman's face was pale with fear. Khurshid pulled Lalli's head down to her chest and covered it with a blanket, 'Don't worry, daughter, nothing will happen. These rogues will go away very soon.' Lalli anxiously put her arms around her unborn child.

Looking at Rehman and Khurshid Nathji stammered, 'Move the tonga forward. It isn't safe to stop here.'

As the rioters came closer Rehman pulled the reins of the horse, 'Tih...tih..tih, well done Sultana, well done. Come on my tiger.' But Sultana or tiger, unimpressed by the praise, jibbed at the downpour and the noise of the mob and when Rehman pulled harder at the reins she reared up and started kicking. Rehman was in a quandry. What should he do? If he waited, the troublemakers would be upon them. If he tried to drive away, Sultana could overturn the carriage with her bucking and if anything happened to Lalli, he might as well be dead. Caught between the devil and the deep sea Rehman, in desperation, turned to Lalli, 'Hold on to the arm of the seat tightly, sister. Once these sons of ...move away then....'

Nathji was helpless, with one hand he patted his sister, trying to reassure her and with the other tried to save the pots of curds from getting smashed.

Two burly men, who were almost mowed down by the tonga, shouted, 'You idiot, you want to kill yourself? Don't you know you have to attend the rally today?' One of them banged his staff on the wooden shaft of the tonga, the other moved towards the wheel, 'Break the wheel, the bastard will understand when everything crashes to the ground.'

A six-footer dressed in a pathani salwar kameez, snatched the reins away from Rehman, 'Get down you…who is sitting at the back? Open the tarpaulin, you mother….'

Rehman barely escaped being elbowed off the tonga. Khurshid now took command, 'Brother, I am taking my daughter to the hospital. She has started her pains. Let us go for god's sake. All of you have sisters and mothers.' Lalli broke into soft sobs under the protective tarpaulin. The six-footer moved the tarpaulin and peeped inside the tonga. Lalli, enveloped in her burqa, clung to Khurshid and Nathji and whimpered with fear.

'You don't believe me? You want to pull off the burqa and look at your sister's face?' The broody hen prepared to protect her chick fiercely, 'You don't believe me. God has given you eyes, take a look and satisfy yourselves.'

The tall man, taken aback by the challenging note in Khurshid's voice, looked at her face, taut and red with anger as she clutched the sobbing, expectant mother protectively to her side.

'Let them go,' the man gestured to his companions. The tone of his voice had changed completely and become calm.

Lalli's tears, Khurshid's threatening tone, the miracle of a woman about to become a mother (or perhaps rioters in those days had some scruples!)—Rehman was instructed by the lathi wielder, 'Not this way, go back via the Sathu bund. The procession will be coming this way.'

'Thank God.' Khurshid raised her hands in gratitude. 'Turn the tonga around and go with confidence. Now there is no fear. The ruffians have gone away.'

A gust of wind blew in and away, leaving behind the dust of fear. Natha slowly released the breath that had been lodged in his throat all this while. 'Why this turmoil, Rehman bhai?'

Rehman coughed, taking his face out from beneath his blanket. This Nathji Kaul would always remain the juvenile Natha! He had no idea what was happening around him. He was lost in his own world, but what could one say, he was a friend after all. 'All these people are going to the Khankai Mohalla. There is a speech today.'

'Wastrels,' Khurshid said angrily, 'An idle person always finds something to keep himself busy. Loitering about early morning! Will a worker worry about his daily bread or will he listen to a lecture and become a leader?'

Nathji looked at Rehman's face. A round cap covered half the eyes above a nose as straight and sharp as a dagger and a tongue perpetually in motion, 'Move ahead, move, slowly, slowly. Don't hurry, we are not going to war.' His voice rose in unprovoked annoyance. Nathji was taken aback. 'Khankai mohalla', the name rang a bell. Yesterday, Kaklal had mentioned something. There was some meeting or rally there today. People were giving lectures about self-rule at various places. They didn't want the rule of the king. There was a strange tension in the air.

The wave of fear had crested and then receded. Lalli was now dozing, resting her head on Khurshid's lap, her body still shaken by soft sobs.

On the birch leaf roofs of the houses the short green grass moved gently in the light rain. The doors and windows were shut tight. Now and again, a thin, wisp of smoke would escape through a crack in a window, a sign that there was life inside. The rain had almost stopped. On the silent wet road, the clip clop of the horse's hooves kept rhythm with the ringing of the bells on the collar around its neck. The tonga splashed through puddles and pools on the wet road raising fountains of muddy water.

Why was Rehman so quiet today? There were lines of tension on his forehead or perhaps the cap was pushing down on his eyes. The very atmosphere was tense, but what did Rehman have to do with it? Why was there a note of unwarranted annoyance in his voice?

'It has never been so cold in the month of Ashadh, sister,' Nathji said, to divert attention or perhaps to push away his own anxiety.

'Yes, the weather has been rather unpredictable this time. It seems the winter ahead is going to be very severe. The signs are not good,' Khurshid commented, lifting the corner of the tarpaulin and looking out at the row of boats moored along the bank of the river.

Silence once again, broken only by the duet of jingling bells and the tapping of horse's hooves. The tonga traversed the bund at Sathu and when it came alongside the temple of Shri Ramchandra, Lalli bowed her head and folded her hands in prayer. The beautiful leaves of the chinar standing in the courtyard wore deep green and whispered in the wind as if conspiring with each other.

Unbelievably empty streets. A stray Pandit with a small towel thrown over the shoulder of his pheran, mumbling some mantras under his breath, was making his way to the Vitasta, or perhaps he was heading to the temple after bathing in the river.

'I can't see any Batnis, going to Hari Parbat today.'

'It's raining.'

'Women who go to pray to the goddess Sharika don't change their routine even when it snows.'

Rehman was silent.

'Perhaps it's because of this meeting.'

'You're probably right.'

'What do you mean, probably? I am right. That *is* the reason. What's a political meeting? Just an opportunity for all the rogues and ruffians to get together. In fact, when they band together, they even forget who their mothers and sisters are. At such times women from good families have no choice but to sit at home or be humiliated if they go out…'

Khurshid's words had little impact. The worm of fear was wriggling its way into everyone's hearts. There was no knowing what disaster lay in wait for them around the next corner. Despite his bravado, Nathji was looking like a scared mouse. Khurshid, however, knew how to sparkle like a lamp in the dark. A brave woman, she looked at Nathji and said, in an attempt to cheer him up, 'Nathjooa, Rehman had his fill of feasting yesterday at the grain parcher's house. His stomach must be hurting. He will only be able to talk once he has relieved himself.'

Rehman smiled faintly, as though laughter was forbidden. Nathji realized that it wasn't just the world around them but also the mind of the normally lighthearted Rehman that was full of turmoil and confusion.

The Curd Ceremony

Ayodhyanath's entire family had gathered in the living room. The men were sitting near the window on carpets and leaning against bolsters, the women sat in a circle on rush mats and namdas spread out near the kitchen. There were separate areas and different limits that were set for men and women. They could always be crossed by men but never by women. These were the traditions of the family, and honour, dignity and happiness were inextricably bound up with them. In this house, whenever two or three men gathered together (something that happened often), no sooner were the preliminaries done that they would launch into heated discussions on everything – the rule of the Maharaja and the merits and demerits of the British masters, the moderates and the liberals and the prospect of self rule, the beautiful spring day in 1919 that turned into a bloody massacre at Jallianwala bagh with the clatter of guns and the hail of bullets.

'Bhai, that is why there was a wave of anger across the country. When Gandhiji suggested non-cooperation in 1921, Lala Lajpat Rai was absolutely against it.'

'That's understandable, after all, everyone was full of anger. There is a limit to oppression, bhai.'

They'd talk about the young rebels. Bhagat Singh, Azaad, Sukhdev, Rajguru. How was it possible that hot blood would not boil over? And the Nehrus – their own people. There was a sense of pride in talking about them: it was the brilliance of Nehru's ancestor Pandit Raj Kaul which prompted the Mughal ruler Farrokhsiyar to invite him to move from Kashmir to Delhi in 1713. He was appointed to a high post and given lands.

'And Motilal Nehru, Jawaharlal's father, was a barrister – what an honour that was! And what a man – despite being born into the luxuries of Anand Bhavan, the pull of the freedom struggle was so strong that he left all that and joined Gandhi. And what a bonfire they made of foreign clothes!' This from Balbhadra, and said with such pride, almost as if he had just set fire to a bundle of foreign cloth himself.

'Jawaharlal's mother Swaroop Rani and his wife Kamala did not lag behind either,' Ayodhyanath added. When Nehru emerged as a new leader, Kashmiris showered blessings on him. What the father could not accomplish, they said, the son has achieved.

Discussions on current affairs were accompanied by fierce intellectual debate. And all this was made so much more enjoyable by the frequent cups of fragrant kehwa, and the chance to take deep pulls of aromatic tobacco.

Today, however, Ayodhyanath was disturbed by the wave of anger sweeping through the city, a dissonance which could grab one by the throat any moment. Some people had revolted against the government and were demanding self-rule. Whether or not their demands were legitimate was not the issue right now. Rather, the problem was that their inflammatory speeches and slogans provided rogues and ruffians with an opportunity to create mayhem and loot and kill with impunity. At such times everyone was vulnerable, women much more so. Which is why everyone would heave a sigh of relief once daughter-in-law Lalli was safely inside her home.

In their homes, as women worked, they exchanged news about everyone, they shared their joys and sorrows, gifts and gossip about the neighbourhood.

'Mohammad, the marriage broker, goes to Jankinath Trisal's house, could you ask him to look out for a suitable match for our Janaki?'

'Arre! What are you waiting for? The girl has almost come of age.'

'Look at that! You know, when they say "A girl is not a burden for her uncle but for the entire village", it's really true. My daughter isn't all that old. With the grace of God she belongs to a prosperous family so she looks older than her age.'

'Arre Behenji, why do you misunderstand me? A girl is like a vine and can grow on the roof overnight, what's there to be upset about?'

'Sister, if you are upset you can pull out my tongue. Isn't your Tulsi just like my Chunni? What I meant was that it isn't an easy task to find the right boy. You have to check the family and match the horoscopes. You are sensible. You know getting a good groom is not as easy as plucking fruit from a tree, you can't bring one down just by throwing a stone!'

'Yes, you are right. Everyone has daughters, everyone knows these things.'

Today, on the occasion of Lalli's curd ceremony, Sona bua, her children, Mangala masi from Vicharnag, various nieces and women from the neighbourhood had all come over for a meal. There were no disturbances on this side of town, merely a hint of discord in the air. So naturally, everyone was discussing Lalli's baby's celebration. Mangala masi waited for the appropriate moment when she could start a discourse.

'When I had my curd ceremony, there was a wazwan, a banquet, in the house. Kaknidedi not only called all the relatives but also sent invitations to the entire neighbourhood from Badyar to Kharyar. Nearly two hundred women came, and for months afterwards they talked about the wonderful feast.'

'We didn't skimp on anything when it was Nanni's turn either.' Baddadi was not going to allow anyone to challenge her status. She still wore a three stranded taalraz and a dejharu, made of nearly five ounces of twenty four carat gold. Anyone looking at her was suitably bedazzled.

'We cooked every kind of dish. Roghan josh, Kaliya, Shami kebab, Tabaqnaat and fifteen vegetarian dishes. Tathya (Ayodhyanath) went personally to Manasbal to buy nadru, lotus root, for the Yakhni.'

'But today we couldn't do much…'

'You are right. In this turmoil it'll be enough if Lalli gets home safely.'

'Prabha, there is some commotion outside, maybe it's Lalli. Arre, children, why are you making so much noise? Sit down and play quietly…'

'All right, ma. Come on, Prabha, let's play okus bokus.'

'Okus bokus tilvan chokus, onum batukh lodum deg.' Dulari chanted as she tapped the fingers of all the outstretched hands till her index finger stopped at Prabha's hand.

'There! Prabha is the thief! Now let's play catch.'

There was a sound outside. 'Who is it…?'

Many eyes and ears were turned towards the door. Jialal masterji, the teacher, came in looking worried and agitated. His brow was beaded with sweat despite the cold.

'People have gone mad! An enormous crowd has collected on Habbakadal bridge. I took shelter in Kishan Bazaz's shop when I heard the slogans. All the shopkeepers pulled their shutters down as soon as they heard angry voices raising the cry of 'Nalaye takbir.' There was unbelievable confusion. Somehow, by the grace of God, I managed to make my way through the crowd. The mob was so agitated anyone could have fallen and been crushed and no one would have cared. What a day you have chosen Ayodhya bhai, for the ceremony! Count yourself lucky if your daughter-in-law gets home safely with the grace of Lord Shiva-Shambhu.'

Ayodhyanath took a long pull at the hookah and handed the pipe to Jialal. Blue veins had started throbbing under the thin skin of his wheatish brow. He was not used to listening to criticism. No one could have imagined that the situation would get out of hand so fast. Even a seasoned, worldly-wise man like Ayodhyanath could not guess the way the wind was blowing. Whatever happened now they would have to deal with it.

Perturbed and irritated, he shouted at Mahdu, 'Is this tobacco or cow-dung? Have you mixed in the khamir properly? What do all of you do the whole day?'

Balbhadra took a deep pull at the hukka. There was nothing wrong with the tobacco, Ayodhya was just worried about his daughter-in-law.

It was a matter of concern, even Mahdu understood that. Lalli was almost in the final stage of her pregnancy. Suppose she got caught up in the crowd and was pushed around? Why were all these rituals so important? This was something he could not understand.

Balbhadra knew how to distract everyone's attention, 'I don't recall anything like this happening during my entire life, Ayodhya bhai. Though I have read about people living through periods of fear and oppression and how they raised their voices against tyranny. But this?'

In other words what were they protesting against this time? It wasn't only Balbhadra but others as well who were troubled by this question. They had experienced the benevolent rule of Maharaja Pratap Singh. Would there ever be another king who cared so much for his people? He wouldn't touch a morsel in the morning before he said his prayers and gave alms to the poor and needy and the Brahmins. And now they had Maharaja Hari Singh. He wasn't as religious as his father but the people faced no real difficulties. Then why this commotion?

It's not as if there weren't any problems though. That, after all, was why people were protesting, and many were also influenced by the turmoil the nation was going through. The cacophony of voices raised against landlords under the leadership of Ramachandra in Maharashtra had spread from Pratapgarh to Bengal like wildfire, taking in Bihar and Avadh on the way. Despite the tyranny of the British, Gandhi and Nehru had also joined the oppressed peasants, so why should our valley hold back? Though it was true that the revolt had taken more than ten years to reach here. The British Residents exercised strict control over Indian princely states and news of the struggle raging through the rest of the country reached the valley only after being censored. Among the many voices which echoed in the valley, the voice that had the sharpest edge was that of Sheikh Mohammad Abdullah. Prem Nath Bazaz said of him that he was the one who taught dumb, oppressed peasants to speak.

People were curious, 'Who is this fearless young man?'

'He is the son of Sheikh Mohammad Ibrahim, the shawl dealer from Saura.'

'He has just returned after completing his MSc in Chemistry from Aligarh Muslim University. He has the fire of youth in his veins and a mind full of revolutionary thoughts.'

'He was a student of Professor Pandit in SP college,' Balbhadra said, adding, 'and he's taken on the task of freeing the state from the chains of monarchy. He is demading equal rights for everyone.'

Freedom? What freedom? From the British or the king? From our own people or from outsiders? The Brahmins shivered with fear. They were a people who had lived in the shadow of fear since they experienced the tyrannical rule of Sikandar Butshikan and the cruelty of the Afghan rulers. Time had tested their resilience again and again. They had found a measure of peace during the rule of the Sikhs and the Dogras. Now what was going to happen?

What was the point of unnecessarily throwing a stone into a calm pool? But if one set of people were comfortable during the Dogra rule what about the others? A difficult question.

The sound of a tonga stopping outside brought all discussion to an end. Sona jumped up and saw Lalli bhabi and Khurshid stepping out of the tonga. She shouted joyfully, 'Bhabi's here Kakni! Lalli bhabi's here!' The men heard her shout and bowed their heads in thankfulness and congratulated each other. Mahdu filled the chillum with fresh tobacco without being asked and started blowing on it. Prithvi Dhar pulled the hookah towards him, praising the first chillum of the morning. Now they drew on the hookah with a sense of satisfaction. The pipe moved from Ayodhyanath to Balbhadra, Balbhadra to Jialal and from Jialal back to Ayodhyanath, filling the room with its fragrance. All worries now vanished from their minds.

'Take the water for the alath daughter,' the elderly Baddadi called out, reminding the ebullient Sona of the traditional welcome ritual.

After circling Lalli's head with a lota full of water three times, Sona bua asked her to put her left foot forward as she stepped into the house. Before taking Lalli to Baddadi she hugged her so hard that Lalli's breath was almost sqeezed out of her. Baddadi thanked Lord Mahaganapati with moist eyes when she saw that her daughter-in-law had arrived safe and sound. She felt as though a heavy weight had been lifted off her chest. Blessings were given. 'May the wishes of both the sisters-in law be fulfilled. Sona is also in the family way. May both children be granted their wishes.' Rehman and Khurshid helped Nathji to stack the platters of curd, the colourful baskets decorated with bells and full of bakirkhani bread, and the trunk with Lalli's clothes in a corner outside the kitchen. Immediately, all the children started hovering around these. 'What's in these? Takhtachi?'

'No, there must be sweet kulchas.'

'No, no there will be crisp bakirkhanis…sugar balls, dates, almonds and apricots.'

Once everyone had settled down, Ayodhyanath asked after Krishnajoo Kaul's family, and about the journey. 'We heard there were a lot of disturbances that side, I hope you didn't face any trouble?'

Nathji raised his eyes heavenwards and folded his hands, 'It was just the blessings of Lord Rama otherwise anything could have happened….'

Khurshid quickly intervened. She took over the narrative and related a spiced up version of the events.

'What can I say Bedmeiji! May any evils stay far away from Lalli, our golden girl. It is almost as though she has been re-born. Those awful rogues stopped the tonga in the middle of the road, lifted the tarpaulin and stuck their heads inside and stared so hard that Lalli's heart started galloping. You could hear it thudding a yard away. To tell you the truth, I felt as though I had no life in me but somehow I gathered my courage for the sake of this child. So, Dedi, I hid Lalli in the folds of the pheran, held her against my chest and shouted so loudly at those ruffians that they were quite taken aback. Then who would have the nerve to touch any of us? I would have hit them. That was it, they ran off like dogs with their tails between their legs.'

Ayodhyanath called out towards the kitchen. 'Is the kehwa

ready or is everyone too busy talking? Make a strong kehwa with lots of almonds and cardamom. Put in some saffron and cinnamon as well. They must be cold after the journey.'

When Lalli sat down on a soft mattress in the circle of women, shielding her eyes with the brocade sleeve of her pheran, all the girls came and surrounded her. Lalli took out fistfuls of sugar balls, dates and almonds and gave them to the children. Sharika, Prabha, Tulsi gazed wide-eyed at their aunt who was behaving like a bride, 'She works around the house everyday, how has she become a bride today?'

Elder sister Shanti explained, 'Bhabi is bringing a brother for little Nanni, that is why she is feeling shy.'

'Sooo…where is the brother? Where?' Tulsi tried to lift Lalli's hem in her eagerness, 'Has she hidden him here?' Immediately she got a tight slap from her mother.

Sona jigri doubled up with laughter as she fetched the kangri from the kitchen with Shanta. The firepot was full of glowing coals and she took a pinch of aromatic Isband and touched it to Lalli's forehead and put it in the kangri. With a sputtering of the seeds clouds of smoke rose and filled the room. 'I want my gift, grandmother! Kakni, open your purse strings. This time Sona is going to ask for a gold necklace, a chandan haar!'

'Yes, yes, why not, sisters-in law have the right to ask for gifts. May there always be elders to give you whatever you ask for. May you always be fortunate.'

Baddadi, Kamala, and the women of the neighbourhood touched the foreheads of the men, women and children with a pinch of Isband and then put it on the glowing coals, 'May all evil be gone, Baddadi, congratulations. Tatyaji, posht, may your daughter-in-law live long and bear sons, may her forehead always be held high….! Felicitations to you too, sister Khurshid and to all the little ones, the young girls and the daughters-in-law. Keshavnath! You are the most important person today, why are you feeling shy?'

In the middle of the hustle and bustle, Baddadi called out, 'If the vaer is ready put it in a thali and bring it out. Place a little bit outside for the birds. Don't forget to put water out for them. They have been hovering around for a long time.'

'Have the children eaten, Janaki?'

'Give the men tea and bakirkhanis, Shanta. We have to see the gifts which have come from daughter-in-law's house as well, Kamala.'

Putting down his cup of tea Nathji took out a purse full of rupees from his pocket. He handed them over to Badadi and started reciting, 'Double atgat –twenty rupees, alath-rupees eleven, salt and bread-rupees fifteen, curds-fifteen trakh, panch jins baki nagad....'

'It is more than enough, may God grant you health. Enough. God bless you. Ask Krishnajoo why he has taken so much trouble. May Lalli's father be blessed with a long life. This is the second shagan after all, not the first. Don't we have daughters too?'

All the ceremonies of the homecoming were complete. Nathji, Rehman and sister Khurshid were urged to eat well. Once they were done, they were given a little money before they left. Khurshid would stay the night. Whatever was happening outside could continue, inside all was well.

And yet, was it really? In a world which changes every moment, how long could this state of contentment last? That day, it was late by the time Lalli went to her room to sleep. Baddadi kept indicating to Sona and Janaki that they should take Lalli away. Her back must be hurting sitting bent over the whole day. She needed to relax a little. But Lalli didn't want to go. The girls drummed on the tumbaknari till late at night and sang auspicious songs. If Lalli had got up in the middle of the gathering while the elders were still sitting, it would have been taken as a sign of disrespect. So she remained there till Khurshid caught her hands and pulled her up from the mattress.

'Get up, don't be stubborn. Baddadi is giving you permission to go! Right now you don't have to think about yourself but about the little one you are carrying.'

Lalli really was very tired. The baby was moving about awkwardly, shifting its little hands and feet. When she got to the room Keshavnath had already been asleep for a while, a sort of broken and unsatisfactory sleep as he waited for his wife to appear. He was also a little angry. The elders have these strange customs, rituals which must be followed even at the cost of one's life. Was this any time to observe these rituals? In any case he felt the curd ceremony was just a farce, announcing to the whole world that your son had proved his masculinity by impregnating his wife.

'This is a custom,' Lalli said as she collapsed on the bed.

'What custom? We have made these customs, we can change them as well.'

'Can you say this to Tathya?' Lalli challenged her husband.

Keshav could not say any of this to his father. He could not register his protest. He just didn't have the courage. Lalli didn't need to be told that the barrier of deference was not meant only for women. Keshav did not even pick up Nanni in front of Tathya. Cuddling her was an impossibility. He carefully tucked the ends of the quilt under Lalli and she could not help smiling.

'Where are you off to, Professor sahib?'

'I am right here. You are tired. You had so much trouble on the way, and I was also getting worried waiting for you. Suppose something had happened to you?'

If anything had happened to Lalli who kept his world secure under her wings, Keshav would have been left bereft and alone under the naked sky. Lalli was the centre of Keshav's universe. Shiv bhaiya often joked, 'It is good that in our family there is at least one man who is a devotee of his wife.'

'It is good,' Shiv bhaiya repeated this phrase with a glance at his wife Kamala which appeared to indicate that there really was nothing good in Keshav's life. After dividing women into separate categories of mother, daughter, sister, daughter-in-law and mother-in-law, the 'wife' remains: despite being captivating and charming to her husband she is just a 'vessel' after all! Shiv bhaiya had the unshakeable belief that this was the role that bound a husband to his wife. Everything else was immaterial.

What could Keshav say, he was a 'henpecked' husband after all, running around after his wife. Keshav himself did not know how much his wife meant to him.

'What could have happened to me?' Lalli held Keshav's hand tightly in hers. 'You were praying for me…'

She kissed Keshav and closed her eyes. Keshav wanted to gather his wife close to him. He could not behave like an ascetic having been away from Lalli for so many months. But he had to curb his passions. Lalli's face was showing signs of fatigue as she slept. A body tired and exhausted with the weight of pregnancy! Keshav softly kissed his wife's forehead and patted her little round stomach.

Once Lalli put her head on the pillow she fell into such deep sleep, that she wasn't even aware of breathing till the morning. The aggression of the rioters, the way they pushed aside the tarpaulin and stuck their heads inside, the blows they rained on the shafts of the tonga, the rude words they used, all these had penetrated into the innermost depths of her mind. She was floating along, buffeted by the waves in a frighteningly huge and labyrinthine lake. Bloated corpses were floating all around her. The sky was full of eagles and vultures beating their wings. With shrieking cries vultures would cartwheel and swoop down on the bodies, tear off chunks of flesh and fly off again. One held an eye in its beak and another a pair of lips. In the middle of this terrifying darkness, the waves in the lake were rising high. Lalli wanted to scream but her voice refused to come out of her throat. Numb with fear, she was also swept along with the dead bodies. Some fearsome demon was doing a dance of death under the lake. Had she descended into some blood-drenched hell? Around her were decapitated bodies and on the shore there was a mob of terrified people stumbling and running desperately. Where were they going, shouting frantically for help? Jalodbhav! Jalodbhav! Strange voices seem to pour into Lalli's ears like molten lead. Has the demon Jalodbhav once again invaded Satisar? Oh! Who is going to kill him? Kashyapa, the father of Kadura and Kayoora's sons, is sitting in deep meditation on the top of the mountain. Is the sea of voices reaching him? 'Arre, help someone, help...'

With a smothered shriek Lalli woke up. The warm rays of the sun were falling on her face through the window. She was breathing heavily and her throat felt completely dry. It had been such a frightening dream, she might even have shouted out. Her heart was heavy with fear. When she noticed that the bed next to hers was empty she got up quickly, opened the window and saluted the Vitasta flowing outside. She narrated her nightmare. The elders said that you should tell mother Vitasta all your bad dreams for she is the one who can free us from all our sins and fears.

She had slept so deeply that she had no idea when Keshav had woken up. She had been dead to the world the entire night, it had been such strange sleep. Her spine was hurting terribly and then this terrifying dream. It was as though the story of Jalodbhav, which she had heard as a child, had come alive. Lalli put on her pheran on top of her kurta and as she went down the stairs her heart almost stopped at the sounds of lamentation and crying coming from the vot. She pushed aside all the fears that filled her mind and tried to convince herself that the voices she heard were just a figment of her overwrought imagination.

But no, her ears had not misheard. As she came down step by step, the wails of Baddadi, Kamala bhabi, Janakimaal and many others assaulted her heart like hammers. With shaking knees the traumatized Lalli made her way down, holding on to the wall for support. This was not a dream. What could have happened so suddenly? Who would it be? The fear of disaster made her dumb. God, have mercy!

Yes, an unexpected disaster had occurred. People said, 'Misfortune doesn't give any indication of its arrival.' why should it have been different this time? Yesterday, at the very moment when Sona was asking God to bless her sister-in-law with a long and happy marriage, asking for gifts and singing celebratory songs on the tumbaknari, terrorists were hacking her husband to bits in the village of Pattan. At dawn Sona's brother-in-law hammered on the door and shouted out the horrifying news from the street.

'Bhai has been slaughtered by the rioters.'

Sona, who was fast asleep, woke up abruptly when she heard her mother screaming. Rubbing her eyes in surprise she looked around. 'What's wrong? Why are you shouting like this?' Beating her breasts, Baddadi called out to her son-in-law, 'What is this thunderbolt that has fallen on us?' So, the mountain fell on Sona. However high her forehead might have been, it inevitably bowed under the blow.

So much had happened and Lalli did not even know.

'How could we tell you child?' Khurshid said sprinkling water on Lalli, who had fainted. She rubbed the soles of her feet and said, 'You are close to your time, God forbid something should happen to you!'

'What can happen to me? Whatever had to happen has happened already. Our daughter Sona is ruined.' The auspicious songs sung by Sona were still echoing in the corners of the house. The manner in which she had jokingly asked for the chandanhaar and how she had hugged Lalli tightly! This dear friend and sister-in-law, who whispered shared jokes in Lalli's ears and filled her life with the warmth of affection, how would Lalli be able to bear her sorrow? It was difficult to control Sona who had been battering her head against the walls ever since she became conscious. Shivnath and Keshav held her by the arms and tried to restrain her.

No one had bothered to change. Everyone was busy trying to look after Sona, though even three people together could not calm her down. It was essential to take her home because the body would be brought there. All the rituals had to be performed, however heartless they might appear. According to custom, the women could not go to Sona's house because mourning had to be observed in her paternal home as well. After all Madhav was the only son-in-law of the house. Khurshid, however, did accompany Sona. But where was the dead body? The rioters had cut Madhavjoo, who was a state official, a patwari, into pieces and it was difficult to gather these together in the middle of all the panic and rioting.

Sona's husband Madhav had been sacrificed at the altar of the anger and resentment aroused by inflammatory speeches on self-rule and the eruption of an illogical desire for instant change. The government belonged to the king and within a few days every government official was being seen as an enemy of the public. Madhav was killed because he was a representative of the king and the government, an official who was bound to follow the rules.

Madhav had gone, leaving Sona behind with his children. The brave little golden bird who used to fly as high as the tallest branches of the kikar tree had lost her voice. Such a claustrophobic cloud arose, like a mushroom sprouting out of the earth, that Sona could not even breathe. Her world, once full of joy and anticipation, would now be under a lifelong pall of mourning. Sona, twenty five years old, the only younger sister of two brothers, a jewel among pearls. Sona, whom her sisters-in-law called the golden girl, whose brocade cap used to be decorated with gold and silver ornaments when she was a child, had been transformed into an inert corpse.

'Who has stolen the sun and the moon from your brocade cap?' Baddadi's laments were heartrending enough to tear open the hearts of the mountains.

Ma mourned for the girl who had been raised with so much love. Tathya would never even allow a fly to settle on her eyelids. Even Madhav had spread his dreams under Sona's feet. So much love that a girl could even forget her parental home. For her wedding, instead of a pheran, she was gifted a sari made from an entire bolt of real brocade. Sona was bent over under the weight of a choker, chapkal, snake headed bangles weighing more than two hundred and fifty grams and a three-stranded taalraz. Viewers were bedazzled. Sona was very fortunate, she would rule over her household.

But the brilliance of Sona's eyes was far more beautiful than the sheen of gold. Once at her in-law's house she was not permitted to spend even two days at her mother's home when she returned after the roth khabar, the traditional gifts of sweet bread, sugar and dry fruits which are sent to the groom's house a few days after the wedding. Messages were sent twice asking her parents to send Sona back. After this Sona was not able to come home for months. Why? Because the girl was already totally engrossed in her household duties. Baddadi would complain, though her eyes reflected her happiness, 'A new bride is expected to travel between her parental and marital homes – after all this is the age to enjoy oneself. Once her family responsibilities increase she won't even have time to look out of the window.'

But what can Madhav do? The entire house feels like a desert once Sona leaves.

His friends laughed and joked and tried to make him understand. His sister-in-law could not really say much, but she often warned Sona, 'This romantic Laila-Majnu kind of love is unlucky for a man, Sona. Why does he get so agitated, it is not as though you are running away. Try to make him understand, you are his wife after all.'

What can Sona do? It is impossible to convince Madhav. Then Madhav was posted to Pattan and everyone heaved a sigh of relief, 'Now he will learn a little patience.'

But who had any patience? Madhav was back home on the third day. Sona was just about to get under the quilt after dinner when she heard the familiar sound of someone clearing his throat outside the window and there was Madhav with his bag, on the verandah! 'There, he has arrived, even the snow can't stop him. Such impatience!' Bhabi would get irritated and bhaiya would smile.

Within five years Sona became the mother of two children. Now after a gap of three years she was pregnant again. In this condition, how could she live alone in the village with two small children? This was what the elders felt. But Madhav argued that he would worry about the children while he was away.

Bhabi said, 'Do I trouble your beloved? Just ask her.'

'No, no bhabi,' Madhav would touch his ears in apology. 'It is nothing like that, its just that I don't feel happy without the children.'

'Take your golden bird with you this time. Don't make the children an excuse. Why don't you just say that you are like Nagrai in the folk-tale and can't live without your Himal? You have a nursemaid already and you can employ a cook. You are an officer after all. Don't keep travelling miles and miles through storms in a tonga! I will get into trouble if anything untoward happens. Everyone will blame me and say that I couldn't bear to see your happiness. No bhaiya, there is no need for all this!'

But Sona never joined Madhav. She kept making preparations that were rejected by fate. Who can understand the workings of destiny? The fate of Sona, who had a voice as sweet as honey, was written with coal. Everyone had his or her opinion. The world changed for Sona.

Shivnath and Keshav went, under police protection, with Madhav's brother, to the village to collect Madhav's remains. The dismembered body was put together on the bier in the shape of Madhav. Sona wailed, beating her breasts till they were bloody, 'Let me see his face. Why have you covered it with a white shroud, he won't be able to breathe.' Pulling at the cloth she insisted on seeing her husband's face. Even a prisoner condemned to death is permitted his last wish, why has Sona's family become so hard hearted? She just wants to have a last glimpse, just one. Allowing her just a glimpse of Madhav's intact right hand, her terrified and grieving sisters-in-law forcibly picked her up and pulled her away from the corpse. Suppose she touches it in her anguish and the dismembered parts fall to the ground, how will Sona be able to bear it? They were not stone hearted, how would they be able to control her?

But Sona was not a prisoner condemned to hanging and her life did not end once her last wish had been granted. Nor was she such a child that she would not recognize the ugly face of reality. A mother of two children with a third on its way, Sona realized she had to survive without Madhav. With Madhav's children as her only support. But she could never fill the gap between knowledge and acceptance. She never became the Sona she was earlier. Moving ahead step by step she embarked on a long tiring journey and was never at ease till she drew her last breath. Days passed and the years slipped through her fingers like sand but Madhav's memories did not leave her. She could not forget. With whom could she share the sorrow and agony of her mind and body? Who can one blame if the pearl necklace around one's neck is stolen? Her heart and mind continued to mourn.

Efforts were made to bring peace to Madhav's soul. His ashes were immersed in Haridwar, shradhs were performed, alms given to Brahmins, food to the poor, clothes, food, diyas were distributed and thousands of shanti paths or prayers for peace were held. Anand Bayu himself came and recited the first eighteen adhyayas of the *Bhagvatgita* within a month of Madhav's demise. On the thirteenth day all the members of the family gathered in the large hall to hear a discourse on the Gita.

Why have you abandoned me, my beloved. Come back to me. You took off on your blue horse without realizing that I, who was walking, would never be able to catch up with you. Sona kept walking till her feet were bloodied and the rider of the blue horse spread his wings and took off into space. Her grief threw a pall of gloom over Ayodhyanath's house as well. Baddadi could not bear the sorrow of her granddaughter but even those wise people who accept death as the final truth cannot stop the march of time.

The Birth of a Girl

Flowing along in this stream of life, Lalli went into labour. For two days she grappled with mild cramps and intense bouts of excruciating pain. And then everything came to a standstill. Lalli thought that perhaps she had caught a chill. Her Kakni called these false pains. It was better not to trouble anyone needlessly. Khurshid was a great talker, she would create a furore if she had even a faint idea of her condition.

When her mother-in-law noticed Lalli's drawn face she asked, 'When did the pains start?' Lalli kept quiet. Khurshid looked into her eyes and scolded her affectionately, 'I have fed you my milk, my child! And the four children which God has been kind enough to give me, were not born out of my ear!'

Khurshid fetched Rehman tongawallah's mother Ashi, the midwife, 'She will check you out, it can't do any harm, she is quite experienced.'

Lalli grit her teeth and bore the pain. Ashi felt around with her fingers and then raised an alarm saying Lalli should be taken immediately to hospital as the child could be a breech baby. When Ayodhyanath heard, he raised a commotion, 'When will you women use your brains? What is the point of keeping quiet on such occasions? Didn't you even think that our daughter-in-law may lose her life? Khurshid sister, you are sensible, why didn't you inform me?'

Lalli was taken to the women's hospital in Navakadal. 'The Englishwoman Dr Gabbe is there, she is an experienced gynaecologist. No unqualified hakims or unhygienic local midwives,' Tathya scolded the women as he left.

Khurshid understood Ayodhyanath's anxiety. Respect made her keep quiet. Tathya is the elder of the house. What is the point of arguing with him?

Despite Tathya's efforts and care Lalli had to bear her share of pain. Notwithstanding the injections and the glucose drip, she was in intense pain for two days. Moving through the dark tunnels of creation till she was exhausted, finally, with a loud scream, she gave birth to a round chubby baby.

The baby yelled, its loud cry piercingly announcing its arrival on this earth, When the sound issued out of the delivery room, Kamala bhabi and Khurshid who were standing with their ears glued to the door, congratulated each other. Mother-in-law asked in a subdued voice, 'What is it?'

The nurse came out and announced with an English accent, 'It is a Lakshmi.'

'A girl?'

'Yes, sister, another daughter.'

There was disappointment in one voice and consolation in the other. 'Oh! Children come with their own destiny! If He gives a beak, He will also provide food. This is an old saying, who are we to worry?'

'Ye...s. That is true.' The acceptance of fate.

When Ayodhyanath heard, he thanked the doctor and noted the time of birth, the day, month and year in his diary:1931, bhadramas shuklapaksh ashtami, two minutes after six in the evening. Now her horoscope could be cast. Janakimaal was instructed, 'Offer roth and sweet laddus to Mahaganapati. Our daughter-in-law has been re-born.' Khurshid wanted to go and whisper in Lalli's ear that a tiny little beautiful daughter had been born but then she thought better of it. It would have been a different matter if it was a son. And then Lalli's mother-in-law also seemed to be upset.

In the courtyard the voice of the child, who was untouched by the psychological impact of the birth of boys and girls, kept echoing intermittently. When the sound reached a crescendo the nursemaid was unnerved. The baby's bath water was a bit too hot. 'Oh, God!' The Christian nurse made the sign of the cross on her chest.

The doctor and the nurses were busy taking care of the new mother and there was no need for the family to distribute any sweets on the birth of a second daughter. Unconsciously, the lack of enthusiasm for the child must have made them disinterested. All the fasts and prayers for a male heir who would carry on the family name and perform the final rites had been ineffective. Perhaps this was why the nursemaid was a little careless. She too had lost the opportunity of getting a substantial gift. But the child created a commotion. You may not celebrate my arrival but you cannot treat me with disregard and indifference. That was why its little scream echoed through the corridors of the hospital and reached the open courtyard outside. Women in labour heard the scream with bated breath. The white nurse, moving about carefully in the wards with the douche tray, raised her eyebrows in surprise, 'Such a tiny little thing and such a loud scream!'

Munni touched the earth with this scream. There was no atmosphere of peace or happiness either within the house or outside it to welcome her arrival. At home an unspoken sense of disappointment prevailed, 'Oh! Keshav has another daughter? He is so young and he already has the responsibility of two girls!'

No one articulated these thoughts out of respect for Ayodhyanath, but their hopes had certainly been dashed to the ground. Saraswati nani, Lalli's mother, sighed as she took out tiny little frocks in pastel colours made of rafal and kurtas made from soft makhanjean, 'May the child be lucky, may she bring a brother after her.' Krishnajoo sensibly added, 'Sons and daughters are born because of one's past deeds. It is all the will of God.'

As soon as he got the opportunity to be alone with her, Keshav answered all the unasked questions he could see in his wife's eyes by kissing her forehead and congratulating her. He reassured her cheerfully. When a smile appeared on Lalli's face he even told her some old stories related by Anand bayu, 'After creating the world, the gods handed the task of having children to man, but he just couldn't handle it! He could not possibly bear the responsibility of creation and carry a baby in his womb for nine months. So after a lot of deep thought the task was finally handed over to women.'

'Truly, Lalli! The process of creation is a great battle which only women can handle.'

Those days, along with the wave of change, there was an increasing tension in the atmosphere. Anticipating an outbreak of communal riots whipped up by Abdul Kader Pathan's inflammatory speeches, the government had arrested him and many other troublemakers. On the thirteenth of July rioters attacked the central jail and threw stones at the police. The

police retaliated with a lathi-charge and then opened fire. The
agitated crowd then moved into the localities of Vicharnag,
Maharajganj and Alikadal, spreading fear and panic everywhere.
They burnt houses belonging to non-Muslims, looted shops.
What had never happened before, happened this time. The
atrocities which were committed against non-Muslims during
Muslim rule were perpetrated by the rulers, the people had
no part in them. But this time brother turned against brother.
According to the poet Mahjoor, as the foundations of the
Muslim Conference were laid in the valley, invisible walls arose
between Muslims and Hindus who had so far mingled with
each other like milk and water. The process of change was
gradual but unmistakable.

But life? In the words of Anand Bayu the flow of life does
not cease even after death, so how could social and national
upheavals bring it to a halt? So respected Anand Bayu noted
the exact time, day and month of Munni's birth (according
to both the Gregorian and the Hindu calendars) and cast her
horoscope with great care. With a smile as pure as the fragrance
of sandalwood on his face, he gathered the men and women of
the house together and gave them a few details such as the fact
that the child was born at an auspicious moment and her sun
sign would be Leo. She would be lucky, intelligent, confident
and of a serious disposition. She would live in good company.
Oh yes, like others belonging to her sun sign, she would be
intolerant of criticism. 'I will recite some mantras in the prayer
room and give you a small taveez, a talisman, put it in a locket
around her neck.'

The family priest chose an auspicious time. This year
Ayodhyanath's family will observe all rites and rituals but there
will be no banquets because they also share Sona's grief. So,
Dina Bayu, who performed all the more mundane rituals,
determined the auspicious dates for the mother's first bath
and the child's naming ceremony. 'Shukla paksh chaudas, the

seventh day, is auspicious. On the eleventh day you can perform the child's Kahnethar. Finish all the bathing rituals early in the morning. You are all experienced, there isn't anything new that I need to teach you.'

'Which alphabet does her name have to begin with, Panditji?'

'The letter M. It would be good if the name began with M. Otherwise, whatever you like. A girl has two names, two homes in her destiny, ultimately she will retain the name given to her by her in-laws after her marriage.'

Whatever Saraswati Krishnajoo may have felt on the birth of a second grand-daughter, she nevertheless sent many blessings for the child's ritual ceremonies.

Kamalawati lit the fire at midnight and heated the water in huge cauldrons with Kahzaban, ginger, black cardamoms and lots of herbs to prepare the special post-delivery bath. The boiled water, which was poured into buckets to cool, gave off a lovely fragrance. Lalli's limbs and back were scrubbed with the herbs which had been boiled in the water. 'God knows what cold things the foreign doctors feed patients in the hospital so that the women can't stand up straight for the rest of their lives.' Baddadi felt that all new-fangled ways of doing things were mere foolishness. 'Our herbs are sanjeevanis, life giving, how can those red faced women understand their worth?' After her bath, Lalli was wrapped up from head to toe and quickly tucked into bed. She was given paranthas cooked in butter and liver fried with red chillies. Eating hot things would get rid of any lingering cold in the system and she would never suffer from headaches or backaches. The naming ceremony was also conducted under the guidance of Baddadi, 'Birth and death are in the hands of Shri Ganesh! One can stop neither of the two and the rituals connected with both are equally necessary.'

Waving the burning Bhojpatra over Lalli and the baby's head to ward off the evil eye, Kalawati and Janakimaal named the child. Keshav liked the name Katyayini, a fact that was conveyed to Baddadi through Shivnath. Baddadi smiled into Keshav's eyes, 'So …the boy already feels affection for the child!' She gracefully gave her consent. 'It is a nice name. Katyayini Devi. But we have to respect her horoscope as well so she will be called Munni.' Janaki served the sondar bath in seven thalis and the ritual was complete. No jokes, new clothes or banquets. The wound of Sona's grief was still quite raw. Katyayini's naming ceremony was a very quiet affair.

The sixth month feeding ceremony was equally subdued. For any function, the first invitee is always the daughter of the house, and Sona was imprisoned in her house for a whole year. When Lalli dipped her finger in the kheer garnished with almonds, raisins and dates and touched it to the baby's lips, chubby Munni gurgled in delight, tasted the sweetness of the food and looked at her mother with laughing eyes lined with antimony. It tasted good! Lalli secretly kissed the baby's rosy lips. The child chuckled, hitting her mother's chest with her plump fists and Lalli's loose kurta was drenched with milk.

And so Katya grew, inch by inch. Her first word was, 'Ma' which she enunciated by repeating the alphabet 'm' with clenched lips. Trying to express herself in her lisping words, Katya began to understand the meaning of the sounds and murmurs around her. When her mother came into the room she would raise her tiny arms with the unspoken conviction that her mother would pick her up and kiss her, clutch her to her chest and feed her. Katya learned to welcome the spring sunshine with blinking eyes. She would listen closely when the birds would chirrup from within the branches of the trees. Sounds, movements and new shapes, a huge new world unravelled in front of her eyes like a ball of wool.

In the meanwhile Sona gave birth to a son. Baddadi took on the responsibility of looking after him. Sona almost lost her wits when she saw the child. On the seventh day after he was born she squeezed him so tightly to her chest that he nearly choked. If Sona's sister-in-law had not forcibly freed him from Sona's arms, anything could have happened. The panic stricken sister-in-law wrote to Baddadi, 'Sona is the queen of the house. She is my responsibility, but how can I look after the house and also keep an eye on her? Today, thanks to my good luck, I saw her just in time to stop her, but suppose something happens tomorrow how will I face anyone? What answers will I give to people's questions?'

Baddadi took the hint and brought Sona home. Kanu, Madhav's son, started growing up alongside Katya. Who knows, perhaps Madhav had been re-born as his son. Baddadi told Sona, 'The yogini Lalleshwari was born in the village of Seempore near Pampore in the fourteenth century. Do you know she had the power to see events that had occurred in past births. When she was married to Sonapandit of Drangbalmahal at the age of twelve she turned to her guru Siddh Shrikant during the ceremony and said, 'My husband was my son in my previous birth.' This was the reason why Lalli refused to consummate her marital relationship.' Therefore, after consultations with elders, astrologers and knowledgeable people it was decided that the boy would be named 'Kanhaiya.' He couldn't be called Madhav after all, that would have caused too many psychological problems.

Daima Khurshid

Subhan, the boatman sang gleefully as he rowed across the Jehlum, 'Ya illah, La illah, kaliyaar, baliyaar, pir dastgir, khaliko, maliko....' Boatmen were in the habit of conversing with the waves in song. He was remembering God but Khurshid was quiet. Khurshid, who was crossing the river in the boat, watched the rise and fall of the waves. Rows of houses were standing shoulder to shoulder on the banks of the Vitasta. There was no movement in the lifeless structures of brick and wood. Arrows of smoke rose skywards from the cracks and crevices in the roofs of the barges standing on the river. The pungent smell of the asafoetida used in cooking the haaq greens was accompanied by the fragrance of boiling rice. Work never stopped. Labourers toiled from morning to evening just to fill the empty space in their bellies. But the turmoil in Khurshid's mind did not allow her to rest in peace. Was this because she now had two grown up sons and no longer had to worry about earning her bread? Because she now had time to think?

Forty days after Katya's birth, once Lalli's sutak was over and she had come home, it had suddenly struck Khurshid that things were no longer the same as before. The feeling of being an outsider would often raise its head without any reason and leave her feeling completely drained. Why did her own people now seem to be strangers? No one had said anything to her. When Lalli came to her parent's home twelve days after childbirth Khurshid also returned with her. There was no difference in Saraswati's behaviour. But the atmosphere had changed. There were external reasons for this feeling, Khurshid knew. Perhaps these were now creating cracks in age-old relationships. The wave of desire for their own state and self-rule had become a flood that threatened to overwhelm the mass of people. There was sloganeering and skirmishes in streets and lanes. The police would mercilessly beat up the sloganeers and lock them up in the police station. Kingship required subservience, how could it tolerate the challenges of those who demanded their rights?

Khurshid had heard that the British and even some other foreign powers were involved in trying to foment trouble and encourage communal tension. The result was that people were misled and there were riots and demonstrations. Some troublemakers burnt the houses of the Bhattas in Vicharnag. Poor Mangala's four-storeyed home was reduced to ashes. The shops of the Khatris in Maharajganj were ransacked. Warm blood began to boil. In such confusion, turmoil and looting, who can distinguish the guilty from the innocent? Mangala and Dina Kak moved with their family into a rented house. They got no assistance from anywhere. They lost their well established home and were reduced to penury. Age old affections were alienated. Brothers turned away from each other. Wasn't this enough to wound the heart?

Rehman started avoiding his friend Nathji. Hakim Suleiman and Subhan Dar, the shawl seller almost stopped visiting Ayodhyanath's house. Khurshid's husband, Subhan mallah, the boatman, a god fearing man who said his namaz five times a day, advised his wife, 'Times are bad, don't stay out late in the evening.' Khurshid would probably have ignored her husband's advice but she remembered that Ayodhyanath had also said something similar to her, though in a different context, 'Sister Khurshid, the police is patrolling the streets, there are skirmishes and fights at every street corner and a curfew as well. Stay at home for a few days, we worry about you.'

'Where do I have to go? Who is waiting for me?' Khurshid felt a pang in her heart at the thought of not being needed any longer.

In any case, there was no shortage of servants in Ayodhyanath's house. After all he was a lawyer and a munsif. Then there were the mothers of the children in the house, the grandmother and the great grandmother. Perhaps no one felt Khurshid's absence but her heart still felt tied to that house. She was more attached to Lalli than to her children. Saraswati's third born, Lalli. Saraswati lost two children before her. Lalli was born after a caesarian operation and her mother was confined to bed for a year afterwards. Saraswati lost a bucketful of blood.

She was reduced to a living, breathing skeleton. Krishnajoo used to feed her glucose with a teaspoon. Lalli was deprived of her mother's milk. Saraswati's mother-in-law consulted Ashi, the midwife and it was on her recommendation that Khurshid came into the house.

Khurshid remembered every single incident. Wali was a year old. He used to eat a bowlful of milk and rice and Khurshid's kurta would be drenched with milk. Saraswati had looked at her so beseechingly, 'This tiny little being is dependent on you, sister Khurshid. I merely gave birth to her, you must think of her as your own child.'

At the age of 25 Khurshid, the mother of three sons became a wet nurse. Her heart was filled with tenderness for the whimpering little baby. Saraswati's mother-in-law would coax Khurshid to have milk, 'Please drink Khurshid, there are two lives that depend on you and you must promise to let me know what you would like to eat.'

Lalli also started recognizing her very quickly. She would raise her tiny little arms as soon as she saw Khurshid and nuzzle around with her lips and tiny hands. Lalli, the daughter of Pandit Krishnajoo Kaul became the daughter of Khurshid. Ashi had spoken bluntly to Krishnajoo, 'Khurshid is the wife of Subhan, the boatman. She has three sturdy sons with the grace of Allah. Subhan earns his bread by his own efforts. He doesn't ask anyone for help. If they agree it will be as a favour to us. I can't think of any suitable Batni, pandit woman.'

'Sister Ashi, Lalli throws up any top feed, she can't survive on water. This is what God wills. Please try and persuade Khurshid.'

Khurshid became a mother as soon as she cradled the baby in her arms. There was no discussion about religion. Wet nurses were not uncommon. In times of need, Muslim women would breastfeed Hindu babies and would be called 'Dod maij' or wet nurse. Even if some people saw anything wrong in the practice, the needy would accept it as the will of God and bow their heads. Following a line of thought Krishnajoo, the devotee of Sanatan Dharm, would ruminate that Subhan Bhatt and Ghulam Mohammad Pandit must have been his co-religionists at one time. They may have been forced to change their religion because of the oppression of Sikandar Butshikan and the Afghan rulers, but they all belonged to the same race. Othodox Hindus did not allow them to subsequently reconvert to Hinduism, but the same blood flowed in their veins.

Beyond religious arguments and debates, Khurshid was just a mother feeding a tiny child. She would rock her gently, crooning a lullaby, 'Koori, koori, tabasheeri, Panaen koori... lageyae....' 'Daughter, daughter, my sweet daughter...may you be safe from all evils....' She could see the scene in front of her eyes just as if it had happened yesterday. Khurshid looked at her husband who was rowing rhythmically across the water. The lifelong habit of simplicity and hard work was unchanged, though a fine network of lines had traced the passage of years across his face. The embroidery of time. Subhan's life was static. Rowing from one shore of the Jhelum to the other, helping people cross from Khanyaar to Kathleshwar. Without any exception, dipping oars in the water morning to evening, 'chulak chap, chulk chapp' he spent his time exchanging greetings with his customers, 'Are you well? Are the children all right? Thanks be to God.'

Daily routine, daily habit, picking up his oars after having his early morning shirchai, salt tea with sesame studded bagels bought from Mage, the baker. Sun, rain, snow, he would not stay at home in any weather.

Finally, Wali asked him one day, 'Don't you get bored doing the same work every day, baba? Rowing people across the river from Khanyaar to Kathleshwar?' What a question for a son to ask!

Subhan scolded his son gently, 'Take the name of God, Wali,

my son! This is my work, my bread. Where does the question of boredom arise? Just because you are educated have you lost the ability to understand basic truths?'

'No, baba, actually I want you to come to my houseboat. We are also capable of something now, by the grace of Allah…but my friends say you are still not willing to give up your shikara.'

'Do you feel ashamed? Does it embarrass you Walia? Tell your friends the old man has become senile. Say whatever you like…'

The situation would have deteriorated if Khurshid hadn't intervened. She knew Subhan Mallah was not the kind of man who would live on the earnings of his children. Allah and his boat, Subhan had complete faith that these were the two things that would stay with him till his last moments.

Though there had been fewer excursions and holidays in the last year, one had to earn one's living. In fact, once or twice, Subhan's shikara, 'Gulistan' had even danced across the Dal lake carrying English tourists. Sinking into the springy cushions of the shikara, which was decorated with bright curtains and namdas with yerma embroidery, these English tourists would coo like doves as they enjoyed the breeze on the lake and the reflections of the tall surrounding snow-covered mountains in the mirror-like water. During the summer the melting snow would flow down the mountains in cascades. Subhan would explain the sights to the tourists, 'These Shalimar gardens were laid out by the Mughal emperor Jehangir, sir! Very big king, sir!'

'Garden? Nishat Garden?'

'Yes, garden, sir. King Shahjehan made Nasim bagh, isn't it beautiful, sir?'

'Wonderful.'

'The hill you see up ahead, that is Pari Mahal, sir.'

'Pari Mahal?' The English tourists would look at the ruins curiously through their binoculars and try to figure out what they used to be.

'Sir, it was made by Dara Shikoh, for his guru, his ustaad.'

'Ustaad? What ustaad…?' The red-faced one didn't understand.

'Oh! Teacher, yes, for his teacher, Akhund Mullahshah. It was made for him.' Would the idiot understand?

There was a lot he wanted to say. He knew so much, Subhan Mallah, but unfortunately language let him down. What could he say and how could he say it? There was a piercing desire inside him …if only he had been educated.

The English couple gazed at each other fondly and dipped their fingers in the waters of the Dal. Whenever Subhan Mallah's gaze fell on the entwined pair he would mutter, 'Muhammad ur Rasool Lillah' and hold the oar a little tighter. The boat would dance across the waves and the sun would crimson the surface of the water. Caught in the middle of the intoxicating colours of the water and the sky, Subhan Mallah would hum sufiana songs: 'There is an ornament on my beloved's forehead and jewels in her ears, today she is visiting my dwelling.'

'Nice song.' The couple would look up at Subhan Mallah and tip him a few rupees. His voice was so sweet.

'Thank you sir, thank you, may God give you plenty.'

Subhan knew how the winds blew and he was not afraid of them. In all his years as a boatman he had not allowed even a single mishap to take place, at least not while he had an oar in his hand and Allah's name on his lips. Krishnajoo often remembers the incident when Subhan managed to prevent an accident. It was a beautiful spring day. The sky was a deep blue and there were just a few clouds playing hide and seek with the mountains. Krishnajoo climbed aboard Subhan Mallah's boat along with the children of his family. They all enjoyed themselves singing as they floated on the waves of the lake which was filled with cool, clear water from melted snow, and the perfume of lotus flowers. Fresh green vegetables were growing on the floating islands around them. The lotus seedpods with their numerous eyes peeped at them from among the rosy lotus flowers. The shikara slid with a gentle rocking motion through the lotus leaves which covered the surface of the lake, as it moved from the Kotarkhana towards Untkadal, the camel bridge. Suddenly Subhana, who had been gazing intently at the clouds hovering above the mountains behind Chashmeshahi, surprised Krishnajoo by turning the shikara towards one of the backwaters.

'What is the matter, Subhanjooa? Why have you changed direction?'

The children had planned to visit the Shalimar gardens.

'I can see signs of bad weather in the clouds. We will have to take shelter near the shore.'

The shikara was tied to the sturdy trunk of a chinar tree growing near the bank and Subhana took Natha, Saraswati, Bhadra batni, Radha and Lalli to Ganikraal's house nearby. Subhana was a respected man. Fata, the potter's wife, gestured to the wood burning stove, sugar and tea leaves and requested the girls to make tea for themselves in their own pot. In the meanwhile the sudden storm and lashing rain had wrenched away the curtains of the shikara. The poplar trees growing on the banks of the canal groaned as they were flattened by the wind.

The storm abated only after midnight when a pale and wan looking moon could be glimpsed in the tiny slice of intensely blue sky visible between the piles of cotton spread across the heavens. Subhan Mallah and Natha fixed the shikara as best as they could. Once the heaving of the waves had quietened down, Subhan Mallah took up his oar to transport Krishnajoo and his family safely back home. 'Ya peer dastgir, khaliko-maliko…' In such circumstances how could one help being impressed by Subhan Mallah's ability to gauge the winds?

These days Khurshid tossed and turned in her bed for a long time. Sleep generally eludes the aged, and as she mentally climbed up and down mountains Khurshid thought of the past when mutual understanding and faith were the basic tenets of life. There were separate beliefs and religions, yet there was an invisible thread linking people to one another.

Courtesy, deep affection and a recognition of each other's place in the scheme of things. Dependence on each other, an age-old habit, whether it was the landlord Baljoo or the farmer Suljoo. Content in their own homes. Mutton roghanjosh in one house and greens and rice in another, but no one spied on anyone else's kitchen. Both were happy in their own space. If the potter Ghulam did not make the different pots and terracotta figurines how could the lawyer, munsif Shyamlal Bhat celebrate the festival of Shivratri? Everyone accepted these symbiotic relationships as the basis of life. But now? Suddenly there was doubt and fear when they looked at each other.

Khurshid felt unsettled if she did not see Lalli for a few days. What the elders said was true, that the pain of bringing up a child was more intense than that of giving birth. One didn't notice the gradual but inexorable passage of time. Lalli married and settled into her new home. Her lap was filled with two children – Ali, Gani and Wali also grew up and set up their own homes. Khatji's cousin asked for her hand in marriage. Everyone got busy with their work, by the grace of Allah. Ali and Gani worked for Sultan Dar of Alikadal doing carvings on walnut wood. They learnt the skill thanks to Sultan Dar. The brothers took some loans and bought a small houseboat for Wali. He was also doing well, thanks to the free-spending and generous English tourists. Khurshid had spent all her savings on the marriages of her children. God is kind, what more can one ask for? Khurshid was pleased that her daughters-in-law took care of her. They were good girls who tried to make her feel respected and important by asking for her advice and guidance. 'Moaji, mother! Tell Baba to send Shabir to school. It will be good for him to learn a few alphabets. No one listens to me!' Ali considered it his birthright to scold his wife whenever he felt like it, 'She is crazy, moaji, she gets influenced by all these new ideas. Someone just mentions something to her and she starts eating my head. Maulvi sahib is teaching Shabir isn't he? What more do we want? He will also learn our work when he grows older. He is not going to become a king is he?'

'All right child,' Khurshid tried to intervene before a war erupted. 'it is all right, we will send him to school once he finishes his religious education. He will do well, the light of our eyes. The government now gives scholarships to students. I will talk to Keshavnath, don't fight, the two of you.' Khurshid took care of the entire household. The young Wali often tried to convince his mother to give up work. 'Moaji, you should rest at home now. Play with your grandsons. You have worked enough. The world is changing.'

'All right Wali, my child. Has the world changed so much that an egg can give instructions to a hen?'

'It isn't that, ma. You don't understand, things really are changing now. There are a lot of discussions about religion. If someone misbehaves, the entire community is held responsible. Suppose something happens to you?'

'Don't worry about me son. Allahtala takes care of everyone. I have never discriminated between you and Krishnajoo's Lalli. God knows I have been faithful to those whose salt I have eaten. Yet, I have remained a Mussalmani and Lalli has remained a Hindu. If my faith has remained strong till the end of my days what is going to happen now? Don't think I am weak, Walia. Worry about yourself. Young blood boils very easily and takes hasty decisions as well.'

The son thought his mother had become senile. Wasn't there a saying that people's wits became addled once they crossed sixty? Khurshid doesn't understand how much times have changed. Her daughters-in-law said, 'Well moaji is quite old now isn't she?'

But Khurshid proved their statements about age quite wrong. Sometimes she felt sad that even those dear to her could not plumb the depths of her heart. What could she expect from strangers?

Talking of age, Khurshid didn't look a day over 40. She might not wear pashmina but she did have printed pherans with piping and embroidered raffal shawls. There were heavy silver bangles on her arms, dozens of hoops in her ears and fine braids on her head which was covered with a clean white scarf. Added to all this was an erect carriage, a neck held high and a confident walk. She might not wear a kasaba but her presence would awe any kasaba wearing woman. Nature had blessed her with an alabaster white skin and sharp features. She was never careless about her appearance or her speech.

Even if no one else had imbibed the manners and courtesies of Krishnajoo's house they had become part of Khurshid's behaviour. She moderated her speech according to the situation. She knew how to express herself in front of elders, how to maintain an affectionate control over youngsters and could deliver a stinging reproof if anyone raised his or her voice needlessly. She was always in demand at any important occasion in Krishnajoo's house. New clothes, gifts of money, salt, bread etc, it was Khurshid's unchallengeable right to accompany all these to the homes of the daughters-in-law. But lately Khurshid had been feeling disturbed. Whatever was happening around her was wrong, she couldn't accept it and time was passing by so quickly.

Lalli gave birth to Munna after Katya. There were joyous celebrations in Ayodhyanath's house. Baddadi's last wish was granted. Khurshid carried Munna around in her arms the whole day singing lullabys, 'I will rock you in a cradle decorated with bells/you were born at midnight/ lord Shiva himself cast your horoscope/You will have a long life/I have seen it written in your horoscope.' Khurshid stayed with Lalli in the hospital. Saraswati Krishnajoo sent gifts of money, clothes, and grain to

Lalli's in-laws with Khurshid. Krishnajoo presented Khurshid with a raffal pheran and a dozen pure silver earrings.

'Sister Khurshid, it is due to your blessings that our home has been blessed with a son. Ask for anything you want. Today I will not refuse you.'

'May the years of my life be added to the baby's age. As God is my witness, you have always been generous to me,' Khurshid replied with genuine feeling.

When Lalli went home from the hospital Khurshid came to see her in the morning and then returned home before evening. The grandmothers wouldn't let Munna out of their sight for even a minute. There was no shortage of people to take care of him. This time even Saraswati did not beg Khurshid to stay overnight. How relationships change with time. Lalli, however, would complain sometimes, 'Now my Khurshid has gone far away from me. She doesn't love me as she did before.' Khurshid would turn away these complaints with a smile, 'Daughter, your Khurshid is no longer the same age she was when she used to come running from Kraalkhod to Sathu to breastfeed you.'

'Yes, sister Khurshid,' Saraswati would chime in, 'now my back is bent and my joints and knees hurt as though the life has been squeezed out of my body.'

One didn't know if the women who complained about their backs blamed time for bending their backs or for creating barriers between hearts. Maybe these were events beyond their understanding because they were uneducated, unfamiliar with the history of their valley. Slogans, riots and ruffians – these were all new to them. The result of living in Kalyug or the curse of nature. If they had been familiar with history they would have known that ever since the twelfth century, political scheming, betrayals and assaults had disturbed the peace and contentment of the people in the valley. During the reign of queen Kota, the ambitious Rinchinshah, who had run away from Tibet, and later the Tartar, Dulchu from Central Asia, had sowed terror and destruction everywhere in the valley. It was the common man who was the victim of political machinations and oppression. People had also forgotten Sikandar Butshikan, the destroyer of idols, the Afghan Karimdad Khan who smothered Bhattas with the smoke of burning cowdung to force them to pay the 'Zarre Dudah' tax and Jabbar Khan who once gave the command that the festival of Shivratri should be celebrated in summer and not in winter.

But they remembered the stories. Generation after generation, stories passed down by grandmothers about how when Shivratri was celebrated in summer there was such a heavy snowfall that summer became winter. People remembered Badshah, the king of kings, Sultan Zainulabdin who respected every religion. Sikandar Butshikan was buried and forgotten in his grave but his son Badshah's tomb became a dargah, a holy place, visited and revered by both Hindus and Muslims. And why not? After all, he was the one who called back the oppressed Battas who had fled their homes and re-settled them. He created an atmosphere of peace and justice by giving every person their rights. People forgot the evil and remembered the good. Except that now that peace was being destroyed.

The Wilful Daughter and Tathya's Half-baked Arguments

Katya was about six years old when Didda scolded her, 'If you don't listen to me, you will cry.'

'Cry? But why should I?' Katya questioned her sister as she combed the hair of the rag doll her grandmother had made for her. Then she answered her own question, 'I don't cry.'

It may have been the obstinacy in Katya's voice or the lack of respect in her attitude that upset Didda. Acting like this in front of Didda who is the darling of the house, the first born of Tathya's Bhabaji? Didda was always conscious of being the eldest and the most cherished child.

Glaring at her sister, Didda said, 'You will cry once I tell Tathya. Do you know, when you were born you were put in a tub of hot water because of your obstinacy? And Baddadi didn't eat anything that day. She was very upset she said, 'Why has she come? We didn't ask for her?''

Katya's became tearful. It was as though Didda had placed a heavy stone on her soft heart. Why did Baddadi get upset with her? Just because she was born? Why didn't she scold Didda? Why her? A scream of anger rose within her. Baddadi had passed away or, as Tathya would say, she'd gone to heaven two years after Katya's birth and two months after Munna was born. Katya couldn't recall her face clearly though there was a photograph of her in the prayer room.

In Katya's imagination Baddadi looked like the witches in fairytales. A long nose bent at the tip, unruly hair as though a basket of jute had been upturned on her head, holding a witch's wand in her hand. Grandma witch! In her anger Katya couldn't decide what to do. She clenched her fists. She thought of tearing her hair and screaming but gave up the idea. Grandma witch was not even alive any longer. Witch! Witch! If she hadn't been a witch she wouldn't have been angry with Katya. She would have loved her. Katya chucked her doll into a chest and went off to interrogate Tathya, 'Tathya! Did Baddadi get upset when I was born?'

She didn't mention Baddadi's fast. Being upset was bad enough. And without reason too! How could she tell Tathya about the witch? She was afraid, after all he prayed to Baddadi. In the midst of idols of Shri Ganesh, Shankar bhagwan, Reginya devi and many other gods in the prayer room, there were photographs of Baddadi and Baddada, and every morning Tathya would bow low before them and offer flowers.

Tathya had to smile at little Katya's queries, 'No, my little one, your Baddadi loved you a lot, why would she be upset with you? Yes, she did have a great desire for sons. When you brought your brother after you she was very happy, she said, 'Munni has brought a brother to play with.''

But Katya had been hurt. How could she be mollified so easily? 'Didda says you put me in a tub of hot water as soon as I was born!' Katya burst into tears, her heart was bleeding even though her body was unhurt.

'No, no. Good children don't cry. Didda was mistaken, I will scold her. Why are you crying? You are Tathya's dearest child. I will buy you beautiful things for your hair and a satin frock with flowers!'

Taking out a sparkling white handkerchief from his pocket, Tathya wiped Katya's wet cheeks lovingly as though he was removing a dew drop from a rose petal. He sat her on his lap and explained, 'The nurse didn't check the temperature of the water when she was bathing you, it was just a mistake. You screamed because you found the water too warm. We came running as soon as we heard you shouting. We scolded the nurse and bathed you ourselves with lukewarm water.'

Katya was happy. Tathya had washed away her grievances with his love though his beard had tickled her when he kissed her. Tathya also gave her an anna to buy something for herself. Not just two paise but a whole anna! Katya would buy lots of nadrumonji, lotus stem fritters, and eat them in front of Didda.

She jumped out of Tathya's lap, went to Didda and, with the authority of an emperor sitting on the Takht-i-taus, thundered, 'Did you hear Didda? Tathya bathed me with his own hands.

Not you, not even Bhaiya, just me. His Bitto. He also scolded the ayah! And see, one anna! Just for me. For you, nothing!'

Actually Didda was a very well-behaved girl. Mother would put perfumed oil in her hair and comb it. She would braid her silky, knee-length hair into intricate plaits and put red ribbons at the ends. Didda would swan around looking like a doll, wearing a beautiful starched satin frock and a garara. Katya hated to get dressed up. She disliked it when her mother tried to oil her hair or when she pulled Katya down on her lap and tugged at her unruly hair as she combed through it with a fine wooden, thousand-toothed comb. Lalli attempted the task by using various strategies, including entreaties, threats and cajoling to make Munni sit down so that her hair could be combed but her machinations invariably failed.

'My Munia's hair will grow so long, just like Sonkesri's, below the knees, like a sheet of satin. Longer than Didda's, shiny, just wait and see. And then a handsome prince will come along riding on a white horse....'

But Katya wasn't planning to get married. She would keep saying, 'Ouch, ouch, ouch' and shift around every minute so that her plait was braided crookedly. Lalli would finally give up and before she could thump Katya on her back in dismissal the child would guess her mother's intent and slip out of her grasp like a wet fish. She didn't want her hair combed or braided. She didn't want shiny hair like Didda's nor did she want any prince!

Lalli would surrender, 'If you run around with unruly hair like the sadhu babas with their dreadlocks, then no one will marry you, I will be stuck with you for the rest of my life!'

'Yes I will stay here,' Katya would tap her mother's chest affectionately, toss her unruly hair and run away to join her band of monkeys. She hated gararas. One could only hang about the house looking like a doll and playing with rag dolls if one wore a garara. You got your dolls married, arranged for the reception of the baraat, the groom's party, and sang and played the tumbaknari on the bride's mehndi ceremony. You couldn't play with tops, spin around, skip rope etc., with your friends.

Once Ma had made her wear a bright, shiny garara with red and green flowers, velvet hair ornaments and god knows what else – all stuff Tathya had brought from Indore. The garara felt very soft, just like a downy little chick, but when she ran to the courtyard to skip rope her toe got caught in its hem and it unravelled and she fell head over heels. Oh! Her knee was badly scraped and not only did the garara get dirty but it also tore near the knee. Katya went crying to Tathya to show him her knee.

In the sitting room Tathya was busy chatting with some of his friends and colleagues. There were legal discussions about court cases, appearances, evidence, court dates, sentences and verdicts. If Lalitashwari's husband beat up his wife despite the intervention of elders then why did this become a legal matter, if Iqbal Krishan brings another woman home while his wife is alive, under which law will he be sentenced to jail, if Balji, the landlord doesn't give Ahdu the farmer his payment for the year, do we need to bring it to a court of law? Many legal matters would be discussed and many conclusions would be reached. But now the topic of discussion and debate had changed. The new developments which had taken place in the last few years had destroyed everyone's peace of mind. 13 July 1931, the day was long past, but its wounds were still fresh.

Complaints, accusations, reproaches

The taste of Ayodhyanath's hookah had changed. Dinananth was a victim anyway.

'During British rule a riot enquiry committee was set up to enquire into disturbances. The state minister Mr. Wakefield did go to Nowshera….' one person would begin.

'He went, but what happened? Did non-Muslims get back what they had lost? Wazire Khatri's shop which was full of merchandise was burnt, did he get any compensation?'

'Wakefield Sahib did not even bother to visit those who suffered in the riots in Vicharnag. What help could he give?' Dinanath had lost everything in the disturbances. His anger refused to cool down. 'The British government is openly using a divide and rule poicy. I have been reduced to nothing. Not only was my house burnt but everything my ancestors had collected over the years was looted by the troublemakers. Mangala has almost lost her wits. Who can we complain to, there is no one who will listen! Even God has become deaf to our woes!'

In such a serious atmosphere, the shrill shouts of the children would often distract Tathya. At times, he would get up just as a high pitched wail began to rise from the bottom of the stairs. He would listen to the children's sorrows, sometimes he would enquire into the matter and pronounce punishment. When Katya went to him after she tripped he washed her knee with Dettol and water. He put some tincture Iodine on the wound, blowing on it all the time to take away the sting, and instructed Lalli not to make Katya wear a garara again. She was too young for it anyway. Lalli kept quiet but Janaki muttered under her breath, 'So, is she going to go around showing her knees and legs even when she grows up? Doesn't she have to learn any manners? She is a girl after all.'

Janaki was upset by Katya's tomboyish habits – they disturbed the atmosphere of the house. She would try to scold her, 'Don't stamp around so loudly Munni, it will become a habit.'

'You laugh so loudly, like a hoyden. Suppose someone hears you what will he think, hmm? He will say we haven't taught you any manners, won't he? And it is not seemly for a daughter of the house to laugh at every little thing.' But what was the use? As the old saying goes, 'no fruit grows on sandy soil.' And then, Tathya was also a bit too indulgent towards the children. He looked at his wife with slightly raised eyebrows as if asking, 'What did you say?' and then he issued the edict, 'We will see when she grows up. She is barely six years old. And listen, all this stuff about being a girl, don't keep repeating it. Girls are the pride of the house. They are like the goddesses Lakshmi and Saraswati.' Dadi, grandmother, could do nothing except bear Tathya's scolding quietly.

Tathya went back into the sitting room to catch up on the unfinished debates. Matters were, however, becoming more and more tangled despite the unending discussions and suggestions. Something invaluable was being lost in the leap towards something new. In this transitional period, people fumbled around, looking for some ray of hope.

Balbhadra was praising Sher-e-Kashmir, 'Sheikh Mohammad Abdullah is very far-seeing, he realised that the name Muslim Conference had religious overtones so he changed the name of his party to National Conference.' If Subhanjoo, the shawl dealer had been there he would have nodded his head sagely like an elder and said, 'Yes, brother. That was sensible. It won't disturb our composite culture. The demand for democracy is for the good of the entire public, not just for one community.'

If one has been wounded and wants to hit back one has to do it subtly. Dinanath would remark, his face bland, 'You are right, brother, but we have two parties anyway, the Lions and the Goats. Now there is tension between these two every other day.'

'Not just tension, there are all out fights very often.'

'Yes. Unnecessary confrontations. The Muslim Conference remains a religious organization, the National Conference has become a secular party.'

Those who had complaints against the administration advocated democracy, others who were government employees or had received benefits argued that there was no need for any change as the general public was being well taken care of anyway. Professor Pandit spoke about the inevitability of change, 'This is the law of nature, brother, the only worry is the way in which religious fervour has become linked to the desire for change.' Balbhadra was not willing to accept that the divisive policies of the Maharaja's government were responsible for creating barriers between different religions. The reasons for religious intolerance lay elsewhere. Ayodhyanath talked of the statement sent by R.K Bhan to the Riot Enquiry Commission which highlighted the rules and laws of the state in order to throw some light on the present situation.

'During the last eight years or so, the administration has taken many steps to improve the lot of the common man, from waiving loans given to farmers to making primary education compulsory. The poor have been offered a lot of incentives to encourage them in the field of education. There is reservation for the poor and preference has been given in government jobs on the basis of necessity rather than capability. There is no reason why Muslims should have any complaints about their Hindu brothers. According to the report, only 20 non-Hindus were unemployed whereas over 600 Hindus were without jobs.'

Bhalbadra was angry, and with reason. 'With the grace of God, you all know my son Somji. Tell me, has he ever got anything less than a first division? He even had a distinction in English, but what happened? There was a farce of an interview and the post was handed over to a third divisioner in the name of reservation. As if it is a crime to be a Batta.'

'Well, things like this will happen in the name of giving help to weaker sections of society, there is no need to give up hope.' Professor sahib tried to give some solace, 'Your son is intelligent, there will be no shortage of jobs for him.'

'With your good wishes and the blessings of Shiva Shambhu I don't need to worry. I merely mentioned it. In any case everyone knows that a Batta has always been associated with learning and education, he is not capable of doing trade or business. He can work in an office or become a collector, teach in a school or college. He doesn't discriminate between a Hindu pupil and a Muslim one, he is a God fearing man.'

'Don't get upset, brother Balbhadra. People tend to blame each other when things get bad. Otherwise everyone knows that Hindus and Muslims are inextricably linked. Do you recall the terrible flood of 1903 when thousands of homes,and lands were washed away?'

'You mean the time when Kashmiris from Uttar Pradesh set up a relief fund? Pandit Motilal Nehru donated a thousand rupees to the fund. How can one forget that?'

'Even more recently, when there was a loss of life and property during the floods in 1928-29 the government immediately provided help.'

'At that time poisonous differences disappeared in thin air.'

The poison had been spread by the policies of the British. Ayodhyanath is quite knowledgeable. 'You know Abdul Kader Pathan, he came from Afghanistan disguised as a cook and then started working for a British army officer.'

'The officer probably had no idea who he was.'

'What are you saying Jia? He definitely knew. He was playing a crooked game. Create divisions and rule. That is what they did. Whenever they sensed any danger to themselves they oppressed the people. Where they did not perceive any threat they became lax, allowing people to fight amongst themselves. Look at what they've done in the rest of the country.'

'You are right, brother.' Professor sahib remembers the day when Mahatma Gandhi was imprisoned by the British, 'Arre, that day Kashmiris raised such loud slogans in support of Gandhi that the entire police force was put on alert. There were all sorts of restrictions. The newspaper *Ranvir*, published from Jammu, was shut down for fear that Kashmiris might join the non-cooperation movement.'

'And when there were riots and looting in Vicharnag,

and houses were being burnt, at that time the police was nowhere to be seen. They arrived only after everything had been destroyed and did nothing. All this is mentioned in R.K. Bhan's report.'

Government officers considered it their duty to praise their superiors. For the Brahmins it was unthinkable that they should disobey or oppose the king. Krishnajoo Kaul, who was very familiar with the Puranas, often recited the shloka from the Neelamath Purana which says that Kashmir is the country of Sati, the wife of Shiva. This was why Kashmir should be considered a part of Shiva. Anyone who wished for the prosperity of Kashmir should never oppose the king. There would always be attempts to defend the Maharaja.

'The Maharaja will do anything for his people but these red faces control everything. He has no choice.'

They doubted whether the sloganeers would ever become rulers. 'These troublemakers? How will they run the administration? Will they be just to the populace? God protect us, the day they occupy the seat of power, the people will not even get two square meals. They will die of hunger.' Balbhadra Dhar was troubled by the changing environment. He could not forget the past and the greatness of rulers like Maharaja Pratap Singh. 'Apart from a few occasions, the kings who have ruled the valley have been quite fair and just.'

'Most of the progress that happened in the state was due to the kings, wasn't it? Our sculpture and architecture bear this out. The temple of Martand constructed by King Lalitaditya in the eighth century must have been a great wonder of its time.'

'It isn't only Martand. Look at the temple of Avanteshwar on the banks of the Vitasta in Zabror. Avantivarman's capital Avantipore was somewhere close by. Now, of course, there are only ruins.'

'Yes, the ruins tell their own stories. Though subsequent attacks destroyed almost everything but these temples must once have been amazing examples of Gandhara art. Symbols of religious tolerance, temples of Shiva and Vishnu. The Taj Mahal is no patch on them!'

Professor Pandit changed the subject, moving from temples to Avantivarman's minister Suryabhatt, 'It is said that once during a terrible flood he changed the course of the Jhelum river and saved the valley from being inundated. After the Bhagirath, it was Suryabhat who showed that it was possible to change the course of a river. Even the ministers at that time were extremely intelligent.'

Once the discussion turned to intelligence and wisdom a long list of kings, maharajas, learned pundits, historians, astrologers, sufi saints and philosophers would be drawn up. Somananda's Shivadrishti, Abhinavgupta's Tantralok, Kalhana's Rajtarangini, Somadeva's Kathasagar, LalDed's Vakh, Nund Rishi's Shrukh! Literary creations all.

The conversation carried on as the evening deepened till Mukundram, the cook, appeared at the door to ask for permission to spread the dastarkhan, the dining sheet. The friends would be startled into departure....

'Oh! We did not even realize it was time for dinner.'

It was evident that the wives had been napping, waiting patiently to serve the food. Annapoornas or providers of food could be made to wait up all night but food could not be kept waiting, that would be a sin.

In other words, the day's gathering was over.

Mahadjoo

Childhood! A time of freedom! A vast, open sky where the imagination can soar free. No domestic cares or tensions, happy within the seemingly endless boundaries of childhood, innocent of differences and barriers, Katya loved to drink tea: the fragrant shirchai that Mahdu made on the brick chulha in the corner of the courtyard. This was much better than the creamy milk she drank at home. The pink tea with sattu in it, which Mahadjoo would drink very decorously in a blue-flowered cup. As though it wasn't a mere cup of tea but some rare heavenly nectar that it would be an insult to drink sloppily.

Mahdu would wash and wipe the cup carefully, making it shine. Almost with the same care that Ma washed utensils for use in the pooja during festivals. Katya loved the smell of the fragrant steam rising from the boiling tea, it always made her hungry. And the thought of telvorus, the small round bagels covered with sesame, from Sula the baker's shop, would make her mouth water.

'Give me a little tea, please, with a piece of that telvoru.'

Mahdu would hesitate, 'If your mother finds out, both of us will be in real trouble. Go in and drink your milk. Children are not supposed to drink tea.'

'No, I won't drink milk! I don't like it. Please give a little shirchai, just a little bit! Aha! The lovely smell of sattu! Give me just two sips from your china cup!' Tea made by Mahdu and drunk from Mahdu's cup! Did the little girl who belonged to a Sanatan Dharam, Brahmin family have any idea what the effect of those two sips could be?

Finally, when he could see no way out, Mahdu would look around furtively and pour a few sips of tea into a clean cup, 'Drink it up quickly and go. Let me drink my tea. Wipe your mouth properly, so no one gets to know.' Victorious, Katya would run off with the speed of an arrow. No one ever had any inkling of what had happened. But Mahdu was not only the source of shirchai. The everchanging stories he told her were no less of an attraction. It was true that Prem bhaiya would scoff and say that all these stories were just made up, but even he listened surreptitiously while Mahadjoo was narrating them.

'So, children! Once I saw a lion in the jungles of Chandanwadi!'

'Lion or cheetah?'

'No, It was a lion – he was so regal.'

Whether any other child questioned him or not, Katya definitely had a million questions to ask. Mahdu was the final authority. He was used to encountering ghosts, spirits, rahchok, lions and cheetahs in the village. Where else would he have got the stories from? He wasn't educated like Rehman Gada's Gul Mohammad who used to read aloud stories written by others, stories about Alladin and his lamp, Alibababa and the forty thieves and Hatimtai. Madhu's were created in his brain. If this hadn't been true, he would have remained Mahamodoo, just an ordinary servant of the house. Who would have addressed him with respect as Mahadjoo? So sometimes Mahadjoo would squat with folded hands in front of the lion in his story, hiding his thumb within his fist (because it would be disrespectful to show one's thumb to the king of the jungle). At other times he would climb up a tree and spend the night shivering, repeating the name of Allah, begging for protection till his mouth ran dry until finally, he was saved. The climax of the story would change according to the situation or the curiosity level of the children.

Mahdu had travelled so far from his village, Chandanwari, which lay at the foothills of the mountains, just beyond Pahalgam, to the city which was so full of noise and chaos. It was all fated. A man had to go where he was destined to earn his bread. How can he explain this to the children? Once

Mahdu had taken the children to his village where they went riding. Mukundram and Mahdu accompanied them just in case a horse bolted and the children fell off, in which case it would be the end of Mahdu. The city children who were used to living in brick and wood boxes almost went crazy when they saw the open fields and farms in the village, the green pastures and the hillsides covered with trees.

'Arre, you had sheep and goats as well?'

'Yes, just a few.'

'You must have spent the whole day grazing the animals.'

Satisfying and encouraging the curiosity of the children, Mahdu would become a hero. He would narrate how he played gulli-danda with his friends and wandered right up to the snow bridge. He took tourists for horse rides around Chandanwari.

'Really, Mahadjoo?'

'I have even been to Amarnath many times working as a porter.'

'What is a porter?'

'Someone who carries the luggage of the yatris, pilgrims. These plains people get out of breath walking up the mountains, how can they possibly carry their luggage?'

Chandanwari was like a fairground months before the Shravan Poornima when the Amarnath Yatra took place. The pigrims who accompanied the holy mace would camp in the open for the night. Sadhus and their followers would play their tambourines and sing religious songs. Food would be cooked on portable stoves. The sleepy valley would wake up with a start. The demand for horses and mules would increase. Mahdu gave the children a detailed account of the Amarnath Yatra.

Mahdu's own life was hardly less interesting than any story. He was the son of a landless farmer who worked as a coolie and a labourer. He had had a very eventful life. Perhaps if these events hadn't happened he would still have been grazing cattle, sitting in the shade of a fir tree, dangling his legs in the bubbling Lidder river or watching the crowns of snow melt on the mountains in the warmth of the sun, listening to the priceless music of the mountain rivulets.

'Wow! Having fun the whole day. Roaming around without having to worry about strict teachers or failing exams.'

But Prem bhaiya saw nothing of interest in Mahdu's daily routine, 'What is so interesting about roaming around the whole day doing nothing?'

'I mean there is no cinema in the village and no theatre either. Won't one get bored just staring at the mountains and rivers the whole day?'

'No, bhaiya sahib! We never got bored. There used to be so many foreign visitors. Lots of milk-white, beautiful foreign women. They looked like fairies from paradise. The red-faced foreigners would sit with them, listen to gramophones, drink and make love....'

There! Mahdu has learnt to make love without seeing even a single movie.

'What is love?' A new word was added to the children's vocabulary, love. When the children asked such questions Mahdu became alert and looked around carefully, hoping that no one had heard.

He went back into the past, digging deep into his memories to offer more stories to the children. He remembered how he spent a year almost floating on air after he married his cousin Khatiji. Whenever Khatiji went to the spring to fill water, Mahdu would follow her on some pretext or the other. He would almost go crazy when the sun, playing hide and seek behind the pine and deodar trees, suffused Khatiji's face with light. He often told Khatiji stories about the memsahibs. He thanked God that his father had caught him spying on the memsahibs and had decided to marry him off, otherwise he would still have been a lonely peeping Tom building castles in the air. At times he did try to make love to Khatiji the 'English' way but Khatiji would just make a face and laugh at him. She never understood the longings and desires in Mahdu's heart. Mahdu's love reduced him to Khatiji's slave but then everyone has his own destiny, who can Mahdu blame?

Sometimes Mahdu would talk to Prem bhaiya about destiny, 'I have really bad luck, bhaiya sahib! Because one day Khatiji went to the spring to fetch water and she never came back.'

'Didn't return? Why didn't she come back, Mahdu?'

What can Mahdu say? That his life was too simple for her beauty? That she hungered for a richer life? How could Mahdu afford that? He was not a princeling. His wounds would reopen whenever he recalled the past and there would be a sharp pain in his chest.

'Some witch cast an evil eye on her, bhaiya sahib.'

'An evil eye? Why are you making up stories, Mahadjoo?'

'Yes bhaiya sahib! She used to go to the spring late in the evenings. That is when someone must have cast a spell on her.'

'Then?'

'Then what? Baba said marry someone else. He wanted a grandson. But my heart wasn't in it.'

Even Mahdu himself did not know why his heart wasn't in it. How could he explain it to others? When Prem bhaiya asked him why he didn't marry again since he was allowed three wives Mahdu said, 'Perhaps God doesn't will it.' God willed that Mahdu should come to the city but how he landed in Ayodhyanath Raina's house was another story. However, once he arrived there, he got along so well with the children and the elders that he soon became a member of the family. Filling Tathya sahib's hookah, mixing the tobacco, cleaning the house and playing with the children, all these became a part of his daily activities.

'Mahadjoo, we want to go to Pratap park,' one child would make a request.

'Today let's visit Shankaracharya hill,' another would chip in.

'Someone is selling chestnuts outside. Please get us some!'

'I want roast corn, nice and warm.'

'We want to hear a story…'

Mahdu could distract the others and they would listen to him, but Katyayini? Mahdu had no choice except to fulfil this wasp's demands. If he refused she would immediately go to the foot of the stairs and shout – 'Taaataaa,' with so much pain in her voice as though someone had beaten her up. So it was better to give in to the little one's demands than to get a scolding from Tathya.

'Yes, tell me, which story do you want to hear?'

'The one about the Amarnath cave. You said the cave was discovered by a boy from the Malik family didn't you? Tell us, how he found it?'

'Thaaaat one!' Mahdu would close his eyes and go back into the past. 'Many, many years ago, one day a boy from the Malik family of Anantnag came to the pastures around Chandanwari to graze his cattle. While the cattle were grazing he lazed around in the shade of a deodar tree close by. It was summer. The cool breeze and gentle shade soon lulled him into deep sleep.'

'Was there a spring close by?' Sharika asked curiously.

'Don't interrupt! Listen to the story of the cave. So, children, may God be merciful, when the boy woke up in the evening he counted his animals. A few were missing. The boy got worried that he would get a beating for his carelessness. So he set off to find them. He thought they might have wandered towards Neelganga and so he crossed the snow bridge and wandered off far into the mountains. He kept walking on but he couldn't find his sheep. The mountains were very steep and there were fields of snow. Finally he saw what looked like a cave ahead.'

'A cave in the snow mountains?'

'Yes, children! He was amazed when he saw the cave at such a height after so many steep hills and fields of snow. He wondered if he was imagining it. What kind of cave was this located in the midst of a barren snow field and who did it belong to?'

'Do you know, children, what he saw when he went inside?'

'Hmmm… he must have seen a lion, no a cheetah.'

'No, no he saw a bear with long hair.'

'We know! It must have been the home of a rahchok, that frightening creature with eyes like lamps that lives in the snows.'

'No, my dears! There was a Shivling in the cave. What kind of a Shivling? It was neither on the ground nor in the sky, it was suspended in midair. The boy was amazed but also scared as he tried to figure out what this insubstantial thing was which was hovering in the air.'

'So, the boy returned to his village and told everyone what he had seen. Some people believed him, others thought he was making up stories. He was good at telling tales anyway. But there were some wise Brahmins in the village who visited the cave along with the boy. After the steep climb they were rewarded not only by the sight of Shivji but they also saw a pair of pigeons who lived in the cave.'

Later when Katya and Didda heard the story of Amarnath in detail from their maternal grandfather Krishnajoo or Kathabab they were convinced that Mahadjoo didn't only tell imaginary stories, he also knew some real ones. Naturally this increased their respect for him. Pandit Krishnajoo's corroboration of what Mahdu said would inevitably increase Mahdu's stature.

Somadeva's Descendants

Pandit Krishnajoo and Balbhadra often argued with each other. When four people are discussing a subject it inevitably gets stretched in all directions. Balbhadra respected Krishnajoo who was, after all, one of the few graduates in the valley. While Pandit Nandlal Kitru was the first graduate from the valley, Krishnajoo belonged to the number of those who followed him including R.C Pandit, Madan, Kazi and others. He was knowledgeable about religion and philosophy and though he wasn't a lawyer, munsif or landlord, his intelligence and wisdom could not be faulted. However Balbhadra couldn't always understand his philosophy.

For instance, recently they had been discussing the possibility of marrying Chunni to Niranjan Raina's son. When Balbhadra asked Krishnajoo's advice about the boy who worked in Krishnajoo's office, he said, 'Go ahead, he is a very good boy.' Balbhadra, however, was a little unsure because the boy's grandfather had been a baker. When he mentioned this fact to Krishnajoo, the latter lost his temper, 'Yes bhai, he was a baker, not a thief. There is no sin in working hard to rise above poverty. Now the family is blessed by both Saraswati and Lakshmi.'

But Balbhadra was worried about what the world would say, 'One has to think about ancestry and antecedents as well. If that wasn't the case, then Dina bayu's son Omkar could also have been a good choice. The parents are gentle and the boy is earning well. But one can't even think of it, because 'gors' or brahmins of the priestly class and Karkun brahmins can never marry each other.'

'You are an educated man and yet you blindly follow these beliefs. Think, it is these 'gors' who have protected and preserved our culture. During the rule of Zainulabdin, when the Hindu brahmins who had been banished from the valley returned, the Sultan employed some of these Bhatts as advisors and salaried officials. These brahmins learnt Persian and were called Karkuns. Others were asked to record and preserve Sanskrit manuscripts and ancient texts, and they were the people who subsequently came to be known as 'gors'. With the passage of time Karkuns and gors became separate castes. So, where does the question of superior and inferior arise?'

Balbhadra had his own ideas about religious beliefs. There can be no argument about them because beliefs are undebatable. They are a part of tradition, that's it! For instance brahmins are allowed to eat meat but they can't touch eggs. Alms are given to poor brahmins on the occasion of Sakranti but if anyone sees Sula, the sweeper, approaching he quickly turns into another alley to avoid any contact with the man.

Krishnajoo enjoyed pulling Balbhadra's leg 'Balbhadra. Gandhiji calls these people Harijans. He also advises everyone to clean their own toilets. He does so himself, but if you had your way you would build a separate road for Sula so that there would be no fear of your coming across him.'

Balbhadra rose to the bait, 'Look at this, now bhai sahib has become obsessed with Sula, the sweeper. Once he is over this he will move on to Gandhiji. But one doesn't become a Gandhi just by repeating his name. Gandhi attends the Round Table Conference wearing just a thin dhoti and a shawl, he does satyagrah and goes on fasts, he suffers the blows of the English lathis. We are only capable of repeating his name, nothing else.' Ayodhyanath mediated and rang the bell for tea. When Mukundram appeared with the fragrant Kehwa and warm Bakirkhanis, the bitterness of the argument was washed away by the sweetness of the tea. There was no rancour left. Both Balbhadra and Krishnajoo were good friends of Ayodhyanath. Krishnajoo was also related to him because his daughter Lalli was married to Ayodhyanath's son. Ayodhyanath had great respect for Krishnajoo. His liberal thinking and endearing behaviour had made him popular at home and in the office, among children and elders.

The children surrounded him whenever they saw that he was free.

'Tell us a story, Babba, a fable, Nanaji.'

Ayodhyanath thought of the wealth of stories that Krishnajoo knew. 'He is definitely a descendent of Somadeva.'

Krishnajoo never tired of telling tales and stories. Stories from the *Panchatantra* and the *Puranas*, stories from history, stories about geography and stories from a thousand years ago. He firmly believed that knowledge of one's culture and traditions was passed on to women by men and to children by their elders. And weren't stories the best medium of instruction? The result was that almost every evening Kathabab, or 'story grandpa' would be surrounded by the children with their demands for more and more stories. One evening, when the children were drawn by their love of stories to Kathabab, he was talking about the worsening political situation with his neighbour, Vishambhar. The children heard him saying, 'Jalodbhav has once again invaded Satisar.'

When the story-telling session began Katya tried to satisfy her curiosity by asking her maternal grandfather, 'Nanaji, who was Jalodbhav? How did he get into Satisar? How did he breathe in the water?'

Her younger brother had an answer, 'Why shouldn't he be able to breathe? He must have dived straight down to the palace in Pataal, the netherworld, which is full of treasures guarded by giants with long teeth. Isn't that so, Babba?'

'Silly,' Didda thumped her younger brother playfully on the back.

'Jalodbhav didn't dive, he actually lived in the water.'

Krishnajoo wanted to satisfy the children's curiosity. He asked Nathji to bring the hookah, took a few pulls at it and sat down comfortably, cross-legged. 'My little ones, all of you sit on the floor and listen carefully. Today I will tell you the story of how Kashmir came into being.'

'But what about Jalodbhav?'

'He will also appear in the story, just keep quiet and listen. If you have any questions save them for the end. I don't like being interrupted.'

'All right children, many many years ago at the beginning of the first age, our valley was a huge lake called Satisar.'

'Why Satisar?' Little brother wanted to know.

'Because it is the land of the goddess Parvati, who is also known as Sati, that is why it is called Satisar. Once, a giant called Jalodbhav came here and started harassing the Nagas, people who lived in the foothills of the mountains.'

'Nanaji , why did he go into the water, he could have walked around in the open. He wasn't afraid of anyone. He could make himself grow as tall as the sky.'

'Babbaji, the Nagas would have run away when they saw him. They must have slithered away into their holes under some rock...' Munni also refused to keep quiet.

'It wasn't like that Munni! How will you understand anything if you ask questions in the middle of the story? Listen. Jalodbhav did great tapasya. He prayed and did penance, till Brahma granted him three boons: one, that he could live in water, two, that he would be very powerful and three, that he would have mastery over illusion. Jalodbhav lived in the water to protect himself and remember, the Nagas were not snakes. Nagas and Pishachas were people just like you and me. The Nagas would come to live in our valley in spring and would go down to the plains of the Pir Panchal mountain range as soon as it snowed in winter. The Pishachas used to stay on in the valley even during winter.'

'So, my golden children. It is said that when people got tired of Jalodbhav's tyranny they went and appealed to Kashyapa rishi, the ascetic, who was the father of the Nagas. They said, "Father, please save us from this demon. We are very unhappy." Kashyapa listened to the woes of the people and tried to find a solution to their problems. The *Neelamath Purana* says that Kashyapa rishi prayed to Lord Shiva for a thousand years at Naubandh near Haripur. The lord was happy and he sent Vishnu and Brahma to kill the demon. Now, children! Jalodbhav couldn't die while he lived in water. Brahma himself had granted him this boon. So, Lord Vishnu gave instructions that a cut should be made in the mountains near Baramullah so that the water from the lake would drain out. When this happened Jalodbhav died and a beautiful valley emerged in place of the lake. Since this great task was accomplished with the help of Kashyapa Rishi, the valley was named Kashyapmar, that is, Kashmir.'

'The rakshasa died, but why did you tell Kakaji that Jalodbhav has entered Satisar once again?' The story had ended but Katya's curiosity had not been satisfied. 'When someone dies they are gone, finished!'

How could Krishnajoo explain to the children that the death of one demon does not mean the end of all the demons in the world? From time to time, they enter the bodies of human beings again and look for occasions to spread terror and create confusion.

'The story is over children, but the sayings still continue to be true. Those who spread fear and chaos in the country and society, who trouble people needlessly, they will be called rakshasas. They will be called demons in any era.'

Who knew how much the children understood and how much was washed away from their minds like water off a slab of ice? It was certain, however, that they were fascinated by stories of rakshasas, gods and goddesses, Nagas and Pishachas. Often, in their dreams, they would see deities wearing golden crowns raining down rays of light on them in blessing or see fierce demons with long, crooked teeth and yard-long moustaches fighting with each other. Then the children would understand that the essence of Nanaji's stories was that evil deeds lead to evil results and one should stay away from evil. The stories did not merely entertain, they also carried a message.

But Krishnajoo did not teach merely through words, his behaviour and social etiquette also set an example.

'Spending lavishly on the marriages of his deceased brother's daughters, making sure they were married into good families, all this could only be done by someone with a big heart, bhai.'

'That is true. Natha is the only one who turned out to be useless despite all of Krishnajoo's efforts.'

'Yes, Krishnajoo has done so much for that boy? He engaged tutors for him and even taught him Mathematics and English personally but if the goddess of learning, Saraswati, withholds her blessings there can be no success however hard one tries. With great difficulty Natha managed to pass the tenth class after which he just came to a complete halt.'

'Well at least Krishnajoo managed to get him a job with the Nanda bus service. That suits Natha's love of the outdoors and his friendly nature.' Ayodhyanath had given up all hope but Krishnajoo felt he had finally managed to repay the debt he owed to his brother. Natha actually managed to impress tourists with his 'yes sir', 'please sir' and soon the Nandas increased his commission and gave him the responsibility of looking after two buses on the Srinagar-Gulmarg route, keeping track of expenses and organizing hotels and skiing and skating for the tourists. Jialal joked, 'Natha is lucky he got a job that suits his temperament. He can hang around for free and in the company of white memsahibs.'

When Krishnajoo heard about the memsahibs from others as well, he sought the advice of Anand bayu. 'He's got the job by a stroke of luck and your blessings, now if we could find a nice girl for him we could fulfil the dearest wish of his mother Bhadra.' Anand bayu nodded his wise head in agreement. He studied Natha's horoscope and judged the effect of the planets, and after everything had been checked, he fixed Natha's marriage to the daughter of Sridhar Bhatt of Anantnag.

The father-in-law to be had expressed some mild doubts to Anand bayu. He said, 'Pandit Krishnajoo is a wise and good man, maharaj, but I have heard that Nathji has not even cleared his matric. I worry that tomorrow, God forbid, if he loses his job what will happen to my daughter? She will have no support.' Anand Bayu felt a little insulted by Bhatt sahib's misgivings. However, he forgave the man and assuaged his fears.

'Think positive Shridharjoo, who knows which moment is 'abhijeth' and Lord Shiva grants whatever you say? You must have heard the story of the weary traveller in the jungle who thought good thoughts and was rewarded with pulao to eat and a soft bed to sleep on but the minute he let negative thoughts enter his mind he was eaten up by a lion.'

'Maharaj, forgive me, after all I am the father of a daughter.' When Bhatt sahib fell at Anand Bayu's feet the pandit was mollified. It was necessary, after all, to explain some things. It was not suitable for the father of a daughter to have too much pride.

'Bhatt sahib, do you know who Pandit Krishnajoo Kaul is? Let me inform you, in case you don't know, that he is the descendent of Dattatreya munishwars.'

In his agitation Anand bayu even narrated the entire story of rishi Atreya and his wife Anusuya, of how Narad munishwar once visited the wives of Brahma, Vishnu and Mahesh and praised Anusuya's devotion saying that there was no other woman in all the three realms who was more dedicated to her husband. Savitri, Lakshmi and Parvati took Narad's claim as a challenge and sent their respective husbands down to earth to test Anusuya. The gods took on the forms of sadhus, mendicants, and asked her to fulfil their wish for food by serving it without wearing any clothes.

'Sati Anusuya was no ordinary woman, maharaj! She realized that these men with their extraordinary request were no common sadhus. She sprinkled water, in which she had washed her husband's feet, over the three and changed them into small babies. Then she breast fed them without her clothes and calmly put them to bed in a cradle.'

'In the meanwhile, the devis were worried at the long absence of the devas. When they got the news from Narad muni they went to Ausuya's hut and enquired about their husbands. Anusuya pointed to the three babies and said, 'Why doesn't each of you pick the one who is your husband?' The goddesses naturally couldn't do so and their pride was destroyed. Anusuya relented and sprinkling on them the water in which her husband's feet had been washed, brought them back to their normal appearance. The gods were impressed with Sati's power and intelligence. Anusuya permitted the gods to leave but only on condition that because she had fed them her milk they should take on a single form and be born in her house. The devas agreed and Dattatreya was born, with three heads and six arms; Vishnu in the center, Shiva on the left and Brahma on the right. Pandit Krishnajoo Kaul is the descendent of this child, who was given to Atreya and who came to be known as Dattatreya.'

Shridhar Bhatt was so moved that he almost started crying and that very instant he decided to marry his only daughter Indira to Nathji. Nathji, however, did not mend his ways. Those days a girl was not inspected like a piece of furniture, it was assumed that since Anand Bayu had seen her she would be all right. But Nathji insisted that he would only get married after seeing the girl. He sent Rehman to Shridhar Bhatt's house with some fish and accompanied him. He covered his head with a blanket, just leaving his eyes open so that he could see his beloved. Rehman shouted out, 'Fish, fish for sale, mahaseer from the Wular lake. Trout fish!' At this, Shobhri, the girl's mother, stuck her head out of the window. She called out to her daughter Indira, who came out with a reed basket, and started checking out the fish as she bargained. Nathji stood under a walnut tree trying to catch a glimpse, even a fleeting one, of his prospective bride, and when he did see her he was spellbound. She looked like an apsara from the court of Lord Indra! She was so beautiful that he forgot to blink, the tourist memsahibs looked like monkeys by comparison.

Nathji's marriage was fixed in this manner and the ceremony took place very soon. Krishnajoo observed all the rituals with great generosity. The wedding tents stayed up from the moment of the shagun and the engagement till the wedding and the phirsaal, the post-marriage dinner. Mohammad qawwal created such a beautiful atmosphere with his 'Sufiana kalaam' that even the men stayed awake the entire night to listen and then Rehman sang some romantic songs. There was a flood of auspicious occasions and rituals and from the very day of the mehndiraat, the henna ceremony, hordes of relatives descended on the household. The girls drew decorative patterns on the doors of the house. Lalli bua sprinkled water at the entrance door to ward off any evil. The walls were decorated with 'krool', designs drawn with turmeric, lime, sandalwood, henna, red and green colours. Lalli wrote the word 'welcome' above the door in a beautiful script. The girls sang all night beating the drum-like tumbaknari, 'Mother Sharda herself has come to join us on the mehndiraat.' Masiji, Natha's maternal aunt, washed his feet, the buas put henna on his feet and hands and then went around the crowded room distributing henna to all the women and collecting shagun money, which was their right.

On the day of the devgoan Natha's mother's family came from Bandipora with new clothes for him. When Natha was getting ready on the day of his wedding, Krishnajoo himself tied the turban on his head. Natha's sisters decorated the saffron coloured turban with a seven stringed gold necklace and a colourful peacock feather. Natha looked like a prince wearing an achkan and a churidar as he stood on the vyuug, the decorative pattern drawn on the ground, and everyone showered him with flower petals.

After Nathji's baraat departed only the women of the house were left behind. Women did not accompany the groom, they could not leave the house unattended and they had their own celebrations at home. They had to perform the ritual of dancing on the vyug, showering flowers on themselves as they turned round and round while other women standing around in a circle sang , 'Our mynah is dancing, covered from head to toe in gold. What does our mynah want as a reward for her dance? A chandanhaar, a choker, a kardan of gold? You will get all of them, just dance.' At every command, the married women laughed and twirled around. Even the elderly women danced, their songs were full of sweet memories they had tucked away in their hearts. They sang,'Parents are like a cool shade in the sandy wastes of life, when I look back at the roads I have traversed, your love and affection calls out to me. My mother, baba, my brothers and sisters, my blessings on you!'

Next day Nathji returned with the bride, Indira. When Krishnajoo, and all the uncles entered the courtyard with the air of victors, voices were raised in song, 'Our dear Mama, maternal uncle has come home with his bride….' Tumbaknaris were beaten with gusto as songs of welcome were sung. The aromatic smoke of burning Isband spread through the house to celebrate the arrival of the bride, the Lakshmi of the house. Rehman's mother danced the Rauf and sister Khurshid welcomed the bride singing, 'Grandmother, your beloved grandson has returned, come and greet him with a cradle decorated with bells.'

The sound of the tumbaknari and the collective voices

raised in song drew the women of the neighbourhood to the house to offer their good wishes and join in the feast. 'Mubarak, congratulations to the women of the house, your son and daughter-in-law have come home.' Bhadra was assaulted by these sweet arrows of good wishes, which she accepted with pleasure as she blessed everyone and invited them to eat their fill. The marriage was over. Krishnajoo thanked God. The happy occasion had gone off without any problems.

Anand Shastri

In the east, streaks of pink brightened the fading darkness of dawn. Dancing lightly across them, the early rays of the sun were reflected in the waters of the Vitasta. Intoxicated by the fragrant pollen of the almond and peach trees, the gentle breeze playfully gusted and rippled the vast mirror of water. Anandjoo stood on the riverbank, watching this grand spectacle of earth and sky, wonderstruck, as though the mysteries of the universe were being revealed to him for the first time.

The journey of the awakening of the mind spans many eons. Where, Anandjoo wondered, had this land of Kashmir been seven eons ago? A great sea after the apocalyptic dissolution of the world at the end of a kalpa, an eon or a day of Brahma. Lord Mahadev himself taking on the form of water, spreading everywhere.

Om Namah Shivay! In Anandjoo's mind's eye the goddess Sati took on the form of the earth on which the vast sweet water Satisar, six yojans long and three yojans wide, spread out.

He saluted Lord Vishnu at whose command, the story goes, Balrama drained this land of water to get rid of the demon Jalodbhav. But how could life exist without water? And so Kashyapa did penance and propitiated the goddesses who agreed to take the form of rivers and springs in this sacred terrain. Lakshmi became the river Vishoka near Kramsaar (Kaunsarnag), Aditi, the mother of the gods, materialised as the river Trikoti near Kulgaam. Shachi appeared as the river Harshpatha and Diti as Chandravati. Devi Sati herself appeared, at the request of the Lord, for the salvation of the people and in the land created out of her own body, as the Vitasta to which the Ganga and the Yamuna bequeathed parts of themselves so that it became a sacred blend of all the rivers.

Anandjoo chanted 'Prabhu Shoolpane, Vibho Vishwanath' and took a dip in the Vitasta. He felt blessed – an unparalleled feeling of benediction. He turned to the east and prayed to the sun, 'Om Mitraye Namah: Om Ravye Nmamah: Om Suryaye Namah.' The battle which had been raging within him since yesterday quietened down. Anandjoo knew how to remain at peace. He was a holy man, but he also bore the yoke of being a householder. He had learnt how to handle the ups and downs of family life. That is why he lingered so long in the prayer room in front of his tiny gods and goddesses. Prayers, chanting, fasts and rituals, all these were a part of his heritage. They helped to calm the mind, wipe out bitterness, and in any case, what is a brahmin without his traditions?

Anandjoo was respected by elders and children alike. No one argued with hm. But now, his own grandson had started speaking an alien language and that was causing him considerable concern. Anandjoo's school was on one side of the sitting room in his house. He had no idea how successful he had been over the years in his attempts to pass on knowledge of religious texts to the neighbourhood children. He was merely justifying his own existence as a brahmin by sowing the seeds of religion, philosophy and culture in the minds of these young children and passing the reins of tradition into the hands of the next generation. His son Nityanand had learnt the early morning chant of the Mangalastrotam and read through the *Ramayana* and the *Bhagvat* sitting in the same class as the other children. He became familiar with texts written in the Sharada script as well as those in Sanskrit. Anandjoo cannot recall a time when his son showed a lack of interest in his studies, but his grandson Moti? Despite sitting in the class from the time he was a child till the age of fourteen and he was never really mentally present there.

At some point Moti informed his grandmother that he had learnt enough mantras, had understood the Gita and would now prefer to study science because he didn't want to study religious texts and become a priest. This message was conveyed to Anandjoo in an indirect manner but he understood its real meaning. He was hurt that his grandson thought of him as just an ordinary priest while so many learned people consulted him to clear their doubts and came to discuss religious philosophy with him. Even Maharaja Pratap Singh included him in the list of great astrologers and sought his guidance at the beginning of any auspicious event. The Maharaja had been so pleased with the brilliance of Anandjoo's father, Vishambhar Shastri, that he had gifted him a piece of good agricultural land in Badgam which was what the shastri's grandchildren and great-grandchildren lived on even today. Were the children of the shastris, who had imparted knowledge of Sanskrit for generations, now going to question the intelligence of their elders? Was this an example of modern education?

Anand shastri spent a restless night. Where had he gone wrong? He was not against English or Urdu. He understood that two hundred years of British rule were bound to have had an impact in their lives. Shastriji knew that the British couldn't bring people over from England to do clerical work and that was why they were educating Indians to make them white collar workers. This was education with a specific purpose. But English and other foreign scholars were also fascinated by Indian religion and philosophy, which is why so many of them visited the country over the ages. Scholars like the Chinese traveller Huen Tsang, U Kong R.L Stein, and Todd had all been impressed by this knowledge. The work of Indian Shaivite scholars, poets and historians had also been appreciated. What knowledge could the British give Indians when they were themselves in need of enlightenment?

Anandjoo made a last attempt to convince Moti. He stroked his head affectionately and spoke about the rich and proud traditions of his ancient culture. Moti just looked down, listening silently to the lecture on religion and philosophy. And when finally Anandjoo asked him for answers Moti tearfully mumbled, 'I am not interested in this subject Bablal, what can I do?'

Despite this Moti continued to excel in his studies. He always scored high marks in Science, English and Mathematics. He used to visit Ayodhyanath's house quite often and was a very close friend of Premnath. This interaction with a socially superior household, in a sense, also muddled his thinking. Where was the comparison between the small shabby house on the banks of the Vitasta, with its group of children sitting in a dark stuffy room repeating Abhinavgupt's 'Shiv stuti' with Moti merely moving his lips, and Ayodhyanath's beautiful airy bungalow surrounded by plants and trees where Premnath sat enjoying stories such as 'Look for me by Moonlight', 'Lochinvar' and 'Horatius'! Both boys were the same age, in the same class and yet their worlds were so different! The day Moti went with Ayodhyanath's family to Gupkar in a boat the mischievous mountain breeze and the perfume of the lotus flowers in the Dal lake filled his mind with a strange unease. The restlessness of freedom! That day Moti asked Premnath some odd questions –'Do your Bhobaji and Kaka Sahib often dress up, wear a saffron coloured turban and visit the Maharaja's durbar?'

'No, when the durbar begins they go with a gift on the Maharaja's birthday. You know the durbar is in Srinagar for six months and in Jammu for six because Jammu has been our winter capital since 1870? Kaka Sahib and Bhobaji are both Gazetted officers that is why they give a gift to the Raja and the Raja also gives them a gift in return.'

'Really?' Moti was amazed. His grandfather was considered to be a great scholar but he has never picknicked in a boat or gone to the Raj durbar.

Pratap, however, told Moti some things he did not know including the fact that Moti's grandfather often used to be invited to the durbar of Raja Pratap Singh. Tathyaji had told them that the Raja always ask Moti's grandfather to advise him on which dates were auspicious for travel.

'Hasn't he told you that he used to given gifts by the Raja?' Pratap asked. Anand shastri had mentioned this fact but Moti had found it difficult to believe his grandfather. It was Pratap who told Moti that his grandfather's great grandfather or an ancestor even further back in the fourteenth century had been forced to abandon his home and country because of the tyranny of Sikandar 'Butshikan'.

'Why did he have to leave his country?'

'Arre, haven't you read that Sikandar 'Butshikan' tried to force Hindus to give up their religion? A lot of brahmins died because of this tyranny and many others left the valley. They even went as far down south as Karnataka and Maharashtra. Ask your Bablal, he will tell you the story of how once, during that time, some Bhatts were lying, tired after their journey, on the shore of the sea in Maharashtra when some local people saw them. They thought the Bhatts were dead and, noticing their sacred threads, took them away to be cremated. But as they moved the bodies the Bhatts began to breathe. The locals were amazed when they realized that the Bhatts were still alive.'

'Those people suffered a lot for the sake of their religion.'

'They were great.'

'Then how did they get back?' Moti wanted to know.

'Sikandar's son the Badshah called the Bhatts back with respect and honour. He gave them important posts and honourable work. Your ancestors wrote commentaries and preserved the ancient Sanskrit texts. They were known as commentators. Even your father and grandfather have written many books. That is why Tathya respects them so much. He says you are the people who are responsible for preserving our religion and culture.'

Moti was delighted to hear his grandfather being praised. Because of this he memorised some important mantras such as the Gayatri mantra, the Brahmi vidya and some couplets from the *Ramayana* together with their explanations. So, in his own way he did try to please his grandfather. Shastriji was happy, he felt that despite everything the boy was rooted in his traditions. Unfortunately he was growing up at a time when tradition and culture were being weakened and challenged by skeptics and by the influence of European thought. Still Shastriji believed he would understand everything gradually. For his part, Moti was trying hard to understand what was happening around him.

1940 was a time of great turmoil in the country. On the one hand, there were furious political discussions between Gandhi, Nehru and Jinnah and on the other, there was the continuing oppression of the English and their false promises. In the valley too things were in upheaval with the rise of the National Conference and the domination of the English Residents. And elsewhere, the Second World War was in full swing. Everything was in a state of confusion and uncertainty.

There was a rising clamour for independence in the valley

with farmers and labourers participating in the agitation. Teachers of Sanskrit and the salaried middle class however, did not play any role in these campaigns. They were also concerned about their country but they could not participate in politics because of the tight control the British had over their state. Youngsters had begun to understand the significance of the word independence and the quest for freedom was beginning at home with cracks fast developing in traditional beliefs, behaviour and accepted modes of thought.

Anand shastri could gauge the direction in which the world around him was heading, so he gave Moti his blessings. Moti completed his B.Sc from Amar Singh College and then left for Benaras Hindu University (Anand shastri felt there were only two real centres of learning, Kashmir and Kashi, that is, Benaras). When Moti returned with his gold and silver medals, Anand shastri welcomed Science into his home for the first time.

Embracing Moti on his success he said, 'we have tried to learn the secrets of creation through the *Veda*s and the *Upanishad*s, you will learn them through Science. There isn't much difference between the two, but, for self-realization you will have to learn to look within yourself and the worship of Shiva will help you, so don't turn away from any kind of learning.' He spoke some more words which others did not hear but then, taking Moti's hand in his, he said something else, more as a request rather than a command, which took all the onlookers by surprise because it was addressed to his grandson rather than to his Sanskrit scholar son, Nitya. He said, 'When I die I want you to recite the Brahmi vidya in my ear.' It seems Anand shastri's eyes filled with tears as he said this.

Masterji: Number One, Two, Three

Ayodhyanth believed in educating the children at home till they reached the fourth or fifth grade, though, of course, he didn't tutor them personally. As a reputed lawyer he barely had time to attend to all his clients' problems so how could he spare time for the children? Nevertheless, he was very particular about their education. The three 'R's', reading, writing and arithmetic, were necessary, as was the study of English (keeping the future in mind), but sowing the seeds of one's culture was absolutely essential. And who could perform this task better than Anand shastri? So, Ayodhyanath handed this task over to him. Anand shastri decided on an auspicious date and determined to impart as much knowledge as the young minds could absorb. On the chosen day the children appeared freshly bathed, as instructed, and sat cross-legged on the floor. Anandjoo then unveiled a framed picture of the goddess Saraswati which was covered in red cloth. He performed a pooja invoking the Brahman and then began by teaching the children the hymn of Saraswati.

But this was not enough. Qualified teachers had to be found to teach modern subjects as well, so Pandit Ishwarjoo, Prakashram masterji and Janakinath masterji also arrived to teach the children. They didn't all appear at the same time but came one after another. No master lasted more than five to six months thanks to the pranks of the children. Ishwarjoo masterji, the first teacher, had a strange habit. He would drink his tea and then lodging the kulcha in his cheek would smoke tobacco and gazing upwards at the sky he would dictate; 'cowwwww, sheeeeep, goaaaat' etcetera. The half-open mouth, unclear sounds and the occasional spray of spit sent the children into fits of laughter and their 'khi khi' could be heard across the room.

'Who is laughing? Should I beat you up? Pay attention to your work and write clearly. Don't scribble on the shlate....'

Masterji would threaten and the children would innocently bow their heads over their slates. Didda, who didn't participate in the general merriment but sat six feet away from masterji with her head buried in her books, would undeservedly earn masterji's praise. One day, however, she told Tathya very clearly that she was not willing to be taught by this 'kulcha masterji.'

Tathya was unnerved by this diktat from his favourite grand-daughter and unhappy about her apparent disrespect and lack of loyalty to her guru. However, being a worldly-wise man, he finally arranged for a new teacher after giving her a scolding.

The next teacher was Prakash masterji. Stocky, well-built, with a round face. He held a carved stick made of walnut wood in his right hand, a symbol of his authority. In Ayodhyanath's house it was strictly forbidden to raise one's hand against any of the children. A scolding was permitted, but that was all. So, masterji would place his stick behind the door as soon he entered the class-room but even this did not detract from his commanding presence.

Actually the children were inordinately impressed by some questions which Prakashram masterji asked them on the very first day. They had come prepared to face some tough queries, including dates and years which were difficult to remember such as 1876, the year Graham Bell invented the telephone, or 1896 the year the Italian scientist Marconi invented the radio. The children were ready, but what did masterji ask them? A very simple, ordinary question which confused the children despite their knowledge of English and taught them the difference between 'I am going' and 'I go'.

The children were impressed by the manner in which masterji demonstrated the difference between the present continuous and the present perfect and quickly got busy writing, 'The cat is mewing, the dog is barking, the sparrow is chirping' etcetera.

Although they were in different classes, Didda, Katya,

Brij bhaiya, Ragya, Sharika and Kanu studied together in the same room which was littered with slates, books, schoolbags, inkpots and bamboo pens. The younger children would recite their tables together. If a child did not complete his homework masterji would sit with him and make him finish his work while the other children enjoyed a holiday. He would just gesture towards the stick but that was enough incentive to obey.

The children were very scared of masterji. The stick was merely a prop, like an elephant's decorative teeth, the fear was based on something else. Masterji had threatened to lock up anyone who didn't do his homework in his rat infested store where there were dozens of big rats. Huge, sharp-toothed, rats! Masterji's house was like a dark basement even in the middle of the afternoon because it was located at the end of a narrow dark alley. The children could imagine ghosts living there, so a dark rat filled room was a definite possibility. If any child entered the room the rats would shred him to bits with their sharp teeth. Hadn't a rat bitten Mahdu's toe once while he was sleeping? He had bled so much, poor man.

The day Katya forgot to do her homework masterji said she would be punished by being locked up in the rat filled room. Katya was petrified. Bhaiya and her sisters also felt the alarm bells ringing. All enmities were forgotten and everyone hovered around Katya, 'Poor thing! The rats will chew up her nose, eyes, ears, everything.'

'They will even chew up her hair.'

'Not just her hair, they will eat her up completely. They are really ravenous.'

It was a moment of grave crisis. The children put their heads together to try and find a way to save Katya who was finding it difficult to complete her work as she imagined rats scampering across the pages of her copybook. Rats in front of her, rats behind her. She thought of huge mustachioed rats staring at her with their shining eyes, evil, biting rats. Rats attacking her from all directions. Her brothers and sisters had already collected their bags and would leave soon, but what about Katya? Masterji would take her to the rat infested room, though at the moment he was having a nap. As masterji's head sank down towards his chest Brij bhaiya thought of a solution. He leapt across, picked up Katya's bag and disappeared from sight. Kanu picked up the wooden writing board and ran, Didda signalled to the others that they should also disappear. But Master Prakash Ram was no ordinary teacher. Aroused from sleep by the rustling sounds of the escaping children he turned his red eyed gaze on them and tripped them up with the curved handle of his stick. Catching Katya's hand he dragged her to the courtyard, 'Now no one can save you. I am definitely going to take you with me. So you were trying to run away, were you, thinking I was asleep? Hm?'

Katya felt totally hopeless and started crying. Mahadjoo tried to intervene on her behalf, 'Please let her go this time Masterji, I shan't try to save her if she misbehaves again.'

Prakash Ram masterji was a little moved by Katya's sobs and let her go because of Mahdu's plea, 'All right, I am letting you go this time but if you ever shirk your work again I am not going to listen to anyone's pleas. Then I will have to take you there.' 'There' meaning the room with rats! Katya, who was shivering with fear at the time, later came to know through Mahdu that there really was no room with rats. It was just a threat used by Masterji to frighten the children.

Prakash Ram masterji was a disciplinarian. This pleased Tathya but there was also a complete lack of softness or affection in his authority. This became evident the day he yelled at tiny Chutku so ferociously that the child screamed in fear and wet his pyjamas. Scared of the thunderous voice and upset by the wetness of his clothes he started crying in real earnest. He was the darling of the household and would get upset even if anyone spoke to him loudly. So, this was the last straw. Tathya was so upset by masterji's behaviour that he got rid of him immediately.

The next in line was Master Anand Pandit. On the very first day of his arrival he was informed about, and understood the reasons for Master Prakash Ram's departure. A very gentle man wearing a pyjama-kameez and a black high collared coat of Pattu with a Gandhi cap on his salt and pepper hair, he followed Gandhiji's principle of non-violence with total faith and gave the children complete freedom in their studies and play. He always seemed to be in the grip of some unnamed, unknown fear. Actually he was in dire need of a job. The children had heard him telling Tathya very humbly, 'Sahib,I am a poor man, you know how little primary school teachers are paid, what do I need to tell you? And then I have the encumberance of a large family....'

The children were not very familiar with the sense in which the word 'encumberance' had been used but it was a new word and they gleefully added it to their vocabulary and immediately christened the new teacher 'Encumberance Masterji'. Encumberance Masterji's knowledge of both English and Sanskrit was quite limited but, to make up for this deficiency, he would tell the children lots of stories. He knew exactly how to handle them. But how long could he succeed in the difficult task of keeping the children happy while maintaining the rules, regulations, codes of conduct and behaviour of the household when teachers like the learned Ishwarjoo and the stern Prakash Ram had failed?

Masterji began well though. The children were spellbound by his narration of entertaining, moving and educational stories about Lal Ded, Badshah and Habba Khatoon. Even their mothers and grandmother would sometimes pause on the threshold of the study room and purify their ears and spirit by hearing a snatch of the story as they were passing by. The girls were especially enthralled when he narrated the story of Lal

Ded of Pampore and described the miracles performed by her. They would imagine Lalli crossing the deep river step by step, her feet barely touching the surface of the water as she walked across to the Natkeshav Bhairav temple on the banks of the river in Zinyapore village. Look! She is coming back carrying a vessel of water on her head. Now her husband is smashing the pot in anger because she has came home late. See, the vessel breaks but the water remains untouched on Lalli's shoulder!

Amazing! Doesn't it seem unbelievable? But that is just what happened! Lalli silently walked in and filled all the pots and vessels in the kitchen to the brim with the water. Then she threw the remaining water in one corner of the courtyard. She didn't say anything, there wasn't even a frown on her face. And the next day people saw that there was a pool filled with water at the very same spot.

'Truly? A pool filled with water?'

'Yes, children, a real pool, which even today is known by the name of 'Laltraag'. This is the same pool into which Lalli's mother-in-law threw the fine cotton spun by Lalli saying it was too thick. It used to be filled with water till a few years ago but now it has dried up.'

Katya would also please Masterji by telling him bits of Lal Ded's story that she had heard from her mother.

'The thread spun by Lal Ded was very fine, wasn't it masterji? That is why the pool was filled with lotus flowers and stems the next day.'

'Yes, you are right Katyayini. When you break a lotus stem, you will find a whole lot of fine threads, just like the threads spun by Lalli.'

'Masterji! Why did her mother-in-law throw such fine spun cotton in the water?'

'A mother-in-law will be a mother-in-law Katyayini, what can I say? It has been like this for centuries. Roopbhavani's mother-in-law, Habba Khatoon's mother-in-law, they were all very cruel to their daughters-in-law. Children, very few mothers-in-law can become mothers. Lalli's mother-in-law was really very pitiless. She used to put a large stone in her dinner plate and serve it to her covered with just a thin layer of rice. She would constantly complain to her son about Lalli. "She spends so much time at the well collecting water, she must be meeting some lover." Lalli's husband also misbehaved. But Lalli bore all this silently.'

'How can anyone bear so much injustice?'

'No, one can't, that is why one day, finally, Lalli left the house and went away. She could not really fit into the life of a housewife. She was an ascetic, a yogini, totally immersed in her love of God. It is said that she used to roam around naked to attain enlightenment. There are many such stories.'

'Please tell us masterji! Everyone likes to hear such interesting stories.'

'They say that one day when Lalli was roaming around naked she saw Samnani sahib, the sufi saint, coming down the street. Lalli said, "A man is coming" and she jumped into a baker's oven nearby. The baker was so scared that he put the lid on the oven. But Samnani sahib had seen Lalli jumping into the oven so he came and took off the cover.'

'Oh! But didn't Lalli get burnt?'

'No, children! She came out dressed in new clothes. When people asked her why she had jumped into the oven she replied, "Because today I saw a real man." Lalli believed that a real man was one who had the true qualities of a human being.'

Masterji recited a few verses or 'vakhs' of Lal Ded and showed the children how beautiful they were. She was a devotee of Shiva who was committed to spreading the message of love and tolerance. Masterji said, 'Lalli was the first poetess of Kashmiri literature. You are still young but when you grow older you will understand the beauty and grandeur of her writings.'

The girls were too young to understand the 'vakhs' but the

stories about Lal Ded's life made them realize that women bore so much of the cruelty they encountered in their marital homes in silence. Katyayini was so upset by this that she told her mother she would never get married. Who knew, her mother-in-law might also serve her a smattering of rice spread over a stone. Katya could not bear to be hungry. She would die. She wouldn't be able to stay quiet. If they kept shouting at her she thought she would run away from home like Lalli.

Ma started laughing, 'You are not Lal Ded nor is your mother-in-law likely to be cruel. Is anyone in our house unkind? Tell me! You know how much Kakni loves me! My dear Munni, Lal Ded's mother-in-law did not understand her. She was a typical housewife who wanted a house full of grandchildren. Lalli was a yogini, how could she become a housewife? This was why her mother-in-law was upset with her, though her father-in-law was very kindhearted.'

Mesmerised by Lal Ded's story, women, who constantly asked God to grant them the same patience as Lalli also wished the same for their daughters. Their daughters would also accept this wish and blessing without question. But the day Katyayini heard the story of Lal Ded, some questions arose in her mind. Lal Ded wrote poetry but Katya couldn't write. Lal Ded bore the persecution of her mother-in-law and husband without protest, but she wouldn't be able to do that at all. Lal Ded could even emerge laughing from the tandoor. Katya was perplexed about this, Kakni was already making her wear a chunni, a long scarf, but Lalli used to move around without any clothes.

A questioning spirit was taken by mothers to be an indicator of the arrival of Kaliyug but Kaliyug had entered Katya's mind very early. This was something the family came to know much later. For the moment, however, let us return to that story of 'encumberance masterji' and the last tale he narrated in Ayodhyanath's house. This was the story of Momma Kukudi. Masterji recounted it in such a manner that the children were in splits. Tatya heard the untrammeled laughter of the guru and his disciples with surprise and subsequently with growing anger.

'Poor Momma! His name was Mohammad but his parents used to call him Momma affectionately. Once Momma grew up he started thinking about earning his living. So, he went and bought a few hens and started a poultry farm. One of his hens was snow white and laid a lot of eggs. Momma would constantly boast about this 'snowy hen' to anyone he met. 'My hen lays so many eggs, she is whiter than snow, look at the way she walks, like a princess, a swan."

After a while people got tired of all this boasting and they started calling him Momma Kukudi. Wherever he went everyone, young and old, would call out Momma Kukudi. Momma finally got so tired of this that he left the village and went to live in the city. There he started a new business and earned a lot of money and fame. People now called him Khan Mohammad and treated him with a lot of respect.

'But look at Momma's luck! After many years he felt homesick and went back to his village to visit his parents. He met a few young boys on the street who did not recognize him. How could they? He looked like Khan, wearing an excellent Pathani salwar, black coat and a Turkish cap. An old woman came up and peered at him, 'Who are you, bhai? Are you a newcomer to the village? Your face looks a little familiar,' Khan Mohammad had just opened his mouth to reply when she patted him affectionately on the back and said, 'Oh, you are Momma, Momma Kukudi."

All his old friends and acquaintances gathered round and Momma was greeted on all sides by voices shouting 'Momma Kukudi has come.'

The children, who were listening to the story, also started clapping and shouting,'Momma Kukudi.' When he heard this noise Tathya came and stood at the threshold of the study room. So this was what they were studying! Shouting like mannerless ruffians. As soon they saw Tathya the children immediately became silent and Masterji could see his future promotion, daily meal and decent salary slipping out of his hands.

He stood up in confusion, uncertain about how he should behave.

'Sit down Masterji, please come and see me before you leave...'

Even the children understood that something was definitely going to happen. Tahtya had a deep affection for the children, but he could not condone indiscipline, especially not in someone who was supposed to be a teacher.

The end result was that the teacher went and the children were admitted to various schools. Katya and Ragya were sent to Maitreyi Middle School, Chutku to Biscoe Sahib's Heddo Memorial School and Didda, Sharika to Vasanta High School which had just opened in the city, thanks to Annie Besant. The girls went to Maitreyi and Vasanta schools so that they would imbibe an education based on Indian values and beliefs. After all, ultimately, they had to become good housewives and mothers. Keeping the boy's future in mind, however, it was essential that he learned English, which would make him eligible for high posts and degrees. Tahtya was also keen to send Kanu to Heddo Memorial school but during this period Sona's brother-in-law was transferred to Ladakh. Her sister-in-law was alone at home so Sona bua had to go back to her in-laws house along with the children. Kanu and Brij bhaiya therefore were admitted to Shri Pratap School where their elder brother Raghunath was already studying in class eight.

The house was suddenly empty after the departure of Raghu, Kanu and Brij bhaiya. Sona was no longer the same chirpy Sona as before, she would spend a lot of time in prayers and rituals. Once in a while from her room one could hear a snatch of a hymn written by Master Zind Kaul or one of Arnimaal's tear drenched songs about the anguish of separation.

Despite the air of sadness about her, the fragrance of her affectionate presence filled the house. But with her departure a cold emptiness permeated and spread its wings over the entire household.

❦

School Admission and the Tulsi Purana

The children enjoyed going to school. Though it did not give them the opportunity to soar into the sky it released them from the restrictions and constant admonishments of life within the four walls of the house.

Katya and Didda attended different schools but Ragya was with Katya. Katya also made a lot of friends in school. Alongside her studies she also had to participate in sports, something she enjoyed very much. At home they could only play catch, hopping on one leg or skip rope and play with gittas, making sure they weren't seen by family members. Kakni would find something wrong with every game, 'Skipping rope? What kind of game is that ? Do you want grow as tall as a palm tree? Then we will have to go and find an equally tall bridegrooms for you.'

'Why are you thumping around in the rooms ? Do you want to bring the house down? Don't you know any dignified games?'

What was a dignified game anyway?

Aunt Kamala would also add fuel to the fire. 'What are these silly games? Now Tulsi, the daughter of those poor neighbours has also started coming to play with you, soon even the boatman's daughter will join in. The way you are going anything can happen' In school one made friends without taking status or religion into account, or perhaps one just did not think about it. Sometimes some fair and white haired memsahibs would visit the school. They would distribute booklets with titles like 'The Gospel by St. Luke' or 'The Real and True God' and try to teach the children about Christianity. Occasionally they would even recite excerpts from the Bible during the assembly.

Once when Katya repeated some of the stories about Jesus related by the mems to Tathya he just said, 'All right, concentrate on your studies' and got up. Later it seems he called the headmaster of the school and asked him not to encourage these Christian missionaries, 'They visit schools to convert people to their religion and confuse the minds of the young school children. Our Hindu religion is the greatest religion in the world, why don't you teach them about that?' Tathya was a member of the School committee, perhaps because of this the mems were never seen in school again. School education had many facets, some good and some bad! During assembly, hymns and patriotic songs were sung and shlokas from the Gita were recited. Songs like 'Saare jahan se achha Hindostan hamara' and 'Vijayi vishwa tiranga pyara....' were compulsory.

In every class the students would chose a neat, well behaved girl as their leader. She had the rights of the prime minister of a country and had to be obeyed by everyone. If a girl bought some peanuts or roast corn she would have to share it with the entire class. Everything was put in the leader's lap and she distributed it evenly to everyone. All decisions were taken together by voting, and everything was very democratic. On the odd occasion that there were a few dissenters, they were quickly dealt with. For instance, once Chunni brought pears from home because her sister-in-law's parents had sent a large basket of fruit to her house and she tried to eat them all alone in secret. When Katya, the class leader, found out she questioned Chunni. Chunn was quite obstinate and replied, 'Ma gave them for me, they are not meant to be shared with everyone!'

Mothers have to be obeyed but friends are friends. They are also special. You can't talk to your mother the way you talk to your friends. If someone was too stupid to understand this she would have to be thrown out of the group and put in quarantine. This decision had quite an impact. For a few days Chunni sat all alone on the bench with her head stuck in her books. No one called her to play nor did anyone share any goodies with her. Finally, on the third day, she surrendered. She apologized to the leader who, in turn, showed her magnanimity by forgiving Chunni, merely reminding her that she must remember to share everything with the others.

'I will.'

'Promise?'

'Yes, promise.'

'No, swear by the knowledge you hold sacred, promises can always be broken.'

'I swear by the knowledge I hold sacred.'

There was nothing greater than knowledge so the punishment was reversed. They made up by touching their index fingers and ran off, arm in arm, to play in the apple orchard near Shitalnath. There was no way the girl would ever again refuse to share anything!

What did the girls talk about in those days?

'Will you play during recess?'

'Yes, we will.'

'Skipping rope?'

'No, cops and robbers.'

'Let's go under the shade of the mulberry tree.'

'No, bhai! Prabhakak masterji is napping there. He'll wake up at the slightest sound and then we'll be in trouble!'

'Oh no! Not that – he's so cruel, he pulls so hard at our plaits that you feel your scalp will come off!'

The girls did not like Prabhakak masterji at all. He was quite weird. He would squeeze and touch the girls for no rhyme or reason or pinch them. But how and to whom could they complain, he was a teacher after all. They were forced to keep quiet.

One day, when Katya was about ten years old, her mother noticed some bruises on her cheeks and asked, 'How did you get these bruises Munni, did you fall down or did you fight with someone?'

'I don't fight without any reason. Uma, Chandra, Tulsi and I had gone to play in Shitalnath, we were a little late in class, that is all. So I was punished.'

'But this bruise?' Lalli still couldn't understand the reason for the bruises.

'Prabhkak masterji punishes us like this, he pinches our cheeks.'

As she was speaking Katya realized that perhaps she shouldn't have said all this to her mother. It was considered very bad to touch a girl's cheeks. Katya was afraid because Lalli's face became pale with anger and shame as she spoke. She scolded Katya needlessly and went off to speak to Bhaisahib.

Another scolding! If you spoke you got a yelling, if you didn't you got a yelling. Very strange!

Who knew what Lalli said to Keshav and what information Keshav passed on to Tathya but the very next day Katya and Ragya were removed from Maitreyi Middle School and admitted to Vasanta High School where Didda studied. Most of the teachers in this school were women. Women's education, which had been neglected since the middle ages and had gradually become limited to the reading of religious texts at home, was being revived by Christian missionaries and Maharaja Pratap Singh. Girls from enlightened households were now attending school in large numbers.

While sending Katya to the new school Lalli explained to her that she was now growing up. She should not behave in a manner that would bring shame to her family or cause any gossip. Katya was affectionately cautioned that she should stop playing games with the neighbourhood boys. The school, of course, had no male students.

So, Katya was admitted to a girls' school and Prabhkak masterji was transferred to a boy's school. This must have been done on Tathya's instructions. He was very influential in the school committee. Later Didda said that initially Tathya was going to throw masterji out of his job, 'He said that anyone who misbehaves in this manner with innocent young girls deserves to go to rorav narak.'

'What is rorav narak?'

'Oof! Don't you know anything Katya? Open your *Kalyan*, everything is shown there. On page eighty there is a horrible picture of a sea of blood, full of alligators, snakes and ferocious sea monsters who chew up the bones of sinners, that is rorav narak.'

The picture of hell was truly horrifying but it was the after-world. Prabhkak was punished in this life as well though Tathya was forced to be lenient because Prabhkak's wife begged him to be merciful.

Even after she joined Vasanta School, Katya did not forget her friend Tulsi. On the contrary, their friendship became stronger with the passage of time. Tulsi lived just two streets away. After wandering through a maze of winding alleys one entered the gloomy corridor of a two-storeyed house through a low doorway. The stairs going up were always dark and Katya would recite a mantra to ward off fear, check every corner and niche carefully and clamber up quickly. She was always apprehensive about encountering a ghoul or a ghost on the next step. When she reached the room, breathless after darting up the stairs two at a time, Tulsi's kakni would scold her affectionately, 'Goodness! Why are you in such a rush? A girl's footsteps should not be heard, you will get into the habit of thumping around!'

Tulsi's mother's hair was snow-white. She looked like a

bag of bones because she had aged early and because of the numerous fasts she observed every week. She also fasted on Ashtami, Ekadashi, Sakranti, the day of the new moon and the full moon. She wore pherans without any brocade borders on her sleeves and would sit on a disintegrating rush mat leaning against an oil-stained bolster as she mended frocks and pyjama-kurtas or spread garlands of turnips, brinjals, gourd and chillies to dry in the sun in preparation for the winter. Sometimes she would give Katya 'yaji' made of rice flour flavoured with cumminseed and salt, which Katya loved.

Tulsi's sad eyes, set in a round face, held such a strange attraction for Katya that she could never stay away from her. She would finish her homework as soon as she got back from school and rush off to Tulsi's house on some pretext or the other. Tulsi, Chandra, Shanta and Katyayini shared a really strong bond. They were trusted friends who shared all their anxieties and concerns and who could discuss anything, including things that were meaningless for others but very meaningful for them.

'Did you hear, Shanta is getting married. Mohammad, the marriage broker, was telling my kakni.' Katya would set off a firecracker.

'Oh! Are you going to get married so soon? I mean one is going to stay married for the rest of one's life.'

'I will have to, if my family insists. A girl can't argue with her elders and say she doesn't want to get married.' This, from helpless Shanta.

'Look at that! Is it you who's getting married or your elders?' Katya was always ready to give a scolding. 'Admit it, you are just dying to wear long dangling earrings, a taal raz and a dejharu.'

'What does your bridegroom look like? Is he really podgy and fat?'

'Don't be silly! He looks like a prince. I saw him in the temple.'

'Oh! You actually met him, you hussy?'

'No, no Katya, I swear by you. My brother said, "Look, your bridegroom is standing on the steps". I just looked at him once and then I ran as though he would come and catch me.'

'He will catch you the day you get married!'

'Not day, you silly girl. Night.' Chandra was more knowledgeable, 'On the night of the satraat you will be fed some curds and then pushed into the bridal room.'

'Oh! I will die of shame.'

Once in a while, Chandra would peep into her brother and sister-in-law's room through the chinks to see what was happening! The next day she would narrate everything to her friends and show off her knowledge.

So what would happen on the first night? How would the bridegroom lift the veil from Shanta's face? What was the first thing he would say? All of them would rehearse the scenario. The true and imagined stories related by elder sisters, the embarrassing acts that acquired sanctity when performed by husbands would be listened to with great curiosity and remembered for future reference. How would it feel? There was a nameless sense of fear rather than any excitement. These young girls, at the threshold of adulthood, would get lost in a fantasy world, a colourful place of marriages and bridegrooms, of love and passion, which had very little connection with reality.

But one day Tulsi shattered this dream cruelly, 'It's all lies. Bridegrooms don't show any love or affection.'

'How do you know? Have you been married? Acting like a grandmother!'

This Tulsi, she always had something negative to say! She wouldn't even let them enjoy the world of their dreams. Huh! When Chandra got upset Tulsi had to give an explanation for what she had said. When her elder sister, didi, was ill, Tulsi's mother had sent her to her sister's house. That's when she got to know the truth.

'What did you see?' Curiosity would not be satisfied so easily.

'I didn't see, I heard. It was dark after all! Didda was crying and saying I am sick with fever and all you are interested in is your pleasure. You are an animal.'

'Pleasure? Meaning?'

'Who knows? Must be that love and affection which keeps all the older people busy at night.'

'Well, he just loved her, he wasn't trying to beat her up was he?' They wanted to know more.

'I don't know. Sometimes he uses really bad words when he's talking to her. I really get very angry with my brother-in-law, he is quite a ruffian.'

'Don't talk rubbish! You are defaming your brother-in-law, you will go to hell.'

'I am not defaming him. He used to trouble me all the time Didda was ill. When I went to give him tea or as I went up and down the stairs, he would grab me every time he found me alone. He would pinch me all over like Prabhkak masterji. Then when I started crying he would try to calm me down, begging me saying, please don't tell your sister but I am in love with you. Crazy man, being mean to his wife but trying to make love to his sister-in-law.'

'Didn't you complain to Didda?'

'I did try but she got angry with me instead. She said you are mad and your mind is full of nonsense, he is like your father. If you malign him like this your tongue will be full of sores. Why can't you cover your chest properly with your chunni?'

'I ran off from that place. I told Kakni I don't care if you chop me into pieces but I am not going there again.'

'Good for you. Don't go there again. Who does he think he is, the great lover! He is just a rogue and a hooligan. Don't go back even if you get beaten up. If you go there you will also end up with seven or eight kids. He loves you, huh! Is it your fault that your breasts are big?'

Katya would get very agitated. She would feel a surge of love for this friend of hers who had been subjected to so much persecution. Prabhkak misbehaved with her in school and then her own brother-in-law tried to grab her. These old men, they only noticed the bodies of young women, not their minds. There must be something wrong with *their* brains, Katya was quite sure about this.

At home, Katya's grandmother and aunt did not approve of her visiting Tulsi's house because Tulsi's family was socially inferior. It was not proper that the granddaughter of the well-known and aristocratic lawyer Ayodhyanath Razdan and the daughter of Professor Keshav Razdan should be seen in the company of such people. But Katya did not seem to understand this simple fact.

'What sort of people Kakni? Tulsi is a girl just like me. In fact she has a much fairer complexion than me.'

'It is not a question of colour, Munni. How do I explain it to you…just try to understand that they belong to a lower class.'

'What do you mean by "lower class" Kakni? Tell me.'

'You're so stubborn and you refuse to understand. Tatya has spoilt you completely. Listen! Tulsi's parents belong to a family who changed their religion many years ago. In other words they converted.'

Katya still did not understand. 'But they also pray to our Gods. They keep fasts and follow the same rituals so how are they irreligious?'

'That's enough! Stop eating my head, go and ask your Tathya, he will explain.' Dadi had run out of answers but Tathya tried to satisfy Katya's curiosity.

'God created all men as equals but because of our destiny we became Brahmins, Munni. Around six hundred years ago, during the reign of the Emperor Sikandar Butshikan, many Brahmins were forced to give up their religion. Some of them became Muslims. Others laid down some terms for converting, including the fact that they would only eat food cooked by a Muslim if it was cooked in a new vessel every day and they could serve the rice themselves. This condition was agreed to, so they ate food prepared by Muslims, but they would serve it themselves and then they would do penance. They continued to think of themselves as Hindus and refused to become Muslims but the more orthodox Brahmins considered them to be half Muslims and refused to consider them to be Hindus. This is why they were considered to belong to a lower and separate caste. Ordinary Bhatts did not intermarry with them.'

Katya was also told how the Razdans became an upper class and renowned family. Razdan meant someone close to the king. Many years ago the Razdans were ministers and advisors to kings and that was how they came by their name. Their gotra and genealogy was high in any case. Who could explain gotras better than Anand shastri? Shastriji, who was so knowledgeable about the *Veda*s and the *Purana*s said that basically all brahmins belonged to six gotras, though now there were one hundred and ninety nine branches and subdivisions. The basic gotras were Dattatreya, Bhardwaj, Paldev, Aupmanya, Maudgalya and Dhaumanya. Initially there were only three surnames, Bhatt, Pandit and Razdan and then followed Kaul, Sopore, Pandit and Raina. Some surnames came to be associated with some special circumstance or reasons but that had nothing to do with the gotra. For instance, Shastriji would relate the story of how Pandit Janardan Teng's surname changed from Kaul to Teng. Kaul sahib had a mulberry tree in his house because of which people started calling him 'tul' or mulberry. He was so annoyed by this that he had the tree cut down so that only the stump or the 'mond' remained but now everyone called him 'mond'. Tired of all these nicknames he finally had the stump removed but this left a hole in the ground, a 'khod' so he was now called 'khod'. This hole was also filled up but now there was a little hill instead, a 'teng' and so all the neighbours started calling him 'teng.' Finally Janardan sahib accepted defeat and resigned himself to being known by the surname of 'teng'!

The final conclusion was that Katya unquestionably belonged to an aristocratic, upper class family. Tathya's great-grandfather and father worked under British officers in the offices of Maharaja Ranvir Singh and Maharaja Pratap Singh, they were known as 'karkuns'. Tathya himself was an influential lawyer, a 'munsi'f. He was regarded with respect by a large section of society and the oil painting covering half the wall in his sitting room was also very impressive. In the portrait Tathya was seated on a beautifully carved walnut wood chair, wearing a black achkan and white narrow pyjamas and holding a slim walking stick, a symbol of pride and position. He had an elegantly tied turban on his head and an awe-inspiring moustache that was as impressive as that of any head-constable. Did anyone in the neighbourhood have a similar portrait? And Tulsi's father! The poor man had a small grocery store at the corner of the street, which was run by his son Amba, after his untimely death. Tathya didn't say anything much but Katya's aunt was delighted to give her a more detailed introduction to Tulsi's ancestors.

'Shop? Huh! It was just a hole in the wall. Mehtab, the grocer, had to keep a lamp lit all the time even during the day. And what did he have in the shop? Mulaithi costing a pice or two, kahzaban for sherbets and small little packets of spices! All his life he wore one piece of clothing regardless of the weather, and used the same cloth as a bedsheet and as a wrap. He wore coarse wooden sandals on his feet, I don't remember him ever wearing any shoes. In summer he would wear a long kurta and in winter he would put on a rough woollen pheran over it.'

'Yes, in his house there was an army of children but how many of them survived? Some died of measles, others of smallpox, till only these two girls and Amba were left.'

Lalli would sigh and add, 'Tulsi's mother Zoonmali suffered so much. First she was laid low by bearing children year after year and then she lost them one after another. Mehtabjoo seemed to have lost his wits due to poverty. Poor half-starved Zoonmali, what could she feed the children and how could she pay for their medicines? Do you remember how she used to fold the dupatta on her head and go from house to house cleaning rice but she never begged for anything? It is good her son is now taking care of the household, at least she will have some comfort in her old age.'

Katya understood the reason for the narration of this saga of Tulsi or 'Tulsi puraan' but she refused to accept that friendship could be circumscribed by differences in financial circumstances, in gotras and family status. It was an inexplicable bond, which became stronger the more Katya's family tried to loosen it. Katya would lie down with her head in her mother's lap and fly away on the wings of imagination as she looked at the moon in the sky. In her mind she and Tulsi walked up the stairs to the moon hand in hand. Sometimes, like Sonakesri in the folk tale, Tulsi would become the wife of a king. Another time she would be like Kavkoor, the woodcutter's daughter who was stolen away and brought up by crows. Then one day, as she sat spinning in the shade of a tree, a prince who was passing by saw her and was so dazzled by her beauty that he fell in love with her. Though the other queens hated her and hatched various plots and schemes to get rid of her, she finally succeeded in becoming a queen. Katya was certain that her innocent and talented friend would also find some good man who would love her, even if he was not a prince.

Unlike Katya, Didda never caused any problems. Her reputation as a well-mannered, gifted young girl was already established. But their younger brother, the only male heir in the family, had started behaving rather strangely. He was different from everyone in the house. He was good at his studies and did not especially want to be different but the excessive love and affection of the household had made him a little spoilt and irritable. He did not like home cooked food, so special butter was brought from Ahdoos for Chote or Nandanji who was also affectionately addressed as 'bhai pyare' by everyone. But the skinny Nandanji, despite all the love and affection lavished on him, would keep the entire household on its toes with his unending demands. He wouldn't eat his dinner if he didn't get his 'plusfours' by the evening. Tathya would cause a commotion, get the cloth, bring the tailor, show him a picture of an English rider wearing 'plusfours' and tell him to make a pair before sunset. Nandanji wants a Karakul cap. Get it for him immediately!

Fortunately, Nandanji excelled in his studies despite being spoilt. His school, Heddo Memorial, had nothing but praise for him except for the admonition that his parents should pay more attention to his health as he was very thin. Nevertheless, due to Lalli and Keshav's good karma the boy finally grew tall and strong. He was chosen to be a part of the school football team and later he won a government scholarship to study engineering in Benaras. The valley did not have an engineering college at the time.

Matayi

Situated on the banks of the lotus-filled blue Manasbal lake, Safapore village woke up to the new day. As sleep began to edge away, Matayi's beautiful voice soared over the darkness of the last watches of the night and compelled the sun to raise its head above the lofty mountains and make its way into people's homes.

Ahad Bande's wife Khatiji felt as though she was listening to the Azaan, the call to prayer. In Prakash Kuryagami's immortal work *Prakash Ramayan* Lord Shiva tells his consort Parvati about the importance of chanting the name of Lord Rama. Matayi had also devoted herself to Lord Rama and had even named her elder son Ramchandra so that whenever she called out his name affectionately she would be repeating the name of Rama. Even Ganika attained salvation by chanting the name of Rama and Matayi after all, was a pure and virtuous woman.

Khatiji only knew how to say, 'La Ilaha Ilalah Muhammad Ur Rasoollillah.' But she was certain that Matayi also chanted something very similar. Without her faith in God how could Matayi bear the humiliation of being treated like a servant despite being the wife of a landowner? Khatiji shook her husband awake, 'Wake up, it's morning, if you leave early you will be able to return from the city with the goods by the afternoon. Can't you hear Matayi's chanting?

Truly, it was Matayi's voice which heralded the arrival of the morning. Ahad Bande put on his pheran and headed towards the fields. He saw a woman who was in a tearing hurry, she was rushing towards Matayi's house, jumping over the embankments in the fields.

'Who is it bhai, so early in the morning? All well I hope?' Ahad Bande called out.

'It is I, Jamila! Our cow is in great pain, she is not calving. I am going to fetch Matayi.' Jamila was Samad Zargar's daughter.

'Do you want me to come?' Ahad Bande was always ready to help.

'No, no. Mother has asked for Matayi, these are women's matters, and then Matayi has a special gift.'

Matayi was stroking Gauri and Sundari's flanks as she filled their troughs with hay and then began to feed them. Matayi was old now but she still fed the cows herself. Nor, under her strict instructions, was anyone allowed to touch their udders except Matayi and her eldest daughter-in-law Kongri. They were not cows, they were Matayi's daughters.

'Matayiiiii…' Matayi was startled by the anxiety in Jamila's voice.

'What is the matter, Jamila? How is Samadjoo? He seemed a little feverish yesterday.'

'Baba is fine, Matayi but Haeri is in pain. Could you have a look please, ma is very anxious.'

'I'll come with you, let's go.' Matayi tightened the lungi around her pheran and went off with Jamila.

As they neared the stable, Haeri's pathetic moans pierced Matayi's heart. She checked the cow's stomach. Putting her cheek next to Haeri's face she rubbed her back with one hand. 'Daa…daaa….' Haeri's eyes were swimming with tears. Oh! The life of a woman! Matayi's experienced hands helped in the delivery, 'Haeri, help! Be brave daughter! Thaaaat's it, you will soon be through, be patient.'

Matayi held the tiny head of the calf and chanted Rama's name. As the cow moaned loudly the calf was pushed into Matayi's arms. Her eyes became wet. Haeri, exhausted by her battle, collapsed in the cold stable, her tired neck drooping to one side.

'Congratulations, sister.' Matayi wiped down the calf with a rag.

'This is all thanks to you Matayi, may God grant you a long life. I had given up hope, she has been suffering since last night and the vet has gone to the city. But then I thought to myself, so what if the doctor isn't available, at least Matayi is here.'

Matayi gently scolded her, 'Don't have so much faith in a human being. These are all miracles wrought by God. Just take care of her feed and water.'

What could Samadjoo's wife offer this woman, who has

never asked for anything except blessings? Samadoo's wife could never forget the day when Matayi snatched Jamila from Sridhar Bhatt's grasp and bore the brunt of the blows herself. Matayi was not just a woman, she was the earth mother herself.

'This goddess has borne so much!' Everyone in the village knew about Sridhar Bhatt's behaviour. Samad Zargar could not control his language whenever he heard Bhatt's name, 'Such an immoral hooligan has bever been born in the village nor will be again. God has settled all past accounts by making him blind. Don't mention him in front of me. He has reaped what he sowed. Matayi is a pure and virtuous woman, if people didn't know her, they would refuse to believe that Ramjoo is Sridhar Bhatt's son.'

The elders sitting around, who believed that family traits were passed on from generation to generation, shook their heads, 'You are right Samadjooa! There is no comparison between Sridhar Bhatt and his son, Ramjoo! They are as different as Sultan Sikandar and his son Zainulabdin. One was called Butshikan, the idol breaker, and the other was known as Badshah, the king of kings! Everyone calls Ramjoo 'devta' or a saintly man but if anyone takes Sridhar Bhatt's name in the morning his entire day is spoilt.'

Matayi must have played some role in making her son such a good human being.

Whenever Ahad Bande's wife Khatiji asked Allah to bless her children and elders she always added Matayi's name. The small shop in the village, where one could buy everything from sherbet, tea, tobacco to coarse khadi cloth and printed fabric as well as small things of daily use, was owned by Ahad Bande, or more correctly, one could say it belonged to Matayi. Khatiji said, 'If Matayi had not given a small piece of her land to Ahad to open a shop and if she hadn't helped him to stock it with goods like tea, sugar etc., how would Ahad Bande have become a shopkeeper?'

But Matayi doesn't agree. This is why, while giving

instructions to her son regarding the shop, she had said, 'Ahad Bande's father worked without remuneration all his life on our lands. We are indebted to him, we are not doing him any favours.' So, Matayi repaid past debts and also atoned for her husband's sins. As soon as her husband became blind, Matayi tore up all those documents and papers on which her husband used to take the thumbprints of tenant farmers and force them to work without pay all their lives in lieu of interest on debts which could never be paid off.

When Sridhar Bhatt passed away, his elder son Ramjoo was ten years old, Krishnajoo was eight and Narayan was five. Durga was still in her swaddling clothes. Matayi sent the children to Pandit Harjoo Shastri for their education. The village school only had classes upto the fifth standard. Matayi told the children enlightening stories from the *Panchatantra* and *Katha Sarit Sagar*. She passed on the knowledge she had gained from her mother and grandmother, the Vakhs of Lal Ded and the shrukh of Nund Rishi, which she now communicated to her grandchildren through the medium of stories.

The villagers were familiar with Matayi's life story and Ramjoo, surrounded by admirers, also acknowledged that,'Whatever I am today is because of Matayi.'

He would get out of bed early in the morning as soon as he heard his mother's melodious voice. Wrapping his dussa around him, he would hum as he picked up his towel and with a fresh kurta slung across his shoulder, walked towards the Manasbal lake.

His village appeared like a beautiful forest in the early hours of the morning. Om Namah Shivay! Ramjoo believed that Lord Shiva resided somewhere close by in the mountains.

After his bath he offered a rose to Bhairav and then, standing on the embankment cast an affectionate look at the crop of rice in the fields. The reaping would begin in about eight days. Looking at the golden ears as they swayed in the breeze Ramjoo never forgot the sweat-drenched bodies of his farm workers. 'Our lands and crops are the product of their hard work and the blessings of the Lord,' Matayi's words echoed in his ears.

As he stepped onto the freshly mopped verandah of the house the smell of shirchai awakened his hunger. Matayi sat in front of her sons as they ate their breakfast. The house was under her command. Taking out a slab of butter, Kongri put it on a corn cob. There was the aroma of warm sattu, each person could eat what he liked and the children also had milk.

Prabhavati and Arundhati were pottering around in the kitchen. Matayi was content that despite having so many members, the house was still united. How long this togetherness would last – Matayi left that decision to fate and time. After breakfast Matayi advised her sons about matters relating to the crops and human relationships.

'The farm workers must get sufficient rice to last them the whole year, there should be no stinginess.'

'Don't worry Matayi, thanks to your blessings our stores will be overflowing even after we have given them enough.'

'Aziz Lone's daughter is getting married, Fazi came to invite us. It would be good if you attended the wedding for a short while. Kongmaal will take a pheran and earrings for the girl. I don't go to weddings any more.'

'Whatever you say, Ma!' Ramjoo always followed his mother's advice.

There was the sound of footsteps at the door and Ganpat looked in., 'Matayi! I am going to be killed, help me, Matayiiiii!'

'What happened, Ganpat? Why are you so out of breath? Come in, Kongmali fetch some tea for Ganpat.'

'What tea Matayi, now it is time for me to drink poison.'

'Don't say inauspicious things early in the morning. Take the name of Lord Rama,' Matayi scolded him.

'What other inauspicious event can happen now, Matayi? Those messengers of death, the revenue officials have arrived early morning. I have a tiny piece of cultivable land, you know I barely manage to grow enough rice for two square meals for my family. I am a landlord in name only!'

'Yes. Yes, but what has happened?' Matayi wanted to know.

'These officers have come to demarcate the land, they are going to add half of my land to Sansarchand's. He's in cahoots with them. Please request bhai sahib to speak to the patwari, I beg of you, I'll lay my turban at your feet. This is sheer injustice, Matayi! I always pay my taxes on time.'

'All right, Ramjoo will talk to them, don't worry. We will think of something.'

It was this readiness to help that had welded Matayi's village together. And Ramjoo had also inherited his mother's generosity. Krishnajoo and Narayanjoo however, did not agree with their mother and Ramjoo's decisions. They protested softly to their brother, 'Bhai sahib, if we become as generous as you, we may be able to manage but our children will definitely be reduced to the level of the tenant farmers.' Narayanjoo felt the future of the landlords was very dim and unsure.

'In any case landlords no longer get the same respect and they aren't as influential either and then Sheikh sahib is trying to get the land transferred to the tenant farmers.'

Krishnajoo also had some complaints, 'Maharaja Bahadur had already begun the transfer of lands to the tenant farmers under the land laws. The "settlement" law reduced the lands of the landlords by half. Every other day the boundaries are drawn and redrawn cutting into the land. Now we are landlords only in name!'

'And then this slogan of "New Kashmir" has addled the brains of the farmers. They no longer show us the same respect.'

Ramjoo could understand his brothers' concerns, 'Krishnajooa! Your Jagaddar and Chakradhar want to become doctors and engineers. Narayanjoo's Vijay has been studying in the city since his childhood. It is obvious that none of these boys has any interst in the land and farming. That leaves Haldhar who helps me in looking after the lands. He is a son of the soil, if he dirties his hands who can steal his birthright from him?'

Ramjoo was the head of a large household. He had to think about the welfare of all its members. This was the tradition that had been passed down the ages. But his brothers complained and cursed the changes that had taken place. Ramjoo, however, knew that it was Matayi herself who had helped to change the village.

Right now the golden ears of rice were swaying in the breeze. People's hearts were full of hope and there was a gleam of lust in the eyes. But who knew how much of this grain would be sacrificed to taxes, how many cold nights would be spent shivering in broken down huts? When the women of the house were forced to desperately search for a few grains in their handis and the demons of hunger bared their fangs as they rushed out to grab you, then one would have to take the road to Jammu via Pindi, go to the Punjab and work as a labourer doing backbreaking work to earn two square meals. Right now, however, everything was fine and Ladishah, sensing an opportunity, was playing his one stringed ektara and collecting a crowd in the middle of the fields. 'Chun, chun, chun, Ladishah has come....'

Standing in the middle of the ring of spectators Ladishah began the story of Nandram the landlord. The story of the small-time landowner who remained in debt all his life, despite paying his taxes to the government. He lived in a rented house and tried to be content, hoping that contentment would bring him happiness. The song satirised Nandram's contentment and portrayed his patience in the face of injustice as cowardice. Ladishah's songs touched people's hearts. He wanted to change the world through his songs.

The folk theatre of the village Baands always attracted an

audience. Matayi invited them to perform at weddings and festivals. Wearing tiger skins, the Baands enacted stories about kings and their subjects in the large hall of the house. Englishmen wearing suits beat poor farmers with hunters and kicked them with their boots. The audience watched, torn between tears and laughter. Matayi got up in the middle of the performance and snatched away the hunter from the Englishman.

'Madam! I am just showing the injustice of the English government to the poor farmers!'

'No, that's enough. That boy is so skinny, if he breaks any bones will your government come to heal him?'

People were surprised. This was just make-believe after all. Matayi may have stopped the performance but she also knew how to look after the Baands. She fed them well and sent them on their way with lots of small gifts and bundles.

It wasn't easy for anyone to understand Matayi, not Ahad Bande, Samadjoo or even her own son. But Ramjoo did know that though Matayi was aging she knew how to change things even without a song and a dance.

Matayi often chatted with Sundari and Gauri. The cows started mooing in protest whenever there was any delay in giving them their feed and water. Matayi would scold them gently, 'Be patient, Sundari! Be calm. Girls should not be so excitable. I am doing your work and when I am no longer there who will look after you? Tell me?'

Sundari came close and licked Matayi's hand, 'Matayi forgive me, I made a mistake.'

'All right, now don't try to show extra affection, go and eat.'

When Durga's children come for a visit from the city they were amazed by this dialogue, 'Babuji, Matayi talks to the cows!'

Matayi sat at the wide window feeding the birds grains of rice and tiny pieces of bread from the palm of her hand. Flocks of bulbuls, sparrows, crows, gathered at the window. They were the ones to whom Matayi related her woes during her days of sorrow. Matayi just had to call out, 'Come and eat....' and an entire orchestra of birds would fill the courtyard.

Matayi's two city bred daughters-in-law could not understand her at all. With the grace of God there was no shortage of anything in the house and yet Matayi would eat buttermilk, rice and mint chutney with every appearance of enjoyment. Drawn by the aroma of mint, her grandsons would also abandon their thalis full of meat roghanjosh and panneer and come running to share her food. It wasn't just her sons, even her grandsons doted on her, God knew what magic spell she had cast on the entire household. Matayi's magic drew the children to her every evening. After feeding them, she tucked them in under the quilt and, in the flickering light of the lanterns she took them on a journey through the magical world of stories.

There were stories about treasure at the bottom of the sea and about horrible demons whose souls were kept safely inside birds in cages hanging from the highest branches of oak and chinar trees deep in the jungle. There were also stories about poor Sudama, Lord Krishna's childhood friend, whose feet were washed by the Lord himself, and about Rama, Sita and Lakshman who wander about in the Dandaka forest obeying the commands of their father. There were Aknandun, Kavkoor, Mahadev Bisht and innumerable others. Among the numerous stories there was also the story of the eternal lovers Himal-Nagraj, which the children would listen to with bated breath.

'Many, many days ago, there was terrible drought in the land,' Matayi would set the tone and create an atmosphere. 'During the drought, there was a learned brahmin who found that one day there was no food at all in his house. His wife gave him a small packet of Sattu and said, 'Go and arrange for some food."

The brahmin left on a long voyage. On the way, exhausted, he went to sleep in the shade of a chinar tree near a small stream. When he awoke he noticed that there was something that was moving about in his bag., He quickly tied up the mouth of the bag and came back home. He thought it was a snake, which would bite his wife and release him from her daily nagging. He handed the bag over to his wife and shut the door. But the snake which came out of the bag turned into a beautiful boy. The brahmin's wife looked after him and brought him up, because she had no children of her own. When he grew up he once again took on the form of a snake and entered the palace of the princess. Then he changed into a prince and he and Himal, the princess, fell in love with each other.

'But who was he? A snake can't fall in love surely?' The children were a little suspicious.

'My dears! That boy was Nagraj, the prince of the underworld. He had many queens all of whom came to the earth to look for him. But Nagraj did not want to leave Himal so he hid himself in water. The queens were also very clever, they also went into the water and found him. Himal was left lamenting, where could she look for Nagraj?'

Listening in the dim light of the oil lamp, the children would be saddened by Himal's sorrow. But Matayi wouldn't allow them to be sad for long, 'So, my dears, Himal met a sadhu, an ascetic who said, "I have seen a strange sight near the Neelnag spring. There was a king's banquet and the queens were putting leftover food in a plate saying, This is Himal's share."'

After getting this clue from the sadhu, Himal reached the underworld in her search for Nagraj. Nagraj was very happy. He whispered a magic spell changing Himal into a piece of stone and put the stone in his pocket. He would change her back into a princess whenever he liked and chat with her for a long time, but how long could this carry on? The queens could smell a human being. Now Nagraj turned Himal back into a princess and told the queens, 'If you trouble her I will leave the underworld and go away.' The queens agreed but they couldn't suppress their jealousy after all. They troubled Himal a lot though she worked for them and looked after their children.

But destiny is great! Once Himal served the children hot milk because of which they died. It was a mistake but the queens refused to forgive her. They bit her and dashed her to the ground.'

'Oh, so Himal died?' Little Pappu started crying.

'O my prince! How can Himal die so easily? A holy man was passing that way, he recognized Himal and used his magic to bring her back to life. Then he adopted her as his daughter and took her home with him.'

'In the meanwhile Nagraj was very unhappy without Himal, he wouldn't eat or sleep. He went looking for her and finally arrived at the holy man's house. Lo! He found Himal sleeping in the hut. Nagaraj became a snake and entered the hut. The sadhu's pupils had no idea who he was so they beat him up thinking he was just a snake. As he was dying he kept lamenting, "Himal, I am dying." When Himal heard his cries, she wept so much that she also died.'

The children didn't like this tragic ending.

'No, no, children, this is not the end of the story. When the two lovers were cremated the gods showered flowers on them. They blessed them saying that their love would be immortal. Lord Shiva himself then told an ascetic, "Put Himal-Nagraj's flowers into Neelnag, they will come back to life." The ascetic followed his commands and the lovers came back to life. They bowed their heads before Shiva, received his blessings and lived happily.'

'So, my dears, this is how real love triumphs.'

Who knows if Matayi ever experienced real love in her life, but no matter. The children were satisfied by the happy ending and they clung to Matayi and went to sleep.

Processions and Meetings

Those days, large and small processions would often flow
into the city streets. As soon as the sound of a crowd became
audible, every window in the bazaar would sprout a number
of heads, all intent on enjoying the excitement and spectacle
of the procession. Women and children would jump out of
their quilts and rush to the windows to see splendidly dressed
bridegrooms riding on horses in the middle of evening, with
everything around them lit up with gas lanterns, mirrored glass
bowls with candles and the fountains of light that lit up the
night sky as fireworks shot into it and exploded. Lalli dashed to
the windows even before Katya-Didda, drawn by the music of
the bands and the shehnai players and by the desire to see the
bridegroom's covered face.

On Janamashtami and Ramnavmi arches made of colourful
Benarasi sarees were put in place to welcome the procession of
the gods. Radha, Krishna, the baby Krishna, Lord Rama, Sita
and Lakshman, with Hanuman sitting at their feet, were carried
past in open carriages, tongas and palanquins decorated with
rainbow coloured red and blue brocade sarees. Hymns filled the
air while baby Krishna, covered with flowers, adorned with a
shining crown of leaves, with his flute at his lips, gently swayed
as he sat in his flower covered swing. The women, children
and old men with rickety knees, who were watching from
the windows, would hail the procession and shower so many
flowers on it that Shri Krishna's face was completely covered
by the time the journey was done.

But the most impressive procession was the Maharaja's river
pageant. Large boats were moored along the river and decorated
with arches. The Maharaja leaned against velvet pillows and
bolsters in the royal boat Chakvari, which was freshly painted
for the occasion. Accompanied by his advisors, soldiers and

ministers he would travel from Shalteng to Shergarhi. There were soldiers in the first motorboat, which was followed by the royal regatta. The seven bridges of the city resounded with shouts of 'long live the Maharaja' and showers of petals rained down on him from the windows of homes along the river. Some petals would fall on the riverbank, others would be carried by the waves of the Vitasta to the Maharaja's boat. With folded hands he would acknowledge the greetings of the people.

The Moharram procession was completely different. Hordes of people would walk alongside the tazias, beating their breasts, crying, shouting 'Hussain, Hussain, maula Hussain, aka Hussain' The palanquin bearers would carry the large decorated tazia. Walking ahead of it, a man carriyng a stick with a silver handle would begin a stanza of a marsiya, an elegy, and two men on either side of him would take up the lament. Some people would express their grief by hitting themselves with chains and daggers, the richer ones would show their grief by beating their chests with handkerchiefs. Rehman, the tongawallah behaved like a crazed man, he would bloody his chest and back, hitting himself with hunters and chains. Women would make their children pass under the tazia and ask for boons. Others would watch from the windows with tears in their eyes. In this grief-filled atmosphere all mothers, Hindu or Muslim felt the pain of loss in their hearts. After all, they said, sons are born from the wombs of their mothers.

Katya and Didda also accompanied Arshi dai to the Imambara once to see the Moharram majlis. Arshi would start preparing for mourning the minute she sighted the Moharram moon. The house would be in mourning for a full forty days. In gatherings, Rehman's wife Zeba would sing the 'nauhe' in memory of Hussain sahib in a voice filled with sorrow and all the women listening would burst into tears.

Troublemakers would also take out processions. There were passionate slogans and sometimes fisticuffs and exchanges of vulgar language between two groups. At times people even went to the extent of hurling kangris at each other. There were frequent confrontations between the lion and the goat parties. Apart from the shouts of 'Nalaye takbir, allaho akbar,' resounding shouts of 'murdabad' and 'zindabad' spread fear and panic. Often there was a police lathi-charge. On such occasions people just locked themselves up in their homes.

It was an occasion like this when there was procession of troublemakers, which became memorable for Katya. That was the day when, without any warning, she suddenly grew up, and in a very awkward way. When she went to sleep at night she was just a playful child, when she awoke she had become an adult. Like Rip van Winkle, it was as though an age had passed between the time she had gone to sleep and to the time she woke in the morning.

Katya didn't know anything. Standing against the window she suddenly felt a warm wetness sliding down her legs. If she hadn't felt a terrible ache in her lower abdomen she wouldn't have noticed the red stains on her white salwar. When she noticed them her heart jumped with fear. Oh! What was this? Shoving Ragya and Sharika aside she rushed to the bathroom. When she saw the red lines on her legs she began to cry loudly. With trembling legs and a piercing ache in her back she just rolled herself into a ball on the floor. But Didda did not leave her alone, she realized something was up and followed Katya. She checked her out and, very conscious of her own status as an elder sister, she instructed Katya on the use of cotton and cloth. She also passed on warnings and directions- 'This is something extremely private and has to be kept hidden, not only from men, but even from other women in the family. No one should know that you have MC.'

'MC?' Katya felt a helpless fear.

'You don't even know this?' Didda frowned. 'You've grown as tall as a palm tree but don't know what is a 'monthly curse'?

Every month after twenty eight days, this red colour and this pain will remind you that you are a woman now, not a carefree girl. Now you can't hang about giggling with boys, otherwise you can get into trouble and then you will have to slash your wrists with a blade.'

'Why, why would I cut my wrist with a blade?' Katya asked, wiping her nose.

'Questions again! Try to use your brain! Didn't Kakni tell you the story of that Kamala, who cut her wrist with a blade? If they hadn't taken her to hospital immediately, she would have died.'

'But why did she cut her wrist?' Katya will not keep quiet till she knows everything!

'Oh! You are really stupid. God knows how you pass your exams. She was pregnant. She used to spend too much time enjoying herself with that ruffian, Moti....'

Katya, listening to her Didda with curiosity and worry, nevertheless felt a sense of wonder at how one could become pregnant by laughing with boys.

There were a lot of questions. Didda would provide some answers at least and Katya had to acknowledge her superior intelligence. Katya didn't know anything, not even the meaning of MC.

Katya tried to remember the instructions about secrecy but she couldn't hide anything for long. Exactly twenty eight days later (Didda's calculations were correct) her body was wracked with pain and she threw up everything so that even the children in the house realised there was something wrong. When Lalli saw her tomboyish daughter writhing in pain she put a hot water bottle under her legs and gave her a tablet of Baralgan with some kehwa. Wiping the sweat from Katya's forehead she hugged her close. Katya saw the sheen of tears in her mother's eyes and heard her murmuring brokenly. 'Oh! The life of a woman.'

The life of a woman! Lalli just muttered these few words, holding her daughter and looking beyond her. How much of what she herself had suffered and endured was encompassed by these words, how much that even her beloved husband could never really understand. Her daughters too had become used to seeing their mother as a busy housewife, a good mother, a daughter-in-law, caught up in the responsibilities of the household. That a mother could have a life beyond this, a private self, was an untold story; no one ever felt the need to think about this in these affluent houses.

Just these few words, 'the life of a woman' were enough to make Katya understand that this was merely the beginning. The beginning of the process of peeling off the layers of black and white emotions. In simple words, it was a warning to stay away from the opposite sex. Thanks to the Baralgan the lower part of Katya's body became numb, the pain diminished but the unease did not. She wanted to talk to someone, to discuss the new questions and feelings rising within her. After a while she slipped out of the house, crossed the road, stumbled across muddy lanes aand reached Tulsi's house. Where else would she go?

The stairs had the familiar smell and coolness of having been freshly smeared with mud. When Katya reached the 'keni', the topmost floor, feeling her way up the steps with her tiny strides she could hear the sound of voices, many voices.

'My congratulations, Zoonmali. The family from Baramullah is well-to-do. They are prosperous and you are lucky!'

'It is thanks to the blessings of the mother goddess otherwise how could I have dreamt of this? I have no wealth at all to my name, sister!'

Katya turned to go back. What was the use? With relatives in the house how would they find any time to themselves? Tulsi must be busy lighting the samovar. Katya went down four steps when Tulsi's brother Amba pounded up the stairs just behind her. 'Arre, Katyayini Are you going? Come up, Tulsi would like to meet you.'

'Why would she like to meet me?' Katya couldn't understand.

'What do you mean why? She is going to get married that's why. The preliminary agreement happened today. The wedding will be on the next full-moon. Go, talk to her.'

Amaranth looked very happy wearing a new kurta-pyjama. Arre! Is he getting married or Tulsi? He is delighted because his sister will be going away. Katya was a little upset. Tulsi will get married but who knows what her in-laws will be like? A witch of a mother-in-law and a foul mothed bridegroom? Just like her sister. Would she and Katya be able to meet again?

As soon as Tulsi caught sight of Katya she leapt up and, putting her arms around her, she began to cry. Dressed in a coral coloured brocade sari her body had acquired new dimensions. She was also looking taller. Katya was pleasantly surprised that her poor friend, who was usually dressed in rags, should have transformed into a beautiful woman as soon as she got engaged.

'All this happened so fast and you didn't even tell me?' Katya protested.

'What could I tell you Katya? How? I barely knew anything myself. All this happened because of Bhailal, my brother. He is the one who was in a hurry for the wedding.'

'What is the bridegroom like? Have you seen him?' Katya tried to cheer up her despondent friend, but Tulsi was too busy crying to answer any questions.

'What bridegroom, it is just an exchange.'

'What?' It was Katya's turn to be surprised.

'Yes, we were looking for a girl for Bhailal. The girl's family said they would only agree to the match if we would marry one of our girls to a boy from their family. I have heard they have a lot of money. Bhai is very happy.'

'This is not fair, will you still agree if their boy is lame or handicapped? What does money matter? You must refuse to get married. Do you want to get married so soon? No, say no to Kakni.'

'No, that is not possible. My brother will not be able to marry if I don't agree. They will refuse to give their daughter to us. We've had a difficult time finding a matching horoscope for Bhailal, and besides, it's a good famiy.'

'But you don't look happy.'

'How can I be happy, Katya? My bridegroom is old, he lost his first wife and he has two children. His elder son is nearly my age.'

'Oh my! And Kakni doesn't know all this.'

'She knows everything, sister. But what can she do? They are asking for me without any exchange of gifts. If we say no to them, other boys are not going to take me without any dowry. There are many things Katya that you will not understand. We are really very poor.'

In other words the poor did not have the luxury of saying no. Bhai was even ready to go to Haridwar and buy a bride for himself. He was not handicapped, and he had grown old waiting for his marriage. How long could his mother keep cooking and looking after the house? She had a cataract in her eyes. Sometimes there was long hair in the food. Tulsi also looked mature for her age. How long could Zoonmali guard her from prying eyes? And then, suppose she died, what would happen to Tulsi? The answer to all these questions was, say yes! So what if he was old? No one bothered about a bridegroom's age. He was the sarpanch of the village and had his own land, cattle and stores full of grain. What was he lacking? The girl would live like a queen. All the relatives persuaded them.

Katya sighed. 'Yes, The old man will get another cow for his cattle shed.' She returned home full of an undefined anger. She hadn't been able to share her own news. What could she have said anyway? People were plotting all around poor Tulsi, how could she be rescued? Katya wanted to do something. It was essential to free her dear friend from her enemies, but how? That Amba was dying to get married after all. Katya's hope that something would happen and Tulsi would be saved from the clutches of that old man did not come true. The old sarpanch got married with great pomp and show.

'Old toothless fellow! He wrapped Tulsi in a beautiful, shiny, silk sari. Not a pheran, a sari. He gifted her necklaces, hair ornaments and twenty-four carat gold bangles weighing forty ounces each. As though Tulsi couldn't live without them. If it had been Katya she would have thrown away the sari and hit the old man on the head with the bundle of gold. And now was Tulsi going to sleep with the old man? Wouldn't she feel disgusted? Poor, innocent Tulsi, she had been sacrificed because of this Amba. What a useless brother! He would have a good time while Tulsi spent her life crying.

But, perhaps Katya was wrong. Tulsi did not cry.

Katya was very saddened by Tulsi's departure. In her mind she roamed the streets of Baramullah. Zoonmali gave a feast when Amba returned with his bride, Lalitashwari. Lalitashwari was a large manly-looking woman with a receding chin, small eyes and a sharp nose. When Katya saw her hands and feet she felt the woman had just returned from digging the fields. So much for being the daughter of a wealthy family!

When Tulsi returned to her mother's house on the occasion of 'roth khabar' she sent for Katya. As she walked along the street Katya thought Tulsi must have been reduced to a skeleton living with that old fogey. He had such a wrinkled face. But Tulsi caught her in a big hug and started talking excitedly about her new home. Katya kept watching her in amazement.

'They have such a big house, Katya, the largest in the village. It doesn't have a roof made of hay or leaves, it is four storeyed and has a tin roof. They are very respected in the village. There are lots of cattle and huge troughs for them to eat in, no shortage of milk or butter, you can eat to your heart's content. They eat

corn bread with lots of butter. There are enough vegetables in
the garden to feed the entire neighbourhood – Kanul greens,
vost haq, huge brinjals, gourds, everything.'

'It feels so good. The huge open courtyard, the farms
and fields! In the morning the sun looks like a round vessel
suspended in the sky. Near the house there is a broad fresh
water stream with cold water. I go with the children to have a
bath there every day and I think of you.'

'I also thought about you a lot,' Katya said emotionally, 'But
what about your bridegroom?' As soon as she mentioned Tulsi's
husband an unknown anger began to grow in her.

'Tell me something more important, did you marry the
house or the old man?'

'Don't say that Katya, he is my husband now.' Tulsi said
softly.

'Are you happy with him?' Katya pressed her.

Tulsi hugged Katya again. 'I don't know Katya. It is a
prosperous household, there is jewellery, clothes, food, milk
and the fact that I rule over the house. Here I once put a little
extra milk into the shirchai by mistake and mother put a hot
tong on my hand. She said if you waste milk like this in your in-
laws' house your mother-in-law will kill you. But there children
drink half a glass of milk and throw away the rest and no
one says anything. I had not imagined such luxury even in my
wildest dreams.'

Katya was not impressed by Tulsi's milky happiness. Tulsi
understood Katya's curiosity, 'Actually he is a good man Katya.
He did not come near me for many days. He told me that if I
wished, he would sleep in another room.'

Katya listened with a frown, 'He is just acting.'

'No, no that's not true. He is really ashamed. He said, "I was
told you were thirty years old but you are not even twenty. But
what can be done now...."'

'All rubbish. You are four years older than me and just

eighteen. That old fogey must be at least fifty years old. The same age as baba.'

Tulsi put her palm on Katya's mouth, 'No, sister, don't say any more, I beg of you. I have accepted him as my husband, he gives me so much happiness.'

What happiness and luxury! Katya felt she did not know her friend at all. Butter in the shirchai had addled her brain. Or, who knows, maybe the old man mixed some magic potion in her milk. Otherwise what was the connection between the sweet innocent Tulsi and the ancient sarpanch with two children?

❦

Mr Jinnah Comes to Kashmir

Jinnah sahib had come to Kashmir, what would happen now?

There was more agitation than curiosity in political circles, with the Muslim League on one side and the National Conference on the other. Khurshid, Ashidai, Noora, Kamlavati and Shobharani's lives, however, carried on undisturbed. As did Subhan mallah and Khurshid's elder sons who were busy earning their daily bread. Others – the educated and elite – anticipated that there would be some trouble. Both League and National Conference members were also anxious. This was the time of the Second World War, uncertainty and rumours were the order of the day.

Ayodhyanath was a disciple of Gandhi. 'Gandhiji gave permission for participation in the war in 1942 on condition that the British promise India independence. Indians should be ready to die for the cause of freedom.'

'And the Cripps Commission? They wanted to divide India. Turn brother against brother. The old English policy of divide and rule!' Ayodhyanath was very upset.

Banta Singh added, 'In 1942 thousands of Indians were imprisoned, and cruelly suppressed. Defenceless Swarajis were beaten up with lathis, trampled under the feet of horses. How much can we tolerate?'

Balbhadra was worried. He feared people would turn against each other in the name of religion. Sultan sahib, the shawl dealer, who was familiar with Sheikh sahib's views, felt Balbhadra's worries were unfounded.

'Brother, It is Sheikh sahib who will prevail in the valley. He has just raised the slogan of 'New Kashmir'. You know he does not agree with Mr Jinnah's philosophy. He is a friend of Gandhi, Nehru and Khan Abdul Gaffar Khan, he is influenced by them.'

'You are right,' Krishnajoo nodded, 'Sheikh sahib is opposed to the two nation theory. Jinnah sahib will not be able to convince him but there is a possibility that all these discussions will create some tension.'

Nadir sahib listened to the lecture given by Mr Jinnah at the meeting of the Muslim conference. Jinnah spoke very forcefully, 'Brothers! Muslims have one forum, one God and one religion. We should all gather under one flag and fight for our rights.'

'So, now will Hindus, Muslims and Sikhs get divided up? Will everyone's rights and responsibilities be different? But friends, how can we be separated?' Banta Singh, the fruit merchant, had his own problems. Should a merchant sell his wares or should he get involved in politics? His customers belonged to every section of society.

'I have heard that Jinnah sahib told Maulavi Yusuf Shah to stay away from politics. He said we need a leader in Kashmir, not a mullah.' Nadir sahib was often privy to inside information.

'The only impressive leader is Sheikh sahib. Jinnah tried to persuade him to come over to his side but he didn't succeed. Sheikh sahib proved his intelligence and farsightedness the day he named his party the All Jammu and Kashmir National Conference and in his presidential address he said that the participation of Hindus, Sikhs, Buddhists and Harijans was essential in order to make a responsible government. He is a secular leader and look at Jinnah sahib, he called the National Conference a gang of ruffians.'

'Yes, it is a case of the grapes being sour!'

'But Mr Jinnah was originally a member of the Congress, why did he leave?' Banta singh was curious.

'Actually he couldn't connect with labourers and workers, the ordinary people. I remember he had initially proposed that anyone who had not passed his Matric exam should not be made a member of the party. At that time he was a member of the Congress.' Bidlal Dhar passed the hookah to Balbhadra.

'Sarojini Naidu even called him the "Ambassador of Hindu Muslim unity," and then he went and joined the Muslim League.'

If someone praised Gandhi too much Ayodhyanath would add a few words of appreciation for Jinnah to provide some balance, 'Jinnah sahib has been an extremely able lawyer and is a good politician. It is said that his ancestors were Hindus, later they became strict Muslims and joined the Muslim League.'

'The Muslim League was also a trick of the British. It was set up with their help in 1906. Its real purpose was to keep the Muslims away from the Congress, that is why they launched a campaign against the Congress party. They also tried to rouse people with slogans like, "Islam in danger".'

'Bhai, the English have very devious minds.' Bidlal Dhar would recount all the clever tactics used by the British since the days of the East India Company, 'How did they get into our country? Tell me? Just like wolves in sheep's clothing? Under the pretext of trade!'

'Actually...' Shah sahib stopped mid-sentence.

'I have heard that Gandhi and Nehru tried many times. They attempted to sit with Jinnah sahib and sort out the differences between the Muslim League and the Congress but Jinnah insisted on the two nation policy. He said you have to accept that the Congress is the party of Hindus only and the Muslim League the party of the Muslims, only then can there be any discussion.'

'But this is clearly impossible. The Congress has many prominent Muslim leaders...'

Sultanjoo, the shawl merchant, said, 'I can only speak for myself and my valley where secular poets like Lalded and Nundrishi have spoken about love and brotherhood and where the words of nationalist poets like Mahjoor and Azad are arousing a passion for freedom in people-

"O bulbul imprisoned in your cage, who are you calling out to?

Who will give you freedom?

The solution to your problems lies in your own hands."'

'Wonderful! What beautiful lines. All his poetry is about affection and comfort among people, about passion and awakening.'

'Azad sahib has composed songs full of the fervour of freedom. He raised his voice against hunger and poverty.'

'Azad posed a question to society. This land that gave birth to sons like Badshah, will its children die of hunger? The water of this land has nourished giants like Kalhana, Gani and Sarfi, who became famous and whose names were recorded in history books, will that water change into poison for us?'

While intellectuals were busy debating, in the streets, in parks and bazaars, people were busy raising slogans. Maulavi Yusufshah's group called the National Conference 'fascists' and National Conference members raised slogans of 'Long live Sher-e-Kashmir' and 'Our demand is New Kashmir.' The opposing parties often came to blows as they shouted at each other. If a person from one group was injured his companions would lift him onto their shoulders and consign the next seven generations of the opposition to hell. The opposition would also respond with verbal warfare. But Jinnah himself was quite disappointed at the outcome of his visit to the valley, but he consoled himself that all this talk of separation had created some fear and doubt in people's minds despite the overall appearance of peace.

Sultanjoo was a wise and mature man who spoke about love and co-existence, but less educated people were often misled into turning away from each other. Rehman had changed completely. These days he could be seen distributing pamphlets in meetings. He went around with a loudspeaker in his tonga, shouting slogans. He had almost stopped meeting his dearest friend, Nathji. Krishnajoo advised Arshi dai to warn Rehman not to get too involved with politics else the police might arrest him and she would be left crying with her head in her hands. But even as he said this, Krishnajoo knew that this new wave of defiance was not going to be suppressed this time.

Rehman said almost the same thing, but in a different tone, to his mother, 'The war has begun, ma, now there is no turning back.'

'Which war are you talking about, son? I can understand a war that is fought for freedom, for one's rights. My head isn't full of hay and you aren't the only intelligent person around. Can you tell me why you scream your lungs out for that Bakra, goat, party of yours? If you have to distribute pamphlets, distribute those of Sheikh sahib's party. He is the one who cares for us. Why are you getting into trouble by getting involved with this League?'

'What are you saying, mother? Tomorrow your son will become a leader and this crowd – the same crowd that today sees him distributing pamphlets – will shout 'long live Rehman'.'

'Don't boast like Sheikh Chilli. God knows what has addled your brain so that you are seeing dreams even in the daytime. Listen to me, and pay attention to your work.'

But Rehman's interest had now become an obsession.and he was not willing to listen to anyone. 'Ma, Sheikh sahib is half a Hindu. We have to fight for our religion. Jinnah sahib has said all Muslims have one flag, one religion and they have to fight for their rights under this flag. We don't want to have anything to do with Battas.'

'You've gone mad! Are you trying to teach me the difference between Battas and Muslims?' Arshi dai lost her temper. 'You wretch, these divisions are the work of outsiders. These differences won't work in our land. How can one separate Hindus and Muslims who are mixed together like milk and sugar? Tell me? I, your mother, work as a midwife, a dai, to earn a few annas. Will I discriminate between a Hindu mother and a Muslim one? Will I say no if a Batni calls me? And if I do this what will I eat and what will I feed my family? Is your father around to feed you? You want to become a leader, you have even given up earning the little you used to make by driving your tonga. And remember whatever happens in Delhi and Bombay, nothing like that is going to happen here. You will burst if you don't talk to Natha for a few more days. Batta-Muslim! Now when Zeba sells her greens and vegetables will she check if her customer is Hindu or Muslim? Will Gafoor the milkman refuse to sell milk to Hindu households? Will the tailor refuse to stitch their clothes? Yes? The boatman won't take them across the river? Tell me?'

Ashi scolded her son but she was actually very worried. Rehman is uneducated, he believes anything he is told. He is destroying his own livelihood. Ya Allah! Grant him some wisdom, he has a family to look after.

Ashi continued to pray as Rehman became more and more involved with the Muslim League, joining processions and shouting slogans like 'Long live the revolution' and 'Allaho Akbar'. It was winter, extremely cold. There was slush on the ground below and from above, an unending rain fell from a grey sky. People said it would snow. With their kangris under their pherans the processionists would challenge their opponents. Someone would hit out in anger and another person would let loose a barrage of swear words. Soon revolutionary fervour was replaced by fisticuffs and fiery kangris were hurled at each other. Someone split Rehman's head with an oiled staff. As the blood flowed Rehman lost consciousness. The police lathicharged and scattered the crowd. Rehman and eight or ten other troublemakers were arrested.

Khurshid was one person who was not troubled by the events around her. Her sons were busy with their own work. The younger son, Wali, did attend some meetings but he never participated in processions. He looked after his houseboat and fulfilled all the wishes of his English memsahibs. His father was right, only concern yourself with your work and your God, that's all. In any case, looking after the houseboat kept him very busy and he earned well. Khurshid thanked God that his work kept Wali so busy, else he would have joined all those useless ruffians and wasted his time shouting slogans.

And Mahdu? Whatever happened outside was not his concern. He was secure in his nest in Ayodhyanath's house. He was content with the familiarity of his daily routine, looking after the needs of the elders, lording it over the children, discussing the minutae of life with the women. By and large his life was moving along smoothly.

The First Snowfall

This year too, like every other year, the snow appeared at the right moment, accompanied by gunmetal clouds, rain and a biting wayward wind. Everyone tall or short, big or small, welcomed the snow. The houseboat dwellers, the hanjis, greeted it as they sat in the open hugging their kangris close under their pherans and those living in houses, welcomed it wrapped in shawls and blankets, sipping at their cups of hot kehwa. Children playing in the streets congratulated each other on the first snow of the season, and elders wrote lines in Persian, welcoming the snow, and asked each other for banquets. A thin layer of the new snow, wrapped in small bits of paper, was gifted to everyone. It was a great occasion to eat, drink and enjoy oneself. How could anyone miss out on the opportunity? Mothers and sisters-in-law placed a little snow in the hands of newly-wed brides, congratulating them on the arrival of the first snow. This meant the bride's family would now have to arrive at her in-law's house with huge baskets of bread and bowls of mutton roghanjosh that would then be distributed among the boy's relatives. This was the traditional way of welcoming the snow, with visits, entertainment and piping hot delicious food.

'And why not?' Anand shastri remarked to Ayodhyanath with a smile as he recited the 483rd and 434th shlokas of the *Neelmath Purana* to explain the manner in which the new snow was traditionally welcomed in the past. Shivnath, one of the listeners, always asked too many questions, 'So Anandjoo maharaj, there were dancing girls in the past and Brahmins, despite their respect for women, used to watch their dances. Did they also drink alcohol?'

'Umm, yes, that is what is written in the *Neelmath Purana*.' On such occasions Anand shastri gave a quick reply and left as soon as possible.

Subsequently, on his way home, Anand shastri thought, 'Our ancestors could not have become such great scholars of the *Vedas* and the *Puranas* despite drinking somras and enjoying the performances of dancing girls unless they were men of great perseverance and discipline. Ordinary men cannot be so focused.' He bowed his head in obeisance to his ancestors.

Days and nights acquired a sameness once the snow began to fall. Eyes would get blurred from watching the incessant snowfall. On his way to court, cocooned in a pheran, monkey cap, muffler, warm gloves, socks and a knee length overcoat, Shivnath would pass through Maisooma bazaar and gaze wistfully at the empty windows of the upper stories of the buildings. He would sigh, 'I wish we could also see the performances of dancing girls and drink somras sitting in comfort at home!'

These two pleasures were far removed from Ayodhyanath's house. The dancing girls had been banished from Maisooma bazaar by Maharaja Ranbir Singh a long time ago, and as far as alcohol was concerned, a teaspoonful of brandy was administered to any member of the house who had a cold or had fainted, and that too under the strict gaze of Ayodhyanath himself. How could Shivnath enjoy the winter under such circumstances? But snow was snow after all. Once it was determined to fall it piled up till it reached the high windows of houses. To make things worse, the frost made the roads so slippery that if one didn't walk with caution one could easily fall and break some bones.

Warming her numb hands on the kangri, Kamala shivered as she saw the swirls of snow being whipped across the sky. 'Oh! I can't recall the last time there was so much snow. Snow is as painful as a co-wife for someone who has to do the household work.'

But the well-protected children of prosperous households and the offspring of hanjis wearing thin pherans and trying to warm themselves with kangris all shared the same desire – that old man snow, sitting in the sky, would wave a magic wand over the vast expanse of whiteness and change all the snow into ice cream or kulfi which they could all enjoy!

School and college-going children built snowmen, rahchok! Two bits of coal for the eyes, a red chilli for a nose and a half-smoked cigarette in the mouth. Boys and girls shoved handfuls of snow down each other's overcoats, there were shrieks and scuffles as the warmth of love enveloped two young hearts. Peanuts were roasted on the warm stoves and romances of Himal-Nagray, Samson-Delilah, Shirin-Farhad and Romeo-Juliet were read with great enjoyment. The warmth of love and snow were inextricably linked with each other.

But Zeba, the vegetable–seller cursed the snow as she bound the green haaq into bundles with her frozen hands, stopping occasionally to wipe her dripping nose. 'Damn this unending snow. It is a curse for the poor who have to earn their living. The cold pierces you like a dagger the minute you step out of the house.'

Janakimaal sympathized with her and sometimes gave her an old kurti or a quilted jacket. Zeba showed her chilblained feet to Lalli and asked her for some medicine, 'May God shower his blessings on you, please ask Boblal to get me some balm or something. My feet are killing me, they burn so much that I feel like cutting them off.'

'Oh! Your feet are swollen, you've bloodied them by scratching so hard. Why don't you get some medicine from Hakim Nooruddin? Maybe you should get some leeches put on your feet to suck out the bad blood.'

Lalli was distressed by the state of Zeba's feet. She gave her some balm and a cup of kehwa. Zeba's eyes filled with tears at Lalli's compassionate words, 'Do you think that hell-bound Noor hakim will do anything unless he is paid? He is not even willing to give away a bit of salve which costs just a few paise. That old man is heartless, he only cares about money.'

'Yes! He is greedy but he is also knowledgeable. He has the Chowbechin herb and God knows what else. He uses Chinese herbs to purify the blood, and his cure for boils is very effective. I've heard he belongs to the family of Maharaja Ranjit Singh's personal doctor Hakim Mohammad Azim, who was very renowned. Once he diagnosed, from afar, the illness of a man whom he saw bathing in the river. He told the man to paste cow-dung all over his body and sit in the sun. When the cow-dung dried up and flaked off the man's illness also disappeared.'

Janakimaal put her hand into her pocket and placed a two anna coin in Zeba's palm. Zeba responded with a string of blessings, 'May God grant you prosperity, health and contentment.'

The varied colours of life! Snow had such a different impact on the lives of different people.

Winter was also the season for feasting, there were so many festivals and rituals. In the month of Paush, Hindu homes celebrated the festival of Khichdi Amavasya. A delicious khichdi was prepared with rice, lentils and lots of ghee. It was accompanied by fish or mutton, whatever was the custom of the household. Yaksharaj was offered the first morsels. A large leaf with servings of all the dishes was kept in a corner, which had been swept and swabbed with fresh mud, in the topmost floor of the house. Katya, Didda and Munna would accompany their mother, leaping up the stairs three at a time to see where Yaksharaj would come to eat his dinner that night. Who will steal the cap on Yaksharaj's head? There would be great competition between the children: they had heard that if you stole the cap Yaksharaj would become your slave. You could ask him for anything and he would fulfil your wish. Katya-Ragya decided that as soon as Yaksharaj bent his head to eat they would sneak up on him and snatch his cap. Then they would hide it under the large stone mortar because a Yaksha could pick up a mountain but he couldn't pick up a mortar. When he pleaded with the children to return his cap the girls would make him grant all their wishes before they returned it.

Prem bhaiya, however, couldn't tolerate the girls' flights of fancy. He arrived at the crucial moment and started scolding them, 'I have never seen girls as stupid as the two of you (God knew how many girls he had seen!). Yaksharaj is not a god. The Yakshas were dacoits. Many years ago men belonging to the Yaksha tribe used to come to our valley to loot and kill, they would terrorise the people. So the elders, after consultation, decided to invite the Yakshas to visit their homes for a feast. The Yakshas agreed. So, on this day they would come, enjoy a great feast and go away without troubling anyone. Since then it has become a habit to celebrate this day.'

'This is an old story. Now there are no Yakshas, Baumyas or Khokas. The cats and mice come at night and eat up the food, that's all!'

In other words, you girls had better give up your fantasy of stealing the cap and asking for a ride in an aeroplane!

Premji was at college so what he said must be correct but the idea of enslaving a Yaksha by stealing his cap was very exciting. He would fulfil all their wishes just like the genie in Alladin's lamp.

So, no one stole the Yaksha's cap. It was a difficult task anyway. The stairs leading to the upper tower were enveloped in darkness, which would be even deeper on the night of the new moon. Suppose a thief was actually sitting on the stairs wrapped in a blanket waiting to jump at you? Like Mahadev Bisht? Better to just leave it be. How does it matter if there are no Yakshas any longer, if there are thieves like Mahadev Bisht around? Didn't Baba say that once Mahadev Bisht pulled the Maharaja's pyjamas right off his legs? He'd warned the Mahraja that he would come at night. 'You can post as many guards as you like.' How could the children find the courage to climb the dark stairs at night in a place where there were thieves like Mahadev Bisht?

There were other festivals like Gaadbatha and Divachkheer. On Gaadbath day, fish and rice were cooked, and on Divachkheer young girls would be worshipped and fed sweet kheer made with rice, milk and dry fruit. In the same month of Paush, Shishur was celebrated for new-born babies and newly-wed brides and all relatives would be invited for a feast. An empty kangri would be placed in front of the bride and all the women would put money into it till it was full to the brim. Even when there was no special occasion Shivnath would have some request or the other. The cold weather could be enjoyed only if the stomach was full of warm food!

Those without any means fought a lonely battle with the cold while those who were more fortunate, who had pashmina, raffal, dussas, warm stoves and servants, enjoyed the winter. During the frosty days the surface of the Dal lake froze. People walked gingerly across the lake, enjoying the feeling of having conquered it. With a kangri inside the pheran how could one be afraid of the cold? This is why it has been said, 'O Kangri, you are more winsome than any fairy or angel.' Even the coldest winter days can become enjoyable if one has a kangri close to one's chest.

The Union of Shivshakti and Swachandnath Bhairav

This time there was no escape from the cold even after winter Anand shastri gathered all the children together and explained the meaning of the festival of Shivratri to them. 'Shivratri is not just an occasion to clean the house, cook delicious food and play with cowrie shells. To understand its significance one has to understand Shaivism, which is very complex and ancient. I will try to explain it in simple terms.'

'Om Namah Shivay,' with this utterance Anand shastri got ready to begin his task. 'Shaivism is explained in the sixth century text the *Neelmath Purana*. Shiva is creation itself. Shiva and Shakti are light and intellect. Shiva is the ultimate truth and Shakti is a part of this truth. Shiva and Shakti are not separate entities though they were separated for a brief while. Haven't I told you the stories of the Daksha yagya, Sati dahan and how the wife of Himalaya gave re-birth to Parvati? Do you remember?'

'Yes, we do.' Anandjoo enjoyed the collective response and carried on, 'Listen carefully then. The *Shri Samhita* of Kashmir clearly explains Shivji's significance in the form of Kaalratri, Mohratri, Harratri, Shivratri and Taalratri. Kaalratri, Mohratri and Harratri, represent the angry aspect of Shiva. Shivratri represents the beneficial aspect. This is the reason why ordinary people celebrate Shivratri. Its aim is to convert ignorance, that is kaalratri, into light. Do you understand this?'

'Yes!' The children signalled their assent.

Anand shastri told them about the *Shivmahimnastrot* and *Tripurarimahimnastrot,* texts written by Mahamuni Durvasa, the founder of Shaivism. He explained that these texts described how, 'there is a difference between our Shivratri and the Shivratri celebrated in other parts of the country. Our festival falls on Treyodashi. We celebrate Shiv Chaturdashi separately and on that day we fast and offer prayers to Shiva. Now you should also understand the significance of Treyodashi.'

'Treyodashi is the evening on which the jwalalingam, whose flames reached all four corners of the earth, scorching everything, materialized. It was so dazzling that everyone was blinded by its light. This jwalalingam is considered a symbol of the inner enlightenment which is described in Shaivite theology.'

'Shastri ji, according to the religious texts, doesn't Shivratri symbolize the union of Shiva and Shakti?' Ayodhyanath was also knowledgeable about religious philosophy.

'Yes. This union of Shiva and Shakti is our Shivratri. The knowledge of Shiva, and consciousness in the form of Shakti inspires humans to live their lives and follow their karma.'

'Shastri ji, which is the best time for the pooja?'

'Jajmaan!' Shastriji cleared his throat, 'earlier pandits were divided into three groups, Dakshachaar, Vaamachaar and Mahachaar. Those who followed Dakshachhar prayed to Shiva in the morning, those belonging to Mahachaar prayed at midnight when the brilliance of the lingam had softened and become more bearable and the Vaamachaaris believed that the pillar of light appeared in pradoshkaal, so evening is the appropriate time to pray... there are different views though.' The children didn't understand this philosophical discussion. Shastriji hadn't left any loophole through which they could enter. But there was a question bubbling inside Katya so she quickly accosted Shastriji.

'Bablal maharaj! We offer prayers to Shivji but why do we cook fish and meat?'

Tathya turned to look at Katya and Janankimaal glared at her but it made no difference. Katya had never learnt to silence her queries and Janakimaal could never guess which ideas would enter her head next. Anand shastri, however, was delighted by the question.

'Asking questions indicates a desire for knowledge – listen Katyayini! In his text, *Shivratri Nirnay* Pandit Shivopadhyaya does say that one should be vegetarian on this festival. But there are many other opinions which you are not familiar with, which is why you have these doubts.'

But Katya would not be satisfied till she was told what these other views were.

'All right then listen, devi! I told you that there is a difference between Shivtreyodashi and Shivchaturdashi. We observe a fast on Chaturdashi. But Shivtreyodashi is called 'bhairav yaag' in our religious texts and it is the custom to offer sacrifice to bhairavs and yoginis on this day. This is why it has become customary to cook meat and fish on Shivtreyodashi.'

'But how is Shivratri connected with bhairavs?' The children were confused. So Anand shastri narrated the story of Swachandnath who lived in the Sundarnalak forest. 'He assumed the appearance of a gigantic bhairav and he and his men troubled and harassed the devis and yoginis. This angered Trikuta Devi and she created a vatuk-like being who appeared out of a lake. This being was sent to attack Swachandnath and protect the yoginis and devis. Trikuta devi also created another bhairav called Raman for their protection and the two together, who are known as the sons of the devi, finally defeated Swachandnath. Since these two appeared out of Kumbhs, therefore on Shivratri day we offer prayers to two vessels that represent the 'vatuk bhairav' and the 'ram bhairav'. They are offered all kinds of food and meat and fish is placed only in these vessels. We put only satvik, pure, foods like milk, yoghurt, honey, cereal in the main Shivratri vessel. We pray to the vatuks because they protect us and we put walnuts in the vessels because no other fruit is available in winter.'

The story was interesting but it was also necessary to know why the 'sunnipatul' was worshipped and what was meant by 'vagurbah'.

'The tradition of worshipping the 'sunnipatul' began during the reign of the Muslims, children! There is no mention of it in the Shastras.'

Ayodhyanath supported Shastiji's statement by referring to history, 'You are right, Shastriji. The Muslim rulers were very impressed by our Shivratri prayers and our Sunni brothers requested us to include the puttul puja in our rituals and pray for their well being. How could the Brahmins ignore a request by their rulers? They may also have thought that these people were forced by circumstances to change their religion but after all they are our brothers. So a small kumbh, a vessel, was included in the rituals and was called the 'sunnipatul'.'

'And what about the 'vagur puja' which is performed on dwadashi?'

'Vagur puja was introduced during the reign of the Sikh rulers. They were very impressed by the Batta's Shivratri rituals. They told their Hindu brothers, "Please include the pure and true name of Vaheguru in your prayers." The Sikhs have always protected the Brahmins so the Battas agreed and began to worship kumbhs, on deodashi, which is the twelfth day of the lunar fortnight and called it 'vagurbah'. This is another ritual which is not mentioned in the traditional religious texts.'

Tathya proudly added, 'Though Shivratri is a purely Hindu festival, yet in our valley it links the Hindus, Muslims and the Sikhs. The inclusions in our puja may have been obligatory during a certain period but even during the rule of the Dogras we continued the puja of the 'sunniputtul' and the 'vagurbah'. This is indicative of our religious inclusiveness and this is what 'Kashmiriyat' means.'

Prem bhaiya wanted to know why prayers were offered to vessels full of water. Anand shastri explained this, 'Shiva represents unlimited energy embodied by the sun and during the month of Phalgun the sun enters the kumbh astrological sign, that is why the kumbhs are worshipped during Shivratri. And then Vatuk bhairav and Ram bhairav were also born from kumbhs weren't they?'

After all this knowledge they only needed to know the meaning of the word 'herath' which is also used to denote the festival. Anand shastri finally replied, though a little reluctantly,

'On this day the lecherous Swachandnath called out three times to Rati-Hey Ratey, Hey Ratey, Hey Ratey! This is why the day is also known as "herath".'

Anandjoo placed the flowers, fruit, incense, clean clay to make the Partheshwar, fresh milk, yoghurt, honey and everything else that was needed for the puja in separate bowls. He arranged the vatuk samagri in the southeast. Lalli brought a large plate, a thali with puffed rice, rice flour, lime and saffron. Tathya sat on the prayer mat facing east and wearing the ring made of kusha grass on his finger.

Anand shastri first drew an Ashtdal and an Omkar on the ground with rice flour. He filled the large vatuk vessel with water and walnuts and decorated it with garlands of flowers. He drew an Om on it with vermilion and placed it on the Ashtdal. The other vessels were also put in their proper places and the puja began. The elders, children, men and women all settled down, holding flowers in their hands.

Sanskrit shlokas rose into the air along with the smoke of incense and touched the gods in the prayer room. The prayers went on for a long time. As the flowers were showered onto the statuettes, little hillocks of petals grew on top of the Vatukraj, Partheshwar and the kumbhs. The voices of Anand shastri, Tathya, Shivnath and Keshav rose together like a pleasing lullaby. Sleep gently stroked the eyes of the children and though they heard some words clearly, most others just sounded like gentle sweet music to their ears. Gradually, apart from Tatya, Shivnath, Keshav and the women, all the children drifted off to sleep on the floor of the prayer room. They were woken up at the end of the puja for the sprinkling of holy water. They took the walnut prasad, put a vermilion tika on their foreheads, tied the red sacred thread around their wrists, drank the sacred water and went off to bed.

But this was not the end of Shivratri. The next day was salaam and early in the morning Tathya sat down with a cash box full of money and small change to distribute 'herath kharch' or spending money to everyone, young and old. The children got five rupees each and quickly sat down in groups to discuss what they would do with the money. The potter, barber, milkman, vegetable seller, tailor and servants all came to give their good wishes. Tathya accepted their greetings and then put some spending money in their hands. Salaam was the day for giving. There was a stream of visitors the whole day. Friends, relatives, Hindus, Muslims, Sikhs, everyone visited the house. Mukundram was kept busy looking after the samovar the whole day, while tea, bakirkhanis, kulchas and katlams were distributed to everyone.

Then it was the day of the new moon, a day the children looked forward to. On this day the women took the vatuk down to the riverbank for prayers. They cut the water with a knife while chanting shlokas and then the first walnut from the vatuk was offered as prasad to the Vitasta which is a form of Shakti or Parvati. Then, blessed by the river, they came back home. But the people in the house shut the door and did not let them enter till they had answered some questions. This was an ancient custom.

What did the women bring with them as a gift from the Vitasta?

As the house was close to the river, Katya and Sharika heard the sounds of Lalli and Kamala jigri's wooden slippers from afar. Looking out of the window the girls saw the women making their way carefully through the snow, balancing their large round vessels on their waists. They were followed by Didda and Sharika holding the smaller kumbhs and sinking into the snow as they walked. Janakimaal couldn't go down to the river bank during the snowfall to perform the ritual of vatuk puja any longer so she had now passed on this responsibility to her daughters-in-law.

Katya-Ragya enjoyed the custom of closing the door.

Janakimaal closed the door. Kamalavati knocked on it saying, 'Dub-dub.'

'Who is it?'Janakimaal asked.

'Rama the cat,' came the answer.

'What have you brought?'

'Food, wealth, prosperity and everything in the world you desire.'

Once she was reassured, Jankimaal opened the door and the women entered.

'Congratulations! Congratulations! To all of you, daughters and daughters-in law! Herath Mubarak.' Kamalavati and Lalli gave the prasad of walnuts and sugar to everyone. The walnuts tasted even better when eaten with tiny, warm, rice flour rotis. With the sounds of walnuts being cracked, the smell of the warm rotis and the aroma of special dishes wafting out of the kitchen, the festival of Shivratri came to an end. This was the biggest festival in the valley, it had a special significance because this is the homeland of Shiva and Parvati.

❧

Gypsy Spring

Mehtab Kaul wass celebrating Navreh by taking his entire family for a boat ride in a doonga to the Nishat gardens. As the doonga danced across the waves, rows of cherry and peach trees full of perfumed white and pink blossoms seemed to accompany it along the banks of the lake. The beauty of the spring blossoms aroused a sweet longing in the hearts of young lovers. The air was heady and intoxicating

Sona always linked the seasons with her memories. Pushing aside the curtains of the doonga she drank in the fresh breeze blowing down from Chashmeshahi. Lotus flowers raised their heads across the surface of the lake and near the Kotarkhana, a pair of quacking ducks passed by. Had nothing changed outside in so many years?

The sound of splashing oars and the voice of the boatman pierced Sona's heart as he sang, 'Come and meet me my beloved.' If Kakni had been there she would have told the boatman, 'Sing some other song Rasooljooa' – even at weddings no one sang about lovers when Sona was around. She had not yet come to terms with her aloneness. Suppose she was reminded of her absent beloved?

Bhabi was busy cooking Roghanjosh, Dhana and Durga were cutting vegetables. Sona insisted on kneading flour and making rotis. Bhabi did not allow her to do much work, 'Rest for a while, Sona. Your daughters are helping aren't they? In any case there isn't so much work here that three women can't handle it, and then you are not even used to it.'

Sona was like a guest in her house. But then, what right did she have over it now? The house was hers only because of Madhav.

The boys were at a playful stage in their lives, they did not understand the emotions churning inside Sona. Today they were in a picknicking mood. They stretched out their hands from the side of the doonga to collect lotus leaves from the lake. Today they would eat their food off these leaves. They were carefree.

Sona turned to scold the boys, 'If you bend over too much you will fall into the lake.'

Prithvi interrupted, 'Don't worry. I am keeping an eye on them.'

Sona kept quiet. This happened quite often. Whenever she cought Prithvi's eye Sona became defenceless. The frozen ice began to thaw.

Prithvi had been visiting the house for the past six or seven years. Tathya had sent him to teach Brij and Kanhaiya. Sona was happy. Her brother-in-law was spoiling them with his affection. But who had imagined that Prithvi would become a part of the family rather than a mere teacher and that he would also become a dear friend of Mahtabjoo?

Sona found Prithvi's presence disturbing. This good man who had silently pulled her towards him a thousand times had challenged her willpower, her ability to say no to a man.

Prithvi does not know how Sona spent fourteen years as a widow. Bathing in the early dawn of winter with ice-cold water, observing fasts, praying and devoting herself to the children, Sona completed thirty eight autumns of her life. Now if she was facing temptation in middle age it was only because of Prithvi!

Sona stopped thinking about Prithvi. Bhabi had packed baskets with mince and rotis, biscuits, barfi, daal moth and lots of other food.

'We are getting close to the shore. Everyone pick up something. The men have to do the work outside the house. We women will only serve the food, that's all!'

'The orders of the kitchen queen will be obeyed.' Mahtabjoo was also in a naughty mood.

'Pick up the pack of cards, Prithvi. We'll play cards in the shade of the royal chinar.'

'Aren't you going to walk around or are you just planning to play cards on a picnic?' The lady of the house scolded. After all she had the right.

'I have brought the harmonium, bhabi. We will sing lots of chakris in the Nishat gardens, "O, potter's daughter! I will weave a garland of flowers for you."'

'Certainly, Prathkaka! But you haven't been able to find a potter's daughter for yourself so far...' Bhabi teased Prithvi, casting a sideways glance at Sona.

Bhabi's glance pierced Sona.She was oversensitive at times.

'Why don't you go for a walk and look at the beautiful roses blooming on that side? We will take care of things here.'

It didn't seem like Prithvi was an outsider.

Bhabi collapsed after climbing up and down the seven levels of the garden.

'Sona, go and get some fresh water in the samovar, we will make some tea. I am really tired.'

Bhabi sat down on the green mowed grass. Sona climbed to the upper level and entered the ruins of the Pandava palace. Something pulled her towards the old Chinar. She was a new bride the first time she came here with Madhav and his family. Madhav had managed to spirit her away to these ruins. She could hear the echo of that old conversation amidst these walls.

'Is it true that these are the ruins of the palaces of the Pandavas? Are they really so old?'

'Yes, Sona. There are so many memories buried here, these ruins bring the past to life.'

'Did the kings ever imagine that their grandeur would be transformed like this in the future?'

'Look at that! My Sona is lost in the past, Arre bhai, one enjoys the luxury of kingship while one is alive, who worries what will happen later? Now please don't waste my time on history and geography. Let me enjoy my kingdom.'

'Whaaat? Your kingdom?'

'What else? That of the Pandavas? See, right now we are in the bedroom.'

'Let me go, what will people think if they see us? You've found a very nice bedroom....' Sona dusted her clothes and stood up, Madhav seemed to have gone crazy.

The sound of birdsong arose from the lacy leaves of the ancient Chinar. Sona looked up – tiny birds and the whispering of the breeze. Trembling green leaves and the golden breeze shimmering in the light of the sun. She looked at the names engraved on the trunk of the old tree- 'Madhav-Sona'.

For a moment Sona felt as though she couldn't breathe. Two names engraved in the bark of the tree: Madhav-Sona. Madhav had carved these words and said, 'See, we are immortal now!'

Sona had traced the letters with her fingers, 'When I die you should come here and remember me.'

Madahav put his hands over Sona's mouth, 'I will strangle you if you say this again.'

Sona touched her lips with the back of her hand. Her lips were dry and chapped.

She had come back to this place after so many years! Why suddenly? Was it something pre-ordained? She trembled. Had she pushed Madhav away from herself?

Sona walked into the waterfall flowing down from the pavilion. She wanted to weep. It had been so long since she cried. Today she wanted to let the stone wall that she had painstakingly constructed inside her melt and flow with the waterfall. Looking around and seeing that she was alone she cried out, 'Where are you?' The sound of her voice was lost in the echoing clamour of the water. Sona looked up and saw a lonely shikara floating down the lake.

She was startled by a touch on her shoulder, 'Who…?'

She turned around, it was Prithvi.

'I was just on my way,' As she got up in confusion her foot twisted as it slipped on the wet stone. She clenched her teeth to hold back the pain.

'Bhabi was getting worried. The children went to look for you in the other direction. I came this side.'

He could see the traces of tears on Sona's wet cheeks and he gently put his arms around her. Sona did not give him permission to come closer, nor did Prithvi ask for it. But the fervour of passion cannot always be disciplined. How had he controlled it for so many years?

Sona pushed herself away quickly, suppose someone saw them?

'Let's go, bhabi must be getting worried.'

'It is 'Navreh' today, one should greet the new year with joy. Wash away the sorrow in your heart, Sona.'

Sona looked at Prihvi for a moment, 'Yes, Masterji.'

'Come on!' Prithvi joked, 'It looks like I will always remain a masterji in this house.'

Bhabi really was getting worried.

'Where were you for so long?' Bhabi started worrying if Sona was out of sight for even a little while. Where was she, what could have happened?

On the third day after 'Navreh' Keshav himself came to fetch his sister, it was the custom. Kaknidedi always cried when she gave gifts to her daughter, an overflow of spontaneous sorrow on her child's untimely widowhood. Their bodies trembled as they embraced each other.

Lalli hugged her so hard that Sona started shouting. She tickled Sona's arm pits till she was forced to giggle. What was the point of always reminding her of the past and making her cry? She had to recover sometime. Don't take away her right to live her own life.

Had Sona really managed to recover from the past? Lalli kept her busy at work when she visited her maternal home. But when she went back to her in-laws there was nothing to do. And then there were the memories of Madhav, which filled every corner of the house. Sometimes Sona fainted suddenly, at other times she cried so much she became inconsolable. It was almost as though she was having a fit. Her sister-in-law was worried, 'Who knows what is wrong with her? She has started getting epileptic fits.' The doctor came and prescribed some medicine. He spoke to Mehtab Kaul, 'Keep her busy. She thinks too much. So much loneliness at such a young age...'

Madhav's death had destroyed Sona's personal life like a small boat overturning in the flooded waters of a broken dam. Her widowhood was the result of her deeds in her previous life and there was nothing one could do except learn to bear it. Even Ayodhyanath's progressive thinking was of no help. He had taken on the responsibility of educating the three children so that Sona would not need to ask anyone for help. Sona received Madhav's pension, but beyond this Brahmin society could only advise her to throw herself at the mercy of the gods.

Sona followed the rules. She understood the social consequences of being a widow. All the brightly coloured, red and green pashmina, raffal and brocade saris were locked away in trunks. They were aired every summer, she put chilli seeds and Kuth roots between the folds to protect them.

'Ma! Why don't you wear the zari shawl? Please wear the coral coloured sari sometime. Must you wear these drab colours all the time?'

Brij was mature but for Kanu it was difficult to assimilate all the rules, restrictions and definitions of good and evil that had been laid down for widows.

'Your brides are going to wear these clothes. This is not my age to wear these bright colours. I am old now.'

'Rubbish! You don't have even a single grey hair.' Kanu was not willing to accept that his mother was old despite the fact that she often behaved like an old person.

Sona read religious texts like the *Bhagvat Gita* and the *Ramayana* morning and evening. She kept numerous fasts, she never laughed and joked and never tried to dress up. She spun cotton on her mother-in-law's old dusty spinning wheel. The world of men was out of bounds for her. If she hadn't slipped on the stairs as she swabbed them on the day of the Sahib Saptami, she would never have exchanged more than a polite namaskar with Prithvi.

It was a superficial wound but it became deadly. Sona bit her lip to stop herself from crying out as she fomented her scraped knees but Prithvi saw the tears swimming in her eyes.

He was teaching Kanhaiya. He got up and came up to Sona. When he saw her swollen feet he called out to Kanhaiya, 'Hold your mother's arm, and help her up, she will have to be taken to a doctor. I will go and fetch a tonga.'

Sona was stunned! How did Prithvi acquire this right? He helped her into the tonga and had her wounds bandaged. He asked about her welfare every day till her wounds healed. Those days Mehtabjoo had been transferred to Sopore. So, bhabi also accepted the situation with equanimity.

But this was where Sona's penance began to fall apart. Prithvi's anxiety, the gentle touch on the forehead, 'How are you today?'

'You are not in pain anymore?' The few chosen words made Sona feel helpless.

'I am fine. Please do not worry about me, I will ask Brij to fetch my medicines.' Sona tried to distance herself. But even as she tried to withdraw she encountered Prithvi in every corner of her being. He was everywhere, just like the Vaman incarnation of Vishnu.

Those nights were full of so much anxiety. Days full of apprehension! The more Sona tried to distance herself from Prithvi the more her heart would pull her towards him. Sona's willpower had collapsed. Initially bhabi thought Prithvi was merely being kind but gradually she became a little suspicious. One day she took the samovar from Sona with a grimace and said, 'Let me take this Sona, I will give Prithvi his tea myself.'

Sona kept looking at her as though she hadn't understood anything.

'This is my fate, I am caught in a dilemma. I can't get rid of Prithvi nor can I hold on to him. Suppose something untoward happens tomorrow, I am the one who will be blamed.'

Sona put her head in Lalli's lap and cried, 'I have committed a sin, bhabi.'

'We are all human Sona,' Lalli stroked her hair.

'After so many years Lalli. I became numb. He barely touched my forehead.'

Lalli listened quietly.

'I tried very hard my friend! I kept reading Lal ded's poetry, the *Ramayan*, *Mahabharat*, the writings of saints and holy men...I scolded Prithvi. I hurt him and also wounded myself. How many years have I spent living a lie?'

'What lie Sona?'

'That renunciation would turn me into a stone, that I would become just a spirit not a body. That the memories of Madhav would fill every corner of my life. I could not control my mind, bhabi, I have felt storms rising in my heart at the thought of Prithvi. What am I going to do Lalli?'

Lalli reassured Sona, 'My dearest Sona be brave. What can I say? Kanhaiya is appearing for his Matric. After his exams there will be no need for Prithvi to come, he will go away.'

'I know. Prithvi won't come, I have hurt him. What could I do, all doors are closed for me.'

Lalli tried to calm her, 'Don't think like this Sona. How many people are happy even while they have husbands and lovers? Munshi Bhavanidas Kachru was a scholar. He wrote a great work like *Behre Tavil* in Persian but he could never give Arnimaal any happiness. She sang songs of separation all her life. A saintly woman like Roopabhavani faced rejection by her cruel husband Harinand Sapru. What happiness did she get? Habba fell in love and achieved her desire but for how long? This daughter of Abdi Rather of Chadhaar was left singing songs of sorrow for her love. On this earth, women have very little happiness written in their destiny, Sona.'

Sona fell ill. She was burning with fever. When Prithvi heard he did not hesitate, he came and kept putting wet cloth on her forehead.

Sona opened her heavy lids and turned her face away.

'Why are you killing yourself? I will go away. Your sons are grown up now. They will look after you….'

Rough words! The fever of a burning sense of belonging, a touch would reduce Sona to ash.

Sona sobbed desperately in Prithvi's arms. Oh! This is Madhav, 'Why did you leave me and go away?' Sona is delirious with fever.

'I won't go away this time, Sona. You will be mine.' Oh! But this was Prithvi.

Sona shivered, 'No. Prithvi! For God's sake please go away. Don't come again while I am here, you must promise me.'

Prithvi went away and did not come back. He kept his promise to Sona. Mehtabjoo sent messages. It seemed Prithvi had been transferred to a school in Shopian. Ayodhyanath also called him after two months but Prithvi did not come. For a few days Sona kept looking out of the window in a daze, but despite her distress she was thankful that Prithvi had not allowed any scandal to touch her. The mother of three young men should be thinking about daughters and daughters-in-law. Her life has drained away like sand through the crevices. A wound remained, which she filled in her loneliness with the songs of Habba. Sona called the marriage broker and started making arrangements for Brij's wedding. Her sister-in-law thanked God, 'Sona has been saved from hell. That rogue Prithvi would have shamed the entire house.'

Sona lived the rest of her life with the support of her sons. Half crazed and half a saint.

❧

Faith and Love

People said that Fatima, the dictatorial and imposing wife of
Sultanjoo the shawl dealer, kept an eagle eye on her daughters-
in-law. Had she not done so, it would not have been long
before the young ladies persuaded their respective mates to set
up separate households. It was the duty of the elders, after all,
to keep the family together. Sultanjoo was a God-fearing man,
unfamiliar with the complexities of human relationships. Ever
since his return from the holy pilgrimage of Haj, he had spent
his days in prayer. He didn't even concern himself with the
business, he left all concerns about profit and loss to his sons.
Fatima, on the other hand, always enjoyed keeping an eye on
her sons and daughters-in-law.

Everything seemed to be going well, with the grace of
God. The sons had bought a new shop in Amirakadal on the
Bund. Shawls, namdas, gabbas, carpets, walnut wood furniture,
papiermache table lamps, the shop was full of so many things.
The entire community was envious of the manner in which
Sultanjoo had dug a gold mine for his sons so that they and
their next seven generations could live in comfort without lifting
a finger. His sons changed the name of the shop from 'Sultana
the Best' to 'Sultana the Worst.' This benefited them in two ways,
firstly it served to ward off any evil eye and secondly it drew in
curious rich foreigners who wanted to see what junk was being
sold inside and in the process ended up buying many things.

These foreign customers paid well. Goods were also sent to
Hindustan and there were orders from Russia and America as
well. Sultanjoo's father was an ordinary, skilled carpet weaver
who had passed on this gift to his son. Sultanjoo did not go to
school or college but he became thoroughly familiar with the
history and geography of his own region. He spent his time with
others who were knowledgeable and skilled. He lit up if anyone

praised a carpet, 'Jenab, this is a very old pattern, who puts in so much effort today? When Maharaja Ranjit Singh was the ruler of the Punjab, he was gifted a beautiful Kashmiri carpet. I believe he was so delighted with it that he started rolling about on it! This pattern is very similar to that one, brother.'

Sultanjoo knew so much. 'May Akhundrehnuma find a place in paradise, he is the one who gifted us this talent of carpet weaving.' If you asked who this Akhundrehnuma was, Sultanjoo would get upset.

'You are fond of carpets and yet you don't know who he was?' Sultanjoo would begin from the time of king Badshah. He would narrate how, during the rule of Jehangir in 1620, a Kashmiri called Akhundrehnuma went for Haj, with the grace of God, travelling through Central Asia. On his return he stopped for a while in Andijan and learnt weaving from the carpet makers there. He brought the implements needed for carpet weaving along with him and taught Kashmiris this Iranian skill. Sultanjoo would add, 'Carpet weavers visit his tomb in Gojwara mohalla even today to pay their respects.'

Sultanjoo said the real Iranian carpet the 'Ardebil mosque carpet' was first woven in Kashan in 1526. This carpet was bought for two thousand pounds by the British and was now displayed in the Victoria and Albert museum in London. Kashmiri carpet weavers later made an exact copy of the same Iranian carpet, which was bought by Lord Curzon for a hundred pounds. Kashmiri carpets were also displayed in 1890 at the World Fair in Chicago. 'Our skills are matchless, no one can equal our ability to weave in beautiful pastel shades.'

The very best shawls were available with 'Sultana the Worst', they ranged from the finest woven 'kani' shawls to the beautifully embroidered 'soznis'. Anyone who looked at them was forced to admire them. Sultanjoo had around twenty shawl embroiderers on whom he showered his affection, he treated them like his sons but he also scolded them for their mistakes.

He explained to them that Kashmiri shawls were famous all over the world for their matchless work. These shawls have been known since the time of the Kauravas and the Pandavas. It is believed that even Julius Caesar wore a Kashmiri shawl.

Sultanjoo was very proud of Kashmiri shawls. At every opportunity he related the anecdote from 1796, the time of the Afghan governor Abdullah Khan, when a blind man, Sayyed Yahya Khan, came to Srinagar from the city of Baghdad. On his departure he was gifted an orange shawl which he in turn presented to the Khadiv of Egypt. The khadiv gave the shawl to Napoleon Bonaparte and he passed it on to the empress Josephine. It was after this that Kashmiri shawls became famous all over the world.

Sultanjoo had now become Haji sahib. When he returned from his pilgrimage Ayodhyanath and Baljoo also went to congratulate him. 'Haji sahib, you are very lucky, you have visited Mecca and Medina. Congratulations on visiting the Kaaba.'

Haji sahib embraced them. 'It is all thanks to the good wishes of friends like you and the blessings of God!'

'It is a very long and difficult journey. I hope you didn't face any problems?' Ayodhyanath wanted to know.

'I didn't really think about difficulties, brother. I was totally possessed by my desire to see the Kaaba. Just longing for the moment when I would raise my hands in supplication in the field of Arafat and mark my presence in the durbar of Allah. And then the governments also help Hajis, both in India and in Saudi Arabia, where a lot of arrangements are made for pilgrims.'

Haji sahib, who had never travelled beyond Jammu, had a lot of incidents to relate. For the first time in his life he saw a train, an aeroplane and a ship. He travelled thousands of miles and met innumerable people. He could relate stories about Prophet Ibrahim and about people who sacrificed themselves for God, about Ma Hajira's search for water in the Marwa hills. Then there was the mosque made by Hazrat Ismail in the Kaaba. Haj was not merely obeisance, it was a prayer and a plea as well as a reminder of sacrifice.

When Ayodhyanath asked Sultanjoo whether he had asked God to fulfil any wish, Haji sahib closed his eyes and appeared to travel back to the Kaaba as he softly sang

> When I first saw the Kaaba
> I forgot about the world
> When I raised my hands in entreaty
> I could not remember what I had thought of
> At the moment of faith
> I forgot everything I had wished for

Ayodhyanath was convinced that God had truly blessed Sultanjoo. He was lucky! After all, how many people in the valley had been able to fulfil their desire to go on the Haj?

Haji sahib invited everyone for a feast. The political situation was a little disturbed, and differences between the National Conference and the Muslim Conference had increased. The influence of the Muslim league was also more evident. But there was a deep friendship between Sheikh sahib and Nehru and the National Conference dominated all the other political parties in the valley. Life continued at its own pace.

At Haji sahib's banquet there were Hindu cooks for the Hindus and Muslim cooks for the Muslims. The wazwaan was prepared observing all the niceties of the different religions. Goshtaba, rista, shamikebab, roghanjosh and a pulao so fragrant with saffron that its aroma spread far and wide. Ayodhyanath, Balbhadra, Jialal, Nadir sahib, Prithvi Dhar, everyone came for the dinner. It was a custom that had to be observed and Haji sahib, in any case, had always stayed far away from all political matters. Though some friends had changed Haji sahib advised them as an elder brother would, 'Friends, Why should we let politics affect our personal relationships? We have to live together, don't we? Islam teaches love and peace brother, it does not want brothers to fight brothers. We will do our namaaz and you do your pooja-prayers, the paths are different but the goal is the same. For the rest, there is no difference between human beings.'

Haji's sons respected their father. They earned and lived well with the grace of God. Everything would have been fine if it hadn't been for the fact that Haji's youngest son, Afzal, fell in love. Fatima bi had no objections to his falling in love, the only problem was why couldn't he have chosen to love someone from his own community? But Afzal was so deeply in love with Dhar sahib's daughter that he refused to change his mind despite everyone's efforts.

With the grace of God Afzal had become a doctor. His brothers looked after the business and let him do what he wanted. In any case what could one say to someone who was two hands taller than his father? Fatima did try, however, she reminded him that they had to live peacefully in their neighbourhood. 'Your father is respected by everyone and he is close to many Battas. Why do you want to become the subject of gossip?' But her son refused to budge, 'We are not dependent on anyone, Ammijaan. We are both adults, we are getting married, not committing a crime.'

'But...different religions...?'

'Love does not consider religion, Ammijaan! Not even beauty. Just think of it as the will of God.'

Fatima bi bowed her head before the inevitable but there was complete turmoil in Dhar sahib's house and in the entire Brahmin community. People started saying this was the result of educating girls. There was no sense of shame or decorum left. If girls were allowed to roam around freely they would inevitably tarnish the honour of their families.

Afzal and Vijaya remained unmoved by all this. Educated

and deeply in love, they were confident of their decision. People called them shameless though they were never seen boating around the Dal Lake in a shikara. Within themselves Afzal and Vijaya had felt the passion and force of the roaring waterfalls that fell from the mountains. They had accepted the inevitable bond between love and suffering. They refused to be like the bee and the narcissus which could never meet. They were like Himaal and Naagray who would always be together in every birth, committed to meeting again every time they faced death.

Perhaps because of his advanced age, Sultanjoo could see his son's obstinacy but he could not understand the depth of his passion. Without worrying too much about the situation, he decided to send his son to England to do his M.D. He thought if the boy really was in love he would persevere despite the distance and the passage of time, otherwise he would forget everything in a short while. Fatima bi felt this was a good idea, Afzal would get busy with his studies and who knows, Dhar sahib might marry off his daughter in the meanwhile.

Haji sahib was quite confident about the future, 'Two years is a long time. He will forget the girl.' This prediction was proved wrong. Six months after Afzal left for England, Vijaya followed him. She was a doctor after all, the daughter of a well-to-do family and she had as much right to do her M.D. Haji sahib gave his blessings when he saw how committed they were to each other, though there was some awkwardness with a few of his Hindu friends. He constantly tried to mend the situation. He would often refer to the number of Afghan and Muslim rulers whose mothers had been Hindu, 'Huzoor, Ghayasuddin Tughlaq and the Sultan of Delhi Ferozeshah Tughlaq! Do you know that both of them had Hindu mothers? And everyone knows of Akbar's wife Jodhabai. These things have often happened in reputed families. How can I blame Afzal, he is in love after all and love is a manifestation of God. ' Fatima bi also bowed before the inevitable though Prithvi Dhar's wife,

Sampatti, almost had a heart attack when she received Vijaya's letter from England stating baldly that, 'Afzal and I have had a court marriage. You can perform my funeral rites if this marriage is unacceptable to you. I cannot live without Afzal and in any case, now it is too late.'

Prithvi Dhar went underground for a few months, hoping that all the gossip would die down soon. But people don't forget so easily. No one had forgotten the earlier incident when a girl called Sarla had run away with her lover Lokeshnath, leaving her plait and a bowl of blood as proof that she had been murdered. The entire community had been shamed by her behaviour.

But this was a different situation. Prithvi Dhar managed to retain his respect and honour in the community. Sampatti sent a dejharu for her daughter with the blessings that may she have a good marriage. In other words, what happened was not good but we accept it since it seems to be the will of God.

When Afzal and Vijaya returned from England with their degrees Haji sahib greeted them with great affection though the celebration was tempered with restraint. Prithvi Dhar's community was worried rather than upset by this marriage and Haji could understand this fear behind which there was a history of religious conversion. The Hindus were worried about protecting their religion though none of their worries proved true as Vijaya never became a Muslim but remained Vijaya Dhar all her life.

In time, the community understood this and soon Prithvi Dhar and Afzal were seen eating on the same dastarkhan while Vijaya's mother served the choicest dishes to her son-in-law. Vijaya and Afzal became renowned doctors in the valley and dedicated themselves to serving the people of their homeland. People sometimes forget the things they want to: forgetfulness makes life more bearable.

The Girls Grow Up

All parents start worrying as their girls grow up and Shivnath and Keshavnath's daughters seemed to be shooting up at a tremendous pace. Kaknidedi put thick chiks on the windows facing the bazaar but boys continued to stop and stare at the shadows flitting across the edges of the chiks. The influence of the planets on Sharika's horoscope was really strong, what could Kaknidedi do? She had some pujas performed on the advice of Anand Shastri. Ayodhyanath, however, did not believe in these attempts to appease the planets. If you said anything he would start talking about the the joys and sorrows, the ups and downs of life faced by Shri Ram and Shri Krishna and repeat the old cliché that what has to happen will happen. Thankfully Shivnath listened to his mother so some efforts were made to find a groom but these proved to be as futile as sowing seeds in sand. Nothing seemed to work.

Sharika may not have been able to study beyond the eighth standard because she wasn't really interested in studying, but there was no doubting her efficiency in household work. She could make delicious grainy Phirni and fragrant Yakhni pulao. She had a pale complexion with eyes as beautiful as the lotus flowers in the lake. A daughter like the goddess Lakshmi, without any faults or flaws. These marriage brokers were useless though, no one could understand their scheming – how could there be any lack of grooms for Tathya's granddaughters?

Kaknidedi would worry every time she looked at the girls. She felt as though the world around her was burning. Sharika was going to be twenty soon. For the last seven generations, in this house, there had been no girl who had remained unmarried at her age. Sharika was almost as tall as the ceiling but there was no groom in sight. And then when a groom was found it was like falling out of the frying pan into the fire! All thanks to

Tathya's legal mind and his dislike of marriage brokers. He said, 'Stop worrying about the planets, don't try to match horoscopes, just place her horoscope at the feet of Mahaganapati. Ganeshji is the remover of obstacles, he will make everything all right. Sharika's marriage should not be delayed any further. The Bhan's son is a good boy, the family is excellent and we have already given them our word.'

'But Tathya, their priest Nandu Bayu has said that the marriage should not take place even if all the arrangements have been made! He says the horoscopes of the boy and the girl do not match at all and Sharika is a Mangalik, she is born under the influence of Saturn! How will she be happy?'

When Kaknidedi heard she was stunned. Which illiterate priest had he shown the horoscope to and why had he sent off the shagun, the gift indicating acceptance of the match? Hadn't he thought before giving a promise to Neelkanth Bhan? Now everyone would talk. The whole house was enveloped in silence. It wasn't only Shivnath, but everyone else too who believed in the planets and horoscopes.

'Well now even the Bhans have taken back their proposal, after all they want their son to be safe and happy.'

Ayodhyanath took a few puffs of the hookah and gestured to Shivnath to stop speaking.

'Leave it be! Neelkanth has now proposed the name of his brother's son, Indra. I am talking about him. All of us want Sharika to be happy but there is no point in being too finicky. In any case let us ask Anand bayu for his advice.'

Lately Anand shastri had become quite weak, he had crossed eighty after all. But he came over as soon as he got Tathya's message. He pored over the horoscopes of Sharika and Indra, checking the planets and the sun signs. When he was satisfied, he turned to the anxious family members sitting around and said, 'Mahaganapati will bless the union, there is nothing to worry about, their horoscopes match very well.'

Putting all their doubts and fears to rest he added, 'Begin the preparations in the name of God. Don't worry about anything.'

Ayodhyanath bowed his head in thanks. Bhan sahib believed in destiny and in custom. He had arranged Sharika's marriage with his brother's son. The promise had been kept and fears had also been allayed. Promises had great sanctity among Brahmins. King Dashrath had to fulfil his promise even though it meant exiling his beloved sons. Kaknidedi was satisfied and the house was full of joy.

Sharika was Kamala's daughter. Kamala had enough gold of her own, different types of necklaces, gold belts, bangles, to divide between her two daughters and still have some left over for her daughter-in-law. Clothes for the in-laws had already been bought and Sharika's headdress was also ready, thanks to Gula the maker of the zojis. The zoji, which was part of the headdress called the Taranga, was made of the finest muslin with a fine mesh and had an intricately worked gold vine embroidered on it. Sharika's mother-in-law would be delighted to see it. Tathya had bought five saris for her from Benaras and there were two saris of Raffal and Pashmina. Lalli herself would take care of Sharika's wedding clothes. She would decorate the veil covering her head with embroidery and beautiful golden flowers. With Nanni's help she would get Sharika ready on her wedding day.

The Zutshis had asked for Didda's hand. She was really fortunate. Kaknidedi took some chillis, waved them around her favourite granddaughter's head and threw them in the fire to ward off the evil eye. Didda's groom was talented and as handsome as Lord Rama himself. Lalji was also lucky to get a wife as beautiful as the apsaras in the court of Indra, the lord of the heavens. But this Katyayini? Till when was she going to roam around without any restraints?

Kakknidedi's worry was understandable given the fact that she was married at the age of ten to Tathya who was only fourteen years old and used to steal dates and sugar balls from her pheran pocket. Kaknidedi would complain to her mother-in-law saying, ' Your son is always emptying out my pockets. If you don't scold him I will complain to my father and get him beaten up.'

'Oh, Kaknidedi, you used to get Tathya beaten up? How sad!'

Kaknidedi would drift back into the past. A warm, mysterious smile would spread across her wrinkled face and then, noticing the impish look on Katya's face, she would look grave and say, 'Quiet! Don't talk too much. You shouldn't talk about elders like this, it becomes a habit. Remember you have to go a different house after your marriage.'

'I have to study Kaknidedi, why don't you just enjoy the weddings of Sharika and Didda?'

'Enough! Enough! I have heard enough! You will never become a man however much you study. You have been born a girl. Remember, in the end, you still have to look after the house and the kitchen.

Lalli would signal to her daughter to stop arguing. It was not seemly to argue with elders. Katya had, in any case, stopped bickering too much because Tathya had dispelled her fears.

How did this happen? Kakni was totally determined to marry her off. She liked Girdhari, the only son of the prosperous Tikku family. When his horoscope did not match with Didda's, Kakni offered Katya's horoscope. There was no shortage of girls in Tathya's house after all!

'Oh! What looks and what qualities! As though Lord Shiva himself has taken the form of Girdhari! And he is so good in his studies!' As if she knew him from the time he was born!

'Arre! Why shouldn't I know him? He belongs to an old family. They may not have their lands any longer but their standard of living is still the same! There is an entire platoon of servants and a four-storeyed house with such large drawing rooms and halls that ten weddings could be held there at the same time. The walls are hung with portraits of their ancestors framed in gold and there are elegant, soft carpets on all the floors.'

'I am telling you, don't reject this match.'

'But Katya wants to study further.'

Janakimaal lost her patience when studies were mentioned.

'Enough! She is too learned already. Look at what the world has come to! Girls as tall as camels roaming around freely with boys! The girl has crossed sixteen already. Send her to her own house, if she wants she can carry on studying for her whole life.'

Tathya set aside his hookah and brought his wife's long-playing record to an end, 'All right, I will think about it.'

Katya went on strike. Lalli tried to persuade her, 'Munnu, you can always study later. We will talk to your in-laws, they will agree. They are a progressive family and they are Tathya's friends.'

'No.' Katya refused to listen to any arguments. They will not allow their daughter-in-law to go to college however progressive they are. And Katya wanted to be a doctor. She cried bitterly as she saw her dreams vanishing before her eyes.

'If you insist I will eat that rat poison lying on the shelf and kill myself.'

'Rubbish! Don't talk without thinking. May your enemies die instead.'

Lalli wiped her daughter's tears and stroked her hair.

'Don't ever say anything like this again.'

Lalli had never tried to limit Katya's horizons. Her mother-in-law grumbled all the time but continued to praise Rajdulari, 'Didda has learnt English, Sanskrit, and no one is as skilled as her at knitting and embroidery. But she listens to everything you say. She is like a gentle cow, content in her life, may God bless her. This Katya, nothing about her is straight. Who knows what she will do if one insists, she is quite obstinate and unpredictable.'

For many days there was tension in the house. For the first time Keshav spoke to Tathya on Katya's behalf. He had a discussion with Tathya's friends, 'The girl wants to study medicine, which college should she apply to? She is good at her studies. S.P College could be the right choice, she has to study biology….'

Keshav kissed Katya's forehead, 'You are the first girl in our house who is going to study in a co-educational college. Remember your honour and the honour of your family.'

Sharika-Didda were busy with their rainbow-hued dreams. They embroidered sheets and quilts and crochet tablecovers. The aim of their lives was to get a good husband, to win over their in-laws and to become efficient housewives, perfect wives, admirable daughters-in-law and good mothers. Katya was irritated with them.

Both the girls started spending more time at home. Didda had done her Ratan, Bhushan and Prabhakar after her Matric, she could even recite the *Ramayana* and the *Mahabharata*. Kaknidedi guarded them diligently, keeping an eye on all their activities. Anything could happen if they met any boys. She scrutinized everyone who entered the courtyard. Who knew what was hidden in anyone's mind?

The girls were no longer interested in the streetside Romeos nor did they bother about the besotted Shyam who sat at his window, gazing at Sharika. Didda had always disliked this hide and seek, she had really scolded Sharika when she saw her peeping at Shyam through the window lattice.

'He looks at you every day and you too?'

'Every day he comes and stands at the window when he comes back from college.'

'How do you know?'

'I just know.' Sharika's face reddened. Who knew when an invisible connection was established through the eyes. Sharika couldn't stop herself. 'I just look at him once and that too from behind the window. He doesn't even get to know.'

'No, this is not right. Once Prediman Lamboo of the Sahib family tried to give me a letter in the street, I just threw it at his face. I would have beaten him with my chappal if he had misbehaved again.'

Didda was like the fearless queen of Jhansi in such matters but Sharika was made helpless by her feelings. She could not bring herself to abandon this routine of peeping out of chinks, sensing the depth of Shyam's love, till the moment of her marriage. Did her heart break a little as she left home? No one was interested in what her feelings were like at that moment. Shyam continued to gaze at the closed windows of Sharika's home for a few days but then perhaps, he also got busy with more important matters.

The house was busy with preparations for the weddings. Sultanjoo, the shawl merchant, sent a bundle of fine tosa shawls home so that the women could choose what they liked. The goldsmith was busy melting and resetting gold according to what the girls wanted.

During this time, one day, Mangala mausi announced that Gandhi baba was visiting the valley. 'A huge crowd of people is collecting at Sheetalnath to see him. Aren't you going?'

Kamala and Lalli were very keen to see the Mahatma. The girls couldn't go because they were engaged now and couldn't step out of the house. 'You go and see the Mahatma. I will tell Shivnath, Keshavnath to take you. I will stay back at home.' Janakimaal was benevolent. She also wanted to meet this Mahatma who wore a thin dhoti and walked miles in the cold to meet people and listen to their problems, a man of whom even the English are afraid. But her knees were giving her a lot of trouble and then there were young girls at home.

Katya insisted, 'I will go, I am not engaged.'

Once they reached Sheetalnath, however, she felt suffocated by the close press of people as she made her way, holding Lalli's hand. There were just heads on every side. A woman's dejharu was stolen in the crowd, another said she had been pinched all over by ruffians, others were heard cursing and shouting. Keshavnath and Shivnath refused to go deeper into the crowd. The police was unable to control the large number of people. Just then there was an announcement over the loudspeaker that Gandhiji would not be able to come today. Shivnath herded them into Ram Munshi's house close by, they would leave once the crowd dispersed.

Masses of people turned back disappointed towards their homes. When half the crowd had dispersed, Bapu's jeep entered the courtyard of Sheetalnath. Katya, Lalli and Kamala ran and sat down in front of the stage. And there was Gandhiji, right in front of them. Thin, frail, wearing a dhoti and a shawl. Deep, wise eyes hidden behind round spectacles, a small bald head and a childlike toothless mouth. As he came on stage with a stick in one hand, resting his other hand on the shoulder of a woman, the hymn 'Raghupati raghav raja Ram, patit pavan Sita Ram' echoed from the mike. All the spectators were moved and for an instant the heavens rang with the sound of 'Ishwar Allah tere naam' and then there was silence. Bapuji did not make a speech. He stood in front of the mike, did namaskar, thanked everyone, blessing them with raised hands. And then he left.

Everyone was silent and pensive on their way home. So this was Gandhiji who spoke about getting freedom through non-violence and Satyagraha! The man who had shaken the British throne and repeatedly suffered violence at the hands of the police. Jai ho, jai ho!

'This is the man who was thrown out of the first class coach in Africa? The British said, "You are black, only whites can sit in the first class coach." The same man?'

'Yes, the same! That is where he started speaking out against racial discrimination.'

'But did he go like this, in these same clothes, like a fakir, to the Round Table conference in England? Just like this?'

'Of course. He stopped wearing suits long ago.'

'He is so thin. This skeletal frame must have borne the blows of so many lathis. How many times has he been to jail?'

'Who's counting? He is not the sort of man who worries about suffering.'

Bapu was the topic of discussion in the house for many days. The son of the Dewan of Rajkot, educated in England, who practised law in South Africa and who had now given up everything for the sake of his country. He was called the 'half-naked fakir'. 'Till now one had only heard of saints but today we have seen one'. Everyone felt blessed to have seen Bapu.

Songs of Freedom

Hundreds of tiny lamps lit up the beautiful palaces of Gupkar, their fairy lights mirrored in the waters of the lake. A gentle breeze stirred the calm waters, and it was almost as if it was whispering to the waves, 'Freedom! The country is free!' In the houseboats, with their outlandish names like 'Paris Beauty', 'Lake Queen' and 'Baghe-Bahar', people watched the lights with curiosity. Could it be that the palace was seeing the birth of another child?

Boatman Mushtaq stuck his head out of the window of his boat to gaze at the stream of lights and, with his eyes almost popping out of their sockets, shouted out the news to Hassan Bande, 'They're saying freedom has come.'

'Who's come, the English queen?'

'The queen has gone and now even the Maharaja is going

to go. Our country is free. That is why there are all these lights and fireworks.'

'What amazing fireworks! I wish freedom would come every day so that our houseboats could be lit up by its light.' This was Hassan Bande's heartfelt wish.

'You ass! Don't get overexcited. We will starve if the British go away. Do you think the local seths have either the money or the generosity to spend money like them?'

Subhan Mallah did not see the lights at Gupkar; instead he saw the ones that shone in Shergarhi on the banks of the Vitasta. He said to Khurshid, 'Perhaps it is good for the country that the British are gone, but it would have been all right even if they had stayed.' What new changes will the seventy year old Subhan Mallah live to see?

Khurshid retorted, 'Have you ever been optimistic about anything? Good or bad, it's all the same to you! See, how the entire country is filled with the fragrance of freedom.'

'Yeeees, you are right. Freedom is special. But Khurshid, remember one thing, the British have taken away our livelihood.'

Subhan Mallah's sons, Ali and Gani, were also worried. Who was going to come and stay in their 'Honeymoon' houseboat now? When the English couples used to go for boat rides in the well sprung shikaras decorated with silk curtains and crewel work cushions, the playful breezes would come down from Pari Mahal to touch them. Subhan Mallah would burst into Sufiana songs like a waterfall springing out from a hillside. Now when dark-skinned officials and miserly businessmen sit in the shikara they bargain and give two rupees instead of ten and that too so reluctantly.

In the city, there were animated discussions: people were excited, elated, and fearful. No one knew what would happen. On the 5th of August 1947 Ayodhyanath, Balbhadra, Jialal and Prithvi Dhar got together to listen to the radio broadcast of

Nehru's speech in Parliament, 'When the world sleeps, India will awaken to freedom.' The light of freedom illuminated the mysterious depths of the lake. Maharaj Bahadur had not only lit up the valley but also ordered illuminations in Jammu and Ladakh. Yet what did the common public know about the hundreds of plans that had been made and the joys, anxieties, hope and uncertainty that were standing shoulder to shoulder in the valley at that moment?,

And there was a 'human earthquake' as people began to flee their homes to head to the new countries for India had been partitioned into two. Nehru was shocked by the violence and inhumanity, the looting that followed. Perhaps Bapu had a premonition about what would happen which is why he opposed Partition till the end. Ayodhyanath's forehead was furrowed with anxiety.

'Yeee…s you are right! Nehru ji has said, "Independent India will never again become dependent. There will be no Pakistan and there will be no communal tensions!" but this Partition has proved all these conjectures wrong.'

'I have heard that trains full of dead bodies are coming from Amritsar and Lahore to Delhi and in return thousands of corpses are being parcelled back… hordes of people have fled their homes in the night with their belongings packed in bundles. Hey Ram! What kind of freedom is this?'

'Many camps have been set up in Delhi to help the refugees.'

With the creation of Pakistan another worry began to creep into the minds of the educated people of the valley: would Maharaj Bahadur join Pakistan or Hindustan?

There were other uncertainties as well. 'Mirwaiz Maulvi Yusufshah has been made the leader of the Muslim Conference. I have heard there are many confrontations between him and the leaders of the National Conference.'

'This is quite worrying. There are many opposing forces at work in the state.'

'Chaudhari Hamidullah had asked the maharaja to leave Kashmir as early as 10 May 1947. He said we should declare Kashmir a free country. Leave Kashmir! Remember how much turmoil there was? So many politicians were sent to jail.'

'Lord Mountbatten visited the valley just a month after that.'

'I have heard he asked the maharaja to take an independent decision, but the maharaja was unwell at the time.'

'Yes, that's what I have heard too. God knows what the truth is.'

'What will the maharaja's decision be?' Everyone was anxious.

'Whatever he decides he will keep the welfare of the people in mind, after all we are his subjects!' Banta Singh did not lose heart.

The Brahmins had a lot of faith in the maharaja. He was their guardian, but they also understood that it was a difficult decision.

'Yes, it seems Gandhiji met the maharaja during his visit to the valley in July or August. They must have discussed everything, including the wishes of the public.'

'There must have been some consultations, Balbhadra bhai, that is why Ramchand Kak was removed from his post as Prime Minister as soon as Gandhi left and Major General Singh was appointed in his place. This just happened on the 10th of August.'

'There is also a rumour that Jinnah sahib is very keen to know the maharaja's decision. He wants to make Kashmir a part of Pakistan on the basis of religion.'

The very mention of Pakistan made Banta Singh anxious. The violence of Lahore and Amritsar immediately came to his mind. Ayodhyanath reassured him.

'Don't worry, Kashmir will not be handed over to Pakistan so easily. Sheikh sahib is not fond of either the Muslim League or Jinnah Sahib. He is Nehru's friend. He is a real patriot. He will ensure that we remain a part of India. There is nothing to be concerned about.'

It was true however, that the intellectuals were concerned. The question uppermost in their minds was 'What will happen to us?' Mahdoo, Khurshid, Lassa the tailor, Sula, the cobbler, Fata the potter were all busy with their daily routine. They didn't know anything much about Hindustan and Pakistan. One was an old country and the other was a new one. There was some trouble there, or at least that is what they had heard. But these were matters concerning the world beyond Banihal. 'What has to happen can happen on the other side, here all will be well.'

They were protected by the armour of their beliefs. Rehman had switched over to Sheikh sahib's party after seeing his growing popularity. And in Rehman's heart there was a growing desire to become a small-time political leader at least. On Independence day Rehman attended the local committee meeting and despite being unfamiliar with difficult words like imperialism and aristocracy he was happy thinking that just as India became free after the British left, similarly the king would leave and farmers and workers would rule the valley under the guidance of Sheikh sahib.

When he praised Sheikh sahib even his friends teased him, calling him a turncoat. They asked if he had been bribed to switch sides by the party and that was why he had become an admirer of Sheikh sahib overnight. Rehman was sometimes shamefaced and sometimes irritated. 'It takes time to understand politics, my friends. You have to be ready to make changes. And as far as bribery is concerned, I will feed all of you Goshtaba-Rista once we form the government. Pray to God that day comes soon.'

Ashi dai was not very impressed by her son's boasting, after all she had washed his nappies! She was happy that he had joined Sheikh sahib's 'palty'. But she was of the view that a person's status also played a significant role in politics. Rehman should pick up the reins of his tonga and pay more attention to looking after his family's welfare. His wife worked in four houses to earn money. His mother was also growing old. She could not go out to attend on pregnant women in the cold of the Kashmiri winter. Also, lately, even the poor had started preferring doctors and nurses. They said midwives are not clean enough, there was fear of 'fection.' These are new beliefs, what can one say? Let's leave things to Allahtala, He will take care of everyone. The same belief in Allah and the thunderous voices of the leaders filled Rehman with the hope that something would happen, that his luck would change.

But suddenly things took a completely different turn and everyone was stunned. How could this have happened? It was the month of October. The plants and trees were feeling the approach of winter. It was as if the leaves of the Chinar, with their wonderful russet and gold, were on fire. Despite the beginning of winter, the rush of tourists had not abated. In the homes of educated people there was an awareness that intermittent skirmishes were taking place between the armies of Pakistan and India on the borders, in Poonch-Rajauri, Muzaffarabad and from Gilgit to Mirpur. These minor disagreements were inevitable now that one nation had been divided into two. The army had to keep itself occupied.

It was the day of Sharika and Didda's henna ceremony. Would Ayodhyanath's family ever forget this day? Kashi was performing and singing 'bacchanagma' for the women. Sona bua no longer accepted any gifts for performing at rituals but she started the celebrations by playing the tumbaknari and singing a few lines of a traditional mehndi song. She handed over the task of mixing and distributing the henna to her cousin, Shanta. The men sat in the next room, discussing the arrangements for the wedding, enjoying enticing glimpses of the women and listening to snatches of romantic songs.

When Kashinath gestured to the older women to let the young girls come forward and dance, the newly married brides laughed softly with lowered heads and the elder women ribbed him with gentle taunts, 'Look at him, he has lost his senses. Do you think we are old, Kashinatha? Yes?' Laughter, jokes, the resounding rhythm of the Chakri, hymns, romantic songs and the general tumult of a wedding. Today all was forgiven!

Mahdu had called a troupe of performers from his village, the women were in splits watching the antics of the folk theatre performers. Sitting in the midst of the women with their hair left open, hands and feet decorated with henna, surrounded by the perfume of burning isband, Sharika and Didda were lost in their dreams. As the rhythmic drumming of the tumbaknari spread the message of celebration in the neighbourhood, Leelavati's sister Shobha suddenly stormed into the room. Distressed, upset, her face reflecting fear, worry and anxiety.

'Arre, Shobhavati! When did you come from Baramulla? Is everything all right? What have you done to yourself?'

But Shobhavati was in no condition to answer these questions. No sooner had she entered the room that she started beating her breast and shouting, 'They have reached Baramulla. People are being killed and you are busy playing tumbaknaris? They will be here by morning….'

'Who has reached Baramulla, Shobha? What are you talking about? What's wrong with you? Why are you destroying such an auspicious moment?'

Kaknidedi felt Shobha had suddenly lost her senses. Her clothes were in complete disarray and she herself was in a real state. 'Those …Kabailis are coming. People are running away. We also ran away without even stopping to put on our shoes. I just stepped into my house for a moment and then rushed to tell you. They have captured Muzaffarabad. Sona's brother-in-law is in Mohra, Kamala bhabi's sister has left Baramulla, God knows what has happened to her. Those people are misbehaving with women. It is such a calamity and you don't seem to know anything.'

The women started crying and lamenting. The men were stunned. Someone's son was posted in Uri, someone else's entire family was in Baramulla! Sona's brother-in-law had recently been transferred to Mohra. Leelavati had come to Srinagar seven days ago along with her children to attend Sharika-Didda's wedding and lend a helping hand. And now this thunderbolt!

Leelavati was almost paralysed with shock. Tulsi's mother started crying and beating her breast, who knew what would have happened to Tulsi? Balbhadra's brother is a forest ranger in Muzaffarabad. People are posted all over the place. Dear God! What is this sudden calamity?

Within moments celebrations were forgotten as people wailed and wept. There was a pall of gloom. Men and women rushed home in the middle of the night, desperate for news of their loved ones, worried and yet supportive of each other. Would they see another sunrise, they wondered.

Food that had been cooking on slow fires all night was taken off, the fires doused and the cooks, servants and helpers sent off to their quarters. Ayodhyanath gathered the weeping women, the frightened brides, the children and his worried sons together in the sitting room. They discussed the situation, as nothing was secret any more.

'The Kabailis have invaded our valley. This is a difficult time but worrying will not serve any purpose. Stop crying, we have to be brave. Whatever happens we will all face it together.' Ayodhyanath advised everyone.

Shobha's husband lived in the neighbourhood. Shivnath went to his house and came back with more information. 'I believe they are extremely brutal. They molest women. They lined up Pitambar Bhatt's entire family and killed them with a single gun.'

'They were looting brass samovars and utensils, mistaking them for gold, they are completely ruthless,' said Shobha who had escaped from Baramulla with her two daughters and her husband, Somnath. 'God bless Yusuf Lone who helped us escape. He put us in his truck and drove us out of the village without worrying about his own safety.'

What should be done now? The wedding was stopped midway. The brides, with their hennaed feet and hands, sat crumpled and pathetic in a corner. The Kabaili invasion became a reality for the residents of Srinagar when the looters occupied the Mohra power house. The entire valley was suddenly enveloped in darkness. The night of 25th October 1947 was a night of terror for people living in the valley. How could one have a wedding when the Kabailis might arrive in the city the next day? Who knew what the fate awaited the women of the house? Even Ayodhyanath's usually logical and legal brain had stopped functioning. Shivnath and Keshavnath were busy collecting any possible weapons, including knives, canes, thick pestles used to grind wheat and sticks. Tathya's sword, which reposed in its velvet scabbard for the entire year, and was used only when he visited the court on the occasion of the Maharaja's birthday, was also taken out of its case by Shivnath, who sat and sharpened its blade. It was rather heavy with a solid handle and who knew whether he would actually be able to use it? For hours Ayodhyanath's family sat waiting for the night to end. Indeed, it wasn't only this family but the entire city that seemed to be waiting, in fear and apprehension, for the morning.

The brides had worn themselves out weeping. Kaknidedi held them close and tried to quieten their sobs. In her heart she asked all the myriad gods why they had chosen this very day for this disaster. Was it necessary to destroy the happiness of these innocent girls? What mistakes, she asked, what omissions have I made in my prayers to you, O God?

Tathya had more serious worries. If the Kabailis reached Srinagar wouldn't it be better to die than see our women dishonoured in front of our eyes? What choice will we have? Wouldn't it be better to give the women poison? But wouldn't that be murder? Torn between right and wrong, honour and dis-honour, Tathya bore the brunt of that terrible night.

It was ridiculous to imagine one could fight bullets with knives and swords. The only option was to run away, but where and how? Men would find it impossible to cross the snow covered Banihal and the peaks of the Pir Panchal range, the women and children would just get buried in the snow. Suddenly, at midnight, the valley had been caught in an unexpected whirlpool. And now it was waiting, fearfully, cowering in the lap of the mountains.

But one cannot abandon hope and no action should be taken in a hurry. The men of the house kept talking and clutching at straws. 'The maharaja will definitely try to do something. After all it is his duty to protect his subjects.' Shivnath and Keshavnath would say a few words that would disappear into the silence around them like a frog jumping into a well.

'Yes, you are right. But….' This was Ayodhyanath as he took a deep pull on his hookah.

'But what, Tathya?' The fear of losing the last vestiges of hope.

'Right now the people are against the maharaja.'

'So? Does that mean he will just abandon us?'

'Our maharaja knows that the great king Lalitaditya was treacherously killed by his own people. He will try to save himself first.'

Lalli, Kamala, Katya and Ragya started reciting the Indrakshi shlokas, at a moment of helplessness one could only appeal to the invisible powers!

One day had changed everything. The 26th of October was a

day of rumours, and fears. The women of the house rose with heavy hearts and took control of the kitchen. One has to eat even in times of crisis. Mukundram had run away to his village at dawn.

Ayodhyanath sent a message through Shivnath to the girls' in-laws saying that the 'devgon' ceremony should be postponed for the moment. Who knew what the situation would be like tomorrow? On the night of the 27th there was some rumbling in the sky. People looked up in disbelief at the planes circling above. 'So, the Indian army has come to our help.' It was as though Lord Shambhu himself had come to help them. 'Hail to you, mother Sharika. You have answered our prayers.'

It was a miracle. People were weeping in relief. Those who had thought of running away, drowning themselves in the Vitasta or fighting the enemy with spears and swords suddenly felt as though they had been granted a new life. Others who had gathered together all their gold and silver, and planned to escape across Banihal put down their bundles in relief. Mother Parvati had protected her subjects. Ayodhyanath took the women to the roof and showed them the aeroplanes performing acrobatics in the sky.

'Look, there are flames and smoke rising from the direction of the airport! Can you see them? The Kabailis have reached Badgam. They will all be finished! Not even one of them will survive!' Thosands of people in Srinagar saw the fighter planes dropping bombs on the airport and Shalteng. Flames rose as high as the sky and smoke billowed up to hide the black clouds overhead.

The Kabailis first occupied Muzaffarabad and then came down via Baramullah and Mohra to Shalteng on the outskirts of the city. They were about to take control of the airport when the Indian army arrived and pushed them back.

'Now everything will be all right. Gandhiji and Nehruji have sent the army for our protection. We are their subjects after all, they won't allow anyone to harm us.'

Ayodhyanath now set out to visit the parents of the bridegrooms. He took with him a basket of almonds and crystallized sugar. How could he visit the girls' in-laws empty handed the first time? He was confident the moment of peril had passed.

'Bhai sahib! God has been kind! The maharaja has sent a request that Kashmir should become a part of India. I believe the viceroy has already agreed to it.' Tathya held forth on the current situation in the country.

'Yes, that is why the Indian army came to our rescue. If they had been late even by a day the entire city would have been razed to the ground.'

'Everything was just touch and go! I have heard the water in the spring at the Khirbhavani temple had turned black.'

'The planets were very adverse, we have survived with the grace of God.'

'Yes! All is well that ends well. The wedding ceremonies were interrupted so suddenly – but now, what do you suggest?'

The girls' in-laws had daughters of their own, they congratulated Tathya and told him to get ready to welcome the grooms after performing the 'devgon' but on condition that the wedding should be performed in a sober fashion and without unnecessary ostentation.

So, Tathya's beloved granddaughters were married very simply. Their aunts helped them wear their dejharus and five gold ornaments during the 'devgon' ceremony. Only close relatives attended the wedding and each of the grooms was accompanied by just twenty people. However, prayers, rituals and the havan were performed properly. The women sang tearfully, blessing the girls and wishing them well as they departed. The grooms were showered with flower petals. Kaknidedi, Kamala and Lalli made roths and bowed their heads before Ganesh in gratitude,

'You have been kind to us now we pray that the girls may have long and happy married lives.'

A Narrow Escape

The Kabailis left behind a trail of violence, loot and arson, and terrible trauma. But even as people dealt with these, there was a sense of a new awakening in the valley, a feeling that change was in the air and many shrugged off the snow and stood up with new enthusiasm and vigour.

Young women and men gathered at the exhibition grounds for firearm training. In the words of the poet 'Azad' the girls snapped the bars of their cages and decided to march in step with the times. This was impact of Sheikh Abdullah's leadership.

'What is the world coming to? Now girls will abandon all shame and learn to use guns together with boys. They will become "volunteers"!'

Neighbourhood committees were formed all over the place.

'Enemies beware! Kashmiris are alert!' New slogans! New enthusiasm! The valley was startled. This was the first time in its history that this had happened.

Even the lazy Prem ji accompanied Shivnath and Keshavnath on their nightly patrols. People took on the responsibility for guarding their neighbourhoods, those who knew how to use firearms procured licenses and bought guns, for who knew when they would be needed? One can't depend on the government for everything. This was the subtle impact of the past when the maharaja's army had been unable to protect his subjects. It was a new lesson in self-reliance. One male from each household would take a turn to do guard duty.

There was a new wave of communal harmony. People said, 'This miracle has happened because of Sheikh sahib! People have blended together like milk and sugar.'

'That is true. If he had not protected us who knows what would have happened, we might not even be alive!'

Ayodhyanath also accepted this bitter truth while sitting with his friends, 'Maharaj bahadur just signed the deed of accession with India and left the valley, handing over charge to Sheikh Abdullah. If we are safe today it is all thanks to Sheikh sahib!'

Balbhadra agreed. 'Absolutely right, bhai. Sheikh sahib is full of energy. He went to jail for his country so many times and he is close to many important leaders. Do you remember the 'quit Kashmir ' agitation? The 20th of may 1947 was when he was arrested. Remember how Pandit Nehru came to Srinagar from Delhi against the wishes of the maharaja to have Sheikh sahib released?

'Yes! How can one forget that day? There was such turmoil in the valley. The maharaja imprisoned Nehru but he just didn't care.'

'Yes, Nehru ji is a true friend! None of us ate anything that day, we were so shocked that Nehruji should be imprisoned in his own home by his own ruler!' This incident created an irrepairable chasm between the maharaja and Nehru but it also cemented the friendship between Nehru and Sheikh sahib.Together with praise for Sheikh sahib there were a few unanswered questions that were troubling the minds of the intellectuals of the valley.

'At the time of Independence, when the country was divided, the maharaja should have taken a decision about whether he wanted to join India or Pakistan. Why did he try to sign an agreement with both countries?'

'Why did he let Kashmir's fate hang in the balance? What did he want?'

'The maharaja's royal priest Swami Santdev had predicted a brilliant future for him. But then, instead of advising the maharaja to stay on in the valley, he also went off with him to Jammu on 28 October.'

'Pandit Ramchand Kak was his advisor, couldn't he suggest anything?'

There was no one left to answer these questions or to address the uncertainties of the Brahmins for whom the king was a reincarnation of God. Their belief was shaken. How could the Maharaja abandon his subjects like this? How could this unprecedented situation have arisen? Now there was only the unquestionable, bare reality. Half-naked, traumatized refugees from Muzaffarabad, Uri, Bramullah, Mohra and all the villages that had been looted and terrorized.

'I have heard that the invaders are vicious Kabailis belonging to the Afri and Masood tribes. They have no pity whatsoever. They picked out Hindus and Sikhs and slaughtered them. Dinanath was telling us what he saw with his own eyes.'

'This is all the handiwork of Pakistan. The invaders acted as they were instructed and then they were joined by some local ruffians as well.'

'These Kabailis are absolutely ruthless and slow-witted! They even stole brass utensils mistaking them for gold.'

Rajrani couldn't stop crying. 'We said, take everything, just spare our lives. We took off all our jewellery and handed it over to them. But they didn't listen. They dragged out women who were hiding in the barns and haylofts, they stabbed people to death with their bayonets. They lined up the men and shot them. What crime had they committed? May these Kabailis rot in hell!'

Mohini, one of the teachers from the Saint Joseph Convent in Baramullah, did not know how she would ever repay her debt to Samad Dar. Despite opposition from his own people, he had sheltered her in his house as his daughter, covering her up in a pheran and burqua, hiding her from the looters. Would a relative have done as much?'

'Well done Samad Dar! You have shown what humanity truly means,' said Balbhadra.

Mohini was petrified, the events that occurred in the convent were frozen in her memory.

'Those men killed the nuns, they raped those women of God! Their white habits were stained red with blood.'

'Those rogues were held up by their greed for women and money otherwise they would have headed straight for Srinagar. Who was there to stop them?'

Dinanath couldn't stop lamenting, 'They burnt villages and houses, they reduced the mansion of the Sumbalis in Sopore to ashes. We could see decapitated heads with staring, wide-open eyes lying about on the roads, Ayodhyanath bhai! I cannot forget all those terrible sights.'

As the mature and experienced Dinananth spoke, his voice shook and his eyes filled with tears. The stories narrated by Raghav Pandit and Makkhan Singh who had escaped from Muzaffarabad were no less heartrending.

'Our forces were just not ready for the attack. A huge mass of Kabailis entered Muzaffarabad on the 23rd of October. Arson, looting and killing…they terrorized the entire city.'

'My beloved mother!' Makkhan Singh started beating his forehead. 'When my mother saw them coming she jumped off the side of the mountain. The screams of so many of our sisters and mothers were lost in the roaring waters of the Krishnaganga. How they must have suffered! O God! Why didn't you protect your people?'

'Be strong Makkhna, be strong sardara! Who can fight destiny? Just be thankful for those who managed to survive.' Balbhadra stroked the Sardar's back trying to comfort him, 'How did you manage to escape?'

'Don't ask, bhai sahib! Just the thought of how we made our way to Uri, with terrified crying women and children, makes me shiver. Rain, hail, stones rolling down from hillsides! The fear of wild animals in the jungles! As we ran over fallen leaves we were scared of making even the faintest sound in case the enemy was close by and heard us! We walked through the nights dragging our swollen feet and legs that felt like they weighed a ton. When my one-year old daughter Nikki started crying from hunger, I tied up her mouth with Surinder Kaur's chunni, there was nothing else we could do. May Vaheguru forgive me!' Makkhan Singh hit his hands on the floor as though he was trying to punish them.

'Makkhan Singh was right. The child's cries would have given us away to the enemy and they would have shot both our families! One forgets all kindness and faith when one is confronted by death.'

'We spent the second night in the hut of a Gujjar goatherd. His wife was a good human being, she opened Nikki's mouth and fed her milk drop by drop till the child recovered. At break of day she put us in a truck and sent us off. I would have become the killer of my own child.'

Ayodhyanath praised the Gujjar woman but he was surprised at how so many invaders had been allowed to enter Muzaffarabad. Why hadn't the government made any arrangements to protect the state?

'Jinnah sahib announced an economic blockade as soon as Pakistan was created and stopped the supply of salt to Kashmir. Who can forget those days and how much difficulty everyone faced?'

'How can we forget, Balbhadra bhai? We used to soak a small piece of crystallized salt in our rice and yoghurt and then wash it and set it aside to be used again the next day. Hindustani salt rasped like sand in our throats. They had closed the Rawalpindi route, couldn't the government gauge their intentions?'

'If the bridge across the Krishnaganga had been blown up they couldn't have stormed into our backyards with such ease.'

A host of questions were buzzing around in the heads of the local intellectuals, 'But where was the dynamite? This is why the Kabailis reached Baramulla so fast. When the Maharaja Sahib realised how critical the situation was, he finally asked the Indian government for help.'

'The help arrived, but we suffered whatever was written in our fate.' Dinanath's brother had been shot in front of his eyes.

'Yes, there was a lot of violence. I believe around thirty thousand people have died, that is what the *New York Times* says.' Shivnath kept track of the news.

At this moment of sorrow they were all disturbed by one question: why had accession not taken place earlier? If that had happened Pakistan would never have had the courage to attack the valley in this manner.

'Brother! In September 1947, when the road between Jammu and Srinagar was improved and there was a proposal to build a bridge on the Ravi river, it seemed that Kashmir would become a part of India. At that time the maharaja could have done whatever he wanted. We would have had no objections.' Prithvi Dhar completed what he had to say but there was no solution for the questions bubbling inside him. The killings, looting and arson that happened on the night of the 24th of October in Poonch and Rajauri would never have happened if the government had adequate forces at its command.

Thankfully the accession had now taken place and the danger was past. Mountbatten accepted the accession of Kashmir with India though Nehru added a condition.

'Condition! What kind of condition? Did our Nehru demand this or was it the Viceroy?'

'Who knows? I believe he has said that a plebiscite should be held once peace is restored.'

'But why? We are speaking about a willing accession. What do ordinary people know about political strategies?'

All sorts of questions came crowding into the mind, 'Is this thanks to Nehru? To his blemish-free and honourable image? No one should be able to say that the decision was forced upon us.'

'Ah! Force! But didn't we ourselves go to him for help? If he hadn't sent his army then wouldn't this state of ours, this thorn in Jinnah's and and Liaquat Ali's flesh, have been reduced to rubble?'

'The Viceroy was an outsider, why would he share our pain? But Nehru belongs to us, couldn't he understand the feelings of his own people?' What could be more disappointing than this? These political mazes were easy to enter but difficult to get out of and Kashmir, somehow, seemed to have found its way into one of these.

So, without waiting for any specific outcome, people gradually learnt to live with uncertainty. Sharika and Rajdulari were happy with their in-laws. The valley was under the protection of the Indian army. Many important national and international strategists and thinkers were pondering over the fate of the people of the state, after all Kashmir was a ' strategic point', very significant politically. Katya was very worried about Tulsi. What could have happened to her? There was no news of her. Where was she and in what condition?

She was not a little girl any longer who could wander around at will. A sixteen year old girl those days, according to Kakni, 'would be looking after two or three children of her own.' So, there was no way she could run away from home as often as she liked to go to Tulsi's house and ask for news.

Katya tried to persuade her mother, 'Can I go to Tulsi's house, Ma? God knows what has happened to her.' She would cry so much that Lalli did not have the heart to stop her from going. However, Nandan was sent along with her.

When Katya knocked on the disintegrating wooden door precariously suspended from half-uprooted hinges Tulsi's sister-in-law looked out from the window of the 'vot' the living room, 'Who is it?'

As soon as she saw Katya she burst into tears.

'What has happened bhabi, why are you crying? Is everything all right at home?' Katya shivered with apprehension.

'My sister-in-law's life is in ruins, Katya, Tulsi's husband is dead. Those brutes killed the entire family!' Katya was stunned into silence as she held on to Bhabi's large frame and tried to comfort her wordlessly. Tulsi was sitting in a corner of the dark room, completely covered from head to toe, sleeping with her head resting on her knees. As soon as her mother saw Katya she started lamenting and beating her breats,' Your Tulsi 's life is over, Katyayini, the unfortunate wretch will have to spend the rest of her life in mourning.'

Tulsi was awakened abruptly by her mother's cries and for a moment she looked uncomprehendingly at her mother and Katya.

'I thought her fate had made her a queen. It must be my evil eye which has destroyed her life, I am the one to blame ...'

Katya looked at her friend who was looking stunned in the midst of her mother's laments. Tulsi's eyes were pools of fear. Was this the same Tulsi who, despite being married off to an old man, went around chirpily talking about her husband all the time? The one who refused to allow Katya to say even a single word of criticism against him saying, 'Katya, sister, promise me you won't say anything against him, he is my husband now and he tries to make me happy.' The period of Tulsi's happiness had been so brief!

Katya tried to put her arms around her her but Tulsi moved away,'No, no, don't touch me.'

'My body is untouchable, I am a sinner....'

'This is what she keeps saying, the unfortunate girl!'

'Her world has been destroyed. They attacked the village head, the Sarpanch's house first. They were prosperous people, with young daughters and daughters-in-law. Everything is finished! My son-in-law, his two sons, those young children, they were killed. She managed to escape with this little one but she is ruined forever. How can she face anyone now?'

Katya fetched a glass of water from the kitchen. 'Drink some water, Kakni! Wash your face. If you are going to behave like this who will look after Tulsi? Don't talk about sin and morality. Others have also had tragedies in their lives...' What could Katya say? She wished she had brought her mother along, Lalli would have handled the situation much better. Katya was too inexperienced.

The baby, wrapped in rags, was woken up by the noise. First he whimpered and then he cried out so loud that the blue veins on his white neck became visible.

'He cries all the time, the unfortunate one. We try to feed him cow's milk with a spoon but he just spits it out. She doesn't even pick him up, at least she could try....'

Katya took the baby from bhabi and put him in Tulsi's lap.

'If you care for me Tulsi you have to feed the baby. What has he done, the poor little thing??'

Katya's voice was heavy with tears. Tulsi waved her aside and started crying with her head between her knees. The touch of affection finally melted the glacier.

'Tulsi, on my life, you have to pick him up. Look how upset he is, he is looking at you so innocently.'

Katya took the 'khasu' of warm milk from bhabi and touched it to Tulsi's lips. She put her arms around Tulsi and wiped her eyes as her own filled with tears. Both of them cried as they held on to each other and their heavily burdened hearts became lighter as they wept.

'For the sake of this little one, sister! I couldn't even die because of this child, I couldn't surrender my barely alive body to the Vitasta. He loved this unfortunate baby so.' Tulsi's lament melted away into sobs. Together, the two friends wept, pouring out their grief and coming to terms with what had happened.

'There is nothing left, Katya! They killed my husband and the boys in front of my eyes. He died trying to save my life. His eyes were looking at me right till the end. There was so much love and pain in those eyes.' Sorrow was rooted very deeply in the depths of Tulsi's heart.

'Take hold of yourself, Tulsi! Be patient, sister. Don't make misfortune the touchstone of good and evil. You have to live and you can only live by forgetting the past.'

'How much can I forget, Katya? Those invaders devoured my soul, not just my body....'

'Enough, Tulsi, save your soul which is much more important than your body. Don't say anything else! Think of it as the fury of the Gods. You are not the only one who suffered. Think of the others...'

But Tulsi was guilty despite being innocent. In a society that considered rape to be the fault of the victim, she was not 'pure' any longer. She was beyond redemption because she had been in the hands of the Kabailis for two days. Society was willing to be kind to women who had been exploited and assaulted but it was not willing to accept them within its rigidly demarcated folds. The attitude of the so-called moralists towards women, who were suddenly demoted from being goddesses of the home to being disgraced, was very cold and conventional.

But such women could not be abandoned either. It was a difficult situation. The result was that some women accepted lives of shame and dishonour and got used to the humiliation and degradation after a while. 'Isn't this the same woman? The one who was kidnapped by the Kabailis?' There were very few women who emerged from this black cave of ignominy and humiliation and were able to make a new life with their heads held high.

Katya admired women who belonged to the second category. So, she tried to convince Tulsi's mother as much as she could.

'Don't keep calling her unfortunate, Kakni. Her only fault is that she came home to you thinking you were her only shelter....'

'Yes, you are right! I was fated to see all this. Even death has not come for me,' Kakni sighed.

Katya visited Tulsi almost every day. Her grandmother was upset, 'Pity is all very well child, so is friendship, but that girl stayed with Kabailis after all. You have to think a little about religion and morality.'

It was as though Kaknidedi had hit Katya with a hammer! She cried out in pain, 'Kakni! Don't be so harsh for God's sake. The whole village was destroyed, who remained unblemished? Are you calling someone who managed to escape from that hell, with a little child, a sinner? Would you have thrown me out of the house if I had been in her place?'

'Don't talk such evil, girl! You have no control over your tongue, you just speak without thinking. Lalli! Take this girl away from my sight. Education has turned her head.' Dadi was boiling mad.

Lalli tried to calm her daughter's anger. 'We will do whatever we can for those people, Munni! Your grandfather is a member of the welfare committees that have been set up. Gopi Krishna ji, Vakil sahib, Ramjoo Pandit, Sudarshan Langoo and many others from good families are busy collecting money and clothes for all those who have been displaced. If he was not concerned why would he have brought Niranjan home after his village Mohra had been destroyed? Hasn't he lived up to his promise of sending Niranjan, who is an intelligent boy, to college? Tulsi is not the only one suffering, there are entire villages which have faced ruin, you know that.'

'But giving Tulsi clothes is not enough Ma!'

Katya wanted to do something for Tulsi. Her friendship had now become a debt that she had to pay off if she wanted any peace.

Tulsi would not spend her entire life cowering and smouldering beneath the pity of others, living at the mercy of her brother and sister-in-law. She would not spend the rest of her life mourning the loss of a brief interlude of comfort and joy. Once Tulsi had recovered a little from her sorrow of losing her loved ones Katya made a suggestion, 'Why don't you take my books and resume your studies, Tulsi? You have already studied till the ninth grade, why don't you appear for the Matric exam as a private student?'

Tulsi's shoulders had become rounded because of her habit of sitting with her head bent over her knees. She answered questions with a simple yes or no without looking up. Her backbone hurt if she raised her neck to look at anyone. She answered Katya's question with a no, bending over and scratching the floor with her nail.

'Look here! I am not going to listen to you. Look up, straight at me, and say yes.'

'I can't do it Katya. I don't have the confidence....'

'Quiet! I am not interested in you confidence,' Katya scolded her, asserting her right as a friend. 'I will come in every other day to teach you. Sometimes you can come over to my house and ask bhaisahib to help you with mathematics. I have always been terrible at Math.'

Katya was determined. She did not want Tulsi to be weak and dependent. She tried to persuade Amarnath who muttered, wearing his importance as the only male member of the house on his sleeve, 'Which accountant office is she going to go to now? Studying won't change her destiny. She has to suffer her fate. At least I won't let her starve till I am alive.'

'That is not the issue bhaisahib, studies will keep her busy. She just cries all the time. How long can she survive like this?'

'She can do whatever she likes.' Perhaps Amarnath saw Katya's sympathy as unnecessary interference in the private affairs of his family. He said irritatedly, 'Have I ever said no? We are all suffering equally.'

Katya didn't like the long face Amba was pulling, nor did she appreciate his constant references to fate and destiny. Without arguing about who was really suffering, she extracted a promise from Tulsi's mother that she would look after the baby and allow Tulsi to pursue her studies.

Tulsi began rebuilding her ruined world brick by brick with Katya's help.

The heaps of snow piled outside the windows during winter would see the two friends bent over their books. The men who were shovelling off snow from their roofs to prevent their houses from sinking under its weight would glimpse Katyayini and Tulsi through half-open windows, struggling with copies, slates and pens.

In deep winter, long radish like icicles were suspended from the roofs. Tiny birds tried to find shelter from the keen arrows of icy winds under the eaves of houses. Katya would leave the warmth of her house and, wrapped in a pheran, scarf, gloves and socks, would trudge through the streets to Tulsi's house. College was closed for the vacation and in any case schools and colleges had been shut for a long while because of the uncertain conditions.

Tulsi's Kakni would keep a kangri and a hot cup of kehwa ready for her. Sometimes she would worry about Katya. 'Don't neglect your own studies, Munni, it doesn't matter if Tulsi doesn't study for two days. If you fall ill in this cold what will I say to Janakimaal?'

Sometimes when Amaranth saw his wife working in the kitchen while Tulsi was busy with her books, he felt that she was being treated like a servant. Sitting at the threshold of the kitchen he would mumble to Tulsi and his mother, 'Who knows whether Vakil sahib's grand daughter is motivated by the love of education or by a desire to do some social work. I think Tulsi is just wasting her time with these books. It would be better if she helped her sister-in-law who slaves away the whole day like a donkey.'

His words suddenly made Tulsi aware of her changed status. A married daughter, who should have lived out her entire life in her marital house had come back to her childhood home, how could she possibly expect to occupy the same place which she was hers earlier?

Tulsi divided up the work with her sister-in-law, 'I will do the cooking in the evening, bhabi! I will also wash all the utensils. I can't break my head over books the whole day! Why don't you rest a little now.'

Tulsi may not have been able to evoke any pity from her brother but she did not want to cause any friction and unhappiness either. He was her only brother after all. Katya could help her to sharpen her brain but she could not wipe off the stain from her forehead. She would have to unravel the tangled knots of relationships all by herself.

Normally, Katya did not give her any time to think. She would allow her to wander freely through the limitless world of books, to speak with anyone, question anyone. Premchand, Sharat, Jainendra. Mahadevi…. Katya spread sheets of paper on the mud shelves in Tulsi's room and filled them with books from her library. Tulsi won't wallow in self-pity if she is busy reading about the joys and sorrows, the concerns and hopes of the larger world around her.

Gorky's *Mother*, Pearl Buck's *Good Earth*, Maupassant's short stories! She must read and Katya has no shortage of books.

Like Sona bua, Tulsi was also a victim of militancy though with a difference. But unlike Sona bua she would not become half crazy and half a saint. This may not have been Tulsi's decision but it definitely was Katya's resolution.

The Martyrdom of Bapu

It was a bitterly cold January that year – even the brutal winters of the past few years paled by comparison. Men and women tried to warm their bones by wrapping themselves in woollen quilts, comforters, and Bandpur blankets piled one on top of the other. But the damp seeped through the quilts. The heat of the kangris held close under the pherans singed stomachs and thighs with burns, turning the skin an angry red.

One day Balbhadra stomped into Ayodhyanath's house, wearing heavy boots, swaddled in a thick blanket and with a monkey cap on his head.

'Ayodhyanath bhai! Shivnatha! Where are you? Have you heard? Mahatma Gandhi has been killed….'

Without even removing his muddy long boots, Balbhadra started talking as soon as he entered the verandah. He was breathless as though he had run miles. Ayodhyanath's family was already gathered in a circle, mourning for Bapu. It felt as though an earthquake had shattered their lives. No one had drunk even a drop of water since hearing the news. Their throats felt raw like sandpaper. The men and women of the house were all participating in the national mourning.

'Friends and comrades! The light has gone out of our lives, and there is darkness everywhere. The light has gone out, I said, and yet I was wrong. For the light that shone in this country, was no ordinary light…that light represented ….the eternal truths, reminding us of the right path, drawing us from error, taking this ancient country to freedom.'

Nehru's voice, steeped in sorrow was echoing in the ears of the family gathered around the radio. It seemed as if he was trying to give solace to himself and to the nation through his words. 'Even in death Bapu taught us to pay attention to the important and significant aspects of life. He showed us the path to truth. If we follow the path of truth and remember it, then India will prosper.' Balbhadra felt as though he has been orphaned again. That skeletal frame riddled with bullets. What did that killer Godse gain from it? Arre! This humane man who hated the British government even showed friendship towards the British….'

Ayodhyanath tried to comfort him, 'He was much greater than us. We couldn't understand him.'

'This partition just broke him, brother Ayodhya. He could not bear so much brutality. He opposed violence from the beginning. He was so agitated after the Chauri-Chaura episode. Do you remember he cancelled the public agitation that was at its peak just because he was so upset and disturbed by that event? Nehru and Motilal were also upset but Gandhiji just couldn't accept it.' Talking about Bapu helped soothe his feelings a little.

'You are right about that Balbhadra.'

'Bapu was happy with us.' Shivnath was referring to the valley. 'During the partition there was so much violence in north India but we were a shining example of communal brotherhood, that is why Bapu said, "I see a ray of hope in Kashmir." This is why Bapu was so dear to the Kashmiris.'

'So much has happened in the past few months.' Ayodhyanath turned his head slightly and looked over his shoulder, 'The Pakistan sponsored Kabaili attack, their annoyance at the attack being repulsed, accusations and counter-accusations! Jinnah sahib's insistence that India should remove its army from

Kashmir and hold a plebiscite under the supervision of the United Nations… so much has happened….'

'Pakistan really created a shindy over this mediation by the United Nations. An internal matter was thus turned into an international issue.'

Shivnath gave a summary of the entire matter. How Sardar Patel and Nehru refused any mediation by the United Nations. On the 26th of December, 1947, Nehru even informed Lord Mountbatten that, 'Pakistan is accusing India wrongly and trying to cover up its own plans of aggression. It is necessary to teach it a lesson.' He was prepared for plebiscite but first there should be peace.

'Yes Shivnath!' Ayodhyanath agreed with his son, 'But finally Bapu had to agree to U.N. intervention even though he did it reluctantly. Actually, this was a step taken under the 'appeasement policy'….'

'On the first of January this year this matter became entangled in international politics, this was not good,' Keshav gave his opinion. 'Bapu did so much to satisfy Pakistan. He even went on a fast when it was suggested that the amount of fifty five crores, which had been decided upon during the partition, should be given to Pakistan only after the Kashmir issue was settled. He fasted till the 13th of this month, insisting that the condition be removed and the money be given to Pakistan. He had such a big heart! He forgave them despite their bad intentions.' In his agitation, Ayodhyanath took such a deep draught of the hookah that the smoke went straight into his lungs. Keshav rushed to the kitchen to fetch a glass of water.

'In other words, while this proved his generosity it also sowed the seeds of his death.' Ayodhyanath started speaking again once he had recovered, 'Yessss…there is no shortage of madmen in this country.'

The women started crying, blowing their noses, their voices roughened by tears.

'Bapu died a martyr.'

Keshavnath referred to the death of Swami Shraddhanand in 1926, 'Bapu himself wished to die fighting for communal harmony. He said swamiji's death is unbearable but I wish that I would also die fighting for humanity like him....'

Ayodhyanath quoted Dinanath Nadim, the poet, who said that Bapu had a heart like a serene ocean and a brilliant personality. When the talk turned to Bapu it was inevitable that innumerable incidents and happenings would come to everyone's mind.

❦

A Sprinkling of Fresh Colours

When schools and colleges reopened after the long vacation there was a new buzz in the air. The valley of Kashmir had heard the term 'democracy' after centuries of oppressive rule. People were eager to learn their new obligations and rights under this new system of governance. Democracy meant freedom from feudalism. Democracy meant that the tillers would now own the crops they grew. Democracy meant freedom from taxes, debts and rasoom. It meant a government of one's own.

Sheikh Abdullah was the new leader. Poets, writers and social workers started work on cultural and social fronts. The voices of writers like 'Mahjoor', Noor Mohammad Noor, Amin Kamil, Ghulam Mohammad Fazil, Nandlal Ambardar, Chamanlal Chaman, Dinanath Nadim and others echoed in the valley. There was an urgent need to arouse new hope and optimism amongst people who had just been freed from oppressive rule. The poets took on this job with great enthusiasm.

When Katya went back to college after the holidays, she felt there was a change in the air. There was a new excitement, a new awakening and a new agitation. When she had begun college last year she'd felt hesitant and uncertain in the unfamiliar environment. She was excited at the novel experience of studying in a co-educational institution – there would be attractive boys after all – but the demarcation of strict boundaries for girls right from the moment of their birth was something she had internalized. There was such a contradictory mixture of attraction and constraint that girls and boys did not quite know what to do if they came face to face. Girls from conservative homes had managed to get permission to join co-ed colleges only after going on extended hunger strikes or threatening to commit suicide by eating rat poison or some other leathal drug. The fathers accepted this new wave of freedom and progress with a sense of resignation while the worried and anxious mothers cursed this new world.

'The girl has returned home safely today, but suppose tomorrow some ruffian kidnaps her in Maisooma bazaar what will we do then?'

Despite Shivnath's repeated assurances that Maharaja Hari Singh had already closed down the brothels in the bazaar long ago, Kamlavati was not convinced. 'Yes! I am sure they will close their shops. And their pimps? Suppose they persuade and tempt young girls and push them into this profession, what will happen to their families?'

Janakimaal was also worried. 'This freedom is very strange! When we were young we did not even look at our elders as we spoke to them. And these girls walk around and pass by the Exchange Road without covering their heads! Didn't our Rajdulari study Hindi-Sanskrit and the religious texts at home? What great exploits of Hatimtai are these girls going to accomplish now?'

Despite all these obstacles girls had emerged from their homes
in search of their own piece of sky. Katya was very fortunate
because she had Tathya, Keshav and Lalli on her side.

Admission to college opened a new world for Katya. The
vast courtyard of the college where boys and girls walked
around or sat in groups, was shaded by Chinar and Poplar trees.
The student's eyes were filled with visions of the future and
their minds with the determination to achieve their dreams.
Katya felt that the long, 'Jack and the Beanstalk' staircase which
led 'Sonakesri' up to the moon began right here. Like the prince
in the fairytale about the golden water only the person who did
not look back would achieve his or her goal while anyone who
did would turn into stone. Among those who didn't look back
were brave women like Kamala Madan, Kamala Zadu, Prabha
Ganjoo and Prabha Labroo, some of them became doctors.
Mehmooda Ahmed Ali Shah, Mrs Qureshi and Barkat Begum
had also set out to chart a new course for themselves.

The girls from the central and lower parts of the city walked
through the streets with their bent heads covered decorously
but those belonging to the upper areas such as Wazirbagh,
Amira Kadal, Hazooribagh walked confidently through the
streets and into college with their heads uncovered and their
dupattas neatly folded on their shoulders. Their ancestors had
come from the Punjab and settled in the valley during the
reign of Ranjit Singh and Gulab Singh. They were not affected
by the rules and regulations which constrained shy Brahmin
girls or the burka-wearing Muslim daughters who had heard
heart-rending stories of atrocities committed on women by the
Pathans and the Afghans.

Normally girls and boys moved in separate groups but
occasionally, when they came across each other in the narrow
corridor behind the science lab or sitting in the shade of a
Chinar tree, their hearts would start hammering, as if in the grip
of an unknown fear. The boys understood well the language of

the lowered eyes and it took them no time at all to get ensnared by them. As a result, everything – lawn benches, treetrunks, bathroom walls – was engraved with the eternal legend, 'I love you' and lines from popular romantic songs.

The girls would giggle as they passed by, 'Katya, Tribhu must have written this for you.'

'No, Tribhu is not that kind of boy, it looks like Bhushan's work.'

'Must have been written for Shobha. I don't encourage anyone. She is the one whose hand shakes as she disssects frogs in the lab, poor Bhushan has to complete half her dissection. It looks like his handwriting….'

College is meant for studies not for affairs of the heart. This was something their professors would often reiterate. Looking at the girls and addressing the boys they would say, 'Your parents pay for your education with their hard earned money, they don't send you here to enjoy yourself. You must bring honour to them and to the college. Do you understand?'

But lately there'd been a change. When the new term began, a slew of cultural festivals and new programmes livened up the atmosphere. The arts section put up performances of *Othello*, *King Lear*, *The Merchant of Venice* and other Shakespeare plays. Though science students had little time to spare for plays because they were kept busy in the labs they took part with great enthusiasm in the 'chakris', group songs and folk dances like 'rov'. There was a sense of excitement in the air.

Songs of national pride and communal harmony rang in the air, there seemed to be a sort of cultural revolution taking place. When the quiet bookworm Tribhu sang, 'I have to keep my country free, I have to make a new Kashmir, I have to spread love and togetherness' in a thunderous voice during the cultural festival, Sheikh sahib called him after the function especially to give him a pat on the back. He also said, 'We need young men like you who are full of enthusiasm and zeal.'

Katya liked Tribhu's fervour as well as his melodious voice, she thought she would congratulate him as soon as she got an opportunity. This praise had such a profound impact on Tribhu that he started consorting with 'comrades'. Mixing with them he began to read books by Lenin and Marx. Dinanath Nadim, who would recite his poem, 'I am filled with the passion of youth.' in a booming voice in poetic gatherings, became his favourite poet. The fervour of young blood in his veins, Tribhu began to speak about oppression and the oppressed in small gatherings and found himself turning into a small-time political leader. One day, as he was marching with the comrades near Habbakadal, he was confronted by a group of Jansanghis. They came to blows. The Jansanghis, who were toughened by daily exercise, hit the delicate Tribhu so hard that he started bleeding from the nose and bruised his forehead.

When Sula, the grocer, saw this he left his shop and picked up Tribhu from the road. The compounder, Brij, cleaned the wound with Dettol, tied a bandage around his head and advised him, 'You are a student. Why are you getting involved in all this useless stuff, wasting your time and destroying your parents' hopes and aspirations? Go home and rest. Once you are standing on your own feet you can take part in as many agitations as you like. You are not yet old enough to dabble in in politics.'

When Tribhu entered the courtyard of the college after two days with a bandage wrapped around his head he really did look like a hero. His friends hugged him and patted his back. How can one become a leader without shedding some blood? Those who joined Subhash Chandra Bose's Azad Hind Army and fought against the British were no less important than the followers of Bapu's non-violent methods. But students who confined themselves to their studies told each other, 'He thinks he is Rustom-e-hind. Ganpat Taploo just hit him twice and look how he came crashing down to earth! '

That day, for the first time, Katya went and asked Tribhu how he was feeling. Tribhu gave a slight smile and shook his head, 'Oh! It's nothing. It is just a scratch, that's all! I can't hide at home because of this little thing.'

Katya didn't ask, 'What happened?' But she liked Tribhu's attitude. She wanted to praise him for his courage but the boys and girls around her were looking at her, surprised by her unexpected enthusiasm. So, saying, 'get well soon' she postponed a more intimate conversation and turned back. Tribhu gave her an intense glance and said, 'Thank you.' As she walked home, Katya could feel Tribhu's gaze on her back. The words, 'Thank You' kept echoing in her ears.

For some reason Katya didn't sleep well that night. A pale moon was making its gradual way across the star-studded sky, which was visible through the window which opened towards the Vitasta. A tiny boat in a vast blue ocean. Where was Katya's unreasonably dejected heart wandering as she sat in that boat? Why was her heart constricted by a miasma of unease? The world around Katya is peacefully asleep, who has stolen away her rest? What has happened to her today, suddenly? She has not spoken to anyone, there were no jokes, nor had anyone put a secret letter in her bag.

Could Tribhu be the reason for this restlessness? Holding on to the railing of the window she suddenly remembered Mangala Masi's daughter, Tara. On Navreh, their local new year, they had all dressed up in new clothes and, full of enthusiasm, had decided to go to Hari Parbat for a picnic. Katya-Tara had wandered off to admire the Badamvari and the almond blossoms. A boy holding two red roses, who was standing in the shade of trees laden with the white and red apricot and almond blossoms, beckoned to Tara. Katya looked at him disapprovingly but Tara's face became rosy. She said, 'You just don't have the guts to fall in love,' a conclusion she seemed to have reached after studying Katya's apprehensive face.

Was Katya truly incapable of falling in love? It was not as if she had never been in situations where the seeds of love could have been planted. She could recall two or three such occasions. Why did the memory of those occasions give her so much pleasure today?

The first occasion – when Prem bhaiya's friend, the effeminate looking, fair-skinned Jawahar, had handed her a thick envelope on the stairs without any explanation. When she opened it, she found he had quoted some romantic dialogues of Suraiya and Rehman from the film *The Victory of Love* and had added, in a cursive, elegant script, 'Katyayini, your eyes are like two lotus flowers, your braid is like a sinuous snake hanging on your slender neck and your walk is as graceful as the gait of a gazelle....I wish I could spend all my days and nights with you.'

Katya's first instinct was to hand the letter over to Tathya so that Jawahar could be made to smell the perfume of shoes and slippers instead of roses, but the fear of the ensuing chaos prompted her to keep Tathya away from this unsavoury episode. Instead, she wrote back to Jawahar, 'I have read, brother, that when God had made man he ran out of material but he still had to make woman, so he borrowed a few things from nature. He took some attributes from flowers, vines, deer, singing birds... but he also took some qualities from fire and lionesses. Jawahar bhaiya, I may be ignorant, but I do have the roar of the lioness and also its claws.'

Jawahar never wrote another letter after this. But he would sometimes greet her with a 'Hello lioness' as he passed by her.

Two months after this episode Jawahar married. When Tathya invited the new bride for a 'dapanbata', the feast for newlyweds, Jawahar's 'shy' bride Radha soon shared the secret bubbling in her stomach with Katya that Jawahar had been in love with her. Katya was totally taken aback on two counts, first she was surprised by Jawahar's eagerness to reveal the story of his unsuccessful love to his bride on the very first night of their marriage, and second, she was bemused by the complete lack of jealousy shown by the new bride who was happily narrating this story of Laila-Majnu, unsuccessful as it was, to the woman her husband had fruitlessly pursued. What could one say in such a situation?

Katya laughed it off saying, 'No, no... there was nothing like this.'

'No, he wouldn't lie to me, would he?'

Absolute faith in her husband from the very first day! Katya did not want to cause any cracks in this wall of faith but she was irritated, 'Your husband has tried to create an impression on you the very first day. Men are often like this. If you listen to my advice you won't have such unquestioning faith in everything Jawahar bhaiya says.'

The second occasion was when Chandra apprehensively handed over a letter from her six feet tall 'horse-faced' brother saying, 'I wouldn't have given you this letter but my brother said that the two of you have met many times, that he has your photograph and that your Tathya has agreed to the marriage.' Katya was so taken aback by this unexpected outburst that she shouted at Chandra and reduced her to tears.

Once she had calmed down she explained to her friend, 'Look, Chandra, tell that brother of yours that if Tathya hears any of this rubbish he will come to his house and and beat him up. Does he think he is some hero from a fairytale like Alladin that Tathya will hand me over to him just like that? And why are you getting involved and behaving like the maid of the princess in the story? Why doesn't he come forward and fight his battles himself?'

Both the girls burst into giggles after this dialogue and another love affair bit the dust.

The third occasion was more recent and concerned her classfellow, the hunchbacked Dayal. The boy walked with a limp and his classmates often teased him, calling him 'Ashtavakr'. Katya felt sorry for him and even got into arguments on his behalf. Sometimes she would sit with him and help him write his Biology notes. One day during the course of a conversation Dayal told her how hurt he felt when the other boys teased him and called him 'Ashtavakr'. Katya tried to console him by telling him the story of the brilliant Ashtavakr, who was the son of the sage Kohad. How he was cursed by his own father for pointing out a fault in his pronunciation. How he freed his father from imprisonment by a scholar of the Vedas. At the court of king Janak when all the courtiers burst into laughter when they saw him, Ashtavakr said, 'All the lovers of flesh who are present here are ignorant.' When the king asked, 'How?' Ashtavakr explained that those who are truly knowledgeable are aware that it is not the flesh but the soul that is of the greatest importance.

Katya added, 'So, why do you allow yourself to be hurt by what these uncouth, ignorant people say?'

However, when this attempt at sympathy and illumination was interpreted by Dayal as love, Katya was completely taken aback. She couldn't do anything much but on the day of the Rakhi festival she tied a thread around Dayal's bony wrist saying, 'Brother, I have long journey ahead of me, I need your affection and support.'

Could any intelligent boy ever fall in love with a girl who had this kind of a history? Tara wasn't wrong. But strangely today the memory of these episodes gave Katya a lot of pleasure. The unaccustomed pain within her felt good. Perhaps this is where the possibility of love begins. Katya tried to sleep. Closing her eyes, she tried all the tricks taught by her mother and started counting sheep. But she couldn't shake the thought of Tribhu form her mind. The sad songs of Habba khatoon and Arnimaal kept echoing in her head. When she did fall asleep, she descended into the subconscious where she was confronted by strange, frightening faces. Tribhu's bleeding forehead and hands reached out for her. When she leant forward to help him her ears were filled with faint voices, 'Thank you, thank you, Katya! I love you!'

Katya wanted to run away but her feet refused to move. The sound of voices came closer. They disappeared after pushing her into a green meadow. In front of her a white narcissus flower was looking around with its big eye. Katya was clammy with sweat. A black bee was buzzing around her face. The intoxicating perfume of the narcissus was wafting through the air. As the perfume spread, the bee circled around faster and faster. Suddenly there was a storm, a cyclone. Dry leaves were rustling in the dust-laden wind. Narcissus? Where had the narcissus disappeared?

Even in her sleep Katya was aware that the narcissus and the bee would never meet. Lalli had told her their story so many times. Katya woke up, drank some water and tried to go back to sleep. This time she did not try to count sheep or trees but she went over every inch of the green meadow looking for the narcissus.

The Gateway Across Banihal

The exam results were out. There was fear, uncertainty, doubt, excitement and celebration all rolled into one. Professor Bhan arrived at Ayodhyanath's house early in the morning. He asked Lalli to make a strong cup of Kehwa and then gave them the good news: 'Katyayini has brought honour to the family. She stood first in the entire state.'

Katya's heart seemed to jump out of her body. She had written her papers well, but the first position?

Tathya kissed his granddaughter, 'I knew our daughter would win a gold or silver medal.' Shivnath and Janakimaal looked skeptical, 'This girl? This girl has stood first? You must have heard wrong! She hardly ever opened her books. Ask me! Every day without fail she would go off to tutor Tulsi for two hours.'

Sona bua's Kanu and Shivnath's daughter Ragya had passed with a second division. Shivnath scolded Ragya a little and praised Katya. 'Learn something from Katya! You used to sit with your head in your books all the time, you are the one who should have got a medal. Who knows what you really think about while you pretend to study? How can anything get into your brain?' There was a searing pain inside him. He had always lagged behind Keshav in everything, now even as far as the children are concerned.

Keshav blessed both the girls, 'Katya-Ragya have opened new horizons for women's education in this house with their success in the examinations.' Lalli hugged her daughter and pointed at the moon, 'You wanted to touch the moon, didn't you? Look at it, there it is, looking over the wall saying, here, come and touch me!' On convocation day, when Katya received her medal from the Education Minister, she felt the moon was really within her grasp now.

Before she knew it, it was time to say goodbye to college. Those wonderful friendships, those days filled with fun and laughter, arguments and discussions – these would soon be a thing of the past. Two years had passed in the blink of an eye and now it was time for tearful farewells and affectionate good wishes. Now everyone would follow their own paths and when they looked back on their college days it would be with the sweet ache of nostalgia. The memories of a first love that grew in the corridors behind the labs will make them recall the places they left behind. The bench under the shade of the Chinar will be forlorn and the Bulbuls in the branches overhead will forget to sing. Will Katya forget the words spoken by Tribhu at the moment of parting, 'For a whole year I haven't been able to say what I wanted to say to you. Now that you are going I want to tell you Katya, I love you and I will miss you a lot!'

'Me too, Tribhu! Me too!'As the tears fell from her eyes she silently conveyed all that she wanted to say. And that was it! The end. An unexpressed, unspoken love which ended before it began. Before they could open their eyes and recognize it, the time had come to say goodbye. As Tara had said, she really wasn't capable of falling in love. Now it was the same story of the bee and the narcissus who were fated not to meet at any time or in any circumstances! Despite Katya's unhappiness Tathya and Keshav were happy that their major worry was over. Katya had been admitted to Agra Medical College. She had to join soon.

All the preparations, advice, suggestions and good wishes done, Katya reached the bus terminal along with her family. Keshav accompanied his daughter to Agra: there, arrangements had to be made for a hostel, a local guardian had to be appointed; Katya was a girl after all, and she was going to be far away from her people. There had to be someone to help her out if she had any problems. So many worries. Ayodhyanath wrote to Dr Katju whom he knew quite well. Dr Sahib was known to help members of his community who were visiting Agra.

'Have you kept a surahi with you daughter?'Ayodhyanath asked her. 'The bus stops only at a few places, and then you can't be sure that the water will be clean. As soon as you cross Banihal the problems begin! Yes, remember to fill the surahi with water at Kud….'

Janakimaal handed her a basket of food. Lots of fried and roasted stuff, 'Remember to eat a few pieces of Roghan josh with paranthas at Qazigund. Though if you go to Lassaram he will definitely be hospitable, but why depend on others....'

'Eat your lunch on the banks of the Chandrabhaga at Banihal. The bus stops there, it's a beautiful spot...'

Nanaji, who travelled down to Jammu every six months when the Darbar administration shifted, suggested, 'Don't get down alone from the train, Katya. Stay with Babuji. You have written the Agra address on your luggage haven't you?'

'Look after the child on the way, Keshavnatha! She is travelling by train for the first time. There are always rogues and ruffians around to trouble girls. Strange, unknown people, who knows who they are? If you let your guard down even for a minute....'

Keshav accepted the advice given by his father, mother, brother, father-in-law, seated his daughter next to him in the bus and reassured them. 'Don't worry! God will take care of us.'

Katya hugged her mother, aunt, grandmother, Nandan and Ragya repeatedly. The mothers kept wiping their tears as they bid goodbye, 'You have to cross Banihal. It is a very steep climb! Don't be scared, child, God will look after you. We are putting you in His care....'

'After the creation of Pakistan the Rawalpindi road was closed. Your Tathya used to travel to Lahore on that road by tonga.'

'Once you cross Banihal, Mahaganpati will look after you the rest of the way.' The road ahead was narrow, winding, covered with snow for the better part of the year, then there was Ramban and the Khooni Nala near Ramsu where the brittle, shale hillside kept coming down in landslides. There were majestic mountains on one side and on the other the rushing, frothy river Chandrabhaga. Deep gorges and ravines. 'He Shriram, He Shambhu! Look after the father and the daughter.'

'Don't forget to show your permit in Lakhanpur. They will

check the luggage there. Be careful when you open your trunk. The checkers create confusion in their hurry….'

Nathji handed over a bag full of walnut kernels. 'Matayi has sent these from Safapore, specially for Katyayini.'

Till the bus left the family, loaded in two tongas, kept giving advice and suggestions. And then it was time for farewells, 'OK badshaho!', 'Goodbye, brother!', 'Namaskar, Kaklal!' 'May God be with you!' 'I will write as soon as I arrive. Don't worry!'

'Study hard, Katya,' the voices followed her for a long while. Niranjan looked on with sad eyes and kept waving till the bus was out of sight.

Durganag, Shankaracharya temple, the Dal lake with its boats and houseboats, Hazratbal dargah, Hari Parbat, they all glanced in and looked at Katya. The bus passed Badami bagh and started travelling on the highway. The poplars lining the road on both sides waved goodbye and whispered their good wishes and congratulations. You've got what you wanted, the rest is up to you. The golden orioles swinging from the branches of the chinars called out to her, don't forget us friend! As the city receded her heart filled with sorrow. Lalli, Nandan, Tathya, Ragya and Tulsi. She was leaving all her loved ones behind. How would Katya be able to stay so far away from them?

Dark clouds started racing across the sky above the mountains. Kalidas's clouds. The ruins of Martand, Avantipur, were outstanding examples of architecture. Inscriptions engraved on the surface of time by Lalitaditya and Avantivarman. The women gathering flowers in the saffron field of Pampore and working in the fields as they sang folk songs whizzed by.

Katya rested her head on her father's shoulder. She was filled with a wave of sadness and tried to hold back her tears. She wouldn't be able to achieve anything if she kept grieving like this and there was so much she wanted to achieve. She would have to stay apart from the family for at least five years. I have to stay strong, she thought, if I am to achieve my dreams.

The driver stopped the bus in Qazigund.

'Have some tea everyone, refresh yourselves. We will stop here for half an hour.'

The smell of petrol in the bus was making her sick even though Tathya had made her take a tablet of Avomine before starting. There were also some lemons and pomegranate seeds to help with the nausea. Mukundram's brother, Lassaram, had a vegetarian hotel near the bus stop in Qazigund. Lassaram was delighted and surprised to see Katya and Keshavnath together.

'Arre, Bhobaji! What are you doing here! Come, come child! I am so lucky, God has come to my house! What will you eat? Nandlal, hey, Nandlala! See who has come. Take this child upstairs. She will have a wash and freshen up. Go, child, go. Consider this your own house! I live upstairs, your aunt is also there....'

'Laskaka the lorry will only halt for a little while! I want to have some of your kehwa. Mukundram had instructed us to have our tea only in your shop....'

Lassaram fed them egg bhurji and paranthas along with the tea. You can't cook eggs in a vegetarian hotel. Vegetarian visitors are put off by the smell of meat and eggs. So the eggs were made upstairs. After all, his own people had come to visit, if he didn't look after them properly for the rest of his life people would say that Lassaram did not know how to treat a guest. When they left, Lassaram's wife gave them eight or ten milky, sweet roasted corn cobs, 'They will taste good with walnuts. Eat them on the way and think of this aunt of yours.'

When the driver honked to gather all the passengers a good-looking young man walking towards the bus greeted Keshavnath with a 'Salaam aleikum'.

Responding politely with 'Aleikum salaam' Keshav tried to place the boy, 'Aren't you Wali Mohammad's son?'

'Yes, I am Imran! Isn't this Katyayini aapa?' The young man knew both of them.

'Yes, yes, this is Katya, you are right. I am seeing you after ages. You haven't come home for a long while.' Gentle displeasure.

Keshav enquired about Khurshid's welfare. He was told she had become quite weak, that it was to do with age. And Imran was going to Aligarh Muslim University to do his MSc.

'Very good. But your father owns some houseboats doesn't he?'

'My brothers will look after his business. I want to study and become a lecturer in a college.'

'Wonderful! May God help you to fulfil your wishes!'

They met Imran in Banihal as well, he looked in through the bus windows trying to locate them. In Banihal they sat by the banks of the Chandrabhaga and ate their meal together. Meeting Imran brought back many memories. Imran laughed and took the Roghanjosh. 'My Ammijaan has made ristas but I won't offer them to you, Babuji!'

'I am definitely going to eat ristas.' Katya opened Imran's tiffin box and helped herself to a piece.

Keshavnath was impressed by Imran's sensitivity. He seemed to be an intelligent, honest boy. Keshav realized that things were bound to change with children stepping out of their homes into the larger world – all these divisions of faith and identity would probably change too.

They were informed that there'd been a landslide near Ramban-Ramsu. Groups of labourers were busy clearing the road with spades and shovels. A military convoy was also held up. The bus driver had been told that everyone would have to stay in Ramban for the night. They rented a room in the Hillview Hotel on the banks of the river with windows that opened out onto the river. Sleep arrived stealthily as Katya listened to the Chandrabhaga's muted roar.

The bus left for its next destination as the early streaks of dawn lightened the sky. The same narrow, winding roads again. The high mountains of the Pir Panjal. The fear of landslides

at Nashri Nala and Khooni Nala and roads made slippery by
flowing streams. On the way they tried to locate Hastivanz and
Bhattgajin. These historic places must be somewhere within
the folds of these high mountains, they thought. The journey
was long and arduous. Keshavnath kept his daughter busy with
his stories. He found that Katya had never heard the name
Hastivanz.

'You have heard of Mihirkul haven't you? During the rule
of the Hoons around 528 A.D this vicious, brutal Turkish
raider attacked the valley. It is said that he was finally defeated
by Baladitya of Magadh and Yashovarman of Central Asia.
Mihirkul was extremely cruel and inhuman.'

'How did he come to Kashmir?'

'Actually he came here in search of sanctuary. Since the
kings of Kashmir considered it their duty to protect anyone
seeking shelter they allowed him to come. But Mihirkul plotted
against him and took away his kingdom. It is said about him
that once he threw a hundred elephants into the deep gorges of
the Pir Panjal just to enjoy hearing the sound of their screams.'
Katya shivered with revulsion,

'Laughing at the misery of dumb animals! This is the work
of a madman. Like the crazy arrogance of the Roman emperor
Nero.'

'Yes child, a man loses his mind when his desires cross all
boundaries. It is said that he ultimately committed suicide.'

Clusters of darkening clouds were touching the high peaks
of the Pir Panjal. Sometimes it looked as though the clouds had
decapitated the heads of the snow-clad peaks – how strange
and wonderful nature was.

'Babuji! Our Hindi teacher used to say that the great poet
Kalidasa was born in Kashmir. That was why he could write
such realistic and vivid descriptions of mountains, and lakes
and waterfalls and the various aspects of nature. *Meghdoot* could
only have been written by a Kashmiri poet.'

'Yes, child. Some people do believe this. Pandit Lakshmidhar, the former head of the Sanskrit Department in Delhi University who is a great scholar also agrees with this belief. And then Kalidasa was also influenced by Shaivite philosophy. *Meghdoot* and *Shakuntalam* are proof of this.'

'If this is true then why did he leave Kashmir?' Katya asked with simple curiosity.

'It is believed that Kalidasa was born towards the end of the fifth or in the beginning of the sixth century. At that time the valley was ruled by the Hoons. It is possible that he left the valley for Ujjain because of their oppression or there may have been some other reasons. But it is indisputable that one can't write such beautiful descriptions of nature unless one has lived in its midst and loved it with all of one's heart.'

Keshavnath now tried to keep Katya's mind busy by explaining the meaning of the term 'Bhattgajin' to her. 'You must have read in History that the kings of Kashmir had become quite corrupt around the thirteenth century. Murders, violence and the proliferation of plots to capture the throne had weakened the kingdom. At this time an invader called Dulchu or Zulich terrorized the valley. There was killing, loot and arson. King Sehdav ran away to Kishtwar. Dulchu burnt the city of Srinagar and took away thousands of Hindus as slaves. On his way back, however, he was caught in a snowstorm and died along with all the Bhattas he had imprisoned. This is the spot which is known as Bhatgajin or the tandoor of the Battas.' He wondered how many more stories these towering mountains had gathered over the centuries. Keshavnath then drew Katya's attention to the waterfalls that intermittently gushed out from the mountains- 'You won't find these waterfalls in your Agra.'

Looking at them he started humming, 'Every inch of my Kashmir is hospitable. Even the stones by the wayside offer me water... This is a couplet written by the Kashmiri poet

Brijnarayan Chakbast. All right, now tell me who said these lines, 'If there is a paradise on earth, it is this, it is this, it is this'.'

'Hmmm…I know…It was Jehangir.'

Ahead there was the beautiful climb towards Kud and Batote. Thick forests of deodar, pine and Himalayan oak. The trees stood in rows like sentinels, waiting to welcome Katya. There was a faint fragrance of pine in the air. A heady aroma of wild flowers floated about them.

As the bus headed towards the plains, the tiny villages of Udhampur and Jammu districts rushed to greet them. They saw the hills of Katra and the mountain range of Trikuta Devi. The travellers bowed their heads in obeisance. 'Jai Sheranwali' they shouted, hailing the mother goddess. Keshavnath promised Katya that when she came back for her holidays they would spend a day or two with his friend Harikrishan Wakhloo in Jammu.

'Your mother also wants to go on a pilgrimage to Vaishno Devi. She is really very keen. We will all go together.'

The pinnacles of numerous temples began to shine from afar. They spent the night in this city of shrines. In the morning they left for Pathankot, the city of Jambulochan, after visiting the Raghunath and Shiva temples. Katya saw a train for the first time in Pathankot. Passengers, coolies, carts, lame and blind beggars, women wearing churidars, their dupattas covering them almost down to their waists, the station platform was teeming with all these. Passing trains rushed by whistling loudly and there was a cacophony of shrill and soft voices. Passengers sitting on bundles, boxes, bags, coolies balancing four holdalls on their heads with travellers running after them, holding on to wives and children, scolding, irritated! A strange confused and jampacked milieu!

Katya watched with amazement as the crowd desperately tried to push its way into the train compartments. New experiences, new situations! She was thankful when they got a place to sit in the train.

As the train gave a shrill whistle and began chugging along, the crowds on the platform, the kiosks for tea, the carts full of luggage, the railway bridge and even the platform seemed to accompany them for a while. Then the train picked up speed and soon it was rushing through the sunbaked plains where, here and there, you could see cattle being herded along by farmers.

When Katya stuck her head out of the window to look at the landscape, a speck of coal from the engine went into her eye but Babuji soon removed it with the corner of his handkerchief. At Ambala, Keshavnath got down at the station to refill the surahi with water and the train started moving while he was still waiting his turn. Katya looked around in desperation, she shouted and screamed and then finally pulled the red emergency cord. The train stopped and Keshavnath got in, breathless. Katya burst into tears. Despite the ticket checker's scolding, both of them were smiling, relieved that they hadn't been separated. 'This was your first lesson, Katya,' Keshavnath said for some obscure reason. Katya just lay quietly with her head resting on her father's shoulder. Whenever a new platform arrived a wave of noise would assail them: chai, chaiiii… Katya, her eyes shut, conjured up the shady Chinars, silently, she called out to the pines, the cypresses and the doedars. Where had they gone? They have abandoned Katya to this world of dust, sunshine and sweat. Her father did not let her get down during the entire journey. Suppose they lost each other again? As she sipped the strange tasting lukewarm water, Katya remembered the fresh water of her home, which was as cool and tasty as the waters of the Chashmeshahi spring. The call of the cuckoo, which used to perch in the mulberry tree, echoed in her ears. Katya is not there any longer, who will listen to the little bird's lament now?

Wife and Companion

Dinabayu was singing a hymn to Lord Ganesha, 'Om Shri Ganeshaye Namah' and grinding sandalwood paste on a piece of stone when a bunch of children pushed open the main door of the temple and swept in like a river in flood, yelling, 'Cockur, cockur.' In their midst, a woman with matted locks cursed all of them roundly as the corner of her sari, which had roosters printed all over it, trailed on the ground.

'Yes! Yes! I am mad. I am your mother you hooligans! Go and tell your Kakni that the madwoman is hungry! Put some coals in my kangri! See, even my nails are turning blue with the cold!'

The woman opened her mouth wide and started howling and beating her chest. The children who, in kabaddi style, were darting in to touch the roosters printed on her sari, drew back, startled. She might just throw them on the ground! The devotees circumambulating the temple forgot their prayers and stood still in shock. Who was this woman?

Even if Dinabayu knew the answer, would he tell? After all, he had faced enough accusations and suspicion when he tried to help Zaidedi who now lay in a dark corner in the dharamshala, the hostel for pilgrims. Poor Zaidedi, she gets two handfuls of rice in return for cleaning the temple premises. She doesn't concern herself with anyone or anything but she is a woman, so Dinabayu has definitely had to answer some questions. It seems there can only be one relationship between men and women nowadays. The world has forgotten the meaning of pity and compassion. But what can Dinabayu do about his heart which cannot bear the pain and suffering of others?

'Who are you? Where have you come from? Look at the state you are in!' These questions were on the tip of Dinabayu's tongue when Surajbhan's mother recognized the stranger.

'Arre, you? You are the wife of Gopal, the baker aren't you?. Why are you creating such a commotion? Why don't you go home? Aren't you ashamed?'

The stranger, who seemed to have a screw loose somewhere, stopped her crying and looked at Surajbhan's mother, puzzled. Then suddenly, as recognition dawned, she jumped and ran back towards the temple.

'I am not going home! He will tear me to bits. He will burn me with a hot branding iron, he is a monster.'

Her eyes were full of fear. She squatted and clung to a temple column, afraid that someone would forcibly take her away.

'He Shambhu, protect us!' Dinabayu appealed to God.

But despite numerous attempts to cajole, threaten and persuade her, the woman refused to move. A large crowd gathered and then gradually dispersed. Then it was time for the evening aarti, and a crowd collected again. Voices rang out singing the aarti, and as the elephant-headed Ganapati looked down upon the woman, she too hesitantly joined in the aarti, singing 'Om Jai Jagdish Hare'. Later, when Dinabayu came to close the doors of the temple, he found her still sitting on the floor near the column. She did not seem to have moved even an inch.

'Listen, sister, you can't stay here for the night. Go home now and come back in the morning.' Dianabayu appealed to her.

'God will rest here at night, here take some puris and laddoos, eat them and then go home. Disagreements do happen...' In reply, she just shook her head and started stuffing herself with puris.

Dinabayu watched her for a while. 'She is hungry, poor woman! Hunger can drive a human being to do anything. Even immorality and sin. Where will this woman go if she doesn't return home? She doesn't seem to be very old.'

Before Dinabayu could become more philosophical the woman lay down on the floor. She pillowed her head on her arms, pulled her legs up to her chest, spread the end of her sari over her face and went to sleep.

'Oh God! Have pity!' Dinabayu felt the woman was like a little child. Was she mad or just very unhappy? If she sleeps in the open like this she will freeze by the morning. It looks like she has been abused.

Dinabayu felt helpless. What should he do? He stealthily walked into the kitchen of his house. When he was returning with the old blanket that was used to keep the rice bowl warm, he found his wife standing before him like a question mark.

'I will bring it back in the morning, all right? She is an unhappy woman.' Dinabayu said.

His wife sighed. She could do nothing except bemoan the actions of her simple and innocent husband. She didn't ever say that she also wanted to earn merit by doing good deeds but mother Lakshmi, the goddess of wealth, had forgotten to visit her house. Often, she cooked rice in the morning and in the evening satisfied the children's hunger by feeding them puris offered as prasad in the temple. How could she explain the limitations of his own prosperity to Dinabayu? But Dinabayu could not control the generosity of his heart, even his wife understood this.

Some enquiries were made in the morning. Volunteers of the Brahmin association found the address and went and knocked at the door of Gopala's house. At that time Gopala was busy picking out lice from his shirt. The enthusiastic devotees tried to lecture him and convince him in the name of religion. 'If she dies of cold you will have committed the sin of killing a Brahmin, brother. You will suffer for seven reincarnations. She is your wife after all, the mother of your children....'

'Chidren?' Gopala spat towards the window, 'This unlucky woman has only borne daughters all her life. Four daughters. If she wasn't unfortunate why would she have fallen ill at this time of her life? Even if she had given birth to a male chick I would have looked after her. I scorch my face and hands to earn barely enough for two meals. No, my friends. Please forgive me, I can't look after a patient at this age.'

The pleas of the Brahmin group went unheard. Gopala was not moved at all. 'Gopala! Where will that poor woman go? She doesn't have any parents otherwise we would have taken her there. Be a little kind and humane.' They made a last attempt. They threatened him with hell. Tried to persuade him that a woman deserved to be given shelter in her home, but Gopala was adamant.

'Let her go to hell! I don't care. Let her suffer for her sins! Am I supposed to take care of a mad woman or try to earn a living? Why are all of you wasting your time worrying about this mess? Just go close to her, her body stinks. Don't call me. If you want to earn merit, let her stay in the temple, she can live on prasad and puris. She is not going to survive very long, why should I rot with her?'

Nathji Zadu stopped Gopala, he felt like beating him black and blue. 'Arre she is your wife, she has been by your side in good times, will you abandon her when she is ill?'

The elders told Nathji, 'Forget that reprobate, he will reap what he has sowed. Even if you force him to come he might give her some poison and send her to sleep permanently. Let us see what can be done….'

The next day, as she circled around the temple, she left streaks of blood on the ground, revealing the nature of her illness.

'Trahi, trahi! You luckless woman! Now you will earn the anger of the gods for desecrating the temple.'

Some devotees raised objections, 'Move her away from here.'

Others suggested she should be admitted to hospital. She

would be fine once she got proper medical attention. Nathji Zadu did a good deed, he took her to the hospital himself. But a few days later the 'Cockur' madwoman appeared in the temple once again. Dinabayu was exasperated when he saw her. He tried to send her away by shouting at her but she just clung to the door of the Shiva temple. Now how could one get rid of her? There wasn't a shovel in existence that could be used to move her from that spot while she was alive.

A crisis, a real crisis! Like a bone stuck in the throat which you could neither swallow nor spit out. Dinabayu consulted with the members of the Brahmin association and other intellectuals. After all this was the place of God, you could not deny anyone sanctuary. But you couldn't allow the temple precincts to be desecrated either. What should be done? Dinabayu found a via media. She could stay with Zaided in the little room on the lower floor of the dharamshala, if she agreed. No one was going to keep her at home. At the hospital they just handed her some medicines and told her to go away.

'Go on woman, are you going to stay here all your life for free? You will get better if you eat well. We have other patients to take care of, we need the bed so go home.'

But where was the madwoman's home? Gopala had thrown her out from his tiny little room after she had slogged in his house for more than twenty years. He told her never to return. If she had parents would they have forced her to live with a monster like Gopala?

The Brahmins were very perplexed when faced with such an insoluble problem. What should be the fate of a woman who has been thrown out of her house?

A lot of changes had taken place in society. People were trying to intervene and find solutions to problems created when women were harassed because of dowry or by cruel husbands and in-laws. They would try to counsel and help in finding amicable solutions, and if these didn't succeed there would be

meetings and processions, But many women also took to heart
what they had been told, that household affairs should not be
discussed in public, and so they remained quiet.

Dinabayu was worried though. Suppose the two mad
women started fighting with each other? But he need not have
worried. After initially eyeing each other with suspicion the two
became good friends. Sitting at the only window, which looked
out over the Vitasta, in the small dark room Zaided shifted
her gaze away from the boats swaying on the river and stared
at the stranger whose skeletal frame was shivering in a thin
sari, and whose eyes reflected all the pain of the world in their
frightened depths. Was this a woman or a goat on its way to
being slaughtered?

Zaided was the first person to ask this woman, who was
called 'cockur madwoman', what her name was.

'I am called Zaided, and you?'

'Durga.'

'Durga! Come and sit here, near the window, you can see the
Vitasta from here.' Zaided made room for Durga. Both women
sat and watched the river for some time. Silently. Dinabayu
moved away from the stage. He was satisfied, they would
manage.

'I am not mad,' Durga broke the long silence, 'They are
telling lies, but I am sick.'

Zaided kept looking at her silently.

'Look, look here! Durga moved her petticoat from her legs
and showed her the wounds on her thighs, 'It oozes. The lower
part of my body becomes numb and I don't realise when I need
to go to the bathroom. He didn't take me to a doctor. He just
said I was mad and threw me out of the house.'

Zaided pulled down the petticoat and covered her legs.

'You are also disgusted?' Durga looked crestfallen.

'No,' Zaided shook her head twice.

'My husband used to shove me into a small room. I gave

birth to eight children, eight full term and the ninth half.' Durga counted on her fingers. 'Four of the girls survived, the rest died one after the other.'

'At that time he used to follow me around because he desperately wanted a son. The ninth child died in the womb. They had to operate. God knows, maybe they left a wound, these doctors use so many instruments….'

'Does it hurt? Does it hurt a lot?' Zaided's eyes brimmed with tears.

'I don't feel anything, but the bed gets wet, what can I do? I go to the bathroom ten times a day, still. I can't sit in the bathroom the entire day…'

Zaided caught Durga's hands in a tight clasp, her lips trembled and her tears silently rolled down from her eyes. Durga watched her in disbelief, stunned.

'Why was this woman, who was stranger to her, crying at her suffering? What relationship did she have with her? A mother, a sister? The mice scurrying out of their holes in the dark room rattled the utensils as the two women sat there crying. Durga wiped her eyes with the corner of her sari, 'What is wrong with you? You seem to be all right, you are not even ill.'

Zaided turned her head away and looked at the flowing Vitasta, 'I am mad, I broke his head.'

She moved towards the stove in the corner and put some tea to boil.

'You are not mad,' Durga said, examining her closely, 'why are you telling lies?'

Zaided apologized, 'No you are right, I am not mad, but sometimes I pretend to be. It is necessary for a woman who is alone….'

In that dark little room, the two suffering women whom society called crazy, told each other everything they had kept secret and unsaid till now

'You had nine children, I had none.' Zaided poured kehwa into two khasus.

'Didn't you have any medical treatment?' The warm kehwa comforted her body as it went down her throat, 'This is very good.'

'Your bones have been affected by the cold, drink up, here take a little more from my khasu.'

'No, that's enough. May Shambhu relieve you of your pain. So, you didn't tell me....'

'I tried everything, what can I tell you? My mother-in-law took me to some tantric who lived in the cremation grounds. I even ate a chapati baked on the burning pyre of a dead man but nothing happened, so she sent me to Jatadhari babaji.'

'Then?'

'Then what? He wasn't really an ascetic, he was just a crooked imposter. He said, "Come early before dawn, after having a bath, and I will give you a mantra." When I went to his room, which was filled with the smoke of cannabis, I was trembling with fear. He said, "Make me happy, if Siddhbaba is happy the seed will take root." His entire body was shaking. I was scared and when he pulled me towards him I used all my strength to break free and ran away...'

'Dear God! It is imposters like these who give ascetics a bad name. I hope he goes to hell.'

'I don't know, but I was very angry with my mother-in-law. Why do women go to people like him to ask for children? Is he a god? Actually my husband was very simple. Very good, but very weak. The doctor had said he had a problem but my mother-in-law wouldn't listen, she kept saying I was barren.'

'Your father-in-law, brother-in-law?'

'What can I say about my brother-in-law, he also passed a lot of sarcastic comments. Finally, this sorrow killed my husband.'

'Oh God!'

'The younger one became a bull after his brother's death.

He would grab me every time he found me alone at night. He thought I was barren and no one would get to know. I complained to my mother-in-law but she also blamed me. She said, "You are a witch from Kishtwar." My husband had brought me from Kishtwar you see. She said, "You women practise all sorts of witchcraft. First you killed my son and now you want to eat your brother-in-law's heart. You are a witch.'"

'Your mother-in-law is the one who was a witch, she harassed you for no reason. She didn't scold her son. She must have been afraid of him because he earned money and supported her. He was an evil man.'

'Aah!' Durga released the pain inside her with a sigh, 'A woman's life is full of sorrow. She is afraid of men all her life. Father or husband, and even the one she has given birth to! Come, don't be sad. What happiness did I get from giving birth to nine daughters? What would have happened even if I had borne sons? Don't they say that a woman with seven sons was eaten by dogs?'

'What was your fault if your womb could not bear fruit?'

'No.' Zaided wanted to shift the stone that was lying across her chest. 'I did bear a child. There was nothing wrong with me. But it was the child of my brother-in-law. The mother and the son said abort it, you are an immoral slut. And many other things. But I refused to agree, I said I wouldn't destroy any life. They kicked me with their legs and hit me with sticks. I was really mad at my brother-in-law. He was putting the blame for his sins on others and pretending to be a saint. I picked up the grinding stone and hit him on the head.'

'Did you kill him?'

'No, he survived. Then they said I was mad and threw me out of the house. They told the neighbours that I was crazy, that I used to become violent.'

'The child?'

'It didn't survive.'

'Did you abort it?'

'No, I wanted to have the baby. To tell you the truth I had started feeling maternal towards the child. I wanted to experience how a woman becomes fertile like the earth, how she becomes a creator like Brahma. But it wasn't in my destiny.' Zaided seemed to be narrating someone else's story.

'I slipped on the stairs while fetching water from the Vitasta. When Gula, the hanji's wife, helped me up there was blood everywhere! Dinakak took me to hospital. He is a good man. He bore the brunt of the anger of Brahmin society, they alleged that it was his child. But he is a saint. '

'Did you see the child?'

'I saw a mass of flesh covered with cotton wool in a bucket. I begged the nurse then she showed it to me. A woman's heart after all, sister! It melted. She said it was a four or five month old boy. His face was already formed!' Zaided's voice was cold.

'Think of it as God's will and forget it! The result of our bad deeds in our past lives what else?'

'Yes. Dinakak bore the anger of the Brahmins along with me but he consoled me and said, "Throw yourself at the feet of Lord Shiva, he is merciful".'

'People thought I was mad. I kept quiet. Who will understand you when your own people don't?'

'You are really unhappy, sister,' Durga's brown eyes filled with affection.

'No, What is happiness and sorrow? I live in the service of Lord Shiva.'

Zaided got up and dusted the quilt. She swept the tattered mattress, 'Come! Lie down! It is filled with cottonwool, you will be warm.'

'What about you? Where will you sleep? No, no you come here, I will lie down down in that corner over there.' Durga pointed to the door, 'You know I have to get up a few times at night.'

'No, you will freeze over there. If we sleep close together we will be warm and sleep well.'

'I have a wound in my body, sister. You may catch an infection.'

'You wrap a sheet over you. Nothing will happen to me. It is very cold. '

'All right! ' Without any further arguments Durga crept under Zaided's quilt.

'Pull the quilt up to your forehead and go to sleep. Hakim Mank Fayal lives just behind the temple. He is very gifted. We will ask him for a salve. You will be all right. I will speak to Kamalavati and Lalleshwari when they come to the temple in the morning. Lalleshwari is very kindhearted. She will help. Don't worry. Leave everything to Shivanath…'

'You are right. He is the only one who will help us.'

Both the women curled up and lay down. When Zaided saw Durga's skeletal frame she sighed, 'She is so unhappy, poor woman.'

She suddenly felt like reaching out her arms and holding Durga close. Perhaps the desire to feel another living soul nearby. She has been alone in this freezing cave for so many years, feeling worthless, wishing for death. Today the desire to stay alive is raising its head. 'This Durga! Let her be all; right. Then, let what has to happen, happen! He Shambhu! You know everything!'

Through the slats in the window. the cool shadow of the moon touched both the women, unable to decide which of the two was less unhappy.

The Inheritance of History

A new place, new people, a new land, a new environment. Katya felt that even the sky was different in Agra. The college campus, the hostel with its extensive, open roof, the mango, fig and banyan trees everywhere – these were all new. There were pink and yellow oleander flowers growing between the lantana and tikoma hedges, but there was no sign of her beloved, shady Chinar. Apple, apricot and pear trees laden with fruit were a distant dream. The sun and the moon, who played their games of hide and seek in the mountains and through the barred windows of homes, had also retreated to distant corners of the sky. Instead there were hot, dust-laden winds that caused you to break out in a rash.

The sound of the azaan from a nearby mosque broke through her sleep in the morning like a call from the Shah Hamdaan. 'Allah-o-Akbar!' It immediately recalled the Vitasta and the emotion-filled voice of the priest standing in front of the image of the goddess Mahakali on its banks: 'Ya devi Sarva Bhuteshu....' A temple and a mosque on the same river bank. Katya would automatically fold her hands in obeisance and begin her day with her sleep-laden eyes.

Students from different states with different languages would mingle in the mess or common room. Tied together by a common interest, they had much to share and talk about; they created new friendships as they confronted big and small problems and difficulties together. Days were filled with educational tours to hospitals, museums, morgues. The smell of Formaline made Katya feel giddy and sick. The sight of the half developed, handicapped foetus in the anatomical museum of the Civil Hospital traumatized her for many days. A boy with a third eye on the forehead, a fleshy hole in place of a nose – how strange nature was. She often wondered: what world was this that she had entered? From a protected, affectionate cocoon, she had been catapulted, full tilt, into the brutal, naked world of reality. A world where there was no place for emotion, a place inundated with the smell and the presence of naked human flesh. She felt she needed to be strong to face this new world.

And time passed at its own pace. Whenever there was a free moment the students would gather in the common room and share their joys and sorrows. Worries about being thrown out of the hostel because the money hadn't arrived from home, or the humiliation of not being able to pay one's mess bill! They were always ready to help each other if the problem could be solved by some minor borrowing or lending between them. A close relationship had grown between all of them now and Katya loved being there. She had just one problem: she would occasionally, and suddenly, become very sad and depressed. Her friends would guess, rightly, that she was feeling homesick, and they would do their best to cheer her up.

'All right, Katya, tell us what does your state have apart from its natural beauty which keeps it in the news so often?'

Katya would smile at Bhardwaj's question and pointing to the glass of water in front of her would say, 'The water!'

'The climate is also excellent but apart from Chashmeshahi even the water in the ordinary neighbourhoods is so good that you can digest a plate full of food by drinking just two gulps!' Neela Rajpal from Jammu had lived in Srinagar.

'Thank God!' Surendra Singh raised his hands in thankfulness on hearing this praise, 'If we had water like that here the mess cooks would collapse rolling out chapatis for us day and night!'

Amidst shouts of laughter and general bonhomie, the sadness would disappear. Whenever a few people sat together and discussed politics, Kashmir was mentioned and Katya always took part in the discussion.

'Bhai, there must be some reason why the entire world

has made Kashmir an issue and is busy creating confusion,' Bhardwaj would begin the discussion.

Ajay Kashtkari was more knowledgeable. Kashmir was his homeland. He was a year senior to Katya. 'Strategic point brothers, strategic point. All of you know that on the eastern side of the valley there is Gilgit, then there are the Himalayas and the Karakoram ranges, all very important from the army's point of view. It is all a matter of self-interest, not merely a question of personal animosity.' One of the subjects that constantly came up for debate was the Dixon Plan – a United Nations initiative to 'solve' the Kashmir problem – but Owen Dixon's suggestions were not acceptable to either Pakistan or India, or indeed to Sheikh Abdullah.

'Brother, who will agree if you suggest dividing a state into three parts on the basis of religion and propose to hold a plebiscite in one of the divisions?'

'These are all political strategems. Kashmir has merged with India. Now even the superpowers have started taking an interest in this issue.'

All sorts of subjects came up for discussion – the growing unrest within the Congress, the selection of the President of Independent India and the relationship between Nehru and Sheikh Abdullah. 'Nehru wanted to make Rajagopalachari the president but Patel insisted on Rajendra Prasad. Nehru was worried and then the Kashmir issue was another headache for him. In 1945 Nehru had said, that only Sheikh Abdullah could deliver the goods in Kashmir.

But now the situation was changing rapidly. The calm surface of the lake belied the disturbance that lay beneath.

'Katya, I have heard that in 1950 Sheikh sahib told Owen Dixon that apart from defence affairs and communications he did not want any interference by India in Kashmir. Doesn't the public protest against these changes in policy?'

'The people of Kashmir have chosen Sheikh sahib as their

leader. They have faith in him.' Katya often spoke of the role played by Sheikh sahib during the Kabaili raids.

'That is true, but this attitude indicates that Sheikh sahib is dreaming of an independent Kashmir.' Surinder Singh was well known for his bluntness.

'Nothing is clear in politics. Sheikh sahib spoke about "strengthening secular India" in the Assembly and then on the 11th of April 1952, he criticized India at a speech in Ranbirsinghpora. On the 13th of July, on the occasion of "martyrs day," he said interference by the central government would not be tolerated.'

'This was the beginning of the 'Appeasement Policy'.' Goyal spoke about the agreement reached between the centre and the state in August 1952.

'The Delhi agreement was actually a gift given by Nehru under the policy of appeasement. It included provisions for the end of hereditary rule, the granting of special citizenship to the people of the state as well as the permission to address the Chief Minister as Prime Minister and to fly a separate national flag, concessions which evidently did not please the other states of India.'

The slogan of the Praja Parishad, which started the movement against these in Jammu, was, 'We will not allow two constitutions, two symbols or two prime ministers in one country.'

Virtually every free moment was spent discussing politics. At the national level, the Jana Sangh was opposed to the Delhi agreement. There were protests throughout the country. The President of the Bharatiya Jana Sangh visited Jammu-Kashmir defying the 'permit laws'. He wanted to stop this movement but he was put in prison on the 11th of May 1953 and died in custody on the 23rd of June. This event shook the country.

Ayodhyanath's family was also stunned by the sudden

death of Shyama Prasad Mukherjee. Katya was home for the holidays. The local Jan Sanghis were all stirred up by the news. The government kept Mukherjee's death a secret. When Katya's friend Tulsi, who had become a nurse in a hospital, came to meet her she seemed very frightened. She whispered to Katya, 'Mukherjee Sahib was ill, I was on duty that day. He felt very uneasy at night and I pressed his forehead and gave him the medicines he asked for. He needed a specialist. I could not do anything, the place was guarded very closely.'

Tulsi's eyes were full of tears, 'He called me daughter. Such a great man, completely alone and he died in police custody.'

'People got to know about his death only when a large crowd participated in his last rites in Calcutta.'

Katya asked Ayodhyanath, 'Didn't the local politicians know how gravely ill he was?'

'He was in police custody. The doctor used to visit him. Your Tulsi was with him, no one knows anything more than this.'

'But, Tathya! Politics is all very well but humanity is also very important. This is sheer carelessness.'

What could Tathya say? Nothing was clear. There was confusion everywhere. The papers were full of strange news related to the future of a people who, despite being in the centre, had been pushed to the margins. On the fifth of July 1953 *The New York Times* had even printed a map, which showed Kashmir as an independent country. The Kashmiris themselves were unsure of their own position. But gradually communal tensions began to surface in minor skirmishes, processions and meetings.

Katya returned to Agra in a very disturbed frame of mind. Though her family members tried to pretend all was well, they were quite worried. Nandan had also come home for the holidays. He was more saddened than surprised by the sloganeering and the cracks developing between the communities. His friend

Triloki lost out to a third class graduate for a job despite having a BSc with distinction. Reservations were also gradually getting affected by communalism.

Nandan told Tathya clearly that he would look for a job outside the state once he became an engineer. Tathya and Keshavnath were stunned by their son's decision. How could people who were so closely attached to their valley even think of going so far away?

But a new beginning had been made. Unknowingly and unrecognizably. Ayodhyanath had also started worrying about the future of his grandchildren. Suddenly he had started thinking about the causes and compulsions that had motivated families like the Nehrus, Katjus, Kunzrus and Saprus to settle outside the valley many years ago. He believed that the Kashmiri Pandits who left their homes between 1707 and 1753 in the hope of better opportunities and jobs had lost touch with the soil and the houses of their ancestors forever. But were they really able to distance themselves from memories of their homes?

The migration which happened during the reign of Sultan Sikandar was enforced, an unplanned exodus motivated by the desire to protect their religion. In the eighteenth century many pundits left the state because of the cruelty of the Afghan rulers but there were others who continued to stay back and follow their religion despite their sufferings. There must be some reason why a man is drawn to the fragrance of his soil and wants to become a part of it after his death. Traditions? Nund Rishi and Lalleshwari? The teachings of Sufi saints or the patience and determinism of the Hindu religion? Or the debts owed to the soil of one's ancestors? Or merely financial compulsions?

Ayodhyanath was not a frog in the well but he could not bear the thought of living far away from the land whose fragrance was an inalienable part of his being. He believed that even after death, he would continue to hold the place he had occupied in his lifetime in the society around him. Outside the valley he would have to live like a stranger and he could never reconcile to the feeling of alienation. But had those who left the valley been able to forget their valley?

Ayodhyanath would think of the pain that was so evident in the lines written by Brijnath Chakbast who lived in Lucknow:

It is an age since I left that garden

And yet the story of its love remains fresh in my heart.

Prithvi Dhar, who lived on the ruins of the glorious past of his landowning ancestors, nevertheless advised his children to do their Bachelor's and Master's degrees from any distant corner of the world. He would often make fun of Ayodhyanath's patriotism and his contentedness. He was delighted to hear about Nandan's decision.

'Bhai sahib! I honour your views. You are older and therefore deserve my respect, but whatever Nandan has said today is not wrong. Everyone has the right to look for a better future. What did you and I gain from our attachment to this soil?' Ayodhyanath looked at Prithvi in surprise.

'What are you saying Prithvi bhai? We don't have any complaints. We got whatever we deserved.'

'No, bhai sahib. You are speaking the language of courtesy. These barristers who have settled in Delhi, Agra, Allahabad, people like Pandit Bishan Narayan Dhar, Bar-at-Law, Tej Bahadur Sapru, Law minister, Motilal Nehru, Barrister etc. You were not inferior to them, but you can say that like frogs in a well we did not recognize the vastness and the possibilities of the world outside.'

'These people were brilliant. There are no two opinions about this, and they earned their high positions because of their capabilities.' Ayodhyanath was very proud of the achievements of his community.

'But did we ever get the opportunity to exhibit our

capabilities? We are enclosed within four walls. Within fixed limits and boundaries. And on top of that there are these reservations and quotas. How many seats are there for the minorities? Nehru rightly said in 1940 that Kashmiri pundits only want a free and fair environment in which they can show their talents and abilities. A free and open field for talent and ability. During the time of the Hindu kings or the reign of fair and just kings like Zainulabdin we have produced Shaivite scholars and poets like Mammat, Kallat, Mankh and Abhinav Gupt, historians like Kalhana, Jonaraj, poets like Lalleshwari, Habba and Arnimaal. But now our talents are becoming blunted and dull.'

'Pandits got the opportunity to flower and progress outside Kashmir, like Raj Kaul with the Mughals, Gangaram in the court of Maharaja Ranjit Singh, or Mohanlal Kashmiri, Ayodhyanath Kunzru, Radhakrishan Sapru and Shambhunath Pandit etc., during the time of the British. Kashmiri Pandits got the opportunity to show their talents only once they left the valley.'

Ayodhyanath could understand Prithvi Dhar's sorrow, the sorrow of realizing that his comfortable life was changing. Democracy had shaken the foundations of the palaces of the rich landlords. Now the tiny piece of land, which remained as a mocking reminder of his vast landholdings, barely produced enough grain for a year. Prithvi Dhar's hopes had been destroyed. He called his sons and told them to take up any jobs they could find and take on the responsibility of looking after their own families. Baba now had nothing left except the bare minimum on which he could survive.

Ayodhyanath tried to be philosophical and said, 'Change! Change is the rule of nature. It includes sunshine, shade, warmth, cold, everything. The new government is trying to look after the welfare of the needy. This is a good thing.'

But despite these philosophical statements, Ayodhyanath

was worried about the changing situation in the state. He remembered that incident in June 1948 when some boys, who had gained top positions from Punjab University, Solan, had met Sheikh Abdullah and asked him to help them get jobs in the state on the basis of their merit. Standing on the steps outside Neelam Hotel, Sheikh sahib had replied, 'The doors across Banihal are open for you, but where will the Muslims of the valley go in search of jobs?' Since then Hindu boys had been forced to leave their homes in search of employment.

On the other side, the Anglo-American combine wanted to see Kashmir as an independent state. On the 11th of November 1953, Clement Attlee gave a statement saying that Kashmir should be a free state and and not a part of India or Pakistan. Perhaps Sheikh sahib was also thinking along these lines. But there was dissension among his ministers. Nehru was very worried by this turn of events. He wanted to talk to Sheikh Abdullah but nothing substantial was happening. The people got to know about these internal struggles the day Sheikh sahib was arrested by the Sadr-e-Riyasat in Gulmarg.

The 7th and 8th of August 1953 were days of surprise, fear and sorrow for the valley. The streets were full of violent hooligans shouting slogans and creating chaos and confusion. People were worried and frightened, waiting behind closed doors and windows in anticipation of the unexpected. Ayodhyanath, Keshav and Shivnath had heard the rumour that the deputy chief minister, Bakshi Ghulam Mohammad, and a majority of the cabinet had accused Sheikh sahib of 'creating doubts and uncertainty in the minds of the public.' The Sadr-e-Riyasat tried to convene a cabinet meeting but Sheikh sahib left for Gulmarg. He was imprisoned there and on the 9th of August Bakshi Ghulam Mohammad took the oath of Chief Ministership. The imprisonment of Sheikh sahib was a great shock to his followers. There was violence on the streets of Srinagar and a number of people were killed. A procession carrying their bodies, shouting slogans 'Long live Sher-e-Kashmir' was taken out from Safakadal to Amirakadal, crossing all the seven bridges. There were skirmishes between the opposing groups but Bakshi dealt firmly with the situation. The rioters were arrested and curfew was declared in the city.

The state became a subject of discussion. Those living far away became anxious about the welfare of their loved ones. Katya sent a telegram to Tathya to enquire about the family. Ayodhyanath himself wrote a long letter to Katya explaining the situation.

My Dearest Katya

It seems that you have become anxious because of all the reports in the newspapers. But my brave daughter, you know the history of your state. Political upheavals, conspiracies, the aspirations of politicians and the resulting difficulties which the public has to bear, these are problems which we have dealt with for a long time.

Life does not come to a standstill because of these. It has been our gift to be able to remain steadfast in the midst of clear or confused circumstances. Believe me, life is carrying on as normally as ever. Marriages, thread ceremonies, celebrations, everything. Yes, people were stunned by Sheikh sahib's arrest, they were also disappointed by the sudden changes, but Bakshi sahib has taken control of the situation very ably. In his radio broadcast after taking over the post of Chief Minister he said, 'The welfare of the nation was being betrayed. The slogan for freedom was dangerous. A free Kashmir under the aegis of an imperialistic nation would pose a danger to both Pakistan and India, a situation like the one in Korea could be created here.'

Don't worry, my child! Bakshi sahib has promised to bring peace and prosperity to the state. The situation is becoming normal. Don't worry. Concentrate on your studies. Become a doctor, come home and cure your grandmother's rheumatism before it becomes untreatable. Everyone at home sends you love and blessings.

It is the apple season these days. I am sending a box of delicious Ambri apples for you. Think of us when you eat them. God Bless you.

Your Own

Tathya

Rehmanjoo

Lately Rehmanjoo had come to realize that God had not really granted him the opportunity to make something of himself. All his life he had been like the washerman's donkey, the more he ran towards his goal, the further his destination seemed to recede. He had thought that there was a faint possibility of some of his hopes being realized. There was a chance that he would get a ticket for the election but then suddenly the situation had changed. Who could have imagined that anyone – in fact his own friends – would have the courage to imprison a lion? But then this was politics. What could one say?

Rehmanjoo was stunned by this event. He even got into an argument with members of the Bakra party in Nawakadal. He spent the entire night twisting and turning restlessly. What had he actually achieved in life? Rehmanjoo's father was one of those unlucky souls who did not get anything easily in life. He was a farmer in Lar and one year his entire crop was destroyed by hailstorms and floods. There was no food to eat. He shifted to the city with his family to earn a living. He came with a recommendation from Neelkanth Bhatt of his village who told him that Gopal Bhan needed an honest servant. Bhan Sahib first asked him to look after his horses, their grooming, their feed etc. Abba spent his life driving Bhan Sahib's tonga and thus supported his family. To tell the truth, even the house they lived in was paid for by Bhan sahib.

In his childhood Rehman spent his days playing 'gulli-danda' with his idle friends, swimming for a few hours with Mohammad Mallah's sons Jamal and Kamal, or chasing stray dogs in the street. Sometimes Abba would box his ears for running around so much because it would make him so hungry that he wouldn't be satisfied with a handful of Sattu. At other times, when he handed over the few coins he had got from visiting English memsahibs, Abba's eyes would sparkle and he would pat him and send him off once again to play on the banks of the river. Abba had learnt new ways of surviving in the city but the other shikara boys would often beat up Rehman, saying that they had first right over tips given by the memsahibs.

Ammi did not like to see Rehman begging so she took him, without Abba's knowledge, to Bhan sahib's wife Rajrani. She begged her, 'Keep the boy with you, he will do small jobs. He will press your legs, fill up the master's hookah, he is your own child. If he stays here he will learn some manners, may God give you prosperity.'

No one kept track of how much etiquette Rehman actually learnt. But yes, he did reap some benefits from living in Bhan sahib's house. For one thing, he got enough to eat, sometimes even a piece of Roganjosh, and for another, as the servant of Bhan sahib's son Shyam Sunder or 'Kingji', he sometimes got to smoke a cigarette butt or two and visit the circus in the exhibition grounds. That was where he met Kingji's friend Nathji, a meeting that slowly matured into a friendship.

Rehman became devoted to Kingji because of the circus. What amazing tricks he saw there! A black mem who rode a motorcycle in the Well of Death! A man who climbed a tall spiral stairway, set fire to his clothes and jumped off the top into a small pond, emerging absolutely unscathed. A girl sitting on a lion, boys swinging in mid air, beautiful white mems wearing tiny red and yellow skirts who rode bicycles on high ropes.

Some strange thoughts also came into Rehman's mind while he was staying in Bhan sahib's house. Looking at his mother's patched pheran, when she came to the house to clean rice, he wished that she could also wear colourful raffal and silk pherans like the ones worn by Rajrani.

One day he said as much to Ashi and she sighed as she replied, 'Everyone has his own destiny, son.' But when Abba heard this, he gave him a solid slap and made him understand that, 'They are our masters, our gods and we are their subjects. Don't forget that they are the ones who feed us.'

Abba did not live very long. He caught typhoid from God knows where. He had diarrhoea, vomited and that was the end. It was during this time that Ashi learnt midwifery from someone and became a dai. She strung her dupatta across her room to make another space where she would sometimes 'check up' some women after cleaning her hands with a red soap.

The ten year old Rehman once peeped through a hole in the curtain to satisfy his curiosity. A woman with white thighs was lying down and his mother was checking something between her round stomach and thighs, causing her to scream constantly. Rehman was really worried that day. Suppose the child sleeping inside jumped out because of his mother's activities? Ashi yelled at Rehman for his mischievousness. Her last recourse in times of trouble was Rajrani. She went to her and begged, 'Mistress! Find some permanent way out for this luckless, fatherless child. There is nothing I can do.'

Keeping Abbu's honesty and Ashi's misfortune in mind, Rajrani decided to teach Rehman how to handle responsibility. He sat with the groom and learnt how to drive the tonga, and take care of the horses, the work his father used to do. Later, after Gopal Bhan's death, when Shyam Sunder left for England to study, Rajrani handed over the entire job of driving the family tonga to Rehman. She added that since her knees were giving her trouble, she could not move around too much and she had no objections if he used his free time to ferry other passengers around and earn a few rupees. But he must always drive the tonga carefully.

When Shyam Sunder returned from abroad he bought a second hand car from some Englishman. The tonga was quite old by now. So, he handed it over along with the old horse to Rehman, thus gaining some merit and also helping Rehman gain a livelihood.

Rehman would have remained a tonga driver all his life if the banner of freedom had not been raised. Now he was a responsible man with a family but the wound caused by the contrast between his mother's torn pheran and Rajrani's silk and raffal still troubled some corner of his psyche. This was also one of the reasons why he joined the struggle for freedom and why Sheikh sahib became his leader.

During the last twenty years Rehman had witnessed the changing colours of his party men, their internal squabbles, attempts to pull each other down and a lot more. Distributing party pamphlets and broadcasting news about party meetings over the loudspeaker attached to his tonga, he had started to consider himself to be a small time leader. Listening to the vigorous speeches of leaders in the Idgah and Gol Park the illiterate Rehman had learnt the history and geography of his country. People said that Sheikh sahib wanted to become the independent emperor of the state. As far as Rehman was concerned he was already the uncrowned king of the valley. And what was wrong with that? In the past, many emperors had looked after the welfare of the poor. Even the children in the street have heard the name of Badshah. How he brought back the Battas who had been exiled. The Afghan sultans were cruel but in 1810 A.D. Ata Mohammad Khan constructed the buildings in Chirar-e-sharif, encouraged trade and spread the name of Nund Rishi, these were all good things. Sheikh sahib also ensured that poor farmers were given their rights. Rehman's children are well settled today thanks to him. The elder one got a government loan and became an apple merchant. The younger one took his matric exam and was appointed as a school teacher in the primary school in Khanabal. The father did not even get to study his religion but the son could speak English. Sheikh sahib said your children will remain slaves all their lives if you don't educate them. Rehman had celebrated his daughter Zeenat's marriage with a lot of pomp. Zeba was no longer a servant girl, she has become a queen. Ashi was also comfortable in her old age. Who was all this due to?

And now everything seemed to be coming to an end. Ashi was trying to read her son's face with cataract dimmed eyes, 'Don't worry. God will fix everything.' Ashi raised her hands in prayer but Rehman was disturbed by the thought that in all honesty he should have also accompanied Sheikh sahib to jail. He should have made a sacrifice for the sake of his party. The tenth pass son could not bear to see his father wallowing in sorrow and regret.

'Baba. Despite being familiar with politics for the past ten or twenty years are you unnecessarily thinking of going to jail because you think that the government will reward you for your honesty by freeing you and your leader? You are not Mahatma Gandhi, whose Satyagraha frightened the British.'

Rehman glared at him. The son modulated his voice and attitude, 'Revolutionaries like Bhagat Singh and Ashfaqullah were martyred in the fight for India's independence. Even Gandhiji could not save these men who died for their country. And when the head of the party has himself been arrested, can you imagine what could happen to you? Baba! Important leaders are well looked after even in jail. People like us get beaten up by the police and if we are disobedient we are even branded with hot irons.'

His son's words upset Rehman but he kept quiet because he felt there was some truth in what the boy was saying. He had learnt to speak the truth, this was the gift of education. The boy proved how educated he was when, pressing Rehman's aching knees, he addressed him in a honeyed voice. 'Baba! Please forgive me, I am too young to be saying this but you have served the party for twenty years. You are an employee of the party and you have always been loyal. Leaders keep changing. First Sheikh sahib was the leader and now Bakshi sahib has become the new leader, so now he is our master isn't he?'

'Hm!' Rehman grunted. He didn't say anything but a voice in his mind said your son is definitely going to become a politician sometime in the future. You remained just a mouthpiece distributing pamphlets all your life. This realization inspired Rehman to set aside his illness the very next day. He bathed and put on a new white salwar. He wore a coat that was kept for special occasions and made his way to Bakshi sahib's door.

'Sir! I have served your party for twenty years....'

Bakshi sahib was extremely astute. He heard Rehman with a smile. This man could be useful. He promised to entrust him with some important party work. He said expansively, 'Rehmanjooa, admit your grandchildren in school, open their eyes. We have promised free education upto MA-BT The scheme will soon be put into effect. Education is essential for the development of the state.'

Rehman returned home full of hope. Arre! He is speaking the same language as Sheikh sahib. The same sweet words about protecting knowledge and the country. Rehmanjoo bowed his head before Allahtala. 'This is your beneficence, you protector of believers! You close one door and open another. Nothing is impossible for you.'

His heart was full of hope once again. Inshallah! Perhaps

one day, Rehmanjoo might also join the ranks of the junior ministers.

❧

Step by Step

How much the valley had changed in just ten years since Independence! The gentle warmth of the rays of the sun still melted the cold, snowy peaks of the Harmukh mountains, creating gushing waterfalls. Waterfalls similar to those which flowed during the time of the Mahabharata when the future ruler of Kashmir, Gonind the second, was still unborn in the womb of Yashovati, the queen of Kashmir. Whether it was the Budh Viharas made by emperor Ashoka 273-232 years before Christ, the sky high golden pinnacles of the Martand temples made by the Hindu king Lalitaditya in the eighth century or the ziarats of the sufi saint Bulbulshah, Shah Hamdan, or Badshah Zainulabdin which were constructed later, the seasons weighed all creation with the same measure.

With the advent of winter, snow covered the plants, trees, fields and houses with a white blanket. Lalli, Kamala, Fatima-Zeba covered the nests of the ababils, the arctic terns, which had taken shelter in the house to protect their new born chicks. Feminine hearts!

Then, when spring slowly awakened, rubbing its eyes and looking around at the fresh new world, all the youngsters rushed out to enjoy the sight. Leaving their kangris and pherans behind, they went off to enjoy the beauty of the Nishat and Shalimar gardens.

The breeze was full of the intoxicating perfume of narcissus flowers and the scent of the newly revealed earth. Velvety, striped, yellow butterflies hovered over beds of roses and pansies. Pangs of love re-awakened in hearts and the air echoed with the sound of the beautiful songs of Habba khatoon and Arnimaal.

'The spring has awakened the flowers
My discontented beloved, come back to me now.'

But away from the entertainments and outings the farming families of Mahadjoo and Matayi were getting ready with their ploughs, bullocks and seeds as soon as the earth emerged from beneath the covering of snow. The efforts of the new rulers had improved the city. Wide roads, new tall buildings, rows of three star and five star hotels on the boulevard. Ancient Pravarpur, established centuries ago by king Pravarsen the Second which today was known as Srinagar, had really developed a lot. New colonies, new districts, a university, a fast expanding city! Sheikh sahib's place had been taken by Bakshi sahib. One loses and the other gains! Losses and gains did not matter much to ordinary people, while the ambitions of politicans shook the educated and the elite.

Crowds of people came to the Hazratbal dargah from towns and villages to listen to Sheikh sahib. Namaz and the pleasure of hearing Sheikh sahib! Speeches about freedom, about rights, about religion! 'Ya Illaha Illalah, Mohammad Urrasoollalah! Nala-e-Taqbir, Allaho Akbar!' The waves on the Dal lake echoed with the shouts.

But knowledgeable people like Ayodhyanath the lawyer, Balbhadra, Santokh Singh and Haji sahib were disappointed and surprised by the ambitions of the leader, by his political machinations and by the changes in the atmosphere in the state. He was the same leader who had been made the head of the emergency interim government by Maharaja Hari Singh and to whom Prime Minister Nehru had entrusted the future of the people of the state by making him its Prime Minister on 4th March 1948. Why was the leader of the people gradually distancing himself from the concerns of the public? Why was he speaking about opposition in his speeches? Everyone had questions. The minorities were very worried.

'Why is Sheikh sahib moving away from his trusted friend, Nehru, who insisted on his approval when the proposal for making Kashmir a part of India was moved in 1948?'

'Nehru has always agreed to Sheikh sahib's demands. Jammu and Kashmir were granted special status under Article 370.'

'The state got its own constitution in 1951, but there was no end to the demands.'

'There was the Delhi agreement in 1952. It marked the end of hereditary rule, granted special citizenship, a separate state flag, and gave the chief minister the title of Prime Minister.'

The Praja Parishad in Jammu protested against the Delhi agreement. 'Why the demand for a separate flag, when our state has acceded to India? A separate constitution, a separate Prime minister! What does this mean? Will our future be different from the future of the rest of the country?'

'Who knows about the future, Jialal?' Balbhadra shared his concerns, 'In the meanwhile it is a fact that our youngsters have started crossing Banihal in search of jobs. There are no jobs for them here.'

There was a moment's silence at the mention of crossing Banihal. This was a new era of being exiled from home. The sons of families belonging to the minority community were being pushed to leave their homes for higher studies and jobs. Jialal changed the subject, 'Bhai sahib! This Delhi agreement is a gift given by Nehru to Sheikh sahib under the appeasement policy. Nehru believes that it is only Sheikh sahib who can keep our boat afloat under these circumstances. Only he can deliver the goods.' A blue vein began to throb on Nazir sahib's forehead.

'We are thankful to Netaji, bhai, he saved our lives during the Kabaili raids. But now he is using this as a trump card....'

Santokh Singh was perturbed. 'Sheikh sahib gave a speech in Ranbirshighpora in which he accused India of being communal and yet Nehru has been sitting quietly.'

Balbhadra agreed with Santokh Singh, 'He's right, Tathya! In 1952 Sheikh sahib even said that the interference of the centre in state affairs would not be tolerated. And what did Nehru do at that time? Lately the influence of the Jamaat-i-islami is also increasing. Something or other happens every other day.'

'Bad manners and lack of civility are also increasing. Ruffians pass all kinds of comments at college-going girls. There is no law, or fear of God left at all.' Santokh Singh, the fruit merchant had a shop in Maharaj ganj. He was thinking of closing it down and migrating to Jammu. 'But Jammu is also quite disturbed these days.' Jialal hates all this talk of going to Jammu or Punjab. When someone leaves home, how often do they come back? This is how brothers are separated from brothers and homes are broken.

'In Jammu, there were a lot of disturbances when the Praja Parishad protested against the Delhi agreement. The police injured many processionists with their lathis. What peace and quiet will you find there?'

Haji sahib had grown old. His eyesight had dimmed and his face was webbed with wrinkles. But he wasn't so old that he could no longer gauge the ambitions that breed in the heart of an individual. He always read the headlines in the newspaper. He had even seen the map, published in the *New York Times* that showed Kashmir as an independent country. It made him think of Sheikh sahib's promises, his friendship and understanding with Nehru. All these were gradually becoming a joke. Sheikh sahib was going against his assurances because of his desire for power. What was happening?

Nehru continued to have faith in the friendship but he accused the Anglo-Americans of using his friend as a pawn in their game of chess. Kashmir shares its borders with China and Russia and it was evident that America wanted to make its defence bases in Kashmir. But Nehru did not remain deluded for long. On 13th July, 1953 Sheikh sahib openly declared that it was not essential that the state should be a part of India or Pakistan. A strange situation! Now there were no Pakistan supporters like Premnath Bazaz or supporters of Kashmiri freedom like Ramchand Kak left in the valley. Sheikh sahib discussed the idea of an independent Kashmir with Shivnarayan Fotedar, the leader of the minorities, but he did not show any interest.

Sheikh sahib was preoccupied and the administration became lax. In a lecture at Hazratbal he declared that it was the people and not the ministers who would decide the future of the state. The cabinet ministers didn't agree with his statement and voices began to be raised against the leader. The Sadr-e-riyasat ordered Sheikh sahib to convene a meeting of the cabinet but he did not comply. And in August of 1953 he was arrested at Gulmarg along with Mirza Mohammad Afzal Beg and other companions. Bakshi Ghulam Mohammad became the new Chief Minister of the state.

There were disturbances in the valley every day. There were riots, processions and confrontations between the supporters of Sher-e-kashmir and Bakshi sahib. It was a strange time. Some people lost hope while others dreamt of climbing the ladder of success.

Rehmanjoo was injured during a riot. When he came home his son, a teacher, bandaged his head and asked his father, 'Bakshi sahib, our new chief minister, used to have implicit faith in Sheikh sahib, but now he has forced Sheikh sahib to give up his post....' Rehman however, thought of Bakshi sahib's speech over the radio in which he said that it was essential to take this step for the welfare of the nation.

Anand Shastri said, 'The wheel of life turns constantly like the change of seasons. Always moving on its axis!' This was an unlucky time for Sheikh sahib and a good time for Bakshi sahib. And the wheel of time? Did it ever stop for anyone? When Katya returned after becoming a doctor her grandmother, who could recognize her footsteps and would come running with her flour smeared hands, had passed away. Her maternal grandfather who used to call her 'my doctor daughter' even before she got admission in medical college was also no more.

❦

The Labyrinths of Life

'What has anyone ever got from being born on this earth, daughter? Wise people have said that this is just a rented house which everyone has to leave at some time.' Janakimaal hugged her stunned and heartbroken granddaughter and consoled her, 'Who stays here permanently, child? Your grandmother was Annapoorna, the goddess of plenty. All her life she wished, 'He Shambhu! Grant that I may come to you before my husband!"

Katya's body shook with sobs, 'She didn't even wait till I came back....'

'Does time wait for anyone, child? Don't be so upset. You are an intelligent educated girl.'

'But both nana and nani together...! Nanaji was really looking forward to my becoming a doctor....'

'Yes, child. They died within a few days of each other. The day your nani passed away the Panchak had just started and it soon showed its effect. This is the influence of the planets, child. There was hardly any gap. Saraswati passed away on the afternoon of the Phalgun Shukla Paksh Pratipada when the Panchak had just begun and Krishnajoo passed away in his sleep on the night of Telashtami.'

Katya, stunned by the maya of the planets, kept searching for the faces of her nana and nani. Janakimaal drew a long sigh almost like a sob, 'Krishnajoo was fine in the evening. Yes, he didn't seem to be very hungry. He told Bhadra, "I will just have a khasu of milk. I don't feel like eating rice, I am feeling a little feverish."'

'Yamraj, the lord of death was knocking at the door after all.'

'For a long while he watched the children burning the old kangris and reed baskets in the courtyard of Sheetalnath to bid farewell to the winter. Who knows which hills and mountains he was climbing? It is very painful to lose your lifelong companion in your old age, child. Even if a man does not really value a woman while she is alive.'

After a moment's silence grandmother started speaking once again, 'He told Bhadra, "Your kakni used to save up old kangris and baskets just for this occasion because her doctor daughter was so fond of joining in this fun!" That was it, he said nothing else.'

'You thought of me nana!' Katya's voice became rough with tears. She remembered the Telashtami's of her childhood. She would go to Sheetalnath with her nana and, tying a rope around an old burning kangri, would twirl it round and round.

'Two deaths within eight days, both Ma and Baba!' Dadi said suddenly.

'Lalli did not express her sorrow at all. She did not even call out to her Ma and Baba. You take care of your mother child. After all who can replace a father and a mother?'

Katya looked at her mother. Her cheekbones had become

more prominent. Mother and daughter held each other and cried. Lalli was like a strong building which crumbles under the impact of an earthquake. Katya had never seen her mother so lost and broken.

'Child, I have lost my childhood home with nana-nani's death!'

'Why didn't you call me, Ma?'

'Kathbab nana! How much Katya used to trouble you, by being stubborn, sulky, unreasonable. The torment of affection! Nanaji tell me a story, nanaji take me to Sheetalnath.'

'You were preparing for your final exams. Your nana himself refused to let us call you. And then he hardly gave us any time to think. We didn't even get an opportunity to look after him…'

Kakni was really moved by their tears. She took her handkerchief out of her pocket and wiped her eyes, 'Lalli was the only daughter. She has no brothers or sisters and now she has no paternal home to call her own. And then this golden child even went and gave away everything that her parents had left for her to Natha. Lalli was the only heir to Krishnajoo's entire estate. She could at least have locked up her father's room and gone there whenever she missed her parents and got some solace from the fragrance of their memory. She didn't need any utensils and other things, it was good she gave all those away….'

'Kakni! What are you saying? What solace could she get from a room when nana-nani are no longer there?'

Katya said these words but there was a fragrance embedded in her memories, which she could smell even now. The smell of her nani's pheran, the smell of sweat and love! A fragrance that still leapt towards Katya with arms wide open.

'She would have been even more lonely if she had locked up the room. Ma and Baba never thought of Nathji as an outsider, that is why they didn't make a will. They were very wise.'

Lalli tried to pull herself together. The world only sees the tip of the iceberg of sorrow, its largest portion is hidden from view, to be borne all alone. Janakimaal had seen a lot of the world,'Your Tathya knows more about inheritance and property affairs, munni. That is why he explained everything to Lalli. He told her about the rules of courts and the laws regarding property. Bakshi sahib is also Tathya's friend. Nothing was impossible but your mother insisted, "I don't want to lose my brother and sister. What will I do with bricks and mortar."'

'Perhaps she is right. After all, one leaves everything behind finally. Whatever Ganapati desires.' Janakimaal gave up gracefully. She moved from the earthly plane to the spiritual one, 'Sufi's and saints have said a lot of wise things, Munni.'

Truly, Nathji treated Lalli as his real sister till the day he took his last breath. He would send gifts, walnuts, roths and kangris on every Shivratri, Navreh, Janamashtami, first to Lalli and then to Radha and Batni. He also observed all the fasts and obsequies for Krishnajoo and Saraswati. Lalli's gesture became a topic of discussion among all the relatives.

'Look at the lawyer Ayodhyanath's daughter-in-law! She gifted everything away to her uncle's son Natha. Does anyone give away even an inch of earth nowadays? Brothers come to blows over one utensil.'

'Everyone knows the Mahabharat that is taking place among Amravati's daughters-in-law and her elder son, Bhaskar, sleeps with the key of the store tied at his waist. He doesn't even have any faith in his own children.'

'Bhaskar's wife Arni is also quite miserly, she measures out rice and sugar to her daughter-in-law. The daughter-in-law is equally clever. She feeds the neighbours all sorts of delicacies without telling her mother-in-law. Even if she is sitting there starving!'

Katya would interrupt the women's gossip with her questions, 'Mausi are you only going to blame the daughters-in-law? Or are the boys totally incompetent? And what you are saying about Bhaskar uncle, is that really correct?'

'Who knows what the truth is daughter? A daughter-in-law is the bedrock of the family. She is also the one who gets the blame. Who is going to check if Bhaskar really keeps the key with him? It is the women who are answerable after all.'

'No, Mausi, a son and daughter-in-law build or destroy a house together. Why don't you learn to respect your own sex? Why do you keep digging up your own roots?'

Katya was a doctor, she earned more than many boys. So, the women would nudge each other and keep quiet. But the older women were really troubled.

'Oh, that Jaya Kazanchi! The same one who used to play "tuley langun tulan chas" in Baljoo's courtyard with her hair open! Yesterday, in the middle of the afternoon, she was roaming around Habbakadal with her head uncovered, giggling with some boy. And the hussy is looking really pretty these days!'

'At least she is a young girl. Have you seen Arni's daughter-in-law? She is a clerk in a bank, and mixes with all sorts of strange men. Then there is that Phoolkumari, she flirts with her father-in-law and talks about setting up house with him...'

Arni was really unlucky. She still had to obey her brothers-in-law. After all, with older people in the house, how could she even dream of setting up house separately? The gossip went on.

Five years after Subhan Mallah's death Khurshid called her sons and daughters-in-law together to discuss the division of the property. How long could she forcibly keep her family together by telling them about the benefits of sharing the same kitchen? When Ali's wife's brother came to visit, the smell of kebabs being grilled on a heater wafted out of his room. Gani's wife was not going to be left behind so she cooked scrambled eggs and roghan josh for her friends on a stove in her room. Anything that was cooked in the common kitchen was meant for everyone. Khurshid wisely put an end to this clandestine cooking and hospitality.

'You lived together while Baba was alive. This made him very happy. Now during my lifetime I want all of you to have your own kitchens and be free to cook whatever you like. Look after your own guests and live in harmony. As far as I am concerned, I am still able to cook a handful of rice for myself.' The daughters-in-law were delighted. Ali, Gani and Wali were really upset, 'You are going to cook for yourself while we are still living, mother? If you think your daughters-in-law are dead, please believe that we haven't gone to meet our maker yet.'

'May God preserve you! May my years be added to yours! Don't say such inauspicious words!' Khurshid was moved by the innocence of her sons. It was decided that she would eat with each of her sons for a month, till God permitted. Now everyone was happy.

She thought, how much time do I have left? I already have one foot in the grave, this will happen after I am gone. But Sona did not share the same happiness. Raghunath, Brijnath and Kanhaiyalal were all working now. There were daughters-in-law in the house. Sona became a grandmother. She pulled out long forgotten tales from her hoard for the little ones. The clever monkey who distributed the butter while sorting out the quarrel of the two cats and kept helping himself to one slice after another, finally eating the last piece of butter as payment for his help! The greedy mouse who ate the entire bowl of khichdi under the pretext of checking its taste. The dusty lullabys she had folded away poured out as music from Sona's throat. She visited the lanes of her childhood once again and swayed to the rhythms of her forgotten youth! She bloomed on seeing her womb becoming fruitful once again. She was needed once more.

Two of the daughters-in-law adjusted well but unhappiness stepped into the house with the third one, Shama. The beloved daughter of the Zutshis, a lecturer in the girl's college, why would she dirty her hands with mud and ash to wash utensils? She couldn't wash the sweaty, smelly, soiled clothes of the entire household. There were so many servants in her house who ran to obey her commands in the blink of an eye...

When Brij's wife, who was a school teacher, heard this she stopped helping Raghu's wife with the chores in the mornings and evenings. In this game of oneupmanship Raghu's wife continued to labour all alone. The eldest daughter-in-law of the house who had merely passed her matric, carried the weight of the entire household on her tired shoulders. Suppressing her anger, she washed the soiled clothes of Brij's children and looked after the guests, making shirchai and kehwa.

Finally, the inevitable happened. Badki, the eldest daughter-in-law, could not take it any longer. Raghu heard his hitherto docile wife's ultimatum. She was not going to work as a servant for for her sisters-in-law. She had done enough. From now on the two delicate darlings, with their Cutex painted nails, would have to wash the oil and gravy-coated utensils because she wanted to rest her aching back for a few hours in the afternoon.

Raghunath handed his wife a jar of Vaseline as a cure for her chapped hands and feet and gave her a lecture on sacrifice, generosity and being an ideal housewife. But Badki had already done her share of sacrificing and she pulled up the quilt and turned away, refusing to speak to him.

After a month of this silent treatment when Raghu finally appealed to his mother, she woke up. She was already aware of the cracks that were gradually developing and had tried to help in small ways to keep the household together. But the desperation written on Raghu's face filled her with a deep tiredness. When relationships begin to seem like restrictions it means the rot has already set in.

Sona could not prevent her house from breaking apart. Where had she gone wrong? These days she spent most of her time in prayer. Despite living in a joint family she viewed the internal tensions and relationships as though from across a wall, shielding herself from the daily bitterness and dissension.

Sometimes she would go with Kanhaiya to hear the discourses of the Shaivite scholar Lakshmanjoo at Ishbar. The rest of the time she lived closed up within herself, following the dictum 'I am in the world but I am not a part of it.'

Sona was not a customer in the bazaar through which she was passing just now. The sweet milky smiles and sleepy yawns of her grandsons had created ripples in the still surface of the pool but Raghu's dejected face reined in her hopes. Which way are you going? Your road lies here.

What kind of a bazaar was this where it was the custom to drown the longings of the wayward mind in prayer and hymns? Where there were pre-determined rules to discipline the burning desires of the body? Where fasts, and rituals were prescribed as a means to control oneself.

Why should anyone have any attachment to this transient body? It was ultimately going to be reduced to a handful of ashes after all. All creation was the work of Shiva and ultimately it would become a part of him, that was the ultimate truth. But before merging with Shiva, Sona had to withstand a number of earthquakes. The three brothers almost became strangers after setting up separate homes.

Kanhaiya went to Calcutta to work for Hindustan Motors. The three daughters-in-law fought over who Sona should stay with because all three of them needed her. The elder one had always dedicated herself to her mother-in-law's service and did not want to give up the goodwill she had gained so far. Brij had two small children and a working wife. Who would look after the children in their mother's absence? Kanhaiya's Shama was pregnant. She had to be careful. It would be so convenient to have someone of one's own close by. Among all these reasons Sona unsuccessfully looked for someone who wanted her for her own sake. Was it not enough that she was their mother, someone who, since the age of twenty-five, had chosen to live a lonely life for the sake of her three children? She forgot that like Prometheus, Masterji had brought warmth and fire into her life to melt her cold and lonely existence. She did not punish Masterji like Prometheus, she bore the punishment herself.

Patwari Madhavjoo's four storeyed house echoed with the sounds of carpenters and labourers as the house was divided into different parts. Walls went up all over. Sona agreed to the wishes of her daughters-in-law. Utensils, carpets, namdas, gold, silver: Sona did not touch anything. The division was done after consulting Tathya. Sona herself did not become an object of division. Only a void remained inside her. No resentment at all. She had stopped losing her temper a long time ago. Raghu would regularly bring Madhav's pension money to her. 'Ma, this is your money.'

'Buy me some rice and dal with this money, son. What will I do with money?'

Brij's wife would bring a small katori of peas and cottage cheese, in the evening the eldest daughter-in-law would come with a bowl of kheer.

Sona would return everything, 'No, children. I prefer to cook khichdi for myself.' Sona made this purity, this desire to eat only what she cooked herself, an excuse to maintain her honour and that of her sons.

'Ma, take my dussa, it is made of Pashmina.' Raghu would beg her.

'Ma, I will put a bukhari in your room. Then you will not feel the cold,' Brij would express his anxiety.

'No, son, I have so much. I will ask if I need anything else. I am comfortable.' Madhav's dearest Sona, Sona the mother of three sons! How could she have any problems!

So much! A blanket, kangri, a mattress, a quilt, a small coal stove and two dishes. A small vessel for tea. One meal a day. Prayers for the rest of the time. Sona chose to stay in the prayer room, which had a window which opened out at the back towards 'Vir van' where an old decrepit boat floated on the silted marshy waters.

Tathya said, 'Come and stay with us. The children are grown up now.' Sona shook her head, refusing the offer. When her own children have not been able to understand their mother what respect and understanding could she expect from brothers and nephews? Tathya read the pain in Sona's lowered eyes and was wounded to the heart. Janakimaal became ill. Golden girl, how many more tests will you have to face?

Lalli, Kehsavnath and Shivnath would visit her two or three times every week bringing, fruit, vegetables, sweets and flowers for her prayers. 'Tathya has sworn that you will see him dead if you refuse these fruits and flowers.' Lalli would hug her and insist. Katya combed her hair, made tea for her, 'Look bua, I have had my bath and come, I am not even having my periods. I am absolutely pure! So let me make some tea for you.'

'You crazy child! You are always pure! Aren't you Lalli's daughter after all? I never learnt to be a good mother from my friend and sister-in-law.' Sona's eyes filled with unshed tears. Sona could not refuse their affection but the sorrowful pity that she saw lurking beneath the serious faces of her brothers hurt her all her life. She was deeply wounded and clutched at the shreds of pride which remained with her.

'Lalli bhabi, I have three sons, why does Tathya still worry about me?'

Raghu and Brij's children would sometimes wander in to meet their grandmother in the hope of hearing a story. Sona would fill their hands with fruit and sweets and give them her blessings. And for the rest of the time, Sona remained enclosed within her room from where sounds of hymns and the fragrance of flowers and incense would waft out of the chinks in the door. Sometimes they would hear the sorrowful lines by Shah Gafoor:

One gains nothing by being born in this world
Just keep the thought of Brahma, Vishnu and Maheshwar
in your mind.

Heart rending sobs would accompany the last line. So
this was what one gained after an entire lifetime! On the next
Baisakhi, something happened in this little prayer room with
its single tiny cage-like window that looked out on the muddy
thatched roofs of the houses of boatmen and a decrepit,
abandoned boat. What happened was that in front of the
idols of Goddess Sharika of Haari Parbat, Laddu Ganesh, the
goddess of Khir Bhavani, the photograph of Madhav Patwari
and his three children, between the flowers and in front of the
burning clay lamp, Sona was found lying in full obeisance on
the ground, dead.

But this happened in the future, after Kanhaiya became the
father of a little girl in Calcutta. It seems he was so delighted at
the birth of the first daughter, he ran to send a telegram to ask
his mother to come and visit and was crushed under the wheels
of a car. The next day some Kashmiri friend identified his body
and informed the family. That day, amidst the lamentation and
the screams, it was unclear whether Sona had heard the news.
The sons and daughters-in-law only remembered their mother
when the smell of burning accompanied by a thud came from
her room. Badki ran and opened the door. She saw the smoke
rising from Sona's hair and threw a blanket over her mother-in-
law's body. When she dusted her hair with the corner of her sari
all the hair came off. The distraught daughter-in-law screamed
and tried to stick some of the hair back on Sona's naked scalp.
Her chest filled with emotion, 'Maaaa...' This was the beautiful
hair which Janakimaal used to decorate with gold and silver
ornaments.

When Madhav died Kanhaiya was just a little infant. Sona
had spent her entire life in sorrow. Once Kanhaiya went, Sona

became silent and sat immobile in front of the idol of Krishna-Kanhaiya. She had already finished her quota of tears in her passage through the bazaar of life.

New Concerns

Tathya's backbone was no longer as straight as it used to be. The pain of Sona's passing brought a whole array of illnesses with it. His eyes were also dimmed by diabetes. But a lion, however old he may be, is still the king of the jungle. He continued to command the same respect in society. He just mentioned to Bakshi sahib that his daughter wanted to serve her people. Bakshi sahib congratulated him saying, 'We desperately need good doctors,' and gave Katya a permanent job in a government hospital. Tathya couldn't stop praising Bakshi sahib. 'Bakshi sahib is a great leader. A strong leader of the people, secular minded, cheerful, charismatic. Always ready to help anyone in need. And administration? Even better! He is a true Indian. You must have heard about his peace brigade?'

Katya would express her disagreement sometimes. 'Tathya, this peace brigade police which moves around in civilian clothes, it does catch a lot of hooligans, but it also violates the rights of citizens sometimes. I mean these peace brigade guys sometimes violently disrupt the gatherings of rival parties. After all everyone should have the right to have his say in a democracy.' Tathya agreed with his granddaughter's opinion but he also presented his political views.

'Politics is very complicated, Katya. Bakshi sahib is strictly trying to suppress the anti-India campaign that provides shelter to a lot of antisocial elements. But at the same time he has also endeared himself to the ordinary man. Just see, he came with a garland of flowers when we invited him for Prem's wedding. He even gave a gift to Vijaya as though he was a member of the family.'

Prem's wife Vijaya was a sweet round-faced girl. She didn't look like the mother of two children. She spoke very little but had smiling eyes. Kamalavati was satisfied because she was not like the brazen girls of today who clawed you like cats if you criticized their family. Vijaya belonged to a reputed family. 'It must be because of my good karma that I have a daughter-in-law like Vijaya. She follows all the religious rituals, knows how to distinguish between what is pure and what is impure. She makes such fabulous roths that even older women cannot compete with her. During the Pan pooja when she narrates the story of Bib Garaz Ma, with her eyes closed, holding grass and flowers in her hand, she looks like the goddess herself.'

Who knew whether Prem still thought the same way. He became an Assistant Engineer in the Public Works Department after getting a diploma in engineering and was now busy raking in money, though he still continued to enjoy himself roaming around with friends. He would prefer to have a wife who looked like Saira Bano rather than Bib Garaz Ma!

He often pulled his wife's sari pallu from her head to tease her. When he stoked her cheeks Kamalavati pretended she hadn't seen anything and looked out of the window. She did not hold her daughter-in-law responsible for her son's embarrassing behaviour but blamed it on the times. She, the middle-aged wife of lawyer sahib, did not have the guts to speak directly to her husband in front of Tathya or even her mother-in-law. And here was this young lady who got an invitation to see a movie from her princely bridegroom right under her mother-in-law's nose.

Kamalavati didn't remember any occasion when she had gone alone with her husband for a movie. However Tathya did take tongaloads of friends and relatives to see *Ram Rajya*, *Bharat Milap* and *Mela*. May he have a long life! If he hadn't taken her how would she have seen mother Sita lamenting in the forest? Or that test by fire and the way she descended into the earth? Kamlavati had been so moved. Kamalavati saw life only in two colours, black and white. She was not concerned with the other beautiful colours of the spectrum. Lalli's case was different because Keshav understood her wishes and desires without even asking her. According to Kamalavati this was also the result of past karma.

'What else can it be? Lalli's children have also turned out so well. Our Prem got a seat to study for a diploma only after Tathya's efforts. Nandan left for America after his engineering to do his M.S and now he is working there. There is very little possibility of Nandan's coming home. He's got used to that life. He is not interested in home food or an Indian girl otherwise wouldn't he have got married by now? Who knows, he may have already got involved with some mem over there. Who is going to check? He is free to do what he likes and he can get away with anything.

'Didn't Lassa Zadu's son get married to some English monkey over there? And this while his poor wife Sati kept waiting for the day when her wayward husband would return home. And that fellow? He would write home two or three times a year and send a calendar with pictures of white women for his children! And later, not even that! He never came back. His poor father passed away after a lifetime of writing letters to his son. The old man even organized the weddings of his grandson and daughter. It seems Lassa sent some money for the children and that was the end of his obligations. His wife, of course, did not exist for him. There was no question of his coming back. He had children by his English wife and there was no way she was going to let him come back.

Katya is two years older than Nandan. She is a doctor. But she is also sitting around unmarried. People started passing comments when my poor Ragya had barely crossed nineteen. "Shivnath's daughter is grown up." Now there is a mature girl of twenty eight sitting at home but no one has the guts to talk about her. Just because she is a doctor. Yes....She will earn and look after others, so why should she bear the restrictions and limitations of marriage? Why should she tolerate the arrogance and bluster of a husband? Even Lalli does not discuss marriage with her these days. And mother-in-law? Who listens to her mumbles? In any case she has become a little senile. Her daughter Sona has almost broken her spirit.'

Katya was busy with her work. The desire to colour new horizons left very little time for her to think about unimportant matters. Hospital, patients, medicines, diagnoses, operations. Katya was stunned to see how beautiful young women changed into what the French naturalist Victor Jacqemont called, 'ugly witches' when they became sick with disease.

'You are my mother, Doctor sahiba, please give me relief from this suffering. I beg you in the name of Allah....' Celebrations at the birth of a son and dejection at the arrival of a daughter, this was common. Katya would stop for five or ten minutes near the beds of women who had daughters. She would caress the baby, 'What a lovely child you have. Look at the way she gazes around. She is just like a statue of goddess Saraswati! What are you going to name her?'

'This is her third daughter, doctor sahiba! What name can we give her? She is destined to bear only daughters, what can I do? I have tried so many mantras and prayers, tried everything but each time she gives birth to a daughter. Everyone has started taunting her.'

Katya would become rigid with anger, 'Why do you women

speak so ignorantly? It is not the woman who determines whether the child will be a girl or a boy.' If the woman was educated Katya would explain the role played by X and Y chromosomes in determining the sex of the child. 'Look, if you want to blame someone for the birth of a daughter blame the man.'

'We agree doctor sahiba, but who is going to explain this to our community? Scientific explanations cannot overrule ancient beliefs so easily, it will take many years and till then we have to bear this….'

'No, sister. This argument about bearing it seems very stupid and ignorant. I am not asking you to revolt but you can rid your minds of any feeling of inferiority and give your daughters a good education. Then they will fight for their own rights. You can do this, at least.' Katya tried to wake them up. She felt a deep anger as well as immense compassion for women who were being gradually frayed and torn apart physically and mentally. Women with dry yellow skin, skeletal weak bodies, dishevelled hair, irregular periods, high-low blood pressure, back pain, coughs and the burden of bearing a child every two or three years. The victims of dirt, poverty and ancient traditions, these broken women, who were never given an opportunity to think about themselves, when would they awaken from their centuries-old sleep?

But Katya didn't have too much time to think. Doctor Avtar rushed into the room. 'Doctor Katya there is an emergency case, you are needed, come quickly.' Katya picked up her stethoscope from the table and moved towards the emergency room with him. She opened the door and looked at the woman lying on the table, the face looked familiar, but no, this wasn't ….'Is it Fazi?' Katya wanted someone to say it wasn't Fazi.

'Yes, the patient is Fazi. She has had a miscarriage in her sixth month of pregnancy, it seems she took some wrong medicines, her entire body is full of poison. She was in terrible pain. We have given her a Morphia injection.' A blue, almost darkening body. Messy hair, full of sweat and dirt and plastered to her face and forehead. Her rosy lips were swollen and slack. Was this the same Fazi whom Katya had called a fairy when she met her for the first time? 'Me? A fairy?' Fazi had curled up in embarrassment and her cheeks had been flooded with crimson.

'Truly, Fazi. It was after seeing a beautiful girl like you that, many years ago, an Englishman, Andrew Wilson, had called the women of Kashmir beautiful fairies. Are you sure it wasn't you he saw? No, you aren't that old, must have been in your last birth.'

'Doctor sahiba I feel embarrassed when you say things like this.'

Katya had liked Fazi, clever, sprightly and full of life.

'Will you work with me in the hospital?'

'What work do I know, Doctor sahiba? I can clean and swab and sweep.'

'Yes, all these small jobs. I need a nurse anyway to help me when I examine women patients. An additional girl will be a big help to me and you will also get some work.'

'I will ask Abba, Doctor sahiba.' Fazi could not believe that she would be working with Doctor sahiba. Katya wanted her to train as a nurse but Fazi's Abbu did not agree. His responsibility was getting his daughter married, not giving her any training or work. So, Fazi was married and had two children within three years. Now this was the third, which had not reached full term. When Fazi came for her second child's delivery Katya told her, 'No more children, Fazi. At least not for another three years. You have become very weak.'

But she was pregnant again before her son was three months old. Katya had not been able to recognize Fazi that day either. With messy hair half covered with a dirty dupatta, and with a yellow face she had sobbed in front of Katya. She'd had a recurrent pain in her lower abdomen since her second pregnancy. Katya had told her to be careful, 'Don't go anywhere near your husband. He doesn't have a brain.'

Fazi started crying, 'I cry all through the night. He just doesn't care. If I say anything he threatens me that he will get another wife.'

'So, let him get another one, at least you will be at peace….'

Some sediment of emotion darkened Fazi's face. Two beautiful children and her own prematurely decaying body. She must have also loved her husband, otherwise why would she be frightened by the threat of another wife? Katya prescribed injections and medicines but she couldn't abort the child. She thought she would make Fazi agree to an operation after her delivery. But Asad the ironsmith called himself a simple follower of God, family planning was forbidden for him. He just kept staring down, frowning at the floor.

In other words, doctors should not interfere in matters of religion. Just take care of the patient, that's all. There is no shortage of doctors in the city. It was Fazi who had insisted on coming to Dr Katyayini. She was a stubborn, stupid woman. How many people can Katya educate? Daya, a patient of epilepsy, was almost beaten to death by people who thought she had been 'possessed'. When she collapsed after the beating, her father-in-law thanked the shaman thinking he had accomplished something great. He went to the shaman's house with a basket of fruit but shied away from any suggestion of medical help.

It was a combination of poverty and ignorance which prevented people from seeking medical help. Where would they get money for expensive medical care?

Katya froze in front of Fazi's blue body. She took out the dead child after an operation but Fazi never regained consciousness. Once it seemed her eyelids moved, but then nothing. She kept staring at Katya with her eyes open.

In the corridor Fazi's mother was trying to console the two

crying children in her arms while she herself was shaken with sobs. Fazi's husband stood there, head bowed, staring at the door of the emergency room.

'Take her away.' Katya couldn't say anything else. Not even two words of sorrow or sympathy. Nothing!

It was raining outside. The sky was merging into a black sea of rain and fog. Dense fog which seemed to be settling inside Katya's chest. Her head was bursting with pain. She thought, I will go home, take an Asprin and rest for an hour or two.

But where was the rest? Mangala Mausi was waiting at home with another headache inducing problem. Tara! She was one or two months pregnant with a child which must be aborted immediately at night by Katya before any neighbours or relatives got to hear about it. The shameless Tara might not be too worried about the impact of the news spreading and Mangala Mausi would keep her lips sealed, while cursing herself for having given birth to such a daughter, but Tara's father Dinakak would either kill both of them or he would commit suicide if he heard. Katya was exhausted but Mangala's desperation was stronger than her tiredness. She reassured her aunt and called Tara into her room to listen to the details.

'Nothing is hidden from you sister Katya. There is nothing that I can deny.'

'But what have you done? Did you ever think what a disaster this would be for your family?'

Tara was ready to explode. She burst out, 'I am not bothered about my family or honour or decency. I have not been brought up in your kind of environment, nor do I have your background or education. All I know is that I am imprisoned in a house. There is a woman there who, every afternoon, shuts herself up with some strange women in a room, after ordering me to make tea and pakoras. She has not given me the right to know who I am serving or why. Father? He sits in a corner of the vott, the sitting room, wrapped in a blanket, smoking a hookah. When his asthma troubles him he shouts, 'daughter, daughter' and asks me to rub his back and make some kehwa for him. For the rest of the time I do not exist. But yes, I do have brother, who is an invalid, confronting death everyday while he is still alive. I live in the midst of this stink of death. Is this a home, a family?'

'Tell me sister, Katya! Would you be able to live in this house even for a day?'

❧

Spirits of a Haunted House

The weather could be wayward and changeable but in winter, it crept into the folds of the old decrepit houses standing shoulder to shoulder in the narrow lanes and settled down, refusing to take its leave.

Tara said, 'I have never been outside my street. Here it is always winter which sits shivering under a blanket throughout the year.' Mangala, who efficiently performed all her household chores in the dim light of a zero power bulb, was very unhappy when she first came to this neighbourhood. These narrow streets filled with the stink of dead fish, early morning sounds of curses and fighting, shouts of hawkers, and the noise of animals being taken to the slaughterhouse, were so very different from her cool and tree shaded house in Vicharnag where the early morning breeze wafting across the Vicharnag lake, carrying the sounds of hymns from the temple, would awaken her so gently.

Tara said the house was haunted, but Mangala was not afraid of spectres and ghosts. How could she be, she was a ghost herself!

Katya felt this was a bit too much. She had heard that Mangala and Dinakak used to live in a four storeyed house in Vicharnag. Their father had handed over the house to his three sons. A well settled home where three brothers lived with dignity, where the *Bhagvatgita* and the *Ramayana* were recited every day....

'And that house was burnt down during the riots in 1931. They were hardly given any compensation!'

'Katya, I am glad I didn't see all that. Had I seen it I wouldn't have been able to live in this contaminated environment at all. I would have run away as soon as I could. How would I have got used to this poverty?'

Poverty! A well settled home! This poverty had not allowed Prabha didi, who was married into a well-to-do home, to rest in peace because in that house she was constantly taunted about her poverty.

Her father-in-law held his forehead in his hands and said, 'The goddess of wealth, Lakshmi, has left us ever since this girl from a poverty stricken home entered out house.'

'Tara, don't forget Prabha's in-laws themselves came and asked for her hand.'

'True, because my brother-in-law was besotted by her lovely face but as soon as she entered the house he forgot all his responsibilities towards her. He never seems to be aware of anything that is happening around him in the house. A gentle, good, woman like Prabha didi is born only to bear pain and discomfort. And she too will never make the mistake of opening her mouth to protest about anything.'

'She should talk to Jijaji, he could speak to his mother and father...'

'Had I been in her place I would have taught my mother-in-law to respect me. Poor didi is trying to live up to the old traditions... Almost as though she is possessed by the ghosts of these traditions.'

'And you, of course, are the rani of Jhansi,' Katya would joke.

'I could have been, but the warrior woman inside me was stifled in this haunted old room. I should have gone to Delhi or Bombay with my uncles. At least I would have been able to enjoy a smidgeon of fresh air and sunshine.' Katya was familiar with Tara's stifling, dark world and she could understand the desire of the caged bird to escape into the open sky, but running away from home was not the answer to Tara's problems.

Tara, however, could not think of any other solution. 'The ones who went away escaped this dismal world. Both the uncles left. One to join the army and the other one was taken to Bombay by a friend to make him a film star. That left Babuji, who had grown old before his time paying off the government loan. Then there was his asthma as well as the burden of his son's illness. Now he sits in the corner of a dark room, gasping and groaning, annoyed with the world, cursing his family.'

'But Mangala Mausi is a very good housewife and hostess, Tara. She maintains relationships with everyone. She doesn't let any visitor leave without a cup of tea. She doesn't have a list of grievances like you.' Katya was quite impressed by Mangala mausi.

'Some tantric sadhu has told Ma that she shouldn't let any visitor leave without offering him tea. She is under the influence of spirits and if a spirit or ghost visits her in the form of a guest it might forgive her because of her hospitality.'

Katya scolded Tara. 'She is your mother, and since when have you started believing all this rubbish about ghosts and spirits?'

But Tara wouldn't be silent. She herself had seen ghosts, she had heard knocks on the door in the night. A childhood memory was indelibly etched in her mind. When she was very small, one day she was awakened by deep, grunting sounds which were coming from her mother's room. With a loudly beating heart and shaking legs she tried to peer in through a chink in the closed door. Babuji was not in his bed. The demon was bending over Ma grabbing and shaking her.

She was barely ten years old at that time, she couldn't even shout. Suppose the demon heard her and grabbed her? At that time the army uncle and his daughters Nikki and Gudiya still lived in the house. When Tara told them the story about Ma's room they were also quite confused.

'Who could it be? Mushran? No, he comes looking like an old man wearing torn old rags. Was he old?'

'I don't know.' Tara had just heard voices.

'It could be a ghost. It shouts and cries at night to frighten people.'

'But it wasn't crying....' Tara was sure about this.

Nikki was quite knowledgeable. Her nani had told her a lot about ghosts. She even knew about wicked spirits like 'Rihs' and 'Dayans'. But these spirits only tried to capture men, not women. They tried to entrap them by taking on the form of a pretty woman. Nani knew everything.

In the end Nikki gave up. She tried to reassure Tara and told her not to be afraid. She said there were a lot of ghosts and spirits in the neighbourhood but they wouldn't come into their two-storeyed tiny little house because they needed a lot of space to march around. Yes, the 'greh devta', the residing deity, lived in every house. Aunt must have committed some sin so it had come to catch her. The 'greh devta' wants the house to be pure doesn't he?

'Greh devta? The one who steals the clothes of sinners and knocks on the door at night if the people living in the house do anything wrong?'

'Yes, that's him.'

'You are right, you wretch! I remember Ma wasn't wearing any clothes.'

Katya burst into laughter when she heard this, 'You crazy

girl! It must have been your Babuji, not any greh devta. This Nikki has also lost her senses.'

'Perhaps.' Tara seemed to agree with her but as she grew older and saw men taking on the form of demons she decided she had to get rid of them.

The first time, Tara thought of getting rid of Sudarshan, that red eyed, ugly demon with his fleshy mouth and moustaches, who came to the house in the afternoon or evening under the pretext of giving medicines and injections to her ailing brother. A man for whom Ma would run and fetch warm bakirkhanis and ask Tara to make kehwa with almonds and cinnamon. Tara felt like throwing up when she looked at the doctor's eyes, they looked like they were drooling! Once, seizing the opportunity, she had sent him away from the door saying that, 'There is another doctor upstairs who has come to see bhaiya, Bapu says now he will take care of him.'

When the doctor did not appear for a week after being sent off Mangala went to his clinic to request him to come. On her return she gave Tara a solid beating for what she had done and also burst into tears. Tara realized that if Doctor Sudarshan did not treat Ajay bhaiya he would die. Ma would have to make some payment for all the free medicine samples, bottles of medicine and injections because Bapu had no money. What did Mangala have except her body? A body that, even in middle age, was fair and well built, which had not darkened despite her bending over a smoky fire while cooking greens and rice everyday.

Mangala would hold her only son close to her as he coughed incessantly, she would put her face next to his and wipe the dirt from his fair fever warmed face. If only she could take her son's illness into her own body! Mangala could not stand by helplessly watching his body waste away at such a young age.

Ajay's illness was no ordinary problem. He needed medicines, injections, fruit, milk. Dinakak would hand over the hundred and fifty rupees of his pension money to Mangala but that was all he could do. He did try to approach some of his friends and neighbours for tuitions but they expressed their sympathy and said, 'Dinakak! You are so frail and your chest is racked by asthma. Sit at home and rest, now. This is not the age for you to be working.'

Dinakak became even more dispirited and shrunk into a corner in his dark room. Mangala did not go anywhere to ask for anything because she was well aware of the decorum of a reputable family. 'Will she disgrace the family by going from house to house sifting rice?'

'Has anyone in your past seven generations ever washed anyone else's dirty dishes?'

But Mangala will not allow her son's life to wear away. She bowed before God, 'I don't know what is right and what is wrong, I just know that my son Ajay has to live.'

Ajay had to be saved. No one knew how many times the cheerful, jovial Mangala moved through dark blind alleys, how often she came close to the door of death and moved away through narrow lanes and crossed the limits of her body. She had left all explanations, definitions of sin and goodness, life and death at the threshold of her God.

'You know Shambhu! You know everything! I have surrendered everything before you!'

'Doublefaced, hypocrite! She will rot to death.' Tara closed her fists in anger. 'She has one foot in the grave and she is still thinking of physical pleasure.'

Physical pleasure or the pleasure of moving beyond the body? Who was going to ask Mangala? She was a demon after all! But Tara's veins were boiling with a lava of complaints. Tara was not sent to college. She was not allowed to go out anywhere. She was given two sets of clothes that she had to wash and wear alternately. She was handed some skeins of thread, and was told to sit and embroider some sheets. They will be part of your dowry and the bridegroom will materialize from somewhere. In the meantime take care of the cooking and waste your youth away!

Those days even the sky seemed to look sad and grey, burdened with sorrow. Tara would lie down opposite the kitchen window after washing the utensils. Looking for a sliver of blue where memories of childhood would fly around joyfully. The younger uncle was fond of measuring the vastness of the sky. Why and for how long would he be content to stay on in this dingy haunted house?

Her memories of childhood were linked with Nikki and Guddi. The dusty courtyard bore the marks of their feet as they twirled around playing their games. Then uncle was posted to Poonch and Nikki and Guddi also went away. And with them her childhood. While she attended school, the companionship of her friends helped her to survive. Tara even had one or two minor love affairs of the filmy kind. But these experiences were wiped out by Ajay's illness. All that remained was a dark abyss inside.

'Then what is all this?' Katya heard Tara's story patiently and then came down to brasstacks. 'Who is it?'

Tara kept quiet. As though the story had suddenly come to an end. But Katya would not rest till she knew the truth.

'What can I say, didi? Whatever I thought was right turned out to be wrong. And it seems it is my fault. I am the one who has to bear the punishment.' Tara's voice broke.

Katya put an arm around her shoulder, 'I am your sister, Tara. I will try to help you if you tell me the truth. Tell me the facts without any fear. Do you love the boy?'

'I had become like Devdas's Paro. I would linger about the roof for just one glimpse. If I heard his voice the lane which stank of fish would fill with the fragrance of flowers.'

'You haven't told me his name, Tara.'

'Bhaiya's friend Pushkar. If you really need to know. '

'Dr Wali's son? The one who is studying engineering in Punjab?'

'How…how did you meet him?'

'He came here during his vacation. I met him a few times last year. This time he came to meet bhaiya almost every day.'

'And you gave yourself to him just like that, without thinking about anything? You seem to know a lot about affairs of the heart, Tara!'

Tara didn't lose her temper.

'I understand what you are trying to say, didi! You are thinking of that boy who, years ago, came to meet me at the Badamwari near Hari Parbat. Actually that wasn't love, it was infatuation. Just a means of getting a reprieve from the boredom and loneliness of home. I was very lonely after Nikki and Guddi left. During that time I met him in the street while passing through. Pushkar is the only person I have ever loved.'

'Has he promised that he will marry you?'

'Katya, I did not calculate before falling in love. It just happened. Those days I would be sitting near bhaiya either putting cold compresses on his forehead or cleaning up his spit and phlegm. It was not an ideal situation for love. Pushkar would take a piece of cloth from my hand and put it on bhaiya's forehead and just glance at me. He would never say a word.' Katya did not interrupt Tara's flow of words.

'To tell you the truth, he did not promise me anything. This time when he came he took me out of the house two or three times on some pretext or the other. He was worried that I might also catch T.B living in that damp and closed atmosphere. He would take me out on the pretext that I needed sunlight and fresh air.'

Katya wanted to know, 'Do you still love Pushkar?'

'Didi, Pushkar is a part of me. It is a strange fire which has consumed my heart and body. There are no regrets or complaints. I have no resentment against Ma either. I really don't know when I handed myself over to him. But I have no regrets for what has happened. I was crazy, didi, he was on my mind all the time. The breeze would be perfumed by his touch. If a crow called sitting on the parapet I would leap up to open the door in case he came and turned away without knocking on the door.'

Katya hugged Tara. Love really loosened all the knots inside and taught a person to flow. Tara had never before seemed so sincere, so true.

Katya met Pushkar first and then Dr Wali. Doctor sahib was an open minded man, he also respected Dr Katya though he could not really understand the need for such a hurried wedding. Dinakak finally moved out of his dark corner into the light of the wedding and gave his daughter away. He was very worried, how would everything be arranged? But Mangala stood delighted in front of her God with her hands folded, 'Whatever you do is for the best, Shambhu! What do we ordinary people understand of your reasons?' Mothers after all begin to make preparations for their daughter's weddings much before their fathers notice that the girls have grown up.

Katya stayed with Tara till the day of the wedding and watched astonished as Mangala rushed around. She had to admire Mangala mausi's intuition and X Ray vision when she whispered in Katya's ear, 'The child will be born seven months after marriage won't it? My Ajay is also a seventh month baby....'

The neighbours were stunned. Who could have guessed that Mangala would be so wise? She had held up the crumbling walls of her house on her shoulders. Looked after her ailing son and married her daughter in a good family! Now Dinakak also walked around proudly, had his asthma been cured as well ?

Even those people who objected to doctor Sudarshan's frequent visits had to accede that Mangala had guts. The intellectuals referred to the story of King Tujin and said it proved that if a woman was wise she could save not only her home but an entire kingdom. Patience and courage! What else does one need to fight against adversity?

Katya tried to imagine what else Mangala must have done to fight against illness and to save her empty house. She also wondered what her next step would have been if Katya had not managed to convince Dr Wali. An illegal abortion?

But Katya could not think of anything because Mangala had left everything to God. Her deliverance, her death, everything was less important than the family. After all, her home was Mangala's first priority, her greatest responsibility. In her words, 'God has said, 'Do your duty' and he will take care of the fruit of your actions.'

❧

Gauging the Depths

O my beloved, sanwariya! Hold me close, my Natwar Giridhari!

The desire for the beloved Krishna trembled on the waves of melody sweeping through the sleeping neighbourhood, piercing through the dome of the sky. Sanwariyaaaaa!

Words that may have sounded childish during the day touched a soft warm corner of the heart in the silence of the night. The restless moon sailing across the sky began to slip into the arms of the Vitasta.

Lying on her bed Katya watched the innocent play of the moon and the waves through the wire mesh window. As though she were seeing it for the first, no, the second time! Years ago, as she stayed awake at night, feeling restless after meeting Tribhuvan, her nerves had experienced the intoxication of the play of the sky and the earth. She had dreamt of the narcissus and the bee. But since that day so much water had flown under the bridges of the Vitasta. Now, she was a successful resolute doctor, who was earning the affection and praise of older members of her profession. Today she had the courage to try and soothe the wounded heart of a doctor like Kartikeya. But this sudden upsurge of pain? Was there some reason for this discomfort of the heart and mind? For this voice arising from some lonely corner of her being? Was it Kartikeya? Or was it still Tribhuvan? Whose memory was this call bringing back to mind? She just could not sleep.

After her MBBS Bakshi sahib had sent her, at government expense, to the All India Institute of Medical Sciences to do her specialization in Gynaecology.With the understanding that after completing the course she would return to her state to serve her people. Katya was happy about this and she came back and got a job in the government hospital. And now after so many years the past had come back to haunt. It wasn't as if she had never thought of Tribhuvan in all these years but she had almost forgotten to think about herself in her enthusiasm and preoccupation with her new job.

Today, during this unexpected meeting after so many years, Tribhuvan had taken the liberty of addressing her as 'Doctor No nonsense!' Suddenly all those days which she had kept safe for years, like goldfish in an aquarium, had seemed so worthless! Merely immature emotionalism!

In the gynae room Katya had completed the check up of a heavyset female who suffered from high blood pressure and asthma and who had become the mother of three children in five years. Giving her some necessary instructions Katya had expressed a desire to meet the woman's husband.

'My husband? Should I call him?' The woman stammered with the fear and apprehension that have always been a part of the heritage of her gender.

, 'Don't worry. I am not going to complain about you nor will I give him an opportunity to scold you.'

Katya tried to cheer up the woman and added jokingly, 'After all your husband has done a praiseworthy job by making you give birth to three boys in five years, aren't you going to give us the opportunity to meet him?'

When Tribhuvan made his appearance as the husband of the woman Katya was taken by surprise.

'Namaste.'

'Namaste, you?' From where did he appear suddenly?

'Yes, it is I, Tribhuvan. I thought you might not recognize me.'

He should have been delighted to see a friend after so many years but here there was just a faded apologetic smile. Katya put her stethoscope on the table and pulled the pad towards her to write the prescription. She needed a few moments to pull herself together.

'I am seeing you after many years, though I have been hearing a lot about you.' Katya's voice was noncommittal.

Tribhuvan scratched his ear. Had he remembered something? But Katya did not even want to remind him. 'Is she your wife?' she asked.

'Yes.' Tribhuvan spoke without looking at Katya.

'Please sit, comrade Tribhuvan!'

Katya looked at the man standing before her. This well fed man wearing three or four rings with different gemstones on his fingers, whose tiny pot belly was an indicator of his prosperity, was the husband of this asthma and blood pressure ridden, weary looking woman. For some reason Katya's voice became brusque. Anger? Tiredness? Or awkwardness in the face of the unexpected? But Katya is a doctor.

'Your wife is extremely anaemic. It isn't easy to give birth to three children in five years. This is also a form of oppression, comrade.'

Katya emphasized the word 'comrade.' This was the height of negligence towards his wife. Wonderful, comrade! What happened to your philosophy? All that talk about the equality of women and their rights? Katya had heard the story of the death of the comrade and of how an ambitious, opportunistic man had taken his place. A man who, immediately after intermediate, had married the only daughter of Aftab Kaul, the tehsildar of Baramullah, so that along with gold, silver, utensils, suits, transistors, watches etc., he could also demand a fat cheque to pay for his engineering studies.

'Tribhuvan has found a rich match.' Chandra had teased Katya, 'You were very impressed by him in college. You should ask him if that progressive philosophy, that enthusiasm, the lectures were just meant to impress fellow students.'

Katya remembered what Chandra had said. She glanced at Tribhuvan as she was writing the prescription. His forehead was furrowed. He hadn't liked Katya's statement. But Katya hadn't really said anything much. She had merely reminded him that he was supposed to fight for the welfare of the oppressed.

'So, all your sympathy for the downtrodden only lasted till the end of college. I was under the impression that by now you would have joined Sadiq sahib and become a politician or a leader.'

A shadow passed over Tribhuvan's face. He was not used to being reprimanded. Trying to make light of things he said, 'Good! You still remember your college days. But since then the state has been through a lot of turmoil. A politician like Sheikh sahib is languishing in jail and fear of Bakshi sahib's police officers like Goga and Ganderbali has made it impossible to speak up in rallies and gatherings. Giving a lecture is impossible. The Peace Brigade has been created to destroy any opposition. Progressive newspapers have almost been banned.'

'But Sadiq sahib was the president of the Constituent

Assembly and later he even became a minister in Bakshi sahib's cabinet…' Katya wanted to understand Tribhuvan's mindset. What did he really think?

'How long could an experienced comrade leader like Sadiq sahib last in Bakshi sahib's cabinet? Setting aside Bakshi sahib's efficiency and good nature, the Bakshi Brothers Corporation dominated our politics and their repressive measures ensured that our groups would not be able to bond together. Finally Sadiq sahib and his group including D. P. Dhar, Mir Kasim and others resigned and created the Democratic National Conference. But despite this Bakshi sahib continues to assert his dominance.'

Tribhuvan became agitated. When his voice took on the stridency of an argument Katya decided to change the topic. 'Comrade, for centuries people have played complicated moves in the chess of politics, some of which are right and others that are wrong. In that world our individual inclinations or faith cannot play a very significant role but we can keep our personal lives clean. If we compromise here then we are squarely responsible for our actions.' Tribhuvan's face hardened. He felt that Katya was trying to put him down.

'I don't know which personal choices you are talking about. If it is wrong to be ambitious then I have been wrong. I wanted to become an engineer. I got a seat in Benaras Hindu University but my father wasn't a lawyer Munsif. You should be able to understand that Dr No Nonsense.' There was a sting in his words but then Tribhuvan was naturally upset by the fact that Katya had brought up the topic.

Katya started smiling. That is what her friends in college used to call her. Miss No Nonsense.

'I can see that you also remember a lot of things from our college days. What you seem to have forgotten are the passionate lectures inspired by progressive philosophy, the rousing sounds of "The ardent blood of youth runs through my veins," and how you were injured in Habbakadal trying to stop the strike called by the Jan Sanghis …Tell me, am I wrong?'

Katya's smile lessened the tension in the room. 'I haven't forgotten, but it is true that our group disbanded quite soon. The leaders got busy with their own selfish concerns. Actually the entire atmosphere changed. And perhaps even I gave in to circumstances. But you will have to agree that at least I chose to steal from a millionaire! Even Marxism doesn't forbid this.' Tribhuvan gave a hollow laugh, 'See, I am carrying the burden of his daughter. Give and take. And it is quite a weight!'

Katya was thankful that Tribhuvan's wife was sitting outside. She did not want Tribhuvan to be one of those who insulted their wives for no reason. Her face reflected her annoyance.

'I know we are free to interpret any thought or philosophy in the manner in which we like but nevertheless I don't agree with these lofty thoughts of yours.'

Katya wanted to close the discussion. It was of no use. Bashing your head against a wall and wounding yourself. She advised him about tonic injections and dates for future checkups.

'Now that you are carrying her as a burden you may as well pay some attention to her health, she is extremely anaemic. Her blood pressure is also very high. This time we will have to have a caesarian operation. One more thing! Though it should not have been necessary to say this to you. Please think about family planning after this delivery.'

Katya glanced up. Tribhuvan nodded his head slightly. He picked up the prescription with a clenched smile.

Katya rang the bell for the next patient to be shown in.

Shameless! Brute! She wanted to say but she stopped herself. She realized that walking along a path where 'everything goes', Tribhuvan had gone beyond the limits where he could listen to or understand anything. At night, as she rested her head on the pillow, she remembered her college days. A small incident related to Tribhuvan had given her the first taste of the pain of love. In Agra she had waited for his letters for a year. When they had parted he had said, 'I love you and I will miss you a lot.'

First love! It is never very easy to forget and Katya had not been able to put it out of her mind. It was like a pang that arose from a corner of her heart. Katya wrote many letters. She wrote them and then tore them up anticipating that her unsaid words would somehow reach Tribhuvan. The immature expectations of youth! But there was silence for a long time and the empty corner of her heart gradually filled up with the sands of time. In her pride and obstinacy Katya allowed her nascent emotions to dry up and dedicated herself to her studies. She was not going to become a supplicant.

When Katya returned as a doctor she became so invoved with her work that she almost forgot the time when she had experienced a warm rush of emotions. And now? An unexplained restlessness. But something had definitely happened. In an unexpected manner, without her knowledge. Kartikeya had suddenly come into her life. And Katya had started thinking about herself.

She was busy in her work and wanted to test her own capabilities. She had already won the affection and cooperation of her fellow doctors. Even her seniors were impressed by her skill and her dedication. Dr Hafizullah, Dr Prabha Labroo, Dr Kaul would often ask her to assist them during operations.They would discuss the problems of the patients. When Bakshi sahib came to visit the hospital a few days ago, Dr Hafizullah had pointed towards Katya affectionately and said, 'Soon, patients are going to forget about me and ask for this new doctor. She is becoming very popular.' Katya might have been upset with Bakshi sahib's thuggish 'gogas' but she admired his openness, his good humour and his determination to strengthen ties with the central government.

Bakshi sahib did not allow the poison of dissent to spread.

He used his workers to deal strictly with any revolt but the humanity and big heartedness of this relatively less educated, strong leader was also unmatched. Katya remembered his confrontation with the Plebiscite Front, how he imprisoned politicians yet ensured that their families were taken care of. How he had recently released Sheikh sahib from prison despite all their past disagreements. If Sheikh sahib had not been associated with the Kashmir Conspiracy case why would he have been sent to jail once again? Bakshi could never tolerate any rebellion against India.

Some people said, 'He is a politician. He knows how to get along with everyone and even gather the goodwill of the opposition. Otherwise why would he allow the Plebiscite Front to hold a meeting?'

Others praised him, 'Look at the integrity with which he has implemented the Delhi agreement and then look at his kindheartedness, he helped Farooq, the son of his political rival to get admission into medical college.'

'And his hospitality? He will stuff a Goshtaba into a guest's mouth without even waiting to check whether the person is a vegetarian.'

Was it softheartedness or some emptiness in a corner of the heart? What was it? What forced the elderly Bakshi sahib to marry a girl, Khurshid, who was much younger than him? The same empty corner! Similar to the one in Katya's heart though she believes it is filled with the sands of time.

Tathya also wanted his daughter to take a decision, whatever she liked. Keshav had faith in his daughter. Whatever she does will be right. But it was surprising that even Ayodhyanath Raina, a staunch follower of the rules of Sanatan Dharma, did not scold his granddaughter, order her or insist upon an answer.

Does success create walls between people? Or had Katya left no room for questioning because of her abilities and achievements? Or were these believers in destiny waiting in the hope of some miracle? Katya had no reason to offer for not getting married. Just a disinterested attitude, it will happen, what is the hurry? There was so much else occupying her mind right now. She had forgotten her own dreams while dealing with a world groaning with the pain of illness and suffering. If she did look around her then she was filled with anger and despair at the suffocating lives of women in society. Even educated women unquestioningly accepted the primacy of men once they were married and walked on the path of compliance. Katya did not want to live a life like that.

What could Katya say if her elders questioned her? That sometimes, inexplicably, a simple conversation or the fleeting touch of the hand becomes imprinted on the soft corners of the heart ....Though her relationship with Dr Kartikeya was one of simple understanding yet it gradually made its way into the very depths of Katya's heart. How could Katya, who never took a step without first thinking about it, assume that Kartikeya would be prepared to forget the pain of his wounds and make a new beginning? The two of them did not ask any questions or look for any answers but Katya nevertheless started losing herself in dreams. Does time provide the answer to all questions?

Tribhuvan and Dr Kartikeya' s paths had never crossed. Tribhuvan was close to her once, but Katya could not equate him with Kartikeya whose arrival had once again aroused the desire for companionship within her. She no longer felt the need to agonise over the past. Kartikeya gazed unblinkingly at Katya. God knows what he was searching for but Katya was helplessly drawn towards him. What was there in his face, what did Katya see in his eyes which seemed to envelop her entire being? Who had ever imagined that someone would come into Katya's life and take possession of her?

Kartikeya had almost lost his mental balance due to an unexpected blow, an unthinkable calamity. That day as he entered his house he had called out to Babloo and the crowd collected in his house had responded with sobs and cries of sorrow. Kartikeya had looked around him, his heart full of foreboding, had these people come to meet him or to reveal some terrible happening? Unnerved, he had called out to his wife Sunaina. But where was she? The fortitude which had held the whole family together so far had dissolved in tears. 'Son, Sunaina will never come back again. She has taken Babloo and gone far away from us.'

'Be strong, my child. You were only meant to be together for a short while.'

'Who can change destiny?'

Consolation, sympathy, a helpless coming to terms with life. Kartikeya had lost the ability to hear anything. But the people around him narrated the story. Babloo, Sunaina and the Kishtwari servant, Munnu, all three of them had been burnt to death in the shrine of Tula mula. On the very night of the holy festival of Jyesht Ashtami! It was fated to be, otherwise why would Sunaina's sister insist on taking her along? Why had she referred to miracles performed by the goddess and persuade Sunaina that, Babloo who was becoming weaker every day, would be cured if she placed him at the feet of the goddess Ragya?

Sunaina performed her pooja with devotion and stayed awake the entire night. Early in the morning she took Babloo and the servant boy with her to the dharamshala so that both the boys could sleep for a few hours. She would also have a nap, then they would bathe in the stream, perform their pooja and return home. But it seemed as though their desire to sleep was just a ruse used by Yamaraj, the god of death, to lure them to their end. Within half an hour a huge ball of fire arose from the boiling oil filled cauldron in the sweetmeat seller's shop below their rooms and set fire to the entire dharamshala.

The mantras being recited in the temple and the voices of the supplicants raised in prayer were soon interspersed with screams of fear and anguish. The birds nesting in the chinar trees screeched as they flew off into the hollow of the sky.

By the time the stunned crowd had doused the flames with buckets of water and the fire brigade arrived in the courtyard of the temple, there was nothing left in the heaps of ashes except a few pitiful blackened bones. Twelve people died in a matter of minutes –including Sunaina, Babloo and Munnu. Kartikeya almost went crazy after the terrible deaths of his wife and his one year old son.

'Couldn't you even find the ashes of the mother and son?'

'Why didn't she wait for me to come back? I was going to return in three or four days. Why didn't any of you stop her? I would have gone with her.'

Sometimes he would ask questions and then answer them himself. 'Naina used to get blisters in her mouth even if she drank hot tea. She must have really suffered ...' His voice would thicken with tears as he spoke.

'Babloo was as soft as butter. He used to smile and show his milk teeth when I threw him up in the air.' Kartikeya would start sobbing.

'Naina must have called out to me. Why didn't I hear her voice?'

Dr Kak told Katyayini, 'Dr. Kartikeya was my colleague. He had just opened his own private hospital and was doing very well. He was a gifted doctor. Very happy with his small family. Full of laughter. And now, look at him! This accident destroyed his entire world. He had gone to Delhi for a week to attend a medical conference and this calamity happened while he was away.'

Katya had met him once or twice before going to Delhi. An

attractive, smiling face. A wide brow with dark golden coloured, slightly curly hair and eyes which appeared to look into your very soul. He had returned from England just two years ago after specializing in surgery and married a girl of his choice. His son was barely a year old...

Katya was very upset to hear about the accident. She had gone with Dr Kak to express her condolences. But once she was there she realized that it is not possible to share in every sorrow. Kartikeya was lost in some dark, deep space inside himself. Any words of sympathy were meaningless because they never reached Kartikeya.

Her voice full of pity, Katya had gently tapped on his door, 'Dr sahib!'

It was no use. Only the echo of her own voice responded to her. 'Dr Kartikeya!' The doctor's tangled hair had spread over his forehead, his face was as white as chalk.

Katya was not ready to accept this immobility, this stony look. It was an unexplainable resolve. There was some movement in the doctor's eyes that were focused on some faraway point. For a while, Katya looked at his fists, which were clenching and unclenching. Suddenly the half closed window in the room was snapped open by a gust of wind. A few chinar leaves were blown into the room from the lawn. The doctor continued to sit like a statue.

Katya got up to close the window. The interior of the room was silent while outside the wind shrilled and whistled through the leaves. When the silence became oppressive Katya had placed her hand on Kartikeya's restless fists to stop their movement. 'Please, Dr sahib.'

Kartikeya felt the touch.

'Sorry, when ...when did you come ?'

'You were lost in your thoughts. I have been sitting next to you for fifteen minutes.'

'Oh, sorry, I didn't realize.'

'Will you tell me what you were thinking about?' Katya suddenly felt a sense of affection. A realization of Kartikeya's sorrow and suffering.

'No, what is there to think about?' A faint frown appeared on his face and then dissolved.

'Something! Won't you share your thoughts with me?'

Kartikeya tried to articulate the storm raging inside him.

'Katyayini! When the atom bomb was dropped on Nagasaki the clouds of fire covered the sky but no eyewitnesses survived who could tell us about the pain of those who were burnt in that fire...'

Katya held the doctor's hands in hers, hands which were freezing cold! The doctor's eyes focused on Katya's face.

'Don't you think, in such a situation, the victim just dies of shock? I mean Naina and Babloo would not have experienced the pain of burning.' The famous, talented Dr Kartikeya wanted some reassurance. Why couldn't someone assure him that Naina and Babloo did not have to endure the hellish torture of being burnt? Why couldn't someone tell him that they stopped breathing and died peacefully in their sleep?

A surgeon, who had often comforted patients and cured them with his healing touch, was now wandering about like a child in a crowd looking for those he had lost. Suddenly, something had happened to Katya. A wave, a flame of emotion passed through her. She felt like clasping this lost and lonely child to her bosom and wiping away all his fears and worries, saving him for herself. She looked at Kartikeya, he was looking at her with hopeful eyes. Katya bent over, kissed his clenched fists and left.

Kartikeya had quietly participated in all the rites and rituals of mourning without protesting about belief and unbelief. Perhaps in the hope that some of these rituals would give peace to the souls of the deceased. A hope which was so blind that it did not look for any scientific, logical proof. A similar illogical belief, that Kartikeya would become part of her life, gradually began to settle in Katya's mind. By placing her lips on his hands she had, perhaps unknowingly, passed on to Kartikeya the assurance that he was not alone.

❧

A River Must Flow

Kartikeya's father, Kameshwarnath, who was staying with his younger sons in Lucknow, came to live with Kartikeya when he heard about the tragic deaths of his daughter-in-law and grandson. An intensely religious man, he bowed his head before whatever joys and sorrows came his way, accepting them as the will of God. A man sustained by his unbreakable faith in destiny, God was Kameshwarnath's strength and his limitation. Everything that happened was His will.

Kartikeya's mother had passed away many years ago during her seventh pregnancy. How would she have consoled her first born at this moment if she had been alive? Within a few months of the tragedy Kartikeya's brothers and sisters demonstrated their farsightedness by suggesting, though in muted tones, that their elder brother should marry again, he was still quite young after all. Parents of eligible girls were thus immediately galvanized into action. When Janakimaal heard about the marriage proposals being sent to the doctor's house, she heaved a sigh in memory of Sunaina.

Everyone accepted the fact that Kartikeya would remarry. He had to re-establish his household. One cannot accompany the dead after all. But Janakimaal did not live to see, or even hear, that he would marry Katyayini. Kartikeya took a long time to recover and when he did and people saw Katyayini working by his side in the Sunaina hospital they remarked, 'So this is what was brewing all this while! We had no suspicion at all!'

All this gossip reached its climax the day Kartikeya's father Kameshwarnath himself went to call on Tathya, Ayodhyanath Raina. Chanting, 'Om namo Bhagvate Vasudevaye' under his breath, Kameshwar greeted Ayodhyanath and narrated the story of his dream. It seemed that the night before the goddess Sharika appeared in Kameshwarnath's dreams and ordered him to marry Kartikeya to Keshavnath's daughter Katyayini. This was their destiny.

Tathya was quite impressed by Kameshwarnath's piety and faith, he also respected him for having been an honest and dedicated officer during his tenure as a forest ranger, but he felt it was essential to ask Katyayini for her views on the subject. Tathya himself had given her the right to decide her future, so he expressed his inability to make any promises in a hurry, also adding that it was not yet six months since the demise of Katya's grandmother, Janakimaal. If God willed, the marriage could take place once the year of mourning was over. The saintly Kameshwarnath agreed with him, understanding the delicacy of the situation and the bindings of religious observances on Ayodhyanath. As he crossed the threshold on his way out he turned back and addressed Ayodhyanath once again, 'Bhabi's soul will also find peace in this union, after all it is the wish of Mother Sharika.'

Lalli stroked Katya's hair, 'Do you have anything to say, Munni?'

Katya's mind was in turmoil. As though her brain had stopped functioning. A strange lassitude seemed to flow through her veins.

'Say something, my child!'

Katya's voice was filled with an uneasy eagerness, 'He is very lonely, Ma!'

Lalli understood. There was a reason why Kartikeya's loneliness troubled Katya.

'But tell me about yourself, child! Caring for others gives life meaning but everyone has to keep aside some dreams for oneself as well, Katya.'

Katya looked at her mother, where had she hidden her bundle of dreams?

'Have you ever had any dreams for yourself, Ma?'

Katya's question was unexpected. Lalli felt a stirring inside her. She smiled, 'I put my dreams in my children's laps. I want to see them coming true in your eyes.'

Katya insisted, 'Ma, come on, tell the truth.'

'To tell the truth, there was never anything very personal in our dreams, daughter. Throughout our childhood we played with dolls and our dreams were about home, marriage, bridegrooms, jewels, clothes, dreams of wearing new shimmering clothes, chandanhaars, bangles, or of marrying a handsome young man! What else ? Even our dreams were confined, restricted.'

'What about wishes, desires, revolutionary dreams?'

'There were only instructions given by elders, teaching us about morality, family traditions. The ideals of women like Sati-Savitri, the chants of the five sisters, how we should grow, everything was decided for us in advance. Childhood blessings that we should be good daughters-in-law, good wives, good mothers taught us to be obedient once we were married, to walk with our eyes lowered, with our ears shut, obeying the instructions of our elders. Toeing the line was the secret of success. Even our wishes were related to the appreciation of others.'

'Didn't your heart ever want to revolt?'

'Sometimes, but we had to control ourselves, otherwise we would bring dishonour to our families. Those who broke the taboos of society were punished and even their families were ostracised. But let's not tak about the past. Things have changed now, they are not the same anymore.'

'And you, Ma? What did you do?'

'I would just say yes to everything. Because my father had allowed me to study till middle school. Bad-dadi was very fond of me but once in a while she would pass a sarcastic comment. Oh she, she is middle pass. In other words I was definitely going to revolt sometime. So…what could one say?'

'Ma! I think women still haven't changed. Even today a woman is merely a medium to help others achieve their dreams. A necessity in the home. Someone who sits on the left side of her husband during poojas and rituals, like aunt Shanta who has the right to sit next to uncle on religious occasions but whom he treats worse than a dog the rest of the time.'

'That isn't true, child!' Lalli tried to speak on behalf of uncle.

'Let it be, Ma. It is only someone like Manini who has the guts to express her anger by staying in her parent's home for a year. How many women are there like her in our community? They grovel at their master's feet like puppy dogs even after being beaten.'

Lalli heaved a sigh, 'It is true your uncle is the one who has filled Shanta's smiling cheerful world with disillusionment. Leave it be. You father has always been so good to me.' Lalli changed the topic.

Katya smiled, 'You are so good Ma, Babuji doesn't have a choice.'

'All right, stop teasing me and tell me what you think of Kameshwar's dream?'

Katya blushed, 'What can I say Ma, I had thought I would never fall in love but the doctor seems to have captured me.'

'What did he say? Did he talk about marriage?'

Lalli wanted to know more. Kartikeya seemed to be suitable in every way to be her daughter's life-partner.

'He hasn't said anything, but if I am late reaching the hospital he walks around restlessly in the corridor, waiting.'

How could she tell her mother that she herself had been wounded while tending to Kartikeya's pain? If she was not around he lost himself in thoughts of Sunaina, surrounded by shadows of death and that was why Katya always rushed to be by his side.

'For two or three days I put some roses and ferns on his table but then I got busy and forgot to do it. One day, I scolded the gardner for not putting the flowers on the table, he replied, "Dr sahib has forbidden me to do it. He says you will do it yourself." When I teased Kartikeya about this he replied very innocently, "I don't know what has happened to the gardner these days. He puts a bush instead of a bouquet on my table."'

'I don't know why the staff of the hospital have started looking hopefully at me. They are very happy their beloved doctor is getting well. But the doctor himself doesn't say anything.'

Katya stopped for a minute, 'Does everything have to be said, Ma?'

'No, child. I can see that you have become a necessity for him. Something has taken birth within you which you are unable to articulate.'

'Perhaps you are right, Ma,' Katya agreed.

'Kameshwarnath spoke about seeing the goddess in his dreams and her command to marry the two of you. You may laugh at this but this is his way of conveying his wishes, child! He has gauged the depths of his son's heart. After all he is a father.'

Katya was quiet. The depths of the heart! The piercing pain of loneliness. Katya had begun to understand it to some extent, that was why she liked to stroll on the hospital lawns with Kartikeya. In his company the beauty of the white asters and the black roses was revealed gradually, layer by layer. Sitting on the verandah, watching the green earth beneath the rain, the gap between her and Kartikeya sometimes seemed to be a mile wide. She enjoyed drinking coffee with him on the lawn at four o'clock. It was becoming a habit, taking sips of coffee and watching the rays of the sun melting along the sides of the snow-covered mountains behind the shady chinar tree. Katya exclaimed like a child, 'How beautiful!' If Kartikeya looked at her with smiling eyes she was overcome by the desire to clasp him to herself. Katya's being was filled with so much passion that she dissolved at his slightest touch.

Relatives were stunned by Katya's plans to marry because of a command given by the goddess in a dream. This obstinate girl who had challenged family traditions and the dictates of elders, who would have preferred to live alone, how did she give in so suddenly and get married? And that too so quietly, without any celebrations? Only a few people guessed that the secret of Katya's transformation was the dawn of an emotion within her, the emotion that has overwhelmed the hearts of lovers since the days, of Adam and Eve. Tara finally got the opportunity to rub it in, 'I always knew that in such a situation one can do nothing except go with the flow. Now even you will have to agree.'

Katya agreed that she had been so overwhelmed by emotion that she had lost herself and for this she would always be graeful to Kartikeya.

❦

The Meadows of Yusmarg

Night was lying abandoned, asleep in the meadows of Yusmarg. The gentle heat of the bukhari had made the room in the Dak bungalow warm and comfortable.

His thighs were aching and sore with the effort of climbing and descending from Nilanag on horses and perhaps this was why Kartikeya shut his eyes as soon as he lay his head down on the soft pillows. Katya found this a little strange. This nap could have been postponed at least for today. But perhaps this was not merely sleep. It was not physical exhaustion but some inner sorrow that had drained Kartikeya and he did not want its awareness to become a drag on Katya's happiness.

She did not have the courage to challenge this weariness. For a while she lay on the bed next to Kartikeya's, waiting. No, tonight she will not allow him to lose himself in the sorrows and disappointments of the past. The reflection of the faint moonlight coming in through the window spread across the bedsheet. The room filled with voices of the night, the rustling of the leaves, a screech accompanied by the beating of wings, the distant whining of mangy village dogs and then, silence. Katya tried to close her eyes but without success. She felt suffocated. A strange emotion filled her being. She wrapped a shawl over her nightie and came out on the verandah.

This was not an ordinary night for Katya. Why did this long wait seem like a limitless desert filled with shifting sands? Katya had deliberately forgotten herself in her desire to apply balm to Kartikeya's wounds, always hoping that she would finally reach the shores of this sandy waste. Cleaning out the dusty corners of Kartikeya's mind, she wanted to access the depths of his heart. Was she merely deluding herself? Was she being overconfident?

She sat down on the stool in the verandah. A cold blast of wind shivered across her back like a snake. Had their love reached its acme once their relationship received the stamp of social approval? And now were they merely content with the rights that they had gained over each other? Did they have absolute faith in each other or had Kartikeya gone back to the past and was he reliving his first night with Sunaina even as he lay next to Katya?

She was even willing to share Kartikeya's sorrows but why had he distanced himself from her now? After marriage were they following a policy of taking each other for granted rather than of discovering each other? Would they struggle with their loneliness individually all their lives? And love? What of it? Would it gradually become just a boring routine after being converted into a relationship? A numbing realization smothered Katya's emotions. What was the point of a wave that could not touch both the shores as it swept along?

The day had been really pleasant. Not just the day, for the past week Kartikeya had followed Katya like a shadow. But all these intensifying emotions seemed to have been stifled on this beautiful night. Suddenly, without any reason. They had a simple marriage a year after Katya's grandmother's death. Katya had felt her absence very deeply. Nandan had come from America and Mahadjoo came with his sons, Gula and Rasoola, to give his blessings. Tathya had sent him off to his village some years ago after gifting him a piece of fertile land, 'Go look after your family. You have taken care of us for many years.' But Mahadjoo could not forget the children even after he went home. He had brought up Katya and he came to bless her. When Katya saw him she felt she like had gone back to the days of her childhood.

Bhadra, Nathji, Indra and their children came with gifts from Katya's mother's family, saris, a dejharu. Memories of her grandparents filled Katya's eyes with tears. Tathya and Katya wanted social reform but now Bhadra had taken Katya's maternal grandmother's place, how could they refuse her gifts? Wouldn't she be hurt if she were made to feel like an outsider?

The very next day Kameshwar went to visit the temple of his family goddess at Hari Parbat along with the new bride and his close relatives. It was essential to take the blessings of mother Sharika the first time the bride and bridegroom stepped out of the house together. The rituals of Brahmin families had to be observed. Bowing his head before the saffron coloured cliff Kameshwar chanted the prayer to mother Sharika along with the priest. Katya wore a small gem-studded gold dejharu in her ears and a ring with Kartikeya's name on her ring finger. This was the extent of the festivities. Her beloved husband stood by her side, what else did she want? The rhythmic chant of the Sharika stuti echoed from the almond orchards below the temple to the fort situated on top of the hill.

Sitting at the base of the mountain with his son and daughter-in-law and his relatives Kameshwarnath talked almost without stopping. He was deeply satisfied now that his son had begun to emerge from the depths of sorrow and dedicate himself to his work. Kameshwar could narrate stories of interest to atheists as well as believers. He recounted a story related to Hari Parbat. When the gods drained out the water of the lake Satisar near Baramulla, the goddess Durga assumed the form of Sharika and crushed the giant Jalodbhav under a rock that, with the passage of time, came to be known as Hari Parbat. Ever since that time pilgrims come here to pay their respects to this goddess who destroys all perils. The cliff in Chakreshwar, smeared with vermillion powder, has inscriptions written in some ancient script. It is a remnant from the Stone Age, which, because of earthquakes, landslides, floods and other natural disasters, has lodged itself on this hilltop as though it was embedded there with the help of some miraculous machine.

Kameshwar also knew a lot of historical facts. How many people were aware that the fort of Hari Parbat had been constructed by the Afghan governor, Sardar Ata Mohammad Khan for his protection? Or that the long wall that enclosed both the mosque of Akhund Mullashah and the Padshahi gurudwara was constructed in 1596 by the Mughal emperor Akbar?

With the feeling that all was well with the grace of God, Kameshwarnath sent off the newly married bride and bridegroom, 'Go to Yusmarg for a few days. The trip will cheer you up and your tiredness will disappear in the fresh cool air of the pine and fir laden mountains. It is a very peaceful place.' Kameshwarnath did not mention the word honeymoon. They were sensible, they would understand. The car drove through Lal Chowk, the bazaars and lanes, Durganag, Shankracharya and then raced along through the countryside after leaving Badami Bagh behind.

Katya covered herself with a shawl. There was a nip in the early morning air. When Kartikeya saw her shivering he reached out and placed his arm around her shoulders. A wave of warmth spread through every pore of Katya's being. Because of the warmth of the arm clad in a black cardigan or the inviting and intoxicating male fragrance, Katya rested her head on Kartikeya's shoulder and relaxed. Outside the window the passing trees, bushes, meadows and fields seemed to be giving their blessings. The songs of birds filtered in through the chinks in the windows.

Ahead were the winding roads full of red-brown dust. A slight jolt on every curve and the gentle pressure of Kartikeya's arm reminding her of his presence. Santokh Singh, the driver, stopped the car when they reached Chirar-e-sharif.

'Sahib, ask for anything you desire, every wish is granted here. I will just go and pay my respects.'

'Do you want to ask for anything?' Kartkeya probed.

'What can I ask for? I have to give thanks for what I have got.' There was a glow of contentment in Katya's eyes.

'Sahib, my Satinder was barren, we tried all kinds of medicines and finally gave up. Then someone suggested we go and make a wish at the dargah of Nund Rishi. That was it! The heir to the family was born within a year followed by a row of young ones!' Santokh Singh smiled.

Kartikeya's face looked grey. The son and heir! He got his son without asking. Who had snatched him away?

Katya spoke up quickly, 'It is said that even the emperor Badshah participated in the funeral procession of this saint Nuruddin Sheikh.' Kartikeya was still lost in thought. Kameshwarnath had named Babloo Kuldip, the light of the house. That young and innocent light now lay buried under tons of earth.

'My mother used to tell me a lot of stories about the miracles performed by Lal Ded and Nund Rishi when I was a child.' Katya once again tried to distract Kartikeya's attention.

'It is said that when Nund rishi was born he refused to drink his mother's milk. Then Lalli came and told the infant, "If you didn't feel any shame in being born then why are you ashamed to drink your mother's milk?"'

'Yes, what?' Kartikeya seemed to awaken from sleep,'what were you saying?'

'Sahib, I was talking about Nund Rishi. A man who was not only a sufi-saint and a pir-aulia but also a social reformer and poet. But you aren't paying attention to my nonsense!'

'No, no! I was listening, but I don't know anything about the poet.'

'The shrukh written by Nuruddin are very similar to the vaakh's of Lal Ded. You must have heard her vaakhs, papa quotes them so often.'

'Yes.' Kartikeya remembered his father's love of poetry and smiled.

'Papa appreciates poets and shayars. I came here with him once when I was very young. Papa said that the two storeyed mosque next to Nund Rishi's tomb was built by the Afghan governor Ata Mohammad Khan. It is made of poplar wood.'

'But I have heard that it was built during the reign of Emperor Akbar.'

'Many rulers must have renovated it. Oh yes, you were talking about shrukhs.'

'Lal Ded's vaakhs and Nund Rishi's shrukhs are so similar.

Even experts can make a mistake in identifying their authors. Look how beautifully and seamlessly two religions have come together in them.'

'There are reasons for this Katya. Nuruddin Sheikh's ancestors were descended from the Hindu rulers of Kishtwar. During the disturbances around 1320 two of the brothers ran away and settled in Kashmir. Later, one of their descendants, Salarsanz, came under the influence of the Muslim saint Saiyad Husain Samnani and converted to Islam, changing his name to Sheikh Salar. Nuruddin was the son of this Sheikh Salar and his wife Sadarmaiji and was born in 1373. There were no religious distinctions in his life, how could they become a part of his vision and thinking?'

'His wife Zaided was also a Hindu. She too was buried in Khaimu.' The winding road slipped by as they chatted. The royal chinar trees growing between the firs on the hillsides waved their leaves in greeting.

Kartikeya gradually relaxed. Sitting next to Katya, he looked at the young herdsmen with torn pherans and bare legs who were descending the hills with their herds of goats and sheep and wondered how much the lives of these people, living in the lap of bountiful nature, had changed. Despite Sheikh sahib and Bakshi sahib they were still exactly where they were before. Struggling from morning till night in sunshine, rain and snow to earn their meagre daily bread.

'There have been changes, the city is full of new hotels, buildings, wide roads. There is free education, schools, colleges, a university. There is so much that is new.' Kartikeya was not pessimistic.

'And the fabulous bungalows of the Bakshi brothers, the relatives of Sheikh sahib and other political bigwigs! What about those?' Katya interrupted looking at huge houses with spacious lawns.

'Yes, the politicians have become prosperous and this has made Srinagar more impressive.'

'It is good that Karan Singh, the former heir to the throne and the present Sadr-e-riyasat leased his ancestral palace Gulab bhavan to the Oberois giving Srinagar its first five star hotel.'

At times Katya would stop the car near a shallow gurgling stream and splash around standing knee deep in water. Kartikeya would quickly open the door of the car and get inside.

'You are just like a child.'

Katya wished that she could remain a child and bask in the warm sunshine of the smile that had appeared on Kartikeya's face. Ahead were the beautiful meadows of Yusmarg lying in the shade of the majestic fir and pine trees. As soon as they arrived, they were surrounded by local men with horses for hire, 'Please hurry if you want to go to Neelnag. There is a possibility of getting caught in a storm if it gets too late. It is a steep climb through a dense forest. It is advisable to return before dark.'

Katya was full of excitement seeing the dappled, white and black horses. 'Why don't we go just now? I will ride this white horse, and you? That dappled one. It is magnificent.' Katya answered all the questions before Kartikeya could attempt any replies. She quickly took out the mince and paranthas they had brought along. Santokh Singh fetched some water.

'Let's have something quickly. Okay?'

'Why don't we first go and drop our luggage at the hotel?'

'Santokh Singh will take it. We will be back by the evening won't we?'

Kartkeya once again felt that his companion was not Doctor Katyayini but a young vivacious Katya, a little impulsive and very happy. They tightened their shoelaces, put their feet in the stirrups and set off.

Riding through the dense forests on the narrow serpentine path sometimes Katya would move ahead and at other times Kartikeya's horse would take the lead. 'Let's ride side by side please!' Katya beckoned him closer, not wanting even a brief distance between them. A silent, brooding pine and cedar forest. The path covered with dry leaves and pine needles and the wind whistling through the trees. Ishhhhh….ishhhhh! Today Katya has set out on a new path, looking, searching for a new life.

With a slithering sound some animal slipped across the path and lost itself in the twisted and knotted roots of the dense forest. The sliminess of its black skin left her feeling shaken. 'Kartik!' Katya screamed.

Perhaps Kartikeya had also seen it. He brought his horse close to hers.

'I must say you are really brave! You just see a snake and start screaming. Suppose you had seen a lion or a cheetah, then?' He put his arm around her to reassure her.

As they moved ahead the smell of dense vegetation almost made her dizzy. She looked up at the tops of the trees which pierced the sky, the sunlight filtering through the leaves dazzled her eyes. Katya held on to Kartik's arm. Companionship was not enough today! The potent male aroma of her beloved was intoxicating her. Katya could not recognize herself today. The birds were flying around the forest, filling it with their varied chorus. Auspicious sounds! An invitation!

Neelnag was full of lotus flowers and their wide, velvety leaves gazed up at the sky and the cloudds that were slowly gathering. Were those droplets of water on the leaves or beautiful noserings? Were those thickets of trees or a platoon of soldiers standing at attention? The mustard fields wre bathed in light, and the breeze was gently rocking the restless waves on the blue waters of the lake. A sweet intense ache pierced Katya, this was a strange pleasure the like of which she had never experienced before! Why was Kartik so far away?

Kartik was more down-to-earth, more practical.

'It is believed that Nagaraj used to lived in this lake once upon a time.'

'I wish I could swim across the lake from one end to the other.'

'Please, don't even think about it! This lake is forty feet deep and more than a hundred yards wide and it is full of water weeds and water snakes. Even the best swimmers don't have the guts to swim in these waters.'

Kartikeya doused her newfound enthusiasm.

'Yes, I haven't swum across the Wular. But if I drown you will save me, won't you?'

They sat down on a bench nearby and gazed at the waves rising on the lake, agitated by the emotions stirring inside them. Their minds and hearts were thrilled by the gentle caress of the mountain breeze.

'Sages and ascetics must have lived in places like these. There is such a sense of peace amidst these trees, mountains and the greenery. Quiet. And yet expressive despite its silence.'

'Really! And what does it say, tell me, I can't understand anything.' Kartikeya joked.

'Listen carefully! You will be able to hear and even touch.' Katya touched Kartikeya's lips with her finger. He leaned over and kissed her neck. The warmth of his breath almost made Katya's heart stand still. As though molten wax was running through her veins. She held Kartikeya's bent head with her arm. If she did not hold him they would both be swamped by the molten river and swept away and there was no possibility of that in this place. People were already staring at them.

The graceful branches of a willow tree dipped into the water and a bluejay hiding among the leaves flew past them.

'Good luck!' Katya gathered up her dishevelled hair.

'Same to you!' Kartik reached out and ruffled the hair back into disarray.

Both of them started laughing. The laughter spilt across the surface of the lake.

The horse owner interrupted their thoughts, 'Sahib! The sky

is becoming overcast. We should make a move now.' Katya and
Kartikeya got up, bowing to necessity, but they felt as though
a beautiful moment of life had just slipped out of their hands.

Going downhill carefully, the owners of the horses kept the
reins in their hands.

'The horses are familiar with the terrain, Sahib, but there is
always the fear of stumbling on the slippery pine needles.'

'Arre! Don't worry, we aren't such novices.' Kartikeya
stroked the flanks of his horse. 'I have ridden very often in
Khilanmarg....'

'That is true, Sahib, but this girl will get scared.'

Katya was touched by the concern of the elderly man. He
chatted with them as they moved along. Suddenly lightning
crackled through the forest. 'Ya, Allah! Save us!' The old man
muttered. Drops of rain started falling on their faces, arms and
hands. 'It is just a small cloud, it will soon move away! Look!
The sun is shining on the lower slopes of that mountain!' The
man pointed to the sunshine that had lit up the valley.

The wonders of the mountains. Sunshine on one side and
rain on the other! A rainbow across a lush green landscape.
Katya became talkative, enroute she told Kartikeya stories
about Neelnag.

'My maternal grandfather was very knowledgeable about
the *Neelmath Puran*. He told lots of stories about the Nagas and
the Yakshas. It is possible that, during the early period of
civilization, there was settlement in this place where Neel, the
king of the Nagas, lived. After all it was the Nagas who lived
here before the arrival of the Aryans.'

'You are right.' Kartikeya agreed.

'It is believed that earlier when the Nagas, Pishachas and
other aboriginal tribes lived in the valley, the Brahmins used to
spend six months of the year here and the other six in the plains.
Once when a Brahmin, Chandradev, stayed back in the valley
during winter, a Pishacha picked him up and threw him into the

Neelnag. Chandradev related his tale of woe to Kashyapa's son, king Neel, who lived in the lake. Neel consoled the Brahmin and giving him a manuscript of the *Neelmath Puran*, told him to follow its directions in his daily life. Be religious, do your duty, be charitable and do good deeds! All your sorrows will disappear and you will be able to live in the valley forever.'

'This *Neelmath Puran* is supposed to be written by king Neel right? Papa also recites shlokas from it sometimes. He says the Brahmin behaved exactly as he was asked to do by Neel and after that Brahmins lived together with the Nagas, Pishachas, Yakshas and other tribes in the valley.'

'Our festival of Khichdi Amavasya is also connected to this story. There are so many legends, stories and beliefs associated with Neelnag.'

'The true happenings of the time of the *Puranas* have become a part of legend. Gradually, with the passage of time, the truth enters the collective consciousness as myth and legend. If you go deep into it you discover the truth of history. Apart from what is said in the *Neelmath Puran*, even geographical research has confirmed that the Kashmir valley was a vast lake once upon a time. Archeologists believe that the water was drained away by a massive earthquake or sinking of the land. Naturally it must have taken years for the water to dry up completely and that must have been the reason why people migrated to the warm plains for six months every year.'

'Yes, the environment and climate must have changed and gradually people must have settled down and started farming.'

Kartikeya kept trying to find some scientific basis for legends from the *Puranas* and giving information about the original inhabitants of the valley. He quoted Sir Francis Younghusband who felt that Kashmiris resembled the Jews. Some people even believed that Christ himself lived in the valley for a while.

It was two friends and not two lovers who chatted about history, geography and politics as time flew by.

They returned to the Dak bungalow and once Kartikeya had his dinner and lay down he suddenly became distant.

'A blanket is not enough. Take a quilt. It gets very cold at night.' Kartikeya was behaving like a guardian.

'No, it is enough. The bukhari is also lit. Are you feeling cold?'

Katya was little surprised by this mundane conversation. Words can separate people just as easily as they can bring them together.

'No, I am just a little tired. I will go to sleep. Why don't you rest as well? You are not used to riding, your back must be aching.'

'O.K. Goodnight.'

'Goodnight.'

Kartikeya had said her back must be aching. But he didn't try to soothe her pain with his caresses. It could have been a magical moment. A golden day, a starry night, the mist on the mountains, the clouds, Sohni crossing the Chenab clinging to an urn, Nagray searching for Himal, Farhad destroying the mountain, all these could have woken up and come to life in this silent warm night close to Kartikeya and Katya. But nothing happened. The word 'goodnight' put a wet blanket on a beautiful day. Was this the long awaited destination towards which they had been moving with such anticipation? This sad, lonely, colourless night?

And was this the moment when Kartikeya would be overwhelmed, pierced by his memories of the past?

Kartikeya had spoken about being tired. But Katya could traverse the world despite this tiredness. For more than a year Katya had been trying to help Kartikeya heal his wounds. They had become necessary to each other and become companions. Kartikeya had also moved along with the flow but suddenly, at this moment, he had withdrawn. This retreat was very difficult, very painful for Katya. Perhaps also for Kartikeya.

It was very painful, even insulting for a companion. What was the point of having a friend who would not help to ease your pain? These were the thoughts that raced through her mind. Kartikeya's wounds are deep. But for how long is he going to carry the past with him, returning to its painful moments again and again? Kartikeya can share those moments with Katya, why does he cling to them alone? What happened, however tragic it was, should not be allowed to disturb the present. It was wrong. Kartikeya should not allow the past to bring his present to a standstill. This night belonged to Katya. She wasn't looking for any embellishments but she did want to share a few simple moments with Kartikeya. She would not stifle her budding desires under a blanket of understanding and compromise.

An insistence very different from the obstinacy of childhood! It might seem stubborn but Kartikeya would have to take the first step. Katya pulled the shawl up to her forehead, she felt very lonely surrounded by the forest of Deodar trees. The wind seemed to pierce her ribs. Why had the turbulence which had melted the boulder in her heart quietened down once the rituals were over? Was this inevitable?

In the east, ash coloured clouds were interspersed by golden rays. Soon the sun would be up trying to spread warmth into the depths of the valley. The birds in the woods were exhilarated by the fresh morning breeze. The night had come to an end.

Katya had fallen sleep sitting on the stool. She woke up startled by the chirruping of the birds or the force of the breeze. Kartikeya was standing before her, with his hand on her right shoulder.

'Were you sitting like this the whole night?' She was touched by the emotion in his voice.

'No, I like looking at the forest in the silvery moonlight.'

Kartikeya was looking guilty.

'Why didn't you wake me up, I would have also enjoyed the moonlight with you.'

A knot inside Katya refused to unravel.

'Never mind, let's leave it. I can be moody and behave quite childishly sometimes. You were tired and you might have caught a cold....' The politeness was a measure of their growing distance.

'How could I feel cold with you next to me?' Kartikeya's words were making her weak.

'Even when I was a child I used to be called crazy, I would keep doing such weird things.' Katya's voice trembled or at least Kartikeya felt it did.

'Please Katya, please dear! Forgive me!'

Kartikeya came closer, 'I don't know why I was feeling tired. I fell asleep as soon as I put my head down on the pillow. I didn't even remember that you were still awake! I am really sorry....' Katya got up to go back into the room.

'Arre, come on, what happened...why are you so upset? The night is meant for sleeping after all....'

Katya couldn't find the right words. Her anger flowed from her eyes and she stubbornly turned away. She wasn't so weak that she would melt on being cajoled. Kartikeya stopped her midway and clasped her in his arms. Katya couldn't say anything because Kartikeya had placed his lips on hers. He wiped away her tears of wounded pride with his lips.

'This night was not meant for sleeping. I was a real boor.'

'What were you supposed to do, go lion hunting?' Katya tried to behave normally.

'Come on let's go, I need to sleep some more....'

'It is morning, the bearer will be here soon with the tea.'

'I have put a 'Do Not Disturb' sign on the door.'

'Please, Kartik.'

'Are you still angry? I said sorry!'

'I wanted to talk about you tonight.'

'But the night isn't over yet. Tell me, where should I begin?'

'Don't joke. Today I only want to hear about you.'

'I am not joking, I am serious.'

Whatever Kartikeya may have been, he was definitely not a fool. By sitting on the verandah, shivering the whole night, Katya had pulled him from the past into the present, a present in which Katya was his beloved bride, beckoning him with passion, love, hope and unspoken reproach.

Katya found herself melting. Kartikeya's arms had caused confusion in the very fibre of her being. Like the pre-anaesthesia agitation and then the gradual numbness which pervades the whole body. Kartikeya's hands kept awakening her body as his lips measured the warmth of her passion. Moving from her neck, chest and navel to the very source of her being, climbing the heights, gasping, slathered in sweat and then slipping down into the valleys of Yusmarg. Katya's body was rigid with tension. Breathless! Kartik kept his passion under check, again and again. Untangling knots, peeling open layer after layer until Katya decided to go with the flow to save herself from the flood. She clasped Kartik in her arms.

Bathing in the spray, splashing each other, they arrived at the point where passion and fervour were transformed into tranquil contentment.

'You wanted to say something?' Kartik recollected his promise.

'Um, not now.'

'Tomorrow?'

'Yes!'

They slept in each other's arms satiated and sweaty in the gentle breeze of the morning. A bluejay flew in and sat on the windowsill watching them with wonder.

Outside the sun was peeping from behind the pine trees, but here the night had not yet come to an end.

Butter, Tea, Chang and Gompas

Vijaya would never have gone to Ladakh if a three-year stint at
the frontier had not been compulsory and if she hadn't been
worried about how Prem would manage for food while he was
there. Hadn't Kathbab nanaji told her how, when he and nani
went to Leh, they travelled over hazardous roads for fifteen
days on horseback, carting their luggage on mules? Miles and
miles of barren mountains and the Zoji La pass. The paths cut
into mountains were so narrow that if a horse shied away, it
would roll down into the abyss on the left. Nani's thighs were
raw by the time they finally arrived at Leh, passing Sonamarg,
Kargil, Lamayuru, the river Sindh and god knows how many
other places. And her screams of fear were lost in the roar of
the Sindh river the time Nana disappeared around a bend in the
mountain leaving her completely by herself in that lonely spot.
Vijaya stated categorically that if something similar happened
with Premji then only her dead body would reach Ladakh. She
would definitely have a heart attack.

Prem teased her, 'Arre bhai, which world are you living in?
Now aeroplanes, buses and even jeeps go to Ladakh. Why
should you have to ride a horse? This is unnecessary panic. And
I will be with you. I will even scare Death away.'

There was another reason for Vijaya's reluctance, Pamposh
and Bulbul. She knew Ma and Babuji would not let them go and
she couldn't live without them. However, it was necessary to go,
and her fears came true. Pamposh and Bulbul stayed back with
their grandmother. Kamalavati said, 'No, I will not send the
children there. It is bitterly cold and what will you do if they get
chilblains? You people go, I can't stop you, it is a job after all!
You can cook for Premji. Go. Mahaganapati will look after you!'

Vijaya cried as she got her luggage together. Her mother-in-
law handed over a lot of bundles and bags. You won't get this

there, you won't get that there! There was a bundle of dried greens. You will long for vegetables there. As they were leaving, Vijaya held the children close to her chest.

On the way, she wept as though she were being sent into exile. Prem was also upset but he couldn't sob like Vijaya. The mountains beyond Sonamarg were frightening. It would be the end of them if they hit a bus or jeep coming round the blind corners. Deep crevasses, canyons and gorges and the roaring sound of the river. Vijaya was so scared that she closed her eyes and leaned back against the headrest of her seat. Prem tried to keep her busy by chatting with her. Vijaya opened her eyes and then closed them, just mumbling yes and no to his chatter. Through the noise of the moving bus she heard the story of the brave general Zorawar Singh who had swept through this rough terrain 'in those days' and managed to conquer Ladakh and make it part of the Dogra durbar in 1839. She also heard about the Amritsar Treaty between the Dogra durbar and the British in 1846, which made Ladakh a part of Jammu and Kashmir.

Prem also mentioned that the people of Ladakh were racially close to the inhabitants of Tibet. But Tibet had been taken over by China. Vijaya knew about the Chinese invasion of 1962, she had donated two gold bangles for the war effort. She knew that China had already occupied Tibet at that time. She was completely shaken up by the time they reached Kargil and cried silently, resting her head on Prem's shoulder. How would she stay so far away from her loved ones in this barren empty land?

Prem tried to comfort her, and kept giving her lemonade to drink. He spoke about the history and geography of Ladakh, narrated incidents about Gilgit, which was surrounded by the mountains of the Himalayas and the Karakoram. He told her how in 1947 the Muslim officials of the area were incited by Pakistan to rise in revolt and imprison the governor Dhansharsingh. Vijaya halted her sniffling for a moment to raise her head and look in the direction of Gilgit, which was now a part of Pakistan because the British official Major Brown had raised the Pakistani flag there.

But she couldn't see anything in this rugged land surrounded by China, Russia, Pakistan, and Afghanistan except a vast, boundless desolation. There was no sign of greenery. How would she spend three years in this place? Just the thought of it was frightening. Wouldn't she feel suffocated?

But Vijaya wasn't stifled at all. Engineer sahib received a warm reception on his arrival in Leh. When they reached their lodgings there was a reasonable sized crowd of eight or ten Kashmiri families awaiting them. The postmaster's wife Sampatdedi, appeared to be their leader. Junior Engineer Kaul's wife had brought a five-tiered tiffin carrier stuffed with food.

'You have gone to so much trouble....'

Vijaya didn't know how to express her gratitude to these strangers. She had not expected such an amazing welcome. Sampatdedi insisted that they have tea and paranthas and also established some connection with Kamalavati!

In the morning the postmaster's daughters, Nimma and Vima, knocked on the door as soon as Prem left for office.

'Bhabi! Ma has asked you to come over.'

'Just let me finish my work!' Vijaya gestured towards all the stuff lying around.

'Why should you do the work, Bhabi? What is the use of the servants?'

Vima explained that Vijaya only had to call out and servants would immediately be at her service. After all she was the wife of Engineer sahib. In this place even the headmaster had one or two servants.

Now there was no scope for loneliness. Today there was a shirchai party at Sampatdedi's. Bhotanis, Ladakhi women, had come to sell real pearls. The junior engineer's wife Rupavati had bought four strings of pearls for her daughters. Such beautiful pearls and as cheap as pieces of glass! Vijaya would also get a pearl necklace made for Pamposh. Sampatdedi had bought two Lhasa carpets from a Ladakhi for her two daughters. Now Lhasa had been captured by China and there was no possibility of buying anything.

'Real pearls, good quality carpets, wool, silk…you can buy anything.'

Nimmi was an irritable girl who was also quite forthright. 'Engineers have a great time here, Bhabi. There is a budget of crores for digging tunnels and cutting roads through the mountains. How many roads are made, how many are washed away and how many are accounted for on paper, even the planners themselves do not know. The people here are very simple, credulous, happy that at least something is being done. Who is there to keep account?'

'Hm!' Vijaya wasn't too happy to hear this.

'Now Bhabi, if the engineers and overseers don't get some small offerings from this amount then what is the point of their coming to this barren land?'

'But everyone is not the same,' Vijaya couldn't restrain herself.

'Everyone might not be the same but people are influenced by each other. And the entire department is taken care of. There are very few honest people like Mukundjoo, overseer, who stuck out like a sore thumb. He wore a tika from his nose to his forehead, recited the Vishnu Strotam and Bhavani Sahastranam and went home in six months without having earned anything. He was of no use here. He wouldn't make any money himself nor would he let anyone else earn it. '

Vijaya looked carefully at Nimma. Big eyes, wheatish complexion, slender build. It was difficult to guess her age, between twenty five and thirty perhaps. Unmarried. Vimma seemed to be a few years younger than her and hadn't yet lost her ability to laugh. Postmaster sahib came home merely to sleep. He was out the whole day. Sampatdedi was the one who performed the roles of the mistress of the house, caretaker, consultant and gossipmonger for the entire neighbourhood. She, naturally, found it necessary to give some advice to Vijaya.

'I am delighted by your concern for your husband but there are some things you have yet to understand. After all you are still young. Who does your husband work for? His family. But has any man ever been capable of looking after a household? Tell me. So, whenever the opportunity arises set aside two or three hundred, maybe even four hundred rupees. You are going to spend that money on your family aren't you? And it doesn't feel good to ask your husband for money all the time. Then at moments of need when you take out the money even your husband will be impressed by your common sense. A woman is like a bank, bahu! Always ready to help in times of difficulty.

Vijaya listened to Sampatdedi as she went on, 'And that Chunni, Master sahib's daughter. She is mentally unbalanced. She was involved in a love affair with the son of a millionaire. May God burn my tongue! I too have daughters and daughters-in-law, but I cannot deny the truth. It is impossible to hide it. I believe she was expecting his child.'

Vijaya had seen Chunni. A veil drawn over her forehead and two vacant looking eyes. As though the plateaus of Leh had formed a barrier between her and that rogue who promised her that he would marry her but never returned. His mother had said she would kill herself. An engineer son! Did he want to make a fool of himself by marrying the daughter of an impoverished schoolmaster? Chunni sits by the window of her two-storeyed house, looking down at the bazaar and the road, humming to herself, 'O swimmer, dive down into the depths of the lake of love and find my diamond which has been lost.' Hope did not die easily but where had the love gone which was meant to be their reason for living? Vijaya was overcome by sadness. Prem tried to cheer her up.

'Come on let's go and visit the gompas. You will feel more at peace. Why do you waste your time with these idle women?' They visited Spitok, Rejong and the viharas of the tantric lamas. They heard the prayers of the lamas in their monasteries. Chanted the mantras 'Om Mani Padme Hum.'

They went on horseback to see the fair at Hemis, twenty five miles from Leh. Prem had always been fond of riding. In Hemis they saw the masked dance of demons. Pamposh and Bulbul would have been frightened, the masks were ferocious. Vijaya was overawed as she bowed before the two-storeyed image of the Buddha in the Leh monastery. But she was also filled with a sense of peace. There was a glow of contentment on the face of the Bodhisatva. A peace beyond life, death, happiness, sorrow, infirmity or anguish. During the circumambulation they also rotated the brass prayer wheels. Vijaya was surprised to see that even their horses did not move ahead without going round the gompas.

Shaven headed lamas, wearing long robes, were sitting in the huge domed hall of the gompa with the radiance of the supreme spirit on their expressionless faces. The breathy sound of voices rising and falling in prayer seemed to come from another world, where man did not indulge in violence and where everyone loved peace.

Life went on as usual. On Navreh, the Kashmiri new year, Doora came with some prasad and chatted with Vijaya for an hour. Her conversation was very different from Sampatdedi's instructions and inquisitiveness. Vijaya liked this sensible woman. As they were chatting she suggested that Vijaya could teach some older women if she had an hour or two to spare. Doora taught the latest knitting patterns to some Ladakhi women. The women here worked with wool anyway, they just needed to be taught different designs.

Doora explained, 'These women knit sweaters, gloves etcetera. I send these to Srinagar and help to sell them. They earn a little money this way. They are very hard working, but they are exploited a lot.'

Doora was not educated. She narrated her story without being asked. Sometimes relationships grew almost on their own, without any effort. It was the same age old story of the troubles of a widowed daughter-in-law. But here the difference was that Doora was not willing to stay and listen to the constant taunts and scoldings of her in-laws about her being unlucky and ill-fated. She decided to marry Trilok, the compounder, though she had no idea that the Hindu Code Bill, which legalized widow remarriage had been passed. Both of them needed each other.

Doora told her the story of Sampatdedi's son's ill-fated marriage, which lasted only one night. Vijaya felt sympathy for the aging woman who had two young marriageable daughters. Every morning she would open the trunks filled with clothes for her daughters and air them and put Phenyl and Kuth to protect them. Some day, a beautiful bridegroom would come and marry Nimma and Sampatdedi would go and bathe in the Ganges to thank the gods.

Nimma was becoming thinner and more irritable. Vimma had managed to protect herself but for how long? She went to Masterji for tuitions as she was appearing for her B.A. privately. Quayum also went there to study. But apparently Quayum's father had been transferred to Rajauri so he would be leaving. Would Vimma be able to hold on to her smile? Soon she would also be sitting by the window looking out at the empty road, waiting endlessly. Her mother would alternate between hope and despair, collecting dowries for her daughters.

In the wordless silence of the night, the king's palace looked forlorn sitting on the hill. Sampatdedi persuaded her daughters, 'Nimma, Vimma, why don't you take Bhabi to see the palace?'

Vimma was always ready to go, 'Let's go tomorrow, Bhabi! Diddi you will also come along, won't you?'

Nimma shook her head, 'No, I don't want to go.' Why was Nimma so stubborn?

'There is nothing there, just a crumbling palace. Not a single human being around. Just owls and bats. I feel uncomfortable in such a lonely place. It is very depressing.'

'No one lives there today, but just imagine some time ago, the king and his courtiers must have stayed there. It must have been full of pomp and luxury.'

Vimma's eyes sparkled. She dreamt of the king. Nimma could only see the ruins and her mother merely wanted to assert the fact that there were palaces once upon a time. Nimma taught in a girls' school. Sampatdedi had not been able to find a suitable bridegroom for her despite all her efforts. The girls were languishing in this desert, waiting.

Vijaya taught for two hours every day in her house. The bhotanis, ladakhi women, took her to their homes a few times. They gave her gur-gur, salt butter, tea to drink. 'Be careful, blow on it before taking a sip or you may get some hairs in your mouth.'

'What? Hair….?'

'No, no, don't worry. The butter is kept in a pouch and sometimes the fibres from the pouch get mixed with it….' Doora explained.

Prem was busy designing roads and bridges and supervising the construction of roads. He went everywhere in his jeep. Mountains over eleven thousand to sixteen thousand feet above sea level. Hazardous roads! Borders guarded by army pickets. Prem was astonished by the spartan lives and the bravery of the soldiers. He wrote long letters to Tathya.

My dear Tathya,
I can't tell you how much your daughter-in-law has changed since she came here. She cried incessantly for the first few days after our arrival. But now she has innumerable friends, sisters and sisters-in-law. She has also taken

on the responsibility of teaching some bhotanis and has become quite an efficient teacher!

Tathya, I am also very comfortable here. The local people are very hard working, simple and religious. They love their culture and blindly worship their lamas. But they are backward. Ladakhis are very far behind the rest of Jammu-kashmir as far as education is concerned. Nor do they have enough medical facilities. Why does the government give them this step-motherly treatment?

Tathya, the soldiers posted here have very difficult lives, one really feels like bowing one's head in respect to them. They come from the plains, far from their families, passing through desert plateus, mountains and passes to protect us, but do we really take care of them? My hair stands on end when I recall the Chinese aggression in 1962, Tathya! Krishna Menon and Bijji Kaul were partly responsible for the incomplete information and suggestions but even the other political leaders played a role in the debacle. Here in Ladakh there are Chinese pickets in the areas near Chipchip. They have occupied the Aksai Chin plateau and it is obvious that they have stashed a lot of arms and ammunitions there. I am surprised by the naivete of our leaders who claimed that they would throw out the Chinese if they ever crossed the international border. Our soldiers were badly equipped, there were no roads which could be used to supply them with rations and arms. I think we were so busy with our domestic problems after Partition that we did not pay any attention to the security of our international borders. All this compounded by Nehruji's unshakeable faith in the Chinese, which was shattered by those he considered his friends.

Tathya, the people of Ladakh are very close culturally to Tibetans. Kushak says that when the Chinese occupied Tibet over five hundred Ladakhi monks were being trained in Lhasa. It is hair raising to imagine how the Dalai Lama and his attendants were spirited away in the space of one night, and what difficulties they faced as they made their way through the rugged mountains in order to reach Tawang. They must have been constantly afraid that the Chinese would appear at any time.

There are a lot of problems here, Tathya. The local leaders are worried about the preservation of their culture. Masterji, Sridhar Dullu, has tried to awaken the people and Ladakhi young men respect him a lot. Kushak Bakula is upset that Ladakhis have not received benefits related to the panchayat and agriculture. I feel Ladakh will never receive fair treatment till it is given the status of an Autonomous Hill Council.

Everything else is fine. Don't worry about us. I am busy with my work. I don't do anything wrong, though I do drink a little chang with Kushak sometimes. It is necessary in the cold. Chang is drunk during religious festivals, consider it to be Somaras, the drink of the gods! I hope you won't be annoyed.

Tathya, I hope Pamposh and Bulbul don't trouble you? Give our love to Ma. With respect and love

Yours

Prem

Vijaya and Prem had a good time in Leh and perhaps would have continued to enjoy their stay if it hadn't been for a couple of incidents, one of which almost turned Vijaya into the destructive goddess Kali. Actually Prem was a little drunk that day and in his inebriated state he groped a Ladakhi woman who had come to the house. Vijaya had gone to Doora's place for some work and when she saw her husband swaying around fiddling with the woman's robe she just went up in flames. Prem immediately came to his senses and apologized to the woman. Vijaya made him grovel for a week, making him sleep alone, having his meals served by Rasoola and giving him the silent treatment before she magnanimously decided to forgive him.

The second incident had a far greater impact on their lives. What happened was that two Junior Engineers and a senior officer were dismissed from service for taking bribes. Prem was not accused of anything but he was transferred out nevertheless. Not to Srinagar, which would have made him jump with joy, but to the Poonch sector in Jammu. Prem felt the warning bells ringing in his head and decided that he would give up his job with the state government. Anything could happen here at any time. He could be falsely implicated in someone else's crime. Perhaps it was time for him to leave.

Khudai Manzil

> Humpty Dumpty sat on a wall
> Humpty Dumpty had a great fall

Little Daisy, her shoulder-length hair decorated with red and yellow ribbons, was clapping and singing, as she and her friends made a circle around the roly poly Shabbir Mian, alias Bablooji. Sitting on the verandah of the bungalow, Zeba was shelling peas and keping a watchful eye on the children. Grandmotherly concern.

She remembered the games of her childhood. Friends holding hands and whirling around, leaving footprints in dusty courtyards, dancing, laughing, breathless, singing songs filled with the notes of mynahs, not this Humpty Dumpty rubbish. A loud scream accompanied the line, 'Had a great fall'. Zeba pushed aside the basket of peas and scrambled up, but by the time she finally managed to get up, the girls were wiping the slippery grass from Bablooji's grazed knee and threatening him even as they cajoled their little brother.

'No one cries when they are playing. If you are such a sissy don't become Humpty Dumpty next time, we will make Thabloo Humpty Dumpty! Cry baby! Cry baby cry. Put your

finger in your eye, and tell your mother, it wasn't I!' Daisy
started chanting to tease Babloo.

'Ya Khodaya! What a stupid game. You silly girls, you are
really brainless! Couldn't you find anyone except Babloo to
make into a scapegoat in your game? Move aside....' Zeba
scolded the girls.

When Babloo saw his grandmother coming towards him
with open arms his screams gave way to sobs and he ran and
threw himself into her lap as she tried to soothe him. At the
other end of the huge lawn Rehman sahib, sitting in a lawn
chair, heard the scream and, abandoning his hukkah, came
towards the children followed by the gardener and the guard.

Babloo was picked up and taken into the bungalow so that
some Dettol could be put on the graze. It was a minor wound,
Allah be praised! Children often hurt themselves while playing.
There was nothing to worry about. Inside, the daughter-in-law
called up her husband, Babloo's father, and received a small
scolding for not looking after the children properly as well as
instructions that Babloo should be taken immediately to the
dispensary for an anti-Tetanus injection.

Rehmanjoo, who has now become Rehman sahib, shook
his head and watched Babloo being transported to the
dispensary. These days Rehman sahib often felt depressed for
no reason. There was no shortage of anything. It had taken
seven generations of poverty for Rehman the tongawallah to
become Rehman sahib. It was the grace of Allahtala. Could
Rehman ever have dreamt of such luxury? Whatever he had
been unable to do, his son had done. A bungalow with three
cornered gables, lattice work verandahs and carved ceilings.
Standing alone and unique in its beauty like a lovely woman
in purdah covered with sweet smelling jasmine! Its slanting
brown roof and stained glass windowpanes looked down
benevolently on passersby on the road that led from the Tourist
Reception Centre towards Shankaracharya. If only Ashi had

lived to witness the luxury of Khudai Manzil, the prosperity of her son and grandson and heard her grandchildren chattering in English.

Childhood had also changed with time. Even today Rehman remembers the two roomed hut with mud walls and a roof made of burj patra where he used to spy through the holes in the curtain as Ashi examined pregnant women. Now there was a solid, bewhiskered guard in a pathani suit guarding the main gate of his house.

Rehmanjoo spent half his life distributing National Conference party pamphlets. He finally understood politics in the fourth quarter of his life and, with the blessings of Bakshi sahib, became a member of the Mohalla Committee and, for a brief while, an officer in the Municipality. But it was his son Kasim who contested the elections, became a member of the Assembly and enjoyed power in the real sense of the term. Kasim respected his father. He entered the party after completing his studies and was given a ticket to fight the elections. It was his duty to fulfil the unfinished dreams of his father.

The house was full of life. Now there were Shabir, Murad, Babloo, Thabloo, Hasina, Sugra and Daisy. The cousins who numbered almost twenty were all studying in Burnhall on the Convent and spoke fluent English. God had blessed their home, Khudai Manzil. The daughters-in-law wore salwar kurtas not pherans. They wore gold ornaments. Ashi wore silver earrings, even in old age, but Zeba was lucky enough to wear gold in the autumn of her life. The younger daughter-in-law sometimes wore saris at parties though thankfully, she hadn't completely given up the veil. The granddaughters wore short skirts and walked around looking just like foreigners.

It was good. The clothes people wore had to change along with the passage of time. Rehman was aware that this change was not merely because the world around him had changed, but also because his status was now different. The only thing he regretted was the fact that the children had forgotten the old greetings. Good morning and good evening were all very well, but one's own customs, manners? Were they then to be forgotten?

Rehman's sons Quayoom and Kasim studied in the local 'jabri' school. Ashi insisted on sending them to school saying that they would at least learn how to read and write. These free 'jabri' schools were started by Maharaja Pratap Singh for those children whose parents could not afford to educate them. Quayoom did not study beyond class five but, thanks to Sheikh sahib, Kasim was admitted to the Government High School. He passed his Matric, became a school teacher, but he was destined to join politics and become a leader.

The elder son became a prosperous fruit merchant. His sons also studied in the Heddo Memorial School, his daughters were now grown up and studied in the Women's College where Miss Mehmooda was the principal. It was good. The state had made progress. The boys and girls were getting a good education thanks to Bakshi sahib. Rehmanjoo was happy. But he was also a little upset. He did not feel he was in sync with the world around him. In fact, he felt somewhat alienated. This was the time of Sadiq sahib. Rehmanjoo belonged to an earlier era. What could be done? After serving Bakshi sahib for ten years he found it very difficult to change sides.

Smoking his hookah, Rehmanjoo often discussed the situation with his friends and elders. He was an experienced politician and knew that no relationships are permanent in politics. One person's beliefs were different and another person's justice was different. Those who were friends today could become enemies tomorrow.

Whether it was Maharaja Pratap Singh, Sheikh sahib, Bakshi sahib or Sadiq sahib, their relationships were as changeable as the colours of a chameleon. And the behaviour of kings and rulers could be even more astonishing. It was said that, in the tenth century, Queen Didda even killed her own grandson! And what could one say about the sultans and Afghans? In the fourteenth century Sultan Sikander's mother, Hoara, assassinated her own daughter and son-in-law. The Ladakhi Rinchin took shelter with King Sehdev and later killed his vazir Ramachandra and took over the throne.

Rehmanjoo set aside the hookah and went into the bungalow. Zeba was busy in the kitchen, giving instructions to the cook. The drawing room door was open. The room was strewn with soft carpets from the shop 'Subhana the Worst' and an antelope head mounted on the wall glared at passers by. The exquisite carving on the walnut wood centre table was evidence of the talent of Kashmiri craftsmen. He had seen this kind of luxury in Gopal Bhan's house in his childhood. There was nothing lacking in this house. It was an indicator of Kasim's standing in society. Ministers and other important people often came to the house for banquets.

Rehmanjoo thanked Allahtala once again. He lay down on his bed thinking he would have a short nap but he couldn't go to sleep. His memories unwound before him like a movie reel in motion. The Kamaraj Plan! God knows what that was meant to be! Kamaraj sahib, who belonged to Tamil Nadu, suggested that the chief ministers and cabinet ministers of the state should resign from their posts and work for the Congress Party. God knows whether the Plan was meant to strengthen the Congress Party or whether it was meant to create problems for Morarji Desai so that he couldn't take over as Prime Minister after Nehru. The same political plotting! Rehmanjoo could not think so far ahead.

Since the Congress Party had no presence in the valley, the Plan could not be put into action in Jammu and Kashmir. But look at the wonders of destiny! Despite this, Bakshi sahib, in his wisdom, went off to Delhi and handed over his resignation to Nehru who immediately accepted it.

Rehmanjoo felt upset. He was convinced that Bakshi sahib's

resignation was harmful for the state. He was such a great man. Whatever people might say, he had definitely made a place for himself in the political history of the state and in the hearts of the people. After this resignation there had been a lot of turmoil in the valley. The Secretary of the National Conference, Bakshi sahib's cousin, Abdul Rashid, opposed it very strongly. There were processions, meetings, slogans demanding that he take back the resignation. Not surprisingly, those members of the Conference who leaned towards Pakistan suddenly changed their stance and approved of the resignation. The Sadiq group of the National Conference stayed in the background, pleased with the developments. Despite Bakshi sahib's friendship with Sadiq sahib, there was internal rivalry between them.

Finally, after all the trips back and forth between Delhi and Srinagar, Bakshi sahib had proposed that Khwaja Shamsuddin be the new Chief Minister and he was duly elected by majority vote. Before relinquishing his post Bakshi ji announced, in the Legislative Assembly, that henceforth the Sadr-e-Riyasat would be called the Governor and the Prime Minister would be called the Chief Minister. But how long did Shamsuddin sahib manage to rule?

The chinar leaves, which could be glimpsed from the window, were blazing. This was autumn's gift. When the fire inside became uncontrollable, even the greenery started reflecting the blaze. There was a swing suspended from a thick branch of the chinar for children. The plank of wood was swaying in the breeze. There was a carpet of golden leaves below the tree. Rehmanjoo leaned back and enjoyed the celestial game of changing seasons reflected in the falling of the old leaves and the birth of the new ones.

He has witnessed many blazes in the past. The riots after Sheikh sahib was arrested in Gulmarg were such a calamity – there were hundreds of deaths. Arrests, beatings, people shouting Zindabad, Murdabad! It seemed the state would never recover, but it did. Bakshi sahib took firm control of the state though he was shaken by the riots that followed the Sheikh sahib's arrest. He spent three days in his house surrounded by guards. Sensible patriots like Ghazi Abdul Rehman, Ghulam Mohammad Sofi and Saifuddin Makhdoomi led a huge procession through the city which was joined by more Muslims than Hindus. What slogans they shouted! 'Long live Hindustan', 'Long live Bakshi Ghulam Mohammad!' Sadiq sahib addressed the rally when it reached Polo ground. He gave a rousing speech, told the people to have faith in democratic India and justified the arrest of Sheikh sahib. The procession went to Bakshi sahib's house to assure him that the people were with him. He came out of his house and addressed them, explaining why certain events had taken place. And then, ten years after that day Bakshi sahib resigned and Shamsuddin took over. But for how long?

Rehman remembered that unfortunate day, 27th December, 1963. How could anyone forget it? The sacred Moye Muqaddas was stolen form the dargah of Hazrat Bal.The news spread like wildfire. Crowds of people came from Anantnag, Baramulla, Shopian, Sumbal, Shadipore, Miraj, Kamraj and many other places. Religious sentiments were jolted. Men, women, children gathered in the dargah.

How did anyone have the courage to touch the sacred hair from the beard of the Prophet which was kept safely in the dargah and which was only shown to the believers gathered in the mosque on special occasions? It seemed a thief had broken a window of the mosque and taken away the Moye Muqaddas. The valley was filled with grief, and mourning almost to the level of madness. People turned against Shamsuddin and even Bakshi sahib himself. His shops and cinema hall on Residency road were burnt down. The Kothi Bagh police station was burnt to the ground.

Shamsuddin sahib was completely at a loss. An 'Action

Committee' was constituted under the leadership of Mohammad Said Masoodi and Sheikh sahib's son, Farooq sahib, also became a part of it. The search began.

That night no one ate anything in Rehmanjoo's house. The entire valley was covered with black flags. Rehman recalled the Sadr-e Riyasat, Karan Singh's visit to the dargah to pray for the return of the holy relic. Many of the old men present fell at his feet saying, 'Our king has come. He will do something, now we will get back the Moye Muqaddas.'

Many senior officials were sent to the valley by the Government of India including B.N Malik, the director of the Intelligence Bureau. Lal Bahadur Shastri also came. A plan was made. All guards were moved away from the Hazrat Bal dargah for twenty four hours to give the person who had stolen the holy hair the opportunity to put it back quietly. And a miracle happened! The holy relic was found back in its place on the fourth of January.

The Pakistani Radio Azad Kashmir however, kept spewing venom, claiming that the hair was a fake. Then, to confirm the authenticity of the hair, the 80 year old devout Sufi, Mirak Sheikh, took the tube with the hair out into the bright light in the packed hall in the mosque. Lal Bahadur Shastri, Karan Singh and many other dignitaries were also seated in the hall. Rehman sat in one of the last rows, holding his breath, waiting for Sufi Sahib's decision. After inspecting the relic minutely, Sufi Sahib finally declared, 'It is real! It is real!' The entire nation started to breathe again! Kitchen fires were lit in homes! Bakshi sahib declared, 'This was the handiwork of the enemies of the nation.'

Sitting in jail, Sheikh sahib made many accusations against Bakshi sahib and called Shamsuddin his stooge.

Someone said, 'Bakshi sahib's mother was ill and she expressed a desire to see the Moye Muqaddas. It is possible that her son arranged for the relic to be removed to fulfil her wish.'

The Jamaat-i-Islami turned completely against Bakshi. Some people claimed it was the work of Pakistani agents. Whatever it may have been, Shamsuddin had to resign, and Bakshi sahib had to suggest Sadiq sahib's name for the new Chief Minister.

So, these were the varied colours of politics that Rehmanjoo had experienced. While you were sitting in the chair you were the boss, the benefactor. And once you were removed, no one recognized you.

Sadiq sahib was an educated, sensible, secular leader. But it was during his rule that relations between Hindus and Muslims began to deteriorate. Drawing room politics, this was what the people who knew Sadiq sahib called it. You couldn't run a state from your drawing room!

Numerous incidents took place during his rule.

Rehman can't forget 11th September, 1964. A group of boat dwellers attacked the houses of the Battas in Chinkral mohalla. They dragged the Batnis out, cut off their dejharus and molested them. The fight began over a piece of land. Why would anyone steal away their land? The hajis, the boat people, wanted to construct a shed and this became the reason for the fight. It was just an excuse, nothing else.

The Matt hajis incited other Muslims to join the fight. Mahanand Kaul Pir from Malapore appealed to Sadiq sahib and explained the situation. But there was no justice. The matter went up to Lal Bahadur Shastri. Nehru had passed away. Many Battas openly said that it was dangerous for them to stay on in the valley. Barriers began to grow between people.

At that time people began to recall Bakshi sahib's administration. Would such an incident have ever occurred during his rule? Then there was the incident of Parmeshwari, the daughter of a poor widowed woman from Rainawari, who ran away with Ghulam Rasool Kant, in 1967. That had really created a lot of ill will. The Pandits had meetings, took out processions saying that a young, immature girl had been forcibly converted to Islam. The entire city was gripped by tension. The Pandits appealed to India. Our religion is in danger.

Rehmanjoo had spent his life in the company of Pandits, eating with them, living with them. He did not like this mutual enmity. If the girl was not an adult then why was she forced? The politically aware Kasim argued with his father, 'Abba, the girl is going to be eighteen. She wants to marry Ghulam Rasool who works as a cashier in a department store. She herself has taken the decision to convert.'

Rehmanjoo said, 'Hindus and Muslims have inter-married earlier, why weren't there any riots at that time? When Jaya became Jamila Bano there were no processions. It is a different matter that her parents were very unhappy. Whatever has happened this time is not correct. Keeping a poor girl confined in the store till late, threatening her, all this seems to have been done deliberately. When an F.I.R. was lodged then the Battas should also have been included in the enquiry committee. There has been unnecessary bloodshed and relations between communities have been spoilt.'

'Babba! But many attempts were made to find a solution. The Congress President, Mir Kasim sahib said that the girl should be lodged with a third party till the investigations were complete....'

Rehmanjoo took a deep breath, 'God knows what is true and what is false. But a lot of questions remain unanswered, my son. The enquiry committee never gave its report. It said, "The girl converted to Islam on the 20th of July. She married on the 28th and was abducted on the 3rd of August. How could she live with her Hindu mother after changing her religion?"'

'The real thing is that the causes for this Batta agitation are deep rooted. This was, in effect, a call for justice. They were worried because the seats reserved for them in education had been decreased and they also felt their religion was being threatened. And those who were killed in the riots, are they ever going to come back?' Rehmanjoo remembers that terrible moment when ruffians pelted the funeral processions of Maharaj Krishan Razdan and Lassakaul Badam with stones.

Rehman was wounded the most by Nathji's demise. By the fact that his friend died in this agitation and Rehman could not do anything. Bhabi Indira was left alone to mourn for the rest of her life. Her elder son had got into bad company and had already run away to Punjab, no one knew where he was. Her younger daughter was a nurse in the hospital, and she took care of her mother and her younger brother. A really independent young girl. How can one fight destiny?

Rehmanjoo couldn't do anything. His son Kasim refused point blank, 'Abba huzoor! Don't do anything that will make people look at your son with suspicion. I am a part of politics and you know, that in this world there are no loyalties.'

But Rehmanjoo did visit Indira bhabi once to offer his condolences. He cried like a child when he placed his hands on the children's heads. Politics had not made him forget his basic humanity. Indira bhabi handed him a glass of water and with tears in her eyes said, 'He never forgot you! He used to tell me so many stories about your childhood together. Then you went into politics….'

That day Rehmanjoo felt truly regretful that politics had given him material wealth but it had taken away his true, heartfelt relationships. He had lost a dear friend like Nathji because he was too preoccupied. Lost in his thoughts he did not realize that the sun had set and night had fallen. He had travelled very far into the past.

The cook came to call him, 'The dinner is laid, huzoor!'

Rehmanjoo got up, supporting his knees. These days his knees were giving him a lot of trouble. His bones were also creaking.

His son was sitting at the dinner table waiting for him. Thank God. Rehman must have done something good, otherwise which son waited for his father these days? There were beautiful carved silver dishes and Rehman and his son sat and chatted as they ate. Every morning and evening. During the days his son was busy with politics and had no free time.

'Abba, did you put any balm on your knees? Tomorrow I will talk to the Orthopaedic surgeon. We must meet him.'

'Arre, this is nothing, child, it is just old age. Don't worry. Creaking bones, gout, sciatica etcetera are gifts of old age. They are healed only in the grave.'

'You will live for a hundred years. Even your beard isn't white yet.'

'What will I do for a hundred years? I have already established my roots, with the grace of Allah.'

'We have to send Shabboo sahib abroad to study, Daisy has to be married....'

The elder son Qayoom didn't talk much, if he spoke at all it was only to discuss profit and loss.

Questions often arose in Rehmanjoo's mind for no reason. Perhaps because he knew that, like politics, in life also there were no permanent solutions or answers.

❧

Floods

A dark and fearful night. The full throated roar of the Vitasta pierced through the silence of the night and did not allow Tathya to sleep. Sleep does not come easily when one is old and this destructive avatar of the river, as it rushed along eroding its banks, added to the disquiet in his mind. Who knew when this flood of muddy water seeping into homes through chinks in windows and doors would swallow up the entire neighbourhood?

Tathya closed his eyes once he grew tired of staring into the dark. Suddenly, he felt as though an invisible hand was shaking his bed. The window shutters vibrated and the chains rattled. It was an earthquake! Om Namah Shivay! It had become a habit to call out to Shiva in moments of crisis. Tathya tried to get up from the bed. As he stood up shaking his benumbed right leg, Shiv and Keshav flung open the door and rushed in, 'Are you all right, Tathya ?'

Keshav offered his arm in support. 'It was just a mild tremor. I hope you weren't afraid?' As though Tathya was a little child. When their grandmother was alive, Tathya was still the elder.

Kamli and Lalli insisted on going down to the entrance, 'The flood has weakened the foundations of houses. One or two more tremors and there will be a disaster….' Kamala got very agitated. She ran screaming into the courtyard if there was even a mild tremor. Lalli embraced her sister-in-law, 'We are all together, aren't we?' In other words, what is there to worry about? You are not alone. But then who is not alone?

'He, Shambhu!' Kamala's eyes filled with tears. 'Our household is scattered! Our children have left us ….'

She was upset that Prem had left for Calcutta with his family. Now he would never come back. Sharika had left the valley even earlier. Kamala, who longed to hear the voices of her grandchildren, was also pained by the thought that when she died none of her children would be around to put a few drops of the pure, sweet water of the Ganges on her tongue.

'You crazy woman! Think of pleasant things! Shivnath! Send a telegram to Prem tomorrow. He can take leave for eight or ten days. Kamali will feel more at peace once she sees him.' Tathya tried to console her.

There was a lot of commotion on the other side of the river. The dongas, boats and barges had risen higher and higher in the water and had to be tied down and secured with strong ropes. People had come out half-dressed and half-awake. Om Namah Shivay! Allah have mercy! If the water didn't recede people would have to take shelter in temples, mosques and on the open roadside.

Shiva and Keshava returned to their rooms after settling Tathya down. The elders had handed down the tradition of caring for each other, though the new generation was wandering far and wide in search of livelihoods. Tathya could see the household disintegrating around him and he didn't want to accept it. Even in the midst of change it wasn't easy to give up the desire for a cohesive joint family. Tathya remembered his schoolmaster father, Bablal, Lakshmanjoo Raina, who was so knowledgeable about the *Vedas* and *Puranas*. A man who used to recite, as a blessing, shlokas from the *Atharva Veda* that said that one should never scatter but stay together and flourish. Stay linked together for a greater cause. The basis of this being together was the joint family, in which one cared not only about individual freedom but also about the welfare of the entire family. But now all that was left behind. Tathya could not prevent change from taking place. It was a time which had already become history! Tathya had finished performing his role.

No one could stop the flow of time. Bablal lived the life he wanted to, he looked for new avenues while paying obeisance to tradition. Filled with pride at being a Pandit, he would often tell his son stories and incidents which would make him proud of himself. 'Ayodhya, everyone is not lucky enough to be born in this land of rishis. We have made contributions to religion, philosophy, the shastras, literature, medicine, astrology and in many other fields. The manuscripts created by our ancestors can be found not only in our country but even in Japan, China and Germany.'

'We have had a very unfortunate history, and yet we have given birth to the Sufi-Rishi tradition as well as to Sahaivite philosophy. We have followed our customs without accepting defeat. We have never given up!'

'We have faced so many difficulties. Read Younghusband, he has written that, "In spite of the splendid Mughals, brute Pathans, bullying Sikhs and rude Dogras, the Kashmiris ever remained the same!"'

Babba was a real Pandit. He chanted Shiva-Shambhu, Ram-Ram, He Krishna as he went up and down the stairs. After his prayers, meditation and pranayam, he would perform his duty as the elder of the house by blessing the children and giving instructions to the women of the household. Together with observing birthdays, shradhs and sacrifices he would also praise the king. 'Lieutenant General His Highness Maharaja Sir Pratap Singh Inder, Mahender Bahadur, GCSI, GC-IE, GB, ILLO… our king was no ordinary ruler!'

'Oh, Babba! Was there any end to his string of degrees?'

'Arre! There has never been another king like him on this earth. '

'He was fair to his poor subjects. He appointed Sir Walter Roper to work on Land Reforms and promulgated the "Settlement of Kashmir Valley" law to give the farmers the rights to their lands. He ended the custom of "begar", unpaid labour. He fought wars in Nagarkot and Chitral and stopped the looting on the Karakoram highway which was obstructing trade.'

Babba never forgot to thank God for his daily bread and butter. 'Your deeds, son, your deeds are important. Do good if you can, sorrow and happiness are merely the result of your actions. You experience heaven and hell in this life. The rest is just imagination. Don't you remember what Lord Krishna said in the Gita?'

Babba was always the focal point in any gathering because of his stories and jokes. Stories about the wisdom of his community and its wit. As proof of the capabilities of Pandits,

Babba would repeat Aurangzeb's words as quoted in the 'Rukte Alamgiri', 'If there were any Kashmiris here we would appoint them in our offices.'

Tathya also agrees that there was something that had kept the Pandits alive even though they were reduced to a mere eleven households at one time. Something which set them apart even when they were far away from their own land.

Scattered far away from the home that they had vowed never to leave, they moved to Delhi, Agra, Lucknow, Allahabad. Sometimes they were propelled by necessity, at other times by ambition.

Tathya turned over in his bed. Many faces came to mind, many names surfaced in his memory, including the Nehrus who became famous throughout the nation, Mir Munshi Mohanlal Kashmiri who travelled to Persia and Afghanistan with Alexander Burns, Sir Gangaram who was invited to Ranjit Singh's Durbar, Shambhunath Pandit, the first Indian judge of the Calcutta High Court appointed in 1861, Bar-at-Law Vishwanarayan Dar and Tej Bahadur Sapru who was Law Minister in the cabinet of Lord Reading. There were so many of them.

During the rule of the Mughals, Pandits who knew Urdu, Persian and English, realized which way the winds were blowing and left the valley. They settled in clusters through the land, adopted the habits of the aristocratic nawabs and indulged in poetry, but they never forgot their home, their religion or their people.

Nandan had said, 'Tathya, now there is nothing for us here. I don't want to be lost in a blind cave, I want to achieve something.' Nandan had felt slighted when the Hindu boys, full of hope in the new democratic world, had gone to the leader for guidance and had been told, 'You are promising young men! The whole of India here belongs to you, but where will these poor Muslim boys go?' Nandan said, 'There is no future for our community in this new dispensation. These people will build a

wall between your Lalded and Nund Rishi, indeed, they have
already begun. We will have to go Tathya. How long can we
hide our heads in the sand and deny the truth?'

'Perhaps you are right, Nandan. But those who have left
are constantly pained by the memory of their homeland. It
isn't so easy to abandon the home of one's ancestors. You are
still a child. Your absence is the reason for Keshav and Lalli's
silence. The way their hands halt midway through their meals.
Their desire to feel the touch of cool fingers on a fevered brow.
The question, 'Why, for what reason?' You are untroubled
by questions but as you run ahead it is not always possible to
forget those you have left behind, son. The day you realize this,
the softest corner of your heart will be bruised.'

Tathya felt overwhelmed by grief. Why was it so difficult for
him to accept realities of the changing times?

Outside, black clouds were colliding with each other like
angry bulls locking horns. Many of the mud and wattle houses
of the boatmen would be washed away by morning. If the
Vitasta did not recede soon even Tathya would have to abandon
his home, and suppose it was washed away in the night? Another
Wular lake would have absorbed an entire settlement within its
womb! It was said that the Wular lake came into existence only
after Kalki Rishi cursed the cruel king Sundersen and his city
was drowned in its waters. This valley had borne the brunt of
floods and earthquakes for many centuries.

People living on the banks of the river were terrified. Even
Tathya, feeble and unable to stand on his two legs, was afraid.
At his age he was totally dependent on his sons and daughters-
in-law. Would they save themselves or Tathya? He did not want
to be responsible for putting them in any danger. 'He shambhu!
Protect us.'

But why this fear? Was Ayodhyanath Raina still bound by
attachment at an age when he should be lost in contemplation
of the divine? Two eyes, full of compassion, were gazing at

Tathya in the dark. The reassuring voice of Swami Lakshmanjoo echoed through Ishbar ashram after touching the snow-clad summits of the mountains.

When had Tathya first seen those compassionate eyes? He had been shattered by Madhav's death and Anand Shastri had taken him to this young ascetic who had gained enlightenment at the age of twenty. Tathya was very impressed by this young philosopher, the son of Narayan Das Raina and the pupil of Swami Ramji who had learnt Shaivism from Mehtab Kak. There was something in his gaze that seemed to look into the innermost layers of a man's being, transporting him beyond pain and suffering. Tathya has felt a similar peace and contentment in the hills of Nagadandi, which were the abode of the gentle Swami Ashokanand. A strange aura surrounded him like a radiance. Were the rishis and ascetics who did penance in these Himalayan ranges hundreds of years ago just like him? As the melting snows transformed into rushing streams, the last vestiges of pride dissolved and melted away, and a strange, not unpleasant feeling of nothingness took over. Habba Khatoon called it 'Fanaa-fila.'

Nagadandi was a place of cool breezes washed by the melting snow, filled with the fertile scent of pine and fir trees. Clouds touched the mountains and then peered through trees and bushes coming down so low that they seemed almost within reach. And the rushing waters of the river seemed to quarrel with the stones and rocks as they hastened along.

Perhaps this northern part of the land of Kuru was Alkapuri once upon a time? The cloud messenger of Kalidasa must have sailed over these mountain ranges. Perhaps this was the land of Kalidasa's 'Kumarsambhava'? Sitting there, Tathya had felt that the Hemkunt mountain, which was mentioned by Matli to Dushyant in the seventh section of the 'Abhgyan Shakuntalam' as the place where Kashyap rishi did his penance, must have been located somewhere nearby. This was the land of ascetics like Marich, Dakshayini and Shaklya. One felt at peace here, more perhaps than in heaven.

Tathya thought that Kalidasa Yakshya must have belonged to this place. The story of this land of demons, yakshas, demi-gods and their ruler Kuber, survives even today in the feativals that are celebrated in every home. But the clever experienced lawyer Ayodhyanath Raina could not guess where this land, once hailed in the *Vishnu Puran* as 'Kartaswarakar' or the land of gold, which had become a democracy after passing through Brahmin, Buddhist, Pathan, Afghan, Sikh and Dogra rule, was headed. He could only watch all the tamashas happening outside his house silently. Something was crumbling within Tathya. Even the iron-willed Nehru was crushed when his faith was betrayed.

Nehru's death shattered Tathya. He felt Nehru died the day his remaining hopes were shattered. The twentieth of October 1962, the day on which the Chinese, reiterating their friendship for India to the last, launched a strong attack on Namkachu valley and Dongli in Ladakh. That thirty-day war! A war fought in the icy heights of the Himalayas by unprepared, almost weaponless soldiers. Hasty instructions. The sacrifices of the brave but defenceless soldiers had shaken the nation. Bakshi sahib had given many brilliant lectures. Money was collected for the National Defence Fund. Women donated their gold bangles and jewellery. Katya and the nurses sent parcels of woollens knitted by them to the frontier. Boys and girls were trained to handle weapons in schools, colleges, parks and parade grounds. Filled with shame and anguish, the peaceloving leader who spoke of Panchsheel and friendship paid his respects to those defenceless brave soldiers who were facing the mortars, machine guns and modern weapons of the Chinese. Nehru had accepted the defeat of his principles.

Lord Montgomery had said, 'If ever a man has the hallmark of greatness, it is Nehru!' That hallmark suddenly became faint and faded away.

Tathya felt smothered by his tears. He had become a fan of Nehru from the time that this man, who grew up in absolute luxury in Anand Bhavan, chose to dedicate himself to the fight for freedom. Ayodhyanath, who belonged to a profession which could prove white was black and vice-versa, gave up his suit and tie and started wearing a Nehru jacket, achkan and churidars. Babba had gauged the agitation in his son's mind. He had smiled, 'Ayodhya, today you look just like Jawaharlal. It is good, it suits you. Freedom is a good thing. If the maharaja didn't have this red-faced Resident lording it over him he could have done so much more for his people. ....'

But Ayodhya was completely dedicated to Nehru. He would discuss each word Nehru said or wrote and every activity of his with great enthusiasm. 'Nehru did not remain inactive even in jail. Read Shivantha! Read *The Discovery of India*. Nehru says that it is man's soul, his unconquerable energy and his reasoning which is the basis of his ability to survive the difficulties of life.' Nehru prevented his soul from being blemished though he did make mistakes despite his wisdom. Tathya made Kamala Nehru, Sarojini Naidu, Ba and Swaroop Rani the role models for the women of his household. He gave them the freedom to see the world outside the four walls of the house. During Babba's time the women had been acquainted with the *Bhagvadgita*, *Bhavani Sahastranam* and with Parmanand and Krishnajoo Razdan at the most.

On this night of floods Tathya was beseiged by memories. Nehru passing the seven bridges of Srinagar city in a flower bedecked shikara. The Vitasta decorated with buntings and streamers like a bride. The banks full of shouting crowds who have gathered to catch a glimpse of this son of the valley and shower him with flowers. Their eyes full of affection and with blessings in their hearts! A man deserving more affection and respect than any past maharaja. There is a flood of people who have gathered to catch a glimpse of his ashes in the

Gadadhar temple on the banks of the Vitasta. Ayodhyanath and his family are sobbing in grief. The dear son of the valley has passed away.

After the defeat by China, Nehru said that he felt he was losing touch with the essential reality of the world around him. That day Tathya had felt his ideals were crumbling all around him. Why hadn't Nehru, who was so knowledgeable about history, learnt from it? Gandhi had handed the administration of the nation to him saying that he was, 'truthful beyond suspicion.' Despite all their differences the Mahatma knew that after him it was Nehru who would follow his path. But didn't the fact that the nation had to face a shameful defeat during the period of his rule prove that Nehru's faith in humanity was misplaced? Didn't the fact, that he included a clause regarding plebiscite during the accession of Kashmir to India, provide proof of the same beliefs?

How did this man, who was never content to be average, who wanted to move his nation beyond the boundaries of superstition and orthodoxy into the field of science, retain his faith in the friendship of the two-faced brutal Chinese who had attacked Tibet in 1950? Did he convert friendship into enmity by giving shelter to the Dalai Lama? Like the rest of the nation, Tathya wanted to understand the reasons for Nehru's actions. Perhaps even Jawaharlal himself had come to realize the hollowness of his beliefs, but no one could understand the invisible pain of betrayal. For Tathya, the sleepless night was filled with memories.

Krishna Menon resigned after the Chinese war and there were murmurs that Nehru should have done so too. Tathya thought perhaps it was easier to accept defeat before the public and resign. Krishna Menon, General Thapar and Bijji Kaul got absolution to some extent by doing that. But it was only possible to accept the defeat of one's ideals by giving up one's life. This is what happened to Jawahar. His ashes, which were scattered over the mountains, rivers and valleys, carried the last message of the apostle of peace all over the land. War was the truth and humanity was an illusion. Life was real only as long as it lasted. Who had seen the other world?

The early light of morning was glittering on the window panes. The dark of night has dissipated.

'The night has come, O Poshnool bird
Gladden the heart with your sweet voice.'

Where had Janaki's voice come from? Tathya looked around rubbing his eyes. Janaki! She passed away more than four years ago. Tathya felt as though he were carrying a heavy load on his head. His body was aching. Had Janaki come to call him? Suddenly? He hadn't slept well at night. Where had he travelled? His mouth felt parched. He needed some water. There was a tumbler of water on the bedside table but his arms were too weak to move.

'Keshavnath....' Tathya called out.

'Shivnatha....' Why had his voice become so feeble?

Lalli had cleaned the hookah and left it next to the bed. Whose fingers were these touching his forehead? Ma! Is that you?

'Who is it? Prem?' Tathya knew his mother passed away many years ago. It was just the sensation of her touch that had returned.

'Tathya, it is I, Lalli! Your forehead is warm. Should I put some balm? Didn't you sleep at night? I think you have caught a chill. You were fine yesterday.'

The pressure of her fingers on his forehead was very pleasing.

'Bahu, daughter-in-law! Get me some water and send Keshav to me. Has Prem come?'

'He will come, Tathya. I will send for Katya, she will come and take a look at you. Don't worry, there is just a slight fever.' Lalli had become a mother.

'Yes, yes,' Tathya was mumbling to himself, the fever was high. Keshav and Shivanath were worried.

'Sit here,' Tathya indicated they should sit on the bed.

'Call Prem, and Shiva, Ragya and Sharika as well. Rajdulari is in Jammu, right? Then she will also come. But Nandan? Won't I be able to see him?' Tathya's voice was becoming feeble. Lalli felt a lump in her throat.

'Your son has gone very far away, Lalli.'

'It would be good if he came back. One's country is always better than any foreign land. Even if he stays in Delhi or Bombay he will be connected to his home. Living abroad makes you feel cut off. Tell him, tell him on my behalf.'

'Tathya was fine at night, why is he talking so strangely today?'

'What is that noise outside, Shiva? Have the waters gone down?'

'Yes, Tathya, the flood is receding, don't worry.'

'Then why this commotion? Has someone drowned?' Tathya wanted to know.

'No, Tathya. A few houses of the boatmen across the river were washed away. They are trying to retrieve their things and planks of wood. Thankfully no lives were lost.'

'Yes. If there is a flood it will definitely sweep something away with it.'

Shiv gazed at his father. Why was he looking so pale? His forehead was burning. Keshav had gone to fetch Dr Katya and Kartikeya. Tathya was an old man. He was not going to last very long.

Tathya breathed out as though he was uttering the word Om. Lalli felt that he had converted a long sob into the holy word.

Shiva went to fetch the girls. Ragya and Katya were close by. If it was just a simple fever Tathya would be fine in a few days. Still, it was necessary to call Prem. And Nandan?

Hadn't Tathya said that it wouldn't be possible for him to see Nandan?

੬

Tathya Sahib

Tathya passed away. Lawyer Ayodhyanath Raina had lived a long, full life. His son, Shivanath, despite being the eldest in the house, found it difficult to fill the yawning gap left by the death of Tathya, who had sheltered them like an umbrella, keeping both the sun and the thunderstorms of life away.

Emptiness and grief roamed through the house and everything around it was enveloped in a sort of haze. Even after the daily gatherings of Tathya's friends had come to an end, the house was filled with the voices of children, but now? Lalli and Keshav in one corner of the house, Shiva and Kamala in another. Tathya had divided the house while he was still alive saying, 'I am doing this so that later on you or your children do not turn against each other for the sake of this framework of brick and cement.' And even as he left them he reiterated the message from the *Rigveda* taught by grandfather, 'always walk together.'

Shivnath was well aware of Tathya's quiet stubbornness. Born in 1885, during the illustrious reign of Maharaja Pratap Singh, in the middle class home of the orthodox religious Pandit, Master Lakshmanjoo Raina, Ayodhya would normally have retired after an unremarkable life spent teaching in Pratap or Tyndale Biscoe school. But he had dreams and aspirations that appeared almost unattainable. He was impressed by the successes, fame of all those Kashmiri lawyers, judges, bars-at-law who had done the impossible and carved a place for themselves in the history of the nation.

After all, Ayodhya was also a son of the valley just like them. He was also a part of the glorious tradition of Kalhana and Bilhana. Ayodhya got scholarships in school and college and as he studied he collected money by giving tuitions to help him study for the degree of Bachelor-at-Law. In those days the Pandits of the valley were filled with pride at the achievements of Motilal Nehru. Ayodhya may not have been born with a silver spoon in his mouth like Jawaharlal but he had ambitions and the zeal to fulfil his desires. He would think that if Ayodhyanath Kunzru, a lawyer of the Allahabad High Court, could become the chairman of the Indian National Conference in 1888 then why should his namesake, Ayodhyanath Raina, be content to become a master or a clerk and grow old correcting copies of schoolchildren or bent over files?

For Ayodhya's schoolmaster father, who believed in cutting one's coat according to one's cloth, the idea of seeing his son becoming a Bar-at-Law was almost like seeing a vision of heaven. His Brahmin upbringing, traditional knowledge, academic discipline and experience of life had made him a contented man who did his work diligently without any expectation of reward. His son's ambitions were like a dream as far as he was concerned.

One evening, while he was pressing his father's feet, Ayodhya placed all the money he had earned through tuitions at his father's feet with the words, 'Babba, tell me what I should do.'

Master Raina was startled at first, then he smiled once he saw the determination on his son's face. Obviously, studying for the bar exams and that too in Lahore, could not be financed merely with the tuition money. The necessary amount was taken on loan with interest from Damodar Bhatt. Without any fuss Masterji, bowed under the weight of obligation, gave his blessings and Ayodhya left for Lahore via Rawalpindi. As he travelled, he was saddened by echoes of his mother's tear-drenched words, ' How will I be able to eat a bite without you? Who will feed you and look after you so far away…' His father had merely raised his hand in blessing and said, 'Go son, and come back once you have accomplished something. We will wait for you.'

One doesn't know if Ayodhya met the lawyer poet and social activist Shivnarain 'Shamim' in Lahore but he did return with a distinction in law. He did not give in to dreams about achieving fame in Agra, Calcutta, Lucknow. His father's words about living together had made a deep impression on him. He consoled himself, thinking there were a lot of things one could accomplish in the Valley. Ayodhyanath began practising during the Dogra-British rule. He dedicated himself religiously and honestly to his work, during imperialism and democracy. When he did not feel comfortable with the administration he left his job and went into private practice. Till the end of his life he advised people and helped them solve their problems.

But he could not prevent his family from disintegrating. In the evening of his life he had to bear the sorrow of seeing his joint family drifting apart. With Nandan's departure abroad, the tradition of living together started to crumble. Nandan would come home every three or four years. He would enjoy the company of the crowd of brothers, sisters, uncles and friends who gathered around him. He would insist on going out in a donga for a visit to the lakes and the gardens, 'Tathya, it is such fun to go for a boat ride together. Cooking meals and eating food off lotus leaves. Doesn't it feel like we are back in the old days? We will hear Mohammadjoo singing his quawwalis as well, won't we?'

'There are such wonderful places to see in America, there

is nothing here except these lakes and gardens,' Prem would dampen Nandan's enthusiasm.

'I am certain that when Ghulab Singh bought the Valley for 75 lakh Nanakshahi rupees from the British during the 1846 Amritsar pact, he must have been really disappointed to realize that three quarters of it was mountains and water and just one part was land.' Those days Prem was very irritated by the administration of the Valley.

Tathya tried to placate Prem, 'The world has changed drastically in the past hundred odd years. Our state is no longer the same as before.' At the end of every long lecture he didn't forget to repeat the words, 'There is nothing like one's own homeland.'

'Yes, Tathya,' Nandan said without thinking, ' Everything is great there except for the fact that all of you are missing....'

'Then come back, Nandan, live in your own land, think about it!' Tathya's voice had melted as he said the words. 'Do you abandon your mother if she is old and sick?'

'I will think about it, Tathya.'

But Tathya realized that Nandan would never come back now. Perhaps Prem would keep the family together.

But Prem left and joined Sharika in Calcutta even while Tathya was alive. On his return form Leh he used Tathya's influence to get a job as an Assistant Engineer in the Salal Project, Riyasi. There he had a disagreement with the Resident Engineer Ghulam Rasool, resigned from his job and came back home.

Shivnath was angry, 'This is not the way to do a job, Prem. You lost your temper, fought with your seniors and resigned. What were you thinking?'

When Tathya questioned Prem about the reason for his resignation he replied, 'Tathya, does a doing a job mean that one should give up one's ideals and accept things which are wrong?'

'No, that is not correct!' Tathya's brows drew together in deep thought.

'But that is the way it is here, Tathya.'

Sharika's husband called Prem to Calcutta, got him a job with Lever Brothers and Prem and his family also left the fold. Tathya kept quiet. He didn't make any comment but he felt as though another cornerstone of the house had disintegrated.

The air in the Valley had been hazy over the past few years, as though a volcano was smouldering somewhere deep inside. Shivnath had become aware of this haze the day he saw strange faces and a row of Jinnah caps as he passed through Lal Chowk. He was surprised. 'Suddenly there are a lot of Jinnah caps around.' Prem laughed and said, 'The Valley is full of tourists from every corner of the world, many of whom wear caps.'

But a few days later he had brought home an Urdu pamphlet entitled 'Declaration of Independence.' Shivnath read the pamphlet. It had been printed by the Sada-e-Kashmir Press on behalf of an organization called the Revolutionary Council of Kashmir. Shivnath knew that there was no printing press by this name in the Valley and now he understood the meaning of the Jinnah caps as well. The people Prem thought were tourists were actually Pakistani infiltrators.

There had been skirmishes between the Pakistani and the Indian armies in Kutch since April 1965. The prime minister of Pakistan had started giving hostile speeches and in Kashmir, Maulana Farooqi's Awaami Action Committee had started an agitation for self-determination. Every now and again, there'd be an incident of arson, or an inflammatory speech, and everyone wondered who was behind these. It emerged that thousands of Pakistani infiltrators, disguised as local citizens, had been distributing pamphlets and urging people to fight against 'Indian imperialism'.

Things came to a head when Pakistan launched an attack with fifty tanks in the Chamb Jurian sector. Rajdulari called from Poonch sounding very worried, 'Tathya, there's bombing at the border, people from Rajouri are taking shelter in Jammu.' Sadiq sahib could not stop these guerillas from infiltrating the state, he and the home minister, DP Dhar were not even aware of the infiltration. But the Indian army retaliated and occupied some pickets across the Line of Control in Kargil and also launched an attack on the Jammu Sialkot border. Indian forces managed to occupy some land in Hajipeer and Sialkot between Poonch and Uri while the Pakistani army took a part of Chamb.

The people of the Valley did not help the guerillas, a fact which shocked Pakistan. Everywhere, there was talk of war, though the toughest battles were being fought in the plains of the Punjab. There, women helped take care of the wounded, they brought home-cooked food and fed the soldiers as if they were their own children.

Lalli, Kamala and their daughters donated their bangles and earrings to the National Defence Fund, the men donated a few days' salary. Mangala mausi gave away her twenty carat gold ring saying she was too old to be wearing jewellery and that she wished she could give away the remaining years of her life to the young men who were fighting to save their country. At the end of September, a ceasefire was declared after the intervention of the international super powers and the United Nations,. Tathya and Shivnath were very disappointed when it was decided that the armies would revert to the positions that they had occupied on the 5th of August 1965. Had the efforts of the army and the sacrifice of the young soldiers been futile?

Mangala cursed Russia and America, especially when the slender yet strong-willed Prime minister, Lal Bahadur Shastri, who Sheikh sahib thought was 'a weak man' proved his bravery and courage. Tragically, he died of a heart attack in Russia shortly after signing the Tashkent Agreement, plunging the entire nation into grief. Mangala did not eat that day.

The guerillas went back across the border, but voices began to be raised against India in schools and colleges. Though Maulana Masoodi, Ghulam Mohammad Kara and their companions had been arrested and sent to Jammu for indulging in anti-national propaganda, terrorist activities increased. Sporadic incidents of arson and throwing of bombs continued. The remaining trained Pakistani agents kept disrupting the peace of the Valley and the administration was unsuccessful in weeding them out.

All quiet outside and boiling lava inside. If Prabhavati tried to sort through vegetables at the shop at the corner of Habbakadal the shopkeeper would shout at her, 'Go away Batni, go somewhere else. You can't pick and choose the vegetables. You will have to take what I give you...' There was a sudden feeling of being despised, of being treated with contempt. Who was spreading this poison quietly behind the scenes?

One day Shivnath was reading out the newspaper to Tathya. In an article in *Economic and Political Weekly* Romesh Thapar had referred to Governor Karan Singh's views on Jammu and Kashmir. He wanted Kashmir to be a single language state. Jammu should be merged with Himachal Pradesh, Ladakh should be centrally administered and the area on the other side of Banihal should become a new state within the union of India.

Tathya was neither a Communist nor a Jan Sanghi though he was influenced by the philosophy of Nehru and Radhakrishnan. He felt a strange reaction to this suggestion. It was as if Karan Singh had denied the very existence of Kashmiri Pandits and shaken their remaining faith. He had pushed his thoughts away.

Shivnath handed the hookah to Tathya.

'Tathya, Karan Singh says Battas have received the correct amount of representation in government jobs but Ladakh and Jammu have not. '

Tathya took a long pull on the hookah.

'Jammu and Ladakh should definitely get the correct representation.'

'Tathya, do you feel that the problems of Kashmiri Pandits have been solved merely by their getting a few government jobs? There has been a very sharp reaction to these views in the Pandit community.'

Shivnath wanted to hear Tathya's views.

'Now our children will have to go abroad or outside the state to look for jobs. Sadiq sahib has also split the Muslims and Hindus into a 70/30 proportion. Now jobs and admission in universities will be given on the basis of quotas, not merit. Our boys will have to go into business. That is the way things are, now.'

'Tathya, our children are wandering all over the country and abroad. Kulbhushan went all the way to Hyderabad for a chemist's job. There he was asked during the interview that, 'India is spending so much money on Kashmir why do you come here to ask for a job?' '

'Our children are facing humiliation everywhere. They are told 'No Indian is allowed to settle in Kashmir, why are you coming here to live?' What answers can our boys give?'

Tathya tried to pacify Shiv. 'Our boys are capable, they don't have enough avenues for growth in the state. They will prove their worth wherever they go. Stop worrying needlessly. Tell me, what is happening in court nowadays?' Tathya tried to change the topic.

'The same politics is happening there as well.'

'Was there any investigation on the report which Mahandjoo gave to Sadiq sahib about the Chinkral Mohalla incident?'

'What investigation could there be, Tathya? Even the police doesn't want to catch the rioters. Ramji even appealed to Shastriji but who is prepared to give evidence in such matters?'

'Hm!' Tathya said thoughtfully, 'Sadiq sahib is the leader of the progressive group. He has promised justice. He has also proved that he wants to fight the group advocating plebiscite in the political arena by withdrawing the conspiracy case against Sheikh sahib and releasing him from jail.'

'Tathya, this also seems to be a political conspiracy to me. On the one hand, he arrested Bakshi sahib and sent him to Tara Mahal and on the other he released Sheikh sahib to prove how liberal he is.'

Tathya agreed, 'That is true' and tried to lighten the atmosphere. 'Don't you get any more cases like the Rajkumari case nowadays?'

'Rajkumari case?' Shivnath repeated.

'Arre, have you forgotten Raghavjoo's daughter, Rajkumari? The one who called head-constable Dwarka's son home on the pretext of feeding him pakoras and upturned a cauldron of boiling oil on his hands?'

Tathya started laughing and Shivnath looked embarrassed. He remembered Rajkumari's innocent statements, 'Tathya sahib, he grabbed me a few times in the alley and when I gave him a tight slap he started spreading rumours about my morals.'

The head-constable's son was gazing down at the ground and the head-constable's hands were itching to thrash Rajkumari. If it had been the time of Maharaja Gulab Singh he would have flayed the skin off the girl for this terrible offence.

At the time, he could only say, shaking in anger, 'Lawyer sahib! This girl is a liar! What proof does she have that…that…'

Rajkumari interrupted him to offer proof, 'Tathya sahib! If you like I can show Kakni the bruise marks made by this ruffian….'

'There is no need for all that,' Tathya had measured the truthfulness and courage of the girl with his eyes.

'But didn't you think that the boy could have lost his life when you threw the boiling oil at him? Why did you take the law into your own hands ? You could have complained to your father or brother…. They would have handled it.'

In her forthright way Rajkumari replied that she wanted to teach this ruffian a lesson herself. And she didn't want to kill the boy, she just wanted to frighten him, that is why the oil was lukewarm! Tathya threatened and soothed the petitioner and the complainant and sent them away. He patted Rajkumari on her back as she left and said, 'Next time use some other method to punish the culprit, not hot oil!' Rajkumari became famous in the neighbourhood, 'She is just like the goddess Chandika.'

'Tathya, people are saying that you are encouraging girls. They are getting out of control as it is.' Tathya became serious, 'Girls are educated now and are conscious of their rights. It is a good thing that now girls won't be killed by being burnt by a stove like Masterji's daughter.'

The memory of Masterji's daughter filled the room with the smell of death. As she was consumed by flames the seventeen year old girl had kept screaming, 'Save me someone, sell my Dejharu, take me to my father....' That young mother-to be had to be cremated by pouring kerosene oil on her half burnt body in that frozen snow-bound month. In the midst of alien people, in an alien place. Her father, Pandita Sahib, crumbled away in his old age even before death could claim him. The entire Pandit community gathered behind him.

'If the girl died because a stove burst, why weren't her parents informed? The city was barely thirty kilometers away.' It was decided that Pandita sahib's son-in-law should be taught a lesson. Ayodhyanath himself went to meet Pandita Sahib. But it was as though the man had been turned to stone by some curse. When he was pulled out of his reverie by the crying of his grandson he burst into tears like a child, 'Sahib! Even if the law condemns my son-in-law to death that will not bring back my daughter. Will this child get back his mother?'

Pandita Sahib did not agree to any legal action despite Ayodhyanath's persuasion. His tired old body had barely enough strength to fight for dual guardianship of his grandchild and ensure that the mother's bank account was transferred in the child's name. That was all. Katyayini and Ayodhyanath went to

Shopian to conduct an enquiry, but the villagers refused to say anything. The engineer son-in-law had bribed everyone. And then the petitioner himself was feeble and weak.

Tathya always regretted the fact that he could not punish the culprit. He couldn't give justice to the girl. That day he vowed that he would always fight on behalf of women even though members of his community muttered behind his back complaining that lawyer Ayodhyanath had lost his wits in his old age. Instead of teaching girls to be gentle, hesitant, polite and diffident he was encouraging them to become Chandikas. The Rajkumari case was just a small example of this resolve.

Unfulfilled Wishes

From the open window she could look over the tops of the houses and see the wall of the Hari Parbat fort raising its head towards the sky. The lake in front of the mountains, where tourists in shikaras and houseboats drank in the clear air was, however, not visible. But from where she stood, the land of Hari Parbat and of so many wish fulfilling temples, mosques and gurudwaras could just be glimpsed – it looked rather like a brown platter held up by a supplicant towards the heavens. When she had done the circumambulation around Chakrishwar as a child, Neelu remembered how she'd been filled with the desire to visit the fort but her mother had refused to allow her to do so.

'No, not there! What do you want to see? It is inhabited by the ghosts of soldiers, cruel kings and bloodthirsty men. No one ever goes there.'

Ma had heard that this fort had been constructed by the Afghan governor, Ata Mohammad Khan, in 1810. The Afghans were very cruel rulers. The incidents narrated by her father-in-law, Krishnajoo Kaul, about Taimur, Zamanshah, Karimdad Khan, Jabbar Khan and other Afghans bore this out. But there were also plenty of stories about their internal bickering, of their plots and rebellions and of how Taimur's sons had put out the eyes of the Afghan ruler Zamanshah. The stories were frightening.

Papa had laughed, 'Her father-in-law must have told you about our Indrani, about the good deeds done by the Afghans along with the bad ones. This Amirakadal bridge and the wall of Shergarhi were also made by an Afghan governor named Mohammad Khan Jawan Sher Kizalbash.'

'Your mother is afraid, Neelu. There are no ghosts. Anyone who dies is gone forever. They will never come back.'

Just as Papa went away forever once he died and Raja bhai decided to go away while he was alive and never come back. And Uday? Papa did not come back even in dreams to talk about him.

Ma was influenced by the spirits of the elders of the family, especially the spirit of grandfather Krishnajoo Kaul. She would sigh deeply and lament, 'What can one call it except fate or destiny that Krishnajoo Kaul's family which was so prosperous and renowned at one time was destined to be reduced to nothing. '

I never met my grandfather. Among the dusty faded photographs of our ancestors hanging on the wall, I had always liked his photograph with his heavy turban, martial moustache, far-seeing eyes and an aura of dignity and power. Perhaps this was because he used to tell a lot of stories to children, some of which were narrated to me by Ma and Papa and Raja bhaiya. True stories, which included the tale of Kota Rani, the brave daughter of Raja Sehdev's prime minister who lived at the beginning of the 14th century. A woman who married her father's killer, Rinchin, in order to save Kashmiris who were oppressed by the constant attacks and cruelty of the Tartar Dulchu from Central Asia. She was also clever enough to have the invader Achala killed. Papa said she was a born politician, clever and skilful. Kota Rani had a weakness for power and romance, though, but when Shahmir came from Swat, and, took over the kingdom by deceit and wanted to marry her, why did she walk into his room and kill herself with a dagger? I didn't ask Papa this question because I felt that he would not bother to understand the secrets of a woman's heart and would merely see her as a defeated woman, a view I was not ready to agree with. If grandfather had been around, I would have asked him. According to Ma he was omniscient. The house hummed with life and prosperity while he was alive.

'Now what is left? Just silence and emptiness.'

I thought to myself, 'But Papa is there, and so is Raja bhaiya with his multitude of friends, and the tiny smiling Babboo. There are rooms and courtyards full of the clamour of children playing, mimicking their teachers. Then there are plays about Satyavan and Savitri and Satyavadi Harishchandra performed in Shitalnath, the fairs held at Ramchandra Gardens every Kashmiri New Year and unending conversations with the moon which peeps in through the windows or rocks gently as it reclines on the clouds.'

Raja Bahiya was born ten years after Papa's marriage. The son and heir of the house. And Papa put the entire weight of his expectations onto Raja bahiya's shoulders. Such a heavy burden that Raja bhaiya couldn't carry it and stumbled.

'I couldn't study enough, but my Raja will fulfil all my dreams. Won't you? You will become an engineer like Nandanji or appear for the IAS like Ratan Bhan and become a Collector or a Commissioner. Your sister will become a doctor....'

Papa would check Raja bhai's homework and school report, 'Arre! Just eighty marks in Math? Next time you must get a hundred. I will ask master Nandlal to tutor you for an hour.'

In his haste Papa used every trick he could think of, like the clever statesman Chanakya. 'Look! Your sister has come first again this time. Just look at Babboo's notebook, he has got so many "goods"! What has happened to your handwriting? Are these letters or dead flies?'

Initially Raja bhaiya got angry, he would glare at me and Baboo, shout at us for no reason. Then gradually he lost interest in his studies. When he failed in science in his Matric exams Papa was really upset.

'Rehman's son has cleared his Matric and our young man hasn't even managed to get a passing grade in science.'

Raja bhaiya failed in his second attempt as well. Papa stopped Raja bhaiya's pocket money. The house became devoid of joy, a dull place. As if on cue, Raja bhaiya became quiet. He would come home late, eat and lock himself up in his room. If I knocked on his door he would send me away saying, 'I am sleepy.' The smell of cigarettes and cannabis seeped out from his room. Once mother found a wad of cannabis in his shirt pocket. The next day when Papa was leaving for office he asked Raja bhaiya to come with him, 'Get up, throw your books into the Vitasta and come with me. You are incapable of studying.'

'I will go and beg my boss. He may give you a job in the Tourist Centre and perhaps later you can get a contract for buses and trucks.'

Raja bhaiya's voice reflected his revulsion, 'I am not going to go around shouting, "any service, green bus" to attract passengers.'

Papa kept his emotions in check, 'If you had cleared your Matric, I would have sent you to Madras to do a diploma in automobile engineering, like Ratan Labroo. You can train to become a mechanic, if you like. You have to have some means to support yourself in the future. I haven't eaten the Sanjivani plant so I can't live for ever….'

'You will be happy when you see me covered in oil and grease.'

Papa's patience began to run out. He gritted his teeth.

'You don't want to do any physical work and you can't study. So what kind of a job do you expect to get?'

'I have spoken to Sukha Singh about a hardware shop. It requires an investment of fifty thousand rupees. His father will contribute twenty-five and I have to arrange for the rest of the money.'

Raja bhaiya's didn't sound as if he was making an appeal, instead it was more like a demand. Papa replied, his voice flat 'Both of you are inexperienced. Sukha is the son of a businessman. Even if I can manage this amount, it would be stupid on my part. If you really are interested why don't you work in Gopi Munshi's hardware shop for a while and learn the ropes? He is the biggest hardware merchant in the state today. We can think about the shop once you have learnt the work. I will talk to Gopi.'

'You won't give me any money but you are willing to beg other people. You always think I am useless.' Raja bhaiya rushed out of the house angrily.

His rebellion became stronger. He would come in late at night, Ma would be sitting up waiting for him, stifling her yawns. She would rush to open the door at the slightest sound, wait to hear the sound of his footsteps in the middle of the lonely nights and nap with her head buried between her knees! Ma had almost become a symbol of patience. It was around that time that money started disappearing from Papa's pockets. First just ten or twenty rupees. But the day a hundred rupee note disappeared Papa caught Raja bhaiya by his collar, 'Who has taken money from my pocket?'

Raja bhaiya maintained a stubborn silence. He was so intoxicated he could barely keep his eyes open. Papa was already upset. Yesterday Radheyshyam Trisal had very solemnly expressed concern about Raja bhaiya, 'I met Raja bhai in Amrish Talkies today. He's always hanging around the Bund with Asad Ahmed of the Al-fateh, why don't you say something to him? His friendship with these ruffians can cause problems for the whole family.'

Papa kept quoting Radheyshyam as he thrashed Raja bhaiya, 'These are the friends for whom you steal? Take drugs? Tell me? Why are you quiet now?' Raja bhaiya was silent.

Papa picked up the hookah, Ma leapt up to try and stop him. 'This boy, the grandson of Krishnajoo Kaul doesn't want to work like his father, so what will he do, steal? He doesn't want to be a doctor, an engineer, not even a peon. He will become a thief and a gambler. He will destroy the honour of the entire family. Why should I want to even look at his face?'

As Papa smashed the hookah down on Raja bhaiya's back he screamed, 'Oh! Maaaaaa! I am dying!'

It was a terrible night of sorrow. Who had died? Beliefs, hopes and the little life and joy that was left in the household? No food was cooked that night. Everyone disappeared into the nooks and crannies of the house. Baboo was sleeping, hidden in a corner behind piles of bedding and trunks, his body shaking with suppressed sobs. This was Papa's weakness. He could even kill someone in anger but once he calmed down he would always regret what he had done.

'Did I expect too much from all of you? Was I too strict? All I wanted was that my children should achieve what I couldn't. That's all.' It was this 'wanting' which lay at the root of all troubles. Papa finally understood this, but by then it was too late. That night when I was awakened by the sound of dogs baying I felt a shadow move through the darkness in the room. I held my breath. Was Papa returning from Raja Bhaiya's room? Had he gone to say something? Or to check the wounds on his back? Ma crept into the kitchen as stealthily as a cat and came out carrying a bowl. Warm oil? No, muted sounds of groans kept emerging from Raja bhiaya's room.

My eyes were heavy with tears. I don't know when Ma came back. In the morning I came awake suddenly either because of the touch of the rays of the sun straining through the wire mesh in the window or because of the sound of Ma's lamentation. It seems Raja bhiaya was not in his room, he had disappeared from the house. Papa sat there like a criminal listening to Ma wailing. The defeated soldier was standing in the dock. Papa left the house to look for Raja bhiaya, to persuade him, to ask forgiveness for what he had done. The same son whose face he had decided not to see again just the day before.

He roamed the streets like a madman. Repeatedly visiting the police station, searching desperately through the crowds emerging from America Talkies, Paladium, Neelam Talkies. He looked for Raja bhiaya in Ahdoos hotel, Punjabi dhabas, the Ganesh temple, Jama Masjid, Nishat, Shalimar and in the homes of friends and relatives.

Our maternal uncle came from Anantnag and Haldhar mama from Matayi's village, Shivnath, Keshavnath and Rehmanjoo also searched everywhere. Where did he go, after all? Rajdulari called from Jammu, 'He came to my place once. He had a beard. He told me, "I am going to Bombay, Teja's brother has promised to get me some work in films."'

Papa went to Bombay. With Raja bhiaya's photograph in his hand, he searched through strange bazaars, streets, slums and the crowds on Juhu beach for that beloved child who had been sent on a rough, difficult path by his father so that he could achieve success for himself and his family. Papa was the culprit. Finally, after a month, Papa returned empty-handed from Bombay. He looked like a skeleton and had aged at least twenty years.

Papa's mind became unbalanced. Sometimes I wonder: had he not been killed during the riots in the Parmeshwari episode would he really have been alive in any sense? A tired, defeated father, guilty of having lost his son! Our father was sacrificed at the altar of his own ambitions.

Ma's being was consumed by the memory of her son crying out,'Oh Maaaa! I am dying!' She would go crazy if she heard anyone crying, 'Raja must be thinking of me! Dear God! Please return my Raja to me. He Mahaganapati! Protect my child...'

'You will go mad, you whore!' Papa would shout at her. Perhaps it was his own helplessness, or his conscience pricking him that made him shout out thus, or perhaps it was just his inability to express his feelings. Who could he talk to and to whom could he show his wounded heart?

Raja bhai did not come back when Papa died. People reached their own conclusions. Must have died somewhere. Memories of Raja bhaiya nestled in various nooks and crannies of the house.

I think, if Raja bhaiya had returned, Papa would have forgiven him and held him close. Raja bhaiya could have come back, studied hard and become successful, or he could have established his own business and become a 'hardware king' after training with Gopi Munshi. He could have built houses in Wazir bagh and Jammu. All this could have happened. But he could also have been arrested for stealing and the police could have brought him to Papa to establish his identity and Papa, like Pyare Kaul, could have refused to recognize his son in order to save his family from disgrace. Anything was possible. What happened and what could have happened were two different things – there was no escaping that.

With his lacerated face Papa searched for Raja Bhaiya for the last time as he lay dying. All of us felt the pain of watching hope fade in those brown eyes. Did Papa see a glimpse of Raja bhaiya in Baboo as he put the drops of Ganges water in his mouth? Why did I feel that his tears were mixing with the blood that had dried at the corners of his eyes?

I did not become a doctor, I did fairly well in Biology in my Inter exams, but Papa passed away before the results were declared. Even though our house had never been free of disasters, Papa's death triggered off an avalanche of accidents. And as we mourned, our community also debated the need to react to the threats they saw growing around them. The Action Committee approached the Chairman of the Legislative Council, Pandit Shivnarain Fotedar, for justice. Rioters had thrown stones at the biers of the Hindus who had died in the riots. Hridaynath Mattoo of Rainawari had been attacked by ruffians at Navpora while he was on his way home from office. Gopinath Handoo, Avtar Krishan Khushoo…. so many people had died untimely deaths in these riots. But Fotedar sahib had been unable to do anything. It seems he had been warned by some members of the Congress not to get involved in this affair. Congress President Syed Mir Qasim even stated in the Legislative Assembly that 'The state does not merely consist of Habba Kadal or Rajendra Bazaar.' In other words, all is well here. There has been no intimidation anywhere.

Some Muslims, emboldened by the attitude of the government, even sent a petition to the Home Minister YB Chavan, on behalf of 'responsible Muslim citizens ' saying that 'the Hindus of the valley want to wipe out all the Muslims.'

It was a strange situation. Not only were the voices of the pitifully small minority drowned out by the clamour of the majority but the Hindus were declared to be the rioters and their houses were raided by the police to check if they were gathering weapons.

Once again the Hindus in the valley were convinced that they were not safe either in their homes or in their own state.

And Ma had also become unstable. She didn't weep or

mourn. She just stopped eating and would sit by the window till late at night waiting for Papa to return. She refused to believe that Papa had passed away. In the dark mist she would look around wide eyed, 'Look, Neelu, isn't that your father? I can recognize his walk but I can't see the face clearly. Babboo, son! Go, persuade him to come home, he left the house in anger.'

If she left the window she would start washing Papa's sheets, towels, kurtas. We didn't know what to do. Kartikeya jija suggested a change of place. Ma was becoming more and more confused living in a house full of memories.

Mama and mami came from Anatnag. Ma refused to move away from the window but they somehow managed to put her in their car. They took Baboo to Mattan, Pandrethan and the temples around Brijbehara to pray for Papa's soul. They made Ma give alms to the priests in Papa's name hoping this would convince her that he was dead. But it was as though she was participating in a stranger's funerary rituals. She was not really there, her eyes dry and vacant.

Ma's maternal cousin, Haldar mamaji, came from Safapore and took us home with him. 'We will go to Matayi's village, You will come, won't you?' He spoke to Ma as though he was talking to a child. Ma accompanied him quietly.

Matayi had passed away three years ago and even her eldest son, Ramjoo, was no longer alive. His two brothers Krishnajoo and Narayanjoo have gone to live with their sons in Delhi and Bombay. The village has also changed a lot. Matayi's four-storeyed house, which once stood proudly in the village, had become an irritant for some envious people. It was burnt down one night during the Kabaili raids. Ramchandra had built a small house from the debris of the old one. Now Ramjoo's eldest son, Haldar mama lived with his wife Pitti mami in that house. Mami had two cows, Lalli and Sundari. There was a small farm and an orchard with pear and walnut trees. It was Pitti mami who brought our mother back to us through her efforts. She awoke

Ma's childhood memories. Gathered her old friends together. Sitting on a rug under the plum tree, we ate sour plums with salt and pepper. Pitti mami roasted tender corncobs plucked from the fields while Ma dug out the sweet kernels from green walnuts with a knife. Mami made fragrant bread from rice flour for Ma and gradually Ma returned to normalcy.

One day when Ahad Bandey's wife, Khatiji, pierced the ears of the cat with a needle in front of Ma, she screamed, 'What are you doing?' Khatiji looked at her searchingly. In her childhood Ma used to put silver earrings in the cats' ears but she couldn't bear the sound of the cat, shrieking. Ma was distressed when Khatiji handed her the cat saying firmly, 'Here, Indrani. Now you can put in the earrings. I have pierced its ears.'

'Indrani!' Ma's lips trembled, she looked around. Papa's term of affection! There was a storm of emotion within her. Either the word 'Indrani' or the memory of the cat's shriek brought her back to her senses. The dam burst and she wept. Haldar mama wiped her tears as Pitti mami cried silently. Those tears made us feel as though a weight had been lifted off our chests.

Once Ma was better Katya suggested that I should apply for a medical seat, 'You have good marks. If you don't get a seat we will file a "writ." We will also apply for a loan.'

A medical degree meant studying for five long years and a lot of expense. A Pandit girl was not very likely to get a loan according to the quota, because no matter that she might be poor, she did not fit any of the government categories that were eligible for loans. If someone was a Batta, how could he or she be needy? Maqbool Sahib said, 'Battas cannot be poor. They have ruled over us for decades.' And what will happen to the house for five years? How will Babboo complete his education?

I did a diploma course in nursing instead. I was grateful to Lalli bua, Bhobaji and Katya for what they had done but how long could I carry the burden of their kindness? Doctor didi got me a job in her hospital. Because of her kindness, I was also able to do short training courses without feeling burdened by a sense of obligation. She kept me by her side while she conducted operations. Within three years I became an indispensable part of the hospital. I wanted Baboo to do engineering but he preferred to do his B. Com and work in a bank. I guess he also had his sense of pride. I felt defeated. Baboo said almost apologetically, 'I am going to stop studying didi. I will appear for M. Com privately. How long are you going to struggle all alone for this house?'

Ma stealthily stitched clothes on her machine. 'I don't know how to pass the day, Neelu. What can I do? I might as well stitch some clothes.' But if she heard anyone at the door she immediately covered the machine with a sheet. She was afraid that if the neighbours saw her using the machine they would start calling her a seamstress. In our Brahmin community which good family would ever agree to a marriage alliance with a tailor, a baker or a cook? In some corner of her mind, Ma was thinking of Uday as a future son-in-law.

'Ma, we are fine as we are. There is no need to hide anything from anyone.'

'Your Papa also liked Uday,' she said calmly. 'His mother, Rajrani Zutshi even spoke about an engagement....'

I liked Uday too, very much. We were young then and young people like to dream. Whenever we met Uday would start, 'Neelu, I will become an engineer, you become a doctor! My father is going to send me abroad to do my M.S. You will wait for me, won't you?'

'You are a daydreamer like Sheikhchilli' I would tease him. 'First you need to sell the milk, then buy many goats, then sell their wool and earn a lot of money and after that you can build your palaces and bungalows.'

'And then? What should I do after that?' Uday wanted to hear about the two of us.

'What then? Don't shake your head. If the pot of milk topples over, all your plans will be shattered. Then don't blame me.'

'I will hold on to the pot tightly with both my hands. You will see. I hope you won't say no, my beautiful blue fairy.'

We were just sixteen years old and in our dreams we would plan everything from the honeymoon to two or three children, keeping the government family planning slogan in mind.

But the milkman in the story shook his head and the pot broke. It was made of mud after all! Uday did engineering from Chandigarh university. At that time most middle class Pandits dreamt that their sons would become engineers and their daughters would study medicine. What was the harm in dreaming? But by that time I had become a nurse. Zutshi Sahib questioned his son sharply, 'Would you like to marry a midwife?'

Uday returned from abroad after completeing his M.S. He met me. He was disappointed and very upset, 'You destroyed your career in a fit of emotion. Even now if you want....' But I did not want that which others wanted from me. Papa's desires had taught me this much. I wish Uday had wanted me. But he wanted a doctor, not Neelu. Especially now that he was 'foreign returned'. I returned all my stored memories of Uday to him, and got busy cleaning up the untidy courtyard of my house. There was a strange smell seeping through the house. The stench of rotting wounds.

Kaderjoo, the servant of the house, had become quite old now. He had been handling the responsibility of the house for the past twenty years. His children had started small businesses and felt it beneath them to work for Battas. Kaderjoo could not leave the house despite being aware of the changes that had taken place around him. He was not a servant but almost a member of the family. He had looked after us in our childhood, how could he abandon us now in our moment of difficulty?

One good thing that happened was the fact that Baboo

found Sangeeta, the third daughter of Master Kriparam Kalla. God knows how many potential in-laws came to inspect this half-dead looking girl and, not finding her to be a beauty, went back after feasting and being entertained. The worshippers of blue-throated Shiva cannot imagine a dark girl as their daughter-in-law. How can any one be beautiful without being fair? But Baboo had become inextricably entangled with Sangeeta the day he saw her crying hunched over a ledger after the bank manager shouted at her for making a mistake. Baboo saw her crying, worrying about what she would do if she lost her job because of the manager's anger. An untouched corner of Baboo's heart melted, 'Don't cry, I will take care of you! Tell me the problem. Oh! so much commotion over a misplaced zero?'

Despite a few minor hurdles Baboo and Sangeeta finally married.

Ma gave them her blessing and detached herself from everything. She felt this marriage had added another patch of coarse thread to the fine pashmina shawl of Krishnajoo Kaul's family. Now her chances of arranging her daughter's marriage were even slimmer than before. Radha and Batni bua were annoyed with me, 'Now there is even a daughter-in-law in the house. When are you planning to get married? Soon you will be too old.'

'Bua! don't worry, I will find an old man for myself!'

Perhaps I spoke too sharply. Ma was annoyed with me. After all, the aunts do care about us. There is no shortage of sympathizers even in the hospital. 'When are you going to get married, Neelu?' I don't know if they are afraid of my being unmarried or worried at the thought that if this fatherless girl grows old she will die without ever having married.

Baboo was transferred to Jammu. There was an effort to get Sangeeta shifted there as well. Ma refused to leave me and go. 'The world is unsafe for women especially for a young woman who is alone.' I finally burst out, 'Please, no one's going to kidnap me and I will not run away with anyone. Nowadays girls work and support their families.'

Ma doesn't say anything to me now. I am stubborn and might give a rude reply or perhaps like Raja bhaiya….I put my arms around Ma. I wanted to say, 'Why do you worry? All doors are not yet closed for us! And even if they are, can't we open new windows? There are two of us, aren't there? We can take care of each other.' But some obstruction pushed the words back in my throat. I wanted to say something but I said something else instead.

'Ma! Look at Hari Parbat from this window! So many gods and goddesses live there and we can look at them while we are sitting at home! Next Sunday, Ma, we will go to Chakreshwar. On our way back we will go for a shikara ride in the Dal lake. Just you and I! Is that O.K? We will vist the Kotarkhana, Sonalank and eat our food off lotus leaves. You make some mince koftas and I will make some paranthas…' Ma understands me well. I do not want her to sit mourning at the window. We will definitely go for a boat ride on the sun-dappled lake. If there is a storm we will tie the boat to the strong chinars in Sonalank. Papa has taught me how to row. Ma knows I am not afraid of storms.

What had to Happen, Should have Happened

The undulating hills of Gulmarg, its flat meadows and valleys were covered with a blanket of snow. The cotton carder in the sky had thrown bagfuls of snow on the golf course too, and on the cedars, firs, hotels, lodges and the low roofs of the tiny settlement.

'The skiers are having a great time, sahib. It has snowed so heavily! This time there will be great winter sports and lots of Indian and foreign tourists will come here.'

Ayuba joyfully dusted off the flurries of snow on his pheran. Premji wanted to enjoy the sight of the falling snow from the comfort of his warm hotel room, cocooned cosily in his quilt. The cold was piercing. It penetrated through ten layers of clothing and froze the ribs.

But Pamposh, Bulbul, Dhara, Nandan, and their kids, Pinki, and Chintu were ready to sally forth wearing fur jackets, overcoats, long boots and ear muffs. Nandan had come home after four years, during the Christmas vacation, with Dhara and the children. The children were becoming strangers to their family, it would be good for them to spend some time together. When Pamposh and Pinki insisted on going to Gulmarg, Nandan suggested, 'Why don't we go skiing? Pinki is a very good skater as well.' Shivnath called up and made reservations in a hotel. Somnath, the lawyer, lived in Gulmarg: he would take care of the children.

Now, here was Gulmarg, spread out before them with its carpet of snow. Inviting them to roll on it and enjoy themselves. Pinki and Chintu were sliding around on thin strips of wood, putting creases on the unblemished sheets of snow. Pamposh and Devika cautiously stumbled down the smaller slopes hand in hand, falling again and again, dusting off the snow, giggling and laughing at their own clumsiness. Ayuba, the helper, ran alongside Bulbul. With his Pattu pheran, which he was wearing on top of two or three shirts and a quilted waistcoat, swinging about as he ran, he looked like a bazooka swaying in the wind. Pinki and Chintu twisted around in dancing poses.

'Come on Pamposh, follow me, it is fun, heyyyyy!' Brij was also very confident. He resembled Kanhaiya from afar. The same sort of build. Kanhaiya was crazy about the snow but he wasn't there anymore. Prem felt sad thinking about him, the youngest and the most intelligent. Why was Time so cruel?

Ayuba was happy that there was so much snow this time. 'More snow means more winter sports, more tourists, and that means more income. In other words warm rice with a piece of meat, a new pheran and a pair of longboots with the grace of Allahtala!' The snow seeped in through the unravelled seams of his boots as he ran around and wet his socks. Wearing wet socks was a surefire way to get painful chilblains. Bulbul slowed down when Ayuba stopped to dust his boots.

'What happened Ayuba, are you tired?' Bulbul had become friendly with Ayuba.

'No, sahib, my right foot is troubling me a little, I am not tired.' Ayuba constantly asked the boys, 'Are you enjoying running the sleigh on the snow, sahib?'

'Very much! It's wonderful!' A few strands of hair had slipped out from under the brim of Bulbul's cap.

'Lots of big heroes come here, sahib. From Bombay, for shooting. Shammi Kapoor, Saira Bano! Have you seen the film *Junglee,* sahib?

'Bulbul jumped, shouting, 'Yahooooo!' like Shammi Kapoor and dashed against two girls who were stuck in the snow.

'Hey, junglee! Behave yourself!' The girl with the red cap was quite annoyed.

'Sorry girls!!' Bulbul laughed and begged pardon.

The other girl was more gracious, 'OK carry on, Shammi Kapoor junior!'

Pamposh and Devika doubled up with laughter, 'Ayuba! Find a Saira Bano for this junglee. There is still time....'

Running, slipping, falling and balancing, with cheeks reddened by the touch of the snow. Their caps were covered with a thin film of snow, which was falling in thick flakes from the trees.

For a while Premji watched in silence. Pinki and Chintu were dancing on the snow with confidence, but Pamposh, Devika, Bulbul were crawling like tortoises. During his college days Premji had visited Khilanmarg, Baba Rishi, Al pether, Afarbat and so many other places. He won medals for hiking, riding and mountaineering. And now his children were floundering in the snow as though they are seeing it for the first time!

Premji suddenly took the children by surprise by grabbing a pair of skis and jumping onto the snow. He was a little unsteady at first then he balanced himself and slithered across the snow slopes like a snake disappearing from sight. Just as the children were starting to worry he appeared on the next slope. 'I have been watching you kids crawling around like tortoises. You are my children, come on, I will teach you how to ski.'

The girls and boys skidded around with Premji: happy, laughing, full of life. Premji felt as though he had suddenly gone back in time. Brij reminded the children about their father's past achievements, 'Mamu bhaiya has skied on the three mile long slope which descends from the 'Lily white shoulder' situated at a height of twelve thousand feet down to Gulmarg!'

The warm hotel room seemed very welcoming when they returnd from frolicking in the snow. The children took off their extra clothing, boots and socks and as they settled down around the wood stove with their quilts and kangris, a bearer entered with a samovar filled with fragrant hot kehwa.

'Sahib, the owner has sent this, he wants to meet you.'

'Right now?' What could be the reason?

'Let him come, what difference does it make? Perhaps he is an old friend of yours.'

Premji couldn't recall which of his friends owned hotels, but when he saw the man Premji's face lit up with recognition. He jumped up to greet him.

'Ehsaana, is it you? When did you become the owner of this hotel?'

'My friend, now you have become a Calcutta and

Bombaywalla, why would you remember your old friends?'
Ehsaana complained. Premji and Ehsaan Malik revived their
memories of college days as the astonished children watched
the two old men returning to their youth. They had their meals
in the room and roasted peanuts and corn on the stove.

During the course of their conversation, Ehsaan Malik told
them that his father had sent him to Bombay to do his MBA
but he had no idea how he survived those two years. Not only
did he find the heat and the humidity unbearable but he also
longed to eat homecooked rice and greens. Bulbul interrupted
the conversation, 'But uncle! Bombay is the city of film stars.
There is the sea, Juhu beach, Elephanta caves, the Nehru
planetarium, the Taj hotel near the Gateway of India…'

'But son, there is no Gulmarg and no Hotel Firdaus!'

Ehsaan made such a face that Bulbul burst out laughing.

'Truly, friend! There is no other place like our Valley
anywhere in the world. My brother goes to Goa for business
but he comes back home after one or two months. I just can't
understand how you manage to live in that heat and dust. Our
food, our language, our way of life is completely different. This
land of ours is a paradise. Come back home my friend. Live
with your own people, even if you earn a little less.'

Premji and Nandanji heard him out, 'You are right! When
you visit Baba Rishi the next time, please ask him to give us his
blessings though I don't think we are destined to earn a living
here any longer!'

The conversation suddenly became serious, perhaps even
a little pointed. Why spoil the atmosphere of the picnic?
They were meeting after so many years. Ehsaan called for a
tumbaknari and a round pot, a ghara. Everyone was ready for
a chhakri.

'My friend! I won't be able to bear separation from you/I
will die if I am far away from you…'

When the beat of the chhakri stopped the room suddenly

became silent and just then the beautiful notes of a flute pierced the darkness outside like a ray of light. The room seemed to heave a long sigh.

'Who is playing the flute at this time Ehsaana?' Prem wanted to know.

'He is a Gujjar. He works for me.'

'Bakarwal?'

'Yes, he is a herder. On the way from Gulmarg to Janub there is a place called Garjan Dhok at a height of eleven to thirteen thousand feet.'

'Where there are five small lakes which are generally frozen?'

'Yes, in the summer there are some beautiful flowers that grow around the shores of the lakes. There are green grazing grounds where the bakarwals take their flocks. We have been there once.'

'But there aren't any settlements there...'

'Just below that is Bachan dhok, where the Gujjars have some huts and further down is Achhan dhok to which our gujjar belongs. When the grazing fields are covered with snow in winter, the bakarwals come down to the villages below. This boy has been working for me for the past three winters. He is very quiet, but never says no to any work. He plays the flute every evening without fail.'

'Sounds like the starcrossed lover Majnu. There is pain in his music.'

'Yes, his story is something like that. He is in love with some girl but he won't marry her. He is afraid that if he does she will die.'

'Amazing! Why is he so afraid, brother Ehsaan? These people are normally very hardy.' Nandan found it hard to accept Ehsaan's story.

'They are hardy but they are also very superstitious.' Ehsaan told them the story of the Jamdeyal tribe, who had migrated to Bachhan Dhok from Kafiristaan hundreds of years ago.

'At that time this area was completely barren. One day Tora, a girl belonging to the tribe, had a vision of the god 'Raksu' and found herself near a huge tree that appeared to have an image of the god on it. Tora started praying to the god and the tribesmen built a temple to the god. All was well till, one day, Tora fell in love with a stranger. Her people did not like this relationship. Tora was the priestess of the god, she was not allowed to fall in love with a human being. So, they killed both the lovers and buried them. It is said that their graves can still be seen in the same spot.'

Pamposh did not like the ending of the story, 'Papa do tribes still follow these old, outdated laws? Why is it that people who see God in trees and stones and pray to them cannot love flesh and blood human beings? Isn't this something like the situation of the devadasis?'

'This is absurd, Papa!'

'But how is this story connected to the gujjar?' Dhara couldn't understand.

'It's because the gujjar's beloved is also a priestess of the god. The gujjar is afraid that if they marry, his tribesmen may kill his beloved as well. He is not worried about himself but about the girl.'

'Can't anyone explain to the tribesmen?' Nandan was amazed that in this day and age when man was ready to land on the moon, there were people who were unable to free themselves from the shackles of these old beliefs.

'Brother Nandan, tribesmen like the Bakarwals, the Gujjars and the Gaddis have their own laws. The beliefs of many tribes about rituals, ghosts-demons, life and death, resemble those found in the *Zendavesta*, the holy book of the Sumerians and the Persians. These tribals are wanderers, they move around with their flocks in search of pasture. They go to towns to sell cheese, milk, wool but they carry their laws with them.'

'Doesn't the government do anything for them?'

Nandan felt that since the Indian government gave so much money to the state some of it should be used to help these tribes as well. There should be schools and medical facilities for them.

'Arre, brother! You are talking about schools and colleges? The government is cutting down so many trees in the name of development that many hillsides are getting eroded. Not only are these people losing their grazing lands but even their huts are getting destroyed by landslides. They are straightforward simple, hardworking people. They don't know any worldly tricks but they face a lot of hardship. May Allah protect them.'

The piercingly sweet sound of the flute echoed in their hearts till late evening. Majnu gujjar! Pamposh was sad that he would never get his beloved. In this romantic atmosphere Ehsaan started narrating the story of the legendary lovers Yusuf Shah Chak and Habba Khatoon. 'You know, Prem, Gulmarg was discovered by Yusuf Shah Chak and Habba Khatoon. Later it became the playground of the British. They came here for riding, golf, mountaineering but Yusuf Shah is the one who found it. It seems Yusuf and Habba were very fond of wandering, and it was while they were searching for places that were naturally beautiful that they arrived here one day. There is even a little hillock named after Habba Khatoon here. We will take the children there sometime.'

At the urging of the children, Ehsaan narrated the sad story of Habba Khatoon. The story of Zoon, who was born in the house of Abdi Rather in Chandhaar village near Pampore, and who faced so much sorrow and pain before she became Yusuf Shah Chak's queen and came to be known as Habba Khatoon. Yusuf Shah Chak loved her with all his heart and soul but they were not destined to be together for too long. Yusuf Shah was a king and became separated from her by internal strife and intrigue. In 1585 he surrendered before the Mughals and left Kashmir forever. Habba could not bear his absence and she composed songs about the anguish of separation. The mountains and forests echoed with her songs. She wandered about looking for her beloved till she reached Basok where she died. In Basok there are two graves side by side, the graves of Habba and Yusuf.

'Lovers are fated to be separated.' Ehsaan concluded.

'This is what old legends and stories seem to tell us. Take any story....Shirin-Farhad, Laila-Majnu, Bambur-Lolar. Love always seems to come to a sad conclusion.'

'Oh God! So many tragic endings! It seems that our elders are trying to warn us, using these folk stories. Be careful! Don't follow this path, there are a lot of dangers if you go this way.'

In the morning the grey skies had cleared after the rain. Premji and party loaded their luggage on mules and set off for Tangmarg on foot. Ayuba accompanied them for a while and Ehsaan came with them till the taxi stand. 'Friend! Come back soon next time. You visited this place after twenty-two long years. That is far too long. You came home but didn't come here. I remember the last time you were here Bakshi had Sheikh Sahib arrested right here in Gulmarg.'

How could Prem ever forget that year? The scenes of twenty-two years ago swam in front of his eyes. The entire valley had gone up in flames after the arrest of Sheikh sahib. 'That friend of ours, Amir Ali, was killed in the riots. He was a good friend, may he find place in paradise.' Prem was upset thinking about Ali.

'Bother, ordinary people can't understand the machinations of politics. But one thing is clear now, that Sheikh sahib is the true leader of the Kashmiris. The prophet of the public. He is returning after twenty-two years once again as our defender. Things should improve now if Allahtala wills it.'

As they returned home in two taxis Premji and the rest of his party felt that the ordinary Kashmiri thought of Sheikh sahib as the only arbiter of his destiny.

There were piles of snow on either side of the road. In the bazaars small groups of labourers and peasants had gathered with their kangris and were raising slogans: 'Babba (Sheikh sahib) will do whatever has to be done, whether it is good or bad, Babba will do it.' Nandan was surprised that a leader who had spent twenty-two years in and out of jail had such charisma that the people had raised him to these heights. Prem offered his opinion, 'Sheikh sahib is a leader of stature, Nandan. He has always supported the downtrodden. He fought against the monarchy. This is the image which people still carry in their hearts.'

'Prem bhaiya, we are all aware of Sheikh sahib's good qualities but it is equally clear that, after the rule of Maharaja Hari Singh ended, he did have ambitions to assume control of the state. These were the ambitions that made him forget even the promises he had made to a friend like Nehru. He even forgot that the accession of the state with India was a necessity for us.'

'That is true. Nehru tried to maintain his friendship with Sheikh sahib. He did not even pay attention to the warnings of eminent leaders like Sardar Patel and Shyama Prasad Mukherjee. To agree to Sheikh sahib's demands he even entered into questionable agreements like the one in Delhi in August 1952. But what was the result? Sheikh sahib continued to maintain contact with England and America. Even after being released in 1958 by the Bakshi government he became a part of the 'Kashmir Conspiracy' and repeatedly went to jail. And see, now the discussions with the Indira Gandhi government are being conducted in such a congenial manner that it seems we are close to an agreement.'

'Nothing happens so quickly, Nandan!' Prem referred to the chequered history of the state to show how the ambitions of past rulers and sultans had influenced events.

'Minor events can create explosive situations and circum-stances can force the greatest leaders to bend. This is politics. Forget the past, look towards the future and improve the present.'

'Yes, bhiaya! The division of Bangladesh and Pakistan, and

Pakistan's defeat in this war, have changed the situation. After surrendering with ninety thousand soldiers, Pakistan signed the Shimla agreement so what can our people expect from them?'

'Bhutto destroyed any remaining hopes by stating that Kashmiris had lost their right to self-determination in 1947, because they agreed to accede to India.'

They had reached the Srinagar bus stand. As the taxis drove homewards, familiar neighbourhoods and the Vitasta became visible. Nandan asked Prem something that had been troubling him, 'Prem bahiya? I often think that if our senior leaders had taken the accession seriously and instead of giving in to ambitions of becoming autocrats had concentrated on solving the problems of the poor then the situation would have been very different today. We, at least, would not have had to come home like visitors.'

'But sometimes ambitions don't merely harm an individual, they even change the destiny of a nation.' Prem felt the history of the Valley proved this. Then, feeling that they had become too serious, Prem tried to lighten the mood. 'Brother Nandan, had the situation been different then you would have been serving the government of your state rather than working in America. What else? You would be showing off your engineering talents in the Jawahar tunnel or in some hydel project. And yes, you would carry on Tathya's tradition of going for trips, excursions, picnics in the gardens and like Nazir, the governor during Dogra rule, you would also sing songs in praise of the Valley.'

Nandan smiled, 'Prem bhaiya, you didn't mention any local poets. Mahjoor, Nadim, Rahi! You have been their fan. Does that mean you have also lost all hope? That you have accepted that there are cracks in our sufi-rishi traditions of Lalded and Nundrishi?'

'There are no cracks yet in the hearts of our friends, Nandan. Didn't you feel Ehsaan Malik's affection? Yet politics has caused a lot of damage. This is our misfortune.'

Brijnath, who had quietly been listening to the conversation of the two brothers, decided to jump in and register his presence as soon as there was a break in their discussion.

'Mamu bhai, I believe in Nadim sahib's hope that our tomorrows will be bright. We haven't given up hope completely yet that is why we are still here. '

'Very good, Brijnatha! Hope keeps one alive.'

'Yes mamu. There seems to be some hope of settlement. The sad thing is that the leaders took so long to accept the truth. Why did they add the rider of 'plebiscite' to the accession which happened in the time of Nehru and the Viceroy?'

'Unfortunately our leaders have linked even religious places to politics,' Nandan added.

'Once again what is the point of thinking of the past? If it hadn't happened then today Prem mamu would be humming this couplet by Ghulam Nabi Nazir instead of quoting "governor" Nazir.'

You light the lamp in the temple of the Goddess,
I will call out the azaan in the mosque.
I will take shelter in the Kaaba
And you will take refuge in the temple.
You are my brother and I am yours.
The taxis stopped in front of the house.

Return

There was no possibility of return from this journey but I did come back. Not as Ragya Raina or Ragya Munshi but just Ragya.

The journey from Ragya Raina to Ragya Munshi was a brief one, full of flowers, blessings, mantras and Vedas. A journey that merely lasted one and a half or two hours. It included the rituals of Saptapadi, Athvaas and Kanyadaan performed with the fire as witness. During this ceremony Vimal was Shiva and I was Parvati. Our elders showered us with so many flowers that they piled up into small hillocks!

My departure was accompanied by flowers, blessings and instructions. Do this, don't do this and the typical observation of the followers of Sanatan dharma, 'May God look after you', a saying whose real meaning it took me twenty wasted years to unravel. Actually the implication was quite clear, bear everything with fortitude or cease to exist, just don't come back! All mothers-grandmothers repeat the same basic mantra at all times to their daughters; that a daughter, from birth, belongs to someone else. She is just a temporary guest in her parents' home.

I did not want to become a stone. I had locked up all that I had learnt or earned in a box and set off with the wisdom imparted by my family on a pre-determined, predictable path. But one day I suddenly felt as though I had come to a halt. When I looked down I saw my feet were embedded in the earth. Static, unfeeling! All around my feet was land filled with the detritus of twenty years, barren and lonely. Many of my friends had moved far ahead of me in the new climate of the Valley. I should not have looked back, my dear ones shook their heads in sorrow, 'According to the story, the prince turned into stone when he looked back.' I became petrified. I became a menhir buried under the soil in Grofkal and Burzhom. Dear God! How did this happen?

What remained in the house was a daughter-in-law who was more a maid than a princess. One who would cook roghan josh, yakhni, make kehwa-shirchai, wash the nappies of her lecturer sister-in-law's children and warm her husband's bed at night!

She would also bear in silence the taunts which were aimed at her if the roghan josh wasn't perfect, if the shirchai was not the correct pink colour, or if she was bad mannered enough to read a book in front of her mother-in-law.

Perhaps I would have continued to remain half-buried if my young daughter, Devika, had not sprinkled some magical water on me one day. It was the annual day at Devika's school. The chief guest had given Devika an award for her excellent acting as Portia in 'The Merchant of Venice'. Handing the shield over she looked at me as though seeing me for the first time.

'Mama didn't you act as the Rani of Jhansi in a play?'

'Why are you asking me, child?' In other words, why are you raking up the past?

'Mama, you also used to take part in a lot of debates, didn't you? You never mentioned it.'

Before I could reply, she shot another question at me, 'Once, in an inter-college debate you spoke against the motion on the topic, "woman is what man makes of her" and the education minister himself congratulated you for your progressive views.'

Devika was very angry. As soon as the director of schools, Mrs Razdan had seen Devika, she had asked her if she was Ragya Raina's daughter. She said Devika resembled her mother, not only in looks but also in intelligence. And Devika did not know her mother at all.

'I can't believe it, Mama! Mrs Razdan said she was a classmate of yours. She said nothing was impossible for you.'

'These are all old stories, Devika. Everything changes after marriage. It is almost like a death and a new life.' I had no answer to give to Devika.

'No, Mama! How can a girl who wants to touch the sky go back to the time of her grandmother? Don't tell me this rubbish about death and re-birth! Look at doctor masi!'

Devika was agitated. She shook her head. She wanted to

get to know me once again and she had a lot of questions. Mrs Razdan became a director of schools but Mama became a hunchbacked housewife who spent her life following outdated instructions. Why?

I was shaken by this restless question, 'why?' Something happened inside me. It wasn't sudden but a slow, gradual process that had been going on for a while. Devika's questions merely became the reason for bringing it out into the open.

I started looking for answers to the questions that arose inside me. Am I going to hand over everything I learnt from my mother and grandmother just as it was to my daughter? The same mantra about all the long-suffering women who were venerated because they could bear so much pain stoically?

Where had everything that I learnt myself disappeared after my marriage? In the debate I had said, 'How can a man create a woman? It is the woman who nurtures him in her womb, gives him shape, substance. Right from the embryonic stage of mankind, man is what woman makes of him!'

My mother frowned at my logic, 'History says that man made woman. She behaved as she was instructed to by him. This was the right given to him by the shastras, the holy books and ancient texts.'

I replied, 'That wasn't creation. Man took the power into his own hands to protect his rule because he was afraid of the abilities of women. Man has always used woman.'

Finally, there was an explosion one day. It wasn't the atom bomb thrown on Hiroshima-Nagasaki or the napalm dropped on Vietnam, it was a silent detonation. I had heard a lot of taunts in my time but this time a shower of fiery words rained down on my head. 'What is she so proud of? Her father's importance or her insignificant job as a teacher? She could only give birth to one daughter, that's all, no sign of any son and heir. If my son hadn't been such a simpleton he would have taken another wife long ago.' That day I had been busy correcting my students' homework and dinner was slightly delayed, the first time something like this had happened.

My blood started boiling, 'Ma ji that's enough. I am not willing to listen to your ranting any longer. Please tell your son whatever you have to say….'

This was my first revolt. I knew it would be explosive. Vimal had gone to Jammu. I was waiting for him, maybe he could find a solution and free me from these daily taunts and scoldings. Perhaps he could convince Ma and Papa that Devika had fulfilled all our desires for a child. Perhaps….But Vimal did not even want to hear my side of the story. My last hopes were dashed. Vimal was tired after the long hill journey of ten hours. His heart held very little warmth towards me anyway. The destructive notes of his mother's laments enraged him, 'All my life I have had to listen to my elders, now I cannot bear to hear this young woman's abuses.'

Vimal kicked at my door in anger, 'How did this woman get the courage to abuse my mother? If she is proud of being the daughter of an important man, she can go back to live with him.' I was stunned. I didn't move, open the door, or reply. There was no question of it in the face of so many challenges and accusations. Vimal kept banging on the door. Devika clung to me in fear. The thunderous sounds continued for a while and then became quiet. I stuffed some essential clothes into a bag and left the house holding Devika's hand. Devika was sobbing but my eyes were dry. I left home.

The road was misty. The pale sun, tangled in the branches of the chinar-kikar, hung like a dirty rag. Walking towards my father's house I knew that I had embarked on a journey. But towards which destination? I did not know. Devika put her arms around me. I wanted to close my mind but it was full of different images rushing along at top speed.

'A daughter-in-law is like the cornerstone of the house, if it shifts the entire edifice will come tumbling down.' My mother, grandmother, aunt everyone said this. Who knows when the foundation shifted, when the first cracks developed and who had collapsed.

I look back and see a lot of young girls full of enthusiasm. There is a youth festival in Delhi.

I ask my father, 'Papa can I go?'

He hands me the ticket money and says, 'Go and get your father-in-law's permission. After marriage you need his permission, not your father's.'

My father-in law's fair face becomes grey, his nostrils shake with anger.

'What is this nonsense? Are the daughters-in-law of the Munshi family going to dance and act in front of strangers now? Does freedom mean a complete absence of shame?'

I felt like I was sinking into the ground. But I was really vexed when my sister-in-law, Jaya was given permission to go. In her case she was participating in a cultural show not dancing and singing in public! That was the day an ember of silent revolt first ignited within me. Why different rules for a daughter and a daughter-in-law? Is this why there has always been a tradition that the whiplashes of in-laws fall on daughters-in-law? Is this tradition going to carry on further?

For many nights my silent tears soaked the pillow. The sad narcissus went down on its knees and wept in the yellow lights of the stage.

Was I looking for Jayant in Vimal at that time?

Nadeem sahib said, 'One must rebel against oppression.'

But mother said, 'There has been oppression for decades, and it will continue. Some statements are just true on paper, others are the lived reality.'

It had rained at night and the potholes on the street were filled with water. As the auto moved ahead, it scattered muddy water as it dipped in and out of the puddles. A big glob of smelly mud spattered across my sari. Ma will definitely say that the mud can be washed off your sari but how will you wipe out the disgrace you have brought to the family?

In '48 when I had seen girls learning how to use rifles alongside boys in the exhibition grounds I had begged, 'Tathya, I want to learn how to use a rifle.' Among the girls there was Uma Razdan, Kaushalya, Krishna Misri, Zainab Begum...there was the fragrance of freedom in the air and hearts were full of hopes and enthusiasm. The slogan, 'This Kashmir is ours, we will protect it. We will rule over it.' had echoed through the Valley.

Premnath Pardeshi had said, 'Every citizen is a soldier of his country. Why should women be left behind?'

The winds of change were blowing through the Girl's College as well. Nadim Sahib had told the girls to step out of their cages. They were now playing cricket. Mohini was the captain of the hockey team. Shanta was performing the role of Habba khatoon in a play and Uma was acting as Yusuf Shah Chak! Ragya was King Lear....

Prem bhaiya teased me, 'Ragya will become a jack of all trades, master of none!'

Papa was disappointed, 'Katya is going to become a doctor, but this girl can't manage anything. She is totally uncontrollable. Good for nothing.'

The day he was handed the piece of paper with my poem written on it he gave up hope altogether. The first time he became suspicious about the relationship between Jayant and me, he could feel the souls of the last seven generations of the Raina family writhing in agony. Papa decided that this evil had to be uprooted before it spread any further.

God knows how evil it was, that fluttering of the heart. Running up the stairs, to catching a bare glimpse from the attic window of the restless young man with curly hair standing in the backyard for whom one was willing to sacrifice everything in life! On the river, alongside the bund, young lovers sat in the shade of the swaying curtains of the shikaras. The air was filled with the maddening perfume of peach and cherry blossoms.

I had met Jayant only once in the shade of these intoxicating flowers. That meeting, perfumed by the peach blossoms, had permeated our very hearts and bodies. The breeze saw us and the roses smiled in pleasure. The mynah bent down to sing its sweet melody in our ears. What had Jayant said in that eternal interlude of half an hour that had made the milky streams rushing down the hills of Ishbar spill over?

All I remembered was the perfume, filled with the teasing ache of the love stories narrated by Farmaroz to Lallarookh. The prince of Iran joined the caravan of his betrothed. It had been decided that the wedding would be held in the beautiful valley of Kashmir but Farmaroz felt it was necessary to gauge Lallarookh's heart first. Or did he want to awaken the thirst for love in her heart?

Reciting Thomas Moore's poem, Jayant was the prince of Iran who had taken on the disguise of Farmaroz in order to test Lallarookh.

'My "reward", Lallarookh? You promised.' It was Farmaroz speaking to Lallarookh, not Jayant to Ragya.

'Reward?' Lallarookh had become Ragya. She didn't posses any treasure, what could she give?

Jayant had burst out laughing. His smile had captivated Ragya. Jayant said, ' You have everything.'

Then, submerged in the perfume of the roses, they had come together for the first time. Without thinking they had kissed each other gently. That innocent experience of a seventeen year old had flowed like a warm waterfall through her veins for the twenty years of her marriage, spreading like a healing balm over the wounds of Vimal's ill-tempered, mechanical and self-centered love-making.

'You know the meaning of touch. You aren't poor!'

That magical world had faded as soon as she reached home.

Someone had seen them walking hand-in-hand, laughing. A male hand, a female hand (that too a girl's), shared laughter, open sky! What would happen to the family's reputation? This meeting fell on my mother like a thunderbolt. She howled and beat her breasts till she became unconscious. Papa was more practical. Within two months he found Vimal Munshi and sent me off. Vimal was a promising young engineer working for the PWD who was expected to become a famous chief engineer sometime in the future after he had constructed numerous bridges, dams, temples and mosques, not merely in the state but in the country and abroad.

Tathya first expressed surprise and then objected to the undue haste, 'Shiva, let the girl finish her BA exams at least! It is not as if she is growing old!

'Your daughter-in-law is insisting, Tathya! Just give your blessings. Her future in-laws will allow her to complete her studies. It is a good family and the boy is promising. What else do we need?'

My mother-in-law would be happy one moment, 'May your father live long, he has sent the Goddess Lakshmi to my house!' The next moment she would be saddened when she remembered Muthoo sahib, 'Muthoo sahib has a really generous heart. It has never happened before, but when he returned his son-in-law's horoscope he had encased it in gold and put it in a ship made of silver!'

This ostentatious act of Muthoo sahib's had become quite a topic of discussion among the community. Those who had become prosperous under the new rulers were trying to find new ways of spending their money. Whereas earlier even the well-to-do middle classes gifted their daughters just five sets of clothing and some utensils on their marriages, now it was becoming socially acceptable to expect half-a-dozen attaché cases and trunks, furniture, gold, silver and cash.

Vasanta was right when she said, 'Ragya, I wish we also had

a dowry system like the Banias. At least they decide on a definite amount. Here, there is no dowry, merely an unending series of expectations. Even when the daughters are old enough to become grandmothers and mothers-in-law their parents have to keep sending gifts on different occasions. And if their parents are no longer alive then their brothers have to shoulder the burden.'

My binoculars now focus themselves on the city of Jammu some years after my marriage. The Girl's College at the Parade Ground: Rita, Vinod and Kailash are trying to persuade me. 'Come on, come with us today. We will be back by lunch time.' Our class is going to Bahu fort for a picnic.

'I will be in real trouble if I am late! Ma ji's eyes are always glued to the clock.' I try to refuse.

'We won't be late! Is it your home or the cellular jail? Will the heavens fall if we are delayed by an hour?'

The girls climb up to the fort, giggling and out of breath. Colourful chunnis flutter in the breeze. The pleasant sun makes everyone's cheeks rosy. My eyes are fixed on the hands of my watch. Is it fear or a blameless guilt? I haven't taken permission for this trip from my in-laws. There is an explosion as soon as I step into the house. My father-in-law takes off his turban and lays it at my feet, 'Here, daughter-in-law, you are bent on destroying my honour, why don't you just complete the job?' My mother-in-law is raging like a captive lioness,' If anything like this had happened during my time, my mother-in-law would have called the barber and shaved off my hair!'

I can't understand what crime I have committed but the ground seems to have shifted beneath my feet. The sky has fallen because I did not think it necessary to take permission from my elders. My first mistake has become a challenge for them. It may be an indication of future insubordination! I feel as though I hadn't merely gone for a picnic but slept with a man. Wouldn't my father-in-law have been dishonoured if I had run away with someone?

That night, after I had almost cried my self to sleep, a dry barren sun-baked desert started gradually growing inside me. More than sorrow it was the sharp pain of humiliation that was killing me slowly like a goat being sacrificed. For what crime was I being punished? Which century had I been pushed into? There were four months left for Vimal's return. I gave in and wrote a letter to my mother. 'I want to stay with you till Vimal comes back. I can't bear it any more, Ma!'

In the seventeenth century Habba Khatoon had begged her parents to rescue her from the tyranny of her in-laws, 'I am not happy with my in-laws, please help me!' How much had we really changed despite claims of progress?

Ma used Niranjan as a messenger and sent back a letter along with a basket of fruit. The letter was full of the usual sentiments and references to the tolerance and patience of women like Lalded and Roopded! When Lalded's mother-in-law served her a mere handful of rice spread over a piece of stone, she quietly ate the rice, washed the stone and put it back in the kitchen. Her husband accused her of immoral behaviour, broke her pot of water but she did not protest. That is why the pond filled with lotuses and lotus stems with her fine spun yarn. God finally heard her prayers and she became a yogini. And Roopbhavani? Did she have any less to bear? Ultimately her mother-in-law realized her mistake and regretted her earlier behaviour. In other words, some day even my in-laws would be shamed by the accusations they had made. I should be patient. These were merely testing times. The same story. It had happened before and would continue to happen in the future. But I did not posess either the patience of Lalded or Roopbhavani nor their yogic powers. It was impossible to explain to Ma that examples from the fourteenth and sixteenth century were of no use to me in the twentieth century. I decided to keep quiet.

Vimal became an engineer. I felt things would change now as I accompanied him to Agra and Jaipur. I had one or two miscarriages and when I was expecting again Katya didi came to take me away with her, 'Ragya needs bed rest for three months. Let her come with me.' Vimal was unhappy at Katya's interference. He shrugged his shoulders, 'My mother husked grain almost till the moment her children were born. Every woman becomes a mother. I don't know what the problem is.'

But Katya kept me under her supervision. When the six pound little girl looked at me with her almond eyes my breasts overflowed with milk. I let Devika suckle on my milk and forgave the world all its excesses against me.

Vimal went to America to do his MS. He did not want to spend his life as a Junior engineer. I returned to my marital home. Nothing had changed for me in the house even though there were many changes in the world outside.

New residential areas were being constructed under Bakshi sahib's administration. After Karan Nagar now there were Jawahar Nagar, Rawalpura, Barzulla, Santnagar etc. etc. When government employees were offered plots at concessional rates my brother-in-law also bought land in Rawalpora and constructed a house. My sister-in-law was finally freed from the ranting of our mother-in-law and our joint family disintegrated. I took Tathya's support and applied for admission in MA Hindi. I picked up my books again six years after completing my BA I was not ready to sit idle for two years waiting for Vimal to return. My mother-in-law was enraged, 'The older one broke up the house and went away and now the younger one has started her studies again. Am I supposed to take care of everyone? Give me some respite now.' Tathya invited my father-in-law home and said, 'We will take care of the child. Please allow Ragya to continue with her studies.'

My father-in-law couldn't refuse Tathya though he couldn't understand why I wanted to study. If I had to do my MA why didn't I study English or Math? What would I do with Hindi?

Tathya smiled and explained the importance of Hindi

literature, its significance in our culture and its connection with Sanskrit. Not that it was wrong to study English, after all we earned our daily bread because of our knowledge of it. But Hindi was our national language.... My father-in-law did not argue with Tathya. It was beyond him to argue with a lawyer.

Tathya had done a lot of work to try and spread the knowledge and use of Hindi in the state. After independence the government laid greater emphasis on Urdu and Hindi was sidelined. Then Shivnath Kaul's son Tribhuvan Nath and his daughter Vimla Kaul established the Oriental College and started classes from Kovid to Prabhakar in Hindi. Tathya also joined this mission along with Kashyap Bandhu, Sridhar Dullu, Shambhunath Parimoo, Kamala Parimoo, Professor Shrikanth Toshkhani, Chamanlal Sapru and RC Pandit. Sharika and Dulari, my elder sisters also studied in Hindi.

Vimal joined the engineering college on his return. I insisted on doing my Doctorate. 'Do what you want but don't neglect your household duties. I don't want the Mahabharat war happening every day at home.' Vimal agreed with a warning. I accepted the challenge. With Bhobaji's help or because of his influence I got a job in the Girl's College. For the first time I felt confident of myself.

Apart from the four or five hours spent in the college I continued to perform the same role as before in the house. My status remained the same. Yes, sometimes the chores would be delayed if I got late and minor skirmishes continued. Vimal's status, however, increased day by day. There were drink parties outside the house and sometimes friends started dropping in for drinks at home as well. I did not object to Vimal's drinking but I did to his getting drunk and throwing up. One day I refused to clean up the mess. Then I objected to his desire for physical intimacy while he was inebriated. I had started looking worn out. He had only one suggestion, 'Why don't you leave the job, rest a little, after all you are just teaching Hindi?' I started resenting Vimal's touch. I gradually grew away from him.

'I don't feel like it, please. Some other time, not today.'

'Just close your eyes and lie there. You don't have to do anything. Let me do the work.'

Vimal would start snoring once he was done. I would scream inside. Was this a marital relationship or rape? I was just an object, nothing more.

The next morning Vimal would remind me, 'Don't forget, you are my wife.'

'Are you a husband or a rapist?' I was also becoming savage.

'That is my right, my dear wife! I didn't kidnap you, I married you with all the rites and rituals!'

My body gradually turned to stone. It would not awaken even if I tried. Even the desire to find out how much this rubberized body satisfied Vimal, irritated him or turned him off, had died.

Ma had said, 'A woman is just a vessel.'

'To keep a man pure and satisfied.' I imagined a dirty commode and felt disgusted.

Ma! You have pushed me into a blind alley with your definition of a woman's duties.

The door of the house was in front of me. The women going to the river bank with their prayer baskets turned around to look at me. The lawyer's daughter has come home for a visit. At that time it was becoming a little cold in the evenings. Behind the houses with the slanting roofs on the banks of the Vitasta, the tired rays of the sun had bent down to the snow-covered peaks to slake their thirst. The dome of the temple had become bronze in colour in the fading light of the evening.

As I crossed the courtyard and stepped into the verandah I saw my mother coming out of her room carrying a full commode. The thought came to my mind that all her life Ma has merely remained the cleaner of commodes for Papa. At that time I did not know that Papa had had a paralytic attack at night and that now Ma really would have to clean his commode.

The room was full of family and acquaintances. Katya, her husband, Brij bhaiya, Raghunath bhaiya, Niranjan.... Katya hugged me and Devika, 'It is good that both of you have come. We were just about to send Niranjan. Papa needs to be taken care of.' The famous lawyer of the valley, Shivnath Raina, was lying inert and motionless. There was just a little bit of movement on his left. My mother, who was so used to being scolded constantly by her husband, burst into tears as soon as she saw me. 'His angina had increased. He was already hypertensive....' People were talking softly, 'He suddenly fell down yesterday and then he couldn't get up...'

Papa made us serve him for a month. One night there was a muffled sound from his room. I woke up when something fell with a crash on the floor. I looked into his room. Papa was fumbling for something on the side table. As he searched, the glass of water on the table fell and broke. Ma had a headache last night. She had taken a tablet. She was irritated by the sound...

'What do you want? Do you want to go to the toilet? I was just taking a nap, my head is bursting...'

I asked Papa, 'Do you need anything?' He pointed at the Amrutanjan with his finger, 'Should I put some on your forehead? When I picked up some balm on my finger he pointed at Ma and mumbled, 'I wanted it for her...' Ma looked at Papa in disbelief, understood and burst into tears. 'I am fine now, I have taken some medicine. Now go to sleep.' All her life Ma never forgot this tender gesture. He did give Ma her due, even if it happened only at the end of his life.

Papa's grandfather had chosen the daughter of Lassabhatt of Bandipora for his grandson. He had given his word without consulting his son. Pandit Lakshmanjoo's promise was like the word of king Dashrath. But for Papa this was a lifelong sentence. Papa wanted a delicate doe-eyed wife with wavy hair like Kamala Nehru. An educated woman who could converse in Hindi and English. Ma had to bear the brunt of Papa's anger against his parents and the entire world. The girl who used to roam around freely like a baby goat in the fields of her village, had to learn the rules and customs of the lawyer's home, and learn enough Hindi to be able to read it and write letters. But Papa had kept her standing in the dock all her life.

Ma however, remembered only his hand reaching out for the Amrutanjan. She was satisfied that her penance had been rewarded. But I had nothing to remember. I had broken out of the dock. After a month I spoke to Bhobaji about a transfer. 'If I am transferred to Anantnag or Baramulla, I can take Devika with me and go. I don't want to stay here and become a topic of discussion. '

Ma cried softly. Before Bhobaji could say anything Lalli ma took me in her arms and scolded me gently, 'Since when have you become so thoughtless that you can think of leaving your mother alone? We are also living by ourselves here. You can stay with us and look after us. Remember, only those people who have done something wrong worry about gossip. You have faced so many tests in the past twenty years.'

Katya said, 'You have been living in fear for a long time, now stop being scared. All will be well.' My in-laws came to express their grief at Papa's passing away. They sent messages once or twice for me to return, but I was not planning to go back. I signed the divorce papers. I wanted to erase every incident, every moment of the past twenty years from my mind.

Days, months and seasons passed. I would come out on the balcony if a melancholy melody played on a flute wafted across the Vitasta on a moonlit night. Some Lochinvar would call out to his beloved, 'Look for me by moonlight/I will come to thee by moonlight/Though hell should bar the way.'

My pen would start racing across the paper. My mind would run towards that Lochinvar whose name was Jayant. Who was imprisoned in his room on the day of my wedding, so that he wouldn't battle with the elements to reach me. His unfortunate father who was just a teacher, couldn't withstand the might of the famous lawyer Shivnath! He had agreed to whatever the lawyer suggested. After twenty years I called out to him in solitude, 'Where are you, Jayant?' My voice froze in the wintry cold: Jayant was long gone – he had left the Valley twenty years ago in anger and despair.

The small room at the back of the temple has become empty. Durga died on one of the freezing winter nights. Dinakak and Jaya covered the body with flowers and consigned it to the flames. After that Jaya left the room and shifted her world to a dark corner of the Shivalaya. Ma would say, 'Durga has gone to heaven. She used to pray to Lord Shiva every night and morning.'

Dinakak passed away. His younger son moved to Bombay. The older one worked in the temple. He had neither his father's faith nor his melodious voice. The Brahmin Mandal had decided to pay him a monthly salary but he seemed more interested in the donation box. No one was attracted to priesthood any more.

Woolly clouds had spread across the sky. Clothes were hanging on the line outside. Ma got up to gather the washing in case it rained. I wanted to write something. I should get up, I thought, there was so much that I had to say.

❧

Shihul Villa

Navreh. Searching for something new in the crevices of time, the new year once again made its appearance, pushing aside the darkness with its silent steps. In the midst of the pink and dark colours of the east, the snow-touched breezes gently kissed the long branches of the towering poplars. Navreh Mubarak! Happy New Year!

Katya, who had slept late, rubbed her gritty eyes and looked at the covered Navreh thali lying on the side table. She lifted the cloth that lay atop it and recited a few mantras. The mound of rice at the center of the platter was surrounded by tiny bowls containing curd, milk, sweets and fruit. There were pictures of Lakshmi and Ganesh, Saraswati and the lunar calendar for the New Year, as well as a bunch of smiling narcissi. Katya picked up a pen and wrote the letter Om with a steady hand on the letter pad. The first and the last letter of creation: Om. She dipped a slice of 'Vay' in a mixture of curds and sugar and touched it gingerly to her tongue.

'Think of it as the herb of eternal life. Taste it on New Year and you won't fall ill the entire year.'

She felt as though Lalli, sitting far away in a foreign land, was gently caressing her hair. She remembered scenes from the past. With the arrival of this festival, which has been celebrated for generations, the Brahmin community got busy with religious and social activities and suddenly the woman of the house became important.

Chaitra Shukla Paksh Pratipada. On this day, she was the one who knocked at everyone's doors at the crack of dawn and showed them the thali filled with food, wealth and images of the gods. With her hands she planted rice and wheat in platters made of mud and invited the goddess Durga, covered with a veil of delicate green grass, into the house with her fasts, prayers and her faith. The goddess was the symbol of prosperity and well being for the entire year. Doctor Katyayini had also been observing this festival for the past twenty years. Despite the preoccupations of her profession and her many unorthodox beliefs, she made time for traditions as the woman of the house. Kartikeya knew that Katya would wake him up before daybreak to wish him a happy Navreh. He barely opened his eyes, bowed before the platter and, pulling Katya close with his right arm, kissed her on her forehead. A gift for the New Year!

The children looked at the thali with half-shut eyes, picked up fistfuls of walnuts and shoved them under their pillows. They wished their mother 'Happy New Year' in sleepy tones, yawning as they pleaded, 'Can we sleep just a little bit more? Please!' And then they flopped back onto their beds. Katya found herself back in her childhood, looking at the fading glory of festive occasions. Time gave a lot but it also took away some things. Laughter, jokes, enthusiasm, all these were gradually fading away with the passage of time.

Time had swallowed childhood. The boats which used to ferry passengers from one shore to another were now used to give rides to tourists around the Dal lake and Nehru Park. No one had the time or the need to use the slow, gently swaying boats to cover distances. Now city buses, taxis, cars or Matadors were more useful to save time.

The atmosphere was full of smoke, dust and noise. Sheikh sahib had become the leader of the state once again after twenty years. The region was making progress. Look at the boulevard, or the magnificent new hotels in Pahalgam, Gulmarg, Sonamarg which raise their heads to the snow covered mountains. New factories had come up. The newspapers said that seven lakh tourists visited Kashmir in 1980. Earlier there had never been more than two lakh visitors.

But the Vitasta had begun to dry up. The mother was becoming pale and emaciated. If only Katya could find a cure for this. The river, however, did not flow through Gogjibagh in front of Dr Kartikeya and Katya's home 'Shihul villa' which adjoined the courtyard of the hospital. When Arjun and Isha awoke they would throw walnuts from their balcony straight into the pool in the middle of the lawn and Sona, the gardner's son, would wade into the water and gather them up.

Sona's sons, Gulla and Sulla, had become Arjun and Isha's friends. When Arjun hit the crcket ball into the rose bushes, Gulla would run and pick it up. And when Arjun thanked him saying, 'Shabash, well-done Gulshera' he extended his tiny little palm for toffees. His eyes were innocent but his voice was naughty, 'Shabash is not enough, bhaijaan!' Sometimes Gulla told Isha and Arjun what he was taught at school. 'Should I read from my textbook? Yesterday's lesson?' Without waiting for their response he ran and fetched his school bag and recited the lesson.

'Little children, be quiet. We will tell you about Islam. You may say that you do not have an army but you still have to fight for your religion….'

'Should I recite some more, bhaijaan?'

Arjun shrugged, 'Okay.'

'We are Kashmiris. Our land is Kashmir. It is surrounded by India, China and Iran…'

When Arjun read Gulla's text book for the first time he wondered who taught children in the third grade to fight in the name of religion. During his time the texts had beautiful songs like 'My desire comes to my lips as a prayer. May my life be like the lamp which illuminates…'

'Which school do you go to, Gulla?' Arjun asked.

'The madrasa in the mosque. Maulvi sahib teaches us.'

Arjun asked his father the same question, 'What are these madrasas that have been started in mosques, which teach little children to fight in the name of Islam? They fill their minds with the belief that they are separate from India by talking about being surrounded by India, China and Iran.'

Kartikeya had heard that the Jamaat-i-Islami group had started teaching Islamic studies in mosques. Preachers came from Pakistan and explained the greatness of the 'Nizam-e-Mustafa'. But one had hoped that religious proselytizing would stop in schools after the return of Sheikh sahib. This hadn't happened. Instead, it was now clear, the Jamaat-i-Islami had started targeting the innocent minds of young children.

'We had heard about the Jamaat-i-Islami Hind which came into existence after independence to improve the condition of Indian Muslims and encourage education among the community. But here the intention seems to be quite different.'

'No, Arjun, this is not the same organization. This one began in our valley in Shopian in 1942. It was Ghulam Mohammad Ahar who laid the foundations of the Kashmiri Jamaat-i-Islami. Its aim is to merge Kashmir with Pakistan. It calls the central government, "Delhi Durbar".'

'This is a strange situation, Papa! First neither Sheikh sahib nor Bakshi sahib allowed any other party to come into existence. Though a responsible opposition strengthens democracy. Praja Parishad and the Jana Sangh faced a lot of opposition for being communal parties but look at what is happening now!'

Kartikeya remembered Sadiq sahib.

'Sadiq sahib laid the foundation of the National Conference in Kashmir, he was quite liberal in his outlook. But immediately after he passed away Mir Qasim reversed the situation. It was during his time that the Jamaat-i-Islami won five seats in the Legislative Assembly.'

'Religious fanaticism has become a part of politics and these madrasas are the result of it.'

Arjun felt a subdued agitation, 'Papa! Don't you think these madrasas could destroy our Kashmiriyat?'

'This education which can destroy the tolerant traditions of Lal Ded and Nund Rishi is far more dangerous than the proxy war Pakistan started in Kashmir after the creation of Bangladesh or the ISI network which General Zia-ul-Haq has spread through the valley.'

Arjun was really upset, 'Today we feel these tiny children

Gulla and Sulla are our own but who knows whether tomorrow religious fanaticism will turn them into our enemies?'

'Don't be so distressed Arjun.' Papa tried to calm him down. 'So far Sheikh sahib has succeeded in tempering down the fires of this volcano. Only time can tell what will happen in the future.'

Time, which was constantly changing, like the seasons. And even that which didn't change, did it remain the same? Just as it was before?

Earlier, everyone visited the Durganag temple on the occasion of Durga Ashtami. They would climb the Shankaracharya hill to pay obeisance to the Shiva lingam in the temple situated at its pinnacle. Children and youngsters would charge up the hill, huffing and puffing, leaning against boulders till they could enjoy the beautiful view of the Dal Lake seen from a height of a thousand feet. They looked forward, with great enthusiasm, to this picnic festival. They would listen to stories about Shankaracharya hill and Zeethyaer narrated by their elders; they heard that two thousand five hundred years before the Christian era, King Sandhiman of the Gunadhya dynasty built the Shiva temple on top of this hill and that it was originally called Sandhiman hill and the temple was named Jetheshwar.

And on Ramnavmi they visited the Rama temple where a huge havan was performed in the courtyard. Outside, the garden was perfumed by the white and pink, cherry and peach blossoms and the aroma of the kehwa brewing in samovars, which refreshed the mind and soul. Sweetmeat sellers put up their small tents, and prepared lotus stem fritters and boiling hot lucchis, making everyone's mouths water. As the new green shoots burst forth from the earth, young hearts filled with longing, intoxicated with the fragrance of the blossoms.

Now the spring passed by with a fleeting touch. There was a sense of freedom in the breeze. Burkas and veils had become symbols of backwardness.

Arjun nudged Isha and Alka, 'What is this, the same old Hari Parbat and Shankaracharya temple! We will spend our new year in Pahalgam next to the Lidder river.'

'We will have to ask Mama,' Alka said thoughtfully.

'Which century do you belong to, you old fashioned woman? You are going to become a doctor after four years but you still don't step out of the house without asking your Mama and Papa.' Arjun made a face.

Arjun and Alka were students of medicine at the university. Their families were friends. Arjun complained that Alka never took any decisions on her own. 'After all you are not a kid!'

'Is there any harm in asking one's elders, Arjun?' Katya sometimes had to intervene.

'That is okay Mama. But why can't these girls be assertive? Don't you agree that they are always anxious and worried, despite their outward modernity?'

'Anxiety and worry are our patrimony, Arjun! It will take us a while to get rid of them. There is some difference in your and Alka's background, son. Alka is the first girl to move out of the protected, enclosed atmosphere of her house. She has to think before taking any step. She has to prove herself.'

'You are lucky, Arjun! You can do as you please. You are a man after all. I have to give an account of every minute I spend outside the house, even today. Papa comes out to look for me if I am even a little late.'

'Bhaiya, don't forget Alka lives downtown in Navakadal. A place where the fresh air of change hardly ever dares to enter. And what about the hooliganism? I wonder how she manages to walk down those streets.' The downtown area was completely under the control of the orthodox Al Fateh and Jamaat-e-Islami. There were incidents every other day. Many Batta families had shifted to the newer parts of town. Alka's father was thinking of taking a house on rent in Karan Nagar.

The minority syndrome was gradually increasing among the Battas. Isha sympathised with Alka.

Katya walked towards Omkar Bhai's room with the filled platter. The early morning sun was shining on the branches of the regal looking chinar which was visible from the verandah. The sound of the fluttering wings of the nightingale and the sleepy, guttural cooing of the Poshnool filled the air. Sati's melodious voice could be heard through the half-closed door of Omkar bhai's room, 'Hey Shiva, grant me the boon that I may never shy away from good deeds....'

She came out when she heard a soft knock on the door. She folded her hands and bowed before the platter.

'Navreh Mubarak, Sati!'

'To you as well, didi, Happy New Year!'

'Here, please take this plate. Show it to Omkar bhai and Tipu when they wake up. I am going to the ward. There was a caesarian yesterday, and it's a slightly complicated case. I will be back soon. I just want to have a look. In the meanwhile, why don't you make the kheer, the milk pudding? The children can have their baths and put on their new clothes. Remember there is a staff party today.'

'Yes, didi. How can I forget? Don't worry.'

Handing over the reins of the day to Sati, Katya stopped worrying about the house.

The other sisters-in-law, full of unnecessary pride at their social status and the positions held by their husbands, made faces when they saw Sati, 'What a priceless diamond our doctor sister-in-law has found in the refugee camp.'

'Hey, didi. Would any beautiful girl from a good family ever marry our crazy brother-in-law?'

'Yes! You are right! God knows how many people pawed her during the Kabaili raid. Now she has been elevated to this position without anyone bothering about what is good, bad, true or untrue. And who can say anything?'

Katya did not refer to religion nor did she reveal the depths of Sati's pain and suffering. She only repeated the sentence that she had said to her grandmother earlier regarding Tulsi, 'Suppose we had been in her place, what would we have done? Jumped into the river?'

The fair faces of the sisters-in-law turned ashen. They thought Katya was irreligious, proud, stubborn and god knows what else. She had employed Noori as a cook and Sula and Gula wandered in and out of her kitchen as they liked. Would all this have happened if their father-in-law, who was such a staunch devotee of Shiva, had been alive?

They chose to forget the fact that it was Kameshwarnath who had gone to Tathya to ask for Katya's hand for his son. Kameshwarnath died soon after Katya's marriage. He did not force his beliefs on anyone. He merely passed on a responsibility to Katya.

'This is Omkar. Your youngest brother-in-law. Don't be misled by his physical appearance. Mentally he is a child. I am certain that you will treat him like your son and teach him how to live.'

Katya lived up to this expectation, which often confronted her in the shape of a challenge.

Surrounded by the rejection and contempt of the family, Omkar appeared to be like the Bodhisattva, alone and isolated. His brothers called him a madman in front of visitors. Omkar bhai never responded to these insults. Not with anger, nor with sorrow. The mentally backward youngest, the last among brothers who were doctors, lawyers, engineers. Kameshwarnath tried very hard to give him some basic education. Omkar learnt some Hindi and Urdu but couldn't understand Math and Science at all.

The father was worried about what would happen to Omkar after him. A person with no consciousness of social behaviour, no recognition of what was good or bad for him. A child's mind in a grown up's body. Kartikeya consulted specialists and tried different kinds of treatment, check ups, tests but without any real results.

The doctors gave up saying, 'Accept him as he is. Thank god he isn't violent. It is possible he may become a little sensible and worldly wise as time goes on. He needs love and care. No medicines. He is physically fit.' Kameshwarnath willed everything he owned to Omkar and made Katya the guardian. He bought a machine for making socks for the boy to keep him occupied and away from bad company. Everything was fine while he was alive. His death left Omkar bhai without any protection. The day after Kameshwarnath passed away Katya brought Omkar with her to Srinagar. As he was leaving, Omkar stuffed things haphazardly into his small case. Things given by his father, photographs, shaving kit, the sock knitting machine and the large photo of Papa in the study.

Katya said, 'Take the photo, but are the other things really necessary?'

Omkar shook his head gravely and holding the case tighter said, 'Yes, Papa gave them to me, that's why.'

Katya melted inside. Omkar wanted to carry his father's fragrance with him. Papa was no longer there but how could Omkar distance himself from his touch, his love, his concern?

Omkar was very quiet for the few days at Shihul Villa. Katya and Kartik tried hard to make him happy.

When Arjun arrived, it was as though Omkar bhai had found a toy. If Arjun cried Omkar bhai would cup his hands and make bird and animal sounds to soothe him. He would tickle the baby, put him in a pram and take him around the garden. He had found a small friend. Even Arjun would open his arms wide whenever he saw Omkar. As the Sunaina hospital grew Kartikeya and Katya found even twenty-four hours too few to deal with all their responsibilities. They followed a set routine and sometimes there would be emergency cases at night. Despite this Katya would cajole Kartik, 'Let's play a game of Carrom with Omkar bhai? He must be feeling lonely, the two of us are so busy.' Omkar would be delighted and would immediately start setting up the game. He was a child after all.

But one day Katya and Katik realized that Omkar bhai really wasn't a child anymore. The head nurse in the hospital, Jani, who had been around for so long that she considered herself a part of the family, hinted to them that something had changed. After all, he was a good-looking young man. Apparently he had tried to tempt Noori into his room with some money. A poor person can always be tempted with money. She was loyal and wanted to alert them in case something untoward happened. Katya felt as though she were being reminded of her oversight.

'A young man sitting alone and idle at home, did you think he was a child?' Katya felt Jani was labouring the point.

'No, Jani, nothing untoward happened, I think Noori may have misunderstood.'

Jani became agitated, 'Dr Sahiba. I have had my suspicions for a while. Noori is a straightforward good girl which is why she told me, otherwise how much time does it take to succumb to temptation?'

Katya spoke to Kartikeya. How did it happen that while dealing with high and low BP's, anaemia, blood sugar, heart problems of their patients they had overlooked Omkar's problem?

They thought deeply on the subject. The conclusion was, marriage!

But to whom? In the community Omkar bhai was considered to be an idiot. 'That crazy fellow? Why don't you just throw the girl into a well, instead of marrying her to him?'

Kameshwarnath had told Katya, ' I am certain you will treat him as your son and teach him how to live.'

That certainty haunted her. 'What now? Where will we find a girl who will agree to marry Omkar despite his shortcomings?' And once they were married who could foretell whether the bedroom would become a haven of peace or a battleground? Katya was worried. Neelu suggested Surinder, 'The girl has suffered for the last twenty years. She is well behaved, intelligent and confident. Talk to her. She might agree. I like Surinder.'

Surinder was an open book. She even revealed things that were not known to everyone.

During the Kabaili attack, the twelve-year old Surinder was separated from her parents and brother one dark night as they were running and hiding in the jungles of Uri. A soldier saw the fear stricken girl, exhausted with crying, hidden behind a cliff. He picked her up in his jeep and took her to the camp. Surinder stayed in the Bageshwari camp. She learnt sewing, stitched clothes and settled down in the house of Prem, the baker.

'For twenty years, didi, twenty black years. I didn't spot my parents anywhere in the streets or lanes.' Surinder choked, 'I was tough, I survived in the hope that I would find my people some day...' Surinder's bad luck followed her everywhere. Both Prem, the baker, and his old mother died in a cholera epidemic. Finding her alone a horde of Prem's relatives descended on her to lay claim to the small room. How could Surinder fight a legal battle on her own?

'I must have done something good that is why I met Neelu didi. Aunt Indira used to get clothes stitched by me and I started visiting her home. Neelu didi has given me a corner in the house. I brought my sewing machine along. What else do I need?' Surinder stopped wishing for anything and continued to stitch clothes. Katya listened to Surinder. A thirty two year old sallow woman whose attraction lay in her voice and her determination not to be defeated. Yes. She was the one. Like Kameshwarnath, some conviction filled Katya. Surinder would be able to take care of Omkar. Katya did not give any guarantees of happiness, nor did she offer any money. She only promised a shelter for someone who was homeless.

'I am handing over a child to you in the form of a husband.

Meet him, we will accept any decision you make. No one will force you.' Surinder listened to Katya with disbelief and started crying silently.

Katya hugged her, 'We need you, sister, we are not doing you a favour.' Surinder met Omkar bhai. The two of them came to some understanding and the marriage took place after a week. Omkar bhai said, 'I will do whatever Bhabi says.'

Surinder said, 'You have shown concern about my welfare. I will take care of you.'

She was grateful. At least someone cared about her.

Omkar bhai was married. He looked handsome as a bridegroom and Surinder also glowed in a pink sari. Katya now called her Sati.

No one knew what transpired between them behind the closed doors of their room, but when Sati became pregnant within a year Kartik gave Katya a meaningful glance. Jani had been right after all. Both of them were even happier when Tipu came into the family. Omkar bhai called out to the child constantly and got busy with a new set of worries and affections. Suddenly he acquired the right to scold Sati, 'Why do you leave him alone in the sun, suppose a cat comes and scratches him, then? What sort of a mother are you?'

At night he would constantly keep checking if the child was breathing properly, worried that the baby might be stifled by a piece of cloth.

Katya was grateful to God for his kindness to the inhabitants of Shihul Villa. She prayed that he would continue to bless them. Sometimes Jani would drop in to play with Tipu and chat with Sati. Sati wouldn't let her go away without a cup of tea. Jani was quite busy now. Katya had made her take a short course and then given her charge of the Family Planning centre. She was capable and well aware of her own capabilities. She would often gather four or five women together and lecture them about family planning.

'Look at this, it is a copper T. Dr sahiba will put it in for you and you won't conceive while it is inside. Take this Nirodh and give it to your husband, he won't have to worry any more. Do you know what is a safe period?'

'No, no this is wrong. We will suffer, children are a gift from God. Who are we to interfere with God's plans?'

Jani would be really annoyed with these illiterate, superstitious women.

'Don't talk about the wrath of God, sister. Is it by the grace of God that your husband loads your skeletal frame with a burden every year?'

Katya would interrupt her, 'Don't talk about religion. Just try and explain things to them. You can get into trouble like this.'

As it was people were apprehensive because of all the rumours about forcible sterilizations in Delhi during the Emergency, this despite the fact that the Emergency had hardly any impact in the Valley.

But Jani wasn't afraid of anyone. She was blunt and straightforward.

She was annoyed with the men and also with the women. When the women who regularly appeared in hospital with their large stomachs every two or three years writhed in pain during delivery she would show no mercy. She would scold them harshly.

'You don't remember these pains when you behave like animals at the bidding of your husbands. He will not use a rubber, you will not have an operation, then you must bear the pain. What is the point of asking for God's help? Rely on your own efforts.' Jani's scolding would have such an impact on the sweating, desperate women that a combination of pain and anger would force them to push out the baby stuck at the mouth of the womb into Jani's waiting hands. Katya would stroke the mother's forehead gently, wipe the sweat and admonish Jani, 'You are also a woman, be a little more understanding.' Jani would not get upset, 'Be thankful Dr sahiba! It is because of my scolding that the delivery happened so quickly, without any injection or operation!'

'That may be true, Jani, but….'

Jani wouldn't let her complete her sentence, 'A woman is just like a dog. Right now she is writhing in pain like a fish on a hot griddle, but if she doesn't appear again next year with a big stomach you can change my name. They are incapable of understanding things that are for their own good. They have been listening to men all their lives after all.'

It was difficult for Katya to explain things to the fifty year old Jani. She would say boldly, 'I have learnt from my experience of life, Dr sahiba, and what can be a better teacher? I don't listen to anyone. I didn't even listen to my husband.'

'So, did you leave him?' Even if someone joked with her she was ready with an answer.

'Yes, sister. I had to. If I hadn't left him I would have given birth to a cricket team! Who knows whether I would even have been alive today? I told him 'Go wherever you want. I am not having any more children.' He threatened me, 'I will divorce you.' I felt as though God had heard my prayers.'

'So, were you happier with your second husband?' The women were inquisitive.

Jani laughed, 'You know how suspicious men are. He said, "If you have an operation you can go around enjoying yourself without any fear." I replied, "Well then why don't you become the martyr, at least you will be assured of my chastity?" It was as if this was a condition for our marriage.'

'What about his children?' The listener would be astonished by Jani's courage.

'He has six. I look after them as well. And look at me, I am having a good time, free from any worries or fears.'

Only Jani knew whether or not she had worries but it was evident that she excelled at her work and in social relationships.

She knew everything about what was happening in the neighbourhood and the world outside. Arjun called her the 'Morning News.'

Early morning when Katya saw Jani she folded up her paper saying, ' Come, Jani, how are you? Do you have any news?' Jani's second husband's eldest son, Majida, had won the last assembly election on a Congress ticket, during the time of Mir Kasim sahib. Now, he had shifted over to the National Congress under Sheikh sahib. It was inevitable that Jani would be knowledgeable about political issues.

She just waited for someone to raise the subject.

'These days the Janta party is in power in Delhi: however, you know more about what is happening here.'

Jani starts with Morarji bhai's visit to Kashmir, 'Do you know Doctor sahiba? Morarji bhai came to meet Maulvi Farooq. There was a grand reception, green flags everywhere…'

'Morarji bhai was greeted with green flags?' Kartik started laughing, 'What are you saying, Jani?'

'I saw it with my own eyes, Doctor sahib! Crowds of women came from villages and towns and started dancing as they sang, "The qazi of Pakistan has come."

'Who would tell those fools that he had not come from Pakistan? They did not even know who Morarji was. They only knew about Nehru. Even their guardian angels aren't aware of the fact that Maulvi sahib is a part of the Janata party nowadays. What do they know about politics, bibi?'

'But Morarji bhai, the ruler of such a large nation, a wise elder, soon realized that the Janata party would not be able to get a toehold in Kashmir. You know what happened in the next elections. Sheikh sahib won all the seats in the valley. The Congress drew a complete blank here and barely managed to salvage their pride with a few seats in Jammu.'

Jani became tearful when she spoke about Sheikh sahib handing over the party leadership to his son Farooq in 1981.

'May God always bless this land of ours, Doctor sahiba. Sheikh sahib's speech in Iqbal Park touched everyone's heart. I was really moved. Sheikh sahib said, "I have shed an ocean of tears for the sake of my people." He said, "I am placing a crown of thorns on Farooq's head." A crown of thorns, Doctor sahiba, not a crown of flowers or jewels.'

Farooq sahib was his father's son after all, he also made a lot of promises.

'You are right.' Farooq sahib said, 'I am ready to lay down my life for the sake of the honour of my people.'

Katya got up to go to the hospital, 'There is one thing I don't understand, Jani! Why was Sheikh sahib in such a hurry to hand over the reins of the party to Farooq? Farooq returned from England only after Sheikh sahib's release from prison. He has spent many years abroad, married an English girl. He still has to get to know his people, understand their joys and sorrows...'

Jani also stood up, 'You are right, but Sheikh sahib is looking for a solution for the revolt which is simmering in his own household. At least that is what I think, bibi! Sheikh sahib's son-in-law, the husband of Khalida Begum, is aiming for the throne. This is the real truth. And besides Sheikh sahib is no longer young.'

'Khalida Begum is Sheikh sahib's daughter, she also has the right to become a leader.'

'Nevertheless, Doctor sahiba, it is Farooq who will be a better leader.'

When Isha, who was jogging in the lawn early morning, heard this conversation, her feminist instincts made her declare war.

'What did you say, Jani? Women don't make good leaders? What is Indira Gandhi? A man? Isn't Queen Elizabeth of England a woman?

'You are right, baby.' Jani tried to save herself from the unexpected attack.

'No, first try to understand things before giving political speeches. Golda Meir, Margaret Thatcher, Bandaranaike... should I name some more? Do you have any idea of the heights which women have scaled?'

Jani rushed towards the gate to save herself from Isha's temper rather than from her argument.

Katya looked back. In the verandah, along with Arjun, Tipu was also gleefully clapping and laughing. It wasn't clear whether he was amused by Jani's sprint or by Isha's attempt to chase her.

Katya felt that 'Shihul villa', sitting encircled by poplars in the gentle morning sunlight, was also smiling.

❧

Journeys

This time Lalli and Keshavnath's trip to the US stretched out longer than unsual. Earlier they would stay for a maximum of three months. There were too many responsibilities that drew them back home.

Prem came back from Bombay soon after Shivnath passed away. He had been made manager of the new unit opened by Lever Brothers in Srinagar. Prem' s son Bulbul, also got married around this time. The son and daughter-in-law were working in Bangalore. Prem's daughter was an architect and worked in Delhi.

Ragya and Devika lived with Kamala. They were a real support to their mother. Nandan and Dhara had been right, in a sense, when they said, 'Now you stay with us, Ma. You have fulfilled all your responsibilities. Now there is no difference

between that house and this house, it's all the same.' Lalli
had listened to them with a smile, but her heart was hovering
somewhere around her home. There was so much there that
needed Lalli's touch.

Had the clothes lying in trunks and almirahs for a year been
eaten by moths? Katya never had the time to put them out in the
sun. This year Kamala must have recited the story of Goddess
Bibgaraz on the occasion of Pan. She must have invited Sona's
daughters-in-law to help make the roths, the sweet breads
with sesame. Hopefully she hadn't forgotten Kanhaiya's wife,
Kshama. She'd been lonely throughout her youth, the girl was
brave but some painful wounds never healed.

Lalli was never free from these minor worries and concerns.
The children were busy with their own lives, what did they know
about all this? However, Nandan and Dhara did hope that their
parents would become so enamoured of this wonderworld that
they would forget about going back. Lalli and Keshav were
fascinated by the technical progress of this new world on their
very first visit. They were spellbound not just by extraordinary
sights but even by ordinary ones. That visit was over in the
blink of an eye. Nandan had chalked out the programme in
advance. They travelled from the East coast to the West, from
New York, Atlanta, all the way to California.

They gazed at the skyscrapers in New York till their
necks started hurting. They were amazed, how did such tall
buildings withstand storms and earthquakes? They took
many photographs leaning against the Statue of Liberty. On
their return home they would be able to relive these moments
that they had spent with the children. In New York they also
met Bhadra Zutshi's daughter, Nina. She was the daughter of
Dulari's brother-in-law and lived in a one room apartment on
the eleventh floor of a building on Chamber Street. Far away
from her loved ones, completely alone in a strange country.
Nina was very moved on meeting them. She had become a

widow only a year after her marriage. She came to America to visit her elder sister Veena for a while and never went back. Veena moved to California later but Nina continued to live in New York.

In response to the question, 'Why do you live alone Nina?' she answered frankly that she was completely wrapped up in her work. Lalli thought for a while then said, 'There are quite a few eligible boys from our community here who would be happy to find someone like you. Why don't you choose one of them?'

Nina burst out, 'Don't talk about boys from our community, aunty. They pretend to be American when they come here but inside they continue to be the same traditional Kashmiri Pandits. Men are forgiven every indiscretion, but women are to be kept under tight vigilance. They shouldn't date anyone, have sex with anyone. Even before their children are grown up they start looking for suitable matches for them within the community.'

'People do become more careful in an alien country. Back home our girls are marrying Punjabis, Marathis, Bengalis but here everyone is holding on to their roots. Perhaps they are worried about losing their identity….'

'There are many tensions aunty, we never really merge with another culture. But at least we are free to live our lives as we like. This is what keeps us back here. No one interferes in anyone else's personal life.'

On their return, as they passed Ellis island, Lalli imagined the boats carrying immigrants from different countries. Where had they come from, with their boxes, bundles, packages and umbrellas? They were not invaders. The soil of this country had absorbed them. They may have found shelter after they had been tortured but what about those left behind? Wouldn't their loneliness have been as tortuous? A question flashed through her mind: who was responsible for this exile and this alienation? Didn't our views and our policies also play a part?

Nina, who had a PhD in Biology, wasn't able to get a full time job, she got only intermittent employment. She started making pizzas in a restaurant along with a Mexican friend. Now she also served Kashmiri Goshtaba and Kathi Kebabs. Americans and Indians enjoyed eating them. Here no one commented on the fact that Nina, the daughter-in-law of a prestigious family, had now become a cook. Here she was just an individual, a successful individual who excelled at her work. It was this joy that had connected her with America. Now Lalli and Keshav did not interfere much in the lives of their children but as the years passed they felt the distance between them growing.

When they had come on their first visit the grandchildren were still young. They would cling to their grandparents. In Disneyland Lalli and Keshav had enjoyed themselves almost as much as Chintu and Pinky. They had also taken photographs with Mickey Mouse, Minnie and Donald Duck. In 'Pirate Island' Pinky insisted that she would sit with grandma and Chintu with grandpa. On their return home Lalli had narrated the story of Sita's abduction and the destruction of Lanka to the children. She had explained the reason why Deepavali is celebrated. The children had imagined Hanuman ji with his burning tail, jumping about in Ravana's golden palaces. They had seen the flames rising as high as fireworks in the sky.

Lalli and Keshav had told the children all the stories from the *Ramayana*, the *Mahabharata* and the old folk tales which they could remember. On their next visit they had bought an entire set of *Amar Chitra Katha* comic books translated into English for them, hoping that the children would remain connected to their culture in this way.

But now the children were grown up. They had moved away from the world of the imagination into the real world of television, videos and computerized games where there was no shortage of entertainment or information. You pressed a button and Alladin's invisible genie appeared with a wealth of information. Who was interested in grandma and grandpa's stale stories any longer?

On their return from school they would say, 'Hi grandma', 'Hi grandpa' and rush off quickly, 'Oh Boy! There's so much homework!' Chintu would take a chicken burger out of the fridge, heat it in the microwave, gulp it down with a coke and rush off to play. Pinky would pour cereal into a bowl, add milk and eat it standing up. If she was in a hurry, she drank a glass of juice, grabbed some chicken nuggets and said goodbye. In the morning Nandan and Dhara left for work before the children went to school. The sounds of the car engines became faint as they drove away.

Lalli and Keshavnath had their baths and sat out on the deck. In front of them the branches of the Dogwoods, Oaks and Poplars swayed in the breeze. Lalli looked up at the trees, trying to locate some familiar birds but she couldn't see any. Her eyes grew tired and weary. She got up and went into the kitchen to cook something for the evening. Keshavnath glanced through the paper, walked for a while on the lawn and then went into his room and switched on the TV. Sometimes the two of them sat on the deck reminiscing about home, Katya's children, Ragya, Devika. Dulari's son had also come to America. Sharika's daughter had been living in California for some years. Lalli felt a pain in her heart. Keshavnath smiled sadly at her, shaking his head. In other words, how could you stop the flow of time? Separation, parting, moving away! All this was necessary.

On Saturdays and Sundays Nandan invited Indian friends over for a meal. A huge crowd of Kashmiri friends got together. They celebrated Shivratri, Navreh, Deepavali. Last time Nandan brought a statue of Ganesha from Orissa. It gave an ethnic touch to one corner of the living room.

Nandan said, 'Ma! We have learnt to retain our culture and heritage despite living abroad. You can see how fluently the children speak Kashmiri!'

Keshavnath smiled and everything appeared fine. Surrounded by one's own people, language, voices, food, it seemed as though one was close to home. But sometimes things turned sour. Like that time in Arlington. When Keshavnath recited the words engraved on JFK's grave Nandan's face became suffused with colour, 'Ask not what your country can do for you, ask what you can do for your country.'

Why did Papa have to repeat those words?

Nandan frequently felt that Papa had never been able to forgive him for settling down abroad, that he considered Nandan to be selfish, someone who thought only about himself, not about his people or his country. In the fourth quarter of their lives Ma and Papa wanted to be close to their grandchildren. Nandan had only been able to give them loneliness though his heart was always with them. Was it a crime to think about the future? What would Nandan have got if he had stayed back?

Papa became silent after reading out the sentence in Arlington. Lalli tried to change the topic, 'Do you know your father is writing a book? He notes down any interesting sayings he comes across.' Nandan's curiosity was aroused and his attention was diverted, 'This is amazing Papa! You didn't even mention it to us. This is really great. What are you writing?'

'After my retirement I thought of writing a book on the socio-political changes in Kashmir. Now I feel I am getting somewhere…'

'Recently a lot of changes have taken place in various countries. A lot has happened in our own state. Family structures have also started breaking up along with the political upheaval. Old traditions, customs, beliefs, are all getting eroded but people are becoming more prosperous in material terms.'

'That is evident, Papa! We no longer have the same values we had at the time of Independence. Also the politics of our state is not isolated from global influences… Keep this in mind as well….'

When Nandan and Dhara returned from work they would sit with Papa and Ma on the deck and, with their chosen drinks in hand, start reminiscing about home and past incidents. In his mind, Nandan kept returning to that time from which he had escaped. Lalli dragged him away from the past to a present in which homes had refrigerators and other modern amenities.

'Don't the daughters of the boatmen dance the Rov on the riverbanks in the evening any more?' he asked.

'Rov is only seen on stage and on TV now. Once in a while it may be performed during a marriage. Where do the girls have the time? They are taking advantage of free education to do their PhDs, and BEds and they have started working in offices, schools, hospitals.'

'Things have changed,' Keshavnath observed gravely.

'You left nearly twenty years ago during the time of Bakshi sahib, now after twenty two years Sheikh sahib has become the chief minister once again. Recently Farooq sahib was named as his father's successor

The conversation turned to politics.

'This dynastic politics is a kind of imperialism, Papa. We seem to be following the old hierarchical patterns of history even in democracy,' Dhara said.

'Yes daughter, it is almost the same pattern. Nehru prepared the throne for Indira, Indira for Sanjay, and Rajiv. Sheikh sahib is doing the same. Why should we blame the kings and emperors, at least they had a claim on their kingdoms. How much has really changed for us after the coming of democracy?'

When the topic of maharajas came up once again they even went back to the era of the *Mahabharat*. But Nandan was not interested in the past, he was concerned about the present which shaped the future.

Keshavnath said, 'History doesn't die, Nandan, it merely repeats itself in different guises. The history of Kashmir can bear witness to this.'

Nandan could be brutally frank at times. 'Whether history repeats itself or not, Papa, there is no end to human aspirations, especially the desire for power. When I look at my own state, its history seems to be merely a quest for power from Maharaja Hari Singh to Sheikh Abdullah. It is this desire that has changed friends into enemies. All the plotting and planning is merely a means to come into power.'

Keshavnath had witnessed the political manoeuvres and clashes from the reign of Pratap Singh to the rule of Sheikh sahib. Accusations and counter-accusations. I am right, you are wrong. Who could be said to be blameless?

He said, 'Look at the period of Dogra rule. Gulab Singh was accused of being greedy. He would only listen to a petition after the petitioner placed a rupee in his hand. And the reason for this is very clear, after all he had paid seventy five lakh nanakshahi rupees for Kashmir. At the beginning of his rule the state was in a deplorable condition. The Afghan-Pathan rulers had reduced the people to beggars. Money was needed to improve the condition of the people and it had to be collected from somewhere.'

'And what about the brutal and inhuman punishment of flaying a man's skin and stuffing it with straw, could that be justified from any angle?' Lalli was revolted by the inhumanity of the punishment.

'If one wants to look for some justification one can say that at that time the policies and rules of the Afghans were still prevalent. Dacoits like Galwan, Bomya, Khoka were still terrorizing the valley. The rulers wanted to create fear in the minds of the people so that they would not commit any crimes. But,' Keshavnath added, 'I agree that flaying the skin of man while he is alive is a cruel and inhuman act.'

'Some of these allegations are true, others were false. Raja Ranbhir Singh was responsible for encouraging the arts, literature and education, he built temples. During his rule there was heavy rain from October 1877 to January 1878. All the crops were destroyed. There was a famine that was so severe that people were reduced to even eating grass. Thousands of people died, many fled to the Punjab. The British accused the king of drowning people in the Wular lake though this was not something a just king like Ranbhir Singh would do.'

'Papa, the reign of Maharaja Pratap Singh during Dogra rule has also been praised. It is said that he was responsible for taking the valley from the medieval ages to the modern age. New laws, land reforms, co-operative movements, education, telephones etcetera, there were many changes. There must be some allegations against him as well.'

Keshavnath laughed, 'Are we only looking for faults today?'

'No, Papa, I am just curious.'

'If you are looking for faults then you can ask why he used to be served forty dishes at every meal when he could have been satisfied with just two. When there was a ban on cow slaughter, why wasn't there a similar ban on the killing of pigs? But one has to be balanced in one's judgement.'

'Pratap Singh was a just ruler. Rigid in his religious beliefs, but fair to his people.'

'No, Papa, I don't want to accuse anyone needlessly. Kings and emperors have always been a little whimsical, though many of them were very able. Not only did they want every luxury in this life they also tried to organize a place for themselves in paradise!' Keshavnath grasped what Nandan was implying though Dhara was confused.

'Rubbish! Who told you they could reserve places for themselves in heaven?'

'Papa!'

Keshavnath narrated the story of the death of Pratap Singh. After the maharaja's death a man was brought from outside the state. His head was shaved, he was gifted all the things which the king used to like and use and then he was escorted out of the state by the police. He was given the king's clothes, vessels, car, bedding etc., in the belief that by accepting them he had taken the deceased king's sins on his own shoulders, thus leaving the king blameless and worthy of a place in heaven.

'It is all a question of belief, Nandan. When the Hair of the Prophet was stolen from the Hazratbal Dargah many people said that it disappeared because Bakshi sahib's ailing mother wanted to see it.' Beliefs are not accusations.

'Hari Singh made a lot of improvements in the state. People only started criticizing him after Sheikh Abdullah became the leader in 1931 and gave the call for democracy. Then they started feeling that the Dogra kings gave high ranking positions only to Dogras, not to Kashmiris. Muslims especially remained very backward and downtrodden. So landless farmers and illiterate workers joined Sheikh sahib's party in huge numbers. They raised their voices asking for justice.'

'The situation did change after Independence, Papa, but did everyone get a fair deal despite the presence of clever leaders like Sheikh, Bakshi and Sadiq? Didn't the differences persist? Though the protagonists had changed?' This was a question to which there was no answer.

'And accusations? Is any political leader free of these?'

'The leaders filled their coffers, the middlemen became rich, the poor got cheap rations and free education. Many people were exiled. How many new avenues of employment were opened up? The leaders were only concerned about Article 370. Who would invest in the state? Considering the amount of money poured into the valley by the central government it should have been thriving and prosperous, but even today the city is full of dirty, open drains. People have built new bungalows with private drainage but the municipality has not been able to improve the drainage system of the city.'

'Some improvements did happen but expectations also grew.' Keshavnath looked at both sides of the coin. But he was aware that even the most passionate leaders were finally dwarfed by their desire for power, and their concern for the common man became fainter and fainter. At such moments he was filled with a quiet sorrow. Had he knowingly or unknowingly expected too much from the independent nation?

But Keshavnath didn't let sorrow overwhelm him. Nor did Lalli. Not even when, despite being very careful, Nandan and Dhara called the parents' views old fashioned and out of date. For instance, it was Ma's habit to get involved with the problems of the whole world. She should have understood by now that people have to find solutions for their problems themselves. There was a common saying here, 'To each his own' But look at Ma, 'Oh! Poor Kshama, she is so unhappy. Why doesn't her daughter get married? Jialal's engineer son has shifted to Madras for work, now his poor parents are all alone in their old age.' Ma should realize that everyone can think for themselves, they have their own difficulties and limitations which they have to deal with. Jialal's son can shift to Timbuktoo if he likes, after all he has to think about his future…

'Actually, Ma, we don't live our own lives, we just interfere in other people's lives creating an internal cesspool of complaints, displeasure and sorrow. I hate this. At least in this country no one interferes in anyone else's life. Each person lives his own life.'

Lalli was hurt by her son's beliefs. Since when had brothers and sisters become 'others'? Since when had worrying about someone become interference? Did life consist of eating, drinking and falling into a comfortable sleep? Keshavnath tried to console her, 'We haven't done anything wrong, Lalli. Our beliefs are becoming outdated like us, that's what it is. Just wish the best for your children, perhaps they are being forced to move with the times, we can't change their thinking, and they have their own problems.'

Many years ago when Nadir sahib had seen Lalli pining for

her son he had said, 'Enjoy the success of your children from afar and be happy, bhabi! Now our children have become like rainbows which can only be enjoyed from far away but never touched when we are in times of need.' Keshav and Lalli were quiet on their return journey. In their minds the unending journeys carried on. Did people who got lost ever return? Only death came again and again separating man from man.

Heer had said to the yogi, 'You are giving me false hopes. I haven't found anyone though I have searched till I was exhausted. The person who has gone never comes back…'

Did anyone who went to the new world ever return to the old one? Lalli thought that Nandan would return home after three or four years. The strings that tied him to his loved ones would pull him back. He loved the play of the moonlight on the Vitasta. He pruned the rose bush crowding around the four walls of the garden himself. He enjoyed trekking to Amarnath and Gangabal, he couldn't eat a meal without the green haaq cooked at home. But today after twenty years Nandan had said, 'Now we are going to stay here, Ma. Don't worry, we will come home every other year and you will also come and visit us. Science has reduced the size of the world so much, and then what is left for us in the Valley now?'

Lalli realized that hearts had definitely shrunk a lot though she didn't know too much about the world outside. Have we increased our sorrows by thinking too much about ourselves? If we had sat with the younger generation, understood and appreciated their dreams then would these distances have grown between us?

Lalli was upset. Separation, departure always filled her mind with sorrow. When they hugged their son at the airport Keshavnath burst into tears. Lalli was stunned. She had never seen her husband breaking down like this. The walls of the dam had cracked and Keshavnath could not stem the tide. When had this loneliness grown within him?

There was a storm in Lalli's heart. She put an arm around her husband and leaned her head on his shoulder. Keshav half opened his eyes and gathered her close. Outside the sky had enveloped the earth. Now it didn't matter how much of the journey still remained.

Flames of the Chinar

Sheikh sahib was no more.

September 8, 1982. Autumn was in the air. Sharp winds gusted down, pushing the leaves off the branches of trees onto their beds on the earth below. The delicate tracery on the leaves of the regal chinars flashed glimpses of fiery, russet autumnal colours. The flames of the chinar! Sheikh sahib had named his autobiography *Flames of the Chinar*.

Many people acknowledged that his personality was as towering as the royal Chinar. Haji sahib was not alive today or he would have spoken about Sheikh sahib's love for his country and how he had lit the flame of freedom adding, 'Huzoor! There was a fire in him which was not quenched even during the twenty odd years he spent under house arrest.' Haji sahib's son, Naseeer, said, 'Sheikh sahib took up the task of changing the miserable lives of the poor people.' Keshavnath also recalled Sheikh sahib's struggle and his battles for freedom, 'There was a tiny little reading room located somewhere between Habbakadal and Fatehkadal. Not very impressive. This was the place from which Sheikh sahib taught his people to raise their voices against imperialism. This was around the thirties, during the reign of Hari Singh.'

'But we have heard that Hari Singh brought in many reforms. What complaints did people have against him?'

Singh sahib passed on all the information that he had about Hari Singh's rule to his friends. The fact that in 1944 a Praja sabha, consisting of members chosen by Hari Singh, was set up, that he included Mirza Afzal Beg and Gangaram in his council of ministers and so on. 'In a sense it was also a kind of democracy, bhai sahib!'

'He had also donated his personal property to the State Treasury,' added Brother De Costa who was a senior teacher in Burnhall Convent.

'But still, brother, it was a feudal system. You have all heard of emperor Lalitaditya Muktipeed who ruled in the eighth century, a man who built temples like Martand, whom Kalhana Pandit called the king of the world. There was prosperity and peace during his rule but Kalhana says that éven during his reign the ordinary man had to live a life of poverty. There were rich landlords and poor landless farmers in Hari Singh's time. A handful of Kashmiri pandits or Muslims were appointed to high posts but the general public still lived a hand-to-mouth existence. Muslims were worse off in any case because they were also uneducated. Sheikh sahib became their representative, their voice.'

'It is said that Sheikh sahib also had his own complaints. He had wanted to study medicine, but the Dogra government refused to sponsor him. When he returned from Aligarh with an MSc degree he was handed an ordinary schoolteacher's job.'

Nityanand said, 'Not just that, they transferred him to Muzzaffarabad! He thought, enough is enough! He resigned and started his campaign for the freedom of his country.'

Prithvi Dhar's son Iqbal Krishan, who had been listening solemnly to this conversation, drew a deep breath and said, 'Yesssss!' After his ancestral lands had been taken away Iqbal had done his BA and managed to get a job as a Postmaster. His friends envied him but Iqbal was transferred constantly from one remote place to another, from Ladakh-Kargil to Kishtwar-Bhadarwah or Poonch-Rajauri. His wife was sick of moving from place to place with their belongings and their children. The kids were intelligent but the constant shift from one school to another, one method of teaching to another, confused them so much that they even failed their exams once or twice.

Iqbal Krishan regretted the fact that he was not Sheikh sahib. He didn't have the courage to resign from his job. He remained a timid Pandit all his life, the contented Batta, who accepted whatever destiny doled out to him, the honest salaried slave. How would he have supported his family if he had left his job? He didn't know any other trade or occupation. So, Iqbal Krishan remained dumb and mute all his life.

In his book *Inside Kashmir* Premnath Bazaz wrote that Sheikh sahib taught millions of dumb people to speak. On the 10th of September all those formerly mute people came out on the streets in their thousands. Women, with their children astride their hips or on their shoulders, beat their breasts and lamented, calling out to Sheikh sahib. 'Where has our lion gone, why has our father left us?' When the children heard their mothers wailing and heard the slogans shouted by their fathers they started bawling. Sheikh sahib's cortege travelled through the streets of the city. The windows of the houses lining its route were like eyes from which the people took a last look at their leader. Flowers were showered from temples, mosques, churches and gurudwaras. There was no distinction between Hindus, Muslims, Christians.

The long procession finally disappeared around a bend in the road. The Sikh Light Infantry, the Naga Regiment, the Ladakh Scouts and many others offered their last salutes to Sheikh sahib. Giani Zail Singh and Indira Gandhi were also part of the procession. The hero of Kashmir, who was now a national hero, was finally laid to rest on the shores of the Nagin lake close to Hazratbal.

The state sank into gloom after Sheikh sahib's death. No one ventured any opinions about whether Farooq would be able to govern the state properly or not. Whatever may have been the public image of the golf playing, partying Farooq who was fond of a good time, he was nevertheless the impressive, tall, beloved son of the chief minister. He had lived in England, married an Englishwoman, but he had been anointed as his successor by Sheikh sahib himself. Those in the know were aware that Gulshah had resigned a month ago and Farooq sahib had taken over as health minister. Why had Beg sahib, Sheikh sahib's lifelong friend and leader of the Plebiscite Front, resigned earlier, followed by the Sheikh's brother-in-law Gulshah? Had they resigned of their own volition or were they forced to resign? No one raised these questions. People just reminisced about all the good work Sheikh sahib had done.

'How can we forget that it was he who saved us at the time of the Kabaili raids?' Nityanand commented.

Makhan Singh, who had been an eyewitness to the slaughter during the raids, raised his scrawny, blue veined neck and, in his thin voice, repeated what he had said many times before, 'Maharaja sahib ran away to Jammu leaving Sheikh sahib to take care of us.'

Nityanand tried to be impartial and say that the Maharaja had been advised to go to Jammu by VP Menon. His life was in danger. But they were mourning Sheikh sahib, this was not the time to defend the Maharaja. Nityanand also felt that a king's primary duty was to protect his subjects, not to worry about his own life. This was what was written in all the holy shastras. Havaldar bhaiji, whose name described his occupation as a sergeant, took the opportunity to mention the story of the extraordinary bravery and sacrifice of Brigadier Rajendra Singh Jamwal.

'I remember the 22nd of October very clearly, brothers.' Havaldar bhaiji's memory was quite sharp anyway. 'The

Indian army had not yet reached the valley. The state force was scattered and disorganized. At that time Rajendra Singh was sent with a force of only a hundred and fifty soldiers to confront the Kabailis! Just a hundred and fifty soldiers!' He repeated the number once again.

'At that critical moment Rajendra Singh promised the Maharaja that the enemy would only advance over his dead body.'

'He was such a valiant young man, he said, "Give me a revolver and leave me here on the road. I will take care of the rest."'

'Three days! Brothers, for three days he stopped the advance of the enemy on the Uri-Dumail road. He destroyed the Uri bridge, and sacrificed his life for his country. Srinagar was saved because of his courage. Otherwise the Kabailis would have happily walked right into Rajgarhi. Who was there to stop them? Rajendra Singh was later awarded the Mahavir Chakra. One must remember his sacrifice as well, brothers.'

'Yes, it took a while for a decision to be taken in Delhi. Mountbatten said the army would be sent only after the accession, the defence committee sent VP Menon to take stock of the situation in Kashmir, then the accession deed was signed. It was only after this that the first squadron of airforce planes landed in Srinagar airport on the 27th of October, in the interim it was brave people like Rajendra Singh who protected the Valley.'

'Politicians get busy with politics, the army is sacrificed and some people who are neither kings nor soldiers prove that they are true sons of their country and make a name for themselves.'

They talked about people like Maqbool Sherwani of Baramulla, who was crucified like Jesus by the Kabailis in the centre of town. They even drove a nail through his forehead. Only because he was against discrimination between Hindus and Muslims, he believed in brotherhood. When one spoke of martyrs how could one forget to mention Colonel Rai? Colonel Rai, who commanded the Sikh regiment and was killed in battle. Just like Major Sharma of the Kumaon regiment who attacked the enemy in Badgam and died fighting. Then there was Brigadier Usman in Nowshera and so many others whom they remembered and saluted. Keshavnath narrated some terrible incidents of looting by the enemy in Rajouri-Poonch, as well as the way they were finally thrown out of the area on the 12th of April 1948.

Jialal was quite convinced that Britain and America sided with Pakistan.

'Who incited the people to revolt in Gilgit? Who encouraged the locals? Major Brown raised the Pakistani flag there, wasn't that a clear indication of their intentions?'

'Even the stupidest people could understand the intentions of the British and the Americans. They also put a lot of pressure on the UN. They stopped the war and a lot of our area was left in the hands of the Pakistanis which they have never returned.'

Jialal took up the topic, 'Thankfully our army, under the command of General Thimayya, had already taken Handwara, Kupwara, Keran and some other places back from the Pakistanis and they'd pushed the enemy beyond Uri. If their petrol had not finished our army would have even reclaimed Muzzaffarabad! Still, at the time of ceasefire we had reclaimed three thousand square miles of territory from the enemy. The area left with them is what is known today as Azad Kashmir and it continues to remain under Pakistani control.'

This was something that upset not only Jialal but Nityanand, Keshavnath, Havaldar bhai and almost everyone else. In hindsight, taking the matter to the UNO was a wrong decision but those in the know were aware that at that time there was no other option. Pakistan was not ready to agree to any terms so Nehru had to perforce go to the UNO for help.

Agreeing that 'Everything happens according to God's

will', they abandoned the topic of India and Pakistan and the UNO and came back to Sheikh sahib. To his leadership and the slogans raised by the members of the National Conference, 'What is the will of the lion of Kashmir-unity between Hindus, Muslims and Sikhs!'

No one mentioned the fact that even while agreeing to the accession, Sheikh sahib repeated his demand for a plebiscite. No one said that the 'plebiscite' was used as a trump card. On the contrary, people noted that at the beginning of his second term as Chief minister in 1974, Sheikh sahib merged the Plebiscite Front with the National Conference saying that it was no longer required. Which meant a firm acceptance of the accession. Without any pre-conditions. Referring to the 1974 Kashmir Accord, Brother De Costa also mentioned the brochure issued by the National Conference, 'Brothers, it says here, "By signing the accord, we once again made Kashmir a willing part of the Indian Union." What more can one say?'

They recalled the friendship between the Sheikh and Nehru. It was on the advice of Iqbal in Lahore and Nehru in Delhi that the Sheikh changed the name of his party from Muslim Conference to National Conference. Then by making Shyamlal Saraf, Kashyap Bandhu, Jialal Kilam, Sardar Budhsingh and others members of the party he set an example of communal harmony.

Suddenly, Havaldar bhaiji started talking about the India-Pakistan war of 1971. Referring to the birth of Bangladesh, the defeat of Pakistan and the Shimla accord he said, 'Brothers, Indira Gandhi showed her generosity by handing over ninety thousand war prisoners and suggesting that the Kashmir issue should be solved through discussion at the Shimla meeting. If she had wanted she could have sorted out the entire issue once and for all right then. Bhutto sahib was both embarrassed and flustered by his defeat. His country had been divided into two. He could have been forced to agree.' Bringing his story to an end he added, 'You will all have to agree that the war of 1971 also cleared away many misconceptions of our leaders. Sheikh sahib was very upset when Bhutto sahib said that Kashmiris had lost the right of self-determination in 1947. The Kashmir accord was, in a sense, the outcome of this falling out.'

And now Sheikh sahib's son Farooq had to win the elections. 'He will definitely win!' Nasir sahib said, 'Inshallah! I am hundred percent sure.'

'Yes! The public will want to pay its debts to Sheikh sahib by electing Farooq sahib.' Keshavnath was of the same opinion.

When the electioneering began it appeared that Indira Gandhi had come to canvass for the Congress candidate.

'Canvassing?' Prem ji, who had gone to Iqbal Park to hear her speech, came back disappointed and somewhat annoyed. 'You are talking about canvassing? There were barely a handful of people in the park, where lakhs of people had gathered to hear Sheikh sahib speak in 1981. The park was almost empty.'

'And to make things worse, a brawl broke out between the Congress workers and members of the National Conference. There was a rumour that some naked people were insisting on meeting Indira Gandhi and the police was busy trying to beat them away with sticks.'

'Whaaaaat? Naked? Did you see anything?' Lalli couldn't believe that anyone could do that.

'No but the police was beating up some people and stopping them from entering. Indira Gandhi was very annoyed. She felt that the National Conference had prevented people from attending her meeting.'

'Whatever happened was unfortunate.' Keshavnath was worried.

'Goondaism is increasing day by day in the state.'

Indira Gandhi never forgot the manner in which she was humiliated in her paternal home. Farooq won by a huge margin in June 1983. The National Conference said the election had been free and fair. The Congress claimed it was rigged. The relationship between Indira and Farooq worsened. People said, 'It was bound to happen.'

Mangala's father, Mahadev Pir, used to work in the Revenue Department during the time of the Maharaja. Dhar Sahib of Nawakadal was like his brother and he used to narrate many stories about the Nehru family. Once he said that Indu had visited their house when she was small, wearing a pheran and with a scarf on her head, the little girl had stared at everyone. And today that same little girl had grown up and become the Prime Minister of the country. But only she knew how much she had lost on her way to this position. First her marital home, then her beloved son, but she had not accepted defeat. There was a fire in her. And this was the Indira who had been humiliated in her paternal home.

Mangala was uneasy. She referred to Indira Gandhi again and again. Ajay tried to calm her down, 'All this is just a part of politics.'

Ajay's son teased his Grandmother, 'Grandma, if you had been educated you would have also become Indira Gandhi. You also know a lot about politics.'

Mangala gently smacked him on the back.

'Grandma you definitely have the qualities which are required.'

'Which qualities are you talking about, Vicky dear?'

'Just that you should have your teeth and your ribs, what other qualities do you need to become a minister or a chief-minister?'

Mangala didn't get angry. She was filled with affection for the child, as well as pride in the manner in which children today were able to understand the world and society around them. Thanks to television, everyone had become knowledgeable. Sometimes, it amazed her to see how much the world had changed. Till he was in class ten, her son Ajay used to be busy with his school books and his friends. The world of childhood was a sheltered world with its own small worries, and mischief. Detached from the big world outside. But his son Vicky talked about ministers and politics. Mangala felt children lost their childhood very early nowadays. Perhaps it was intelligent to know so much at such a young age but it also meant the loss of that magical, carefree world which was as gentle as the perfume of flowers and the colours of butterflies, a world to which one could never return.

Mangala remembered her childhood. Anyone who could draw solace from the memory of a cool spring in the vast desert of life was lucky, because the memory reminded him that life is not merely an unending battle.

It felt good to go back to the past. To the place years ago where the swing, hanging in the shade of the Chinar, swung back and forth. Where the Poshnool and the Bulbul sang from their hiding places among the leaves. Where childhood was carefree, running over hillocks and fields in the free open breezes of Vicharnag. Mangala bathed with her friends in the little pond of the Vicharnag temple. The bigger pond was quite deep, in the middle of it there was a Shivling on a stone platform. Four massive chinars bent over, looking at their reflections in the pond. When the shadows moved, it appeared as though there was another unknown world under the surface. On Janamashtami, Mangala, and her mother and sisters, lit lamps around the circumference of the pond. The tiny lamps floating on pieces of wood seemed to challenge the darkness, little lights dancing on the water.

Mangala's Baba said that it was here, in Vicharnag, that Lord Vishnu thought of creating the universe, and so he created Brahma on the night of the new moon or amavasya. That is why a fair is held here on New Year which always falls on amavasya. One year it didn't rain, the ponds became dry. The girls of the village smeared the mud from the pond on their bodies and walked through the streets and lanes with empty earthen pots on their heads. Kamala, Mangala, Noori, Arshi, Fatah....begging the sky for water 'O sky! Rain your kindness down on us, we are waiting.'

The next day it rained. The mothers said, 'How could the sky bear the sight of the girls smeared with mud and dust?' The empty pots, and the dry ponds were filled to the brim with water. Mangala danced about in the rain with her friends for so long that she fell ill. But till today she remembers the way the rain had seemed to seep into her body and her soul. Her childhood disappeared as soon as she was married. But the hopes of childhood remained. The riots of 1931 changed her life. After the Vicharnag house was looted and burnt, Mangala, along with Dina kak, Tara and Ajay, became refugees, moving from home to home. The roads became more and more rough. But there was a fire within Mangala that kept her alive.

She kept fighting. With herself, with the world, with God. Ajay's illness destroyed all her faith. The stubbornness inside her reared its head. 'I will not let my children die.' People said, 'God knows who she is going around with. How does she manage to keep the house going, buy medicines? Does money rain down from heaven?'

Mangala refused to listen. She never asked anyone for help. She did not retire even in her old age. Her daughter-in-law was working. Her grandson, Vicky, studied in college and her grand daughter Shilpi was in class four. She looked after the children. She still enjoyed cooking. The fragrance of rice filled her soul with peace just like the smell of incense. She did not forget that she ate cold rice gruel for months while feeding others piping hot rice. Cooking it over wood fires first and then on a Janata stove. Now, Ajay has become a doctor. He did his BDS from Madras with the help of Havaldar bhaiji and Lalli Keshavnath. He has opened a small dental dispensary. Now there was a gas stove and even a black and white TV in the house. Now why should Mangala have to stoop?

Ajay's college friends, Shabir Lone and Yusuf Tilwani, often came to meet him. Yusuf had bad teeth so Ajay cleaned his teeth sometimes, did a filling or applied gum paint without charging him anything. Yusuf was fond of politics, Shabir was crazy about movies. When the three of them were together Vicky often joined them on some pretext or the other.

'Shabir saw Farooq sahib in Pahalgam, on a motorcycle. Do you know who was sitting behind him?'

'Who?' Vicky's eyes shone.

'Shabana Azmi.'

'You are joking! Really?'

'Do you think I am telling a lie?'

Vicky was crazy about cricket. He went to the stadium to watch the match between India and the West Indies. There was a lathi-charge, people shouted, 'Long live Pakistan'. Vicky was upset because some people threw pieces of glass and rocks at the pitch. When the West Indians hit a four they rushed down to the pitch to congratulate them but when the Indians hit a six, shouts of 'Down with Kapil Dev, long live Imran Khan.' filled the air. There was such confusion and chaos that Vicky got frightened and came away.

At such moments Shabir Lone would get up to go saying, 'People have gone mad.' Tilwani would say, 'Bye, brother,' and follow him out, leaving a strange uncomfortable silence behind. Ajay would look at Vicky angrily, 'What was the need to come here and say all this? Huh?'

'Papa! I only described what happened in the stadium.' Vicky tried to defend himself.

'You still have to learn what has to be said before whom, Vicky. You are still young. It is better that you don't sit with your elders. '

Vicky was upset and went out of the room.

'There was no need to scold him.' Mangala defended her grandson.

'Ma! You don't know what is happening. You only know about the lions and the goats. Now there are many parties, Jamaat-e-Islami, People's Party, this party, that party. There is a fire smouldering away inside that flares up once in a while. Otherwise where is the need to raise Pakistani flags and shout, 'Indian dogs go back!' in the middle of a cricket match? It is not as if we don't understand. The truth is that we have to keep our eyes and ears closed in our own homes. Every statement of ours can be misinterpreted. It would be good if you could explain things to Vicky, otherwise he will get beaten up sometime.'

Mangala knew there was a fire smouldering somewhere inside. This fire was not the fire of the Chinar, it was the smouldering lava of a volcano which was gradually simmering. No one knew when it would burst forth, not even those who could foretell the future.

Four Friends

The four friends sat in a corner of the lawn, unusually silent. There was a nip in the air and the tall poplars cast long shadows across the lawn. A clutch of crows flew overhead. Their loudly beating wings made the men look up. 'These crows make such a racket. It hurts the ears!' Ashraf said almost in complaint.

The crows flew away behind the distant mountains and silence descended on the men once again. Every now and again a desultory bit of conversation would make its appearance and then settle back into the pool of silence.

'So, give us some news.'

'Everything is OK.' Then, silence.

The breeze stirred the leaves, an occasional one floated down to the ground.

'Where have you been posted, Peter? When are you leaving?'

Peter had come home before joining work. The first people he thought of were his friends. He met Jeetu and talked to Vicky and Ashraf on the phone.

'Why don't we do something exciting, like in the old days?'

'Where?' Jeetu looked at Peter.

Was he aware of all the things that had happened in the Valley in the past year? But Peter was busy chatting away.

'Anywhere, friend! Lets go to Chashmeshahi! We can go swimming at Gagribal point. I feel like doing waterskiing. Come on, it's been an age….'

Ashraf suggested, after some thought, 'Why don't we just chat here at my place?'

Peter was surprised, 'At home?'

Ashraf explained, 'Actually when you called Ammi ordered shami kebabs. And Naseem is at home today. She said, the four of you are getting together after a year so we should have a feast. You know that Naseem works in the Women's Welfare Centre these days, don't you?'

It was an evening in the summer of 1989. The smouldering lava of the Valley had begun to intermittently burst forth in the form of a bomb or slogans. The word 'freedom' scrawled on walls reminded every passer-by that the time had come to make sacrifices for the sake of freedom. There was no more time for picnics.

Though Peter only came home for a month or so every year he was not unaware of the situation. People had not accepted the coalition government consisting of the Congress and the National Conference, which had come to power in March 1987. In opposition many Islamic parties had emerged among the Muslim United Front. Farooq had been accused of rigging the elections.

Even when the four of them had been together at college in the mid-eighties there had been a lot of political upheaval. Growing terrorism in Punjab, the attack on the Golden Temple, Maqbool Bhatt being hanged in Tihar jail, Indira Gandhi's assassination and the slaughter of Sikhs in Delhi. The four of them used to speak up openly against injustice. They believed it was wrong to send the army into the Golden Temple just as it was wrong to pull innocent people out of buses and kill them. The killing of Indira Gandhi by her own guards signified the death of faith but the killing of innocent Sikhs in Delhi was brutal and inhuman. They were truly the children of the sufis but there were growing instances of terrorism and atrocity in the country and abroad as a result of which there were frequent disturbances in the Valley. Life had moved on.

Four friends, each with his own dreams, hopes, complaints and grudges. They were proud of their friendship. But people could not understand them. Two people could be friends but four? Someone saw the four of them laughing uproariously, joking, cuffing each other and named them the 'frisky four'. Others seeing no similarity between their religions, castes or family backgrounds named them the NIG (National Integration Group). The four of them would just laugh at other people's reactions.

They followed separate paths after graduating. Peter went to Dehradun to train at the military academy. Ashraf got a seat in Electrical Engineering on the basis of merit and Vicky got a reserved seat in Chemical Engineering. Jeetu took advantage of free education and did his B.Sc. Sardarji had already told him, 'Look son, ultimately you have to take over my business. For the time being however, you concentrate on your studies, it doesn't matter.'

But whenever the friends met they would enjoy themselves

as though the four directions had come together to embrace each other. They had loved their days in college. Cricket brought them together there and, before they knew it, they had become close friends. In college the four of them took part in every discussion, debate, play or function. All of them were impressed by Marxist philosophy. They believed that every human being would get his due share one day. They argued about national and international politics. America, Russia, the revolution in Iran, Khomeini's orthodoxy, the Taliban in Afghanistan, Che Guevara and Mao.

They would prepare a topic for their next discussion in advance and then impress the girls with their knowledge. Razia, Shehnaz, Nimmi, Diksha! They had included the four girls in their group with the understanding that each one would consider the other's friend his sister-in-law. The result was that none of the girls developed a closer relationship with any of them.

They talked to each other, to figure out new and old formulas for impressing girls. But the girls would drink their cold Limcas after their 'hot' discussions, say goodbye and move on. The restless Romeos would try to douse the flames of passion by singing sad songs or having cold baths.

We are familiar with this generation born after the sixties because Ashraf, who has just become an electrical engineer, is the grandson of our Khurshi benyi, the son of Professor Imran. Vicky is aunt Mangala's grandson, the son of Dr Ajay the dental surgeon (who may have just done his BDS but who is qualified to pull out teeth). Jeetu is the grandson of sardar Makhan Singh who had escaped from the Kabaili attack on Baramullah. In the early days he used to go from house to house trying to sell the bundles of cloth he carried around on his bicycle. Later he bought a small little shack in Amirakadal. With the grace of Vaheguru and with hard work his son, Kripal, became a silk merchant and Jeet Singh is his only son.

Peter will tell us about himself. He is filled with pride whenever he talks about his forefathers.

'Brothers! You must have heard about Reverend Droxy. When he opened a missionary school in the Valley in 1881 he asked my great grandfather to come from Bombay. He said, "Dominic, I need you here!" Greatgrandpa had only two ambitions in life, to be a dedicated teacher and to cross the Wular lake. He managed to achieve both.' Whenever Peter came home he would drag the other three out of their homes. Every Sunday for that entire month they'd go off visiting different places: Gulmarg, Pahalgam, they'd go cycling to Chashmeshahi or swimming at Gagribal point. Last time they had dashed across the lake in a motor boat raising huge waves. And had eaten goshtabas and ristas in Ashraf's uncle's houseboat. Looking at the tiny settlements mushrooming alongside the lake, they were also worried at the thought that, apart from the weeds which were choking the lake tons of phosphorous and nitrogen would also be flowing into it. Ashraf thought of Abul Fazal, 'Friends, if Abul Fazal had been alive today he would have fainted at the sight of the lake which has been reduced in size from 24 square kilometers to a mere ten. At that time he called Kashmir a paradise on earth. I wonder what he would call it now?'.

'Brother, thank god for Jagmohan's attempts to clean the Dal Lake. Now at least you can see the reflection of the sky in the water.' On their way home they even took a trip to the city forest at the foothills of Jatiyar mountain where there were rows and of flowers amidst the dense trees. Gladioli, snowbell and roses. Sitting near the stream they spotted a Hangul staring at them with its big eyes. When Jeetu tried to catch it, it flew into the trees and disappeared from sight.

'Earlier this place was full of garbage, right?' Jeetu remembered.

'Thanks again to Jagmohan. This city forest is his idea!' Peter was delighted.

'Now there is going to be a golf course here. The chief-minister has agreed to this' Ashraf startled the other three with his news.

'Really?'

'Why? Another attraction for tourists?'

'That is not the reason. Tourists don't come here to play golf. They want to visit Gulmarg. There could have been many other attractions. What is the point of snatching away fresh air from people? As it is jungles and forests are disappearing. Look at how many Chinars have gone. God knows what our government is planning.'

'Vicky! You are becoming too sentimental. Look at the flip side of the coin. The government is making new plans and programmes. The Centre has given one thousand four hundred or even two thousand crores worth of funds. There is the Kandi Watershed Development programme, the National Sericulture Project, the new recruitment policy…'

'There might even be a chemical industry where I could get a job. Otherwise I will have to leave all of you and go far away.' Vicky didn't want to give up hope. The friends were saddened at the thought of going away. In a sense Peter had already left. Who knew where he would be posted?

'Vicky, you didn't try for medical.'

Vicky was surprised at Ashraf's statement.

'You are saying this? You know how hard I tried.'

'Trying hard is one thing Vicky, or even relying on quotas. You did not meet the right person at the right time. You have to admit it.'

Vicky looked dejected, 'I didn't have the means.'

Ashraf tried to lighten the atmosphere.

'Hey, Vicky, that Nimmi of yours came to our place yesterday.'

'Nimmi?' The friends were startled.

'Why did she go to your place? She was Vicky's wasn't she?' Jettu said mischievously.

'She has joined Nasim's welfare centre. But it's no use. She has chosen some millionaire.'

'Which millionaire? Who? Where did she find him? She turned out to be very unfaithful. Girls are like that ...fickle... none of them is really committed to love.'

The atmosphere became a bit too gloomy and Peter started feeling uneasy. He went and put a consoling arm around Vicky's shoulder. 'Vicky! Tell me truthfully did you really love that scrawny girl? Such a bad choice!'

Vicky made a serious face and looked up as though in surprise. 'So have you completely forgotten, Peter? Nimmi was your girl. Deeksha was mine. I was feeling sorry on your behalf.' The friends broke into laughter at this complete untruth.

But this time the laughter was missing. Peter had returned home after a year. Papa had already told him everything that had taken place in his absence. Many young men had returned from Pakistan after being trained. On the 14th of August green flags fluttered all over the valley and on the 15th there were black flags everywhere.

The news of Zia's death on the 17th of August led to riots. After the Friday namaaz, prayers were offered for his soul. Slogans were raised against India and there were incidents of arson. Three or four people were killed in police firing. The jehadis had spread the poison of communalism everywhere. People were afraid that there could be an explosion any time. Peter knew it was not possible to laugh at such a time.

They had never supported the sloganeers, they always fought against what was wrong. Why should they be afraid? They had condemned the killers when Indira Gandhi had been assassinated.

When the Sikhs were slaughtered in Delhi, troublemakers in the valley raised slogans, 'Muslims-Sikhs are brothers, Hindus are outsiders.'

'For god's sake! There is a limit to stupidity. Don't these

people know that the Hindus have been living here for thousands of years? Islam was born only in the seventh century.'

Ashraf became agitated.

'Opportunistic idiots! Trying to create divisions between people. Brothers indeed! I have heard that in 1947 the Kabailis killed more Sikhs than Hindus. Terrorists have no religion or faith.'

Peter remembered Guru Teg Bahadur's sacrifice.

'Kashmiri Pandits owe a debt of gratitude to Sikhs. My father says that in the 17th century Pandit Kriparam, unable to bear the cruelty of governor Iftikhar Khan, went to Anandpur Sahib to ask Guru Teg Bahadur for help. And the Guru sacrificed himself to protect their religion. Sikhs helped Hindus even during Afghan rule. What was his name…?'

Jeetu also opened up after hearing his friends talking.

'Birbal Dhar? He went with his son Rajkak to ask the Sikhs for help after Azim Khan ordered him to convert to Islam.'

'We have also read that at that time Abdul Qaddoos Gojwari gave shelter to Birbal's wife and daughter-in-law. The Maliks helped him to get out of Kashmir. It is only now that we have learnt to differentiate between Hindus, Muslims and Sikhs. Kashmiri Pandits do not forget Muslims and Sikhs even on such a holy day as Shivaratri, that is why they keep a Sonyapatul in their pooja and remember Vahe Guru in the Vagurbah. We have provided so many examples of brotherhood and communal harmony.'

Vicky continued the story, 'You could say that we ourselves have given birth to many Jaichands. Maharaja Ranjit Singh accepted Birbal Dar's request and sent his army to free the state from its tyrannical rulers. Abdul Qaddoos Gojawari put himself in danger to shelter Birbal Dhar's wife and daughter-in-law but his own son-in-law Teluk Munshi turned out to be a traitor. He informed the pathans who came and abducted the daughter-in-law while Dar's wife committed suicide.'

These four friends, who were always so cheerful, were afraid this time. The cause of this fear lay not within them but outside and it could not be denied because the jehadis had their eye on Ashraf's house. A few days ago four young men had advised his sister Naseem, who was on her way to the centre, to wear a burka. They also added, 'Tell your brother to stay away from Indian spies.'

'Wear a burka, keep purdah, do your namaaz. Don't ride your bicycle. Don't do anything which is unIslamic.'

Ashraf shared his fears with Peter.

'I am not worried about myself, but for those I love, which includes all of you. Please don't misunderstand me.'

'So, will Naseem wear a burka now?' Peter asked Ashraf.

Naseem was not scared. She thought of all four of them as her brothers, 'I am not going to regress into the past by wearing a burka, Peter bhai! But I have started feeling a little apprehensive about these hotheads. These days they have thought of new ways of persuading people to do as they ask.'

'New ways? For instance?'

'They throw green colour on the faces of girls without burkas. It really burns. It must be something with acid in it.'

'My god! What will you do now?'

'Don't worry. Now we are all getting loose garments stitched which cover us from head to toe. We will cover our heads with scarves. What else can we do?'

'Take care of yourself, sister Naseem! The situation is getting worse every day.'

'Everything will sort itself out, Vicky. This jehadi passion is not likely to last very long. The blood of Sufis and saints runs through our veins. It will cool down very soon. In the meantime our boys are behaving like puppets. The day they understand that they are being manipulated from outside they will be forced to change their thinking.'

Ashraf's ammi made the boys sit in front of her and fed

them. She gave them her blessings. They hugged each other as they left. Vicky was leaving for Rishikesh very soon. A friend of his had promised to get him a job there. He was wary of the situation in the city, anything could happen anytime. Peter was also going to leave the Valley shortly. Jeetu and Ashraf would stay back home but it was difficult to guess how, when and where someone might get hit in the crossfire or be accused of a crime without any wrongdoing.

It was necessary to get home before dark. Curfew was often declared in the evening. Either by the government or the terrorists and everyone had to obey. If you didn't then you could be killed in a hail of bullets like Yusuf Halwai, the block president of the National Conference, who did not obey the terrorists' call for a blackout. The result of his disobedience was death. A piece of paper was stuck on his chest saying, 'Traitor of Kashmir'.

Evidently these four friends, whatever they might have been, were not traitors to their country.

Cracks

Professor Keshavnath's sharp and bright mind had lately become a little muddled. A strange kind of melancholy had overwhelmed him. Even when he spoke his thoughts were so muddled that the listener could not understand anything. Brother DeCosta, Jia bhai and even Imran who was almost the same age as Keshavnath's son, were quite concerned. Advancing age, high blood pressure, diabetes and a half-written book. There was a lot of pressure on Professor sahib. And then the environment was going from bad to worse.

'What does that mean?'

'It means that he has always been proud of the rich culture of Kashmir. He cannot accept this new desire for freedom and jehad which has affected so many people.'

Lalli slept restlessly, she stroked her husband's forehead, 'Do you remember the dense forests in the Vurpash mountains above Nunar? Who goes there to sow seeds? They are blown in from other places, they take root in the earth and grow into tall trees one day.'

'That is it, Lalli! That is what I am saying. Anything can become a reason, a cause. A breath of air, a monsoon, spring, a bird! The wet earth helps the seed to grow and we are not even aware of all this.'

'But of course we are aware of them! Bushes, trees, prickly pears grow all over the place, they don't remain hidden from us.'

'When these prickly pears grow between relationships it becomes necessary to detach oneself from them, however bloodied one might get in the process. Otherwise relationships become like open sores.' This bitter statement had been made by Prem ji in 1986 when communal violence had suddenly erupted in Anantnag. Indira bhabi's brother Roopkrishan had run away from Anantnag with his family and taken shelter with them.

Roopkrishan had left his house in the middle of the night with his wife Sarla and his two daughters. He had narrated a lot of terrifying stories, 'What can I tell you, Bhobaji? The ruffians first attacked all the temples. They pulled out the idols from the Lokbhavan and Danavgund temples and threw some of them into the river. After destroying the temples they attacked the Pandits. We could not understand what had happened. It was like a storm of madness. Looting, arson, killings—so many terrible things.'

Roopkrishan was shaking with anger, 'Prem bhaiya, one thing is very clear, that we are not at all safe in our homes. Anything can happen to us anytime.'

'But didn't any good soul try to stop them?' Keshavnath still had faith in the goodness of human beings.

'Bhobaji, people become animals when they are in a crowd. Do they listen to anyone? People are scared of crowds. Though some people did help us afterwards. A Muslim girl even shouted at the rioters but who will ever compensate us for what has happened?'

Roopkrishan's wife, Sarla, was sobbing, 'Those rogues burnt my house down. My husband only asked them why they were destroying the temples. If Ahmed Wani had not intervened we would have been killed.'

'He is the one who advised us to come to the city for a few days. Those ruffians were just waiting for an opportunity to harm us. Wani said, "Staying alive is the most important thing, go, don't worry about anything. I will take care of your stuff."' Keshavnath thought Ahmed Wani had given the correct advice. He also felt a ray of hope that perhaps everything wasn't over yet.

Roopkrishan said, 'It was like a bolt from the blue. Everything was fine. We have been living peacefully as neighbours for decades. We have no enmity with anyone. Now who knows who these people were, who instigated them to destroy our home.'

Thirty-nine years after independence suddenly the minorities had been attacked openly. The difference was that this time the attackers were not Kabailis sent from Pakistan but one's own people.

'Pakistan wanted to occupy Kashmir but what do our own people want? What is the reason behind this rioting and destruction?' Keshavnath wanted to get to the bottom of this.

'The reason is obvious, Bhobaji, if you don't mind my

impertinence. They're not ordinary people, the troublemakers, everyone knows that. Either they are bigots who hate Hindus and India, members of Al-Fatah, Jamaat-i-Islami or some other fanatics whose purpose is to throw all "unbelievers" out of the valley and create an Islamic state. This is not a secret any longer.' Prem had always been very outspoken.

Keshavnath, however, did not jump to conclusions so easily. He reminded them that, 'It is our Rishi-Sufi tradition which kept us together during the partition in 1947 and made us support each other during the Kabaili attack. We don't have to think too far back, even during the war in 1965 Kashmiris taught Pakistan the lesson that it could not divide us on the basis of religion.'

'How can a few misguided people destroy a centuries-old tradition?'

'Bhobaji, our state has changed completely after 1965 and you know this better than me. Today it is clear that it is Pakistan and the ISI which has helped to spread the poison of terrorism and communalism. Zia Sahib's "Operation Topac" has been successful, the terrorists have AK 47s and Kalashnikovs. But we have also made some mistakes, not just one, but many.'

'By creating the Muslim League in 1932 our leaders inadvertently laid the foundation of an invisible wall between religions.'

'Isn't that the basis of the troubles we are facing today?'

'From 1975 till today our politicians have used underhand means. People were made to promise in mosques that they would vote for National Conference candidates. Even worse, in the 1984 Lok Sabha elections "Operation New Star Poster" was used to project India as the enemy of Kashmir. Religious sentiments were aroused. So many other things happened.'

'Bhobaji, Was there any place in your Rishi-Sufi tradition for fundamentalist parties like the Muslim League and the Jana Sangh? For the Al Fateh and the Jamaat-i-Islami?'

Keshavnath tried to calm Prem down. 'At that time the

Muslim Conference was created to oppose Dogra rule, Prem. The Dogra kingdom was a Hindu kingdom. The Muslim Conference was meant to contest it. But later our leaders accepted their mistake and changed it into the National Conference. They realized that would never succeed in their mission if they divided Hindus and Muslims.'

'It was mere necessity, Bhobaji, all the communities together formed a strong group which could ask the "Kashmir Darbar" to grant its requests.' It seemed Prem was not going to keep quiet today.

'You are also aware that the inspiration for this secular conference was provided by far sighted people like Nehru, Gandhi and Iqbal.'

'It doesn't matter who the inspiration was, it was Sheikh sahib who brought it to life. I remember the first general session of the National Conference took place in this same Anantnag, where fundamentalists are raising their heads today. Even today I cannot forget the words spoken by Sheikh sahib that day, "It is a great revolution that all of us, belonging to different religions have gathered today on the same platform."'

'Yes, Bhobaji, it was thanks to the greatness of all those members of the minority community who decided to forget the wounds of the riots of 1931 and join Sheikh sahib.'

This was the problem with Prem, he never forgot incidents from the past. The words spoken by a leader to young aspirants for jobs about 'you and those poor people' on the steps of Nedous Hotel had drawn a line between two brothers. Prem had not forgotten another statement made by the same politician who claimed to sympathise with the minorities, a statement with a sting that still hurt him. The words spoken by a tall politician, 'God willing! The day will come when the Pandit women whom you serve today will work as servants in your homes...'

These words, supposedly spoken in sympathy with the dalits

and the oppressed, had sown the seeds of an invisible hatred between two religions. Weren't there any Pandit women who lived lives of poverty subsisting on rice gruel?

'Prem ji, politicians often use one community against another to establish their own supremacy. This is the British "Divide and Rule" policy. What is new about it?'

'Now religion is being used as a weapon, merely for personal gain. What has Gulshah's government done? This attack on temples in Anantnag is just one example.'

'But Bhobaji! Why should we only blame Gulshah? Attacks on temples began in 1951. What happened to the Bhakteshwar Bhairavnath temple in Chattabal?'

'Tell me, couldn't the Food Control Division find any other place to distribute rations except the river bank in front of the Bhakteshwar temple? Is there any shortage of riverfronts here? But no, there was mischief in their minds. They anchored the boats carrying rations at the exact spot where Pandits used to offer prayers and perform religious ceremonies. They disrupted the Yagya that was taking place in the courtyard of the temple. If this had happened in any other state in our country wouldn't there have been a storm of violence? But our people kept asking for justice, which no one listened to even after twenty years. We were really rewarded for our non-violence.'

'Yes! That was terrible.' What else could Keshavnath say?

'A lot of wrong things happened, Bhobaji. A priest was murderd in 1972 in the Chakreshwar temple on Hari Parbat. The managing committee wanted to construct a wall around the temple but it was denied permission. I remember, Bhobaji, even the enclosure of thorn bushes which people made was torn down. Fruit trees planted on temple land were uprooted overnight. You will recall that some ascetics were asked to live near the Saptarishi temple to protect it but they were called CID agents and beaten up. Have you forgotten the 7th of June 1984, when the Hanuman temple was attacked? The idol was thrown into the Vitasta. Why did the Hindus bear the brunt of their anger when Maqbool Bhatt was hanged? Because they have always been easy prey, isn't that true? Have our religious sentiments ever been respected?'

'Bhobaji, you still carry on praising the Rishi-Sufi tradition which has been buried by our leaders long ago.'

Leaders and common people—Keshavnath wondered whether leaders were born from among common men and whether they just distanced themselves from common men once they become politicians.

'Global impact.' Shivnath would have said this if he were around. 'We have all become self-centered,' said Keshavnath who felt that the reason for this lay somewhere within our thinking. We have not learnt any lessons from history.

On the 31st of March 1986 Keshavnath was perturbed once again by the headlines in the newspapers. It was written that the Intelligence Bureau had given information about planned terrorist activities to the state and the centre but no one had taken any notice of it.

The Anantnag Temple Management Committee published the story about the troubles faced by minorities in the newspapers. They called for a bandh against attacks on homes and temples. But the sectarians termed this non-violent protest a 'conspiracy against the majority.' Premji was already upset, this news set him off again.

'Are we really living in an independent country, Bhobaji? Now we are not even permitted to protest against injustice.'

Keshavnath was worried. This really was the limit of discrimination. This February there had been two bandhs, and strikes in the Valley for the flimsiest of reasons. One was declared against the Israeli interventions in Arab territory and the other one was called in memory of Maqbool Bhatt.

Even vegetables had disappeared from the market at the time. The press had nothing to say. But the strike against atrocities on minorities in March was called a 'conspiracy of fundamentalists'.

'Journalists are supposed to raise their voices against injustice, do they also want us to go on bearing injustice without protest?'

'Free press!' Prem grimaced. 'Your big newspapers say that Kashmiri Pandits give wrong information to the press. They come here from Delhi, talk to some leaders and terrorists, walk around and then publish a one-sided report in their papers. Who bothers to meet the minorities and listen to their troubles?'

'Bhobaji, even the journalists know that the Kashmiri minority is not a vote bank. Why should they anger the majority by listening to this handful of people?'

Prem had decided to leave the Valley. He was not willing to live as a second class citizen. He was angry, but he didn't really know who with. So he took his anger out on Bhobaji.

'Actually, Bhobaji, we are responsible for our pitiable condition. Our peaceable nature has made us law abiding, meek and cowardly. Especially the Pandits, who have borne injustice because they are afraid of violence.'

Prem was not wrong. The brutality of the Afghans and Pathans taught the Pandits to bear cruelty without protest. At that time opposition or revolt meant certain death. As they had no choice they bowed their heads before fate and destiny.

After independence they mistakenly thought of their political leaders as their saviours. They continued to be victims of injustice while believing in secularism. Their abilities and worth only became evident after they left the Valley. Time passed, and by the time the end of the twentieth century approached, beliefs and hopes began to crumble but the faith the Pandits had in God and the central government did not die. At least not till 1986.

On 5 March 1986 the *Kashmir Times* published a report that said that 'minorities have been discriminated against since 1947 in Kashmir.' The report went on to say that the Pandits were saying, 'If the government does not punish those responsible and give us justice we will be forced to leave the Valley.' The supplicants forecast their own future.

Keshavnath frowned. What a strange way of asking for justice. He could not even imagine that in an independent republic anyone could be forced to flee the home of his forefathers.

'What rubbish! This is what Islamic Pakistan wants. It wants to achieve its purpose through these underhand means after facing defeat in three wars. Won't we be helping them to win if we accept defeat?' History moved the curtain aside slightly and laughed. Look, I am not dead yet.

On 7 March Jagmohan dismissed the Gulshah government. Keshavnath could see a ray of hope. Then events happened with great rapidity. In November there was the Rajiv-Farooq understanding. Keshavnath was surprised by this coalition between the Congress and the National Conference but then his thoughts went back to the past. The Congress government had made Sheikh sahib the chief-minister for the second time. Sheikh sahib filled the cabinet with members of the National Conference. And then Indira Gandhi had the oath-taking ceremony cancelled. Sheikh sahib took the help of Jha sahib to take revenge for this insult. Wheels within wheels, plots, manoeuvres.

Prem had started making a lot of predictions those days.

'Just watch, Bhobaji, the people will not accept this coalition.'

And that was exactly what happened. Maulvi Farooq said, 'Farooq Abdullah has committed "political suicide" by signing the accord with Rajiv Gandhi.' The MUF or Muslim United Front was born and stood up roaring in protest against the accord.

'What has a secular party given us?' They had many complaints.

'The politicians built bungalows, amassed wealth worth crores. Who thought about us?'

Farooq won the election. The people were enraged. There had been open rigging. Dissatisfaction grew. Bombs were hurled, there were attacks on the police. Pakistan, waiting in the wings, realized that the iron was hot and the moment was right to strike. People said, 'Sheikh sahib spent his life in jail for the sake of the Kashmiris and now his son has sold Kashmir to India.' Farooq sahib remained indifferent to the erupting volcano in his home state and spent his time travelling around the country and abroad. Rajiv Gandhi was busy with his own problems. And the volcano started to create fissures in the earth around. Hindustan came to mean the land of the Hindus and because the Pandits were Hindus they became agents of Hindustan in Kashmir. That is, outsiders. Relationships were redefined. It wasn't clear, though, how Keshavnath managed not to lose faith in his beliefs. His non-Hindu friends continued to visit him, there were discussions and debates and friendships stayed constant. The day Ragya received a letter transferring her to a college in Jammu, Prem spoke to Bhobaji, 'Bhobaji, I am going to Jammu with Ma and Ragya. I have had the house in Jammu vacated.'

'Arre! Have you really decided?' Keshavnath felt a hollow sensation inside.

'Sorry, Bhobaji. I can't see a future here. How long can we carry on being scapegoats for Chacha Nehru's secular policies? Jammu is a better place for Ragya and it will be easier for Devaki to visit us from Delhi.'

'So have you accepted defeat, Prem? Have you given up?'

'Forgive me, Bhobaji, I can't live like a dead man encased in the past!'

Two days before Imran had told Keshavnath, 'Uncle, it would be better if Prem bhaiya stayed away from the Valley for a while. Some boys are waiting for an opportunity to do him harm.'

'Why?' Keshavnath did not understand, 'What has Prem done?'

'Bhaiya laughs at their call for Independence. You know people have gone crazy these days.'

Prem had already made preparations for departure. There was no need to say anything to him.

On a misty morning in September, 1988, Lalli, Keshavnath and Katya went to the bus stop to say goodbye to Prem, Ragya, Vijaya and Kamala. A chill wind shrieked through the branches of the Chinars. Ragya couldn't stop sobbing. Katya could have consoled her. She could have said,'You silly girl, you are just going to Jammu not across the oceans. You will be back as soon as winter is over. We will celebrate Navreh, new year, together.' But she felt as though something was stuck in her throat. Standing at the mist shrouded bus stop watching a melancholy looking Prem, Keshavnath suddenly had a premonition that this time Prem was leaving his home forever, that he would never return.

The house was completely empty. After Kamala's departure it seemed to get bigger and bigger each day. Lalli got tired moving from one room to another. Katya suggested that they should shift to Shihul Villa but Lalli did not agree. 'I'm not going to leave my home and go and live with my daughter at this age. Don't worry. Lalram is here and he takes good care of us. Besides you people will also keep visiting often.'

The house could not be left empty. Katya knew this. If Ma left, then who would put the grain out for the birds on the window sill every morning? If the bowl of water for the birds remained empty they would fly away thirsty. Someone had to offer prayers before the idols in the prayer room, place flowers, light the evening lamp. How could Lalli abandon those routines of life and religion which she had followed all her life, especially now when even Kamala was not in the house.

Keshavnath felt he had too much time on his hands. He had

neither Prem nor Ragya around to argue with. He didn't feel like writing anything. Who would print what he really wanted to say? The mist of uncertainty obscured everything. Newspapers and television were full of frightening news that raised the blood pressure and caused heart palpitations.

'Today terrorists killed a boy in Sathu Barbarshah. The boy was going to see his in-laws, he had just got married.'

'The culprit has been caught. He was asked if he had any enmity with the deceased.'

'Nothing. I don't even know him.' The culprit's startling reply.

'Then why did you kill him, you rogue?' Angry questions.

'I had been paid to kill any Hindu.' Direct and unambiguous.

In December: the mahant of Vicharnag temple was shot dead by the policeman appointed to protect him because the priest refused to read the Kalma. The chief minister, Farooq Abdullah, called the incident shameful.

The *Kashmir Times* said, 'The DIG police Wali said that the reason for the spread of terrorism in the valley was the presence of police officers who had links with communal groups like the Al Fateh.'

Lalli woke up suddenly at night. The loudspeakers in the mosque nearby were broadcasting slogans of independence. In the silent, cold night the slogans fell on the chest like whiplashes. Lalli was petrified. Keshavnath held her to him like a child. 'Nothing will happen. Go to sleep. The army is out all over the city. And then we have never done anyone any harm.'

The echoing voices had now become a daily occurrence. '*Hum kya maange? Azaadi!*'.

'Long live the rule of the Prophet.'

'We want Pakistan!'

'Without the Battas but with the Battnis'

How did the days pass? Gloomy days, frightened nights. A hubub of voices. Slogans for independence scribbled across the walls! 'Do the Namaz, observe purdah.' The city had lost its identity. One evening, Iqbal Krishan came to the house, completely breathless. 'Tikalal Tapiloo has been killed by the JKLF bhai sahib!'

'Where….how….' Keshavnath stuttered.

'He was shot right in front of his house. Those people thought he was a spy for the Indian government.'

'God save us!' Lalli's eyes were brimming with tears.

'But the JKLF talks about collaborating with the minorities. They have even included a saffron triangle in their flag to represent the Hindus.'

'That is true, but for them anyone who is in contact with India is a traitor.'

People thought he was killed because he was a BJP leader. It was political enmity. Soon after retired judge Neelkanth Ganjoo became the target of the terrorists's bullets. The minorities thought this was almost inevitable. After all he was the judge who had condemned Maqbool Bhatt to hanging. The JKLF were just waiting to attack him. Some people conveyed their anger to the JKLF, 'You have taken revenge for the hanging of Maqbool Bhatt by killing Ganjoo sahib, now are you also going to kill all those who testified against him?' The reply came soon in the form of the killing of the lawyer Prem Nath Bhatt.

Would anyone ever have the courage to question the terrorists again? The newspapers were full of the slogans of the jehadis. They were determined to achieve their goals.

'The rule of the Prophet will prevail.'

'Indian dogs go back!'

This time the minorities could not find any justification for Bhatt sahib's death. Keshavnath spoke to his friend who was the editor of a regional newspaper, 'Is it necessary to publish the aims of the terrorists?' The editor was imprisoned in his room, 'Professor sahib! Nowadays we only publish what they want. And whatever is published is written in the shadow of their guns.' The editor's brown eyes were filled with fear.

Keshavnath wanted to explain things to the wayward young people. Maybe suggest some other means. Lalli stopped him. 'You will not write anything because right now your voice will not reach those you want to address.'

By now the Hizbul Mujahiddeen had spread out all over the Valley. Allah Tigers, Zia Tigers, Hizbullah. The realm of terror. The poison of separatism was spreading. Today this school was burnt, the next day it was that cinema hall. Destroy all the beauty parlours and video parlours. Secularism is unIslamic. It is a trick of the unbelievers.

Many years ago Sonamali's sons, Gula and Sula had read, in their Class III Reader, 'You may not have weapons but nevertheless, you must fight in the name of Islam.' Gula and Sula were now grown up. They had returned from Pakistan as trained militants, with weapons. They had been brainwashed by the indoctrination they had received in the mosques and madrassas, 'You must fight in the name of Islam.'

'Fight against whom?'

'The unbelievers.'

'Who are the unbelievers?'

'Those people in the Valley who support India. Those who are the enemies of our freedom and of Pakistan.'

Keshavnath sometimes listened to Radio Azaad Kashmir. Anti-India venom filled the room as soon as he pressed the button.

'Atrocities on Muslim brothers in Kashmir.'

'The Indian army is killing innocent Muslims.'

Keshavnath got fed up and switched off the radio. Lalli brought some kehwa. Both of them looked out at the silent row of houses through the window. The river that linked the two shores was becoming narrower. Putting down his cup, Keshavnath decided to lie down.

'My head is feeling heavy, even the tea did not help. Give me an Anacin.'

Keshavnath took the Anacin and lay down. He closed his eyes but sleep eluded him. A series of scenes unfolded in front of his closed eyelids. When Keshavnath had started feeling at a loose end after retirement, Shivnath suggested that he should go to the club.

'Come with me. Play bridge for an hour or two. Or you can learn golf. Your De Costa sahib plays quite often... it will be a good way to while away the time. Just yesterday Gul Mohammad was asking about you.'

Kamala was annoyed.

'Tell Gul Mohammad that Bhobaji enjoys listening to Pushkarnath Mam's radio plays "Zoon Dabba" and "Hero Macham", with his family.' Lalli and Kamala had become essential to each other after Shivnath's death. Ragya and Devika questioned Keshavnath when they found him alone.

'Nanaji, are we Saraswat Brahmins?'

'Yes, we are.'

'Mummy says Saraswat Brahmins are the descendants of those Aryans who lived by the shores of the Saraswati river in the Punjab. But there is no Saraswati river in the Punjab.'

'The Saraswati river did exist earlier, our scientists have just confirmed this fact. After the river dried up the Aryans searched for another place to live and reached Kashmir. They were delighted by its beauty and prosperity and decided to settle down here.'

'Nanaji, the Naga tribes used to live here initially. Then the Pishachas came from Sinkiang. They used to live here during the winter months and go back in summer. I have read this. But I have another question. '

'What is your question?' Nanaji liked Devika's curiosity.

'Nanaji, the Aryas and the Pishachas both came from outside the Valley. With the help of the Nagas, the Aryas threw the Pishachas out and later they dominated over the same Nagas. The Nagas gradually mingled with the Aryas or left and went away. Why didn't the Nagas understand the intentions of the Aryas?'

'Initially the Nagas opposed them. Then King Neel agreed to let them stay on certain conditions. The Aryas must have been strong, that is why the Nagas could not oppose them.' Keshavnath tried to explain.

During the past few years terrorists had spread out all over the valley. First it was our own boys and then the Afghanis and Pakistanis came in. As Ragya was leaving for Jammu she said to Bhobaji, 'Don't you feel, Bhobaji that Kashmiris are going to find themselves in the same situation as those old Nagas?'

'What are you trying to say, child?'

'Bhobaji, today our boys are inviting the Pakistanis. They are helping them to throw out the minorities…finish them off. But tomorrow will these Pakistani-Afghani terrorists allow Kashmir to remain independent? Won't they want to dominate? Even today the Karachi-Sindhi Muslims in Pakistan are known as Muhajirs, what title is going to be bestowed on the Kashmiris?'

Ragya was right. Pakistan did not want the Kashmiris, it only wanted Kashmir. If anyone came in the way, whether the person was Hindu or a secular Muslim, he had to be removed. Even Imran had understood this fact. He had not come over for many days. Keshavnath was worried. Katya sent Jani to Imran's house, 'Is professor sahib all right?' She found out that Imran had gone to Delhi on the pretext of delivering his father's goods.

'So suddenly?' Jani was a little suspicious.

Abbajan explained that some boys had been threatening Imran because he visited Raina sahib. He was discouraged from going there too often. It seems Prem ji used to argue with the boys. He was Imran's friend and they didn't like this fact. 'But even I visit Pandits, no one says anything to me. It is good to spend time with someone your age. Where is the question of likes and dislikes?' Jani made the statement but she was disturbed. Would the boys send a message to Jani as well? Or will they just shoot her?

The next day Ajay Wali was shot at Habbakadal in broad daylight. When she heard a shot being fired, his mother, Taravati, came out on the road with her flour besmeared hands. Crying and weeping, she called out to her son who was lying wounded in the middle of the bridge. Taravati cradled her son in her lap, the wide open eyes on the blood stained face looked up sightlessly at the sky. Ajay could not hear his mother's voice.

Travati begged the gunmen, 'Why don't you shoot me as well, just one bullet. I beg you in the name of Allah.'

The gunmen kicked her away with their boots, 'We won't kill you. Someone has to be left behind to mourn for him.'

There was dead silence in Habbakadal at that time. People were hiding in their homes, someone looked out and saw Taravati holding her son, others were thinking of running away somewhere to save their children before the gunmen came for them. The very next day Katya sent Lalli and Keshavnath to Jammu by car. She didn't ask for their opinion, she just said the winter was too harsh for them.

The doors and windows of Vishni Vatika were shut. Standing inside the closed doors Katya heard voices from her childhood, playing games,'Okus bokus tilwan chokus', songs being sung on marriages, Tathya's stern instructions, Shivnath Kak's last journey. Many scenes passed before her eyes, the last of which was Lalli and Bhobaji's reluctant departure today. She felt a sharp pain in her heart when she remembered the way they kept turning back to look at their home as they left. Katya felt a storm raging in her heart, her eyes were full of tears. At that very moment some innocent soul was being punished at Gavkadal for crimes he had not committed. Katya put Lalli's special Ladhakhi lock on the heavy wooden doors of Vishnu Vatika and returned to Shihul Villa with a heavy heart.

※

First Stop, Jammu

Jammu no longer felt like Jammu.

Lalli could not recognize the city.

'The city is the same one grandma, which was established by King Jambulochan three thousand years ago. The city of "Duggars"!' Riddhi wanted to explain things to her grandmother.

'When you saw it for the first time it was a small little city situated on a hillock, full of temples with golden pinnacles. Now the narrow alleyways and crowded markets have expanded into large neighbourhoods and are continuing to spread out.' Lalli nodded, indicating that she agreed with Riddhi but her eyes were searching in vain for something. Everything was different. Only the peaks of the Trikuta mountain, where Ma Vaishno Devi resided, hadn't changed. They were there earlier and continued to remain in the same place. This gave a little solace to the heart, nowadays. Otherwise everything had scattered. 'Change is an inevitable part of life'. Keshavnath had become philosophical.

Riddhi taught History in the Women's College. She got an opportunity to travel through the past when Lalli started talking about the changes in the city. And then there was no one more knowledgeable and available than grandpa who could be included in this journey. Nanu was the one who told her that the word Dogra came from the Sanskrit word 'Dogirath' which meant two lakes. The two ancient lakes, Mansar and Siroinsar that have existed in this land of the Duggars since ancient times.

'Nanu. It is believed that Jammu was also one of the sites of the Indus valley civilization. This city has also seen a lot of turmoil in its past.'

'Yes, Riddhi, this land is steeped in legends of the heroism of the Duggar kings and stories about the cruelty and brutality of invaders. Jammu was almost completely destroyed after the attack of Taimur Lang in 1398.' Nanu also loved to dabble in history.

'Yes, Nanu! Ranjit Dev re-established the city after its destruction by the Mughals, a task which must have been as difficult as growing crops in sand.'

'You are right, Riddhi. Ranjit Dev changed the very destiny of this state with his intelligence, courage and political acumen. Just think, he took command after defeating twenty two Dogra generals. The Mughal ruler of the Punjab, Zakaria Khan imprisoned him merely on suspicion for twelve years. Thankfully Adina Beg Khan, the Governor of Jalndhar, released him on payment of a fine of twelve lakh rupees otherwise the fate of the state would have been very different.'

'I am amazed at one thing, Nanu. How did Ranjit Dev's kingdom survive despite the fact that the Mughals had left their representatives in the Punjab. And it was a prosperous kingdom.'

'What is strange about this, child? Kings knew how to protect their kingdoms at any cost. They had their own clever ploys, but they also took the welfare of the public into account. Look at Ranjit Dev for instance. He helped Ahmadshah Durrani against Sukhjeevan Mal when Durrani attacked Punjab. This was politics. Ahmadshah was so happy that he granted him a lot of land.'

'Politics or opportunism? It is also said that Ranjit Dev finally became so sick of internal squabbles that in 1803 he merged his state with the Sikh state. Bhobaji, if I am not wrong, the person who took the maximum advantage of the situation was Gulab Singh.'

'Gulab Singh was very clever, apart from being very brave. He showed immense courage when the Sikhs attacked Jammu. At that time he was only sixteen years old.'

'That is why Maharaja Ranjit Singh was impressed with him and took him into his army. He gave land and estates to Gulab Singh and his brothers. Wasn't that a bit too generous, Nanu? He gave Jammu to Gulab Singh, Poonch to Dhyan Singh and gifted Ramnagar to Suchet.'

'Why do you forget that Gulab Singh had also pleased the king by defeating Agha Khan in Rajouri. He was just a governor of the Sikh kingdom in Kashmir, but even there he gave ample proof of his courage.' Keshavnath never got tired of praising Gulab Singh. But Riddhi could not understand his politics.

'Nanu, it is clear that Gulab singh was never really completely aligned with anyone. Sometimes he sided with the Sikhs, at other times with the British. He also mediated between the two, while retaining a rigid stance at other moments. What kind of a strategy was this for a brave soldier?'

'Gulab singh is the one who established Dogra rule in Jammu-Kashmir. He was a favourite of Ranjit Singh but the Sikhs did not treat him well after Ranjit Singh's death. Jealousy. Jawahar Singh even placed him under detention.'

'Yes, I have heard this. He was later released because of the intervention of Dewan Jwala Sahay.'

'He was released but he must have always felt the sting of having been imprisoned. That is why he befriended the British. He helped them by sending his army to attack Afghanistan. But he was never disloyal to the Sikhs. On the contrary he pleased both sides by intervening in the fight in Subraon between the Sikhs and the British. That is why in 1846 Maharani Jindan made him the chief minister of Punjab in recognition of his strength and bravery.'

'Yes, Nanu. The British also recognized his strength that is why they signed so many treaties with him.'

'The two treaties of 1846 changed the map of northern India.'

Riddhi knew that the Sikhs were forced to sign an agreement with the British on 9 March 1946. The Sikhs owed the British a crore of rupees and they had to give Kashmir, Hazara, Vyas and parts of Sindh to them to pay off this debt.

But the other treaty which was signed by Gulab Singh and the British on 16 March 1946 was motivated, to some extent, by Gulab Singh's ambition to become an 'emperor'. That is why he bought Kashmir for seventy five lakh Nanakshahi rupees from the British.

'Nanu, the historian Munshi Mohammad Fauq has rightly said that, because of the Amritsar treaty of 1846, eleven lakh Kashmiris were bought for seventy five lakh rupees.'

Keshavnath never forgot to look at the other side of the coin. 'Fauq is right in a way but it is also true that when Gulab Singh stepped into the flooded valley on 9 November 1946 and saw the terrible condition of the city dwellers, he must have wondered whether he had taken the right decision. But the Kashmiris welcomed him because they were sick of the cruelty of the governor Sheikh Imamuddin.'

'Nanu, there are archeological finds that indicate that Kashmir existed from the time of the *Mahabharat* or even earlier from the period of the *Ramayana*. There have been so many kings here but in my view the greatest Hindu kings were Lalitaditya Muktipeed in the sixth century and Avantivarman after him. Also Kota Rani, to some extent, and Sultan Zainulabdin during the Muslim period. The rest were either weak rulers or ambitious, crafty plotters. Diddarani was a strong queen but she got so entangled in her selfish interests and plots that she ultimately destroyed herself and the state.'

'There are very few areas in the world which have been as

unfortunate in the matter of governance as Kashmir, Riddhi.' Keshavnath quoted Vincent Smith. 'When you read the *Neelmath Puran*, the *Rajtarangini* you realize that the amount of political churning, cultural mixing, attacks from outside and intrigues from within that you find in the history of Kashmir are rarely found anywhere else. And yet no one can deny that we have managed to leave the imprint of our identity not merely in India but in the culture of the world.'

'Yes, Nanu. Kashmir was the cradle of different religions and cultures from the reign of Gonand till the end of Dogra rule. First it was a Hindu kingdom and then the Kusha dynasty spread the Buddhist religion. Lalitaditya of the Karkot dynasty reintroduced Hinduism though he was very tolerant towards Buddhism. After that from Harsh and Didda to queen Kota, the kings became more and more politically corrupt. Yet we managed to produce so many Sanskrit scholars, Shaivite scholars, learned poets, historians and writers from Mammat, Abhinavgupt to Kalhan-Bilhan. The Islamic period which began with Shahmir, Rinchinshah also produced Lalded and Nund Rishi who belonged to the Rishi-Sufi tradition but then tyrants like Sikandar Butshikan and Suh Bhatt were also born here. How many great kings like Zainulabdin Badshah did we produce? And now that we have become independent and won our freedom from kings and emperors, the new political leaders have turned out to be worse than the worst rulers.'

Kamala changed the subject, she did not enjoy political discussions. What had politics given them? It had just thrown them out of their homes. Their hearts were in Vishnu Vatika even while they lived here. The memory of the Vitasta filled the heart with pain. She used to look at it as soon as she woke up in the morning, now where can she find the Vitasta? As far as the eye can see there are half-constructed, concrete and brick houses with a few trees scattered here and there. The shade of the Chinars and the willows has become a distant memory.

Lalli didn't complain, she just looked for the old Jammu she knew, searching for some connection with the past. Earlier when she would come with Bhobaji to Jammu during the 'darbar move' Jammu consisted of Julaka Mohalla, Mast Garh, Bavda Bazaar, Pakka Danga and Dhakkis. 'We used to live in Pakki Dhakki in Sardar Attar Singh's house which we had taken on rent. Every morning we would to go with his wife to "pir kho". We would cross the Tavi river and visit the temple in Bahu fort. We would get wet upto our knees splashing about in the rushing waters of the river as it flowed over stones.'

Lalli's eyes shone as she looked back at the past. Wandering through the winding streets of the Dhakkis, the huge cauldrons of the sweetmeat sellers full of boiling milk and the earthy smell of dabar-bhalle would make their mouths water. At the fairs held at the Shiva temple and Raghunath temple, the proud Duggar women would be all dressed up with round, shining ornaments on their foreheads, their arms full of bangles, wearing long velvet kurtas and tight pyjamas. Meena would sing folk songs in a voice as sweet as the falling rain, Thakur Attar Singh was mesmerized by it. Where was he now?

Dulari had lived in Jammu since her marriage. She built a house in Gandhinagar. In the past forty years everything had changed. 'Thakur Attar Singh's wife passed away many years ago. He married her so-called sister, Behenji, very soon afterwards, Ma. But then two years ago Attar Singh also died in an accident.'

Lalli was upset, 'And what about Behenji?' She was still clinging to her hopes. Maybe there was something still left of that house where Biji used to feed the monkeys and the loud strains of ghazals coming from Attar Singh's drawing room attracted the entire neighbourhood.

'Behenji also left with the youngest son. The house was almost collapsing, they gave it to the Dharamarth Trust. Actually the house started to fall apart after Biji's death....'

The atmosphere became heavy, the air itself still. Lalli became melancholy.

'O, grandma! What are you thinking about? Time always moves forwards, Nani, how can it go back?'

'Come on, we will take you to see the Bahu garden tomorrow. It is just like Nishat and Shalimar and has been made at the foot of the Bahu fort. You can climb the steps and go straight to the temple within the fort. Now you don't have to climb the hill after crossing the river, the car goes right up to the park. Stop living in the past, Nani.'

'Yes, child. The past never comes back. What is the point in complaining about it?'

Both Lalli and Kamala felt a sense of detachment, time had taken so much away from them. 'First the Pandits left their homes in search of jobs. They went to Delhi, Agra, Jammu, Lucknow, all over the country and abroad. They built houses, but their own nests, their own identity remained. Now they have been thrown out of their homes, how will they ever go back?' Keshavnath listened to Lalli and Kamala's laments. He felt he should reassure them, try to make them understand. Didn't they know that we have made and are still making a place for ourselves in the country and abroad as doctors, engineers, lawyers, professors, writers and scientists? If we had just sat at home then…? But now Keshavnath didn't say or hear anything, he just observed and thought. When he tired of doing this, he would just close his eyes and lie down.

In this way he protected himself against Lalli and Kamala's sorrow and Prem's stinging questions but he could not defend himself from those memories that knocked at his closed eyelids. The loud laughter of friends, the sufiana songs of Gul Mohammad, the sound of the azaan from the Hazratbal dargah which touched the heart, the picnics, the joys, Hari Parbat and Shankaracharya. Not merely scenes of natural beauty but interspersed with questions, doubts, a mist-covered past full of memories. Wandering through the green forests, shivering in the water, there was a priceless shard of the past whose fragrance was an inalienable part of Keshavnath's consciousness. He couldn't free himself from it. He didn't know when which scene would appear before his eyes.

Look, where has Maharaja Hari Singh suddenly appeared from? He is sitting in the shooting lodge near Harvan. Is he planning to hunt Hanguls in the jungle? That's the sport of kings. Whatever his heart desires. This is Hokarsar, or is it Hegam? He is aiming at the ducks swimming on the surface of the lake. He was just playing Polo in the Polo ground. Now there is music—Begum Akhtar, Siddheshwari Devi or Mallka Pukhraj singing; '*Abhi to main jawan hoon*...I am still young...no. no...not yet, I am still young....'

Arre! What is this, why have the voices suddenly stopped? The scene darkens. In the dead of the night, Hari Singh is crossing Banihal with a small fleet of cars. In the wagon there is a wheel chair with the only heir to the throne and Queen Tara Devi...the staff officer and the gunman are going with them. The palace which looks down on the lake, the white heads of the ancient mountains reflected in the water, the ducks dancing on the waves, kingship, power and the inheritance of ancestors –everything is being left behind. He doesn't know whether he will ever return home. He knows he has lost Kashmir.

The man on whose coronation treasuries full of pearls and diamonds were thrown open, whose horse was decorated with emeralds costing seven lakh rupees...when his procession floated down the Jhelum the entire Valley gathered on the banks to greet him.... the same person was stealing away from the valley like a thief in the night.

Which unfortunate day is this in 1949 when the Maharaja has been summoned to Delhi? He is still hopeful. How can he lose the kingdom of his ancestors so easily? Nehru and Patel show the Maharaja the face of reality, 'It will be good for the country if you stay away from the Valley for a while.' In other words, the king can also be exiled. The formalities are observed. Karan Singh will be the Regent, look after his father's property. The proclamation is being signed. And then it is goodbye.

Hari Singh is going to Bombay, Tara Devi to Kasauli. Their son Karan Singh will stay with Vishnu Sahay in Karan Mahal. The winds of time have destroyed a home. It's the end of an era. The proud king ignored the call of the times but time is more cruel than tempests and storms. How did the king feel to be cut off from his inheritance and sent far away? Did he merely lose his kingdom? His identity, the earth beneath his feet, the breezes, the remains of his ancestors in the Raghunath temple….didn't he remember all these?

Keshavnath turned over. What were these scenes he was seeing these days? Why does he go so far away? He can see sand and desert all around. Everyone gets the fruit of their deeds, the fruit of their debts, one has to reap what one sows. But what had the entire minority community sown that made them lose the handful of land they called their own? Why hadn't the breeze of the new democracy benefited them? Motilal Saqi had said,

'This beautiful laughing garden, our land!

Our Dal lake embedded with priceless pearls!

Here we will always be able to hold our heads up high.'

And yet why did the Battas have to bow their heads? Who was responsible? Why did the clouds of rust cover the entire Valley?

Nadim sahib! Which song are you going to sing today? Keshavnath was staring into the dark with his eyes wide open…so many great poets who used to make the Valley echo with their voices, why had they become silent? Why didn't Mohammad Amin Kamil say any longer that 'It is always good to be together, come together, become one'? Had he also been silenced by the fear of Kalashnikovs?

Fear was in the air.

Keshavnath waited for letters. He talked to Katya every day and asked her about the situation. He buried his head in the newspapers. Deaths, threats, news of bombings. 'Mohammad Mufti's daughter, Dr Rubaiya Sayid has been kidnapped by terrorists in broad daylight! At three thirty in the afternoon! Three people got down from a blue Maruti van and took her away. The people are angry. Release Rubaiya.' The National Conference government was alarmed. Gujral sahib, Arif Mohammad Khan and many Intelligence officers arrived in Srinagar.

The terrorists wanted five bloodthirsty militants to be released in exchange for Rubaiya.

'Prem! Call Katya.' Keshavnath was looking pale. His voice was shaking. Fear? Why was Keshavnath afraid? What was Keshavnath, the son of Tathya who was as steady as a cliff, afraid of? But he was scared. Lalli was also feeling uneasy. 'Oh God! Keep my children safe.'

Katya reassured them over the phone, 'Bon't worry, Bhobaji, we are absolutely safe. There are security personnel in the hospital. Look after your health. I worry about you.'

On television Rubaiya was clinging to her mother and weeping. The beautiful Rubaiya, who was doing her internship at the Lal Ded hospital had returned home. The Centre had accepted the demands of the terrorists. The militants were celebrating, distributing sweets, shouting slogans-

'Anyone who is Godfearing should pick up a Klashnikov.'

The newspaper *Dawn* had written that the entire kidnapping was 'a bluff that worked.' Prem gnashed his teeth, 'How is such a big country being run by such politicians? It is the eighth wonder as far as I am concerned.'

Keshavnath did not comment.

19 January, 1990. Jagmohan once again became Governor of Kashmir. He took up office in Jammu where he received a tumultuous welcome. But Farooq sahib resigned.

Keshavnath was surprised, 'I clearly remember that in 1988 Farooq sahib was full of praise for Jagmohan, saying that he had done a lot of developmental work and had also improved the system. The people were also very happy with him.'

'How much water has flown under the nine bridges on the Jhelum since then, Bhobaji?' Prem asks.

'Yees! At this time who is bothered about the sparkling, clean surface of the Dal lake or the illuminations which light up the shrine of Vaishno Devi? Their ears are ringing with the sounds of Kalashnikovs.'

The situation became worse soon after Jagmohan's arrival. The telephone rang at midnight. As Prem took the call his face became pale. Keshavnath realized something was wrong. Who was it at this hour? On the phone, the voice of Iqbal Dhar's son Ramesh was shaking.

'Bhai sahib! There is total chaos here! Jehadi slogans are being shouted and the sounds of 'la-ilaha-illah' are echoing like threats from mosques. People have come out on the streets. There are fires on the roads and the houses are shrouded in darkness. I don't know what will happen to us. If we're lucky enough to survive till morning we'll come down to Jammu. Please look for a room for us. We are all scared. Papa has fainted because of the commotion. I hope he doesn't have an attack.'

Many events took place on the next day. Newspapers, TV, the radio were full of news.

'Crackdown in the city on 20 January! Three hundred arrested on suspicion. Thousands of people come out on the roads in protest. A hundred protesters shot in Gawkadal.'

What happened suddenly? How did it happen? Even Jammu was stunned. The news came, 'The crowd which was trying to ransack the Women's Polytechnic, Saidakadal, Mahjoor bridge and Lal Bazaar was dispersed by force.'

Houses were searched on the nights of the 19th and 20th. People were incensed. Jagmohan said he had no knowledge of this, even Farooq claimed he knew nothing. Then who gave the orders for the crackdown? Was it a conspiracy or meant to capture terrorists? Someone said, don't drink the water, the tanks have been poisoned…In this atmosphere full of suspicion and rumours Jagmohan was given the difficult task of maintaining law and order. Four jawans of the Kashmir Armed force were killed by the Paramilitary forces. The Kashmir Armed Guards almost revolted. An eye for an eye! Jagmohan accepted the challenge. He sent the Central Reserve Police Force to the police stations. Prem made a prediction, 'This time Jagmohan will not be allowed to function. There are terrorists in our territory now and rumours and panic everywhere. It is difficult to distinguish between truth and falsehood.'

Pakistan was openly supporting the militants.

Lalji rang up from Karan Nagar, 'Truth-untruth, right-wrong, nowadays one can't distinguish anything. The city is frightened and under curfew. Slogans are broadcast from mosques night and day. War to the end. These people are ready to fight for independence till they die. Roads and lanes have been named after those who have been killed by the security forces. The road named after the militant leader Fayyaz Ahmed Dar is now called 'Martyr General Fayyaz road'. I don't know how long I can continue to stay here…' Lalji's voice faltered and then stopped. Keshavnath held on to the phone for a while. His body was burning. His eyes were drooping.

'Why do you pick up the phone, Bhobaji? You are not feeling well as it is.'

Prem didn't know what to say. How can he explain to Bhobaji that worrying won't help improve the situation.

Prem had strictly instructed everyone in the house, 'Don't let Bhobaji see the newspaper. His health will worsen if he keeps hearing about violence and killings. If you people can't do anything at least put on some cassettes of bhajans, holy songs.

He will feel a little at peace.' Bhobaji was touched. The children were concerned about him. He knew worrying would do no good to anybody but he couldn't stop. Every day busloads of Battas were arriving in Jammu. Many of those who continued to stay on after receiving threats had been killed. There was complete lawlessness. Katya, Kartik, friends, relatives were still in Srinagar. And....

Riddhi stroked Nanu's forehead.

'Will the situation change if I don't get to know what's going on, child?'

Keshavnath asked a strange question.

'How is that possible, Nanu. What has to happen will....'

'Then read out the newspaper to me. Let us find out what is happening where. What steps the Central Government is taking, what policies it's formulating. It is better to be knowledgeable rather than to lack knowledge, Riddhi.'

Riddhi read out the news to Nanu, though no steps seemed to have been taken to bring about any change in the situation. 'On the 24th of January the Akali leader Simranjit Singh Mann went to Srinagar and told Jagmohan, "There shouldn't be another Bluestar in Srinagar."'

'On the 25th of January Squadron Leader Ravi Khanna and four IAS officers who were waiting at the Rawalpora Bus stop were killed.'

'Jagmohan imposed curfew on the afternoon of the 25th.'

Newspapers report Farooq sahib's saying, 'The governor has created a Martial Law situation in the valley.'

'This will happen! All this will happen! Lal Ded had said, "The rivers will dry up and the drains will roar, then the monkeys will rule."'

'Nanu, what are you saying?'

'These people will show the rebellion in Azerbaijan on TV. Mann Sahib will come to Srinagar and talk to the journalists, why didn't he speak to the governor on the phone? The militants will come on motorcycles and in Maruti Gypsies, fire forty rounds and get away safely after killing senior officials. The police will watch the tamasha from the police post close by. And the politicians will keep finding fault. No one will talk of a solution. The rot will continue to spread.' Keshavnath became breathless.

'Nanu, please calm down. Your fever…'

'No, nothing will happen. No magician will come and wave his magic wand. Those people will allow curfew to be imposed. Killers will not be dealt with strictly. Guns will come from across the border, AK47s, rockets, anti-tank mines…. The innocent will die, blood will flow. There will be propaganda, rallies….'

Prem brought the doctor. 'Uncle gets very excited at times. We don't know what to do.'

The doctor checked his blood pressure and prescribed some medicines. 'Keep your mind peaceful, Professor sahib! You are a sensible man.'

'Yes, doctor sahib. I am at peace. These people get worried unnecessarily.'

On the 13th of February the terrorists killed Lassa Kaul, the director of Doordarshan. He was going to visit his sick father. They shot him as he was on his way.

When Keshavnath heard this, he just leaned back and rested his head on the pillow. Two minutes of silence. Lassa Kaul had been one of his favourite students. Lalli brought some water and Keshavnath took the glass.

'Sit down Lalli, here, next to me.' He gestured to her.

'Will you have some tea?' Lalli was frightened by her husband's silence.

Keshavnath's eyelids fluttered. 'Lassa Kaul said he had travelled all over the world for many years. Now he wanted to repay his debt to his motherland. He…he … really wanted to do something, Lalli!' Lalli saw the storm of emotion that was welling up in Keshavnath's eyes.

Mass Exodus

The year 1990. It was only now, in this year that one realized how quickly a small town could be transformed into a big city.

The exodus had begun a while ago but this year the winding roads near Banihal were jammed with melancholy caravans of buses and trucks. In these trucks-buses-matadors terrified Pandits sat with bowed heads—entire families of them, clutching on to any boxes, bags, bundles that they had managed to grab as they left. They were leaving behind homes, inheritances, names which had been theirs for generations. Till Qazigund their eyes looked around carefully like police dogs on the alert for any danger. Their bones trembled with fear and their voices became hoarse. Their backs were tense, almost as though they could feel the Kalashnikovs pointed at them.

They knew they were at fault. They had committed the crime of staying on in their homes even after receiving the orders from the jehadis to 'leave home and disappear anywhere'. Such insolence towards the orders of the jehadis? Naturally the jehadis were angry. They had hung the corpses of ten or fifteen Pandits branded with hot irons, with their eyes put out, bodies sawn in half, on trees. Some bodies had been thrown on the road, others into the Vitasta. Now what do you say? Are you going to leave everything behind and go or do you want to be stuck here mourning the demise of a five thousand year old Hindu civilization?

The screaming winds accompanied the buses as they raced along. Once across the Jawahar tunnel, close to Banihal they stopped and looked back. The Chandrabhaga sobbed. The people stuffed into the buses bid goodbye to the mountain peaks with their snowy caps. It was time to leave their homeland. Though they had no idea where they were going or what would happen next. Right now they were only worried about saving themselves from death. Jammu welcomed these displaced people with open arms. The poor Pandits. Those who always gave to others had now become beggars themselves. People were full of sympathy.

Temples, dharamshalas, guest-houses, hostels started to fill up with refugees. Under construction hostels, government schools, half covered courtyards, when the Pandits saw any place where there was a roof they used sheets, saris, jute matting to create an enclosure. Half-naked elders, young women and children from villages and small towns found a place to rest amidst their utensils, tin boxes, trunks and other meagre possessions. Soon camps were opened around Jammu in Nagrota, Jhiri, Mishriwala, Purkhu, Talab Tiloo, Indira Nagar and ARTC Miran Sahib Force building, Labour Sarai. MAM stadium also opened transit camps for the refugees and life resumed. Refugee relief organizations took up the task of looking after the displaced. The government was warned. Jagmohan himself came to see the people packed together like sardines in the camps. It was the relief organizations rather than the government that helped the refugees get back on their feet. Those who had the means to travel went to Dehradun, Chandigarh, Punjab, even Maharashtra. A large number of refugees arrived in Delhi. But the situation was equally bad everywhere. In Delhi ten camps were opened for three hundred families. The other ten thousand families wandered from place to place. They lived the kind of life that was possible on an allowance of a hundred and twenty five rupees a month in a metropolis. The thirty lakh rupees in the Prime-Minister's Relief Fund were soon exhausted. And then? The Kashmiri Samiti in Delhi fought for the rights of the refugees. But what are the rights and the lives of the displaced? A transit camp was opened in Kashmir Bhavan, in Amar Colony. The Samiti gathered food and some basic necessities and told the government, 'We want justice. We are citizens of this country.'

'Our children are educated, they want jobs. They need admissions in schools and colleges. We need our salaries.'

'Aren't we the descendants of those Kashmiri Pandits who contributed so much to Indian philosophy, theology, history and politics?'

'Have we ever responded violently to all the injustice and humiliation we have suffered? How long will we be tested like this?'

'For how long will it be considered a crime to live with our heads held high in our own country?'

They had many questions. There were seminars and rallies, attempts to find solutions but Delhi was the capital after all. It could not concern itself only with Kashmiri refugees. And that too Pandits. They may have been important in the past but in this changing, globalized world what use were these Pandits who did not even constitute a vote bank? We have to worry about the whole world. In other words, take what you are being given and live or die in the camps. Stand in queues with your children. Get burnt by the sun or drenched by the rain.

George Fernandes, the politician, said the Pandits were the culprits. A small minority and yet they'd monopolized most of the government jobs which should have gone to the majority community. This had given birth to terrorism. Politically knowledgeable leaders pulled a cloak of silence over 42 years of misgovernance and wrong decision making by the central and state governments.

The Pandits were amazed at these wise leaders. Didn't they know that the Pandits constituted a mere two per cent of the population of Kashmir? How many posts could two per cent occupy? Weren't they aware that the basis of Kashmir's economy was the carpet industry, shawl industry, papier mache, wood work, silk factories and tourism? How many Pandits were a part of this vast business which was spread all over the world? A handful? Was there any discrimination there, any injustice? Didn't these leaders know that since 1947 Pandits had been searching for jobs everywhere from Delhi to America? Most Pandits were white collar clerks and teachers in government offices and school. The percentage of Pandits in government jobs was decreasing day by day. Had any of the problem solvers ever thought about these issues?

The Pandits wished these wise men, proclaimers of fatwas, would also keep track of the number of Pandits who, since 1947, had been forced to wander all over the country and abroad in search of jobs and education. They would realize how, in a gradual but planned manner, the Pandits had slowly been eased out of the Valley. They would see that these beggarly looking people, living a makeshift existence in ragged tents, shacks and dhurrie sized rooms had left beautiful homes, gardens, orchards and property worth lakhs behind.

The Pandits started losing faith. They wished that the diplomats, the so-called Kashmir specialists, would critically examine Pakistani diplomacy and the irresponsible behaviour of its leaders. After losing three wars and the creation of Bangladesh, Pakistan had taken its revenge through Operation Topac and used religious fanaticism as a means of spreading terrorism. This was the basic reason for terrorism but our rulers refused to acknowledge it.

'Why don't you people get up, hawk goods from door to door, put up kiosks, after all, that's what the people displaced during Partition did.'

Prem tried to help these displaced people to make a life for themselves. He didn't have any expectations from the government. Why should those people trouble themselves? It was easier to blame the minority and forget about the speeches from the mosques, the rigged elections, the complete disregard of the common man by the corrupt system. Was the Pandit a part of any of these, how did he become a reason, a cause? In other words accept this division and get ready for the future.

In the dead of night the Muthi camp in Jammu looked like a large cemetery. During the day, the children and the elderly spent hours waiting in long queues for their daily ablutions or stood holding boxes, pots, utensils for water and the daily rations. Waiting from morning till night was a way of life here. As the queue slowly crept forward, an inch at a time, the rays of the sun beat down on people's heads. Sansar Chand wrapped a wet towel around his head and looked around for any shade. Was this sunshine or a glowing ember? His breath became uneven. His heart yearned for the snow-cooled breezes of his home in Kupwara. Sansar Chand, who had left the valley for the first time, felt he was stuck in a boiling, stinking hell. Hey Ram! For what sins was he being punished? The retired school master from Shahpore, Ganderbal, had lost his mind. He talked rubbish all the time, 'Didn't I tell you ? But you don't listen to me. There is still time, join the jehad. Take out rallies. At least you won't have to bear the humiliation of having to beg. Teach your children the Kalma. Come children! Say with me, "What do we want?"'

A huge crowd of children gathered around him.

'Say, "azaadi", independence. Repeat after me.'

Neelkanth from Sopore looked murderously at the schoolmaster.

'Stop your nonsense, master! Doesn't your throat ever dry up?'

Kashinath was always ready to intervene.

'Brother, Neelkanth, why do you get upset with masterji? He has lost his young daughter. Who will understand his sorrow apart from us?'

'Kashinath! Who is happy here? Who is there who hasn't lost something? The militants shot me in the leg. I turned out to be a tough guy and I survived. But I can never forget what happened in our Sopore in front of my eyes. Even in my sleep I can see Prof Ganjoo and his wife Prana. They told Ganjoo sahib to go into the river, to walk on it and not look back. He begged and pleaded but did they listen? They shot him even as he was drowning. Poor Prana was gang-raped and her body was cut to pieces. I can never forget that heart-rending scene. The lava of hatred was boiling over in those beasts. If I had been alone I would have killed one or two and died myself, but the thought of my children held me back. I am burning up inside. And then this master goes around spouting rubbish and sprinkling salt on my wounds.'

Hari Krishan, who was listening to this conversation as he tightened the ropes of his tent, tried to console Masterji, 'Did they spare those who read the Kalma? They kidnapped so many girls in Bihom, Shahpura. They married some of them temporarily and then sent them back pregnant. Among the jehadis there are so many Afghani kabailis and Pakistanis who are worse than animals. It makes no difference to them whether someone is a Hindu or a Muslim. Whether it was the General Manager of HMT, Mr Khera, Chowdhury, the manager of the cement factory, Mir Mustafa or Abdul Sattar Ranjoor, they finished off anyone who was a thorn in their side. They didn't even spare the elderly Said Masoodi and what harm had Dr Mushirulhaq done them?'

The two young daughters of Shivji Bhatt of Baramulla were shooting up day by day despite their meagre diet. His wife, Shobhavati wouldn't let them out of her sight. She made them bind their breasts. At night her daughters slept close to her. Shobhavati spread out her sari to try and preserve her daughter's modesty and asked her husband, 'When will things improve? When will we go back home?'

Shivji read the newspaper. Things were going from bad to worse every day.

'On the 21st of May 1990, three militants killed Mirwaiz Maulvi Farooq in his home in Nagin lake. The police fired on the procession which accompanied his body. It is believed that around 50 people were killed.'

Everyone in Muthi camp, the young and the old, was confused. If Maulvi sahib was killed by militants, why would the army fire at his funeral procession? This must have been a conspiracy of the militants, they must have provoked the BSF somehow. People asked, 'Who killed the Mirwaiz?'

Suspicion fell on Jagmohan. Lakhs of people came out on the streets in protest. The inferno kept on raging, the violence continued. Many Pandit homes were burned to the ground. More than a lakh of them crossed the Banihal leaving behind the Valley and property worth crores.

The Human Rights Commission commented on the atrocities in the Valley. The militants opened a press agency, distributed pamphlets, made video cassettes and distributed them. Verses were engraved on the graves of the militant-martyrs, 'You did not bow before injustice/We salute your faith and courage'. On 21st May Jagmohan resigned and Girish Saxena took over as the new Governor.

A deeper darkness descended on the Muthi camp. There was darkness during the day when old Sansarchand was bitten by a poisonous snake. His body turned blue within minutes and he was finally released from the humiliation of having to beg. Two days later Nitya's one-year old daughter was stung by a scorpion. All the Seva Samitis participated in Sansar Chand's funeral. The Shiva worshippers performed a pooja. The government organizations gave assurances, 'The government will provide permanent homes very soon. We will not let you stay here much longer. Twelve hundred and fifty rooms will be built, nine feet by fourteen feet.'

Brijkrishan asked, 'Why, don't we even deserve huts? How will families with as many as eight members live in those tiny rooms? In summer and during the monsoons how will all of us live piled on top of each other in those black holes?'

Wazir sahib, a member of the advisory council, declared, 'There is no question of rights in such situations.' Schools, dispensaries, doctors and medicines were needed in the camp. Brijkrishan's wife gave birth to a child. Her neighbour, Taravati, cut the umbilical cord. There was no midwife available. The child's navel was full of pus. Brijkrishan couldn't bear the cries of his newborn. He would have liked to take him to the city, have him treated by a good doctor, but where was the money? There was a little money in the bank, even that had not been transferred. He kept visiting one office after another for his salary, Baba's pension, the children's school admissions. One headache after another!

The tents had begun to shred, there was no water in the toilets. At one end of the tent some utensils had been placed within a square demarcated by logs of wood. This was the kitchen where Shubhavati and other Anapurnas did their cooking and household work and waited for better days to come.

Gash Kaul from Anantnag often woke up at night.

'What happened Baba? Did you have a bad dream?' Brijkrishan could see his father was anxious.

'No, it wasn't a dream, I felt he was really standing there before me.'

'Who, Baba?'

'It was Premi. Master Sarvanad Kaul Premi. He said, "Read the *Ramayan* I have written". He didn't have eyes, Brijkrishan, and a nail had been hammered through his forehead. But his voice was the same. It was unchanged. He said, "Look after my books. There is the *Mahabharat*, the *Rajtarangini* and also the *Quran*. Make sure no one spoils my books. I have left them for my children…"'

Brijkrishan helped his father lie down on the string cot.

'Don't think about anything, Baba. Premi sahib was a godly man. He must have gone to heaven, just think that he was needed there.'

'Yeees, that is true', Gash Kaul started singing a hymn to Mother Sharika, 'Mother Bhavani have pity on me….'

Kashinath could hear the voices from his tent close by. Saying 'Hari Om' he walked across to meet Gash Kaul. After chatting about this and that he suggested ways to keep oneself peaceful and calm.

'Listen to me, brother, wear rudraksh around your neck. Your mind is full of negative thoughts. Rudraksh has the power to calm you down.'

The next day again the same long lines stretched out in front of the toilets, taps and ration shops.

People held their noses as they went into the stinking toilets. This was something that could not be avoided. Utensils clattered as everyone rushed to fill water. Good looking women began to resemble wicked witches with their open hair flying all over. Combative, unmindful of their own bodies, unaware of men staring lustfully at them.

Kashinath chanted a mantra to ward off danger. Thankfully, Neelkanth bhai was not anywhere close by, otherwise he would have said, 'Kashinath! Is there any evil left which you are trying to ward off with this mantra?'

Jungle Tantra

Flying through the smoky grey clouds, crossing the Pir Panjal range, the plane landed in Srinagar on a gloomy cold October evening. Gusts of wind swept the falling leaves hither and thither. Near the airport, behind the hillocks, under the trees, were a number of little bunkers made of piled up sandbags. Sheltering behind them were soldiers who were keeping a watchful eye out for terrorists. Peter wished them well, these young men standing at attention in bone-piercing cold, who faced the bombs and guns of the militants and did their duty for the nation. Men who had been included in the list of torturers and criminals by the messiahs of human rights, by journalists and terrorists. Men whose mothers, wives and children waited for them in far away towns and villages, apprehensive that their loved ones might never return. The shuttered shops, damaged roads and the branches of trees disappearing into the mist made Peter feel very melancholy. He had come home after two years, this time on duty. He could not feel any sense of welcome. During this period so much had happened that the mere thought frightened him and his friends. Lakhs of people had left the valley and gone to Jammu and Delhi. They included Pandits, Sikhs, Muslims. Vicky was working in Hyderabad. Peter longed to meet Ashraf and Jeetu. He handed in his joining report and immediately left for Ashraf's house. He had to wait a while before the door opened. When Imran Sahib greeted him, Ashraf who had been peering over his father's shoulder, gave a sigh of relief.

'Oh! Peter!'

Peter and Ashraf embraced each other. Ammijan, who was lying in one corner of the room supported by a pillow, sat up as soon as she saw Peter.

'How are you, Ammijan? Did you ever think of me?'

He couldn't see Naseem anywhere. Peter asked a string of

questions in one breath. Ammijan put her head down on her knees and started sobbing.

'Have you come here in connection with a crackdown?' Ashraf asked as soon as they sat down.

'Ashraf! I am your friend.' Peter felt uncomfortable.

'Sorry! Actually....'

'I think my uniform is upsetting you. Did the army really misbehave with you Ashraf?'

Ashraf refused to look at Peter, 'No, it is our God who is angry with us. We don't know who is a friend and who is an enemy.'

Peter wanted to know why Ammijan was crying but he felt hesitant to ask. He felt his friend was not too happy to see him. Peter became subdued.

'Where is sister Naseem, Ashraf? I want to meet her, it is so long since I was here.'

Ashraf became silent. The entire room, the house and the tree that was visible through the window, all became silent.

Naseem was looking out of the window with her back to the door. A little baby was whimpering in her lap.

'Naseem!' Peter was surprised, 'When did this happen?'

Naseem looked up with a start. She turned around: Peter! Her face reflected many emotions, she sat up properly. 'Sit down, Peter.'

'How are you, Naseem?'

Peter was dismayed. Naseem looked very pale, her eyes had sunk deep into their sockets. For some reason he thought of Mushtaq who used to call her 'red rose'. Naseem used to tease him by calling him 'hero Macham'.

Once Mushtaq had recited these lines from Burns for her:

My love is like a red-red rose
That is newly sprung in June
My love is like the melody
That is sweetly played in tune.

Naseem's rosy face had blushed. Peter recalled the incident and reminded Naseem.

'Why has our 'red rose' become so quiet? And where is our friend Mushtaq?'

'A storm blew the 'red rose' away, Peter bhai…'

Naseem's voice broke. A wave of pain arose and was pushed away inside. Peter watched silently.

Later Naseem herself told him the story. She had recently returned home after a whole year. Those people had picked her up from the Welfare Centre. Four men had got down from a blue Maruti. God knows where they took Naseem with them. How many mountains and rivers she was made to cross. She gouged them with her nails, they kept clawing at her body. Naseem bit one of them, in return her chest was branded with a hot iron to warn her that she shouldn't try such stunts of bravado, they should be kept for the welfare centre.

She begged them, pleaded in the name of Allah, explained the meaning of jihad to them. One of them said, 'I will marry you.' With great patience Naseem quoted the Quran and said, 'The Quran considers it to be a terrible sin to force a girl to marry anyone against her will and you call yourselves jehadis….' They called her a 'bastard' and broke her jaw. They showed her that a woman should keep her mouth shut and obey the commands of men. She did not eat for many days. Their commander took pity on her and did 'Mutah', a temporary marriage, with her. The married jehadi wanted to go to heaven after all.

'Now you are my begum, my wife!' He pointed at the other four boys, 'And now they are your servants.'

Begum Naseem endured being pawed and used in cow sheds, hay barns and stables. For many days she went on hunger strike. Her intestines started shrinking. A strange anger crackled through her nerves. She would be swept by a desire to do something brutal but she was helpless in their inhuman, savage hold. Without any hope that anyone would rescue her from their claws. She knew that she was not the daughter of any minister, nor did her parents have any contacts with any jehadi group. She was bound to die. From her window she could only see a forest and trees. She wasn't sure whether she was in Kupwara or Avantipora.

'I tried to run away very often, Peter! But I was caught every time. They tightened the guard and branded my body with hot rods.'

Naseem showed the burn marks on her arm.

'No, Naseem, please!' Peter was unable to look at them.

'What harm had you done them?' He couldn't stop his outburst. He was afraid he was going to break down and cry.

'Who had harmed whom? They just needed a woman, the excuse was that I did not wear a burka. That I mislead girls in the women's welfare centre. That I did not stop riding my bicycle despite being warned. I was a rebel. Initially I tried to make them understand but they only understood the language of bombs, explosives and Kalashnikovs. Their hands were awash with the blood of human beings, Peter!'

'You are a brave girl.' Peter gently hugged Naseem.

'I don't know, Peter! I had lost the capacity to think about life and death. Buried under stones and mountains, I suffered through many seasons, many hells. I proved to be a very tough person.' Naseem became silent as her voice wavered. And God's will, she became a mother in these terrible, harsh circumstances. They looked at her swelling stomach with suspicion and brought a one-eyed, manly looking woman along to examine her.

'Do you want it?' she questioned Naseem with her eyes.

Naseem wanted to be freed from this humiliation. Perhaps there was a chance of freedom, she could destroy this seed of hatred that was growing within her and become free, but Naseem didn't say anything. She would never be free. Those people also did not want any impediments. Naseem would not allow their wishes to be fulfilled. A voice spoke within her though she did not say anything.

'They don't want any problems. But you are lucky, you will give birth to a jehadi. You are going to have a boy.'

Naseem couldn't understand whether she should pummel her own stomach and die along with her jehadi or pull out her hair or do anything else. She just watched whatever happened. Four months later another woman gently felt around and tried to ease out the baby's head as Naseem screamed and wept. She wiped Naseems face, which was wet with tears.

'You have to try yourself, child, may God have mercy on you.'

Naseem put her arms around that kind soul and tried for the last time. Her face stuck in the woman's dirty pheran, her piercing shriek struggled to escape. 'May God have mercy!' The woman kept muttering as she swaddled the baby. A gushing stream of blood came out of Naseem, which soaked all the sheets and rags in the hut.

She opened her heavy eyelids when she felt a soft warmth on her chest. Were they the petals of some flower or a soft warm piece of cotton wool? She felt someone had breathed life into a dead body. Naseem held the pink body close to her chest. A storm arose within her and her eyes filled with tears as streams of milk welled up in her breasts. Ya Allah! What miracle is this? Naseem was amazed, was this how a seedling sprouted from the earth? Regardless of the rain, the winds, the shadow of death?

The next day the child was unwell. She started crying with pain. The commander almost picked her up and smashed her to the ground. Naseem was like a woman possessed. She jumped up and hid the child in the folds of her kurta. It would be so easy to kill this tiny little being. They were worried that some BSF soldier would hear the shrieks of the baby. They had set out to kill others but they wanted to stay alive at any cost. Naseem tied up the child's mouth, 'No, she won't make a sound.' she convinced them. The child whimpered for a while and then became silent. When they moved away Naseem took off the gag. The baby looked at her silently. What sort of mother are you? Naseem put the child to her breast and hugged her close, 'Please forgive me, my heart. May God forgive me.'

Two of their companions had been killed. The other two ran away the day the man who had become her so-called 'husband' didn't return. Naseem felt she had given birth to an angel of freedom.

Stubbornly she forced her emaciated body to get up. When she came out of the cowshed, with the baby hidden in her pheran, her knees buckled. There was a sharp pain in her stomach and some liquid trickled down her legs. She crawled on her knees, picked up a chunni, wrapped it around herself and crept towards the road. Her legs got stuck in the mud on the side of the road and she fell down unconscious. She didn't know who picked her up and brought her to hospital. She didn't know how many days she spent there. Her baby was with her and she didn't have cloth tied around her mouth. This was the only thing that registered in her mind. She wanted to forget everything else.

'One day Rehman's son, Shabir, came to the hospital on some work. He recognized me and brought me home.'

Naseem did not say anything about what her parents felt on her return.

Later Peter asked them whether they had tried to find Naseem.

Given the situation in the valley this question had very little meaning but Ashraf had given Naseem's photographs to the BSF, the army and even Shabir Ahmed. Shabir had resigned from the National Conference and joined the JKLF. He had tried to find Naseem. It was evident that looking for Naseem was as impossible as counting the waves of the ocean. Her parents and Ashraf had tried to come to terms with the fact that she was probably dead.

But new problems arose when Naseem returned.

'Problems?' Peter felt the word was a little harsh.

'Yes, Peter! Now everyone keeps an eye on our house, the militants as well as the neighbours. Do you think they will let us live if they come to know? As far as our community is concerned, you know what the attitude is towards a girl who has been raped. The human psyche is very complex. I told Naseem we would put the baby in an orphnage, God knows whose child it is.... but Naseem doesn't agree, she says, "Tell everyone this is Naseem's daughter. I have given birth to her". She says, "It is the body which is the victim of injustice, not the soul. Rape is a crime like any other crime. Connecting it with chastity is a double injustice against those innocent girls who have been kidnapped by terrorists."'

'She is a strange, stubborn girl. Her experiences have made her obstinate.'

Sitting in the army headquarters, Peter saluted Naseem's stubbornness. This ability to survive the storms of time and circumstance was so necessary for girls from the Valley today. Meanwhile some local boys, who were sick of violence, had started surrendering before the army. But the fight for azadi refused to abate. One went and ten took his place.

On the 6th of November the front page of the *Srinagar Times* carried the news, 'India should be treated like Kuwait on the question of Kashmir. Every inch of Kashmir is drenched in the blood of martyrs. The Muslims of India should fight for an independent nation.' Peter could not find any connection between the deeds and words of the terrorists. On the one hand there was the call for jihad and on the other the raping of innocent girls, drug trafficking, violence.

The BSF had an operations centre on Gupkar road. 'Papa two', where terrorists are interrogated. There was severity during questioning, but sometimes it was just a drama to frighten the other militants. Outside, Peter heard the sounds of whips and screams cross the Gupkar road, reach the Dal Lake, pass by Farooq sahib's house and cross over the Zabarvan hills. Screams, bombs, bloodshed! 'Oh, God! What have you done to my garden?' It was difficult to believe that once upon a time this place echoed with the strains of Sufiana music and chakris.

The news came that terrorists had thrown a bomb at a BSF vehicle in the downtown area. There were many casualties. The army was also trying to perform the role of a peace-keeping force. A sixteen year old had been injured in cross firing. The terrorists were using hit and run techniques. Peter took the boy to hospital along with the BSF soldiers. He had bled a lot and the blood had congealed and formed a crust on his face and nose. Intermittently he cried out, 'Babaaa....Maaaaa. Oh... Oh...!' There was a strange innocence on the boy's face. It was difficult to imagine that this boy could pick up a gun and kill his own brothers and sisters.

The doctor said, 'The boy needs a blood transfusion. We don't have his blood group, B plus, in stock.'

'Somebody has to donate blood. Let us see.'

An army soldier, Yadunath, offered to donate it. 'Sir, my blood group is also B plus.'

Peter looked at the bottle of blood in its sling as the blood dripped down drop by drop. He wondered to himself about the thread which connected Yadunath from Uttar Pradesh to this boy, who said his name was Imtiaz, and who had evidently been trained across the border to kill army soldiers. Imtiaz did not look at them when he regained consciousness. Peter introduced Yadunath to him, 'This soldier has saved your life. You were going to kill him weren't you? And those companions of yours, they just left you for dead and ran away.'

There was a deep wound in Imtiaz's right arm with a bandage around it. His face had darkened with pain. He turned his face away as he cried. Peter looked around him for some representatives of human rights to show them how a soldier can be humane despite doing his duty. But there were only army and BSF personnel around him.

Peter was ordered to go to Kupwara to the Line of Control.

Jeetu's father asked for security. Many Punjabi merchants had been kidnapped by militants. Would Jeetu also leave the valley and go away? Apparently militants had hanged a dead body on the branches of the tree in his garden. There was a haunting silence in the half-burnt, abandoned houses of the Pandits. Peter thought, will the displaced Hindus ever come back? He couldn't believe that this was the same city about which Mahjoor said that here the Hindus were like milk and the Muslims like sugar. Lalli in her Vaakh said:

Shiva is present everywhere

Don't think there is any difference between a Hindu and a Muslim....

In Jammu the migrant Kashmiris raised the demand for 'Panun Kashmir'. They asked that a security zone be made for Kashmiri Hindus near Banihal or Udhampur. The Hindus should be given a homeland north-east of the Jhelum river. They should be given the opportunity to live with dignity in the land of their birth. They didn't want to live degrading lives full of humiliation as migrants stuffed into narrow rooms and tents. On the 26th of December a two-day convention was held in Jammu.

In Delhi, the government was ready to hold talks with the militants. The displaced Kashmiris wanted to participate in these talks, they tried to give a petition to the Prime Minister but they were beaten up by the police.

'Oh God! what is happening?' Peter felt he would go crazy if he thought too much.

The Valley was in the grip of terror, though thousands of BSF and army personnel were deployed there. Ashraf said,

'The ordinary Kashmiri wants their protection but he is also angry because of the crackdowns.'

'What is the solution, Ashraf?' Ashraf looked up at the sky, 'God knows.'

No one expected miracles nowadays but Peter prayed in his heart for the return of Badshah, waited for him. Perhaps he was the only solution to the problems in the Valley.

In the meantime he had to report for duty.

❧

The Sad End of the Rishi Tradition

Two events occurred in Jammu which were not very unusual but which the Raina family felt were rather surprising. During the year 1995 words such as unusual, unprecedented and impossible had been worn out with overuse. Anything could happen anywhere in the world at any time. The sky could develop a hole, the oceans could dry up. Clones could be manufactured and people could think of settling on Mars. People in the Valley had become immune to shock. If a packet of henna was found outside their door they understood that a jehadi wanted to marry their daughter.

Kamala and Vimla's breasts were cut off and hung like dejharus from their ears and in Bandipora a young girl was sawed into half while alive, after she had been raped. So called 'friends' were being bled to death and their blood was being collected and stored in bottles for the future use of some mujahids. Nothing was surprising anymore.

It so happened that on one pleasant November evening, as

Keshavnath was walking on the road in front of his house in an effort to calm himself down, he heard loud noises from the police station close by.

It was such a barrage of sound that Keshavnath was forced to pay attention. He wondered who was screaming. What had he done? When he came closer he realized it was Rasool Ahmed, Mahadjoo's son. With him was a young man whose face looked like a combination of Rajesh Khanna and Shahrukh Khan. Rasool Ahmed fell at Keshavnath's feet when he saw him, 'May God grant you a long life. I was coming to meet you. These people caught me. Please tell them that everyone from the Valley is not a militant.' Keshavnath found that the policemen were questioning Rasool on suspicion because he had been found roaming around the area. Now Rasool Ahmed was sitting in Keshavnath's house telling them why he had come to Jammu. It was not unusual for Rasool to come to Jammu. A lot of Kashmiri merchants and traders used to come to Jammu for work and trade along with the official 'darbar move'.

But Rasool Ahmed was neither a trader, nor a merchant. He was a small farmer from a village. He said, 'You know, Bhobaji, that we have to look after our children. Who will take care of their future besides us?' So, Rasool Ahmed, with the future of his children in mind, had taken up some new work. This consisted of helping those Battas, who had abandoned their homes and come away, to sell those houses. In other words he was a middle-man. His worries were genuine.

'Now the Battas can't ever return to their homes. But they need money to survive in a new place. So, I thought I should help them out a little, after all we are brothers, we belong to the same land, speak the same language....'

His words were infused with the generosity of the Rishi tradition but defined in a completely new way.

Keshavnath was a little confused.

'But we don't want to sell our houses. '

'I know, I know, Bhobaji.'

It was evident that Rasool Ahmed had arrived fully prepared.

'I know there are BSF jawans living in your house, it is close to the temple isn't it? It was a good decision, your house will remain safe and secure because of the soldiers.'

The next moment he started asking about Zutshi sahib, 'How is your son-in-law? I have heard he wants to sell his house. The thing is this boy,' and he pointed towards the combination of Shahrukh Khan and Rajesh Khanna, 'he is my brother's son, he has taken a liking to the house…'

'Hm!' Keshavnath grunted, so that the story would continue.

Rasool Ahmed looked downcast, 'Bhobaji it is good that you decided to leave that place. There is nothing there except violence and bloodshed.'

Rajesh-Shahrukh added his own two bits, 'There is no peace there at all.'

Keshavnath kept grunting, shaking his head and listening. Premji began to detect a glimmer of craftiness behind Rasoola's apparent innocence. Lalli and Kamala were thinking that this was the son of the same Mahadjoo who was gifted a piece of fertile land by Tathya sahib after he had spent nearly half his life with the Raina family. Keshavnath was the one who had persuaded him to send his sons to school.

Rasoola had really accomplished a lot. He had become an agent for selling the houses of the Battas.

Now his brother's son had fallen in love with Zutshi sahib's house.

'I thought why don't we buy it if you are planning to sell it.'

In other words we deserve the first choice.

'How is Mahadjoo? Does he ever remember us?'

Lalli wanted to know whether he also had the same ideas as his sons.

'Baba passed away about five years ago, Lalli mother.'

Lalli was sad. Now she found it easier to understand

Rasoola. He had been freed from the obligations of the older generation.

Rasool Ahmed became emotional.

'All his life he kept talking about you. We even remember all your names.'

He heaved a long sigh, 'As God is my witness, even when he died we found a photograph of all of you in his pocket. He always slept holding it close to him.'

Keshavnath had met Mahadjoo about ten years ago during a trip to Amaranth. He was transporting luggage for the pilgrims, on mules from Chandanwari. He stayed with Keshavnath for the entire trip. His face was exactly the same apart from the network of lines knitted by time. The same old affection, concern and blessings.

Everyone in the house was silent thinking of Mahadjoo.

Lalli served tea. Rasool Ahmed said, 'This tea is nice and strong, my brain is feeling refreshed.' He complained that he hadn't really enjoyed his meals for the last week, just dal-roti and vegetables in various hotels.

'I am just waiting to go home and eat rice and haaq. I even long for the water of Kashmir when I am here…'

'Why don't you have a meal with us before you leave?' Lalli asked him, 'Though the taste lies in the place …'

'I don't eat food in a Batta's house though I do drink tea and I have already had that. May God bless you.'

Now they came down to brass tacks.

'If you can speak to Zutshi sahib, this boy here is ready to give a good price. To tell the truth he really likes the Karan Nagar house. Otherwise you know this whole transaction is quite dangerous. The government has strictly forbidden the buying and selling of houses.'

The boy had a shop selling oil on Nai Sadak. He'd made a lot of money selling either oil or opium or marijuana, who knows? There are many new occupations in the Valley, organizing meetings between militants and journalists, giving inside information to news agencies.

But Rasool Ahmed was not a militant. He had heard the demands for freedom rising from the valley and come to believe that the Hindus were creating obstacles in the path of this 'azadi' because they were agents of Hindustan. So, it was better that they left the Valley. And once they left who had a better claim on their homes, property and jobs than Rasool Ahmed and his nephew?

Keshavnath said, 'I will speak to my son-in-law.'

Lalli remembered the story of the thief of shrouds. Initially, the thief used to dig up the corpses, steal their shrouds and seal them up once again in their coffins. But then a day came when he stole the shroud and just left the corpse lying naked on the ground.

How many such thieves had the Valley given birth to from 1947 till the beginning of the new millennium? First the number of seats for Battas in schools and colleges were reduced. Then jobs became fewer in number and promotions were blocked. Then there was anger that they got jobs in the central government. Finally, one day, there wasn't even enough land and it became the norm to establish a right over anything which remained. Those who went away lost everything and the corpse was left lying naked under the vast sky.

Zutshi sahib said, 'What is the point of holding on to the house when there is no possibility of returning home? In any case that house is now occupied by militants. Let anyone buy it, what difference does it make?' His attitude was totally detached.

Till last year Dulari had refused to sell the house. She had thought they would live in Srinagar for six months every year. The red roses on the fence in the garden would still flower every year. She said that the situation would improve now that there was an elected government.

'After all, the Indian government is not going to hand over Kashmir on a plate to the militants.'

'The problem of Kashmir is not so simple that it can be solved by throwing out the Battas and turning it into an Islamic state. Then how many Pakistans will India be expected to make for the nine or ten crore Muslims who live there?'

'On the one hand, China, Iran, Pakistan want to make the valley their base for geopolitcal reasons, on the other, America keeps an eagle eye on the borders. They might merge Buddhist Ladakh with an independent Tibet and shackle China. Will India be a pawn in this game?'

'How can you forget that India has invested thousands of crores of rupees in the state and now it is not merely a question of prestige but linked to India's very existence?' Prem quoted the chief minister saying that when he was dismissed from office in 1984 by Jagmohan he wanted to teach him a lesson. So even though he was aware of the activities of the militants he pretended to be unaware of them and the situation became much worse. He had also added that he felt India had not treated his father well. This was his revenge; to ignore the spreading tentacles of terrorism, to let whatever was happening, happen.

Some people thought that the situation had improved in recent times. Large numbers of young men were surrendering. They had realized that the gun culture was giving them nothing except devastation. They had also finally understood the fact that Pakistan was not interested in them but only in the Valley. The BSF was quite alert. And people didn't need to take permission from the militants to enter or leave the Valley.

This assurance about an improvement in the situation prompted Dulari and Riddhi to make the journey home. The two of them, along with their young servant Santu, left for Srinagar in a taxi. This journey was very different from earlier journeys, not a trip home, but a furtive attempt to enter an alien land. The BSF conducted a search at Banihal. Sorry! They were polite but they had to do their duty.

The unknown stretched before them like a wall. As they

passed through their lane, friends and neighbours passed them with downcast eyes without acknowledging them or saying anything. The city was in the grip of fear. Family homes, land permeated with the memories of ancestors, the fragrance of the air and even the weather, everything had changed. The house, decorated once upon a time with chandeliers and carpets, looked as though it had been devastated by an earthquake. Quilts and blankets lay in rotting bundles on carved walnut wood beds. A strange, sickening smell permeated the room. Dulari's face became pale when she saw the stains of dried blood and urine on the bedding. Suppose there were some bodies of raped girls lying in this house like those found in many abandoned homes? When they opened the room at the back, they found some ghosts sitting on the chairs. Dulari's legs started shaking with fear.

One of the ghosts, with a French cut beard, greeted them pleasantly saying that they were planning to rent the place and were planning to talk to the owners very soon. Dulari looked around for any luggage, bundles, boxes, any possessions at all. But there were only four young men sitting comfortably in the chairs with their hands behind their backs. What were they hiding in their hands? Bombs, pistols, Kalshnikovs? What were those young men doing hiding in the house? Rakesh, their neighbour who had accompanied them, came and closed the door.

He indicated that they should go back without any argument if they valued their lives. In the meanwhile Riddhi had put some of her grandfather's books into a bag, *Rajtarangini*, *Neelmath Puran*, *Prakash Ramayan*, *Tavareekh-e-Kashmir*….The driver had put Ma ji's heavy trunk into the car already. Suddenly Dulari went and opened the door of the prayer room. Termites had eaten up the frames of the pictures of the gods and goddesses. Dry marigold flowers were stuck to the marble images of Shankar, Parvati and Ganesh.

Dulari picked up the dual image of the gods and put it in

the pocket of her pheran. 'I don't understand what your real plan is but you are going into exile with us.' The roads were more muddy on their return, the mountains had never seemed so cruel and pitiless before. Why were the winds piercing their bones? In Lalleshwari's village, Pampore, the purple-eyed flowers in saffron fields stretching as far as one could see looked for Lalli. The saffron flowers looked lonely, sad and indifferent. Riddhi was mystified by her mother's behaviour when Dulari stopped the taxi in Qazigund and filled it with armloads of Chinar leaves.

Standing near the Banihal tunnel they looked down at the grey downcast looking Valley. A Valley swimming on the surface of water in the lap of the mountains, They felt the water had spread everywhere. Satisar! Where new Jalodbhavs were causing mischief and turmoil. Kashyap rishi was history, the time of the rishis and learned ascetics was over. The Nagas had left the Valley, scared away by terrorism. Now it was the demons who ruled there. Who would come to free the Valley this time?

In Jammu, Lalli made 'roths' and offered them to Lord Ganapati in thanksgiving, 'It is enough that you have returned home safely. Who cares about shawls and dushalas? We can always get more so long as we are alive.' Keshavnath was surprised, 'Rakesh had the keys. He must have known that there were militants staying in the house. He should have informed us.'

Prem was outspoken as usual. 'What would he say? Is this anything new? If a militant puts an AK 47 on someone's neck and asks for shelter, anyone will hide him in the deepest basement possible regardless of whether he is a Hindu or a Muslim. Dulari's house was empty, so it became their property in a sense. And then everyone tries to maintain cordial relations with militants there. Rakesh must have been sure those people wouldn't harm Dulari.'

Lalli said, 'Thank God they didn't shoot you. One doesn't know with such crazy people...'

The end of the story was that Zutshi sahib's house was finally sold for a paltry sum. The papers were signed in Keshavnath's house. Zutshi sahib said that he believed Australia was giving some relief to displaced Kashmiris. 'I might even go and settle down there after retirement. I don't feel like living here any longer. What is the point of living in a country where you get neither concern nor respect?'

The strangest part of this episode was Rasool Ahmed's insistence that he would only accept the papers of the house from sister Dulari's hands and that too with her blessings. Prem asked Rasool Ahmed, 'So, Rasool bhai will you allow us into the house if we ever come there?'

Rasool Ahmed was effusive, 'We will be honoured to have you, bhaijaan. The house is yours, we have been brothers, after all, and will continue to be in the future as well.'

So a very tiny bit of Kashmiriyat still survived. Dulari's heart was full of sorrow and anger. They had left their home for the sake of employment, hoping that they would return home once they had retired. But now the last link with home was shattered forever. She handed over the papers to Rasool Ahmed with the same gravity with which one performs the last rites.

'Give me your blessings, sister!' Rasool begged.

'Be happy, what else can I say?'

Her voice roughened. Questions kept whirling around inside her.

'You are asking for my blessings but you never once asked God to help us return home.'

'You told me, there is no peace there. Innocents are killed. And yet you are buying the properties of poor displaced migrants cheaply because you are concerned about the future of your children. At the back of your mind is the fear that if the migrants retain their houses they may actually return home sometime in the future. You want to destroy this last vestige of hope as well.'

Yet blessings were exchanged. Even though Dulari felt like sobbing and crying.

Prem ji was fascinated. He had to admire this example of Kashmiriyat.

The second incident was not really a surprise. If birth is not surprising why should death be unusual?

Eighty year-old Keshavnath had kept himself busy despite his many ailments. He read and taught others. Maintained good relations with them. He had spoken about the concept of 'Vasudev Kutumbkam' when he had to leave home. Discussing globalization, the computer revolution and international trade agreements, he had consoled his children and told them that they should consider the entire world their home. Lalli felt her husband was losing his mental balance. When Prem commented on Rasool Ahmed's opinions, Keshavnath quoted Marx saying that people are not bad, it is their circumstances that mould them.

'Mahadjoo used to write letter after letter whenever we were away from home telling us to come back because he was missing us and now there is his son Rasoola, who says, "It is good you left that place…."'

'Times have changed.' In other words, in relationships, monetary considerations had become more important than emotional ones. This was the stark truth of our times. Lalli didn't blame Rasool Ahmed.

'Circumstances.' Bhobaji searched for a logical, not an emotional answer.

'Listen, a man makes his history according to the circumstances in which he finds himself. He cannot choose. Mahdoo used to talk about Lal Ded and Nund Rishi, he knew stories about Jain ascetics and Baba rishi. His thoughts were moulded by their philosophy. A philosophy of generosity.

Rasool Ahmed has seen only political scheming, and divisive policies. Pakistani propaganda has filled his mind with the poison of hatred. He believes Hindus and India are his enemies so how can we blame him for his values and opinions?'

'In other words, Bhobaji, you are saying that the new history of Kashmir will be moulded in an environment created by the mistakes, selfishness and failiures of our leaders. These inner deficiencies and the global Islamic movement started by the Taliban and the jehadis, are destroying the valley. In such circumstances, the Hindus of the valley should forget about staying on in the land of their ancestors and hunker down wherever they find place.'

'Perhaps this is what is going to happen, Prem.' Keshavnath sighed.

'Whether it is the earlier Dixon plan or the call for Azadi in the valley today, it is always the Kashmiri Pandit who suffers. The demand for an Autonomous Hill Council for Ladakh may protect the rights of the Ladakhi people and in Jammu, the Regional Council will look after its welfare. But who will listen to the Kashmiri Pandit? He has been exiled from the valley. Now the government speaks about a package for Kashmir but no one talks about the Hindus.' That day the discussion continued late in the night. Riddhi couldn't understand why Farooq sahib intermittently raised the demand for autonomy. 'Article 370 has already granted us a special status, what more do we want?'

Prem called this demand a 'political gimmick'. 'Who wants autonomy? The farmer, the trader, the labourer? No, it is the leaders who want autonomy, especially the dissatisfied politicians. For those people who refuse to accept them as leaders.'

'Kashmir does not merely consist of the valley, it is a state,' Keshavnath added, 'Jammu and Ladakh are also part of it. And they are in favour of a complete merger with India. The Shias and the Gujjars in the valley don't talk about autonomy either. Prem is right, this is just a political gimmick.'

Dulari raised another topic, 'Kashmiriyat.'

Keshavnath looked at his watch, 'It is eleven o'clock. Go to sleep now, Riddhi, you have to go to college in the morning. Kashmiriyat has nothing to do with autonomy, it is our collective culture. It is the product of the collective influence of Buddhist, Hindu, Sufi and Rishi philosophies, it is our code of ethics and our identity. There are historic reasons behind its evolution.'

Prem ji mentioned the fact that Buddha had come to Kashmir along with five thousand monks. In Haervan there was archeological evidence of Buddhist Viharas. The Buddhists did not belive in caste. Kashmiri Pandits did not have any castes either, couldn't this have been due to Buddhist influence?

Lalli also gave three or four examples to show that both Hindus and Muslims believed in Pirs and ascetics.

Riddhi joked, 'Nani, one of my colleagues in college says that Kashmiri Hindus are half Muslims and Kashmiri Muslims are half Hindus!'

Keshavnath smiled, 'This is what Kashmiriyat means!'

'But now even this has become an old story, Riddhi. Kashmir has become an international problem and China and America want to keep this problem alive for their own selfish reasons. The people of the valley will soon forget that Kashmiriyat is the joint heritage of Hindus and Muslims.'

They went to sleep finally around twelve o'clock.

In the morning the telephone rang just as dawn was breaking. Vijay woke up, startled. Prem quickly picked it up. It was Neelam calling from Srinagar. Prem's face turned pale as he heard what she had to say.

'What is it?' Vijaya asked Prem, 'what happened, tell me.' Prem put down the receiver.

'Trouble, what else? Katya and her husband have been kidnapped by militants.'

Vijaya started crying. Prem went to Bhobaji's room to give him the news. Lalli was in the bathroom. Prem called out, 'Bhobaji.' Bhobaji was fast asleep.

'Bhobaji!' Prem tried to shake him awake but he did not open his eyes.

He was fine last night, what happened to him so suddenly? The house was in an uproar. The doctor was called. He checked the pulse, the eyes and said, 'Sorry'.

'It seems to have been a heart attack. Did he receive some kind of shock recently?'

'Shock?' Prem had not spoken about Katya and Kartik to anyone except Vijaya so far.

'I am surprised,' he said, 'he talked to us till around twelve o'clock. He didn't have a heart condition and as far as a shock is concerned…' The doctor put the stethoscope in his bag. He indicated that Keshavnath's body should be placed on the ground and said, 'What is surprising about it, bhai sahib, everyone finally dies of heart failure.' As he laid Bhobaji down on the ground, Prem thought that he must have had some premonition of the calamity that was to befall them.

Ten Days in a Snowy Grave

The trellised window gave onto a huge and beautiful expanse of snow. But the atmosphere was gloomy. Why didn't the snow seem like it used to earlier? 'When we were children the snow used to come down in fluffy drifts of cottonwool. Running along with the wind, playful, it joined in our games.'

There were two dead bodies lying on the vast carpet of snow. One facing downwards and the other looking up at the sky. Its open eyes were filled with snow. 'Now they will end up killing each other, these wretches.' The woman who brought them food had said, 'There are so many factions and they are all ready to slaughter each other.'

It was evident that the JKLF wanted Azad Kashmir also to be independent along with Jammu-Ladakh-Kashmir. This prompted Pakistan to set up the Hizbul Mujahiddeen and created tensions between the two groups.

'Kartikeya where are you? Where are you my Kartik?'

Some birds had made their nest in the shelter of the main roof beam. A small little nest protected and sheltered by sticks and grass, for their tiny offspring who are sleeping, cuddled close to their mother's body.

I was missing Isha and Arjun. My heart sank when I thought of their sad faces. They must be worried about us. Would we meet the same fate as the four foreign tourists who were kidnapped by the Al Faran group? These people didn't seem to belong to that group. Were they Hizbul Mujahiddeen, Al Umar, Al Jehad or JKLF? One couldn't make out. Four of them were Kashmiris but the fifth one who was hit in the leg by a bullet, seemed to be Afghani.

My children! Your mother was not Mufti sahib's daughter Rubaiya, nor was she Soz sahib's daughter Nahida. So the state and the centre will not rush to accept the militants' demands. But perhaps, like the Wakhloos and the Dhars we will also return safely by some miracle.

I've been here for seven days now. I didn't know where we are, I think we are in a small village somewhere near Pulwama, Kupwara or Sonamarg. There was small playful rivulet in Sonamarg that gurgled as it flowed over stones and pebbles. It wasn't visible from here.

This shingled two storeyed house, isolated from its

neighbours, seemed to belong to a family. Sometimes there were voices in the room next door. Soft voices! Instructions, distribution of goods, taking stock, counting, mostly it was the commander who spoke.

'How many Kalashnikovs did you get?'

'Twenty, AK 47's, bombs, rocket launchers....'

'Right! Does everone remember today's programme?'

'Four of you go to Bandipora....'

'It is essential to spread rumours. Say the army is behaving badly with the womenfolk.'

'Incite the people. The support of the public is necessary for jehad....'

'Did you pass on the news to the British reporter?'

'Keep in wireless contact with the Markaz-al-dawa....'

'Distribute cassettes in every lane, hand out the posters in every house, eat something quickly and do your jobs.'

'Some wretches are surrendering. They have to be taught a lesson.'

'Listen, all of you! It is not possible to turn back from the path of jehad.'

'Okay?'

'Okay.' Collective voices.'Al-jehad, al-jehad.'

'Remember, the army officers' heads carry a reward of four lakh rupees. Your families will never be poor again!'

There were a lot of loud noises, clanging sounds as if things were being picked up and put down.

I covered my face with the edge of my dupatta.

There was a tiny little aperture in one wall of the room. The sounds came from there. Those people must have been confirming my presence by looking at me through that window. How could I go away leaving Kartik behind?

The distant roofs which were visible were covered with snow. I would freeze if I stayed here another two days. I don't know whether I will be able to see Kartik. What will they have done to him? My eyes were clouded with the mist of defeat. Tathya sahib used to say there was only one brave daughter in the house who could not be frightened by anybody. I have never learnt to accept defeat. But today I do not have even a shred of hope left. Have I really been crushed? Or am I being punished for my unnecessary bravery?

The fault, if there was one, was mine. Kartikeya was just swept along because of me. I didn't know whether he even had a blanket and a kangri. That hefty fellow had hurt Kartikeya's shoulder quite badly in the ambulance. The desire to hold Kartikeya was like a pain in my chest. I felt I hadn't seen him for years. My heart felt as if it was in a wilderness.

He said, 'Let's send the ambulance to fetch the patient here. It is possible that we might have to operate. And it is evening…'

But I had melted because of the pitiful weeping of the two women who had got down from the matador. They were amazing actresses. They had fallen at my feet as soon as they entered. 'Doctor sahiba! We tried very hard to bring our daughter to the hospital, but she doesn't let anyone touch her. She is writhing in pain. Please save her.' Kartikeya was not willing to go. It was unsafe nowadays, why take an unnecessary risk?

'Why don't you also come along with the ambulance? The house is near Badgam. God will bless you with health and prosperity. We have come with a lot of hope, who knows whether the girl is still alive or not.' They were sobbing.

'All right. We'll come.' I thought the situation was much better now, Kartikeya was worrying unnecessarily.

Neelam put in the emergency operation kit, medicine box etc., in. She was worried, 'Didi! You are not doing the right thing. It is night. Nowadays you can't trust anyone.'

I was wearing a coat. Neelam handed me a shawl as well. 'It is cold outside, didi.'

Katrikeya said, 'I am also coming along.' The driver Ghulam Nabi was there in any case.

No one stopped the ambulance on the way.

Outside the city the night gradually darkened among the rows of poplars lining the road. The woman who was constantly wiping her tears said, 'One minute' and stopped the ambulance. 'I am sorry. I can't hold on any longer. I will be back in a moment.'

All around there was darkness. It was winter. Katikeya felt there was something wrong. He ordered Ghulam Nabi, 'Ghulam Nabi! Turn the ambulance around!' Ghulam Nabi was apprehensive. He also wanted to go back. But as soon as the ambulance turned three men appeared from behind the trunk of a cedar. They stopped the vehicle and sat down on the seats. Their faces covered with kerchiefs, and they were wearing black pherans.

'Doctor sahib! Why are you afraid? We are almost there. There, you can see the house.'

Outside one could see some ruins like those at Mattan, frightening and dark. Now it was obvious that we had been captured by terrorists. Kartikeya tried to stop them and told Ghulam Nabi to turn the vehicle. One of the boys pulled out a gun from his pheran and pushed Ghulam Nabi off his seat, another held Kartikeya roughly by his shoulder.

'Be careful! Don't shout, otherwise there will be unnecessary bloodshed. We are not going to harm you. Our boys have been wounded, we want to save them. That is why we have brought you here. If those wretched BSF soldiers had not been there we would have brought them in to the hospital. We will drop you back as soon as you have finished attending to them.'

Kartikeya held my hand in both of his. His hands were cold and he was shivering. Both of us were drowning in a black ocean, sinking deeper and deeper. I put my arm around Kartikeya and held him tight. At some place they stopped the ambulance and transferred us to a jeep. They blindfolded us and brought us here. They had told the truth. Three of their men had been badly wounded. Kartikeya even removed a bullet from the arm of one of the boys. The entire night we were busy looking after the wounded fighters. There were two Kashmiri boys among them. One man was around forty-five years old and had a brown beard, he was probably an Afghan. Perhaps he was their commander.

They brought me here before it was dawn but they kept Kartikeya back. I begged to be allowed to remain with him. In an impassive voice I was told, 'Go, we will call you when we need you. Fayyaz take her. You also stay there and listen, don't go off to sleep, you have a habit of falling asleep.'

The young blue-eyed boy, Fayyaz, brought me here. He continually walked up and down outside the room holding his gun. A woman wearing a brown pattu pheran came twice a day with food for me. She slept in my room at night. The entire night I heard her snores and the sound of her nails as she scratched herself. She had scabies. I prescribed some medicine for her. She hasn't been scratching for the past two days.

Earlier she wouldn't talk to me but today she spared a minute to ask about my welfare. An invisible thread had started connecting the two of us. I had only one thing to say, 'Where is the doctor? Can't I stay with him?'

She also had only one answer, 'The commander knows. Nothing happens without his orders.'

'What is your relationship with these people?' I asked the woman in the morning. She opened up. She told me that the jehadis had entered her house forcibly. The commander had said, 'Make food for the fighters. If anyone asks tell them we are your relatives.' Actually they were strangers.

'Where does the money come from?' I was curious.

'Who knows, must be coming from outside, like the weapons. But if they put a gun to someone's head he isn't likely to refuse them.'

The woman's anger was becoming obvious.

'We thought they are jehadis but they have dishonoured our girls. God will punish them.'

'Do you like all this, this violence, kidnapping….'

'We are helpless, what is there to like?' She drew a deep breath. Today she told me she was sick of these jehadis.

'Why, don't you want jehad?'

'I wanted it earlier, not any more. But I can't do anything. I am helpless. May God forgive me.'

The hatred inside her erupted, 'It is all a sham. Hooliganism and nothing else. My daughter…went crazy. These ruffians spoilt her life.'

'What happened?'

'She became pregnant, she is just fourteen years old, my daughter Noori. She has lost her mind.'

'Bring her to me!' I felt a tug of sympathy.

The girl was really scared. She wouldn't let me touch her. I patted her, cajoled her—'Come here, I will comb your hair. I will make a beautiful plait. You will see how lovely it looks.'

'No, they will punish me. They will tear me like a piece of cloth!' As I turned her round, innocent face towards me she kept repeating the same words. She allowed me to touch her only after three days. Those animals had really torn her apart. She needed surgery. Her vagina was so badly torn that her urether and her anus had become one.

'Bring her to my hospital once I get away from here. I will operate on her. She will be fine, she just needs some medical care.' I consoled the girl's mother.

I don't know why I was worried about the girl when I did not even know what was going to happen in the next instant. No one knew what they were going to do with me. Not even Fayyaz.

Fayyaz limped while walking. I thought it was a congenital defect. Today, on the eighth day, he sat down in the room and took off his shoes and socks.

His right foot was badly swollen. I looked at it closely. It was all red, swollen, the wounds full of pus.

'It is infected. Get my medical kit. I need some boiled water as well.'

The woman who brought my meals fetched a bowl of hot water. I put on my gloves and washed the wound with warm water and boric acid. He squirmed as he tried to muffle his screams. 'Maaaaa.' he shouted and his eyes filled with tears. 'So you are missing your mother?' I don't know why I asked the question. He kept quiet.

I put some salve, bandaged the foot and gave him some Ciprofloxacin capsules.

'Take this tablet and go to sleep. I won't run away.'

The boy felt a little better.

Now he talked a little more freely. The loathing in his eyes had been replaced by shame.

'How did this happen?' I probed.

'My shoes got stuck in the snow when we were coming from there. They were torn and I kept on running barefoot. I stumbled and maybe that is when I got this wound. I didn't realize because my foot was numb at the time.'

'Didn't you get a chance to show it to anyone? Is killing people more important than your own life?'

'Who would I show it to? We spent four days in the jungle hiding from the Indian army.'

'Can't your patrons across the border even give you new shoes? Then why do you put yourself in danger? Or do you get a fat sum for killing your own people?'

My voice was full of subdued anger.

'We are jehadis. We have set out to martyr ourselves for the sake of azaadi. It doesn't matter even if we lose our lives in this war.' He asserted himself.

'But son, you are killing your own people in this war. Nothing happens to those people.' I don't know why I wanted to pull him out of the quicksand in which he was stuck.

'We help those who are with us. We destroy those who stand in our way.' He replied clearly.

'But will you be able to fight the entire might of the Indian army, the BSF and the lakhs of soldiers? Just think....'

Fayyaz didn't let me complete what I was saying.

'We hate Hindustan. It has sent four or five lakh soldiers to finish us off though we are fighting for our rights. We will never turn back.'

'Which right have you been denied, Fayyaz?'

'The right of self-determinism, the right to freedom! The Indian government had promised the Security Council that it would hold a plebiscite. Why is it going back on its word now?'

'Fayyaz, you are an educated young man, you know the terms of the plebiscite. To hold one, Pakistan will first have to withdraw its forces from Azaad Kashmir, which it is not ready to do. Some parts of Kashmir, which were seized by Pakistan in 1947, including Siachin, some of our territory in Ladakh, Hunza, Baltistan, parts of Gilgit, it has already handed over to China. According to the terms of the plebiscite these areas will first have to be returned, which is not possible. So how can there be any proper assessment of the people's wishes? And then the issue has already been settled by the Shimla Agreement.'

Fayyaz interrupted me again.

'We don't recognize the Shimla Agreement.'

'Doesn't India look after your needs? Thanks to Article 370 our Kashmiriyat is protected and we have also been given more concessions than other states...'

'We are not interested in all that. That stuff is fine for the National Conference members who are only interested in their own welfare.'

Fayyaz spoke about the 1987 elections, 'At that time the Muslim United Front would have won. Sayyed Salahuddin of the MUF stood for election from Amirakadal, but he lost to Mahiuddin Shah because of rigging. He was arrested and put in jail. That was the time when we decided that this was going to be a war to the end. Pakistan helps us in our struggle. After all they are our Muslim brothers....'

'That is true, Fayyaz, but you people are divided into many factions. One wants freedom, the other wants Kashmir to become a part of Pakistan. You have ended up disagreeing with each other, so what is the real meaning of this war?'

I don't know how Fayyaz controlled himself and heard me out but his face reflected his thoughts as I spoke.

'There is one thing which India should understand by now, that we have always been in favour of freedom, right from the beginning. Our leaders have betrayed us and cared more for own their interests than for our rights.'

'I know that Fayyaz!' I tried to calm him down. 'Go to sleep now! You need rest.'

In my mind I thought, it isn't just you alone, even Raja Hari Singh wanted freedom. Jinnah sahib, who claimed that he had created Pakistan merely with the help of a PA and a typewriter, was also probably in favour of granting freedom to the princely states. It was Hari Singh's desire for freedom that ultimately forced him out of the state into exile. In 1953 Sheikh sahib separated Doda from Udhampur district and made it a part of Kashmir as part of his dream about becoming the sultan of Greater Kashmir, a dream that put him in jail for 22 years. Later, he came to understand the situation better and he merged the Plebiscite Front with the National Conference. Then why had this issue once again raised its head, after India had invested crores of rupees in the state and continued to do so? These thoughts kept running through my mind though I did not say anything aloud. Fayyaz would not have spared me if I had spoken. I would also have been branded an 'Indian agent', a traitor to the cause.

Fayyaz had gained his Bachelors degree and was looking for a job when he came under the influence of Pakistani militants. His story was one of necessity, greed and also perhaps a desire for what he thought would be a glorious martyrdom. He joined the JKLF. He raised the cry for freedom but his Baba told him that people in that part of Pakistan which the JKLF wanted to merge with—the state of Jammu and Kashmir, including Muzaffarabad, Kotli, Mirpur etc.—were completely different from the people of the valley in their way of life, thinking, language and culture. They were not familiar with Alamdar-e-Kashmir, Sheikh-ul-alam, Nooruddin Noorani, nor did they know about Baba Zainuddin who meditated for twelve years in a cave in Aishmukam and said, 'Believe in God. Wipe out all differences between people.' Both Kashmiri Hindus and Muslims venerated him, Pakistan and Azad Kashmir had no interest in Lal Ded, Makhdoom Sahib, Hazratbal or all the holy places associated with pirs and saintly ascetics in the valley.

But Fayyaz was angry with Kashmiri leaders, though he was aware that Kashmiri craftsmen sold their wares in India and that houseboat owners, hoteliers, workers and tradesmen earned their living from Indian tourists. Now he had also realized that Pakistan had no love for Kashmiris, it just wanted the valley: for its rivers, and for its own security and for political and military leverage. There were things that made him uneasy. His mind was in such a turmoil, and rumours had become truths.

The next day Fayyaz took the trouble to bring me tea. His foot seemed to be a little better. Feeling a sense of closeness I said, 'Lately many of your companions have surrendered to the army. They have realized that guns are not the solution to their problems and they have got good jobs. They live with their families. Why don't you also start your life anew?'

Fayyaz was annoyed. 'Surrender? Me? In front of those beasts who flayed my brother in the interrogation cell?' You have no idea how cruel they can be. Till today I have not

forgotten the incident in Baramulla in June of 1992. They took
the Principal of the Jamaat-e-Islami school for interrogation
and sent back his dead body after two days. We buried him
like a martyr. Women and children came out on the streets of
Baramulla demanding freedom.'

I wanted to say, you tried to use the women and children
as shields by placing them at the head of the procession.
Why didn't the residents of Mirpur mohalla come out when
the corps commander asked everyone to gather in the Idgah
park for a search? Why did you people fire from the upstairs
windows and initiate cross firing? Isn't it a given that innocent
people die in such situations? As Fayyaz narrated incidents of
BSF brutality, in my mind's eye I saw the bodies of innocent
men hanged from trees by terrorists. These included not only
men like Tikalal Taploo, Neelkanth Ganjoo and Lassa Kaul,
but also the Muslim police officer of Pattan and his brother
who had been killed in their home by militants. There was
Ajay Kapoor, the businessman of Maharajganj, Handoo, the
Assistant Director of Information, the young engineer from
the telecommunication department, BK Ganjoo who tried to
hide in an empty petrol drum and was shot there by terrorists.
His wounded wife cried out in anguish that they should shoot
her as well but her wish wasn't granted.

I kept quiet. I was their prisoner. I did not have the right to
say anything. I could only listen.

He continued, 'Jagmohan was responsible for these
atrocities. He told the Pandits to run away, arranged buses and
trucks for them so that he could wipe us out. But we know
how to retaliate, we can counter his bullets with our rocket
launchers.'

'But Jagmohan took over as governor on 19th or 20th January
1990. A lot of Hindus had already left the valley by that time.
The situation had already deteriorated.' I couldn't help speaking
out.

'No one troubles the Hindu and Sikh brothers who have stayed back. How can we help it if they have a minority complex? We consider them our brothers. But anyone who is a spy, is our enemy. We won't spare him.'

I kept nodding, because I had to think about Kartikeya, not only about myself. But the question 'how safe are those who have stayed back in the valley' troubled me throughout the night, bringing a lot of known and unknown faces to mind. These included the Ganjoo family of Bhana Mohalla. On 17th June 1990 terrorists walked into their house and killed four of the family members, just because they did not want to abandon the home of their ancestors. Were they spies?

Dr Shiban Krishan Kaul and Dr Rajendra Kaul of Rehbaba Sahib, Srinagar, who had been assured of their safety by their neighbours and even terrorists, were killed along with their wives in October 1990 for no reason. What crime had they committed?

Terrorists did not need to give any reasons. 'The Battas ran away'. But why did they run away? Not just Fayyaz but many journalists and even intellectuals made irresponsible, insensitive and erroneous comments. They made statements without looking for the truth. Ma Lalli is right when she says that only someone who has lost his home can understand what home really means. Losing one's home means getting cut off from one's geography, history and collective memory. No one leaves home needlessly or simply because someone else asks him to.

I could not tell Fayyaz to ask those migrants who were surviving in ragged camps, rotting in terrible conditions, what it meant to lose one's home. To ask those proud people living in the midst of disease, psychological problems and humiliation, facing the burning hot winds of summer, what forced them to leave the homes of their ancestors? Were they all really spies? Those simple hardworking farmers who did not ask for anything other than two square meals a day and a life of peace and dignity. Did they also run away because Jagmohan asked them to go?

After ten days a weak and watery sun appeared in the sky.

Fayyaz returned late that night. I asked about Kartikeya as I did every day.

'How is the doctor? Will you take me to him now?'

In other words your wounded soldiers were healed now. Why do you continue to keep us imprisoned?

'I have spoken to the leader. Actually your doctor is slightly unwell.' He replied a little haltingly.

'What's wrong with him?' I became worried.

'Nothing, nothing much. It was his own fault, he tried to run away. The commander shot him. Thankfully the bullet only struck his arm. He took the bullet out himself. He is a good doctor.' There was a muted admiration in Fayyaz's voice.

The doctor was brought to me. After ten days or ten ages? I wrapped him in my overcoat. He was burning. I had never seen such dark circles around his eyes. When had his hands become so wrinkled? Had I slept unknowingly like Rip Van Winkle in the interim? I tried to enfold Kartikeya within the oasis that, during the icy storms of these endless days, I had kept from freezing over in the hope of his return.

I, Tathya's brave, fearless daughter held Kartikeya as I started sobbing. I enveloped him in my arms. 'I thought I had lost you, Katya! That I would never see you again!' His voice seemed to emerge from a deep well. Fayyaz and two boys left the doctor in my room at night and left in the dark. They were in a hurry. The woman who used to bring our meals got some hot kehwa in a samovar along with two pieces of bread from the baker. There was compassion in her eyes.

'Here take this bread and kehwa. Give them to your husband. God knows if he ate anything there at all!' she added, 'Let me know if you need anything else, I will get it for you.'

'I will be grateful if you fetch me a warm kangri. The doctor's feet are cold.' I answered, rubbing the soles of Kartkeya's feet. I felt there was something stuck in my throat, that I was about to break into tears. She could see the flood of tears welling up in my eyes. She went and quickly fetched a kangri. I was comforted. I don't know whether it was because of the hot kangri or because of the dawning warmth that I could sense in the woman's heart.

Early morning Fayyaz knocked at the door.

'Get up, move out. I will escort you to the road.'

I kept looking at him in disbelief. Were we really going to be free? He was in a hurry. Perhaps the BSF had discovered their location.

The woman came forward to help the doctor. As though she had just been waiting for a signal.

Fayyaz carried the doctor on his back for half a kilometere to the road. The woman walked with us, holding my hand. Fayyaz stopped a short distance away from the road. 'Go, doctor. It is your good luck and our misfortune that our leader was captured while crossing the border. We have to leave this place.'

Fayyaz turned back. Kartikeya raised his hand and thanked him. His eyes were wet. I felt like reaching out and hugging Fayyaz, but he had neither the time nor the option to indulge in emotions.

'Look after yourself….son.' He turned back when he heard my voice and then left without saying anything. I couldn't read his face in the dark.

The woman walked with us on the road, giving us her support.

Snow lay in random little piles on the road. We reached a ramshackle looking shop. The woman spread her dupatta on the ground. 'Sit on this, doctor. A lot of BSF vehicles pass this way. They will take you to your destination. Have faith in Allahtala! I have to leave, otherwise suspicion will fall on me. We are in danger from both sides, go, may God be with you…'

She turned away without looking back. I wanted to wrap myself around her and thank her for all her kindness, but I had started shaking uncontrollably. I don't know why. Was it an excess of emotion or the joy of freedom? The realization that a seed of humanity still survived in people or the unexpected happiness of finding that the impossible had become possible?

'You must bring your daughter to my hospital. Remember, I will wait for you...' my quavering voice followed her.

Gleams of light brightened the sky, the white peaks of the mountains gradually became visible as the mist melted away. Both of us continued to sit close to one another, like two children who had been reunited after being separated in a crowd. Afraid that we might lose each other again. In that freezing cold and fog, the open sky and earth were like a dream. Had I ever seen such a vast sky before? After half an hour or so, a military truck appeared a short distance away. I stood in the middle of the road and stopped it.

Two soldiers picked up Kartikeya and laid him down in the truck. Covered him with blankets.

'You are lucky you have come back safe and sound. I would call it a miracle. Otherwise one can never tell with these brutes.'

They were rejoicing in our freedom. For us they were messengers of God. They were asking questions but we were silent. I don't know what Kartikeya was thinking.

The last ten days were playing themselves out in front of my eyes like a film. The commander with the brown beard, the wounded jehadis, the crazy girl, the lady who brought our meals, the freezing cold room, the seemingly endless days and Fayyaz! The blue-eyed, intelligent young boy who was the victim of misunderstanding, rumours and the plots of Pakistani militants, who had lost faith both in India and Pakistan.

I remembered the two women who had come crying to Shihul Villa, the mujahids with their faces covered with kerchiefs, the fearful nights...the slain fighters covered in blood, lying on the snow…the four-month pregnant young girl whose vagina had been torn brutally and so many other things. I had forgotten Fayyaz's arguments but one statement of his was hammering against my brain.

'We don't want Hindustan. We don't want Pakistan. We have come to realize what their reality is. We want freedom. Just freedom.'

I don't know why I had the feeling that if Fayyaz managed to survive the bullets, he would definitely return home one day.

Dark Night of Mourning

Even eight years after Aslam had left home, Aziza continued to wake up at night and check out the sounds of footsteps in the street through crevices in the windows or wait for him by the shores of the Manasbal lake. Her elder son, Altaf, and husband Ramzan Malik, came to the conclusion that she had lost her mind. Friends and relatives expressed their sympathy. They even suggested that perhaps it might be a good idea to have her treated at one of the 'recovery centres' and hospitals which the BSF had opened for psychiatric patients. Aziza might learn to come to terms with the fact that Aslam was never going to come back.

Altaf listened but kept quiet. He wonderered whether there was any hospital which could really cure the sick, the troubled and mentally disturbed people living in this frightened valley. Could it heal the wounded hearts of those mothers who washed their sons' bloodstained clothes on the banks of the Vitasta or cure those fathers who mourned for their own lives as they carried the dead bodies of their sons?

Altaf's mother didn't throw stones, shout or scream obscenities. She just sat in a dark corner of the house knitting a patterned sweater for her absent son. Knitting and unravelling the stitches, she sometimes set her work aside and roamed around the streets of the village. She asked every passer-by the same question: 'Have you seen my Aslam?'

'He has light brown hair. Just as soft as a girl's, like strands of silk! May God protect him from the evil eye but if he goes out in the sun his face becomes rosy. He used to sleep with me. His father used to get angry. He used to tell Aslam, "You are going to get married in two years' time, will you still carry on clinging to your mother's pheran then?"'

'Now tell me, is that the way to talk to a youngster? I think he got angry. Otherwise why doesn't he come back home even in this bitter cold? He hasn't even taken his kangri with him.'

The villagers looked at her with sad eyes. Earlier they used to console her, 'He will come back, don't worry. How long can he stay away from you?' But when Aslam's dead body was shown on TV along with the bodies of other slain militants, they realized he had been killed in cross-firing. Aziza, however, did not accept that her son was dead.

How could the boy on television be Aslam? Her son couldn't even throw a dead rat caught in a rat-trap into the lake. He was not capable of hitting a bird with a slingshot, how could he pick up a gun and kill another human being? Once Altaf had spoken to her a little sharply in order to try and make her accept the truth, 'Ammi! Those people force you. They persuaded Siddiqui's son to go with them. Have you forgotten what happened to him? He had said he wouldn't pick up a gun. I will not kill my own people. Those merciless people broke his right hand.'

All the blood had receded from Aziza's face. She had started beating her chest in anguish. Then Altaf had tried to explain things to her more gently. 'Nothing like this happened to Aslam. Those people sent him across the border for training. Waqar Ahmed told me.' After Aslam's departure there were knocks at the door at odd times of the night. The BSF suspected that they were militants. They would ask one question after another. Search the house at every opportunity. Just in case there were any bombs, explosives or Kalashnikovs hidden in the house.

They did not find any explosives but yes, once they did find four boys who had chosen to hide in Ramzan Malik's house during a crackdown. They had put a gun to Ramzan's head and asked for shelter. When the BSF dragged them out from the basement where they were hiding behind vessels of grain and bunches of hay, Ramzan, with an expressionless face, claimed that they were his relatives. Ramzan's eyes were lowered to the ground but he did want to save the boys. They looked innocent and he remembered his Aslam. Perhaps they had also been misled and forced to become part of some faction. The security forces had taken them away. Ramzan was happy to know that they surrendered before the army and also surprised to hear that they had later joined the police force.

Even the BSF had become more considerate since Aslam's body was shown on TV. Virender Singh kept an eye on Altaf's house. The militants might succeed in winning him over as well. If they could threaten the younger brother why would they spare the elder one? But no one came to take Altaf. He stayed aloof anyway. His Abbu's silence and his mother's strange behaviour had made him feel almost detached from things around him.

Days passed. Days full of news about bomb explosions and deaths. People had gradually got used to these. A bomb exploded in the Secretariat, a BSF vehicle was blown up in Lal Chowk. Ten jawans were killed. Two terrorists were killed in cross firing.

'Pakistani forces retreated from Kargil and militancy in the valley has increased.'

'Pakistan will not let go of Kashmir. Even if God himself, leave alone Bill Clinton, comes and asks them. Kashmir is a do or die issue for them. It is definitely going to take revenge for being defeated three times.'

'Yes, otherwise why have they made the atom bomb?'

But the nights did not pass so easily. Was it a night or a dark inky sea?

Altaf and Aslam's mother, Aziza, peered through the chinks in the closed windows. Within the patches of faint colour in the dark she could see the tiny Aslam waddling along on unsteady legs lisping, 'Mama's lap, mama's lap!' Aziza woke up with a start. She ran towards the window with open arms to pick up her son and hit her head against the closed shutter. There was a swelling on her forehead.

Altaf heard his mother's soft moans from the room next door and descended into the depths of a dark well. A well in which everyone was alone. In the whip-like night, four hefty men riding black horses grabbed Aslam by his arms and dragged him away. Aziza's ears echoed with the sound of her son's pleas, 'I can't do this brother, please have pity on me. I can't even kill a mouse...'

'Don't worry, we will teach you. Give thanks to Allah, you have been chosen for the jehad.'

'Amma, abba, bhai jaaaaaan! Why don't you explain ...'

Aslam went away, only the memory of his screams remained. Altaf could not save his younger brother.

Their neighbour Mushtaq congratulated their father, 'You are a lucky man, your son has gone to fight for his religion. Stop lamenting.'

Mushtaq was the jehadi son of a jehadi father. His family distributed halwa the day he was killed in BSF firing. Their son had been martyred for his religion, for the work of Allah. There was nothing to lament. But the day Aslam's body was shown on television, Ramzan Malik broke down and sobbed. Aziza looked stunned. The tears kept falling from Ramzan Malik's brownish eyes and seeping into his graying beard. No one in the house distributed halwa or shouted 'al-jehad'. Aziza was not even willing to accept the possibility that Aslam could be a militant. A child who was even afraid of a dead rat how could he...?

Aslam was a close friend of Shiban, Haldar Bhatt's grandson. Aslam did not eat anything the day Shiban left the village and went away. For two days he kept wandering around the shores of Manasbal like a madman. When the jehadis cajoled and brainwashed Nisar and took him across the border for training Aslam was really angry. He did not like violence. He watched films with Madhuri Dixit, Mithun and Sridevi. Often Altaf would exercise his rights as an elder brother and scold him, 'Don't you want to study or are you just planning to watch these films?'

'Bhaijaan, I study a lot, you can check with Shiban. But one has to have some hobbies as well, don't you think?'

'Hobbies, what hobbies?'

'Just three hobbies, bhaijaan, just three!'

Number one, playing cricket, number two, swimming in the Manasbal lake and number three, watching Madhuri Dixit's films...

'Bhaijaan look at my medal. My team won against Sopore. They couldn't even make a hundred runs in fifty overs....'

'How many runs did you make, captain sahib? I heard you were out for a duck!'

'Lies, Completely untrue. I made forty-two runs off forty balls. You can check with Shiban....'

Aslam's face had looked stiff on television, his golden hair was soaked with blood. Where had the bullet hit him? Would he have called out to ammi or bhiajaaan?

A silent bullet lodged itself in Altaf's heart. He thought Aslam probably never even learnt how to use a gun.

Ammi also had the same thought. That was why she refused to believe that the body on television could be Aslam's corpse. Cricket captain, Sridevi fan, Shiban's friend, Aslam, who loved to swim in the Manasbal lake.

Altaf couldn't sleep at night. How could he forget Aslam's various facets and moods?

His maternal aunt, mausi, came from Sopore and stayed with them for two months. Ma got very depressed if she was all alone. Mausi took Ma back into the lanes and bylanes of childhood. She switched on the television and put on Chitrahaar. The family members needed to come out of their grief into the world outside. She said, 'We have to carry on living till we are summoned from above, sister.'

They watched television till late at night. Someone had made a film on the Vondhama massacre. Twenty members of a Pandit family had been burnt alive in Vondhama village. The terrorists had been criticized at home and abroad. Altaf had gone to the village and visited Motilal's ruined house. Even today he felt unnerved when he thought of the place. Now after around four years someone had made this film in which the elders of the village were reminiscing about the Pandit family. The women were in tears. The faces of the elders reflected their fear and sorrow.

'Motilal was an angel. He would go running to help if anyone in the village was ever ill.'

The old bearded man with the weak eyes was shaking his head in sorrow, 'They were good people. What happened was very unfortunate. They never quarrelled with anyone. My wife has high blood pressure. Every week Motilal would come with his machine to check her blood pressure.' A twelve or thirteen year old remembered his teacher who, after teaching him in school, would often coach him at home for free. 'Who is going to teach me now?' He was worried.

A woman who was breast feeding her young infant was very

agitated, 'It was a family of twenty people. All of them died. On this land, right here, all their dead bodies were laid out. None of them could be recognized. They had been charred, all of them. All the Pandits in the villages nearby left their homes and ran away. We tried to stop them. All of us used to live together in harmony. Those people couldn't bear that.'

When the film finished Ammi asked Altaf, 'Who was this Motilal?' She was surprised that even four years after the Vondhama massacre the villagers were still crying in memory of someone who was not related to them in any way.

'He was also the son of some mother, Ammi, and his entire family was wiped out by militants.' Altaf spoke without thinking.

'Are those the people who took away my Aslam?'

Ma started shaking with sobs. Mausi held her, 'Cry, sister. Cry as much as your heart desires. Let your voice reach him. Your son was not a militant. Allahtala knows that.'

Ma had a good cry after many years. She might have fallen into a deep sleep at night but Altaf couldn't sleep at all. Outside they could hear some noises in the street. Virender Singh knocked at the window, 'Turn the light off, bhaijaan. It is late. Go to sleep. I will come and listen to some of your poetry tomorrow.'

'Yes, bhai. I am going to sleep.' Altaf switched off the light. 'Come over tomorrow.'

The stranger Virender had become a friend of Altaf's. One night Ammi was sitting by the shores of Manasbal calling out loudly to Aslam. Virender was on night duty. He brought her home.

Since that day he felt some special connection with Ma.

He didn't know whether Aslam was a terrorist or not but he knew that a mother had lost her son. Her sorrow was deep. Virender Singh thought of his own mother. Mothers are mothers! She wanted a letter every week. She worried a lot about her son. Altaf was a schoolteacher. He wrote poetry.

Virender Singh said poets had a very soft heart. Altaf closed his eyes and tried to go to sleep. His eyelids became heavy.

A door opened in front of his eyes. Within, marriage songs were being sung with enthusiasm. There was a puja being performed outside the door. The bride and bridegroom were standing on a dias decorated with flowers. The smiling lips of the bride were visible under the veil. The Muslim women from the neighbourhood were dancing the Rov arm in arm. The scene became indistinct. Smoke rose from the house where the marriage had taken place. Flames rose high almost touching the sky. Shouts…screams. Chaos. The entire village had come out. Buckets and pots of water were being thrown on the fire. BSF jawans were using the fire engines to douse the flames.

Dead bodies were being taken out of the house. The remains of half-burnt young girls. Which of them was that beautiful young bride? The teacher, daughter-in-law and her loving husband? That tiny little boy, Bittu? Kakni, Bhabi and the head of the family? The bodies were laid out in rows in the courtyard. None of them was breathing. A family of twenty two people. Yesterday they were so alive, so full of joy and today it was as if they were all just sleeping there, unaware of their surroundings. The door, grimy with smoke, hung loose below the banners that said, tragically, 'welcome' and 'long live the couple'. Among those charred, distorted bodies, it was impossible to identify that 'happy couple'.

These people had defied the diktat and not left their villages as they'd been instructed to do. What could be a greater crime than that? Altaf tossed from side to side in his sleep. The wind was shrieking outside. There was the sound of running feet. Some clamour and then the sound of firing! 'Aaaaaah!' A scream cut through the darkness and reached Altaf. Altaf was flustered, he opened the window and looked out into the street. Just a few steps from the house a tall man in uniform was lying on the ground in the mud. Altaf felt as though a sharp dagger had been shoved into his heart. Could this be Virender Singh?

He felt giddy and his legs started shaking. He didn't know when Abbu opened the door and came into the room. He came and put his arms around his son. Altaf cried as he leaned into his old father's arms.

'Abbu, those brutes have killed Aslam....'

Ramzan Malik stood there, stunned. Aslam's body had been shown on television many years ago. Today, it was Virender Singh who had been killed by some terrorist.

What was Altaf saying?

Had he also gone crazy, like his Ammi?

❧

Y2K, The Crow in the Pot and Dearest Bittoo Exiled from the Village

So, finally, the year came to an end. Another decade gone. A decade of good and bad changes, communal upheavals, struggles for independence, Gorbachovian initiatives, crumbling institutions, successes and failures. A decade during which the world changed into a global village, and technology showed its might.

We came closer to each other, but we also became more distant. And what happened to our area of interest, the ancient Satisar? The Kashmir of sage Kashyap changed from being a paradise on earth to a bloody hell of bombs and Kalashnikovs, but this was an issue that was somehow lost and forgotten in the midst of discussions on more important national and international problems.

There was a new global concern, Y2K, the fear that computer brains would get scrambled at the beginning of the new millenium. Everyone got busy, frantically trying to prevent the world from coming to a halt. One has to pay the price for being a part of the global village, so we were equally engrossed in finding a solution to this international problem. The result was that our own Y2K concerns were put on the back burner.

However, the Y2K which was causing panic in her homeland remained alive in the mind of the writer who was narrating the story of Satisar. She was troubled by the fear that the number of the original inhabitants of the valley was fast being reduced in their own country. Could politicians, administrators, mediators, middlemen suggest any effective way of dealing with this fear? No. The ordinary people had no hope of getting any viable solution from those who were capable of baking bread on the pyres of the dead.

No ray of light anywhere. Where should one look for a sign, inspiration, an idea?

The writer takes a long leap backwards into the past where the first folk historian of Kashmir, Gunadya, the composer of a treatise of seven hundred and twenty thousand verses, is sitting in a glow of light. But why is the brow of Gunadya Pandit, who inscribed stories he heard from Karnabhooti with his blood, wrinkled with worry and sorrow? Is it because he wrote his stories in the language of the ordinary people and the king refused to listen to them, calling the language of the Pisachas an uncivilized language? Is that why he was so distressed that he contemplated reducing his entire treatise to ashes?

The huge manuscript written by Gunadya remains unavailable today, though in the 11th century the Kashmiri pandit Somadeva did discover some remnants of the *Vrihat Katha*. Based on these he wrote the *Katha Sarit Sagar* for the entertainment of Queen Suryamati. Thus Gunadya stayed alive through these stories, which came to be known at home and abroad and which, even today in the era of Doordarshan and videos, remain alive on celluloid. Their survival also provides comfort to those westernized modern critics and reviewers who fear the imminent death of the story.

Returning now to the story of the last decade, how does one relate such a heartbreaking narrative?

If the writer of the *Rajtarangini*, Pandit Kalhana, were alive today he could perhaps have provided some direction. Historians like him also had the hearts of poets and revealed the story of human destiny while writing their histories. But the writer is not Pandit Kalhana. In this era of fast food, fast music and fast lives she does not want to lose the patience of her readers with a huge treatise written along the lines of Gunadya's *Vrihat Katha*. So, paying tribute to the energy, intellect and creativity of past writers she has decided that now, in keeping with the video era, she will say less and show more. And yes, she will show her story to the ordinary public, not to any king or officer. Peering through windows and chinks in doors, she will reveal whatever glimpses she can, of innocent Abhimanyus caught in the chakravyuha, the web of flatterers, troublemakers, friends and enemies.

Treading carefully, her first window opens straight into Bandipora village. Yes, the same Bandipora, located on the banks of the Wular Lake. A lake crammed full of green water chestnuts, bunches of lotus flowers and broad lotus leaves. This is where 30-year old Abdul Gaffar Sheikh was killed in 1991 during the army crackdown. At that time Bandipora was in the grip of terror. On the one hand, there were baseless rumours spread by the terrorists and on the other, the harshness of the army in its interrogation of militants. Two mad bulls, independence and governance, fighting with locked horns.

The dense fog of rumours spread by the terrorists had obscured the faces of the guilty and the innocent alike. In one case the veiled women, who were produced before the journalists as victims of oppression, giggled all the while holding their veils between their teeth as they accused the army of rape. There was another rumour, that some Kashmiri pandit, in the guise of an armyman, was terrorizing the villagers.

This whole circus was observed by Raghunath Kastur of Kalusa village who had spent his entire life singing chakris based on the sufiana verses of Rasool Mir, Shamas Fakir and Wahab Dar with his friends. He knew that a pandit who spent his entire life in fear and stayed miles away from any violence, a man adorned with the nickname of *dalibatta*, a dal eating milksop, would never have the guts to threaten anyone. Wasn't this the height of invention?

Raghunath saw and heard many things with his own eyes and ears. Riyaz and Javed distributing pamphlets on jihad, the wives of the Hizbul Mujahiddeen shouting, 'Indian dogs go back, Indian spies, may you perish' and other threats that took him totally by surprise. How did so much poison seep into the village? Why did one's friends become enemies? These questions disturbed Raghunath so much that he left the village the very next day. It was no longer a place where peace-loving people could stay.

Raghunath wandered around like a madman in the refugee camps in Delhi as though he were roaming in the fields of Bandipora, among the hills of Deeneshwar or conversing with mother Sharda of Sharda Bal. One day, lost in his song, 'We have come your threshold as supplicants, mother Parvati have pity on us' he mistook a crowd on a Delhi street for a group of bhajan singers of Narain Nag and was crushed by a bus. Lingering in hospital for a few days, he died crooning these heart-rending lines,'The world has changed so much, when will I hear the sweet words and melodious songs of my friends again?'

Niranjan lives in a single storied house in this very Bandipora village in the shadow of the Sonarvanya hill. Let us see what he is doing. It is a long spacious room. Through the window you can see a milky stream cutting across and pouring down the heart of the hillside. The room is filled with the sweet music of the bubbling brook that passes by the door. Niranjan is leaning against a bolster, narrating stories to his granddaughters. What else can he do, a man with time on his hands? He was a school headmaster and retired around five years ago. There is a small *vaer*, a kitchen garden, adjacent to the house where he grows some greens and vegetables.

Niranjan loves to tell stories. When he reached Tathya sahib's house after escaping from the clutches of the Kabailis, he was surrounded by youngsters to whom he would narrate all kinds of true, imaginary, old and new stories. The stories were fascinating, unusual. Why did the fish laugh? How did the daughter of the crow become a queen? Stories of Akhnandun, Sonakesri, Himal-Nagrai, Gulrez, Premchand's Nirmala, Prasad's Madhulika, Hardy's Mayor of Casterbridge, Tess and even the romantic tale of Samson and Delilah. Niranjan would say, 'Stories are not merely meant to entertain, they also give us insights into the meaning of life.' Tathya would agree, 'You are right.'

Katya was very fond of the story of the crow that fell into a pot, to the consternation of the entire village. The *shoga* bird cut off its beard in sorrow, the water in the pond dried up, the cow shed its tail and the bridge dropped one of its planks.

'Goodness, so much commotion for a crow?'

'Yes, yes. The crow fell into the cooking pot and was burnt, wouldn't his friends be upset?'

'This is a story of the past, the Satyuga. In today's Kaliyuga if the crow falls into the pot the cook will just put the lid on it and no one will see or hear the cries of the crow.' This used to be the response of Prem bhaiya. That is, everything changed because of terrorism. Look at what happened to Radhakrishan. The terrorists took him away and asked him to reveal the names of spies. Poor Radhakrishan would have told them if he knew anything. So, he was beaten up with rods the whole night. Next day, like an animal being killed for halal, his throat was slit and he was thrown on the riverbank to die slowly. The blood kept flowing but no one came to help him. Radhakrishan asked a passerby for help, the man first asked him what his name was and when he heard the reply, dragged Radhakrishan by the legs and pushed him into the river to die. It was just his luck that the blood stopped flowing because of the cold water. He somehow managed to crawl out of the river and made his way to the police beat and was taken to the hospital. So, the villagers not only refused to mourn for the poor crow who had fallen into the pot but even tried to put the lid on the pot. Now it is your choice whether you call this Kaliyug or the era of terror.

But today Niranjan is going to narrate another story. Let us hear 'The story of Bittooji's travels'.

Nikki and Munni are listening spellbound balancing their chins on their hands.

'So my dear Nikki-Munni, Bittoo was on his way to visit his in-laws. He was newly married and had to travel to a far off village. His mother gave him directions, blankets, food and provisions for the journey. She instructed him to walk in a straight line and speak only weighty phrases and sent him off.

'The boy was really simple so, taking his mother's words literally, he chose three words, grinding stone, mortar and pestle. As he walked in a straight line following his nose he met an elderly gentleman who asked him, 'Where are you going, son? And what is this nonsense you are muttering?' '

'Bittoo told him the whole story. The old man laughed at the naivete of the youngster and blessed him, "Go safely, *var kar*, with joy and prosperity."'

'A new idea dawned on the young man. He should also say *var kar*. So he started repeating the phrase like a mantra, "*Var kar*, with joy and prosperity."'

'As he walked on he saw some men carrying a corpse. They were very upset when they heard Bittoo saying "With joy and prosperity." One of them stopped the young man and explained that these words were inappropriate, instead he should say, "No, no never."'

Bittoo obligingly started repeating this new mantra. As he walked a few paces he encountered a *baraat*, a joyous wedding procession. Two of the dancing revellers beat him up saying, 'You inauspicious man. You can see a *baraat* is passing by, say some words of cheer and happiness, say, "May it flourish may it increase."'

'The young man started singing this new tune, "May it flourish, may it increase."'

'Everything is the will of God. Just then a man, who was suffering from a painful boil in his arm, passed by crying in pain. When he heard Bittoo's words he abused him roundly, "You bastard...are you cursing me? Say, May what you have disappear, vanish."'

'The boy was totally confused and upset by now but he had no choice, so he started reiterating these new words, "Vanish, vanish."'

'He had just walked another twenty steps when he came across two labourers, slathered with perspiration, who were trying to dig a well. A few drops of water had just started spouting out of the ground when Bittoo passed by repeating his new phrase. The workers beat him up solidly with sticks, "You...you misbegotten one, are you blind? Can't you see that we have just succeeded in drawing a few drops of water in the well after backbreaking effort and you are cursing us saying that the little we have found should also disappear."'

'The boy started crying in pain. They told him don't cry, say "May there be a deluge, may there be floods."'

'But there was no end to Bittoo's saga of woe. He had just walked ahead a little when he met an old woman with a stick in her hand who was drying rice in the sun. When she heard Bittoo repeating, "May there be a deluge, may there be floods." she straightened her back and beat up the young man to teach him the lesson that he must learn to say the appropriate words at the appropriate time.'

'By now, however, poor Bittoo had received too many beatings and had come to the conclusion that none of his words was welcome in the village. With a heavy heart and a bruised body he threw away his belongings and ran as far as he could from the borders of the village. And this is how his story ends.'

Nikki and Munni were upset, 'Dadu, do you mean to say that Bittoo never reached the home of his in-laws?'

Munni seems to be a little more sensible. In her twelve years of life she has heard many stories about running away and being beaten up. Thoughtfully she asks her grandfather, 'Dadu, will Bittoo never return to the village? Just like Kaka, our uncle and Sunil bhaiya? Dadu, they should come back, shouldn't they? We are all waiting for them.'

'Oh! What is this?' So many tears are flowing from Munni's eyes.

Niranjan takes a handkerchief out of his pocket. 'Just look at her, the fairy who sheds tears of pearl. I am going to collect all of them in my handkerchief.'

'Daduuuu…' Munni bursts out laughing at the way he picks up her tears on his little finger and puts them in his handkerchief.

'Look at this, now narcissus flowers will rain down from your laughter. Let me gather these as well.'

Niranjan has never been able to see the children unhappy.

His younger son Shambhu has just returned from the shop. Nikki and Munni, Sahiba, Daddu and Shambhu are sitting on either side of the *dastarkhan*, the dining cloth spread on the floor. Uma, the daughter-in-law is serving steaming hot rice and turnips.

There is a brief dialogue between the father and the son.

'Was there any problem today?'

'No, I didn't even speak to anyone. Just handed over the goods and that is all.'

'Troublemakers…?'

'What will they take from me? They know I am an unimportant man. How can I harm anyone?'

'Yes… but still, it is better to be careful.'

'Why don't you also sit down daughter-in-law?' Niranjan requests Uma to sit. He wants to keep all his near and dear ones safe under his wings like a broody hen. Every moment he is afraid, every moment he is alert. He did not abandon his village even during the worst times but what can he do about the displacement that is hidden inside him?

Niranjan has already lost his wife. His older son Raghunath is living the life of a migrant in Udhampur along with his family. He was an officer in the telecommunications department. The jehadis were after his life. He also ran away from the village like the Bittoo in the story. Just like Bittoo his words, his requests were never appropriate.

Niranjan looks at Nikki and Munni with affection.

'Eat your food, children. Today you must also pray in the prayer room with me. We will ask mother Bhavani to return Kaka and Sunil bhaiya to us. I am sure she will listen to our prayers.'

We know that once everyone is asleep Niranjan will stay up late looking through old photo albums. He will talk to the photographs of his relatives. He will complain to Nandan, Dhara and their children who are settled in the US, to the granddaughters of Sharika's granddaughters, to Prem's grandsons, to his own Raghu and their Billoo-Tilloo who never write letters. After chatting and looking at them to his heart's content, he will close the album. Then, with his eyes shut, he will pray to God to keep all of them safe and happy wherever they are. In this new century, Niranjan finds himself unable to imagine anything beyond this. This is all. An expectation, a prayer and a request.

Niranjan! Standing in the shadow of the Sonarvanya mountains. 'Half buried in the earth/ with his eyes fixed on the peaks of the mountains/ he looks for his past in the archives/ sees the genes of Nagas and Yakshas taking breath.

He does not give up hope. He thinks
Clutching the edges of a disappearing heritage in my fist,
I will not be able to stop the flow of time
I am poised barefoot on the fires of hell
lost in some undefined hopes
I do not know what I am guarding!
Grant me a voice, my unnamed ancestors!

It is only the echoes of our voices that will break through our revisited exile.

Aerial Survey! Conclusion: Waiting for Badshah

Friends! Let us now go for an aerial survey.

There is Kathabab, Pandit Krishanjoo Kaul's house. He Shankar! There is nothing left here except a pile of broken bricks and burnt and corroded bits of the roof. So has this house also been sacrificed? The house is empty. After the death of Krishanjoo Kaul and Saraswati, Bhadra, Nathji and Indira also left. Death had become acquainted with the house, it was not likely to spare anyone.

Raja never returned once he left the house. Babboo is a bank officer posted somewhere in Bhadarwah-Kishtwar. It seems Sangeeta and his children are in Jammu where Sangeeta has a job. Nathji's daughter, Neelam. has chosen to be alone. She lives with Dr Katyayini in Shihul Villa. She spends all her time taking care of the patients. She hasn't married. She has no family. What about that doctor who used to daydream and call Neelam, 'Neelmaal fairy'? Who knows where he is? Does he still remember Neelam?

Here we are, at Shihul Villa. The house and the hospital look the same as they did ten years ago, just a little dirty and depressing. The walls are a little damp because of the melting snow. The slogan written on the wall, 'Anyone who fears Allah, should pick up a Kalashnikov',has faded away.

But even two years after his death it is impossible to forget Omkar bhai. He had lost his temper when he saw the slogan. He had tried to whitewash it and wipe it out. Two days after that his dead body was found lying on the road. The terrorists had cut off both his hands.

Inside Katya and Kartik are sitting close to the bukhari for warmth. Sati and Neelam are working in the kitchen. Sati now speaks much less than she did before. The house feels empty without the children. Isha is in Delhi. Tipu is working in Bombay. What will the house be like once Sati goes away to stay with her son? Katya doesn't want to think about it.

Omkar continued to be Katya and Kartikeya's son even after he became a father. Kartik has also become like blue throated Shiva who drank poison. He can't talk about Omkar nor can he forget him.

'Let me check my e-mail before dinner is served,' Katya gets up and goes into the computer room. Arjun and Alka are in America. They may have sent a mail. She downloads her mail. There are two or three messages.

'We are fine mum. How is Dad? There is good news for you. Alka is pregnant.'

Dr Arjun has sent the news from Illinois that Kartik and Katya are about to become grandparents. Truly? Eight years after their marriage? Kartik will be overjoyed. Katya is happy.

The second message. 'Lalli is not doing too well.' Nandu from New Jersey. A shadow passes over Katya's face.

'Kartik! Ma isn't well.' Her voice is shaking.

'What is the matter? Come here, let us talk.' Kartik puts his arm around her.

'I don't think Ma will be able to wait any longer. Should we send Isha to her grandmother?'

'Come on. Don't be silly. Ma is old now, her health will go through some ups and downs. Let her get a little better and then we can go and bring her back with us.'

Kartik knows how to allay fears.

'I couldn't fulfil my promise, Kartik. I wanted to bring Lalli back to Vishnu Vatika one more time. At this time of life one re-lives and remembers past friendships, relationships and the time spent in one's home.'

'You are right, Katya! For a while it seemed as though things were improving. But militancy has increased again after the Kargil war. Nandu knows that. I am not sure whether Ma will be able to endure such a long journey now….'

Katya is sobbing with her head on Kartik's shoulder.

Why is this brave doctor's heart melting like this?

Is it because she could not fulfil the promise she had made to her mother? Or is it because, despite living with her family in an alien land, Lalli has continued to yearn for her own soil, water, language, the fragrance of her own home and its surroundings? Despite living abroad for so many years Lalli has never been able to forget Rishi Pir, Chirar-e-sharif, Shakaracharya and Tullamulla. Her eyes can still see the peaks of Vishnipad and Brahmashukla.

Katya is saddened by the fact that she could not justify her mother's faith. She had told her mother, 'Lalli! History is witness that we survived even after being reduced to only eleven families. We gradually grew into a community of lakhs and created a new history. You will see that your Katya will also be a part of those eleven families.'

Neelam and Sati have put the food on the table. Someone is knocking at the door.

'Who is it?'

' Ghulam Rasool, doctor sahib.'

'What is it Ghulam Rasool, at this time of night?'

'There is an emergency case, sahib. Yusuf's crazy daughter is in great pain....'

'Oh God! What happened?'

'Even four women can't handle her. She had bloodied herself hitting her stomach. She says she doesn't want a militant....'

'Inform Dr Kiran and Dr Shamim. They should prepare everything for an operation, I will just come.'

Dr Katya pulls her coat over her shoulders and walks with Ghulam Rasool towards the emergency ward. Even Dr Kartikeya cannot stop Katya, nor does he try. Yususf's daughter, who is a victim of the terrorists, is under Katya's care. She is eight months pregnant. Katya will have to operate.

Let us go towards the lakes now, the scene here is very upsetting. There is Khurshid's elder son, Alijoo's, houseboat. Would it be impolite of us to look inside?

Alijoo is sitting on an gabba made in Anantnag and smoking his hookah. He has grown quite old. There are hardly any tourists nowadays. One sees just a handful of them during summer. After the incident, when terrorists killed six tourists in a houseboat, all the visitors avoid staying in houseboats.

Alijoo's sons have now joined their cousins' business. They sell handicrafts in the emporium in Delhi. They even go to Goa to sell their merchandise. Alijoo's son, Saif, has constructed a house at the Delhi-Haryana border. Though it is true that Alijoo felt strange that day, almost as though his son was becoming a foreigner. The only consolation is that he comes home frequently. Saif has said clearly that now we should consider Hindustan as our country, Baba. And like our Batta brothers, we should get into the habit of tolerating the heat and humidity of the plains. Otherwise we will continue to behave like frogs in a well.

'There aren't enough jobs for everyone in the Valley. It is better to make an effort on one's own rather than wait for government help. India is a large country after all. Our destiny is linked to it. Even today there are thousands of young men who are jobless in the state of Jammu and Kashmir. There won't be any miracles even if the state does formulate new policies. So, in other words, we have to move out and look for opportunities.'

Actually the militants have driven Saif crazy with their demands for money. Rehana and Jawahra are also growing up. He is worried about his family. Who knows when someone will leave a packet of henna on their doorstep? But how can his old father find any solace in the last quarter of his life? He is not prepared to leave his house, his houseboat or Mazar Bal. And in the meanwhile he waits for tourists to arrive.

Now should we visit Mangala mausi's house in Chanpora? Mangala passed away long ago, now her son Ajay and his wife Shobha live in the house. Her grandson, Vicky, is in Hyderabad. Shilpi is in Chandigarh with her husband, but they get transferred all the time. The elders are destined to be lonely. Most of the Battas in the valley have sent their children and grandchildren away. They don't have the right to play with the future of their children because of their love for their own home. It doesn't matter what happens to them.

Ajay is sitting in the dark dispensary, waiting, surrounded by medicines, bottles, jars, old and new instruments and assorted stuff. Who is he waiting for? For patients or friends? Or just so that he can exchange a few words with someone? Ajay and

Shobha live in fear, afraid of those terrible voices which startle them within and outside the house. Sometimes Shobha says, 'God knows why we are sitting here. What are we waiting for? I am longing to see the children.'

Vicky asked his father, 'Why are you still holding on to this house now, Papa? You are constantly balanced on a knife-edge of fear. You can't even talk freely to anyone. You don't know when an enemy will suddenly raise his head. Why don't you listen to me, sell the property and come and live with me?'

'Look!' Ajay becomes philosophical as he peers through the gloom, 'Whatever happens is the will of God.'

'The will of God or your politicians?'

Ajay is quiet. He wishes he could look into the future. In the meanwhile, the shop is open. Trigami sahib is coming. He has always had bad teeth. Ajay doesn't take any money from him even today. It is enough that at least someone comes and exchanges a few words with him in this wilderness. A veil of secrecy has fallen over Khudai Manzil, the home of Rehmanjoo's sons. The BSF keeps a watch on visitors to the house. Shabir is linked to the JKLF. He hopes to become the leader of the state one day.

Now how about a flight to Jammu?

Down below we see Trikuta Nagar. There is the home of Keshavnath Raina. No, it is Premji's house. Keshavnath is not alive any more. Kamala also passed away two months after his death. They suddenly discovered that she had cancer, in the last stages. Katya, Kartikeya had come to meet Lalli and Premji after they were released by the militants. Lalli hugged her daughter and son-in-law for a long time.

'Where did those brutes touch you?' Lalli will wash away the scars with her tears.

'No, Lalli. They really had taken us to treat some of their injured companions. They didn't misbehave with me. They were scared themselves. '

Kamala couldn't believe it.

'How can anyone believe that animals who can cut a woman in two would ever let Katya go without misbehaving with her?'

She wept as she spoke.

'You are right, Kakni. Anything could have happened to me but they needed me for other reasons. And even if something of the sort had happened to me it would only have been a terrible episode. But the greatest sorrow and pain that I suffered was my worry for Kartikeya...'

Katya's voice became gruff with tears. Kamala hugged her, crying loudly.

'You have come back to us, child, we don't want anything else.'

Nandan and Dhara had come and taken Lalli away with them to New Jersey a year after Keshavnath's death. 'Don't worry about Dulari-Katya, Lalli! I will always be there for them.' Prem had reassured Lalli as she departed.

'Go, travel a little and then come back. Sharika's sons Aniruddh and Arvind are in Washington, you should spend a few days with them. You must visit Arjun as well, he is in Illinois. You won't even realize how time passes.'

Vijaya cried. Bulbul is working in Bangalore. Pamposh has settled in Pune after marrying a Marathi boy. Lalli's presence was like a benign, cool shade. How is Vijaya going to stay alone in the house now?

Prem is surrounded by friends and acquaintances as usual. He is preoccupied with so many problems, the problems of the entire community, the problems of the migrants, the worries of getting no relief or help from the government agencies. Premji is associated with many relief organizations. The houses of many migrants have been burnt down, some of them are not getting their salaries while for others it is their pensions that have been stopped. Problems related to the schooling of children, medicines for elders, the longing for home, the eagerness to re-connect with what they have left behind are what people are thinking of. And the demand for 'Panun Kashmir'.

Rattan Warikoo still cannot forget Sayyad Shahabuddin's statement that, 'The Kashmiri Pandits betrayed the trust of the Kashmiri Muslims by migrating on the advice of the Governor and they started a propaganda campaign which became the root cause of terrorism...'

Great, Shahabuddin Sahib! That was well said! It was merely on the provocation of the Governor that Kashmiri Hindus, abandoned their homes and properties worth crores of rupees and came to live in tents and hovels, penniless and destitute! What amazing logic!

'Let it be, Rattan bhai. Shahabuddin sahib's house is safe. It is only the homeless, living under the naked sky who can feel the pain of losing their homes. Ask Moti Lal Saqi, in Delhi who says:

Losing your home is like climbing on to a burning pyre while you are alive/or laying yourself down in a grave.

Only someone who has lost his home can understand the pain of this loss.

Rattan bhai is angry. 'We hurt the feelings of our Muslim brothers? We have always tolerated so much. I still remember my childhood when I used to go to play in the Idgah grounds. The boys of the neighbourhood would catch me when I was alone and tease me, "Batta boy, I will catch you and make you take off the sacred thread you wear around your neck, I will make you drink a dog's urine and read the Kalma."'

'Forget that, that was just boyish mischief.' Zutshi wants to calm Rattan down. Why remember a truth that causes pain?

'Even if we do that, how can we forget that the same Sheikh sahib, whom we supported whether he was right or wrong, called us spies and worse in "Atish-e-Chinar"? Shahabuddin sahib should read how, while praising the Pandits, Sheikh sahib then went on to say that they were spies for Delhi and acted as a fifth column. That they had committed many atrocities in the past.'

'If some Hindu and Sikh rulers were cruel then what about the rule of the Pathans, Afghans and Sultan Sikandar? There have been good and bad people in both communities. But if you are unfair to someone, if you close your eyes when you see a murder being committed, then how do you expect others to have faith in you?'

'The gentleman says that terrorism is the result of propaganda.' Maharaj Bhan is trying to keep his anger in check by walking in and out of the room.

'They seem to be unaware of all the efforts made by Islamic fundamentalists to spread terrorism in the valley. To make an Islamic state. To create rifts between brothers. Maulvis came from Bihar, UP, Islamic schools were opened. There was an Islamic exhibition, in which everything, ranging from household goods to trade, industry, language was said to be the creation of Islam.'

'Not only did they reject Shaivite philosophy, they even ignored the Rishi-sufi tradition. All non-Muslims were said to be the enemies of Islam.'

'Maharaj bhai, even today Osama bin Laden openly says that America, Russia and India are the enemies of Islam.'

'Nowadays Iqbal, who wrote "Saare jehan se accha Hindustan hamara", the beautiful patriotic song about India, is called the "Voice of Pakistan".'

'Rattan bhai, there is also a line in the song that says "We are Muslims, the whole world is ours."'

'Leave it be, Maharaj bhaiya. Such statements break my heart. Say something which will mend hearts and bring them together'

'We have Persian songs as well as Bhavanidas Kachru. I can never forget the Krishna Leelas sung by Mohammad Abdul Tibbat Bakal.'

'And our Mohanlal Aima, Prem bhai? He used to recite the Naat-e-sharif in such a beautiful, melodious voice that people of all religions and communities used to be drawn to him.'

Suddenly Maharaj bhai says, 'My Kakni, living this hard life as a migrant, recites the poetry of Samad Mir and cries to herself.'

The atmosphere in the room becomes heavy with grief.

'Maharaj bhai, did Sankalp get a seat in an Engineering college?'

Prem changes the direction of the conversation.

'The Maharashtra government has reserved a number of seats for Kashmiri migrants. Sankalp has got admission in Engineering and Shraddha is doing a diploma in Commerce. Thank God! Baba Sahib Thackrey sympathises with our plight.'

The room is silent once again.

'Did you get any news of home, Bharat? Triloki has gone back to his village.'

'The house has been reduced to rubble. I was thinking of going back to take a look. But the situation seems to be worsening after the Kargil war.'

'Poor Pakistan! They thought they would take control of the Srinagar-Leh road. The Kashmir problem would become an international issue. But they made fools of themselves and even earned the anger of America.'

'Evidently even the US does not want to support Islamic fundamentalism any longer. It is aware that Vajpayee did his best to extend a hand of friendship towards Pakistan by travelling to Lahore by bus. But Pakistan stabbed him in the back. It kept making secret incursions into the Batalik mountains in Kargil. The excuse was that they wanted a line of control to be demarcated.'

The conversation veered towards the Kargil war.

'Actually, Maharaj bhai, the Kargil war was the result of internal squabbles in Pakistan. They had supported the Taliban in Afghanistan. When the fighting there came to an end they sent the militants across to our side.'

'Yes, and they even refused to acknowledge their own dead soldiers to maintain the façade. It is India's largeheartedness which made us bring the Pakistani soldiers to Delhi and bury them with all due ceremony. The Pakistanis treated the bodies of our soldiers with such brutality. They put out their eyes, chopped off their limbs. Who can forget what happened to Saurabh Kalia? Our Havaldar bhai's son, Major Ashish, was also martyred fighting in the Batalik mountains.'

Premji's eyes filled with tears.

'His family members couldn't even recognize his dead body, they had defaced him so badly. He Shabhu! Forgive!' The room fills with murmurs of regret and shock.

'When will all this violence come to an end?' Zutshi sahib draws a deep breath.

'These days there are so many attacks on the BSF and army centres. The blood of the jawans is being spilt in the valley. The human rights people are sitting quietly with their eyes shut.'

'And army officers have opened social welfare centres in so many villages. Their doctors are looking after orphaned children and those needing psychiatric treatment. They have opened rehabilitation centres. The whole of Ahagam was burnt. The army is helping the villagers to rebuild their houses. It is protecting our borders and fighting with the terrorists.'

'Now people have started realizing that these soldiers are dying to protect them. Recently Major Purshottam was killed in broad daylight.'

'Yes! The terrorists haven't spared anyone and they are specially targeting the army.'

'Whether it is soldiers or local boys who die, they are all somebody's children.'

Zutshi is feeling very upset.

'Mothers and fathers carry the corpses of their sons. Farooq

Nazki writes: 'Where mothers wash the bloodstained wedding garments of their sons on riverbanks/Where the dresses of the brides are on fire/where women are weeping/while the Vitasta flows *nisang*.'

This is the valley of Kashmir. A ruined garden with sorrow everywhere.

Take a look at these makeshift, one room tenements which have been home for over ten years to these migrants and refugees. 'Return' is now a distant dream for them. Why, many ask, should they be denied the right to live in their own homeland? Why does the world talk so much about Palestinians, why not about them?

'Should we take up arms? Become friends with the JKLF? In 1992 Sunil Kaul and Suresh Bhan were accused of damaging the examination centre in Jammu. Sunil died. The smoke of disappointment, anger and sorrow did not dissipate with his death, it still smoulders in the hearts of the young.'

'Why are we being deprived of our right to live with dignity?'

'Why doesn't anyone pay attention to our demands?' So many questions.

Prem says, 'We will have to give birth to a Yasser Arafat or a Nelson Mandela. Otherwise, we will have to continue to live with false promises. Our voices will be stifled by the noise and one day we will become silent.'

But Shashi Shekhar Toshkhani believes that, 'Our silence will spread and swell!'

What stifling heat! A little girl is rubbing a cube of ice on her grandmother's chest. Oh! This is Haldhar's wife, Shanta. The daughter-in-law of Matayi who lived in Safapore. The little girl is Haldhar's grand-daughter, Sharada. The grandmother is muttering to herself with her eyes shut.

'There must be a cool breeze blowing there. The waves must be rising in Manasbal. The branches of the walnut tree must be swaying and bending in the breeze. Big pears, juicy mulberries.

Sharda, give me a sip of water, my throat is dry and my palate feels as though it is cracked.'

Sharada fetches a glass of water.

'Aah! What terrible taste! I wish someone could get me a few drops from Chashm-e-shahi.'

'Sharada, move a little! Let some air come this way.' A tired voice grumbles from the kitchen. 'Oh! I feel like I am also being fried along with the fish.'

A tired looking fan is rattling away in the corner blowing warm gusts of wind around the room.

'Let me get some air. I have to study. I have an exam tomorrow.'

Haldhar is sitting close to the door with his eyes shut.

Outside the hot wind is blowing. Haldhar is panting. His bony chest is rising and falling, rising and falling. He does not have answers to any questions.

The television people are here with their cameras and equipment. The courtyard is filled with people. The migrants are going to be interviewed. Their story will reach the public. Sharada runs and stands right in front of the camera.

'Would you like to go back home? Now? Since the situation seems to be improving?'

There is a strange sparkle in Sharada's eyes.

'We don't like it here at all. There are eight of us living in a tiny little room. We can't study, vegetables cost double. We don't even have enough money to buy watermelons. My father did farming back in our village. My grandmother used to feed the goats watermelon.'

Sharada is talking at top speed.

'Please tell the government to get us out of this rotten hole in Jammu.' Sharada's voice is shaking with anger.

'She is just a child. She has no idea how those animals treat girls. What does she know about militancy?'

Sharada, who has been in the camp from the age of four till the age of fourteen, wrinkles her brow.

'Of course I know what militants are like. Like those men who call you "child" and then grab you in the streets and bazaars. When you go to buy anything they ask you to come back, come in the evening, you will get cheap vegetables. They make all sorts of excuses to touch you. May they rot! Militants!'

'Would you like to say something, mister?' The reporter addresses Shiban.

'My name is Shiban. What should I say? Even the honourable ministers need police security. Who will protect us if we return? Other people have been given our jobs. Our houses have been burnt. We have asked for 'Panun Kashmir'. Tell the government to put an end to this militancy. They should punish the militants instead of talking to them. The Kashmir problem will not be solved by shouting for autonomy. The government should make some concrete plan. It expresses sympathy for the Palestinians but none for displaced Kashmiris. Are we not citizens of this country?'

'Cut! Cut! Bhai we can't show this.'

The camera focuses on an old man sitting under an acacia tree.

The man is rocking as he sings. Or is he crying? One can't tell.

> 'Alas! what has happened to me
> Where has my son gone
> I had a home, a life
> Happy, laughing
> Achabal, Nagbal
> Nagin and Dal lake
> They have all become a dream
> Oh Goddess Mahakali
> My hands are empty.'

Oh God! He seems to be a madman.

He is Chaman's father. Chaman was the only brother among five sisters. The militants shot him. It would be surprising if his father hadn't become mad. It isn't surprising that he has. Who knows how many such mad men there are in these pigeon holes?

There is a group of children playing on the other side. What are they playing? How strange! When most children want to watch cartoons on television, these migrant kids are playing 'Ladishah'. Just look how beautifully they pick up the tune!

> They lost the correct path unknowingly
> The innocents were misled by others
> They were shown Kalshnikovs and incited to anger
> The militants led them to destruction

Let us now take our aerial survey towards Delhi.

After all this is the capital of the country. In his story entitled 'In This Metropolis' Hari Krishan Kaul describes the sense of alienation the migrant Kashmiri feels in this city. A different language, a different culture and customs. Sixteen thousand displaced families, each with this sense of alienation....

At that time there were a lot of rallies at the Boat Club. There were seminars. The All India Kashmiri Samiti and Kashmiri organizations and societies in the country and abroad all tried to help the migrants. There were world conferences. They asked for their rights. There was talk of human rights violations and by the end of the decade two ramshackle colonies, named Vitasta and Kongposh in memory of their motherland, had been established in Najafgarh. Here the migrants built shelters for themselves and gradually their hopes of returning home were replaced by hopelessness and painful memories. The magazine *Koshur Samachar* helped to bind the migrant Hindus in Delhi together to some extent.

But the sorrow of exile hurt like a sore even after the passage of ten years.

They had been thrown out of the homes of their ancestors and told to go and live with their guardians.

In the large house outside, their guardians glanced at them, gave them some jute sacks and pieces of dry bread and said, 'Stay a while. You can return home once things improve. Kashmir is an inalienable part of India after all.'

Cold comfort!

Where were we and where have we come? By remaining silent are we becoming a part of the very system against which we had protested? Will getting buried under the rubble become the destiny of the fatalists? 'The Kashmir Research Institute is busy with the task of exploring and investigating the ancient literature and culture of the valley. It is necessary to get rid of the rubble. To look at history afresh.'

Jagmohan tries to raise the morale of the researchers, 'Kashmir is not merely the crown but also the forehead of India.' The forehead will never be bowed.

There are discussions on Shaivism.

Swami Lakshmanjoo, who was a pandit of Shaivite philosophy, has passed away. Now there is Baljinath Pandit, an expert on Spandshastra. It is said that the world is Shiva. Man is just a part of Shiva's creation, a piece of Shiva. The world is not an illusion, it is real. There is just an illusory curtain between man and Shiva. If it is removed man will become Shiva, unconcerned about race, religion or discrimination.

The foundation of the Amriteshwar Bhairav Bhavan has been laid in Sarita Vihar in Delhi and this is where the Ishwar Ashram will be built. Elderly migrant Hindus will be reminded of Swami Lakshmanjoo's Ishwar Ashram near Nishat in the valley. Memories are necessary. They have to be preserved.

But what can the younger people do? They feel as though they are in a vast wilderness. The deceit of the valley is strangling their truth. They are losing faith both in God and in politicians.

They are being forgotten by the state, the country. Who should they depend on?

Prem gets irritated with the word 'hope'.

'Expectations? From whom? The refugees who escaped from West Pakistan after the partition and took shelter in Jammu-Kashmir still haven't succeeded in becoming citizens of the state after five decades. They are also living in hope!'

'In these conditions you migrants have to take charge of your own dreams, aspirations and identities.'

'But something will have to be done.'

'Hundreds of years ago Lalded said that it is essential to raise your voice collectively.' Ratan is not ready to accept defeat.

'An Agni Shekhar, a Shaant, a Maharaj, a 'Majboor' will raise his voice.'

'Prem bhai! Look at the Jews, how they rose from the ashes of annihilation. They were burnished by the fire of Nazi hatred.'

'It is essential to have a survival instinct. One has to save oneself.'

'Struggle is necessary.'

There is long period of trial ahead. Maharaj bhai will continue to hope, Santoshi, Majboor, Halim, Qayoom, Sapru and all other sensitive people will keep searching for light in the haze.

The writer will ask her homeland for the promise that it will look after our footprints because, 'I will return to look for them/to soothe your wounds and our own.'

A new year, a new century.

'We are still waiting.'

'We haven't got Panun Kashmir.'

'The migrants are looking for their history and geography.' Premji, as outspoken as ever.

A tiny little co-operative society called Rajtarangini was registered in 1985 in the Valley. The plan was to construct thirty or thirty-five quarters for army men. But there was loud protest before the project even got off the ground. 'This is a conspiracy by the centre. This is how the Jews made inroads into Palestine, how the East India Company established itself in India.'

The centre decided to drop the plan. It didn't want to lose its vote bank.

'The state needs the security personnel who stand like rocks in its defence.'

'The army and BSF have always had to make sacrifices guarding Kashmir.'

'The terrorists burnt Chirar-e-sharif and it was the BSF which was blamed for it. Why didn't they take action in time? The army can't fire on jehadis inside the Hazratbal shrine. How would it enter Chirar-e-sharif? If it did enter, the human rights authorities would cry themselves hoarse. They would accuse them of orchestrating a repeat of Operation Bluestar. The hands of the security forces are always tied.'

'That's the way it is.'

'On the 2nd of October 1988 a lawyer protested in the High Court about putting up a photograph of Mahatma Gandhi. Protesting about the man who once saw a ray of hope in Kashmir!'

'Forget it. You can only get peace of mind if you forget.'

This is the reason why governments also close their eyes and ears.

'But the Hurriyat, which has links with terrorist organizations, has opened a Kashmir Awareness Bureau in Delhi where the militants can get in touch with the embassies of Pakistan-Iran-Afghanistan. Is this the way to end communalist frenzy?'

'When will this madness end?'

'So far there doesn't seem to be any end in sight.' Ragya draws their attention to the hijacking of the Indian Airlines plane on the 24th of December. Six highjackers forced the plane to fly from Kathmandu to Kandahar and announced that they would kill the hundred and seventy passengers unless the Pakistani militant, Azhar Masood was released.

'The centre is very generous when it comes to things like this, but it is completely helpless in the valley.'

'Can't another Vivekanand, Patel, Bhagat Singh or Gandhi take birth in this country ever again?'

Ragya asks a strange question.

'We are waiting for Badshah,' adds Haldhar's old mother.

'It is good we were thrown out otherwise we would have continued to cling to our soil despite facing all kinds of injustice and discrimination. We may have to struggle here but we can live with dignity.' Why is Shiban from Shilpora so agitated?

One evening the militants took his friend Kanhaiya away to give them directions and the next morning they killed him and left his dead body by the side of the road.

'Where will you go now? They have already laid the foundations of an Islamic world. The land of the Battas has disappeared. Very soon the handful of Pandits who remain will also be dealt with.'

'They have lost their minds.' Ratan is shaking his head in sorrow.

Friends! Now we are going to say goodbye. I will take you back to Shihul Villa.

There is a lot of hustle and bustle in the charitable hospital situated next to the villa. Kartik and Katya have just performed a major operation. They have taken off their masks and gowns in the changing room. Katya's face is glowing despite her fatigue and tension.

'You have done a great job.' Kartik puts his arms around Katya. 'It is a miracle that you managed to save both the mother and the child.'

The clock strikes twelve.

'Happy new year. Today's success is a great beginning.'

'A new millennium! All the best to you as well.'

The corridor resounds with the cries of an infant, louder and louder.

'Oh God! Such a tiny little thing and such a loud voice!'

Neelam laughs, 'There you are, these are good wishes for the new year.'

Katya hears and smiles. Sati has also walked into the corridor to wish everyone.

All of them can hear the loud fearless cry.

'This free, untrammeled voice heralds the birth of the new century.'

'A voice rising from a womb which has borne indignities and pain, a loud, clear voice raised against terror and violence.'

'Amen, Amen!'

A familiar, brash voice echoes in the hospital. Where has Jani's voice come from?

She passed away many years ago.

Is her spirit still haunting Shihul Villa?

Wait, perhaps this voice has emerged from within us?

A voice that keeps hopes, dreams and resolutions alive.

An obstinate voice which refuses to get tired or accept defeat?

Katya leans her head against the back of the chair and closes her eyes. Behind her closed eyes, the voice becomes an arrow of light spreading far beyond the lakes, waterfalls and snow-capped mountains. Thousands of people raise their arms as they turn towards the voice.

Katya looks on in amazement as a ninety-year old woman, leaning on a stick, walks towards her.

Her face is not clearly visible in the darkness.

Is it Lalli?